Bleak House

Bleak House

by

Charles Dickens

Sastrugi Press Classics
Jackson, WY

Bleak House by Charles Dickens

For permission requests, write to the publisher, addressed
"Attention: Permissions Coordinator" Sastrugi Press, P.O. Box 1297, Jackson, WY 83001, United States.

www.sastrugipress.com

CIP Data available
Dickens, Charles
Bleak House / Charles Dickens - Reprint 1st United States edition
p. cm.
1. Classic 2. Fiction 3. Literature

Summary: Bleak House was written by Charles Dickens in 1853 and is considered one of his best works due to the witty, poignant critique of the convoluted British legal system.

ISBN-13: 978-1-64922-101-8 (Hardback)
ISBN-13: 978-1-64922-102-5 (Paperback)

813-dc22

Sastrugi Press Classics
00199

Printed in the United States of America when purchased in the United States

10 9 8 7 6 5 4 3

Publishing Note

The text of the original book has been left as was in the first printing. Some words and spellings have since changed, hyphenated, combined, or otherwise gone out of use during the ensuing century in the English language. We hope you enjoy the experience.

PREFACE

A Chancery judge once had the kindness to inform me, as one of a company of some hundred and fifty men and women not labouring under any suspicions of lunacy, that the Court of Chancery, though the shining subject of much popular prejudice (at which point I thought the judge's eye had a cast in my direction), was almost immaculate. There had been, he admitted, a trivial blemish or so in its rate of progress, but this was exaggerated and had been entirely owing to the "parsimony of the public," which guilty public, it appeared, had been until lately bent in the most determined manner on by no means enlarging the number of Chancery judges appointed—I believe by Richard the Second, but any other king will do as well.

This seemed to me too profound a joke to be inserted in the body of this book or I should have restored it to Conversation Kenge or to Mr. Vholes, with one or other of whom I think it must have originated. In such mouths I might have coupled it with an apt quotation from one of Shakespeare's sonnets:

"My nature is subdued
To what it works in, like the dyer's hand:
Pity me, then, and wish I were renewed!"

But as it is wholesome that the parsimonious public should know what has been doing, and still is doing, in this connexion, I mention here that everything set forth in these pages concerning the Court of Chancery is substantially true, and within the truth. The case of Gridley is in no essential altered from one of actual occurrence, made public by a disinterested person who was professionally acquainted with the whole of the monstrous wrong from beginning to end. At the present moment (August, 1853) there is a suit before the court which was commenced nearly twenty years ago, in which from thirty to forty counsel have been known to appear at one time, in which costs have been incurred to the amount of seventy thousand pounds, which is A FRIENDLY SUIT, and which is (I am assured) no nearer to its termination now than when it was begun. There is another well-known suit in Chancery, not yet decided, which was commenced before the close of the last century and in which more than double the amount of seventy thousand pounds has been swallowed up in costs. If I wanted other authorities for Jarndyce and Jarndyce, I could rain them on these pages, to the shame of—a parsimonious public.

There is only one other point on which I offer a word of remark. The possibility of what is called spontaneous combustion has been denied since the death of Mr. Krook; and my good friend Mr. Lewes (quite mistaken, as he soon found, in supposing the thing to have been abandoned by all authorities) published some ingenious letters to me at the time when that event was chronicled, arguing that spontaneous combustion could not possibly be. I have no need to observe that I do not wilfully or negligently mislead my readers and that before I wrote that description I took pains to investigate the subject. There are about thirty cases on record, of which the most famous, that of the Countess Cornelia de Baudi Cesenate, was minutely investigated and described by Giuseppe Bianchini, a prebendary of Verona, otherwise distinguished in letters, who published an account of it at Verona in 1731, which he afterwards republished at Rome. The appearances, beyond all rational doubt, observed in that case are the appearances observed in Mr. Krook's case. The next most famous instance happened at Rheims six years earlier, and the historian in that case is Le Cat, one of the most renowned surgeons produced by France. The subject was a woman, whose husband was ignorantly convicted of having murdered her; but on solemn appeal to a higher court, he was acquitted because it was shown upon the evidence that she had died the death of which this name of spontaneous combustion is given. I do not think it necessary to add to these notable facts, and that general reference to the authorities which will be found at page 30, vol. ii.,* the recorded opinions and experiences of distinguished medical professors, French, English, and Scotch, in more modern days, contenting myself with observing that I shall not abandon the facts until there shall have been a considerable spontaneous combustion of the testimony on which human occurrences are usually received.**

In Bleak House I have purposely dwelt upon the romantic side of familiar things.

1853

*This referred to a specific page in the printed book. The pertinent information is in Chapter XXX, paragraph 90.

**Another case, very clearly described by a dentist, occurred at the town of Columbus, in the United States of America, quite recently. The subject was a German who kept a liquor-shop and was an inveterate drunkard.

CHAPTER I
IN CHANCERY

London. Michaelmas term lately over, and the Lord Chancellor sitting in Lincoln's Inn Hall. Implacable November weather. As much mud in the streets as if the waters had but newly retired from the face of the earth, and it would not be wonderful to meet a Megalosaurus, forty feet long or so, waddling like an elephantine lizard up Holborn Hill. Smoke lowering down from chimney-pots, making a soft black drizzle, with flakes of soot in it as big as full-grown snowflakes—gone into mourning, one might imagine, for the death of the sun. Dogs, undistinguishable in mire. Horses, scarcely better; splashed to their very blinkers. Foot passengers, jostling one another's umbrellas in a general infection of ill temper, and losing their foot-hold at street-corners, where tens of thousands of other foot passengers have been slipping and sliding since the day broke (if this day ever broke), adding new deposits to the crust upon crust of mud, sticking at those points tenaciously to the pavement, and accumulating at compound interest.

Fog everywhere. Fog up the river, where it flows among green aits and meadows; fog down the river, where it rolls defiled among the tiers of shipping and the waterside pollutions of a great (and dirty) city. Fog on the Essex marshes, fog on the Kentish heights. Fog creeping into the cabooses of collier-brigs; fog lying out on the yards and hovering in the rigging of great ships; fog drooping on the gunwales of barges and small boats. Fog in the eyes and throats of ancient Greenwich pensioners, wheezing by the firesides of their wards; fog in the stem and bowl of the afternoon pipe of the wrathful skipper, down in his close cabin; fog cruelly pinching the toes and fingers of his shivering little 'prentice boy on deck. Chance people on the bridges peeping over the parapets into a nether sky of fog, with fog all round them, as if they were up in a balloon and hanging in the misty clouds.

Gas looming through the fog in divers places in the streets, much as the sun may, from the spongey fields, be seen to loom by husbandman and ploughboy. Most of the shops lighted two hours before their time—as the gas seems to know, for it has a haggard and unwilling look.

The raw afternoon is rawest, and the dense fog is densest, and the muddy streets are muddiest near that leaden-headed old obstruction, appropriate ornament for the threshold of a leaden-headed old corporation, Temple Bar. And hard by Temple Bar, in Lincoln's Inn Hall, at the very heart of the fog, sits the Lord High Chancellor in his High Court of Chancery.

Never can there come fog too thick, never can there come mud and mire too deep, to assort with the groping and floundering condition which this High Court of Chancery, most pestilent of hoary sinners, holds this day in the sight of heaven and earth.

On such an afternoon, if ever, the Lord High Chancellor ought to be sitting here—as here he is—with a foggy glory round his head, softly fenced in with crimson cloth and curtains, addressed by a large advocate with great whiskers, a little voice, and an interminable brief, and outwardly directing his contemplation to the lantern in the roof, where he can see nothing but fog. On such an afternoon some score of members of the High Court of Chancery bar ought to be—as here they are—mistily engaged in one of the ten thousand stages of an endless cause, tripping one another up on slippery precedents, groping knee-deep in technicalities, running their goat-hair and horsehair warded heads against walls of words and making a pretence of equity with serious faces, as players might. On such an afternoon the various solicitors in the cause, some two or three of whom have inherited it from their fathers, who made a fortune by it, ought to be—as are they not?—ranged in a line, in a long matted well (but you might look in vain for truth at the bottom of it) between the registrar's red table and the silk gowns, with bills, cross-bills, answers, rejoinders, injunctions, affidavits, issues, references to masters, masters' reports, mountains of costly nonsense, piled before them. Well may the court be dim, with wasting candles here and there; well may the fog hang heavy in it, as if it would never get out; well may the stained-glass windows lose their colour and admit no light of day into the place; well may the uninitiated from the streets, who peep in through the glass panes in the door, be deterred from entrance by its owlish aspect and by the drawl, languidly echoing to the roof from the padded dais where the Lord High Chancellor looks into the lantern that has no light in it and where the attendant wigs are all stuck in a fog-bank! This is the Court of Chancery, which has its decaying houses and its blighted lands in every shire, which has its worn-out lunatic in every madhouse and its dead in every churchyard, which has its ruined suitor with his slipshod heels and threadbare dress borrowing and begging through the round of every man's acquaintance, which gives to monied might the means abundantly of wearying out the right, which so exhausts finances, patience, courage, hope, so overthrows the brain and breaks the heart, that there is not an honourable man among its practitioners who would not give—who does not often give—the warning, "Suffer any wrong that can be done you rather than come here!"

Who happen to be in the Lord Chancellor's court this murky afternoon besides the Lord Chancellor, the counsel in the cause, two or three counsel who are never in any cause, and the well of solicitors before mentioned? There is the registrar below the judge, in wig and gown; and there are two or three maces, or petty-bags, or privy purses, or whatever they may be, in legal court suits. These are all yawning, for no crumb of amusement ever falls from Jarndyce and Jarndyce (the cause in hand), which was squeezed dry years upon years ago. The short-hand writers, the reporters of the court, and the reporters of the newspapers invariably decamp with the rest of the regulars when Jarndyce and Jarndyce comes on. Their places are a blank. Standing on a seat at the side of the hall, the better to peer into the curtained sanctuary, is a little mad old woman in a squeezed bonnet who is always in court, from its sitting to its rising, and always expecting some incomprehensible judgment to be given in her favour. Some say she really is, or was, a party to a suit, but no one knows for certain because no one cares. She carries some small litter in a reticule which she calls her documents, principally consisting of paper matches and dry lavender. A sallow prisoner has come up, in custody, for the half-dozenth time to make a personal application "to purge himself of his contempt," which, being a solitary surviving executor who has fallen into a state of conglomeration about accounts of which it is not pretended that he had ever any knowledge, he is not at all likely ever to do. In the meantime his prospects in life are ended. Another ruined suitor, who periodically appears from Shropshire and breaks out into efforts to address the Chancellor at the close of the day's business and who can by no means be made to understand that the Chancellor is legally ignorant of his existence after making it desolate for a quarter of a century, plants himself in a good place and keeps an eye on the judge, ready to call out "My Lord!" in a voice of sonorous complaint on the instant of his rising. A few lawyers' clerks and others who know this suitor by sight linger on the chance of his furnishing some fun and enlivening the dismal weather a little.

Jarndyce and Jarndyce drones on. This scarecrow of a suit has, in course of time, become so complicated that no man alive knows what it means. The parties to it understand it least, but it has been observed that no two Chancery lawyers can talk about it for five minutes without coming to a total disagreement as to all the premises. Innumerable children have been born into the cause; innumerable young people have married into it; innumerable old people have died out of it. Scores of persons have deliriously found themselves made parties in Jarndyce and Jarndyce without knowing how or why; whole families have inherited legendary hatreds with the suit. The little plaintiff or defendant who was promised a new rocking-horse when Jarndyce and Jarndyce should be settled has grown up, possessed himself of a real horse, and trotted away into the other world. Fair wards of court have faded into mothers and grandmothers; a long procession of Chancellors has come in and gone out; the legion of bills in the suit have been transformed into mere bills of mortality; there are not three Jarndyces left upon the earth perhaps since old Tom Jarndyce in despair blew his brains out at a coffee-house in Chancery Lane; but Jarndyce and Jarndyce still drags its dreary length before the court, perennially hopeless.

Jarndyce and Jarndyce has passed into a joke. That is the only good that has ever come of it. It has been death to many, but it is a joke in the profession. Every master in Chancery has had a reference out of it. Every Chancellor was "in it," for somebody or other, when he was counsel at the bar. Good things have been said about it by blue-nosed, bulbous-shoed old benchers in select port-wine committee after dinner in hall. Articled clerks have been in the habit of fleshing their legal wit upon it. The last Lord Chancellor handled it neatly, when, correcting Mr. Blowers, the eminent silk gown who said that such a thing might happen when the sky rained potatoes, he observed, "or when we get through Jarndyce and Jarndyce, Mr. Blowers"—a pleasantry that particularly tickled the maces, bags, and purses.

How many people out of the suit Jarndyce and Jarndyce has stretched forth its unwholesome hand to spoil and corrupt would be a very wide question. From the master upon whose impaling files reams of dusty warrants in Jarndyce and Jarndyce have grimly writhed into many shapes, down to the copying-clerk in the Six Clerks' Office who has copied his tens of thousands of Chancery folio-pages under that eternal heading, no man's nature has been made better by it. In trickery, evasion, procrastination, spoliation, botheration, under false pretences of all sorts, there are influences that can never come to good. The very solicitors' boys who have kept the wretched suitors at bay, by protesting time out of mind that Mr. Chizzle, Mizzle, or otherwise was particularly engaged and had appointments until dinner, may have got an extra moral twist and shuffle into themselves out of Jarndyce and Jarndyce. The receiver in the cause has acquired a goodly sum of money by it but has acquired too a distrust of his own mother and a contempt for his own kind. Chizzle, Mizzle, and otherwise have lapsed into a habit of vaguely promising themselves that they will look into that outstanding little matter and see what can be done for Drizzle—who was not well used—when Jarndyce and Jarndyce shall be got out of the office. Shirking and sharking in all their many varieties have been sown broadcast by the ill-fated cause; and even those who have contemplated its history from the outermost circle of such evil have been insensibly tempted into a loose way of letting bad things alone to take their own bad course, and a loose belief that if the world go wrong it was in some off-hand manner never meant to go right.

Thus, in the midst of the mud and at the heart of the fog, sits the Lord High Chancellor in his High Court of Chancery.

"Mr. Tangle," says the Lord High Chancellor, latterly something restless under the eloquence of that learned gentleman.

"Mlud," says Mr. Tangle. Mr. Tangle knows more of Jarndyce and Jarndyce than anybody. He is famous for it—supposed never to have read anything else since he left school.

"Have you nearly concluded your argument?"

"Mlud, no—variety of points—feel it my duty tsubmit—ludship," is the reply that slides out of Mr. Tangle.

"Several members of the bar are still to be heard, I believe?" says the Chancellor with a slight smile.

Eighteen of Mr. Tangle's learned friends, each armed with a little summary of eighteen hundred sheets, bob up like eighteen hammers in a pianoforte, make eighteen bows, and drop into their eighteen places of obscurity.

"We will proceed with the hearing on Wednesday fortnight," says the Chancellor. For the question at issue is only a question of costs, a mere bud on the forest tree of the parent suit, and really will come to a settlement one of these days.

The Chancellor rises; the bar rises; the prisoner is brought forward in a hurry; the man from Shropshire cries, "My lord!" Maces, bags, and purses indignantly proclaim silence and frown at the man from Shropshire.

"In reference," proceeds the Chancellor, still on Jarndyce and Jarndyce, "to the young girl—"

"Begludship's pardon—boy," says Mr. Tangle prematurely. "In reference," proceeds the Chancellor with extra distinctness, "to the young girl and boy, the two young people"—Mr. Tangle crushed—"whom I directed to be in attendance to-day and who are now in my private room, I will see them and satisfy myself as to the expediency of making the order for their residing with their uncle."

Mr. Tangle on his legs again. "Begludship's pardon—dead."

"With their"—Chancellor looking through his double eye-glass at the papers on his desk—"grandfather."

"Begludship's pardon—victim of rash action—brains."

Suddenly a very little counsel with a terrific bass voice arises, fully inflated, in the back settlements of the fog, and says, "Will your lordship allow me? I appear for him. He is a cousin, several times removed. I am not at the moment prepared to inform the court in what exact remove he is a cousin, but he IS a cousin."

Leaving this address (delivered like a sepulchral message) ringing in the rafters of the roof, the very little counsel drops, and the fog knows him no more. Everybody looks for him. Nobody can see him.

"I will speak with both the young people," says the Chancellor anew, "and satisfy myself on the subject of their residing with their cousin. I will mention the matter to-morrow morning when I take my seat."

The Chancellor is about to bow to the bar when the prisoner is presented. Nothing can possibly come of the prisoner's conglomeration but his being sent back to prison, which is soon done. The man from Shropshire ventures another remonstrative "My lord!" but the Chancellor, being aware of him, has dexterously vanished. Everybody else quickly vanishes too. A battery of blue bags is loaded with heavy charges of papers and carried off by clerks; the little mad old woman marches off with her documents; the empty court is locked up. If all the injustice it has committed and all the misery it has caused could only be locked up with it, and the whole burnt away in a great funeral pyre—why so much the better for other parties than the parties in Jarndyce and Jarndyce!

CHAPTER II
IN FASHION

It is but a glimpse of the world of fashion that we want on this same miry afternoon. It is not so unlike the Court of Chancery but that we may pass from the one scene to the other, as the crow flies. Both the world of fashion and the Court of Chancery are things of precedent and usage: oversleeping Rip Van Winkles who have played at strange games through a deal of thundery weather; sleeping beauties whom the knight will wake one day, when all the stopped spits in the kitchen shall begin to turn prodigiously!

It is not a large world. Relatively even to this world of ours, which has its limits too (as your Highness shall find when you have made the tour of it and are come to the brink of the void beyond), it is a very little speck. There is much good in it; there are many good and true people in it; it has its appointed place. But the evil of it is that it is a world wrapped up in too much jeweller's cotton and fine wool, and cannot hear the rushing of the larger worlds, and cannot see them as they circle round the sun. It is a deadened world, and its growth is sometimes unhealthy for want of air.

My Lady Dedlock has returned to her house in town for a few days previous to her departure for Paris, where her ladyship intends to stay some weeks, after which her movements are uncertain. The fashionable intelligence says so for the comfort of the Parisians, and it knows all fashionable things. To know things otherwise were to be unfashionable. My Lady Dedlock has been down at what she calls, in familiar conversation, her "place" in Lincolnshire. The waters are out in Lincolnshire. An arch of the bridge in the park has been sapped and sopped away. The adjacent low-lying ground for half a mile in breadth is a stagnant river with melancholy trees for islands in it and a surface punctured all over, all day long, with falling rain. My Lady Dedlock's place has been extremely dreary. The weather for many a day and night has been so wet that the trees seem wet through, and the soft loppings and prunings of the woodman's axe can make no crash or crackle as they fall. The deer, looking soaked, leave quagmires where they pass. The shot of a rifle loses its sharpness in the moist air, and its smoke moves in a tardy little cloud towards the green rise, coppice-topped, that makes a background for the falling rain. The view from my Lady Dedlock's own windows is alternately a lead-coloured view and a view in Indian ink. The vases on the stone terrace in the foreground catch the rain all day; and the heavy drops fall—drip, drip, drip—upon the broad flagged pavement, called from old time the Ghost's Walk, all night. On Sundays the little church in the park is mouldy; the oaken pulpit breaks out into a cold sweat; and there is a general smell and taste as of the ancient Dedlocks in their graves. My Lady Dedlock (who is childless), looking out in the early twilight from her boudoir at a keeper's lodge and seeing the light of a fire upon the latticed panes, and smoke rising from the chimney, and a child, chased by a woman, running out into the rain to meet the shining figure of a wrapped-up man coming through the gate, has been put quite out of temper. My Lady Dedlock says she has been "bored to death."

Therefore my Lady Dedlock has come away from the place in Lincolnshire and has left it to the rain, and the crows, and the rabbits, and the deer, and the partridges and pheasants. The pictures of the Dedlocks past and gone have seemed to vanish into the damp walls in mere lowness of spirits, as the housekeeper has passed along the old rooms shutting up the shutters. And when they will next come forth again, the fashionable intelligence—which, like the fiend, is omniscient of the past and present, but not the future—cannot yet undertake to say.

Sir Leicester Dedlock is only a baronet, but there is no mightier baronet than he. His family is as old as the hills, and infinitely more respectable. He has a general opinion that the world might get on without hills but would be done up without Dedlocks. He would on the whole admit nature to be a good idea (a little low, perhaps, when not enclosed with a park-fence), but an idea dependent for its execution on your great county families. He is a gentleman of strict conscience, disdainful of all littleness and meanness and ready on the shortest notice to die any death you may please to mention rather than give occasion for the least impeachment of his integrity. He is an honourable, obstinate, truthful, high-spirited, intensely prejudiced, perfectly unreasonable man.

Sir Leicester is twenty years, full measure, older than my Lady. He will never see sixty-five again, nor perhaps sixty-six, nor yet sixty-seven. He has a twist of the gout now and then and walks a little stiffly. He is of a worthy presence, with his light-grey hair and whiskers, his fine shirt-frill, his pure-white waistcoat, and his blue coat with bright buttons always buttoned. He is ceremonious, stately, most polite on every occasion to my Lady, and holds her personal attractions in the highest estimation. His gallantry to my Lady, which has never changed since he courted her, is the one little touch of romantic fancy in him.

Indeed, he married her for love. A whisper still goes about that she had not even family; howbeit, Sir Leicester had so much family that perhaps he had enough and could dispense with any more. But she had beauty, pride, ambition, insolent resolve, and sense enough to portion out a legion of fine ladies. Wealth and station, added to these, soon floated her upward, and for years now my Lady Dedlock has been at the centre of the fashionable intelligence and at the top of the fashionable tree.

How Alexander wept when he had no more worlds to conquer, everybody knows—or has some reason to know by this time, the matter having been rather frequently mentioned. My Lady Dedlock, having conquered HER world, fell not into the melting, but rather into the freezing, mood. An exhausted composure, a worn-out placidity, an equanimity of fatigue not to be ruffled by interest or satisfaction, are the trophies of her victory. She is perfectly well-bred. If she could be translated to heaven to-morrow, she might be expected to ascend without any rapture.

She has beauty still, and if it be not in its heyday, it is not yet in its autumn. She has a fine face—originally of a character that would be rather called very pretty than handsome, but improved into classicality by the acquired expression of her fashionable state. Her figure is elegant and has the effect of being tall. Not that she is so, but that "the most is made," as the Honourable Bob Stables has frequently asserted upon oath, "of all her points." The same authority observes that she is perfectly got up and remarks in commendation of her hair especially that she is the best-groomed woman in the whole stud.

With all her perfections on her head, my Lady Dedlock has come up from her place in Lincolnshire (hotly pursued by the fashionable intelligence) to pass a few days at her house in town previous to her departure for Paris, where her ladyship intends to stay some weeks, after which her movements are uncertain. And at her house in town, upon this muddy, murky afternoon, presents himself an old-fashioned old gentleman, attorney-at-law and eke solicitor of the High Court of Chancery, who has the honour of acting as legal adviser of the Dedlocks and has as many cast-iron boxes in his office with that name outside as if the present baronet were the coin of the conjuror's trick and were constantly being juggled through the whole set. Across the hall, and up the stairs, and along the passages, and through the rooms, which are very brilliant in the season and very dismal out of it—fairy-land to visit, but a desert to live in—the old gentleman is conducted by a Mercury in powder to my Lady's presence.

The old gentleman is rusty to look at, but is reputed to have made good thrift out of aristocratic marriage settlements and aristocratic wills, and to be very rich. He is surrounded by a mysterious halo of family confidences, of which he is known to be the silent depository. There are noble mausoleums rooted for centuries in retired glades of parks among the growing timber and the fern, which perhaps hold fewer noble secrets than walk abroad among men, shut up in the breast of Mr. Tulkinghorn. He is of what is called the old school—a phrase generally meaning any school that seems never to have been young—and wears knee-breeches tied with ribbons, and gaiters or stockings. One peculiarity of his black clothes and of his black stockings, be they silk or worsted, is that they never shine. Mute, close, irresponsive to any glancing light, his dress is like himself. He never converses when not professionally consulted. He is found sometimes, speechless but quite at home, at corners of dinner-tables in great country houses and near doors of drawing-rooms, concerning which the fashionable intelligence is eloquent, where everybody knows him and where half the Peerage stops to say "How do you do, Mr. Tulkinghorn?" He receives these salutations with gravity and buries them along with the rest of his knowledge.

Sir Leicester Dedlock is with my Lady and is happy to see Mr. Tulkinghorn. There is an air of prescription about him which is always agreeable to Sir Leicester; he receives it as a kind of tribute. He likes Mr. Tulkinghorn's dress; there is a kind of tribute in that too. It is eminently respectable, and likewise, in a general way, retainer-like. It expresses, as it were, the steward of the legal mysteries, the butler of the legal cellar, of the Dedlocks.

Has Mr. Tulkinghorn any idea of this himself? It may be so, or it may not, but there is this remarkable circumstance to be noted in everything associated with my Lady Dedlock as one of a class—as one of the leaders and representatives of her little world. She supposes herself to be an inscrutable Being, quite out of the reach and ken of ordinary mortals—seeing herself in her glass, where indeed she looks so. Yet every dim little star revolving about her, from her maid to the manager of the Italian Opera, knows her weaknesses, prejudices, follies, haughtinesses, and caprices and lives upon as accurate a calculation and as nice a measure of her moral nature as her dressmaker takes of her physical proportions. Is a new dress, a new custom, a new singer, a new dancer, a new form of jewellery, a new dwarf or giant, a new chapel, a new anything, to be set up? There are deferential people in a dozen callings whom my Lady Dedlock suspects of nothing but prostration before her, who can tell you how to manage her as if she were a baby, who do nothing but nurse her all their lives, who, humbly affecting to follow with profound subservience, lead her and her whole troop after them; who, in hooking one, hook all and bear them off as Lemuel Gulliver bore away the stately fleet of the majestic Lilliput. "If you want to address our people, sir," say Blaze and Sparkle, the jewellers—meaning by our people Lady Dedlock and the rest—"you must remember that you are not dealing with the general public; you must hit our people in their weakest place, and their weakest place is such a place." "To make this article go down, gentlemen," say Sheen and Gloss, the mercers, to their friends the manufacturers, "you must come to us, because we know where to have the fashionable people, and we can make it fashionable." "If you want to get this print upon the tables of my high connexion, sir," says Mr. Sladdery, the librarian, "or if you want to get this dwarf or giant into the houses of my high connexion, sir, or if you want to secure to this entertainment the patronage of my high connexion, sir, you must leave it, if you please, to me, for I have been accustomed to study the leaders of my high connexion, sir, and I may tell you without vanity that I can turn them round my finger"—in which Mr. Sladdery, who is an honest man, does not exaggerate at all.

Therefore, while Mr. Tulkinghorn may not know what is passing in the Dedlock mind at present, it is very possible that he may.

"My Lady's cause has been again before the Chancellor, has it, Mr. Tulkinghorn?" says Sir Leicester, giving him his hand.

"Yes. It has been on again to-day," Mr. Tulkinghorn replies, making one of his quiet bows to my Lady, who is on a sofa near the fire, shading her face with a hand-screen.

"It would be useless to ask," says my Lady with the dreariness of the place in Lincolnshire still upon her, "whether anything has been done."

"Nothing that YOU would call anything has been done to-day," replies Mr. Tulkinghorn.

"Nor ever will be," says my Lady.

Sir Leicester has no objection to an interminable Chancery suit. It is a slow, expensive, British, constitutional kind of thing. To be sure, he has not a vital interest in the suit in question, her part in which was the only property my Lady brought him; and he has a shadowy impression that for his name—the name of Dedlock—to be in a cause, and not in the title of that cause, is a most ridiculous accident. But he regards the Court of Chancery, even if it should involve an occasional delay of justice and a trifling amount of confusion, as a something devised in conjunction with a variety of other somethings by the perfection of human wisdom for the eternal settlement (humanly speaking) of everything. And he is upon the whole of a fixed opinion that to give the sanction of his countenance to any complaints respecting it would be to encourage some person in the lower classes to rise up somewhere—like Wat Tyler.

"As a few fresh affidavits have been put upon the file," says Mr. Tulkinghorn, "and as they are short, and as I proceed upon the troublesome principle of begging leave to possess my clients with any new proceedings in a cause"—cautious man Mr. Tulkinghorn, taking no more responsibility than necessary—"and further, as I see you are going to Paris, I have brought them in my pocket."

(Sir Leicester was going to Paris too, by the by, but the delight of the fashionable intelligence was in his Lady.)

Mr. Tulkinghorn takes out his papers, asks permission to place them on a golden talisman of a table at my Lady's elbow, puts on his spectacles, and begins to read by the light of a shaded lamp.

"'In Chancery. Between John Jarndyce—'"

My Lady interrupts, requesting him to miss as many of the formal horrors as he can.

Mr. Tulkinghorn glances over his spectacles and begins again lower down. My Lady carelessly and scornfully abstracts her attention. Sir Leicester in a great chair looks at the file and appears to have a stately liking for the legal repetitions and prolixities as ranging among the national bulwarks. It happens that the fire is hot where my Lady sits and that the hand-screen is more beautiful than useful, being priceless but small. My Lady, changing her position, sees the papers on the table—looks at them nearer—looks at them nearer still—asks impulsively, "Who copied that?"

Mr. Tulkinghorn stops short, surprised by my Lady's animation and her unusual tone.

"Is it what you people call law-hand?" she asks, looking full at him in her careless way again and toying with her screen.

"Not quite. Probably"—Mr. Tulkinghorn examines it as he speaks—"the legal character which it has was acquired after the original hand was formed. Why do you ask?"

"Anything to vary this detestable monotony. Oh, go on, do!"

Mr. Tulkinghorn reads again. The heat is greater; my Lady screens her face. Sir Leicester dozes, starts up suddenly, and cries, "Eh? What do you say?"

"I say I am afraid," says Mr. Tulkinghorn, who had risen hastily, "that Lady Dedlock is ill."

"Faint," my Lady murmurs with white lips, "only that; but it is like the faintness of death. Don't speak to me. Ring, and take me to my room!"

Mr. Tulkinghorn retires into another chamber; bells ring, feet shuffle and patter, silence ensues. Mercury at last begs Mr. Tulkinghorn to return.

"Better now," quoth Sir Leicester, motioning the lawyer to sit down and read to him alone. "I have been quite alarmed. I never knew my Lady swoon before. But the weather is extremely trying, and she really has been bored to death down at our place in Lincolnshire."

CHAPTER III
A PROGRESS

I have a great deal of difficulty in beginning to write my portion of these pages, for I know I am not clever. I always knew that. I can remember, when I was a very little girl indeed, I used to say to my doll when we were alone together, "Now, Dolly, I am not clever, you know very well, and you must be patient with me, like a dear!" And so she used to sit propped up in a great arm-chair, with her beautiful complexion and rosy lips, staring at me—or not so much at me, I think, as at nothing—while I busily stitched away and told her every one of my secrets.

My dear old doll! I was such a shy little thing that I seldom dared to open my lips, and never dared to open my heart, to anybody else. It almost makes me cry to think what a relief it used to be to me when I came home from school of a day to run upstairs to my room and say, "Oh, you dear faithful Dolly, I knew you would be expecting me!" and then to sit down on the floor, leaning on the elbow of her great chair, and tell her all I had noticed since we parted. I had always rather a noticing way—not a quick way, oh, no!—a silent way of noticing what passed before me and thinking I should like to understand it better. I have not by any means a quick understanding. When I love a person very tenderly indeed, it seems to brighten. But even that may be my vanity.

I was brought up, from my earliest remembrance—like some of the princesses in the fairy stories, only I was not charming—by my godmother. At least, I only knew her as such. She was a good, good woman! She went to church three times every Sunday, and to morning prayers on Wednesdays and Fridays, and to lectures whenever there were lectures; and never missed. She was handsome; and if she had ever smiled, would have been (I used to think) like an angel—but she never smiled. She was always grave and strict. She was so very good herself, I thought, that the badness of other people made her frown all her life. I felt so different from her, even making every allowance for the differences between a child and a woman; I felt so poor, so trifling, and so far off that I never could be unrestrained with her—no, could never even love her as I wished. It made me very sorry to consider how good she was and how unworthy of her I was, and I used ardently to hope that I might have a better heart; and I talked it over very often with the dear old doll, but I never loved my godmother as I ought to have loved her and as I felt I must have loved her if I had been a better girl.

This made me, I dare say, more timid and retiring than I naturally was and cast me upon Dolly as the only friend with whom I felt at ease. But something happened when I was still quite a little thing that helped it very much.

I had never heard my mama spoken of. I had never heard of my papa either, but I felt more interested about my mama. I had never worn a black frock, that I could recollect. I had never been shown my mama's grave. I had never been told where it was. Yet I had never been taught to pray for any relation but my godmother. I had more than once approached this subject of my thoughts with Mrs. Rachael, our only servant, who took my light away when I was in bed (another very good woman, but austere to me), and she had only said, "Esther, good night!" and gone away and left me.

Although there were seven girls at the neighbouring school where I was a day boarder, and although they called me little Esther Summerson, I knew none of them at home. All of them were older than I, to be sure (I was the youngest there by a good deal), but there seemed to be some other separation between us besides that, and besides their being far more clever than I was and knowing much more than I did. One of them in the first week of my going to the school (I remember it very well) invited me home to a little party, to my great joy. But my godmother wrote a stiff letter declining for me, and I never went. I never went out at all.

It was my birthday. There were holidays at school on other birthdays—none on mine. There were rejoicings at home on other birthdays, as I knew from what I heard the girls relate to one another—there were none on mine. My birthday was the most melancholy day at home in the whole year.

I have mentioned that unless my vanity should deceive me (as I know it may, for I may be very vain without suspecting it, though indeed I don't), my comprehension is quickened when my affection is. My disposition is very affectionate, and perhaps I might still feel such a wound if such a wound could be received more than once with the quickness of that birthday.

Dinner was over, and my godmother and I were sitting at the table before the fire. The clock ticked, the fire clicked; not another sound had been heard in the room or in the house for I don't know how long. I happened to look timidly up from my stitching, across the table at my godmother, and I saw in her face, looking gloomily at me, "It would have been far better, little Esther, that you had had no birthday, that you had never been born!"

I broke out crying and sobbing, and I said, "Oh, dear godmother, tell me, pray do tell me, did Mama die on my birthday?"

"No," she returned. "Ask me no more, child!"

"Oh, do pray tell me something of her. Do now, at last, dear godmother, if you please! What did I do to her? How did I lose her? Why am I so different from other children, and why is it my fault, dear godmother? No, no, no, don't go away. Oh, speak to me!"

I was in a kind of fright beyond my grief, and I caught hold of her dress and was kneeling to her. She had been saying all the while, "Let me go!" But now she stood still.

Her darkened face had such power over me that it stopped me in the midst of my vehemence. I put up my trembling little hand to clasp hers or to beg her pardon with what earnestness I might, but withdrew it as she looked at me, and laid it on my fluttering heart. She raised me, sat in her chair, and standing me before her, said slowly in a cold, low voice—I see her knitted brow and pointed finger—"Your mother, Esther, is your disgrace, and you were hers. The time will come—and soon enough—when you will understand this better and will feel it too, as no one save a woman can. I have forgiven her"—but her face did not relent—"the wrong she did to me, and I say no more of it, though it was greater than you will ever know—than any one will ever know but I, the sufferer. For yourself, unfortunate girl, orphaned and degraded from the first of these evil anniversaries, pray daily that the sins of others be not visited upon your head, according to what is written. Forget your mother and leave all other people to forget her who will do her unhappy child that greatest kindness. Now, go!"

She checked me, however, as I was about to depart from her—so frozen as I was!—and added this, "Submission, self-denial, diligent work, are the preparations for a life begun with such a shadow on it. You are different from other children, Esther, because you were not born, like them, in common sinfulness and wrath. You are set apart."

I went up to my room, and crept to bed, and laid my doll's cheek against mine wet with tears, and holding that solitary friend upon my bosom, cried myself to sleep. Imperfect as my understanding of my sorrow was, I knew that I had brought no joy at any time to anybody's heart and that I was to no one upon earth what Dolly was to me.

Dear, dear, to think how much time we passed alone together afterwards, and how often I repeated to the doll the story of my birthday and confided to her that I would try as hard as ever I could to repair the fault I had been born with (of which I confessedly felt guilty and yet innocent) and would strive as I grew up to be industrious, contented, and kind-hearted and to do some good to some one, and win some love to myself if I could. I hope it is not self-indulgent to shed these tears as I think of it. I am very thankful, I am very cheerful, but I cannot quite help their coming to my eyes.

There! I have wiped them away now and can go on again properly.

I felt the distance between my godmother and myself so much more after the birthday, and felt so sensible of filling a place in her house which ought to have been empty, that I found her more difficult of approach, though I was fervently grateful to her in my heart, than ever. I felt in the same way towards my school companions; I felt in the same way towards Mrs. Rachael, who was a widow; and oh, towards her daughter, of whom she was proud, who came to see her once a fortnight! I was very retired and quiet, and tried to be very diligent.

One sunny afternoon when I had come home from school with my books and portfolio, watching my long shadow at my side, and as I was gliding upstairs to my room as usual, my godmother looked out of the parlour-door and called me back. Sitting with her, I found—which was very unusual indeed—a stranger. A portly, important-looking gentleman, dressed all in black, with a white cravat, large gold watch seals, a pair of gold eye-glasses, and a large seal-ring upon his little finger.

"This," said my godmother in an undertone, "is the child." Then she said in her naturally stern way of speaking, "This is Esther, sir."

The gentleman put up his eye-glasses to look at me and said, "Come here, my dear!" He shook hands with me and asked me to take off my bonnet, looking at me all the while. When I had complied, he said, "Ah!" and afterwards "Yes!" And then, taking off his eye-glasses and folding them in a red case, and leaning back in his arm-chair, turning the case about in his two hands, he gave my godmother a nod. Upon that, my godmother said, "You may go upstairs, Esther!" And I made him my curtsy and left him.

It must have been two years afterwards, and I was almost fourteen, when one dreadful night my godmother and I sat at the fireside. I was reading aloud, and she was listening. I had come down at nine o'clock as I always did to read the Bible to her, and was reading from St. John how our Saviour stooped down, writing with his finger in the dust, when they brought the sinful woman to him.

"So when they continued asking him, he lifted up himself and said unto them, 'He that is without sin among you, let him first cast a stone at her!'"

I was stopped by my godmother's rising, putting her hand to her head, and crying out in an awful voice from quite another part of the book, "'Watch ye, therefore, lest coming suddenly he find you sleeping. And what I say unto you, I say unto all, Watch!'"

In an instant, while she stood before me repeating these words, she fell down on the floor. I had no need to cry out; her voice had sounded through the house and been heard in the street.

She was laid upon her bed. For more than a week she lay there, little altered outwardly, with her old handsome resolute frown that I so well knew carved upon her face. Many and many a time, in the day and in the night, with my head upon the pillow by her that my whispers might be plainer to her, I kissed her, thanked her, prayed for her, asked her for her blessing and forgiveness, entreated her to give me the least sign that she knew or heard me. No, no, no. Her face was immovable. To the very last, and even afterwards, her frown remained unsoftened.

On the day after my poor good godmother was buried, the gentleman in black with the white neckcloth reappeared. I was sent for by Mrs. Rachael, and found him in the same place, as if he had never gone away.

"My name is Kenge," he said; "you may remember it, my child; Kenge and Carboy, Lincoln's Inn."

I replied that I remembered to have seen him once before.

"Pray be seated—here near me. Don't distress yourself; it's of no use. Mrs. Rachael, I needn't inform you who were acquainted with the late Miss Barbary's affairs, that her means die with her and that this young lady, now her aunt is dead—"

"My aunt, sir!"

"It is really of no use carrying on a deception when no object is to be gained by it," said Mr. Kenge smoothly, "Aunt in fact, though not in law. Don't distress yourself! Don't weep! Don't tremble! Mrs. Rachael, our young friend has no doubt heard of—the—a—Jarndyce and Jarndyce."

"Never," said Mrs. Rachael.

"Is it possible," pursued Mr. Kenge, putting up his eye-glasses, "that our young friend—I BEG you won't distress yourself!—never heard of Jarndyce and Jarndyce!"

I shook my head, wondering even what it was.

"Not of Jarndyce and Jarndyce?" said Mr. Kenge, looking over his glasses at me and softly turning the case about and about as if he were petting something. "Not of one of the greatest Chancery suits known? Not of Jarndyce and Jarndyce—the—a—in itself a monument of Chancery practice. In which (I would say) every difficulty, every contingency, every masterly fiction, every form of procedure known in that court, is represented over and over again? It is a cause that could not exist out of this free and great country. I should say that the aggregate of costs in Jarndyce and Jarndyce, Mrs. Rachael"—I was afraid he addressed himself to her because I appeared inattentive"—amounts at the present hour to from SIX-ty to SEVEN-ty THOUSAND POUNDS!" said Mr. Kenge, leaning back in his chair.

I felt very ignorant, but what could I do? I was so entirely unacquainted with the subject that I understood nothing about it even then.

"And she really never heard of the cause!" said Mr. Kenge. "Surprising!"

"Miss Barbary, sir," returned Mrs. Rachael, "who is now among the Seraphim—"

"I hope so, I am sure," said Mr. Kenge politely.

"—Wished Esther only to know what would be serviceable to her. And she knows, from any teaching she has had here, nothing more."

"Well!" said Mr. Kenge. "Upon the whole, very proper. Now to the point," addressing me. "Miss Barbary, your sole relation (in fact that is, for I am bound to observe that in law you had none) being deceased and it naturally not being to be expected that Mrs. Rachael—"

"Oh, dear no!" said Mrs. Rachael quickly.

"Quite so," assented Mr. Kenge; "—that Mrs. Rachael should charge herself with your maintenance and support (I beg you won't distress yourself), you are in a position to receive the renewal of an offer which I was instructed to make to Miss Barbary some two years ago and which, though rejected then, was understood to be renewable under the lamentable circumstances that have since occurred. Now, if I avow that I represent, in Jarndyce and Jarndyce and otherwise, a highly humane, but at the same time singular, man, shall I compromise myself by any stretch of my professional caution?" said Mr. Kenge, leaning back in his chair again and looking calmly at us both.

He appeared to enjoy beyond everything the sound of his own voice. I couldn't wonder at that, for it was mellow and full and gave great importance to every word he uttered. He listened to himself with obvious satisfaction and sometimes gently beat time to his own music with his head or rounded a sentence with his hand. I was very much impressed by him—even then, before I knew that he formed himself on the model of a great lord who was his client and that he was generally called Conversation Kenge.

"Mr. Jarndyce," he pursued, "being aware of the—I would say, desolate—position of our young friend, offers to place her at a first-rate establishment where her education shall be completed, where her comfort shall be secured, where her reasonable wants shall be anticipated, where she shall be eminently qualified to discharge her duty in that station of life unto which it has pleased—shall I say Providence?—to call her."

My heart was filled so full, both by what he said and by his affecting manner of saying it, that I was not able to speak, though I tried.

"Mr. Jarndyce," he went on, "makes no condition beyond expressing his expectation that our young friend will not at any time remove herself from the establishment in question without his knowledge and concurrence. That she will faithfully apply herself to the acquisition of those accomplishments, upon the exercise of which she will be ultimately dependent. That she will tread in the paths of virtue and honour, and—the—a—so forth."

I was still less able to speak than before.

"Now, what does our young friend say?" proceeded Mr. Kenge. "Take time, take time! I pause for her reply. But take time!"

What the destitute subject of such an offer tried to say, I need not repeat. What she did say, I could more easily tell, if it were worth the telling. What she felt, and will feel to her dying hour, I could never relate.

This interview took place at Windsor, where I had passed (as far as I knew) my whole life. On that day week, amply provided with all necessaries, I left it, inside the stagecoach, for Reading.

Mrs. Rachael was too good to feel any emotion at parting, but I was not so good, and wept bitterly. I thought that I ought to have known her better after so many years and ought to have made myself enough of a favourite with her to make her sorry then. When she gave me one cold parting kiss upon my forehead, like a thaw-drop from the stone porch—it was a very frosty day—I felt so miserable and self-reproachful that I clung to her and told her it was my fault, I knew, that she could say good-bye so easily!

"No, Esther!" she returned. "It is your misfortune!"

The coach was at the little lawn-gate—we had not come out until we heard the wheels—and thus I left her, with a sorrowful heart. She went in before my boxes were lifted to the coach-roof and shut the door. As long as I could see the house, I looked back at it from the window through my tears. My godmother had left Mrs. Rachael all the little property she possessed; and there was to be a sale; and an old hearth-rug with roses on it, which always seemed to me the first thing in the world I had ever seen, was hanging outside in the frost and snow. A day or two before, I had wrapped the dear old doll in her own shawl and quietly laid her—I am half ashamed to tell it—in the garden-earth under the tree that shaded my old window. I had no companion left but my bird, and him I carried with me in his cage.

When the house was out of sight, I sat, with my bird-cage in the straw at my feet, forward on the low seat to look out of the high window, watching the frosty trees, that were like beautiful pieces of spar, and the fields all smooth and white with last night's snow, and the sun, so red but yielding so little heat, and the ice, dark like metal where the skaters and sliders had brushed the snow away. There was a gentleman in the coach who sat on the opposite seat and looked very large in a quantity of wrappings, but he sat gazing out of the other window and took no notice of me.

I thought of my dead godmother, of the night when I read to her, of her frowning so fixedly and sternly in her bed, of the strange place I was going to, of the people I should find there, and what they would be like, and what they would say to me, when a voice in the coach gave me a terrible start.

It said, "What the de-vil are you crying for?"

I was so frightened that I lost my voice and could only answer in a whisper, "Me, sir?" For of course I knew it must have been the gentleman in the quantity of wrappings, though he was still looking out of his window.

"Yes, you," he said, turning round.

"I didn't know I was crying, sir," I faltered.

"But you are!" said the gentleman. "Look here!" He came quite opposite to me from the other corner of the coach, brushed one of his large furry cuffs across my eyes (but without hurting me), and showed me that it was wet.

"There! Now you know you are," he said. "Don't you?"

"Yes, sir," I said.

"And what are you crying for?" said the gentleman, "Don't you want to go there?"

"Where, sir?"

"Where? Why, wherever you are going," said the gentleman.

"I am very glad to go there, sir," I answered.

"Well, then! Look glad!" said the gentleman.

I thought he was very strange, or at least that what I could see of him was very strange, for he was wrapped up to the chin, and his face was almost hidden in a fur cap with broad fur straps at the side of his head fastened under his chin; but I was composed again, and not afraid of him. So I told him that I thought I must have been crying because of my godmother's death and because of Mrs. Rachael's not being sorry to part with me.

"Confound Mrs. Rachael!" said the gentleman. "Let her fly away in a high wind on a broomstick!"

I began to be really afraid of him now and looked at him with the greatest astonishment. But I thought that he had pleasant eyes, although he kept on muttering to himself in an angry manner and calling Mrs. Rachael names.

After a little while he opened his outer wrapper, which appeared to me large enough to wrap up the whole coach, and put his arm down into a deep pocket in the side.

"Now, look here!" he said. "In this paper," which was nicely folded, "is a piece of the best plum-cake that can be got for money—sugar on the outside an inch thick, like fat on mutton chops. Here's a little pie (a gem this is, both for size and quality), made in France. And what do you suppose it's made of? Livers of fat geese. There's a pie! Now let's see you eat 'em."

"Thank you, sir," I replied; "thank you very much indeed, but I hope you won't be offended—they are too rich for me."

"Floored again!" said the gentleman, which I didn't at all understand, and threw them both out of window.

He did not speak to me any more until he got out of the coach a little way short of Reading, when he advised me to be a good girl and to be studious, and shook hands with me. I must say I was relieved by his departure. We left him at a milestone. I often walked past it afterwards, and never for a long time without thinking of him and half expecting to meet him. But I never did; and so, as time went on, he passed out of my mind.

When the coach stopped, a very neat lady looked up at the window and said, "Miss Donny."

"No, ma'am, Esther Summerson."

"That is quite right," said the lady, "Miss Donny."

I now understood that she introduced herself by that name, and begged Miss Donny's pardon for my mistake, and pointed out my boxes at her request. Under the direction of a very neat maid, they were put outside a very small green carriage; and then Miss Donny, the maid, and I got inside and were driven away.

"Everything is ready for you, Esther," said Miss Donny, "and the scheme of your pursuits has been arranged in exact accordance with the wishes of your guardian, Mr. Jarndyce."

"Of—did you say, ma'am?"

"Of your guardian, Mr. Jarndyce," said Miss Donny.

I was so bewildered that Miss Donny thought the cold had been too severe for me and lent me her smelling-bottle.

"Do you know my—guardian, Mr. Jarndyce, ma'am?" I asked after a good deal of hesitation.

"Not personally, Esther," said Miss Donny; "merely through his solicitors, Messrs. Kenge and Carboy, of London. A very superior gentleman, Mr. Kenge. Truly eloquent indeed. Some of his periods quite majestic!"

I felt this to be very true but was too confused to attend to it. Our speedy arrival at our destination, before I had time to recover myself, increased my confusion, and I never shall forget the uncertain and the unreal air of everything at Greenleaf (Miss Donny's house) that afternoon!

But I soon became used to it. I was so adapted to the routine of Greenleaf before long that I seemed to have been there a great while and almost to have dreamed rather than really lived my old life at my godmother's. Nothing could be more precise, exact, and orderly than Greenleaf. There was a time for everything all round the dial of the clock, and everything was done at its appointed moment.

We were twelve boarders, and there were two Miss Donnys, twins. It was understood that I would have to depend, by and by, on my qualifications as a governess, and I was not only instructed in everything that was taught at Greenleaf, but was very soon engaged in helping to instruct others. Although I was treated in every other respect like the rest of the school, this single difference was made in my case from the first. As I began to know more, I taught more, and so in course of time I had plenty to do, which I was very fond of doing because it made the dear girls fond of me. At last, whenever a new pupil came who was a little downcast and unhappy, she was so sure—indeed I don't know why—to make a friend of me that all new-comers were confided to my care. They said I was so gentle, but I am sure THEY were! I often thought of the resolution I had made on my birthday to try to be industrious, contented, and true-hearted and to do some good to some one and win some love if I could; and indeed, indeed, I felt almost ashamed to have done so little and have won so much.

I passed at Greenleaf six happy, quiet years. I never saw in any face there, thank heaven, on my birthday, that it would have been better if I had never been born. When the day came round, it brought me so many tokens of affectionate remembrance that my room was beautiful with them from New Year's Day to Christmas.

In those six years I had never been away except on visits at holiday time in the neighbourhood. After the first six months or so I had taken Miss Donny's advice in reference to the propriety of writing to Mr. Kenge to say that I was happy and grateful, and with her approval I had written such a letter. I had received a formal answer acknowledging its receipt and saying, "We note the contents thereof, which shall be duly communicated to our client." After that I sometimes heard Miss Donny and her sister mention how regular my accounts were paid, and about twice a year I ventured to write a similar letter. I always received by return of post exactly the same answer in the same round hand, with the signature of Kenge and Carboy in another writing, which I supposed to be Mr. Kenge's.

It seems so curious to me to be obliged to write all this about myself! As if this narrative were the narrative of MY life! But my little body will soon fall into the background now.

Six quiet years (I find I am saying it for the second time) I had passed at Greenleaf, seeing in those around me, as it might be in a looking-glass, every stage of my own growth and change there, when, one November morning, I received this letter. I omit the date.

Old Square, Lincoln's Inn

Madam,

Jarndyce and Jarndyce

Our clt Mr. Jarndyce being abt to rece into his house, under an Order of the Ct of Chy, a Ward of the Ct in this cause, for whom he wishes to secure an elgble compn, directs us to inform you that he will be glad of your serces in the afsd capacity.

We have arrngd for your being forded, carriage free, pr eight o'clock coach from Reading, on Monday morning next, to White Horse Cellar, Piccadilly, London, where one of our clks will be in waiting to convey you to our offe as above.

We are, Madam, Your obedt Servts,

Kenge and Carboy

Miss Esther Summerson

Oh, never, never, never shall I forget the emotion this letter caused in the house! It was so tender in them to care so much for me, it was so gracious in that father who had not forgotten me to have made my orphan way so smooth and easy and to have inclined so many youthful natures towards me, that I could hardly bear it. Not that I would have had them less sorry—I am afraid not; but the pleasure of it, and the pain of it, and the pride and joy of it, and the humble regret of it were so blended that my heart seemed almost breaking while it was full of rapture.

The letter gave me only five days' notice of my removal. When every minute added to the proofs of love and kindness that were given me in those five days, and when at last the morning came and when they took me through all the rooms that I might see them for the last time, and when some cried, "Esther, dear, say good-bye to me here at my bedside, where you first spoke so kindly to me!" and when others asked me only to write their names, "With Esther's love," and when they all surrounded me with their parting presents and clung to me weeping and cried, "What shall we do when dear, dear Esther's gone!" and when I tried to tell them how forbearing and how good they had all been to me and how I blessed and thanked them every one, what a heart I had!

And when the two Miss Donnys grieved as much to part with me as the least among them, and when the maids said, “Bless you, miss, wherever you go!” and when the ugly lame old gardener, who I thought had hardly noticed me in all those years, came panting after the coach to give me a little nosegay of geraniums and told me I had been the light of his eyes—indeed the old man said so!—what a heart I had then!

And could I help it if with all this, and the coming to the little school, and the unexpected sight of the poor children outside waving their hats and bonnets to me, and of a grey-haired gentleman and lady whose daughter I had helped to teach and at whose house I had visited (who were said to be the proudest people in all that country), caring for nothing but calling out, “Good-bye, Esther. May you be very happy!”—could I help it if I was quite bowed down in the coach by myself and said “Oh, I am so thankful, I am so thankful!” many times over!

But of course I soon considered that I must not take tears where I was going after all that had been done for me. Therefore, of course, I made myself sob less and persuaded myself to be quiet by saying very often, “Esther, now you really must! This WILL NOT do!” I cheered myself up pretty well at last, though I am afraid I was longer about it than I ought to have been; and when I had cooled my eyes with lavender water, it was time to watch for London.

I was quite persuaded that we were there when we were ten miles off, and when we really were there, that we should never get there. However, when we began to jolt upon a stone pavement, and particularly when every other conveyance seemed to be running into us, and we seemed to be running into every other conveyance, I began to believe that we really were approaching the end of our journey. Very soon afterwards we stopped.

A young gentleman who had inked himself by accident addressed me from the pavement and said, “I am from Kenge and Carboy’s, miss, of Lincoln’s Inn.”

“If you please, sir,” said I.

He was very obliging, and as he handed me into a fly after superintending the removal of my boxes, I asked him whether there was a great fire anywhere? For the streets were so full of dense brown smoke that scarcely anything was to be seen.

“Oh, dear no, miss,” he said. “This is a London particular.”

I had never heard of such a thing.

“A fog, miss,” said the young gentleman.

“Oh, indeed!” said I.

We drove slowly through the dirtiest and darkest streets that ever were seen in the world (I thought) and in such a distracting state of confusion that I wondered how the people kept their senses, until we passed into sudden quietude under an old gateway and drove on through a silent square until we came to an odd nook in a corner, where there was an entrance up a steep, broad flight of stairs, like an entrance to a church. And there really was a churchyard outside under some cloisters, for I saw the gravestones from the staircase window.

This was Kenge and Carboy's. The young gentleman showed me through an outer office into Mr. Kenge's room—there was no one in it—and politely put an arm-chair for me by the fire. He then called my attention to a little looking-glass hanging from a nail on one side of the chimney-piece.

"In case you should wish to look at yourself, miss, after the journey, as you're going before the Chancellor. Not that it's requisite, I am sure," said the young gentleman civilly.

"Going before the Chancellor?" I said, startled for a moment.

"Only a matter of form, miss," returned the young gentleman. "Mr. Kenge is in court now. He left his compliments, and would you partake of some refreshment"—there were biscuits and a decanter of wine on a small table—"and look over the paper," which the young gentleman gave me as he spoke. He then stirred the fire and left me.

Everything was so strange—the stranger from its being night in the daytime, the candles burning with a white flame, and looking raw and cold—that I read the words in the newspaper without knowing what they meant and found myself reading the same words repeatedly. As it was of no use going on in that way, I put the paper down, took a peep at my bonnet in the glass to see if it was neat, and looked at the room, which was not half lighted, and at the shabby, dusty tables, and at the piles of writings, and at a bookcase full of the most inexpressive-looking books that ever had anything to say for themselves. Then I went on, thinking, thinking, thinking; and the fire went on, burning, burning, burning; and the candles went on flickering and guttering, and there were no snuffers—until the young gentleman by and by brought a very dirty pair—for two hours.

At last Mr. Kenge came. HE was not altered, but he was surprised to see how altered I was and appeared quite pleased. "As you are going to be the companion of the young lady who is now in the Chancellor's private room, Miss Summerson," he said, "we thought it well that you should be in attendance also. You will not be discomposed by the Lord Chancellor, I dare say?"

"No, sir," I said, "I don't think I shall," really not seeing on consideration why I should be.

So Mr. Kenge gave me his arm and we went round the corner, under a colonnade, and in at a side door. And so we came, along a passage, into a comfortable sort of room where a young lady and a young gentleman were standing near a great, loud-roaring fire. A screen was interposed between them and it, and they were leaning on the screen, talking.

They both looked up when I came in, and I saw in the young lady, with the fire shining upon her, such a beautiful girl! With such rich golden hair, such soft blue eyes, and such a bright, innocent, trusting face!

"Miss Ada," said Mr. Kenge, "this is Miss Summerson."

She came to meet me with a smile of welcome and her hand extended, but seemed to change her mind in a moment and kissed me. In short, she had such a natural, captivating, winning manner that in a few minutes we were sitting in the window-seat, with the light of the fire upon us, talking together as free and happy as could be.

What a load off my mind! It was so delightful to know that she could confide in me and like me! It was so good of her, and so encouraging to me!

The young gentleman was her distant cousin, she told me, and his name Richard Carstone. He was a handsome youth with an ingenuous face and a most engaging laugh; and after she had called him up to where we sat, he stood by us, in the light of the fire, talking gaily, like a light-hearted boy. He was very young, not more than nineteen then, if quite so much, but nearly two years older than she was. They were both orphans and (what was very unexpected and curious to me) had never met before that day. Our all three coming together for the first time in such an unusual place was a thing to talk about, and we talked about it; and the fire, which had left off roaring, winked its red eyes at us—as Richard said—like a drowsy old Chancery lion.

We conversed in a low tone because a full-dressed gentleman in a bag wig frequently came in and out, and when he did so, we could hear a drawling sound in the distance, which he said was one of the counsel in our case addressing the Lord Chancellor. He told Mr. Kenge that the Chancellor would be up in five minutes; and presently we heard a bustle and a tread of feet, and Mr. Kenge said that the Court had risen and his lordship was in the next room.

The gentleman in the bag wig opened the door almost directly and requested Mr. Kenge to come in. Upon that, we all went into the next room, Mr. Kenge first, with my darling—it is so natural to me now that I can't help writing it; and there, plainly dressed in black and sitting in an arm-chair at a table near the fire, was his lordship, whose robe, trimmed with beautiful gold lace, was thrown upon another chair. He gave us a searching look as we entered, but his manner was both courtly and kind.

The gentleman in the bag wig laid bundles of papers on his lordship's table, and his lordship silently selected one and turned over the leaves.

"Miss Clare," said the Lord Chancellor. "Miss Ada Clare?"

Mr. Kenge presented her, and his lordship begged her to sit down near him. That he admired her and was interested by her even I could see in a moment. It touched me that the home of such a beautiful young creature should be represented by that dry, official place. The Lord High Chancellor, at his best, appeared so poor a substitute for the love and pride of parents.

"The Jarndyce in question," said the Lord Chancellor, still turning over leaves, "is Jarndyce of Bleak House."

"Jarndyce of Bleak House, my lord," said Mr. Kenge.

"A dreary name," said the Lord Chancellor.

"But not a dreary place at present, my lord," said Mr. Kenge.

"And Bleak House," said his lordship, "is in—"

"Hertfordshire, my lord."

"Mr. Jarndyce of Bleak House is not married?" said his lordship.

"He is not, my lord," said Mr. Kenge.

A pause.

"Young Mr. Richard Carstone is present?" said the Lord Chancellor, glancing towards him.

Richard bowed and stepped forward.

"Hum!" said the Lord Chancellor, turning over more leaves.

"Mr. Jarndyce of Bleak House, my lord," Mr. Kenge observed in a low voice, "if I may venture to remind your lordship, provides a suitable companion for—"

"For Mr. Richard Carstone?" I thought (but I am not quite sure) I heard his lordship say in an equally low voice and with a smile.

"For Miss Ada Clare. This is the young lady. Miss Summerson."

His lordship gave me an indulgent look and acknowledged my curtsy very graciously.

"Miss Summerson is not related to any party in the cause, I think?"

"No, my lord."

Mr. Kenge leant over before it was quite said and whispered. His lordship, with his eyes upon his papers, listened, nodded twice or thrice, turned over more leaves, and did not look towards me again until we were going away.

Mr. Kenge now retired, and Richard with him, to where I was, near the door, leaving my pet (it is so natural to me that again I can't help it!) sitting near the Lord Chancellor, with whom his lordship spoke a little part, asking her, as she told me afterwards, whether she had well reflected on the proposed arrangement, and if she thought she would be happy under the roof of Mr. Jarndyce of Bleak House, and why she thought so? Presently he rose courteously and released her, and then he spoke for a minute or two with Richard Carstone, not seated, but standing, and altogether with more ease and less ceremony, as if he still knew, though he WAS Lord Chancellor, how to go straight to the candour of a boy.

"Very well!" said his lordship aloud. "I shall make the order. Mr. Jarndyce of Bleak House has chosen, so far as I may judge," and this was when he looked at me, "a very good companion for the young lady, and the arrangement altogether seems the best of which the circumstances admit."

He dismissed us pleasantly, and we all went out, very much obliged to him for being so affable and polite, by which he had certainly lost no dignity but seemed to us to have gained some.

When we got under the colonnade, Mr. Kenge remembered that he must go back for a moment to ask a question and left us in the fog, with the Lord Chancellor's carriage and servants waiting for him to come out.

"Well!" said Richard Carstone. "THAT'S over! And where do we go next, Miss Summerson?"

"Don't you know?" I said.

"Not in the least," said he.

"And don't YOU know, my love?" I asked Ada.

"No!" said she. "Don't you?"

"Not at all!" said I.

We looked at one another, half laughing at our being like the children in the wood, when a curious little old woman in a squeezed bonnet and carrying a reticule came curtsying and smiling up to us with an air of great ceremony.

"Oh!" said she. "The wards in Jarndyce! Ve-ry happy, I am sure, to have the honour! It is a good omen for youth, and hope, and beauty when they find themselves in this place, and don't know what's to come of it."

"Mad!" whispered Richard, not thinking she could hear him.

"Right! Mad, young gentleman," she returned so quickly that he was quite abashed. "I was a ward myself. I was not mad at that time," curtsying low and smiling between every little sentence. "I had youth and hope. I believe, beauty. It matters very little now. Neither of the three served or saved me. I have the honour to attend court regularly. With my documents. I expect a judgment. Shortly. On the Day of Judgment. I have discovered that the sixth seal mentioned in the Revelations is the Great Seal. It has been open a long time! Pray accept my blessing."

As Ada was a little frightened, I said, to humour the poor old lady, that we were much obliged to her.

"Ye-es!" she said mincingly. "I imagine so. And here is Conversation Kenge. With HIS documents! How does your honourable worship do?"

"Quite well, quite well! Now don't be troublesome, that's a good soul!" said Mr. Kenge, leading the way back.

"By no means," said the poor old lady, keeping up with Ada and me. "Anything but troublesome. I shall confer estates on both—which is not being troublesome, I trust? I expect a judgment. Shortly. On the Day of Judgment. This is a good omen for you. Accept my blessing!"

She stopped at the bottom of the steep, broad flight of stairs; but we looked back as we went up, and she was still there, saying, still with a curtsy and a smile between every little sentence, "Youth. And hope. And beauty. And Chancery. And Conversation Kenge! Ha! Pray accept my blessing!"

CHAPTER IV
TELESCOPIC PHILANTHROPY

We were to pass the night, Mr. Kenge told us when we arrived in his room, at Mrs. Jellyby's; and then he turned to me and said he took it for granted I knew who Mrs. Jellyby was.

"I really don't, sir," I returned. "Perhaps Mr. Carstone—or Miss Clare—"

But no, they knew nothing whatever about Mrs. Jellyby. "In-deed! Mrs. Jellyby," said Mr. Kenge, standing with his back to the fire and casting his eyes over the dusty hearth-rug as if it were Mrs. Jellyby's biography, "is a lady of very remarkable strength of character who devotes herself entirely to the public. She has devoted herself to an extensive variety of public subjects at various times and is at present (until something else attracts her) devoted to the subject of Africa, with a view to the general cultivation of the coffee berry—AND the natives—and the happy settlement, on the banks of the African rivers, of our superabundant home population. Mr. Jarndyce, who is desirous to aid any work that is considered likely to be a good work and who is much sought after by philanthropists, has, I believe, a very high opinion of Mrs. Jellyby."

Mr. Kenge, adjusting his cravat, then looked at us.

"And Mr. Jellyby, sir?" suggested Richard.

"Ah! Mr. Jellyby," said Mr. Kenge, "is—a—I don't know that I can describe him to you better than by saying that he is the husband of Mrs. Jellyby."

"A nonentity, sir?" said Richard with a droll look.

"I don't say that," returned Mr. Kenge gravely. "I can't say that, indeed, for I know nothing whatever OF Mr. Jellyby. I never, to my knowledge, had the pleasure of seeing Mr. Jellyby. He may be a very superior man, but he is, so to speak, merged—merged—in the more shining qualities of his wife." Mr. Kenge proceeded to tell us that as the road to Bleak House would have been very long, dark, and tedious on such an evening, and as we had been travelling already, Mr. Jarndyce had himself proposed this arrangement. A carriage would be at Mrs. Jellyby's to convey us out of town early in the forenoon of to-morrow.

He then rang a little bell, and the young gentleman came in. Addressing him by the name of Guppy, Mr. Kenge inquired whether Miss Summerson's boxes and the rest of the baggage had been "sent round." Mr. Guppy said yes, they had been sent round, and a coach was waiting to take us round too as soon as we pleased.

"Then it only remains," said Mr. Kenge, shaking hands with us, "for me to express my lively satisfaction in (good day, Miss Clare!) the arrangement this day concluded and my (GOOD-bye to you, Miss Summerson!) lively hope that it will conduce to the happiness, the (glad to have had the honour of making your acquaintance, Mr. Carstone!) welfare, the advantage in all points of view, of all concerned! Guppy, see the party safely there."

"Where IS 'there,' Mr. Guppy?" said Richard as we went downstairs.

"No distance," said Mr. Guppy; "round in Thavies Inn, you know."

"I can't say I know where it is, for I come from Winchester and am strange in London."

"Only round the corner," said Mr. Guppy. "We just twist up Chancery Lane, and cut along Holborn, and there we are in four minutes' time, as near as a toucher. This is about a London particular NOW, ain't it, miss?" He seemed quite delighted with it on my account.

"The fog is very dense indeed!" said I.

"Not that it affects you, though, I'm sure," said Mr. Guppy, putting up the steps. "On the contrary, it seems to do you good, miss, judging from your appearance."

I knew he meant well in paying me this compliment, so I laughed at myself for blushing at it when he had shut the door and got upon the box; and we all three laughed and chatted about our inexperience and the strangeness of London until we turned up under an archway to our destination—a narrow street of high houses like an oblong cistern to hold the fog. There was a confused little crowd of people, principally children, gathered about the house at which we stopped, which had a tarnished brass plate on the door with the inscription JELLYBY.

"Don't be frightened!" said Mr. Guppy, looking in at the coach-window. "One of the young Jellybys been and got his head through the area railings!"

"Oh, poor child," said I; "let me out, if you please!"

"Pray be careful of yourself, miss. The young Jellybys are always up to something," said Mr. Guppy.

I made my way to the poor child, who was one of the dirtiest little unfortunates I ever saw, and found him very hot and frightened and crying loudly, fixed by the neck between two iron railings, while a milkman and a beadle, with the kindest intentions possible, were endeavouring to drag him back by the legs, under a general impression that his skull was compressible by those means. As I found (after pacifying him) that he was a little boy with a naturally large head, I thought that perhaps where his head could go, his body could follow, and mentioned that the best mode of extrication might be to push him forward. This was so favourably received by the milkman and beadle that he would immediately have been pushed into the area if I had not held his pinafore while Richard and Mr. Guppy ran down through the kitchen to catch him when he should be released. At last he was happily got down without any accident, and then he began to beat Mr. Guppy with a hoop-stick in quite a frantic manner.

Nobody had appeared belonging to the house except a person in pattens, who had been poking at the child from below with a broom; I don't know with what object, and I don't think she did. I therefore supposed that Mrs. Jellyby was not at home, and was quite surprised when the person appeared in the passage without the pattens, and going up to the back room on the first floor before Ada and me, announced us as, "Them two young ladies, Missis Jellyby!" We passed several more children on the way up, whom it was difficult to avoid treading on in the dark; and as we came into Mrs. Jellyby's presence, one of the poor little things fell downstairs—down a whole flight (as it sounded to me), with a great noise.

Mrs. Jellyby, whose face reflected none of the uneasiness which we could not help showing in our own faces as the dear child's head recorded its passage with a bump on every stair—Richard afterwards said he counted seven, besides one for the landing—received us with perfect equanimity. She was a pretty, very diminutive, plump woman of from forty to fifty, with handsome eyes, though they had a curious habit of seeming to look a long way off. As if—I am quoting Richard again—they could see nothing nearer than Africa!

"I am very glad indeed," said Mrs. Jellyby in an agreeable voice, "to have the pleasure of receiving you. I have a great respect for Mr. Jarndyce, and no one in whom he is interested can be an object of indifference to me."

We expressed our acknowledgments and sat down behind the door, where there was a lame invalid of a sofa. Mrs. Jellyby had very good hair but was too much occupied with her African duties to brush it. The shawl in which she had been loosely muffled dropped onto her chair when she advanced to us; and as she turned to resume her seat, we could not help noticing that her dress didn't nearly meet up the back and that the open space was railed across with a lattice-work of stay-lace—like a summer-house.

The room, which was strewn with papers and nearly filled by a great writing-table covered with similar litter, was, I must say, not only very untidy but very dirty. We were obliged to take notice of that with our sense of sight, even while, with our sense of hearing, we followed the poor child who had tumbled downstairs: I think into the back kitchen, where somebody seemed to stifle him.

But what principally struck us was a jaded and unhealthy-looking though by no means plain girl at the writing-table, who sat biting the feather of her pen and staring at us. I suppose nobody ever was in such a state of ink. And from her tumbled hair to her pretty feet, which were disfigured with frayed and broken satin slippers trodden down at heel, she really seemed to have no article of dress upon her, from a pin upwards, that was in its proper condition or its right place.

"You find me, my dears," said Mrs. Jellyby, snuffing the two great office candles in tin candlesticks, which made the room taste strongly of hot tallow (the fire had gone out, and there was nothing in the grate but ashes, a bundle of wood, and a poker), "you find me, my dears, as usual, very busy; but that you will excuse. The African project at present employs my whole time. It involves me in correspondence with public bodies and with private individuals anxious for the welfare of their species all over the country. I am happy to say it is advancing. We hope by this time next year to have from a hundred and fifty to two hundred healthy families cultivating coffee and educating the natives of Borrioboola-Gha, on the left bank of the Niger."

As Ada said nothing, but looked at me, I said it must be very gratifying.

"It IS gratifying," said Mrs. Jellyby. "It involves the devotion of all my energies, such as they are; but that is nothing, so that it succeeds; and I am more confident of success every day. Do you know, Miss Summerson, I almost wonder that YOU never turned your thoughts to Africa."

This application of the subject was really so unexpected to me that I was quite at a loss how to receive it. I hinted that the climate—

"The finest climate in the world!" said Mrs. Jellyby.

"Indeed, ma'am?"

"Certainly. With precaution," said Mrs. Jellyby. "You may go into Holborn, without precaution, and be run over. You may go into Holborn, with precaution, and never be run over. Just so with Africa."

I said, "No doubt." I meant as to Holborn.

"If you would like," said Mrs. Jellyby, putting a number of papers towards us, "to look over some remarks on that head, and on the general subject, which have been extensively circulated, while I finish a letter I am now dictating to my eldest daughter, who is my amanuensis—"

The girl at the table left off biting her pen and made a return to our recognition, which was half bashful and half sulky.

"—I shall then have finished for the present," proceeded Mrs. Jellyby with a sweet smile, "though my work is never done. Where are you, Caddy?"

"'Presents her compliments to Mr. Swallow, and begs—'" said Caddy.

"'And begs,'" said Mrs. Jellyby, dictating, "'to inform him, in reference to his letter of inquiry on the African project—' No, Peepy! Not on my account!"

Peepy (so self-named) was the unfortunate child who had fallen downstairs, who now interrupted the correspondence by presenting himself, with a strip of plaster on his forehead, to exhibit his wounded knees, in which Ada and I did not know which to pity most—the bruises or the dirt. Mrs. Jellyby merely added, with the serene composure with which she said everything, "Go along, you naughty Peepy!" and fixed her fine eyes on Africa again.

However, as she at once proceeded with her dictation, and as I interrupted nothing by doing it, I ventured quietly to stop poor Peepy as he was going out and to take him up to nurse. He looked very much astonished at it and at Ada's kissing him, but soon fell fast asleep in my arms, sobbing at longer and longer intervals, until he was quiet. I was so occupied with Peepy that I lost the letter in detail, though I derived such a general impression from it of the momentous importance of Africa, and the utter insignificance of all other places and things, that I felt quite ashamed to have thought so little about it.

"Six o'clock!" said Mrs. Jellyby. "And our dinner hour is nominally (for we dine at all hours) five! Caddy, show Miss Clare and Miss Summerson their rooms. You will like to make some change, perhaps? You will excuse me, I know, being so much occupied. Oh, that very bad child! Pray put him down, Miss Summerson!"

I begged permission to retain him, truly saying that he was not at all troublesome, and carried him upstairs and laid him on my bed. Ada and I had two upper rooms with a door of communication between. They were excessively bare and disorderly, and the curtain to my window was fastened up with a fork.

"You would like some hot water, wouldn't you?" said Miss Jellyby, looking round for a jug with a handle to it, but looking in vain.

"If it is not being troublesome," said we.

"Oh, it's not the trouble," returned Miss Jellyby; "the question is, if there IS any."

The evening was so very cold and the rooms had such a marshy smell that I must confess it was a little miserable, and Ada was half crying. We soon laughed, however, and were busily unpacking when Miss Jellyby came back to say that she was sorry there was no hot water, but they couldn't find the kettle, and the boiler was out of order.

We begged her not to mention it and made all the haste we could to get down to the fire again. But all the little children had come up to the landing outside to look at the phenomenon of Peepy lying on my bed, and our attention was distracted by the constant apparition of noses and fingers in situations of danger between the hinges of the doors. It was impossible to shut the door of either room, for my lock, with no knob to it, looked as if it wanted to be wound up; and though the handle of Ada's went round and round with the greatest smoothness, it was attended with no effect whatever on the door. Therefore I proposed to the children that they should come in and be very good at my table, and I would tell them the story of Little Red Riding Hood while I dressed; which they did, and were as quiet as mice, including Peepy, who awoke opportunely before the appearance of the wolf.

When we went downstairs we found a mug with "A Present from Tunbridge Wells" on it lighted up in the staircase window with a floating wick, and a young woman, with a swelled face bound up in a flannel bandage blowing the fire of the drawing-room (now connected by an open door with Mrs. Jellyby's room) and choking dreadfully. It smoked to that degree, in short, that we all sat coughing and crying with the windows open for half an hour, during which Mrs. Jellyby, with the same sweetness of temper, directed letters about Africa. Her being so employed was, I must say, a great relief to me, for Richard told us that he had washed his hands in a pie-dish and that they had found the kettle on his dressing-table, and he made Ada laugh so that they made me laugh in the most ridiculous manner.

Soon after seven o'clock we went down to dinner, carefully, by Mrs. Jellyby's advice, for the stair-carpets, besides being very deficient in stair-wires, were so torn as to be absolute traps. We had a fine cod-fish, a piece of roast beef, a dish of cutlets, and a pudding; an excellent dinner, if it had had any cooking to speak of, but it was almost raw. The young woman with the flannel bandage waited, and dropped everything on the table wherever it happened to go, and never moved it again until she put it on the stairs. The person I had seen in pattens, who I suppose to have been the cook, frequently came and skirmished with her at the door, and there appeared to be ill will between them.

All through dinner—which was long, in consequence of such accidents as the dish of potatoes being mislaid in the coal skuttle and the handle of the corkscrew coming off and striking the young woman in the chin—Mrs. Jellyby preserved the evenness of her disposition. She told us a great deal that was interesting about Borrioboola-Gha and the natives, and received so many letters that Richard, who sat by her, saw four envelopes in the gravy at once. Some of the letters were proceedings of ladies' committees or resolutions of ladies' meetings, which she read to us; others were applications from people excited in various ways about the cultivation of coffee, and natives; others required answers, and these she sent her eldest daughter from the table three or four times to write. She was full of business and undoubtedly was, as she had told us, devoted to the cause.

I was a little curious to know who a mild bald gentleman in spectacles was, who dropped into a vacant chair (there was no top or bottom in particular) after the fish was taken away and seemed passively to submit himself to Borrioboola-Gha but not to be actively interested in that settlement. As he never spoke a word, he might have been a native but for his complexion. It was not until we left the table and he remained alone with Richard that the possibility of his being Mr. Jellyby ever entered my head. But he WAS Mr. Jellyby; and a loquacious young man called Mr. Quale, with large shining knobs for temples and his hair all brushed to the back of his head, who came in the evening, and told Ada he was a philanthropist, also informed her that he called the matrimonial alliance of Mrs. Jellyby with Mr. Jellyby the union of mind and matter.

This young man, besides having a great deal to say for himself about Africa and a project of his for teaching the coffee colonists to teach the natives to turn piano-forte legs and establish an export trade, delighted in drawing Mrs. Jellyby out by saying, "I believe now, Mrs. Jellyby, you have received as many as from one hundred and fifty to two hundred letters respecting Africa in a single day, have you not?" or, "If my memory does not deceive me, Mrs. Jellyby, you once mentioned that you had sent off five thousand circulars from one post-office at one time?"—always repeating Mrs. Jellyby's answer to us like an interpreter. During the whole evening, Mr. Jellyby sat in a corner with his head against the wall as if he were subject to low spirits. It seemed that he had several times opened his mouth when alone with Richard after dinner, as if he had something on his mind, but had always shut it again, to Richard's extreme confusion, without saying anything.

Mrs. Jellyby, sitting in quite a nest of waste paper, drank coffee all the evening and dictated at intervals to her eldest daughter. She also held a discussion with Mr. Quale, of which the subject seemed to be—if I understood it—the brotherhood of humanity, and gave utterance to some beautiful sentiments. I was not so attentive an auditor as I might have wished to be, however, for Peepy and the other children came flocking about Ada and me in a corner of the drawing-room to ask for another story; so we sat down among them and told them in whispers "Puss in Boots" and I don't know what else until Mrs. Jellyby, accidentally remembering them, sent them to bed. As Peepy cried for me to take him to bed, I carried him upstairs, where the young woman with the flannel bandage charged into the midst of the little family like a dragon and overturned them into cribs.

After that I occupied myself in making our room a little tidy and in coaxing a very cross fire that had been lighted to burn, which at last it did, quite brightly. On my return downstairs, I felt that Mrs. Jellyby looked down upon me rather for being so frivolous, and I was sorry for it, though at the same time I knew that I had no higher pretensions.

It was nearly midnight before we found an opportunity of going to bed, and even then we left Mrs. Jellyby among her papers drinking coffee and Miss Jellyby biting the feather of her pen.

"What a strange house!" said Ada when we got upstairs. "How curious of my cousin Jarndyce to send us here!"

"My love," said I, "it quite confuses me. I want to understand it, and I can't understand it at all."

"What?" asked Ada with her pretty smile.

"All this, my dear," said I. "It MUST be very good of Mrs. Jellyby to take such pains about a scheme for the benefit of natives—and yet—Peepy and the housekeeping!"

Ada laughed and put her arm about my neck as I stood looking at the fire, and told me I was a quiet, dear, good creature and had won her heart. "You are so thoughtful, Esther," she said, "and yet so cheerful! And you do so much, so unpretendingly! You would make a home out of even this house."

My simple darling! She was quite unconscious that she only praised herself and that it was in the goodness of her own heart that she made so much of me!

"May I ask you a question?" said I when we had sat before the fire a little while.

"Five hundred," said Ada.

"Your cousin, Mr. Jarndyce. I owe so much to him. Would you mind describing him to me?"

Shaking her golden hair, Ada turned her eyes upon me with such laughing wonder that I was full of wonder too, partly at her beauty, partly at her surprise.

"Esther!" she cried.

"My dear!"

"You want a description of my cousin Jarndyce?"

"My dear, I never saw him."

"And I never saw him!" returned Ada.

Well, to be sure!

No, she had never seen him. Young as she was when her mama died, she remembered how the tears would come into her eyes when she spoke of him and of the noble generosity of his character, which she had said was to be trusted above all earthly things; and Ada trusted it. Her cousin Jarndyce had written to her a few months ago—"a plain, honest letter," Ada said—proposing the arrangement we were now to enter on and telling her that "in time it might heal some of the wounds made by the miserable Chancery suit." She had replied, gratefully accepting his proposal. Richard had received a similar letter and had made a similar response. He HAD seen Mr. Jarndyce once, but only once, five years ago, at Winchester school. He had told Ada, when they were leaning on the screen before the fire where I found them, that he recollected him as "a bluff, rosy fellow." This was the utmost description Ada could give me.

It set me thinking so that when Ada was asleep, I still remained before the fire, wondering and wondering about Bleak House, and wondering and wondering that yesterday morning should seem so long ago. I don't know where my thoughts had wandered when they were recalled by a tap at the door.

I opened it softly and found Miss Jellyby shivering there with a broken candle in a broken candlestick in one hand and an egg-cup in the other.

"Good night!" she said very sulkily.

"Good night!" said I.

"May I come in?" she shortly and unexpectedly asked me in the same sulky way.

"Certainly," said I. "Don't wake Miss Clare."

She would not sit down, but stood by the fire dipping her inky middle finger in the egg-cup, which contained vinegar, and smearing it over the ink stains on her face, frowning the whole time and looking very gloomy.

"I wish Africa was dead!" she said on a sudden.

I was going to remonstrate.

"I do!" she said "Don't talk to me, Miss Summerson. I hate it and detest it. It's a beast!"

I told her she was tired, and I was sorry. I put my hand upon her head, and touched her forehead, and said it was hot now but would be cool to-morrow. She still stood pouting and frowning at me, but presently put down her egg-cup and turned softly towards the bed where Ada lay.

"She is very pretty!" she said with the same knitted brow and in the same uncivil manner.

I assented with a smile.

"An orphan. Ain't she?"

"Yes."

"But knows a quantity, I suppose? Can dance, and play music, and sing? She can talk French, I suppose, and do geography, and globes, and needlework, and everything?"

"No doubt," said I.

"I can't," she returned. "I can't do anything hardly, except write. I'm always writing for Ma. I wonder you two were not ashamed of yourselves to come in this afternoon and see me able to do nothing else. It was like your ill nature. Yet you think yourselves very fine, I dare say!"

I could see that the poor girl was near crying, and I resumed my chair without speaking and looked at her (I hope) as mildly as I felt towards her.

"It's disgraceful," she said. "You know it is. The whole house is disgraceful. The children are disgraceful. I'M disgraceful. Pa's miserable, and no wonder! Priscilla drinks—she's always drinking. It's a great shame and a great story of you if you say you didn't smell her to-day. It was as bad as a public-house, waiting at dinner; you know it was!"

"My dear, I don't know it," said I.

"You do," she said very shortly. "You shan't say you don't. You do!"

"Oh, my dear!" said I. "If you won't let me speak—"

"You're speaking now. You know you are. Don't tell stories, Miss Summerson."

"My dear," said I, "as long as you won't hear me out—"

"I don't want to hear you out."

"Oh, yes, I think you do," said I, "because that would be so very unreasonable. I did not know what you tell me because the servant did not come near me at dinner; but I don't doubt what you tell me, and I am sorry to hear it."

"You needn't make a merit of that," said she.

"No, my dear," said I. "That would be very foolish."

She was still standing by the bed, and now stooped down (but still with the same discontented face) and kissed Ada. That done, she came softly back and stood by the side of my chair. Her bosom was heaving in a distressful manner that I greatly pitied, but I thought it better not to speak.

"I wish I was dead!" she broke out. "I wish we were all dead. It would be a great deal better for us."

In a moment afterwards, she knelt on the ground at my side, hid her face in my dress, passionately begged my pardon, and wept. I comforted her and would have raised her, but she cried no, no; she wanted to stay there!

"You used to teach girls," she said, "If you could only have taught me, I could have learnt from you! I am so very miserable, and I like you so much!"

I could not persuade her to sit by me or to do anything but move a ragged stool to where she was kneeling, and take that, and still hold my dress in the same manner. By degrees the poor tired girl fell asleep, and then I contrived to raise her head so that it should rest on my lap, and to cover us both with shawls. The fire went out, and all night long she slumbered thus before the ashy grate. At first I was painfully awake and vainly tried to lose myself, with my eyes closed, among the scenes of the day. At length, by slow degrees, they became indistinct and mingled. I began to lose the identity of the sleeper resting on me. Now it was Ada, now one of my old Reading friends from whom I could not believe I had so recently parted. Now it was the little mad woman worn out with curtsying and smiling, now some one in authority at Bleak House. Lastly, it was no one, and I was no one.

The purblind day was feebly struggling with the fog when I opened my eyes to encounter those of a dirty-faced little spectre fixed upon me. Peepy had scaled his crib, and crept down in his bed-gown and cap, and was so cold that his teeth were chattering as if he had cut them all.

CHAPTER V
A MORNING ADVENTURE

Although the morning was raw, and although the fog still seemed heavy—I say seemed, for the windows were so encrusted with dirt that they would have made midsummer sunshine dim—I was sufficiently forewarned of the discomfort within doors at that early hour and sufficiently curious about London to think it a good idea on the part of Miss Jellyby when she proposed that we should go out for a walk.

"Ma won't be down for ever so long," she said, "and then it's a chance if breakfast's ready for an hour afterwards, they dawdle so. As to Pa, he gets what he can and goes to the office. He never has what you would call a regular breakfast. Priscilla leaves him out the loaf and some milk, when there is any, overnight. Sometimes there isn't any milk, and sometimes the cat drinks it. But I'm afraid you must be tired, Miss Summerson, and perhaps you would rather go to bed."

"I am not at all tired, my dear," said I, "and would much prefer to go out."

"If you're sure you would," returned Miss Jellyby, "I'll get my things on."

Ada said she would go too, and was soon astir. I made a proposal to Peepy, in default of being able to do anything better for him, that he should let me wash him and afterwards lay him down on my bed again. To this he submitted with the best grace possible, staring at me during the whole operation as if he never had been, and never could again be, so astonished in his life—looking very miserable also, certainly, but making no complaint, and going snugly to sleep as soon as it was over. At first I was in two minds about taking such a liberty, but I soon reflected that nobody in the house was likely to notice it.

What with the bustle of dispatching Peepy and the bustle of getting myself ready and helping Ada, I was soon quite in a glow. We found Miss Jellyby trying to warm herself at the fire in the writing-room, which Priscilla was then lighting with a smutty parlour candlestick, throwing the candle in to make it burn better. Everything was just as we had left it last night and was evidently intended to remain so. Below-stairs the dinner-cloth had not been taken away, but had been left ready for breakfast. Crumbs, dust, and waste-paper were all over the house. Some pewter pots and a milk-can hung on the area railings; the door stood open; and we met the cook round the corner coming out of a public-house, wiping her mouth. She mentioned, as she passed us, that she had been to see what o'clock it was.

But before we met the cook, we met Richard, who was dancing up and down Thavies Inn to warm his feet. He was agreeably surprised to see us stirring so soon and said he would gladly share our walk. So he took care of Ada, and Miss Jellyby and I went first. I may mention that Miss Jellyby had relapsed into her sulky manner and that I really should not have thought she liked me much unless she had told me so.

"Where would you wish to go?" she asked.

"Anywhere, my dear," I replied.

"Anywhere's nowhere," said Miss Jellyby, stopping perversely.

"Let us go somewhere at any rate," said I.

She then walked me on very fast.

"I don't care!" she said. "Now, you are my witness, Miss Summerson, I say I don't care—but if he was to come to our house with his great, shining, lumpy forehead night after night till he was as old as Methuselah, I wouldn't have anything to say to him. Such ASSES as he and Ma make of themselves!"

"My dear!" I remonstrated, in allusion to the epithet and the vigorous emphasis Miss Jellyby set upon it. "Your duty as a child—"

"Oh! Don't talk of duty as a child, Miss Summerson; where's Ma's duty as a parent? All made over to the public and Africa, I suppose! Then let the public and Africa show duty as a child; it's much more their affair than mine. You are shocked, I dare say! Very well, so am I shocked too; so we are both shocked, and there's an end of it!"

She walked me on faster yet.

"But for all that, I say again, he may come, and come, and come, and I won't have anything to say to him. I can't bear him. If there's any stuff in the world that I hate and detest, it's the stuff he and Ma talk. I wonder the very paving-stones opposite our house can have the patience to stay there and be a witness of such inconsistencies and contradictions as all that sounding nonsense, and Ma's management!"

I could not but understand her to refer to Mr. Quale, the young gentleman who had appeared after dinner yesterday. I was saved the disagreeable necessity of pursuing the subject by Richard and Ada coming up at a round pace, laughing and asking us if we meant to run a race. Thus interrupted, Miss Jellyby became silent and walked moodily on at my side while I admired the long successions and varieties of streets, the quantity of people already going to and fro, the number of vehicles passing and repassing, the busy preparations in the setting forth of shop windows and the sweeping out of shops, and the extraordinary creatures in rags secretly groping among the swept-out rubbish for pins and other refuse.

"So, cousin," said the cheerful voice of Richard to Ada behind me. "We are never to get out of Chancery! We have come by another way to our place of meeting yesterday, and—by the Great Seal, here's the old lady again!"

Truly, there she was, immediately in front of us, curtsying, and smiling, and saying with her yesterday's air of patronage, "The wards in Jarndyce! Ve-ry happy, I am sure!"

"You are out early, ma'am," said I as she curtsied to me.

"Ye-es! I usually walk here early. Before the court sits. It's retired. I collect my thoughts here for the business of the day," said the old lady mincingly. "The business of the day requires a great deal of thought. Chancery justice is so ve-ry difficult to follow."

"Who's this, Miss Summerson?" whispered Miss Jellyby, drawing my arm tighter through her own.

The little old lady's hearing was remarkably quick. She answered for herself directly.

"A suitor, my child. At your service. I have the honour to attend court regularly. With my documents. Have I the pleasure of addressing another of the youthful parties in Jarndyce?" said the old lady, recovering herself, with her head on one side, from a very low curtsy.

Richard, anxious to atone for his thoughtlessness of yesterday, good-naturedly explained that Miss Jellyby was not connected with the suit.

"Ha!" said the old lady. "She does not expect a judgment? She will still grow old. But not so old. Oh, dear, no! This is the garden of Lincoln's Inn. I call it my garden. It is quite a bower in the summer-time. Where the birds sing melodiously. I pass the greater part of the long vacation here. In contemplation. You find the long vacation exceedingly long, don't you?"

We said yes, as she seemed to expect us to say so.

"When the leaves are falling from the trees and there are no more flowers in bloom to make up into nosegays for the Lord Chancellor's court," said the old lady, "the vacation is fulfilled and the sixth seal, mentioned in the Revelations, again prevails. Pray come and see my lodging. It will be a good omen for me. Youth, and hope, and beauty are very seldom there. It is a long, long time since I had a visit from either."

She had taken my hand, and leading me and Miss Jellyby away, beckoned Richard and Ada to come too. I did not know how to excuse myself and looked to Richard for aid. As he was half amused and half curious and all in doubt how to get rid of the old lady without offence, she continued to lead us away, and he and Ada continued to follow, our strange conductress informing us all the time, with much smiling condescension, that she lived close by.

It was quite true, as it soon appeared. She lived so close by that we had not time to have done humouring her for a few moments before she was at home. Slipping us out at a little side gate, the old lady stopped most unexpectedly in a narrow back street, part of some courts and lanes immediately outside the wall of the inn, and said, "This is my lodging. Pray walk up!"

She had stopped at a shop over which was written KROOK, RAG AND BOTTLE WAREHOUSE. Also, in long thin letters, KROOK, DEALER IN MARINE STORES. In one part of the window was a picture of a red paper mill at which a cart was unloading a quantity of sacks of old rags. In another was the inscription BONES BOUGHT. In another, KITCHEN-STUFF BOUGHT. In another, OLD IRON BOUGHT. In another, WASTE-PAPER BOUGHT. In another, LADIES' AND GENTLEMEN'S WARDROBES

BOUGHT. Everything seemed to be bought and nothing to be sold there. In all parts of the window were quantities of dirty bottles—blacking bottles, medicine bottles, ginger-beer and soda-water bottles, pickle bottles, wine bottles, ink bottles; I am reminded by mentioning the latter that the shop had in several little particulars the air of being in a legal neighbourhood and of being, as it were, a dirty hanger-on and disowned relation of the law. There were a great many ink bottles. There was a little tottering bench of shabby old volumes outside the door, labelled "Law Books, all at 9d." Some of the inscriptions I have enumerated were written in law-hand, like the papers I had seen in Kenge and Carboy's office and the letters I had so long received from the firm. Among them was one, in the same writing, having nothing to do with the business of the shop, but announcing that a respectable man aged forty-five wanted engrossing or copying to execute with neatness and dispatch: Address to Nemo, care of Mr. Krook, within. There were several second-hand bags, blue and red, hanging up. A little way within the shop-door lay heaps of old crackled parchment scrolls and discoloured and dog's-eared law-papers. I could have fancied that all the rusty keys, of which there must have been hundreds huddled together as old iron, had once belonged to doors of rooms or strong chests in lawyers' offices. The litter of rags tumbled partly into and partly out of a one-legged wooden scale, hanging without any counterpoise from a beam, might have been counsellors' bands and gowns torn up. One had only to fancy, as Richard whispered to Ada and me while we all stood looking in, that yonder bones in a corner, piled together and picked very clean, were the bones of clients, to make the picture complete.

As it was still foggy and dark, and as the shop was blinded besides by the wall of Lincoln's Inn, intercepting the light within a couple of yards, we should not have seen so much but for a lighted lantern that an old man in spectacles and a hairy cap was carrying about in the shop. Turning towards the door, he now caught sight of us. He was short, cadaverous, and withered, with his head sunk sideways between his shoulders and the breath issuing in visible smoke from his mouth as if he were on fire within. His throat, chin, and eyebrows were so frosted with white hairs and so gnarled with veins and puckered skin that he looked from his breast upward like some old root in a fall of snow.

"Hi, hi!" said the old man, coming to the door. "Have you anything to sell?"

We naturally drew back and glanced at our conductress, who had been trying to open the house-door with a key she had taken from her pocket, and to whom Richard now said that as we had had the pleasure of seeing where she lived, we would leave her, being pressed for time. But she was not to be so easily left. She became so fantastically and pressingly earnest in her entreaties that we would walk up and see her apartment for an instant, and was so bent, in her harmless way, on leading me in, as part of the good omen she desired, that I (whatever the others might do) saw nothing for it but to comply. I suppose we were all more or less curious; at any rate, when the old man added his persuasions to hers and said, "Aye, aye! Please her! It won't take a minute! Come in, come in! Come in through the shop if t'other door's out of order!" we all went in, stimulated by Richard's laughing encouragement and relying on his protection.

"My landlord, Krook," said the little old lady, condescending to him from her lofty station as she presented him to us. "He is called among the neighbours the Lord Chancellor. His shop is called the Court of Chancery. He is a very eccentric person. He is very odd. Oh, I assure you he is very odd!"

She shook her head a great many times and tapped her forehead with her finger to express to us that we must have the goodness to excuse him, "For he is a little—you know—M!" said the old lady with great stateliness. The old man overheard, and laughed.

"It's true enough," he said, going before us with the lantern, "that they call me the Lord Chancellor and call my shop Chancery. And why do you think they call me the Lord Chancellor and my shop Chancery?"

"I don't know, I am sure!" said Richard rather carelessly.

"You see," said the old man, stopping and turning round, "they—Hi! Here's lovely hair! I have got three sacks of ladies' hair below, but none so beautiful and fine as this. What colour, and what texture!"

"That'll do, my good friend!" said Richard, strongly disapproving of his having drawn one of Ada's tresses through his yellow hand. "You can admire as the rest of us do without taking that liberty."

The old man darted at him a sudden look which even called my attention from Ada, who, startled and blushing, was so remarkably beautiful that she seemed to fix the wandering attention of the little old lady herself. But as Ada interposed and laughingly said she could only feel proud of such genuine admiration, Mr. Krook shrunk into his former self as suddenly as he had leaped out of it.

"You see, I have so many things here," he resumed, holding up the lantern, "of so many kinds, and all as the neighbours think (but THEY know nothing), wasting away and going to rack and ruin, that that's why they have given me and my place a christening. And I have so many old parchmentses and papers in my stock. And I have a liking for rust and must and cobwebs. And all's fish that comes to my net. And I can't abear to part with anything I once lay hold of (or so my neighbours think, but what do THEY know?) or to alter anything, or to have any sweeping, nor scouring, nor cleaning, nor repairing going on about me. That's the way I've got the ill name of Chancery. I don't mind. I go to see my noble and learned brother pretty well every day, when he sits in the Inn. He don't notice me, but I notice him. There's no great odds betwixt us. We both grub on in a muddle. Hi, Lady Jane!"

A large grey cat leaped from some neighbouring shelf on his shoulder and startled us all.

"Hi! Show 'em how you scratch. Hi! Tear, my lady!" said her master.

The cat leaped down and ripped at a bundle of rags with her tigerish claws, with a sound that it set my teeth on edge to hear.

"She'd do as much for any one I was to set her on," said the old man. "I deal in cat-skins among other general matters, and hers was offered to me. It's a very fine skin, as you may see, but I didn't have it stripped off! THAT warn't like Chancery practice though, says you!"

He had by this time led us across the shop, and now opened a door in the back part of it, leading to the house-entry. As he stood with his hand upon the lock, the little old lady graciously observed to him before passing out, "That will do, Krook. You mean well, but are tiresome. My young friends are pressed for time. I have none to spare myself, having to attend court very soon. My young friends are the wards in Jarndyce."

"Jarndyce!" said the old man with a start.

"Jarndyce and Jarndyce. The great suit, Krook," returned his lodger.

"Hi!" exclaimed the old man in a tone of thoughtful amazement and with a wider stare than before. "Think of it!"

He seemed so rapt all in a moment and looked so curiously at us that Richard said, "Why, you appear to trouble yourself a good deal about the causes before your noble and learned brother, the other Chancellor!"

"Yes," said the old man abstractedly. "Sure! YOUR name now will be—"

"Richard Carstone."

"Carstone," he repeated, slowly checking off that name upon his forefinger; and each of the others he went on to mention upon a separate finger. "Yes. There was the name of Barbary, and the name of Clare, and the name of Dedlock, too, I think."

"He knows as much of the cause as the real salaried Chancellor!" said Richard, quite astonished, to Ada and me.

"Aye!" said the old man, coming slowly out of his abstraction. "Yes! Tom Jarndyce—you'll excuse me, being related; but he was never known about court by any other name, and was as well known there as—she is now," nodding slightly at his lodger. "Tom Jarndyce was often in here. He got into a restless habit of strolling about when the cause was on, or expected, talking to the little shopkeepers and telling 'em to keep out of Chancery, whatever they did. 'For,' says he, 'it's being ground to bits in a slow mill; it's being roasted at a slow fire; it's being stung to death by single bees; it's being drowned by drops; it's going mad by grains.' He was as near making away with himself, just where the young lady stands, as near could be."

We listened with horror.

"He come in at the door," said the old man, slowly pointing an imaginary track along the shop, "on the day he did it—the whole neighbourhood had said for months before that he would do it, of a certainty sooner or later—he come in at the door that day, and walked along there, and sat himself on a bench that stood there, and asked me (you'll judge I was a mortal sight younger then) to fetch him a pint of wine. 'For,' says he, 'Krook, I am much depressed; my cause is on again, and I think I'm nearer judgment than I ever was.' I hadn't a mind to leave him alone; and I persuaded him to go to the tavern over the way there, t'other side my lane (I mean Chancery Lane); and I followed and looked in at the window, and saw him, comfortable as I thought, in the arm-chair by the fire, and company with him. I hadn't hardly got back here when I heard a shot go echoing and rattling right away into the inn. I ran out—neighbours ran out—twenty of us cried at once, 'Tom Jarndyce!'"

The old man stopped, looked hard at us, looked down into the lantern, blew the light out, and shut the lantern up.

"We were right, I needn't tell the present hearers. Hi! To be sure, how the neighbourhood poured into court that afternoon while the cause was on! How my noble and learned brother, and all the rest of 'em, grubbed and muddled away as usual and tried to look as if they hadn't heard a word of the last fact in the case or as if they had—Oh, dear me!—nothing at all to do with it if they had heard of it by any chance!"

Ada's colour had entirely left her, and Richard was scarcely less pale. Nor could I wonder, judging even from my emotions, and I was no party in the suit, that to hearts so untried and fresh it was a shock to come into the inheritance of a protracted misery, attended in the minds of many people with such dreadful recollections. I had another uneasiness, in the application of the painful story to the poor half-witted creature who had brought us there; but, to my surprise, she seemed perfectly unconscious of that and only led the way upstairs again, informing us with the toleration of a superior creature for the infirmities of a common mortal that her landlord was "a little M, you know!"

She lived at the top of the house, in a pretty large room, from which she had a glimpse of Lincoln's Inn Hall. This seemed to have been her principal inducement, originally, for taking up her residence there. She could look at it, she said, in the night, especially in the moonshine. Her room was clean, but very, very bare. I noticed the scantiest necessaries in the way of furniture; a few old prints from books, of Chancellors and barristers, wafered against the wall; and some half-dozen reticles and work-bags, "containing documents," as she informed us. There were neither coals nor ashes in the grate, and I saw no articles of clothing anywhere, nor any kind of food. Upon a shelf in an open cupboard were a plate or two, a cup or two, and so forth, but all dry and empty. There was a more affecting meaning in her pinched appearance, I thought as I looked round, than I had understood before.

"Extremely honoured, I am sure," said our poor hostess with the greatest suavity, "by this visit from the wards in Jarndyce. And very much indebted for the omen. It is a retired situation. Considering. I am limited as to situation. In consequence of the necessity of attending on the Chancellor. I have lived here many years. I pass my days in court, my evenings and my nights here. I find the nights long, for I sleep but little and think much. That is, of course, unavoidable, being in Chancery. I am sorry I cannot offer chocolate. I expect a judgment shortly and shall then place my establishment on a superior footing. At present, I don't mind confessing to the wards in Jarndyce (in strict confidence) that I sometimes find it difficult to keep up a genteel appearance. I have felt the cold here. I have felt something sharper than cold. It matters very little. Pray excuse the introduction of such mean topics."

She partly drew aside the curtain of the long, low garret window and called our attention to a number of bird-cages hanging there, some containing several birds. There were larks, linnets, and goldfinches—I should think at least twenty.

"I began to keep the little creatures," she said, "with an object that the wards will readily comprehend. With the intention of restoring them to liberty. When my judgment should be given. Ye-es! They die in prison, though. Their lives, poor silly things, are so short in comparison with Chancery proceedings that, one by one, the whole collection has died over and over again. I doubt, do you know, whether one of these, though they are all young, will live to be free! Ve-ry mortifying, is it not?"

Although she sometimes asked a question, she never seemed to expect a reply, but rambled on as if she were in the habit of doing so when no one but herself was present.

"Indeed," she pursued, "I positively doubt sometimes, I do assure you, whether while matters are still unsettled, and the sixth or Great Seal still prevails, I may not one day be found lying stark and senseless here, as I have found so many birds!"

Richard, answering what he saw in Ada's compassionate eyes, took the opportunity of laying some money, softly and unobserved, on the chimney-piece. We all drew nearer to the cages, feigning to examine the birds.

"I can't allow them to sing much," said the little old lady, "for (you'll think this curious) I find my mind confused by the idea that they are singing while I am following the arguments in court. And my mind requires to be so very clear, you know! Another time, I'll tell you their names. Not at present. On a day of such good omen, they shall sing as much as they like. In honour of youth," a smile and curtsy, "hope," a smile and curtsy, "and beauty," a smile and curtsy. "There! We'll let in the full light."

The birds began to stir and chirp.

"I cannot admit the air freely," said the little old lady—the room was close, and would have been the better for it—"because the cat you saw downstairs, called Lady Jane, is greedy for their lives. She crouches on the parapet outside for hours and hours. I have discovered," whispering mysteriously, "that her natural cruelty is sharpened by a jealous fear of their regaining their liberty. In consequence of the judgment I expect being shortly given. She is sly and full of malice. I half believe, sometimes, that she is no cat, but the wolf of the old saying. It is so very difficult to keep her from the door."

Some neighbouring bells, reminding the poor soul that it was half-past nine, did more for us in the way of bringing our visit to an end than we could easily have done for ourselves. She hurriedly took up her little bag of documents, which she had laid upon the table on coming in, and asked if we were also going into court. On our answering no, and that we would on no account detain her, she opened the door to attend us downstairs.

"With such an omen, it is even more necessary than usual that I should be there before the Chancellor comes in," said she, "for he might mention my case the first thing. I have a presentiment that he WILL mention it the first thing this morning."

She stopped to tell us in a whisper as we were going down that the whole house was filled with strange lumber which her landlord had bought piecemeal and had no wish to sell, in consequence of being a little M. This was on the first floor. But she had made a previous stoppage on the second floor and had silently pointed at a dark door there.

"The only other lodger," she now whispered in explanation, "a law-writer. The children in the lanes here say he has sold himself to the devil. I don't know what he can have done with the money. Hush!"

She appeared to mistrust that the lodger might hear her even there, and repeating "Hush!" went before us on tiptoe as though even the sound of her footsteps might reveal to him what she had said.

Passing through the shop on our way out, as we had passed through it on our way in, we found the old man storing a quantity of packets of waste-paper in a kind of well in the floor. He seemed to be working hard, with the perspiration standing on his forehead, and had a piece of chalk by him, with which, as he put each separate package or bundle down, he made a crooked mark on the panelling of the wall.

Richard and Ada, and Miss Jellyby, and the little old lady had gone by him, and I was going when he touched me on the arm to stay me, and chalked the letter J upon the wall—in a very curious manner, beginning with the end of the letter and shaping it backward. It was a capital letter, not a printed one, but just such a letter as any clerk in Messrs. Kenge and Carboy's office would have made.

"Can you read it?" he asked me with a keen glance.

"Surely," said I. "It's very plain."

"What is it?"

"J."

With another glance at me, and a glance at the door, he rubbed it out and turned an "a" in its place (not a capital letter this time), and said, "What's that?"

I told him. He then rubbed that out and turned the letter "r," and asked me the same question. He went on quickly until he had formed in the same curious manner, beginning at the ends and bottoms of the letters, the word

Jarndyce, without once leaving two letters on the wall together.

"What does that spell?" he asked me.

When I told him, he laughed. In the same odd way, yet with the same rapidity, he then produced singly, and rubbed out singly, the letters forming the words Bleak House. These, in some astonishment, I also read; and he laughed again.

"Hi!" said the old man, laying aside the chalk. "I have a turn for copying from memory, you see, miss, though I can neither read nor write."

He looked so disagreeable and his cat looked so wickedly at me, as if I were a blood-relation of the birds upstairs, that I was quite relieved by Richard's appearing at the door and saying, "Miss Summerson, I hope you are not bargaining for the sale of your hair. Don't be tempted. Three sacks below are quite enough for Mr. Krook!"

I lost no time in wishing Mr. Krook good morning and joining my friends outside, where we parted with the little old lady, who gave us her blessing with great ceremony and renewed her assurance of yesterday in reference to her intention of settling estates on Ada and me. Before we finally turned out of those lanes, we looked back and saw Mr. Krook standing at his shop-door, in his spectacles, looking after us, with his cat upon his shoulder, and her tail sticking up on one side of his hairy cap like a tall feather.

"Quite an adventure for a morning in London!" said Richard with a sigh. "Ah, cousin, cousin, it's a weary word this Chancery!"

"It is to me, and has been ever since I can remember," returned Ada. "I am grieved that I should be the enemy—as I suppose I am—of a great number of relations and others, and that they should be my enemies—as I suppose they are—and that we should all be ruining one another without knowing how or why and be in constant doubt and discord all our lives. It seems very strange, as there must be right somewhere, that an honest judge in real earnest has not been able to find out through all these years where it is."

"Ah, cousin!" said Richard. "Strange, indeed! All this wasteful, wanton chess-playing IS very strange. To see that composed court yesterday jogging on so serenely and to think of the wretchedness of the pieces on the board gave me the headache and the heartache both together. My head ached with wondering how it happened, if men were neither fools nor rascals; and my heart ached to think they could possibly be either. But at all events, Ada—I may call you Ada?"

"Of course you may, cousin Richard."

"At all events, Chancery will work none of its bad influences on US. We have happily been brought together, thanks to our good kinsman, and it can't divide us now!"

"Never, I hope, cousin Richard!" said Ada gently.

Miss Jellyby gave my arm a squeeze and me a very significant look. I smiled in return, and we made the rest of the way back very pleasantly.

In half an hour after our arrival, Mrs. Jellyby appeared; and in the course of an hour the various things necessary for breakfast straggled one by one into the dining-room. I do not doubt that Mrs. Jellyby had gone to bed and got up in the usual manner, but she presented no appearance of having changed her dress. She was greatly occupied during breakfast, for the morning's post brought a heavy correspondence relative to Borrioboola-Gha, which would occasion her (she said) to pass a busy day. The children tumbled about, and notched memoranda of their accidents in their legs, which were perfect little calendars of distress; and Peepy was lost for an hour and a half, and brought home from Newgate market by a policeman. The equable manner in which Mrs. Jellyby sustained both his absence and his restoration to the family circle surprised us all.

She was by that time perseveringly dictating to Caddy, and Caddy was fast relapsing into the inky condition in which we had found her. At one o'clock an open carriage arrived for us, and a cart for our luggage. Mrs. Jellyby charged us with many remembrances to her good friend Mr. Jarndyce; Caddy left her desk to see us depart, kissed me in the passage, and stood biting her pen and sobbing on the steps; Peepy, I am happy to say, was asleep and spared the pain of separation (I was not without misgivings that he had gone to Newgate market in search of me); and all the other children got up behind the barouche and fell off, and we saw them, with great concern, scattered over the surface of Thavies Inn as we rolled out of its precincts.

CHAPTER VI
QUITE AT HOME

The day had brightened very much, and still brightened as we went westward. We went our way through the sunshine and the fresh air, wondering more and more at the extent of the streets, the brilliancy of the shops, the great traffic, and the crowds of people whom the pleasanter weather seemed to have brought out like many-coloured flowers. By and by we began to leave the wonderful city and to proceed through suburbs which, of themselves, would have made a pretty large town in my eyes; and at last we got into a real country road again, with windmills, rick-yards, milestones, farmers' waggons, scents of old hay, swinging signs, and horse troughs: trees, fields, and hedge-rows. It was delightful to see the green landscape before us and the immense metropolis behind; and when a waggon with a train of beautiful horses, furnished with red trappings and clear-sounding bells, came by us with its music, I believe we could all three have sung to the bells, so cheerful were the influences around.

"The whole road has been reminding me of my namesake Whittington," said Richard, "and that waggon is the finishing touch. Halloa! What's the matter?"

We had stopped, and the waggon had stopped too. Its music changed as the horses came to a stand, and subsided to a gentle tinkling, except when a horse tossed his head or shook himself and sprinkled off a little shower of bell-ringing.

"Our postilion is looking after the waggoner," said Richard, "and the waggoner is coming back after us. Good day, friend!" The waggoner was at our coach-door. "Why, here's an extraordinary thing!" added Richard, looking closely at the man. "He has got your name, Ada, in his hat!"

He had all our names in his hat. Tucked within the band were three small notes—one addressed to Ada, one to Richard, one to me. These the waggoner delivered to each of us respectively, reading the name aloud first. In answer to Richard's inquiry from whom they came, he briefly answered, "Master, sir, if you please"; and putting on his hat again (which was like a soft bowl), cracked his whip, re-awakened his music, and went melodiously away.

"Is that Mr. Jarndyce's waggon?" said Richard, calling to our post-boy.

"Yes, sir," he replied. "Going to London."

We opened the notes. Each was a counterpart of the other and contained these words in a solid, plain hand.

I look forward, my dear, to our meeting easily and without constraint on either side. I therefore have to propose that we meet as old friends and take the past for granted. It will be a relief to you possibly, and to me certainly,

and so my love to you.
John Jarndyce

I had perhaps less reason to be surprised than either of my companions, having never yet enjoyed an opportunity of thanking one who had been my benefactor and sole earthly dependence through so many years. I had not considered how I could thank him, my gratitude lying too deep in my heart for that; but I now began to consider how I could meet him without thanking him, and felt it would be very difficult indeed.

The notes revived in Richard and Ada a general impression that they both had, without quite knowing how they came by it, that their cousin Jarndyce could never bear acknowledgments for any kindness he performed and that sooner than receive any he would resort to the most singular expedients and evasions or would even run away. Ada dimly remembered to have heard her mother tell, when she was a very little child, that he had once done her an act of uncommon generosity and that on her going to his house to thank him, he happened to see her through a window coming to the door, and immediately escaped by the back gate, and was not heard of for three months. This discourse led to a great deal more on the same theme, and indeed it lasted us all day, and we talked of scarcely anything else. If we did by any chance diverge into another subject, we soon returned to this, and wondered what the house would be like, and when we should get there, and whether we should see Mr. Jarndyce as soon as we arrived or after a delay, and what he would say to us, and what we should say to him. All of which we wondered about, over and over again.

The roads were very heavy for the horses, but the pathway was generally good, so we alighted and walked up all the hills, and liked it so well that we prolonged our walk on the level ground when we got to the top. At Barnet there were other horses waiting for us, but as they had only just been fed, we had to wait for them too, and got a long fresh walk over a common and an old battle-field before the carriage came up. These delays so protracted the journey that the short day was spent and the long night had closed in before we came to St. Albans, near to which town Bleak House was, we knew.

By that time we were so anxious and nervous that even Richard confessed, as we rattled over the stones of the old street, to feeling an irrational desire to drive back again. As to Ada and me, whom he had wrapped up with great care, the night being sharp and frosty, we trembled from head to foot. When we turned out of the town, round a corner, and Richard told us that the post-boy, who had for a long time sympathized with our heightened expectation, was looking back and nodding, we both stood up in the carriage (Richard holding Ada lest she should be jolted down) and gazed round upon the open country and the starlight night for our destination. There was a light sparkling on the top of a hill before us, and the driver, pointing to it with his whip and crying, "That's Bleak House!" put his horses into a canter and took us forward at such a rate, uphill though it was, that the wheels sent the road drift flying about our heads like spray from a water-mill. Presently we lost the light, presently saw it, presently lost it, presently saw it, and turned into an avenue of trees and cantered up towards where it was beaming brightly. It was in a window of what seemed to be an old-fashioned house with three peaks in the roof in front and a circular sweep leading to the porch. A bell was rung as we drew up, and amidst the sound of its deep voice in the still air, and the distant barking of some dogs, and a gush of light from the opened door, and the smoking and steaming of the heated horses, and the quickened beating of our own hearts, we alighted in no inconsiderable confusion.

"Ada, my love, Esther, my dear, you are welcome. I rejoice to see you! Rick, if I had a hand to spare at present, I would give it you!"

The gentleman who said these words in a clear, bright, hospitable voice had one of his arms round Ada's waist and the other round mine, and kissed us both in a fatherly way, and bore us across the hall into a ruddy little room, all in a glow with a blazing fire. Here he kissed us again, and opening his arms, made us sit down side by side on a sofa ready drawn out near the hearth. I felt that if we had been at all demonstrative, he would have run away in a moment.

"Now, Rick!" said he. "I have a hand at liberty. A word in earnest is as good as a speech. I am heartily glad to see you. You are at home. Warm yourself!"

Richard shook him by both hands with an intuitive mixture of respect and frankness, and only saying (though with an earnestness that rather alarmed me, I was so afraid of Mr. Jarndyce's suddenly disappearing), "You are very kind, sir! We are very much obliged to you!" laid aside his hat and coat and came up to the fire.

"And how did you like the ride? And how did you like Mrs. Jellyby, my dear?" said Mr. Jarndyce to Ada.

While Ada was speaking to him in reply, I glanced (I need not say with how much interest) at his face. It was a handsome, lively, quick face, full of change and motion; and his hair was a silvered iron-grey. I took him to be nearer sixty than fifty, but he was upright, hearty, and robust. From the moment of his first speaking to us his voice had connected itself with an association in my mind that I could not define; but now, all at once, a something sudden in his manner and a pleasant expression in his eyes recalled the gentleman in the stagecoach six years ago on the memorable day of my journey to Reading. I was certain it was he. I never was so frightened in my life as when I made the discovery, for he caught my glance, and appearing to read my thoughts, gave such a look at the door that I thought we had lost him.

However, I am happy to say he remained where he was, and asked me what I thought of Mrs. Jellyby.

"She exerts herself very much for Africa, sir," I said.

"Nobly!" returned Mr. Jarndyce. "But you answer like Ada." Whom I had not heard. "You all think something else, I see."

"We rather thought," said I, glancing at Richard and Ada, who entreated me with their eyes to speak, "that perhaps she was a little unmindful of her home."

"Floored!" cried Mr. Jarndyce.

I was rather alarmed again.

"Well! I want to know your real thoughts, my dear. I may have sent you there on purpose."

"We thought that, perhaps," said I, hesitating, "it is right to begin with the obligations of home, sir; and that, perhaps, while those are overlooked and neglected, no other duties can possibly be substituted for them."

"The little Jellybys," said Richard, coming to my relief, "are really—I can't help expressing myself strongly, sir—in a devil of a state."

"She means well," said Mr. Jarndyce hastily. "The wind's in the east."

"It was in the north, sir, as we came down," observed Richard.

"My dear Rick," said Mr. Jarndyce, poking the fire, "I'll take an oath it's either in the east or going to be. I am always conscious of an uncomfortable sensation now and then when the wind is blowing in the east."

"Rheumatism, sir?" said Richard.

"I dare say it is, Rick. I believe it is. And so the little Jell—I had my doubts about 'em—are in a—oh, Lord, yes, it's easterly!" said Mr. Jarndyce.

He had taken two or three undecided turns up and down while uttering these broken sentences, retaining the poker in one hand and rubbing his hair with the other, with a good-natured vexation at once so whimsical and so lovable that I am sure we were more delighted with him than we could possibly have expressed in any words. He gave an arm to Ada and an arm to me, and bidding Richard bring a candle, was leading the way out when he suddenly turned us all back again.

"Those little Jellybys. Couldn't you—didn't you—now, if it had rained sugar-plums, or three-cornered raspberry tarts, or anything of that sort!" said Mr. Jarndyce.

"Oh, cousin—" Ada hastily began.

"Good, my pretty pet. I like cousin. Cousin John, perhaps, is better."

"Then, cousin John—" Ada laughingly began again.

"Ha, ha! Very good indeed!" said Mr. Jarndyce with great enjoyment. "Sounds uncommonly natural. Yes, my dear?"

"It did better than that. It rained Esther."

"Aye?" said Mr. Jarndyce. "What did Esther do?"

"Why, cousin John," said Ada, clasping her hands upon his arm and shaking her head at me across him—for I wanted her to be quiet—"Esther was their friend directly. Esther nursed them, coaxed them to sleep, washed and dressed them, told them stories, kept them quiet, bought them keepsakes"—

My dear girl! I had only gone out with Peepy after he was found and given him a little, tiny horse!—"and, cousin John, she softened poor Caroline, the eldest one, so much and was so thoughtful for me and so amiable! No, no, I won't be contradicted, Esther dear! You know, you know, it's true!"

The warm-hearted darling leaned across her cousin John and kissed me, and then looking up in his face, boldly said, "At all events, cousin John, I WILL thank you for the companion you have given me." I felt as if she challenged him to run away. But he didn't.

"Where did you say the wind was, Rick?" asked Mr. Jarndyce.

"In the north as we came down, sir."

"You are right. There's no east in it. A mistake of mine. Come, girls, come and see your home!"

It was one of those delightfully irregular houses where you go up and down steps out of one room into another, and where you come upon more rooms when you think you have seen all there are, and where there is a bountiful provision of little halls and passages, and where you find still older cottage-rooms in unexpected places with lattice windows and green growth pressing through them. Mine, which we entered first, was of this kind, with an up-and-down roof that had more corners in it than I ever counted afterwards and a chimney (there was a wood fire on the hearth) paved all around with pure white tiles, in every one of which a bright miniature of the fire was blazing. Out of this room, you went down two steps into a charming little sitting-room looking down upon a flower-garden, which room was henceforth to belong to Ada and me. Out of this you went up three steps into Ada's bedroom, which had a fine broad window commanding a beautiful view (we saw a great expanse of darkness lying underneath the stars), to which there was a hollow window-seat, in which, with a spring-lock, three dear Adas might have been lost at once. Out of this room you passed into a little gallery, with which the other best rooms (only two) communicated, and so, by a little staircase of shallow steps with a number of corner stairs in it, considering its length, down into the hall. But if instead of going out at Ada's door you came back into my room, and went out at the door by which you had entered it, and turned up a few crooked steps that branched off in an unexpected manner from the stairs, you lost yourself in passages, with mangles in them, and three-cornered tables, and a native Hindu chair, which was also a sofa, a box, and a bedstead, and looked in every form something between a bamboo skeleton and a great bird-cage, and had been brought from India nobody knew by whom or when. From these you came on Richard's room, which was part library, part sitting-room, part bedroom, and seemed indeed a comfortable compound of many rooms. Out of that you went straight, with a little interval of passage, to the plain room where Mr. Jarndyce slept, all the year round, with his window open, his bedstead without any furniture standing in the middle of the floor for more air, and his cold bath gaping for him in a smaller room adjoining. Out of that you came into another passage, where there were back-stairs and where you could hear the horses being rubbed down outside the stable and being told to "Hold up" and "Get over," as they slipped about very much on the uneven stones. Or you might, if you came out at another door (every room had at least two doors), go straight down to the hall again by half-a-dozen steps and a low archway, wondering how you got back there or had ever got out of it.

The furniture, old-fashioned rather than old, like the house, was as pleasantly irregular. Ada's sleeping-room was all flowers—in chintz and paper, in velvet, in needlework, in the brocade of two stiff courtly chairs which stood, each attended by a little page of a stool for greater state, on either side of the fire-place. Our sitting-room was green and had framed and glazed upon the walls numbers of surprising and surprised birds, staring out of pictures at a real trout in a case, as brown and shining as if it had been served with gravy; at the death of Captain Cook; and at the whole process of preparing tea in China, as depicted by Chinese artists. In my room there were oval engravings of the months—ladies haymaking in short waists and large hats tied under the chin, for June; smooth-legged noblemen pointing with cocked-hats to village steeples, for October. Half-length portraits in crayons abounded all through the house, but were so dispersed that I found the brother of a youthful officer of mine in the china-closet and the grey old age of my pretty young bride, with a flower in her bodice, in the breakfast-room. As substitutes, I had four angels, of Queen Anne's reign, taking a complacent gentleman to heaven, in festoons, with some difficulty; and a composition in needlework representing fruit, a kettle, and an alphabet. All the movables, from the wardrobes to the chairs and tables, hangings, glasses, even to the pincushions and scent-bottles on the dressing-tables, displayed the same quaint variety. They agreed in nothing but their perfect neatness, their display of the whitest linen, and their storing-up, wheresoever the existence of a drawer, small or large, rendered it possible, of quantities of rose-leaves and sweet lavender. Such, with its illuminated windows, softened here and there by shadows of curtains, shining out upon the starlight night; with its light, and warmth, and comfort; with its hospitable jingle, at a distance, of preparations for dinner; with the face of its generous master brightening everything we saw; and just wind enough without to sound a low accompaniment to everything we heard, were our first impressions of Bleak House.

"I am glad you like it," said Mr. Jarndyce when he had brought us round again to Ada's sitting-room. "It makes no pretensions, but it is a comfortable little place, I hope, and will be more so with such bright young looks in it. You have barely half an hour before dinner. There's no one here but the finest creature upon earth—a child."

"More children, Esther!" said Ada.

"I don't mean literally a child," pursued Mr. Jarndyce; "not a child in years.

He is grown up—he is at least as old as I am—but in simplicity, and freshness, and enthusiasm, and a fine guileless inaptitude for all worldly affairs, he is a perfect child."

We felt that he must be very interesting.

"He knows Mrs. Jellyby," said Mr. Jarndyce. "He is a musical man, an amateur, but might have been a professional. He is an artist too, an amateur, but might have been a professional. He is a man of attainments and of captivating manners. He has been unfortunate in his affairs, and unfortunate in his pursuits, and unfortunate in his family; but he don't care—he's a child!"

"Did you imply that he has children of his own, sir?" inquired Richard.

"Yes, Rick! Half-a-dozen. More! Nearer a dozen, I should think. But he has never looked after them. How could he? He wanted somebody to look after HIM. He is a child, you know!" said Mr. Jarndyce.

"And have the children looked after themselves at all, sir?" inquired Richard.

"Why, just as you may suppose," said Mr. Jarndyce, his countenance suddenly falling. "It is said that the children of the very poor are not brought up, but dragged up. Harold Skimpole's children have tumbled up somehow or other. The wind's getting round again, I am afraid. I feel it rather!"

Richard observed that the situation was exposed on a sharp night.

"It IS exposed," said Mr. Jarndyce. "No doubt that's the cause. Bleak House has an exposed sound. But you are coming my way. Come along!"

Our luggage having arrived and being all at hand, I was dressed in a few minutes and engaged in putting my worldly goods away when a maid (not the one in attendance upon Ada, but another, whom I had not seen) brought a basket into my room with two bunches of keys in it, all labelled.

"For you, miss, if you please," said she.

"For me?" said I.

"The housekeeping keys, miss."

I showed my surprise, for she added with some little surprise on her own part, "I was told to bring them as soon as you was alone, miss. Miss Summerson, if I don't deceive myself?"

"Yes," said I. "That is my name."

"The large bunch is the housekeeping, and the little bunch is the cellars, miss. Any time you was pleased to appoint to-morrow morning, I was to show you the presses and things they belong to."

I said I would be ready at half-past six, and after she was gone, stood looking at the basket, quite lost in the magnitude of my trust. Ada found me thus and had such a delightful confidence in me when I showed her the keys and told her about them that it would have been insensibility and ingratitude not to feel encouraged. I knew, to be sure, that it was the dear girl's kindness, but I liked to be so pleasantly cheated.

When we went downstairs, we were presented to Mr. Skimpole, who was standing before the fire telling Richard how fond he used to be, in his school-time, of football. He was a little bright creature with a rather large head, but a delicate face and a sweet voice, and there was a perfect charm in him. All he said was so free from effort and spontaneous and was said with such a captivating gaiety that it was fascinating to hear him talk. Being of a more slender figure than Mr. Jarndyce and having a richer complexion, with browner hair, he looked younger. Indeed, he had more the appearance in all respects of a damaged young man than a well-preserved elderly one. There was an easy negligence in his manner and even in his dress (his hair carelessly disposed, and his neck-kerchief loose and flowing, as I have seen artists paint their own portraits) which I could not separate from the idea of a romantic youth who had undergone some unique process of depreciation. It struck me as being not at all like the manner or appearance of a man who had advanced in life by the usual road of years, cares, and experiences.

I gathered from the conversation that Mr. Skimpole had been educated for the medical profession and had once lived, in his professional capacity, in the household of a German prince. He told us, however, that as he had always been a mere child in point of weights and measures and had never known anything about them (except that they disgusted him), he had never been able to prescribe with the requisite accuracy of detail. In fact, he said, he had no head for detail. And he told us, with great humour, that when he was wanted to bleed the prince or physic any of his people, he was generally found lying on his back in bed, reading the newspapers or making fancy-sketches in pencil, and couldn't come. The prince, at last, objecting to this, "in which," said Mr. Skimpole, in the frankest manner, "he was perfectly right," the engagement terminated, and Mr. Skimpole having (as he added with delightful gaiety) "nothing to live upon but love, fell in love, and married, and surrounded himself with rosy cheeks." His good friend Jarndyce and some other of his good friends then helped him, in quicker or slower succession, to several openings in life, but to no purpose, for he must confess to two of the oldest infirmities in the world: one was that he had no idea of time, the other that he had no idea of money. In consequence of which he never kept an appointment, never could transact any business, and never knew the value of anything! Well! So he had got on in life, and here he was! He was very fond of reading the papers, very fond of making fancy-sketches with a pencil, very fond of nature, very fond of art. All he asked of society was to let him live. THAT wasn't much. His wants were few. Give him the papers, conversation, music, mutton, coffee, landscape, fruit in the season, a few sheets of Bristol-board, and a little claret, and he asked no more. He was a mere child in the world, but he didn't cry for the moon. He said to the world, "Go your several ways in peace! Wear red coats, blue coats, lawn sleeves; put pens behind your ears, wear aprons; go after glory, holiness, commerce, trade, any object you prefer; only—let Harold Skimpole live!"

All this and a great deal more he told us, not only with the utmost brilliancy and enjoyment, but with a certain vivacious candour—speaking of himself as if he were not at all his own affair, as if Skimpole were a third person, as if he knew that Skimpole had his singularities but still had his claims too, which were the general business of the community and must not be slighted. He was quite enchanting. If I felt at all confused at that early time in endeavouring to reconcile anything he said with anything I had thought about the duties and accountabilities of life (which I am far from sure of), I was confused by not exactly understanding why he was free of them. That he WAS free of them, I scarcely doubted; he was so very clear about it himself.

"I covet nothing," said Mr. Skimpole in the same light way. "Possession is nothing to me. Here is my friend Jarndyce's excellent house. I feel obliged to him for possessing it. I can sketch it and alter it. I can set it to music. When I am here, I have sufficient possession of it and have neither trouble, cost, nor responsibility. My steward's name, in short, is Jarndyce, and he can't cheat me. We have been mentioning Mrs. Jellyby. There is a bright-eyed woman, of a strong will and immense power of business detail, who throws herself into objects with surprising ardour! I don't regret that I have not a strong will and an immense power of business detail to throw myself into objects with surprising ardour. I can admire her without envy. I can sympathize with the objects. I can dream of them. I can lie down on the grass—in fine weather—and float along an African river, embracing all the natives I meet, as sensible of the deep silence and sketching the dense overhanging tropical growth as accurately as if I were there. I don't know that it's of any direct use my doing so, but it's all I can do, and I do it thoroughly. Then, for heaven's sake, having Harold Skimpole, a confiding child, petitioning you, the world, an agglomeration of practical people of business habits, to let him live and admire the human family, do it somehow or other, like good souls, and suffer him to ride his rocking-horse!"

It was plain enough that Mr. Jarndyce had not been neglectful of the adjuration. Mr. Skimpole's general position there would have rendered it so without the addition of what he presently said.

"It's only you, the generous creatures, whom I envy," said Mr. Skimpole, addressing us, his new friends, in an impersonal manner. "I envy you your power of doing what you do. It is what I should revel in myself. I don't feel any vulgar gratitude to you. I almost feel as if YOU ought to be grateful to ME for giving you the opportunity of enjoying the luxury of generosity. I know you like it. For anything I can tell, I may have come into the world expressly for the purpose of increasing your stock of happiness. I may have been born to be a benefactor to you by sometimes giving you an opportunity of assisting me in my little perplexities. Why should I regret my incapacity for details and worldly affairs when it leads to such pleasant consequences? I don't regret it therefore."

Of all his playful speeches (playful, yet always fully meaning what they expressed) none seemed to be more to the taste of Mr. Jarndyce than this. I had often new temptations, afterwards, to wonder whether it was really singular, or only singular to me, that he, who was probably the most grateful of mankind upon the least occasion, should so desire to escape the gratitude of others.

We were all enchanted. I felt it a merited tribute to the engaging qualities of Ada and Richard that Mr. Skimpole, seeing them for the first time, should be so unreserved and should lay himself out to be so exquisitely agreeable. They (and especially Richard) were naturally pleased, for similar reasons, and considered it no common privilege to be so freely confided in by such an attractive man. The more we listened, the more gaily Mr. Skimpole talked. And what with his fine hilarious manner and his engaging candour and his genial way of lightly tossing his own weaknesses about, as if he had said, "I am a child, you know! You are designing people compared with me" (he really made me consider myself in that light) "but I am gay and innocent; forget your worldly arts and play with me!" the effect was absolutely dazzling.

He was so full of feeling too and had such a delicate sentiment for what was beautiful or tender that he could have won a heart by that alone. In the evening, when I was preparing to make tea and Ada was touching the piano in the adjoining room and softly humming a tune to her cousin Richard, which they had happened to mention, he came and sat down on the sofa near me and so spoke of Ada that I almost loved him.

"She is like the morning," he said. "With that golden hair, those blue eyes, and that fresh bloom on her cheek, she is like the summer morning. The birds here will mistake her for it. We will not call such a lovely young creature as that, who is a joy to all mankind, an orphan. She is the child of the universe."

Mr. Jarndyce, I found, was standing near us with his hands behind him and an attentive smile upon his face.

"The universe," he observed, "makes rather an indifferent parent, I am afraid."

"Oh! I don't know!" cried Mr. Skimpole buoyantly.

"I think I do know," said Mr. Jarndyce.

"Well!" cried Mr. Skimpole. "You know the world (which in your sense is the universe), and I know nothing of it, so you shall have your way. But if I had mine," glancing at the cousins, "there should be no brambles of sordid realities in such a path as that. It should be strewn with roses; it should lie through bowers, where there was no spring, autumn, nor winter, but perpetual summer. Age or change should never wither it. The base word money should never be breathed near it!"

Mr. Jarndyce patted him on the head with a smile, as if he had been really a child, and passing a step or two on, and stopping a moment, glanced at the young cousins. His look was thoughtful, but had a benignant expression in it which I often (how often!) saw again, which has long been engraven on my heart. The room in which they were, communicating with that in which he stood, was only lighted by the fire. Ada sat at the piano; Richard stood beside her, bending down. Upon the wall, their shadows blended together, surrounded by strange forms, not without a ghostly motion caught from the unsteady fire, though reflecting from motionless objects. Ada touched the notes so softly and sang so low that the wind, sighing away to the distant hills, was as audible as the music. The mystery of the future and the little clue afforded to it by the voice of the present seemed expressed in the whole picture.

But it is not to recall this fancy, well as I remember it, that I recall the scene. First, I was not quite unconscious of the contrast in respect of meaning and intention between the silent look directed that way and the flow of words that had preceded it. Secondly, though Mr. Jarndyce's glance as he withdrew it rested for but a moment on me, I felt as if in that moment he confided to me—and knew that he confided to me and that I received the confidence—his hope that Ada and Richard might one day enter on a dearer relationship.

Mr. Skimpole could play on the piano and the violoncello, and he was a composer—had composed half an opera once, but got tired of it—and played what he composed with taste. After tea we had quite a little concert, in which Richard—who was enthralled by Ada's singing and told me that she seemed to know all the songs that ever were written—and Mr. Jarndyce, and I were the audience. After a little while I missed first Mr. Skimpole and afterwards Richard, and while I was thinking how could Richard stay away so long and lose so much, the maid who had given me the keys looked in at the door, saying, "If you please, miss, could you spare a minute?"

When I was shut out with her in the hall, she said, holding up her hands, "Oh, if you please, miss, Mr. Carstone says would you come upstairs to Mr. Skimpole's room. He has been took, miss!"

"Took?" said I.

"Took, miss. Sudden," said the maid.

I was apprehensive that his illness might be of a dangerous kind, but of course I begged her to be quiet and not disturb any one and collected myself, as I followed her quickly upstairs, sufficiently to consider what were the best remedies to be applied if it should prove to be a fit. She threw open a door and I went into a chamber, where, to my unspeakable surprise, instead of finding Mr. Skimpole stretched upon the bed or prostrate on the floor, I found him standing before the fire smiling at Richard, while Richard, with a face of great embarrassment, looked at a person on the sofa, in a white great-coat, with smooth hair upon his head and not much of it, which he was wiping smoother and making less of with a pocket-handkerchief.

"Miss Summerson," said Richard hurriedly, "I am glad you are come. You will be able to advise us. Our friend Mr. Skimpole—don't be alarmed!—is arrested for debt."

"And really, my dear Miss Summerson," said Mr. Skimpole with his agreeable candour, "I never was in a situation in which that excellent sense and quiet habit of method and usefulness, which anybody must observe in you who has the happiness of being a quarter of an hour in your society, was more needed."

The person on the sofa, who appeared to have a cold in his head, gave such a very loud snort that he startled me.

"Are you arrested for much, sir?" I inquired of Mr. Skimpole.

"My dear Miss Summerson," said he, shaking his head pleasantly, "I don't know. Some pounds, odd shillings, and halfpence, I think, were mentioned."

"It's twenty-four pound, sixteen, and sevenpence ha'penny," observed the stranger. "That's wot it is."

"And it sounds—somehow it sounds," said Mr. Skimpole, "like a small sum?"

The strange man said nothing but made another snort. It was such a powerful one that it seemed quite to lift him out of his seat.

"Mr. Skimpole," said Richard to me, "has a delicacy in applying to my cousin Jarndyce because he has lately—I think, sir, I understood you that you had lately—"

"Oh, yes!" returned Mr. Skimpole, smiling. "Though I forgot how much it was and when it was. Jarndyce would readily do it again, but I have the epicure-like feeling that I would prefer a novelty in help, that I would rather," and he looked at Richard and me, "develop generosity in a new soil and in a new form of flower."

"What do you think will be best, Miss Summerson?" said Richard, aside.

I ventured to inquire, generally, before replying, what would happen if the money were not produced.

"Jail," said the strange man, coolly putting his handkerchief into his hat, which was on the floor at his feet. "Or Coavinses."

"May I ask, sir, what is—"

"Coavinses?" said the strange man. "A 'ouse."

Richard and I looked at one another again. It was a most singular thing that the arrest was our embarrassment and not Mr. Skimpole's. He observed us with a genial interest, but there seemed, if I may venture on such a contradiction, nothing selfish in it. He had entirely washed his hands of the difficulty, and it had become ours.

"I thought," he suggested, as if good-naturedly to help us out, "that being parties in a Chancery suit concerning (as people say) a large amount of property, Mr. Richard or his beautiful cousin, or both, could sign something, or make over something, or give some sort of undertaking, or pledge, or bond? I don't know what the business name of it may be, but I suppose there is some instrument within their power that would settle this?"

"Not a bit on it," said the strange man.

"Really?" returned Mr. Skimpole. "That seems odd, now, to one who is no judge of these things!"

"Odd or even," said the stranger gruffly, "I tell you, not a bit on it!"

"Keep your temper, my good fellow, keep your temper!" Mr. Skimpole gently reasoned with him as he made a little drawing of his head on the fly-leaf of a book. "Don't be ruffled by your occupation. We can separate you from your office; we can separate the individual from the pursuit. We are not so prejudiced as to suppose that in private life you are otherwise than a very estimable man, with a great deal of poetry in your nature, of which you may not be conscious."

The stranger only answered with another violent snort, whether in acceptance of the poetry-tribute or in disdainful rejection of it, he did not express to me.

"Now, my dear Miss Summerson, and my dear Mr. Richard," said Mr. Skimpole gaily, innocently, and confidingly as he looked at his drawing with his head on one side, "here you see me utterly incapable of helping myself, and entirely in your hands! I only ask to be free. The butterflies are free. Mankind will surely not deny to Harold Skimpole what it concedes to the butterflies!"

"My dear Miss Summerson," said Richard in a whisper, "I have ten pounds that I received from Mr. Kenge. I must try what that will do."

I possessed fifteen pounds, odd shillings, which I had saved from my quarterly allowance during several years. I had always thought that some accident might happen which would throw me suddenly, without any relation or any property, on the world and had always tried to keep some little money by me that I might not be quite penniless. I told Richard of my having this little store and having no present need of it, and I asked him delicately to inform Mr. Skimpole, while I should be gone to fetch it, that we would have the pleasure of paying his debt.

When I came back, Mr. Skimpole kissed my hand and seemed quite touched. Not on his own account (I was again aware of that perplexing and extraordinary contradiction), but on ours, as if personal considerations were impossible with him and the contemplation of our happiness alone affected him. Richard, begging me, for the greater grace of the transaction, as he said, to settle with Coavinses (as Mr. Skimpole now jocularly called him), I counted out the money and received the necessary acknowledgment. This, too, delighted Mr. Skimpole.

His compliments were so delicately administered that I blushed less than I might have done and settled with the stranger in the white coat without making any mistakes. He put the money in his pocket and shortly said, "Well, then, I'll wish you a good evening, miss.

"My friend," said Mr. Skimpole, standing with his back to the fire after giving up the sketch when it was half finished, "I should like to ask you something, without offence."

I think the reply was, "Cut away, then!"

"Did you know this morning, now, that you were coming out on this errand?" said Mr. Skimpole.

"Know'd it yes'day aft'noon at tea-time," said Coavinses.

"It didn't affect your appetite? Didn't make you at all uneasy?"

"Not a bit," said Coavinses. "I know'd if you wos missed to-day, you wouldn't be missed to-morrow. A day makes no such odds."

"But when you came down here," proceeded Mr. Skimpole, "it was a fine day. The sun was shining, the wind was blowing, the lights and shadows were passing across the fields, the birds were singing."

"Nobody said they warn't, in MY hearing," returned Coavinses.

"No," observed Mr. Skimpole. "But what did you think upon the road?"

"Wot do you mean?" growled Coavinses with an appearance of strong resentment. "Think! I've got enough to do, and little enough to get for it without thinking. Thinking!" (with profound contempt).

"Then you didn't think, at all events," proceeded Mr. Skimpole, "to this effect: 'Harold Skimpole loves to see the sun shine, loves to hear the wind blow, loves to watch the changing lights and shadows, loves to hear the birds, those choristers in Nature's great cathedral. And does it seem to me that I am about to deprive Harold Skimpole of his share in such possessions, which are his only birthright!' You thought nothing to that effect?"

"I—certainly—did—NOT," said Coavinses, whose doggedness in utterly renouncing the idea was of that intense kind that he could only give adequate expression to it by putting a long interval between each word, and accompanying the last with a jerk that might have dislocated his neck.

"Very odd and very curious, the mental process is, in you men of business!" said Mr. Skimpole thoughtfully. "Thank you, my friend. Good night."

As our absence had been long enough already to seem strange downstairs, I returned at once and found Ada sitting at work by the fireside talking to her cousin John. Mr. Skimpole presently appeared, and Richard shortly after him. I was sufficiently engaged during the remainder of the evening in taking my first lesson in backgammon from Mr. Jarndyce, who was very fond of the game and from whom I wished of course to learn it as quickly as I could in order that I might be of the very small use of being able to play when he had no better adversary. But I thought, occasionally, when Mr. Skimpole played some fragments of his own compositions or when, both at the piano and the violoncello, and at our table, he preserved with an absence of all effort his delightful spirits and his easy flow of conversation, that Richard and I seemed to retain the transferred impression of having been arrested since dinner and that it was very curious altogether.

It was late before we separated, for when Ada was going at eleven o'clock, Mr. Skimpole went to the piano and rattled hilariously that the best of all ways to lengthen our days was to steal a few hours from night, my dear! It was past twelve before he took his candle and his radiant face out of the room, and I think he might have kept us there, if he had seen fit, until daybreak. Ada and Richard were lingering for a few moments by the fire, wondering whether Mrs. Jellyby had yet finished her dictation for the day, when Mr. Jarndyce, who had been out of the room, returned.

"Oh, dear me, what's this, what's this!" he said, rubbing his head and walking about with his good-humoured vexation. "What's this they tell me? Rick, my boy, Esther, my dear, what have you been doing? Why did you do it? How could you do it? How much apiece was it? The wind's round again. I feel it all over me!"

We neither of us quite knew what to answer.

"Come, Rick, come! I must settle this before I sleep. How much are you out of pocket? You two made the money up, you know! Why did you? How could you? Oh, Lord, yes, it's due east—must be!"

"Really, sir," said Richard, "I don't think it would be honourable in me to tell you. Mr. Skimpole relied upon us—"

"Lord bless you, my dear boy! He relies upon everybody!" said Mr. Jarndyce, giving his head a great rub and stopping short.

"Indeed, sir?"

"Everybody! And he'll be in the same scrape again next week!" said Mr. Jarndyce, walking again at a great pace, with a candle in his hand that had gone out. "He's always in the same scrape. He was born in the same scrape. I verily believe that the announcement in the newspapers when his mother was confined was 'On Tuesday last, at her residence in Botheration Buildings, Mrs. Skimpole of a son in difficulties.'"

Richard laughed heartily but added, "Still, sir, I don't want to shake his confidence or to break his confidence, and if I submit to your better knowledge again, that I ought to keep his secret, I hope you will consider before you press me any more. Of course, if you do press me, sir, I shall know I am wrong and will tell you."

"Well!" cried Mr. Jarndyce, stopping again, and making several absent endeavours to put his candlestick in his pocket. "I—here! Take it away, my dear. I don't know what I am about with it; it's all the wind—invariably has that effect—I won't press you, Rick; you may be right. But really—to get hold of you and Esther—and to squeeze you like a couple of tender young Saint Michael's oranges! It'll blow a gale in the course of the night!"

He was now alternately putting his hands into his pockets as if he were going to keep them there a long time, and taking them out again and vehemently rubbing them all over his head.

I ventured to take this opportunity of hinting that Mr. Skimpole, being in all such matters quite a child—

"Eh, my dear?" said Mr. Jarndyce, catching at the word.

"Being quite a child, sir," said I, "and so different from other people—"

"You are right!" said Mr. Jarndyce, brightening. "Your woman's wit hits the mark. He is a child—an absolute child. I told you he was a child, you know, when I first mentioned him."

Certainly! Certainly! we said.

"And he IS a child. Now, isn't he?" asked Mr. Jarndyce, brightening more and more.

He was indeed, we said.

"When you come to think of it, it's the height of childishness in you—I mean me—" said Mr. Jarndyce, "to regard him for a moment as a man. You can't make HIM responsible. The idea of Harold Skimpole with designs or plans, or knowledge of consequences! Ha, ha, ha!"

It was so delicious to see the clouds about his bright face clearing, and to see him so heartily pleased, and to know, as it was impossible not to know, that the source of his pleasure was the goodness which was tortured by condemning, or mistrusting, or secretly accusing any one, that I saw the tears in Ada's eyes, while she echoed his laugh, and felt them in my own.

"Why, what a cod's head and shoulders I am," said Mr. Jarndyce, "to require reminding of it! The whole business shows the child from beginning to end. Nobody but a child would have thought of singling YOU two out for parties in the affair! Nobody but a child would have thought of YOUR having the money! If it had been a thousand pounds, it would have been just the same!" said Mr. Jarndyce with his whole face in a glow.

We all confirmed it from our night's experience.

"To be sure, to be sure!" said Mr. Jarndyce. "However, Rick, Esther, and you too, Ada, for I don't know that even your little purse is safe from his inexperience—I must have a promise all round that nothing of this sort shall ever be done any more. No advances! Not even sixpences."

We all promised faithfully, Richard with a merry glance at me touching his pocket as if to remind me that there was no danger of OUR transgressing.

"As to Skimpole," said Mr. Jarndyce, "a habitable doll's house with good board and a few tin people to get into debt with and borrow money of would set the boy up in life. He is in a child's sleep by this time, I suppose; it's time I should take my craftier head to my more worldly pillow. Good night, my dears. God bless you!"

He peeped in again, with a smiling face, before we had lighted our candles, and said, "Oh! I have been looking at the weather-cock. I find it was a false alarm about the wind. It's in the south!" And went away singing to himself.

Ada and I agreed, as we talked together for a little while upstairs, that this caprice about the wind was a fiction and that he used the pretence to account for any disappointment he could not conceal, rather than he would blame the real cause of it or disparage or depreciate any one. We thought this very characteristic of his eccentric gentleness and of the difference between him and those petulant people who make the weather and the winds (particularly that unlucky wind which he had chosen for such a different purpose) the stalking-horses of their splenetic and gloomy humours.

Indeed, so much affection for him had been added in this one evening to my gratitude that I hoped I already began to understand him through that mingled feeling. Any seeming inconsistencies in Mr. Skimpole or in Mrs. Jellyby I could not expect to be able to reconcile, having so little experience or practical knowledge. Neither did I try, for my thoughts were busy when I was alone, with Ada and Richard and with the confidence I had seemed to receive concerning them. My fancy, made a little wild by the wind perhaps, would not consent to be all unselfish, either, though I would have persuaded it to be so if I could. It wandered back to my godmother's house and came along the intervening track, raising up shadowy speculations which had sometimes trembled there in the dark as to what knowledge Mr. Jarndyce had of my earliest history—even as to the possibility of his being my father, though that idle dream was quite gone now.

It was all gone now, I remembered, getting up from the fire. It was not for me to muse over bygones, but to act with a cheerful spirit and a grateful heart. So I said to myself, "Esther, Esther, Esther! Duty, my dear!" and gave my little basket of housekeeping keys such a shake that they sounded like little bells and rang me hopefully to bed.

CHAPTER VII
THE GHOST'S WALK

While Esther sleeps, and while Esther wakes, it is still wet weather down at the place in Lincolnshire. The rain is ever falling—drip, drip, drip—by day and night upon the broad flagged terrace-pavement, the Ghost's Walk. The weather is so very bad down in Lincolnshire that the liveliest imagination can scarcely apprehend its ever being fine again. Not that there is any superabundant life of imagination on the spot, for Sir Leicester is not here (and, truly, even if he were, would not do much for it in that particular), but is in Paris with my Lady; and solitude, with dusky wings, sits brooding upon Chesney Wold.

There may be some motions of fancy among the lower animals at Chesney Wold. The horses in the stables—the long stables in a barren, red-brick court-yard, where there is a great bell in a turret, and a clock with a large face, which the pigeons who live near it and who love to perch upon its shoulders seem to be always consulting—THEY may contemplate some mental pictures of fine weather on occasions, and may be better artists at them than the grooms. The old roan, so famous for cross-country work, turning his large eyeball to the grated window near his rack, may remember the fresh leaves that glisten there at other times and the scents that stream in, and may have a fine run with the hounds, while the human helper, clearing out the next stall, never stirs beyond his pitchfork and birch-broom. The grey, whose place is opposite the door and who with an impatient rattle of his halter pricks his ears and turns his head so wistfully when it is opened, and to whom the opener says, "Woa grey, then, steady! Noabody wants you to-day!" may know it quite as well as the man. The whole seemingly monotonous and uncompanionable half-dozen, stabled together, may pass the long wet hours when the door is shut in livelier communication than is held in the servants' hall or at the Dedlock Arms, or may even beguile the time by improving (perhaps corrupting) the pony in the loose-box in the corner.

So the mastiff, dozing in his kennel in the court-yard with his large head on his paws, may think of the hot sunshine when the shadows of the stable-buildings tire his patience out by changing and leave him at one time of the day no broader refuge than the shadow of his own house, where he sits on end, panting and growling short, and very much wanting something to worry besides himself and his chain. So now, half-waking and all-winking, he may recall the house full of company, the coach-houses full of vehicles, the stables full of horses, and the out-buildings full of attendants upon horses, until he is undecided about the present and comes forth to see how it is. Then, with that impatient shake of himself, he may growl in the spirit, "Rain, rain, rain!

Nothing but rain—and no family here!" as he goes in again and lies down with a gloomy yawn.

So with the dogs in the kennel-buildings across the park, who have their restless fits and whose doleful voices when the wind has been very obstinate have even made it known in the house itself—upstairs, downstairs, and in my Lady's chamber. They may hunt the whole country-side, while the raindrops are pattering round their inactivity. So the rabbits with their self-betraying tails, frisking in and out of holes at roots of trees, may be lively with ideas of the breezy days when their ears are blown about or of those seasons of interest when there are sweet young plants to gnaw. The turkey in the poultry-yard, always troubled with a class-grievance (probably Christmas), may be reminiscent of that summer morning wrongfully taken from him when he got into the lane among the felled trees, where there was a barn and barley. The discontented goose, who stoops to pass under the old gateway, twenty feet high, may gabble out, if we only knew it, a waddling preference for weather when the gateway casts its shadow on the ground.

Be this as it may, there is not much fancy otherwise stirring at Chesney Wold. If there be a little at any odd moment, it goes, like a little noise in that old echoing place, a long way and usually leads off to ghosts and mystery.

It has rained so hard and rained so long down in Lincolnshire that Mrs. Rouncewell, the old housekeeper at Chesney Wold, has several times taken off her spectacles and cleaned them to make certain that the drops were not upon the glasses. Mrs. Rouncewell might have been sufficiently assured by hearing the rain, but that she is rather deaf, which nothing will induce her to believe. She is a fine old lady, handsome, stately, wonderfully neat, and has such a back and such a stomacher that if her stays should turn out when she dies to have been a broad old-fashioned family fire-grate, nobody who knows her would have cause to be surprised. Weather affects Mrs. Rouncewell little. The house is there in all weathers, and the house, as she expresses it, "is what she looks at." She sits in her room (in a side passage on the ground floor, with an arched window commanding a smooth quadrangle, adorned at regular intervals with smooth round trees and smooth round blocks of stone, as if the trees were going to play at bowls with the stones), and the whole house reposes on her mind. She can open it on occasion and be busy and fluttered, but it is shut up now and lies on the breadth of Mrs. Rouncewell's iron-bound bosom in a majestic sleep.

It is the next difficult thing to an impossibility to imagine Chesney Wold without Mrs. Rouncewell, but she has only been here fifty years. Ask her how long, this rainy day, and she shall answer "fifty year, three months, and a fortnight, by the blessing of heaven, if I live till Tuesday." Mr. Rouncewell died some time before the decease of the pretty fashion of pig-tails, and modestly hid his own (if he took it with him) in a corner of the churchyard in the park near the mouldy porch. He was born in the market-town, and so was his young widow. Her progress in the family began in the time of the last Sir Leicester and originated in the still-room.

The present representative of the Dedlocks is an excellent master. He supposes all his dependents to be utterly bereft of individual characters, intentions, or opinions, and is persuaded that he was born to supersede the necessity of their having any. If he were to make a discovery to the contrary, he would be simply stunned—would never recover himself, most likely, except to gasp and die. But he is an excellent master still, holding it a part of his state to be so. He has a great liking for Mrs. Rouncewell; he says she is a most respectable, creditable woman. He always shakes hands with her when he comes down to Chesney Wold and when he goes away; and if he were very ill, or if he were knocked down by accident, or run over, or placed in any situation expressive of a Dedlock at a disadvantage, he would say if he could speak, "Leave me, and send Mrs. Rouncewell here!" feeling his dignity, at such a pass, safer with her than with anybody else.

Mrs. Rouncewell has known trouble. She has had two sons, of whom the younger ran wild, and went for a soldier, and never came back. Even to this hour, Mrs. Rouncewell's calm hands lose their composure when she speaks of him, and unfolding themselves from her stomacher, hover about her in an agitated manner as she says what a likely lad, what a fine lad, what a gay, good-humoured, clever lad he was! Her second son would have been provided for at Chesney Wold and would have been made steward in due season, but he took, when he was a schoolboy, to constructing steam-engines out of saucepans and setting birds to draw their own water with the least possible amount of labour, so assisting them with artful contrivance of hydraulic pressure that a thirsty canary had only, in a literal sense, to put his shoulder to the wheel and the job was done. This propensity gave Mrs. Rouncewell great uneasiness. She felt it with a mother's anguish to be a move in the Wat Tyler direction, well knowing that Sir Leicester had that general impression of an aptitude for any art to which smoke and a tall chimney might be considered essential. But the doomed young rebel (otherwise a mild youth, and very persevering), showing no sign of grace as he got older but, on the contrary, constructing a model of a power-loom, she was fain, with many tears, to mention his backslidings to the baronet. "Mrs. Rouncewell," said Sir Leicester, "I can never consent to argue, as you know, with any one on any subject. You had better get rid of your boy; you had better get him into some Works. The iron country farther north is, I suppose, the congenial direction for a boy with these tendencies." Farther north he went, and farther north he grew up; and if Sir Leicester Dedlock ever saw him when he came to Chesney Wold to visit his mother, or ever thought of him afterwards, it is certain that he only regarded him as one of a body of some odd thousand conspirators, swarthy and grim, who were in the habit of turning out by torchlight two or three nights in the week for unlawful purposes.

Nevertheless, Mrs. Rouncewell's son has, in the course of nature and art, grown up, and established himself, and married, and called unto him Mrs. Rouncewell's grandson, who, being out of his apprenticeship, and home from a journey in far countries, whither he was sent to enlarge his knowledge and complete his preparations for the venture of this life, stands leaning against the chimney-piece this very day in Mrs. Rouncewell's room at Chesney Wold.

"And, again and again, I am glad to see you, Watt! And, once again, I am glad to see you, Watt!" says Mrs. Rouncewell. "You are a fine young fellow. You are like your poor uncle George. Ah!" Mrs. Rouncewell's hands unquiet, as usual, on this reference.

"They say I am like my father, grandmother."

"Like him, also, my dear—but most like your poor uncle George! And your dear father." Mrs. Rouncewell folds her hands again. "He is well?"

"Thriving, grandmother, in every way."

"I am thankful!" Mrs. Rouncewell is fond of her son but has a plaintive feeling towards him, much as if he were a very honourable soldier who had gone over to the enemy.

"He is quite happy?" says she.

"Quite."

"I am thankful! So he has brought you up to follow in his ways and has sent you into foreign countries and the like? Well, he knows best. There may be a world beyond Chesney Wold that I don't understand. Though I am not young, either. And I have seen a quantity of good company too!"

"Grandmother," says the young man, changing the subject, "what a very pretty girl that was I found with you just now. You called her Rosa?"

"Yes, child. She is daughter of a widow in the village. Maids are so hard to teach, now-a-days, that I have put her about me young. She's an apt scholar and will do well. She shows the house already, very pretty. She lives with me at my table here."

"I hope I have not driven her away?"

"She supposes we have family affairs to speak about, I dare say. She is very modest. It is a fine quality in a young woman. And scarcer," says Mrs. Rouncewell, expanding her stomacher to its utmost limits, "than it formerly was!"

The young man inclines his head in acknowledgment of the precepts of experience. Mrs. Rouncewell listens.

"Wheels!" says she. They have long been audible to the younger ears of her companion. "What wheels on such a day as this, for gracious sake?"

After a short interval, a tap at the door. "Come in!" A dark-eyed, dark-haired, shy, village beauty comes in—so fresh in her rosy and yet delicate bloom that the drops of rain which have beaten on her hair look like the dew upon a flower fresh gathered.

"What company is this, Rosa?" says Mrs. Rouncewell.

"It's two young men in a gig, ma'am, who want to see the house—yes, and if you please, I told them so!" in quick reply to a gesture of dissent from the housekeeper. "I went to the hall-door and told them it was the wrong day and the wrong hour, but the young man who was driving took off his hat in the wet and begged me to bring this card to you."

"Read it, my dear Watt," says the housekeeper.

Rosa is so shy as she gives it to him that they drop it between them and almost knock their foreheads together as they pick it up. Rosa is shyer than before.

"Mr. Guppy" is all the information the card yields.

"Guppy!" repeats Mrs. Rouncewell, "MR. Guppy! Nonsense, I never heard of him!"

"If you please, he told ME that!" says Rosa. "But he said that he and the other young gentleman came from London only last night by the mail, on business at the magistrates' meeting, ten miles off, this morning, and that as their business was soon over, and they had heard a great deal said of Chesney Wold, and really didn't know what to do with themselves, they had come through the wet to see it. They are lawyers. He says he is not in Mr. Tulkinghorn's office, but he is sure he may make use of Mr. Tulkinghorn's name if necessary." Finding, now she leaves off, that she has been making quite a long speech, Rosa is shyer than ever.

Now, Mr. Tulkinghorn is, in a manner, part and parcel of the place, and besides, is supposed to have made Mrs. Rouncewell's will. The old lady relaxes, consents to the admission of the visitors as a favour, and dismisses Rosa. The grandson, however, being smitten by a sudden wish to see the house himself, proposes to join the party. The grandmother, who is pleased that he should have that interest, accompanies him—though to do him justice, he is exceedingly unwilling to trouble her.

"Much obliged to you, ma'am!" says Mr. Guppy, divesting himself of his wet dreadnought in the hall. "Us London lawyers don't often get an out, and when we do, we like to make the most of it, you know."

The old housekeeper, with a gracious severity of deportment, waves her hand towards the great staircase. Mr. Guppy and his friend follow Rosa; Mrs. Rouncewell and her grandson follow them; a young gardener goes before to open the shutters.

As is usually the case with people who go over houses, Mr. Guppy and his friend are dead beat before they have well begun. They straggle about in wrong places, look at wrong things, don't care for the right things, gape when more rooms are opened, exhibit profound depression of spirits, and are clearly knocked up. In each successive chamber that they enter, Mrs. Rouncewell, who is as upright as the house itself, rests apart in a window-seat or other such nook and listens with stately approval to Rosa's exposition. Her grandson is so attentive to it that Rosa is shyer than ever—and prettier. Thus they pass on from room to room, raising the pictured Dedlocks for a few brief minutes as the young gardener admits the light, and reconsigning them to their graves as he shuts it out again. It appears to the afflicted Mr. Guppy and his inconsolable friend that there is no end to the Dedlocks, whose family greatness seems to consist in their never having done anything to distinguish themselves for seven hundred years.

Even the long drawing-room of Chesney Wold cannot revive Mr. Guppy's spirits. He is so low that he droops on the threshold and has hardly strength of mind to enter. But a portrait over the chimney-piece, painted by the fashionable artist of the day, acts upon him like a charm. He recovers in a moment. He stares at it with uncommon interest; he seems to be fixed and fascinated by it.

"Dear me!" says Mr. Guppy. "Who's that?"

"The picture over the fire-place," says Rosa, "is the portrait of the present Lady Dedlock. It is considered a perfect likeness, and the best work of the master."

"Blest," says Mr. Guppy, staring in a kind of dismay at his friend, "if I can ever have seen her. Yet I know her! Has the picture been engraved, miss?"

"The picture has never been engraved. Sir Leicester has always refused permission."

"Well!" says Mr. Guppy in a low voice. "I'll be shot if it ain't very curious how well I know that picture! So that's Lady Dedlock, is it!"

"The picture on the right is the present Sir Leicester Dedlock. The picture on the left is his father, the late Sir Leicester."

Mr. Guppy has no eyes for either of these magnates. "It's unaccountable to me," he says, still staring at the portrait, "how well I know that picture! I'm dashed," adds Mr. Guppy, looking round, "if I don't think I must have had a dream of that picture, you know!"

As no one present takes any especial interest in Mr. Guppy's dreams, the probability is not pursued. But he still remains so absorbed by the portrait that he stands immovable before it until the young gardener has closed the shutters, when he comes out of the room in a dazed state that is an odd though a sufficient substitute for interest and follows into the succeeding rooms with a confused stare, as if he were looking everywhere for Lady Dedlock again.

He sees no more of her. He sees her rooms, which are the last shown, as being very elegant, and he looks out of the windows from which she looked out, not long ago, upon the weather that bored her to death. All things have an end, even houses that people take infinite pains to see and are tired of before they begin to see them. He has come to the end of the sight, and the fresh village beauty to the end of her description; which is always this: "The terrace below is much admired. It is called, from an old story in the family, the Ghost's Walk."

"No?" says Mr. Guppy, greedily curious. "What's the story, miss? Is it anything about a picture?"

"Pray tell us the story," says Watt in a half whisper.

"I don't know it, sir." Rosa is shyer than ever.

"It is not related to visitors; it is almost forgotten," says the housekeeper, advancing. "It has never been more than a family anecdote."

"You'll excuse my asking again if it has anything to do with a picture, ma'am," observes Mr. Guppy, "because I do assure you that the more I think of that picture the better I know it, without knowing how I know it!"

The story has nothing to do with a picture; the housekeeper can guarantee that. Mr. Guppy is obliged to her for the information and is, moreover, generally obliged. He retires with his friend, guided down another staircase by the young gardener, and presently is heard to drive away. It is now dusk. Mrs. Rouncewell can trust to the discretion of her two young hearers and may tell THEM how the terrace came to have that ghostly name.

She seats herself in a large chair by the fast-darkening window and tells them: "In the wicked days, my dears, of King Charles the First—I mean, of course, in the wicked days of the rebels who leagued themselves against that excellent king—Sir Morbury Dedlock was the owner of Chesney Wold. Whether there was any account of a ghost in the family before those days, I can't say. I should think it very likely indeed."

Mrs. Rouncewell holds this opinion because she considers that a family of such antiquity and importance has a right to a ghost. She regards a ghost as one of the privileges of the upper classes, a genteel distinction to which the common people have no claim.

"Sir Morbury Dedlock," says Mrs. Rouncewell, "was, I have no occasion to say, on the side of the blessed martyr. But it IS supposed that his Lady, who had none of the family blood in her veins, favoured the bad cause. It is said that she had relations among King Charles's enemies, that she was in correspondence with them, and that she gave them information. When any of the country gentlemen who followed his Majesty's cause met here, it is said that my Lady was always nearer to the door of their council-room than they supposed. Do you hear a sound like a footstep passing along the terrace, Watt?"

Rosa draws nearer to the housekeeper.

"I hear the rain-drip on the stones," replies the young man, "and I hear a curious echo—I suppose an echo—which is very like a halting step."

The housekeeper gravely nods and continues: "Partly on account of this division between them, and partly on other accounts, Sir Morbury and his Lady led a troubled life. She was a lady of a haughty temper. They were not well suited to each other in age or character, and they had no children to moderate between them. After her favourite brother, a young gentleman, was killed in the civil wars (by Sir Morbury's near kinsman), her feeling was so violent that she hated the race into which she had married. When the Dedlocks were about to ride out from Chesney Wold in the king's cause, she is supposed to have more than once stolen down into the stables in the dead of night and lamed their horses; and the story is that once at such an hour, her husband saw her gliding down the stairs and followed her into the stall where his own favourite horse stood. There he seized her by the wrist, and in a struggle or in a fall or through the horse being frightened and lashing out, she was lamed in the hip and from that hour began to pine away."

The housekeeper has dropped her voice to a little more than a whisper.

"She had been a lady of a handsome figure and a noble carriage. She never complained of the change; she never spoke to any one of being crippled or of being in pain, but day by day she tried to walk upon the terrace, and with the help of the stone balustrade, went up and down, up and down, up and down, in sun and shadow, with greater difficulty every day. At last, one afternoon her husband (to whom she had never, on any persuasion, opened her lips since that night), standing at the great south window, saw her drop upon the pavement. He hastened down to raise her, but she repulsed him as he bent over her, and looking at him fixedly and coldly, said, 'I will die here where I have walked. And I will walk here, though I am in my grave. I will walk here until the pride of this house is humbled. And when calamity or when disgrace is coming to it, let the Dedlocks listen for my step!'"

Watt looks at Rosa. Rosa in the deepening gloom looks down upon the ground, half frightened and half shy.

"There and then she died. And from those days," says Mrs. Rouncewell, "the name has come down—the Ghost's Walk. If the tread is an echo, it is an echo that is only heard after dark, and is often unheard for a long while together. But it comes back from time to time; and so sure as there is sickness or death in the family, it will be heard then."

"And disgrace, grandmother—" says Watt.

"Disgrace never comes to Chesney Wold," returns the housekeeper.

Her grandson apologizes with "True. True."

"That is the story. Whatever the sound is, it is a worrying sound," says Mrs. Rouncewell, getting up from her chair; "and what is to be noticed in it is that it MUST BE HEARD. My Lady, who is afraid of nothing, admits that when it is there, it must be heard. You cannot shut it out. Watt, there is a tall French clock behind you (placed there, 'a purpose) that has a loud beat when it is in motion and can play music. You understand how those things are managed?"

"Pretty well, grandmother, I think."

"Set it a-going."

Watt sets it a-going—music and all.

"Now, come hither," says the housekeeper. "Hither, child, towards my Lady's pillow. I am not sure that it is dark enough yet, but listen! Can you hear the sound upon the terrace, through the music, and the beat, and everything?"

"I certainly can!"

"So my Lady says."

CHAPTER VIII
COVERING A MULTITUDE OF SINS

It was interesting when I dressed before daylight to peep out of window, where my candles were reflected in the black panes like two beacons, and finding all beyond still enshrouded in the indistinctness of last night, to watch how it turned out when the day came on. As the prospect gradually revealed itself and disclosed the scene over which the wind had wandered in the dark, like my memory over my life, I had a pleasure in discovering the unknown objects that had been around me in my sleep. At first they were faintly discernible in the mist, and above them the later stars still glimmered. That pale interval over, the picture began to enlarge and fill up so fast that at every new peep I could have found enough to look at for an hour. Imperceptibly my candles became the only incongruous part of the morning, the dark places in my room all melted away, and the day shone bright upon a cheerful landscape, prominent in which the old Abbey Church, with its massive tower, threw a softer train of shadow on the view than seemed compatible with its rugged character. But so from rough outsides (I hope I have learnt), serene and gentle influences often proceed.

Every part of the house was in such order, and every one was so attentive to me, that I had no trouble with my two bunches of keys, though what with trying to remember the contents of each little store-room drawer and cupboard; and what with making notes on a slate about jams, and pickles, and preserves, and bottles, and glass, and china, and a great many other things; and what with being generally a methodical, old-maidish sort of foolish little person, I was so busy that I could not believe it was breakfast-time when I heard the bell ring. Away I ran, however, and made tea, as I had already been installed into the responsibility of the tea-pot; and then, as they were all rather late and nobody was down yet, I thought I would take a peep at the garden and get some knowledge of that too. I found it quite a delightful place—in front, the pretty avenue and drive by which we had approached (and where, by the by, we had cut up the gravel so terribly with our wheels that I asked the gardener to roll it); at the back, the flower-garden, with my darling at her window up there, throwing it open to smile out at me, as if she would have kissed me from that distance. Beyond the flower-garden was a kitchen-garden, and then a paddock, and then a snug little rick-yard, and then a dear little farm-yard. As to the house itself, with its three peaks in the roof; its various-shaped windows, some so large, some so small, and all so pretty; its trellis-work, against the south-front for roses and honey-suckle, and its homely, comfortable, welcoming look—it was, as Ada said when she came out to meet me with her arm through that of its master, worthy of her cousin John, a bold thing to say, though he only pinched her dear cheek for it.

Mr. Skimpole was as agreeable at breakfast as he had been overnight. There was honey on the table, and it led him into a discourse about bees. He had no objection to honey, he said (and I should think he had not, for he seemed to like it), but he protested against the overweening assumptions of bees. He didn't at all see why the busy bee should be proposed as a model to him; he supposed the bee liked to make honey, or he wouldn't do it—nobody asked him. It was not necessary for the bee to make such a merit of his tastes. If every confectioner went buzzing about the world banging against everything that came in his way and egotistically calling upon everybody to take notice that he was going to his work and must not be interrupted, the world would be quite an unsupportable place. Then, after all, it was a ridiculous position to be smoked out of your fortune with brimstone as soon as you had made it. You would have a very mean opinion of a Manchester man if he spun cotton for no other purpose. He must say he thought a drone the embodiment of a pleasanter and wiser idea. The drone said unaffectedly, "You will excuse me; I really cannot attend to the shop! I find myself in a world in which there is so much to see and so short a time to see it in that I must take the liberty of looking about me and begging to be provided for by somebody who doesn't want to look about him." This appeared to Mr. Skimpole to be the drone philosophy, and he thought it a very good philosophy, always supposing the drone to be willing to be on good terms with the bee, which, so far as he knew, the easy fellow always was, if the consequential creature would only let him, and not be so conceited about his honey!

He pursued this fancy with the lightest foot over a variety of ground and made us all merry, though again he seemed to have as serious a meaning in what he said as he was capable of having. I left them still listening to him when I withdrew to attend to my new duties. They had occupied me for some time, and I was passing through the passages on my return with my basket of keys on my arm when Mr. Jarndyce called me into a small room next his bed-chamber, which I found to be in part a little library of books and papers and in part quite a little museum of his boots and shoes and hat-boxes.

"Sit down, my dear," said Mr. Jarndyce. "This, you must know, is the growlery. When I am out of humour, I come and growl here."

"You must be here very seldom, sir," said I.

"Oh, you don't know me!" he returned. "When I am deceived or disappointed in—the wind, and it's easterly, I take refuge here. The growlery is the best-used room in the house. You are not aware of half my humours yet. My dear, how you are trembling!"

I could not help it; I tried very hard, but being alone with that benevolent presence, and meeting his kind eyes, and feeling so happy and so honoured there, and my heart so full—I kissed his hand. I don't know what I said, or even that I spoke. He was disconcerted and walked to the window; I almost believed with an intention of jumping out, until he turned and I was reassured by seeing in his eyes what he had gone there to hide. He gently patted me on the head, and I sat down.

"There! There!" he said. "That's over. Pooh! Don't be foolish."

"It shall not happen again, sir," I returned, "but at first it is difficult—"

"Nonsense!" he said. "It's easy, easy. Why not? I hear of a good little orphan girl without a protector, and I take it into my head to be that protector. She grows up, and more than justifies my good opinion, and I remain her guardian and her friend. What is there in all this? So, so! Now, we have cleared off old scores, and I have before me thy pleasant, trusting, trusty face again."

I said to myself, "Esther, my dear, you surprise me! This really is not what I expected of you!" And it had such a good effect that I folded my hands upon my basket and quite recovered myself. Mr. Jarndyce, expressing his approval in his face, began to talk to me as confidentially as if I had been in the habit of conversing with him every morning for I don't know how long. I almost felt as if I had.

"Of course, Esther," he said, "you don't understand this Chancery business?"

And of course I shook my head.

"I don't know who does," he returned. "The lawyers have twisted it into such a state of bedevilment that the original merits of the case have long disappeared from the face of the earth. It's about a will and the trusts under a will—or it was once. It's about nothing but costs now. We are always appearing, and disappearing, and swearing, and interrogating, and filing, and cross-filing, and arguing, and sealing, and motioning, and referring, and reporting, and revolving about the Lord Chancellor and all his satellites, and equitably waltzing ourselves off to dusty death, about costs. That's the great question. All the rest, by some extraordinary means, has melted away."

"But it was, sir," said I, to bring him back, for he began to rub his head, "about a will?"

"Why, yes, it was about a will when it was about anything," he returned. "A certain Jarndyce, in an evil hour, made a great fortune, and made a great will. In the question how the trusts under that will are to be administered, the fortune left by the will is squandered away; the legatees under the will are reduced to such a miserable condition that they would be sufficiently punished if they had committed an enormous crime in having money left them, and the will itself is made a dead letter. All through the deplorable cause, everything that everybody in it, except one man, knows already is referred to that only one man who don't know, it to find out—all through the deplorable cause, everybody must have copies, over and over again, of everything that has accumulated about it in the way of cartloads of papers (or must pay for them without having them, which is the usual course, for nobody wants them) and must go down the middle and up again through such an infernal country-dance of costs and fees and nonsense and corruption as was never dreamed of in the wildest visions of a witch's Sabbath. Equity sends questions to law, law sends questions back to equity; law finds it can't do this, equity finds it can't do that; neither can so much as say it can't do anything, without this solicitor instructing and this counsel appearing for A, and that solicitor instructing and that counsel appearing for B; and so on through the whole alphabet, like the history of the apple pie. And thus, through years and years, and lives and lives, everything goes on, constantly beginning over and over again, and nothing ever ends. And we can't get out of the suit on any terms, for we are made parties to it, and MUST BE parties to it, whether we like it or not. But it won't do to think of it! When my great uncle, poor Tom Jarndyce, began to think of it, it was the beginning of the end!"

"The Mr. Jarndyce, sir, whose story I have heard?"

He nodded gravely. "I was his heir, and this was his house, Esther. When I came here, it was bleak indeed. He had left the signs of his misery upon it."

"How changed it must be now!" I said.

"It had been called, before his time, the Peaks. He gave it its present name and lived here shut up, day and night poring over the wicked heaps of papers in the suit and hoping against hope to disentangle it from its mystification and bring it to a close. In the meantime, the place became dilapidated, the wind whistled through the cracked walls, the rain fell through the broken roof, the weeds choked the passage to the rotting door. When I brought what remained of him home here, the brains seemed to me to have been blown out of the house too, it was so shattered and ruined."

He walked a little to and fro after saying this to himself with a shudder, and then looked at me, and brightened, and came and sat down again with his hands in his pockets.

"I told you this was the growlery, my dear. Where was I?"

I reminded him, at the hopeful change he had made in Bleak House.

"Bleak House; true. There is, in that city of London there, some property of ours which is much at this day what Bleak House was then; I say property of ours, meaning of the suit's, but I ought to call it the property of costs, for costs is the only power on earth that will ever get anything out of it now or will ever know it for anything but an eyesore and a heartsore. It is a street of perishing blind houses, with their eyes stoned out, without a pane of glass, without so much as a window-frame, with the bare blank shutters tumbling from their hinges and falling asunder, the iron rails peeling away in flakes of rust, the chimneys sinking in, the stone steps to every door (and every door might be death's door) turning stagnant green, the very crutches on which the ruins are propped decaying. Although Bleak House was not in Chancery, its master was, and it was stamped with the same seal. These are the Great Seal's impressions, my dear, all over England—the children know them!"

"How changed it is!" I said again.

"Why, so it is," he answered much more cheerfully; "and it is wisdom in you to keep me to the bright side of the picture." (The idea of my wisdom!) "These are things I never talk about or even think about, excepting in the growlery here. If you consider it right to mention them to Rick and Ada," looking seriously at me, "you can. I leave it to your discretion, Esther."

"I hope, sir—" said I.

"I think you had better call me guardian, my dear."

I felt that I was choking again—I taxed myself with it, "Esther, now, you know you are!"—when he feigned to say this slightly, as if it were a whim instead of a thoughtful tenderness. But I gave the housekeeping keys the least shake in the world as a reminder to myself, and folding my hands in a still more determined manner on the basket, looked at him quietly.

"I hope, guardian," said I, "that you may not trust too much to my discretion. I hope you may not mistake me. I am afraid it will be a disappointment to you to know that I am not clever, but it really is the truth, and you would soon find it out if I had not the honesty to confess it."

He did not seem at all disappointed; quite the contrary. He told me, with a smile all over his face, that he knew me very well indeed and that I was quite clever enough for him.

"I hope I may turn out so," said I, "but I am much afraid of it, guardian."

"You are clever enough to be the good little woman of our lives here, my dear," he returned playfully; "the little old woman of the child's (I don't mean Skimpole's) rhyme:

"'Little old woman, and whither so high?'
'To sweep the cobwebs out of the sky.'

"You will sweep them so neatly out of OUR sky in the course of your housekeeping, Esther, that one of these days we shall have to abandon the growlery and nail up the door."

This was the beginning of my being called Old Woman, and Little Old Woman, and Cobweb, and Mrs. Shipton, and Mother Hubbard, and Dame Durden, and so many names of that sort that my own name soon became quite lost among them.

"However," said Mr. Jarndyce, "to return to our gossip. Here's Rick, a fine young fellow full of promise. What's to be done with him?"

Oh, my goodness, the idea of asking my advice on such a point!

"Here he is, Esther," said Mr. Jarndyce, comfortably putting his hands into his pockets and stretching out his legs. "He must have a profession; he must make some choice for himself. There will be a world more wiglomeration about it, I suppose, but it must be done."

"More what, guardian?" said I.

"More wiglomeration," said he. "It's the only name I know for the thing. He is a ward in Chancery, my dear. Kenge and Carboy will have something to say about it; Master Somebody—a sort of ridiculous sexton, digging graves for the merits of causes in a back room at the end of Quality Court, Chancery Lane—will have something to say about it; counsel will have something to say about it; the Chancellor will have something to say about it; the satellites will have something to say about it; they will all have to be handsomely feed, all round, about it; the whole thing will be vastly ceremonious, wordy, unsatisfactory, and expensive, and I call it, in general, wiglomeration. How mankind ever came to be afflicted with wiglomeration, or for whose sins these young people ever fell into a pit of it, I don't know; so it is."

He began to rub his head again and to hint that he felt the wind. But it was a delightful instance of his kindness towards me that whether he rubbed his head, or walked about, or did both, his face was sure to recover its benignant expression as it looked at mine; and he was sure to turn comfortable again and put his hands in his pockets and stretch out his legs.

"Perhaps it would be best, first of all," said I, "to ask Mr. Richard what he inclines to himself."

"Exactly so," he returned. "That's what I mean! You know, just accustom yourself to talk it over, with your tact and in your quiet way, with him and Ada, and see what you all make of it. We are sure to come at the heart of the matter by your means, little woman."

I really was frightened at the thought of the importance I was attaining and the number of things that were being confided to me. I had not meant this at all; I had meant that he should speak to Richard. But of course I said nothing in reply except that I would do my best, though I feared (I really felt it necessary to repeat this) that he thought me much more sagacious than I was. At which my guardian only laughed the pleasantest laugh I ever heard.

"Come!" he said, rising and pushing back his chair. "I think we may have done with the growlery for one day! Only a concluding word. Esther, my dear, do you wish to ask me anything?"

He looked so attentively at me that I looked attentively at him and felt sure I understood him.

"About myself, sir?" said I.

"Yes."

"Guardian," said I, venturing to put my hand, which was suddenly colder than I could have wished, in his, "nothing! I am quite sure that if there were anything I ought to know or had any need to know, I should not have to ask you to tell it to me. If my whole reliance and confidence were not placed in you, I must have a hard heart indeed. I have nothing to ask you, nothing in the world."

He drew my hand through his arm and we went away to look for Ada. From that hour I felt quite easy with him, quite unreserved, quite content to know no more, quite happy.

We lived, at first, rather a busy life at Bleak House, for we had to become acquainted with many residents in and out of the neighbourhood who knew

Mr. Jarndyce. It seemed to Ada and me that everybody knew him who wanted to do anything with anybody else's money. It amazed us when we began to sort his letters and to answer some of them for him in the growlery of a morning to find how the great object of the lives of nearly all his correspondents appeared to be to form themselves into committees for getting in and laying out money. The ladies were as desperate as the gentlemen; indeed, I think they were even more so. They threw themselves into committees in the most impassioned manner and collected subscriptions with a vehemence quite extraordinary. It appeared to us that some of them must pass their whole lives in dealing out subscription-cards to the whole post-office directory—shilling cards, half-crown cards, half-sovereign cards, penny cards. They wanted everything. They wanted wearing apparel, they wanted linen rags, they wanted money, they wanted coals, they wanted soup, they wanted interest, they wanted autographs, they wanted flannel, they wanted whatever Mr. Jarndyce had—or had not. Their objects were as various as their demands. They were going to raise new buildings, they were going to pay off debts on old buildings, they were going to establish in a picturesque building (engraving of proposed west elevation attached) the Sisterhood of Mediaeval Marys, they were going to give a testimonial to Mrs. Jellyby, they were going to have their secretary's portrait painted and presented to his mother-in-law, whose deep devotion to him was well known, they were going to get up everything, I really believe, from five hundred thousand tracts to an annuity and from a marble monument to a silver tea-pot. They took a multitude of titles. They were the Women of England, the Daughters of Britain, the Sisters of all the cardinal virtues separately, the Females of America, the Ladies of a hundred denominations. They appeared to be always excited about canvassing and electing. They seemed to our poor wits, and according to their own accounts, to be constantly polling people by tens of thousands, yet never bringing their candidates in for anything. It made our heads ache to think, on the whole, what feverish lives they must lead.

Among the ladies who were most distinguished for this rapacious benevolence (if I may use the expression) was a Mrs. Pardiggle, who seemed, as I judged from the number of her letters to Mr. Jarndyce, to be almost as powerful a correspondent as Mrs. Jellyby herself. We observed that the wind always changed when Mrs. Pardiggle became the subject of conversation and that it invariably interrupted Mr. Jarndyce and prevented his going any farther, when he had remarked that there were two classes of charitable people; one, the people who did a little and made a great deal of noise; the other, the people who did a great deal and made no noise at all. We were therefore curious to see Mrs. Pardiggle, suspecting her to be a type of the former class, and were glad when she called one day with her five young sons.

She was a formidable style of lady with spectacles, a prominent nose, and a loud voice, who had the effect of wanting a great deal of room. And she really did, for she knocked down little chairs with her skirts that were quite a great way off. As only Ada and I were at home, we received her timidly, for she seemed to come in like cold weather and to make the little Pardiggles blue as they followed.

"These, young ladies," said Mrs. Pardiggle with great volubility after the first salutations, "are my five boys. You may have seen their names in a printed subscription list (perhaps more than one) in the possession of our esteemed friend Mr. Jarndyce. Egbert, my eldest (twelve), is the boy who sent out his pocket-money, to the amount of five and threepence, to the Tockahoopo Indians. Oswald, my second (ten and a half), is the child who contributed two and nine-pence to the Great National Smithers Testimonial. Francis, my third (nine), one and sixpence halfpenny; Felix, my fourth (seven), eightpence to the Superannuated Widows; Alfred, my youngest (five), has voluntarily enrolled himself in the Infant Bonds of Joy, and is pledged never, through life, to use tobacco in any form."

We had never seen such dissatisfied children. It was not merely that they were weazened and shrivelled—though they were certainly that too—but they looked absolutely ferocious with discontent. At the mention of the Tockahoopo Indians, I could really have supposed Egbert to be one of the most baleful members of that tribe, he gave me such a savage frown. The face of each child, as the amount of his contribution was mentioned, darkened in a peculiarly vindictive manner, but his was by far the worst. I must except, however, the little recruit into the Infant Bonds of Joy, who was stolidly and evenly miserable.

"You have been visiting, I understand," said Mrs. Pardiggle, "at Mrs. Jellyby's?"

We said yes, we had passed one night there.

"Mrs. Jellyby," pursued the lady, always speaking in the same demonstrative, loud, hard tone, so that her voice impressed my fancy as if it had a sort of spectacles on too—and I may take the opportunity of remarking that her spectacles were made the less engaging by her eyes being what Ada called "choking eyes," meaning very prominent—"Mrs. Jellyby is a benefactor to society and deserves a helping hand. My boys have contributed to the African project—Egbert, one and six, being the entire allowance of nine weeks; Oswald, one and a penny halfpenny, being the same; the rest, according to their little means. Nevertheless, I do not go with Mrs. Jellyby in all things. I do not go with Mrs. Jellyby in her treatment of her young family. It has been noticed. It has been observed that her young family are excluded from participation in the objects to which she is devoted. She may be right, she may be wrong; but, right or wrong, this is not my course with MY young family. I take them everywhere."

I was afterwards convinced (and so was Ada) that from the ill-conditioned eldest child, these words extorted a sharp yell. He turned it off into a yawn, but it began as a yell.

"They attend matins with me (very prettily done) at half-past six o'clock in the morning all the year round, including of course the depth of winter," said Mrs. Pardiggle rapidly, "and they are with me during the revolving duties of the day. I am a School lady, I am a Visiting lady, I am a Reading lady, I am a Distributing lady; I am on the local Linen Box Committee and many general committees; and my canvassing alone is very extensive—perhaps no one's more so. But they are my companions everywhere; and by these means they acquire that knowledge of the poor, and that capacity of doing charitable business in general—in short, that taste for the sort of thing—which will render them in after life a service to their neighbours and a satisfaction to themselves. My young family are not frivolous; they expend the entire amount of their allowance in subscriptions, under my direction; and they have attended as many public meetings and listened to as many lectures, orations, and discussions as generally fall to the lot of few grown people. Alfred (five), who, as I mentioned, has of his own election joined the Infant Bonds of Joy, was one of the very few children who manifested consciousness on that occasion after a fervid address of two hours from the chairman of the evening."

Alfred glowered at us as if he never could, or would, forgive the injury of that night.

"You may have observed, Miss Summerson," said Mrs. Pardiggle, "in some of the lists to which I have referred, in the possession of our esteemed friend Mr. Jarndyce, that the names of my young family are concluded with the name of O. A. Pardiggle, F.R.S., one pound. That is their father. We usually observe the same routine. I put down my mite first; then my young family enrol their contributions, according to their ages and their little means; and then Mr. Pardiggle brings up the rear. Mr. Pardiggle is happy to throw in his limited donation, under my direction; and thus things are made not only pleasant to ourselves, but, we trust, improving to others."

Suppose Mr. Pardiggle were to dine with Mr. Jellyby, and suppose Mr. Jellyby were to relieve his mind after dinner to Mr. Pardiggle, would Mr. Pardiggle, in return, make any confidential communication to Mr. Jellyby? I was quite confused to find myself thinking this, but it came into my head.

"You are very pleasantly situated here!" said Mrs. Pardiggle.

We were glad to change the subject, and going to the window, pointed out the beauties of the prospect, on which the spectacles appeared to me to rest with curious indifference.

"You know Mr. Gusher?" said our visitor.

We were obliged to say that we had not the pleasure of Mr. Gusher's acquaintance.

"The loss is yours, I assure you," said Mrs. Pardiggle with her commanding deportment. "He is a very fervid, impassioned speaker—full of fire! Stationed in a waggon on this lawn, now, which, from the shape of the land, is naturally adapted to a public meeting, he would improve almost any occasion you could mention for hours and hours! By this time, young ladies," said Mrs. Pardiggle, moving back to her chair and overturning, as if by invisible agency, a little round table at a considerable distance with my work-basket on it, "by this time you have found me out, I dare say?"

This was really such a confusing question that Ada looked at me in perfect dismay. As to the guilty nature of my own consciousness after what I had been thinking, it must have been expressed in the colour of my cheeks.

"Found out, I mean," said Mrs. Pardiggle, "the prominent point in my character. I am aware that it is so prominent as to be discoverable immediately. I lay myself open to detection, I know. Well! I freely admit, I am a woman of business. I love hard work; I enjoy hard work. The excitement does me good. I am so accustomed and inured to hard work that I don't know what fatigue is."

We murmured that it was very astonishing and very gratifying, or something to that effect. I don't think we knew what it was either, but this is what our politeness expressed.

"I do not understand what it is to be tired; you cannot tire me if you try!" said Mrs. Pardiggle. "The quantity of exertion (which is no exertion to me), the amount of business (which I regard as nothing), that I go through sometimes astonishes myself. I have seen my young family, and Mr. Pardiggle, quite worn out with witnessing it, when I may truly say I have been as fresh as a lark!"

If that dark-visaged eldest boy could look more malicious than he had already looked, this was the time when he did it. I observed that he doubled his right fist and delivered a secret blow into the crown of his cap, which was under his left arm.

"This gives me a great advantage when I am making my rounds," said Mrs. Pardiggle. "If I find a person unwilling to hear what I have to say, I tell that person directly, 'I am incapable of fatigue, my good friend, I am never tired, and I mean to go on until I have done.' It answers admirably! Miss Summerson, I hope I shall have your assistance in my visiting rounds immediately, and Miss Clare's very soon."

At first I tried to excuse myself for the present on the general ground of having occupations to attend to which I must not neglect. But as this was an ineffectual protest, I then said, more particularly, that I was not sure of my qualifications. That I was inexperienced in the art of adapting my mind to minds very differently situated, and addressing them from suitable points of view. That I had not that delicate knowledge of the heart which must be essential to such a work. That I had much to learn, myself, before I could teach others, and that I could not confide in my good intentions alone. For these reasons I thought it best to be as useful as I could, and to render what kind services I could to those immediately about me, and to try to let that circle of duty gradually and naturally expand itself. All this I said with anything but confidence, because Mrs. Pardiggle was much older than I, and had great experience, and was so very military in her manners.

"You are wrong, Miss Summerson," said she, "but perhaps you are not equal to hard work or the excitement of it, and that makes a vast difference. If you would like to see how I go through my work, I am now about—with my young family—to visit a brickmaker in the neighbourhood (a very bad character) and shall be glad to take you with me. Miss Clare also, if she will do me the favour."

Ada and I interchanged looks, and as we were going out in any case, accepted the offer. When we hastily returned from putting on our bonnets, we found the young family languishing in a corner and Mrs. Pardiggle sweeping about the room, knocking down nearly all the light objects it contained. Mrs. Pardiggle took possession of Ada, and I followed with the family.

Ada told me afterwards that Mrs. Pardiggle talked in the same loud tone (that, indeed, I overheard) all the way to the brickmaker's about an exciting contest which she had for two or three years waged against another lady relative to the bringing in of their rival candidates for a pension somewhere. There had been a quantity of printing, and promising, and proxying, and polling, and it appeared to have imparted great liveliness to all concerned, except the pensioners—who were not elected yet.

I am very fond of being confided in by children and am happy in being usually favoured in that respect, but on this occasion it gave me great uneasiness. As soon as we were out of doors, Egbert, with the manner of a little footpad, demanded a shilling of me on the ground that his pocket-money was "boned" from him. On my pointing out the great impropriety of the word, especially in connexion with his parent (for he added sulkily "By her!"), he pinched me and said, "Oh, then! Now! Who are you! YOU wouldn't like it, I think? What does she make a sham for, and pretend to give me money, and take it away again? Why do you call it my allowance, and never let me spend it?" These exasperating questions so inflamed his mind and the minds of Oswald and Francis that they all pinched me at once, and in a dreadfully expert way—screwing up such little pieces of my arms that I could hardly forbear crying out. Felix, at the same time, stamped upon my toes. And the Bond of Joy, who on account of always having the whole of his little income anticipated stood in fact pledged to abstain from cakes as well as tobacco, so swelled with grief and rage when we passed a pastry-cook's shop that he terrified me by becoming purple. I never underwent so much, both in body and mind, in the course of a walk with young people as from these unnaturally constrained children when they paid me the compliment of being natural.

I was glad when we came to the brickmaker's house, though it was one of a cluster of wretched hovels in a brick-field, with pigsties close to the broken windows and miserable little gardens before the doors growing nothing but stagnant pools. Here and there an old tub was put to catch the droppings of rain-water from a roof, or they were banked up with mud into a little pond like a large dirt-pie. At the doors and windows some men and women lounged or prowled about, and took little notice of us except to laugh to one another or to say something as we passed about gentlefolks minding their own business and not troubling their heads and muddying their shoes with coming to look after other people's.

Mrs. Pardiggle, leading the way with a great show of moral determination and talking with much volubility about the untidy habits of the people (though I doubted if the best of us could have been tidy in such a place), conducted us into a cottage at the farthest corner, the ground-floor room of which we nearly filled. Besides ourselves, there were in this damp, offensive room a woman with a black eye, nursing a poor little gasping baby by the fire; a man, all stained with clay and mud and looking very dissipated, lying at full length on the ground, smoking a pipe; a powerful young man fastening a collar on a dog; and a bold girl doing some kind of washing in very dirty water. They all looked up at us as we came in, and the woman seemed to turn her face towards the fire as if to hide her bruised eye; nobody gave us any welcome.

"Well, my friends," said Mrs. Pardiggle, but her voice had not a friendly sound, I thought; it was much too business-like and systematic. "How do you do, all of you? I am here again. I told you, you couldn't tire me, you know. I am fond of hard work, and am true to my word."

"There an't," growled the man on the floor, whose head rested on his hand as he stared at us, "any more on you to come in, is there?"

"No, my friend," said Mrs. Pardiggle, seating herself on one stool and knocking down another. "We are all here."

"Because I thought there warn't enough of you, perhaps?" said the man, with his pipe between his lips as he looked round upon us.

The young man and the girl both laughed. Two friends of the young man, whom we had attracted to the doorway and who stood there with their hands in their pockets, echoed the laugh noisily.

"You can't tire me, good people," said Mrs. Pardiggle to these latter. "I enjoy hard work, and the harder you make mine, the better I like it."

"Then make it easy for her!" growled the man upon the floor. "I wants it done, and over. I wants a end of these liberties took with my place. I wants an end of being drawed like a badger. Now you're a-going to poll-pry and question according to custom—I know what you're a-going to be up to. Well! You haven't got no occasion to be up to it. I'll save you the trouble. Is my daughter a-washin? Yes, she IS a-washin. Look at the water. Smell it! That's wot we drinks. How do you like it, and what do you think of gin instead! An't my place dirty? Yes, it is dirty—it's nat'rally dirty, and it's nat'rally onwholesome; and we've had five dirty and onwholesome children, as is all dead infants, and so much the better for them, and for us besides. Have I read the little book wot you left? No, I an't read the little book wot you left. There an't nobody here as knows how to read it; and if there wos, it wouldn't be suitable to me. It's a book fit for a babby, and I'm not a babby. If you was to leave me a doll, I shouldn't nuss it. How have I been conducting of myself? Why, I've been drunk for three days; and I'da been drunk four if I'da had the money. Don't I never mean for to go to church? No, I don't never mean for to go to church. I shouldn't be expected there, if I did; the beadle's too gen-teel for me. And how did my wife get that black eye? Why, I give it her; and if she says I didn't, she's a lie!"

He had pulled his pipe out of his mouth to say all this, and he now turned over on his other side and smoked again. Mrs. Pardiggle, who had been regarding him through her spectacles with a forcible composure, calculated, I could not help thinking, to increase his antagonism, pulled out a good book as if it were a constable's staff and took the whole family into custody. I mean into religious custody, of course; but she really did it as if she were an inexorable moral policeman carrying them all off to a station-house.

Ada and I were very uncomfortable. We both felt intrusive and out of place, and we both thought that Mrs. Pardiggle would have got on infinitely better if she had not had such a mechanical way of taking possession of people. The children sulked and stared; the family took no notice of us whatever, except when the young man made the dog bark, which he usually did when Mrs. Pardiggle was most emphatic. We both felt painfully sensible that between us and these people there was an iron barrier which could not be removed by our new friend. By whom or how it could be removed, we did not know, but we knew that. Even what she read and said seemed to us to be ill-chosen for such auditors, if it had been imparted ever so modestly and with ever so much tact. As to the little book to which the man on the floor had referred, we acquired a knowledge of it afterwards, and Mr. Jarndyce said he doubted if Robinson Crusoe could have read it, though he had had no other on his desolate island.

We were much relieved, under these circumstances, when Mrs. Pardiggle left off.

The man on the floor, then turning his head round again, said morosely, "Well! You've done, have you?"

"For to-day, I have, my friend. But I am never fatigued. I shall come to you again in your regular order," returned Mrs. Pardiggle with demonstrative cheerfulness.

"So long as you goes now," said he, folding his arms and shutting his eyes with an oath, "you may do wot you like!"

Mrs. Pardiggle accordingly rose and made a little vortex in the confined room from which the pipe itself very narrowly escaped. Taking one of her young family in each hand, and telling the others to follow closely, and expressing her hope that the brickmaker and all his house would be improved when she saw them next, she then proceeded to another cottage. I hope it is not unkind in me to say that she certainly did make, in this as in everything else, a show that was not conciliatory of doing charity by wholesale and of dealing in it to a large extent.

She supposed that we were following her, but as soon as the space was left clear, we approached the woman sitting by the fire to ask if the baby were ill.

She only looked at it as it lay on her lap. We had observed before that when she looked at it she covered her discoloured eye with her hand, as though she wished to separate any association with noise and violence and ill treatment from the poor little child.

Ada, whose gentle heart was moved by its appearance, bent down to touch its little face. As she did so, I saw what happened and drew her back. The child died.

"Oh, Esther!" cried Ada, sinking on her knees beside it. "Look here! Oh, Esther, my love, the little thing! The suffering, quiet, pretty little thing! I am so sorry for it. I am so sorry for the mother. I never saw a sight so pitiful as this before! Oh, baby, baby!"

Such compassion, such gentleness, as that with which she bent down weeping and put her hand upon the mother's might have softened any mother's heart that ever beat. The woman at first gazed at her in astonishment and then burst into tears.

Presently I took the light burden from her lap, did what I could to make the baby's rest the prettier and gentler, laid it on a shelf, and covered it with my own handkerchief. We tried to comfort the mother, and we whispered to her what Our Saviour said of children. She answered nothing, but sat weeping—weeping very much.

When I turned, I found that the young man had taken out the dog and was standing at the door looking in upon us with dry eyes, but quiet. The girl was quiet too and sat in a corner looking on the ground. The man had risen. He still smoked his pipe with an air of defiance, but he was silent.

An ugly woman, very poorly clothed, hurried in while I was glancing at them, and coming straight up to the mother, said, "Jenny! Jenny!" The mother rose on being so addressed and fell upon the woman's neck.

She also had upon her face and arms the marks of ill usage. She had no kind of grace about her, but the grace of sympathy; but when she condoled with the woman, and her own tears fell, she wanted no beauty. I say condoled, but her only words were "Jenny! Jenny!" All the rest was in the tone in which she said them.

I thought it very touching to see these two women, coarse and shabby and beaten, so united; to see what they could be to one another; to see how they felt for one another, how the heart of each to each was softened by the hard trials of their lives. I think the best side of such people is almost hidden from us. What the poor are to the poor is little known, excepting to themselves and God.

We felt it better to withdraw and leave them uninterrupted. We stole out quietly and without notice from any one except the man. He was leaning against the wall near the door, and finding that there was scarcely room for us to pass, went out before us. He seemed to want to hide that he did this on our account, but we perceived that he did, and thanked him. He made no answer.

Ada was so full of grief all the way home, and Richard, whom we found at home, was so distressed to see her in tears (though he said to me, when she was not present, how beautiful it was too!), that we arranged to return at night with some little comforts and repeat our visit at the brick-maker's house. We said as little as we could to Mr. Jarndyce, but the wind changed directly.

Richard accompanied us at night to the scene of our morning expedition. On our way there, we had to pass a noisy drinking-house, where a number of men were flocking about the door. Among them, and prominent in some dispute, was the father of the little child. At a short distance, we passed the young man and the dog, in congenial company. The sister was standing laughing and talking with some other young women at the corner of the row of cottages, but she seemed ashamed and turned away as we went by.

We left our escort within sight of the brickmaker's dwelling and proceeded by ourselves. When we came to the door, we found the woman who had brought such consolation with her standing there looking anxiously out.

"It's you, young ladies, is it?" she said in a whisper. "I'm a-watching for my master. My heart's in my mouth. If he was to catch me away from home, he'd pretty near murder me."

"Do you mean your husband?" said I.

"Yes, miss, my master. Jenny's asleep, quite worn out. She's scarcely had the child off her lap, poor thing, these seven days and nights, except when I've been able to take it for a minute or two."

As she gave way for us, she went softly in and put what we had brought near the miserable bed on which the mother slept. No effort had been made to clean the room—it seemed in its nature almost hopeless of being clean; but the small waxen form from which so much solemnity diffused itself had been composed afresh, and washed, and neatly dressed in some fragments of white linen; and on my handkerchief, which still covered the poor baby, a little bunch of sweet herbs had been laid by the same rough, scarred hands, so lightly, so tenderly!

"May heaven reward you!" we said to her. "You are a good woman."

"Me, young ladies?" she returned with surprise. "Hush! Jenny, Jenny!"

The mother had moaned in her sleep and moved. The sound of the familiar voice seemed to calm her again. She was quiet once more.

How little I thought, when I raised my handkerchief to look upon the tiny sleeper underneath and seemed to see a halo shine around the child through Ada's drooping hair as her pity bent her head—how little I thought in whose unquiet bosom that handkerchief would come to lie after covering the motionless and peaceful breast! I only thought that perhaps the Angel of the child might not be all unconscious of the woman who replaced it with so compassionate a hand; not all unconscious of her presently, when we had taken leave, and left her at the door, by turns looking, and listening in terror for herself, and saying in her old soothing manner, "Jenny, Jenny!"

CHAPTER IX
SIGNS AND TOKENS

I don't know how it is I seem to be always writing about myself. I mean all the time to write about other people, and I try to think about myself as little as possible, and I am sure, when I find myself coming into the story again, I am really vexed and say, "Dear, dear, you tiresome little creature, I wish you wouldn't!" but it is all of no use. I hope any one who may read what I write will understand that if these pages contain a great deal about me, I can only suppose it must be because I have really something to do with them and can't be kept out.

My darling and I read together, and worked, and practised, and found so much employment for our time that the winter days flew by us like bright-winged birds. Generally in the afternoons, and always in the evenings, Richard gave us his company. Although he was one of the most restless creatures in the world, he certainly was very fond of our society.

He was very, very, very fond of Ada. I mean it, and I had better say it at once. I had never seen any young people falling in love before, but I found them out quite soon. I could not say so, of course, or show that I knew anything about it. On the contrary, I was so demure and used to seem so unconscious that sometimes I considered within myself while I was sitting at work whether I was not growing quite deceitful.

But there was no help for it. All I had to do was to be quiet, and I was as quiet as a mouse. They were as quiet as mice too, so far as any words were concerned, but the innocent manner in which they relied more and more upon me as they took more and more to one another was so charming that I had great difficulty in not showing how it interested me.

"Our dear little old woman is such a capital old woman," Richard would say, coming up to meet me in the garden early, with his pleasant laugh and perhaps the least tinge of a blush, "that I can't get on without her. Before I begin my harum-scarum day—grinding away at those books and instruments and then galloping up hill and down dale, all the country round, like a highwayman—it does me so much good to come and have a steady walk with our comfortable friend, that here I am again!"

"You know, Dame Durden, dear," Ada would say at night, with her head upon my shoulder and the firelight shining in her thoughtful eyes, "I don't want to talk when we come upstairs here. Only to sit a little while thinking, with your dear face for company, and to hear the wind and remember the poor sailors at sea—"

Ah! Perhaps Richard was going to be a sailor. We had talked it over very often now, and there was some talk of gratifying the inclination of his childhood for the sea. Mr. Jarndyce had written to a relation of the family, a great Sir Leicester Dedlock, for his interest in Richard's favour, generally; and Sir Leicester had replied in a gracious manner that he would be happy to advance the prospects of the young gentleman if it should ever prove to be within his power, which was not at all probable, and that my Lady sent her compliments to the young gentleman (to whom she perfectly remembered that she was allied by remote consanguinity) and trusted that he would ever do his duty in any honourable profession to which he might devote himself.

"So I apprehend it's pretty clear," said Richard to me, "that I shall have to work my own way. Never mind! Plenty of people have had to do that before now, and have done it. I only wish I had the command of a clipping privateer to begin with and could carry off the Chancellor and keep him on short allowance until he gave judgment in our cause. He'd find himself growing thin, if he didn't look sharp!"

With a buoyancy and hopefulness and a gaiety that hardly ever flagged, Richard had a carelessness in his character that quite perplexed me, principally because he mistook it, in such a very odd way, for prudence. It entered into all his calculations about money in a singular manner which I don't think I can better explain than by reverting for a moment to our loan to Mr. Skimpole.

Mr. Jarndyce had ascertained the amount, either from Mr. Skimpole himself or from Coavinses, and had placed the money in my hands with instructions to me to retain my own part of it and hand the rest to Richard. The number of little acts of thoughtless expenditure which Richard justified by the recovery of his ten pounds, and the number of times he talked to me as if he had saved or realized that amount, would form a sum in simple addition.

"My prudent Mother Hubbard, why not?" he said to me when he wanted, without the least consideration, to bestow five pounds on the brickmaker. "I made ten pounds, clear, out of Coavinses' business."

"How was that?" said I.

"Why, I got rid of ten pounds which I was quite content to get rid of and never expected to see any more. You don't deny that?"

"No," said I.

"Very well! Then I came into possession of ten pounds—"

"The same ten pounds," I hinted.

"That has nothing to do with it!" returned Richard. "I have got ten pounds more than I expected to have, and consequently I can afford to spend it without being particular."

In exactly the same way, when he was persuaded out of the sacrifice of these five pounds by being convinced that it would do no good, he carried that sum to his credit and drew upon it.

"Let me see!" he would say. "I saved five pounds out of the brickmaker's affair, so if I have a good rattle to London and back in a post-chaise and put that down at four pounds, I shall have saved one. And it's a very good thing to save one, let me tell you: a penny saved is a penny got!"

I believe Richard's was as frank and generous a nature as there possibly can be. He was ardent and brave, and in the midst of all his wild restlessness, was so gentle that I knew him like a brother in a few weeks. His gentleness was natural to him and would have shown itself abundantly even without Ada's influence; but with it, he became one of the most winning of companions, always so ready to be interested and always so happy, sanguine, and light-hearted. I am sure that I, sitting with them, and walking with them, and talking with them, and noticing from day to day how they went on, falling deeper and deeper in love, and saying nothing about it, and each shyly thinking that this love was the greatest of secrets, perhaps not yet suspected even by the other—I am sure that I was scarcely less enchanted than they were and scarcely less pleased with the pretty dream.

We were going on in this way, when one morning at breakfast Mr. Jarndyce received a letter, and looking at the superscription, said, "From Boythorn? Aye, aye!" and opened and read it with evident pleasure, announcing to us in a parenthesis when he was about half-way through, that Boythorn was "coming down" on a visit. Now who was Boythorn, we all thought. And I dare say we all thought too—I am sure I did, for one—would Boythorn at all interfere with what was going forward?

"I went to school with this fellow, Lawrence Boythorn," said Mr. Jarndyce, tapping the letter as he laid it on the table, "more than five and forty years ago. He was then the most impetuous boy in the world, and he is now the most impetuous man. He was then the loudest boy in the world, and he is now the loudest man. He was then the heartiest and sturdiest boy in the world, and he is now the heartiest and sturdiest man. He is a tremendous fellow."

"In stature, sir?" asked Richard.

"Pretty well, Rick, in that respect," said Mr. Jarndyce; "being some ten years older than I and a couple of inches taller, with his head thrown back like an old soldier, his stalwart chest squared, his hands like a clean blacksmith's, and his lungs! There's no simile for his lungs. Talking, laughing, or snoring, they make the beams of the house shake."

As Mr. Jarndyce sat enjoying the image of his friend Boythorn, we observed the favourable omen that there was not the least indication of any change in the wind.

"But it's the inside of the man, the warm heart of the man, the passion of the man, the fresh blood of the man, Rick—and Ada, and little Cobweb too, for you are all interested in a visitor—that I speak of," he pursued. "His language is as sounding as his voice. He is always in extremes, perpetually in the superlative degree. In his condemnation he is all ferocity. You might suppose him to be an ogre from what he says, and I believe he has the reputation of one with some people. There! I tell you no more of him beforehand. You must not be surprised to see him take me under his protection, for he has never forgotten that I was a low boy at school and that our friendship began in his knocking two of my head tyrant's teeth out (he says six) before breakfast. Boythorn and his man," to me, "will be here this afternoon, my dear."

I took care that the necessary preparations were made for Mr. Boythorn's reception, and we looked forward to his arrival with some curiosity. The afternoon wore away, however, and he did not appear. The dinner-hour arrived, and still he did not appear. The dinner was put back an hour, and we were sitting round the fire with no light but the blaze when the hall-door suddenly burst open and the hall resounded with these words, uttered with the greatest vehemence and in a stentorian tone: "We have been misdirected, Jarndyce, by a most abandoned ruffian, who told us to take the turning to the right instead of to the left. He is the most intolerable scoundrel on the face of the earth. His father must have been a most consummate villain, ever to have such a son. I would have had that fellow shot without the least remorse!"

"Did he do it on purpose?" Mr. Jarndyce inquired.

"I have not the slightest doubt that the scoundrel has passed his whole existence in misdirecting travellers!" returned the other. "By my soul, I thought him the worst-looking dog I had ever beheld when he was telling me to take the turning to the right. And yet I stood before that fellow face to face and didn't knock his brains out!"

"Teeth, you mean?" said Mr. Jarndyce.

"Ha, ha, ha!" laughed Mr. Lawrence Boythorn, really making the whole house vibrate. "What, you have not forgotten it yet! Ha, ha, ha! And that was another most consummate vagabond! By my soul, the countenance of that fellow when he was a boy was the blackest image of perfidy, cowardice, and cruelty ever set up as a scarecrow in a field of scoundrels. If I were to meet that most unparalleled despot in the streets to-morrow, I would fell him like a rotten tree!"

"I have no doubt of it," said Mr. Jarndyce. "Now, will you come upstairs?"

"By my soul, Jarndyce," returned his guest, who seemed to refer to his watch, "if you had been married, I would have turned back at the garden-gate and gone away to the remotest summits of the Himalaya Mountains sooner than I would have presented myself at this unseasonable hour."

"Not quite so far, I hope?" said Mr. Jarndyce.

"By my life and honour, yes!" cried the visitor. "I wouldn't be guilty of the audacious insolence of keeping a lady of the house waiting all this time for any earthly consideration. I would infinitely rather destroy myself—infinitely rather!"

Talking thus, they went upstairs, and presently we heard him in his bedroom thundering "Ha, ha, ha!" and again "Ha, ha, ha!" until the flattest echo in the neighbourhood seemed to catch the contagion and to laugh as enjoyingly as he did or as we did when we heard him laugh.

We all conceived a prepossession in his favour, for there was a sterling quality in this laugh, and in his vigorous, healthy voice, and in the roundness and fullness with which he uttered every word he spoke, and in the very fury of his superlatives, which seemed to go off like blank cannons and hurt nothing. But we were hardly prepared to have it so confirmed by his appearance when Mr. Jarndyce presented him. He was not only a very handsome old gentleman—upright and stalwart as he had been described to us—with a massive grey head, a fine composure of face when silent, a figure that might have become corpulent but for his being so continually in earnest that he gave it no rest, and a chin that might have subsided into a double chin but for the vehement emphasis in which it was constantly required to assist; but he was such a true gentleman in his manner, so chivalrously polite, his face was lighted by a smile of so much sweetness and tenderness, and it seemed so plain that he had nothing to hide, but showed himself exactly as he was—incapable, as Richard said, of anything on a limited scale, and firing away with those blank great guns because he carried no small arms whatever—that really I could not help looking at him with equal pleasure as he sat at dinner, whether he smilingly conversed with Ada and me, or was led by Mr. Jarndyce into some great volley of superlatives, or threw up his head like a bloodhound and gave out that tremendous "Ha, ha, ha!"

"You have brought your bird with you, I suppose?" said Mr. Jarndyce.

"By heaven, he is the most astonishing bird in Europe!" replied the other. "He IS the most wonderful creature! I wouldn't take ten thousand guineas for that bird. I have left an annuity for his sole support in case he should outlive me. He is, in sense and attachment, a phenomenon. And his father before him was one of the most astonishing birds that ever lived!"

The subject of this laudation was a very little canary, who was so tame that he was brought down by Mr. Boythorn's man, on his forefinger, and after taking a gentle flight round the room, alighted on his master's head. To hear Mr. Boythorn presently expressing the most implacable and passionate sentiments, with this fragile mite of a creature quietly perched on his forehead, was to have a good illustration of his character, I thought.

"By my soul, Jarndyce," he said, very gently holding up a bit of bread to the canary to peck at, "if I were in your place I would seize every master in Chancery by the throat to-morrow morning and shake him until his money rolled out of his pockets and his bones rattled in his skin. I would have a settlement out of somebody, by fair means or by foul. If you would empower me to do it, I would do it for you with the greatest satisfaction!" (All this time the very small canary was eating out of his hand.)

"I thank you, Lawrence, but the suit is hardly at such a point at present," returned Mr. Jarndyce, laughing, "that it would be greatly advanced even by the legal process of shaking the bench and the whole bar."

"There never was such an infernal cauldron as that Chancery on the face of the earth!" said Mr. Boythorn. "Nothing but a mine below it on a busy day in term time, with all its records, rules, and precedents collected in it and every functionary belonging to it also, high and low, upward and downward, from its son the Accountant-General to its father the Devil, and the whole blown to atoms with ten thousand hundredweight of gunpowder, would reform it in the least!"

It was impossible not to laugh at the energetic gravity with which he recommended this strong measure of reform. When we laughed, he threw up his head and shook his broad chest, and again the whole country seemed to echo to his "Ha, ha, ha!" It had not the least effect in disturbing the bird, whose sense of security was complete and who hopped about the table with its quick head now on this side and now on that, turning its bright sudden eye on its master as if he were no more than another bird.

"But how do you and your neighbour get on about the disputed right of way?" said Mr. Jarndyce. "You are not free from the toils of the law yourself!"

"The fellow has brought actions against ME for trespass, and I have brought actions against HIM for trespass," returned Mr. Boythorn. "By heaven, he is the proudest fellow breathing. It is morally impossible that his name can be Sir Leicester. It must be Sir Lucifer."

"Complimentary to our distant relation!" said my guardian laughingly to Ada and Richard.

"I would beg Miss Clare's pardon and Mr. Carstone's pardon," resumed our visitor, "if I were not reassured by seeing in the fair face of the lady and the smile of the gentleman that it is quite unnecessary and that they keep their distant relation at a comfortable distance."

"Or he keeps us," suggested Richard.

"By my soul," exclaimed Mr. Boythorn, suddenly firing another volley, "that fellow is, and his father was, and his grandfather was, the most stiff-necked, arrogant imbecile, pig-headed numskull, ever, by some inexplicable mistake of Nature, born in any station of life but a walking-stick's! The whole of that family are the most solemnly conceited and consummate blockheads! But it's no matter; he should not shut up my path if he were fifty baronets melted into one and living in a hundred Chesney Wolds, one within another, like the ivory balls in a Chinese carving. The fellow, by his agent, or secretary, or somebody, writes to me 'Sir Leicester Dedlock, Baronet, presents his compliments to Mr. Lawrence Boythorn, and has to call his attention to the fact that the green pathway by the old parsonage-house, now the property of Mr. Lawrence Boythorn, is Sir Leicester's right of way, being in fact a portion of the park of Chesney Wold, and that Sir Leicester finds it convenient to close up the same.' I write to the fellow, 'Mr. Lawrence Boythorn presents his compliments to Sir Leicester Dedlock, Baronet, and has to call HIS attention to the fact that he totally denies the whole of Sir Leicester Dedlock's positions on every possible subject and has to add, in reference to closing up the pathway, that he will be glad to see the man who may undertake to do it.' The fellow sends a most abandoned villain with one eye to construct a gateway. I play upon that execrable scoundrel with a fire-engine until the breath is nearly driven out of his body. The fellow erects a gate in the night. I chop it down and burn it in the morning. He sends his myrmidons to come over the fence and pass and repass. I catch them in humane man traps, fire split peas at their legs, play upon them with the engine—resolve to free mankind from the insupportable burden of the existence of those lurking ruffians. He brings actions for trespass; I bring actions for trespass. He brings actions for assault and battery; I defend them and continue to assault and batter. Ha, ha, ha!"

To hear him say all this with unimaginable energy, one might have thought him the angriest of mankind. To see him at the very same time, looking at the bird now perched upon his thumb and softly smoothing its feathers with his forefinger, one might have thought him the gentlest. To hear him laugh and see the broad good nature of his face then, one might have supposed that he had not a care in the world, or a dispute, or a dislike, but that his whole existence was a summer joke.

"No, no," he said, "no closing up of my paths by any Dedlock! Though I willingly confess," here he softened in a moment, "that Lady Dedlock is the most accomplished lady in the world, to whom I would do any homage that a plain gentleman, and no baronet with a head seven hundred years thick, may. A man who joined his regiment at twenty and within a week challenged the most imperious and presumptuous coxcomb of a commanding officer that ever drew the breath of life through a tight waist—and got broke for it—is not the man to be walked over by all the Sir Lucifers, dead or alive, locked or unlocked. Ha, ha, ha!"

"Nor the man to allow his junior to be walked over either?" said my guardian.

"Most assuredly not!" said Mr. Boythorn, clapping him on the shoulder with an air of protection that had something serious in it, though he laughed. "He will stand by the low boy, always. Jarndyce, you may rely upon him! But speaking of this trespass—with apologies to Miss Clare and Miss Summerson for the length at which I have pursued so dry a subject—is there nothing for me from your men Kenge and Carboy?"

"I think not, Esther?" said Mr. Jarndyce.

"Nothing, guardian."

"Much obliged!" said Mr. Boythorn. "Had no need to ask, after even my slight experience of Miss Summerson's forethought for every one about her." (They all encouraged me; they were determined to do it.) "I inquired because, coming from Lincolnshire, I of course have not yet been in town, and I thought some letters might have been sent down here. I dare say they will report progress to-morrow morning."

I saw him so often in the course of the evening, which passed very pleasantly, contemplate Richard and Ada with an interest and a satisfaction that made his fine face remarkably agreeable as he sat at a little distance from the piano listening to the music—and he had small occasion to tell us that he was passionately fond of music, for his face showed it—that I asked my guardian as we sat at the backgammon board whether Mr. Boythorn had ever been married.

"No," said he. "No."

"But he meant to be!" said I.

"How did you find out that?" he returned with a smile. "Why, guardian," I explained, not without reddening a little at hazarding what was in my thoughts, "there is something so tender in his manner, after all, and he is so very courtly and gentle to us, and—"

Mr. Jarndyce directed his eyes to where he was sitting as I have just described him.

I said no more.

"You are right, little woman," he answered. "He was all but married once. Long ago. And once."

"Did the lady die?"

"No—but she died to him. That time has had its influence on all his later life. Would you suppose him to have a head and a heart full of romance yet?"

"I think, guardian, I might have supposed so. But it is easy to say that when you have told me so."

"He has never since been what he might have been," said Mr. Jarndyce, "and now you see him in his age with no one near him but his servant and his little yellow friend. It's your throw, my dear!"

I felt, from my guardian's manner, that beyond this point I could not pursue the subject without changing the wind. I therefore forbore to ask any further questions. I was interested, but not curious. I thought a little while about this old love story in the night, when I was awakened by Mr. Boythorn's lusty snoring; and I tried to do that very difficult thing, imagine old people young again and invested with the graces of youth. But I fell asleep before I had succeeded, and dreamed of the days when I lived in my godmother's house. I am not sufficiently acquainted with such subjects to know whether it is at all remarkable that I almost always dreamed of that period of my life.

With the morning there came a letter from Messrs. Kenge and Carboy to Mr. Boythorn informing him that one of their clerks would wait upon him at noon. As it was the day of the week on which I paid the bills, and added up my books, and made all the household affairs as compact as possible, I remained at home while Mr. Jarndyce, Ada, and Richard took advantage of a very fine day to make a little excursion, Mr. Boythorn was to wait for Kenge and Carboy's clerk and then was to go on foot to meet them on their return.

Well! I was full of business, examining tradesmen's books, adding up columns, paying money, filing receipts, and I dare say making a great bustle about it when Mr. Guppy was announced and shown in. I had had some idea that the clerk who was to be sent down might be the young gentleman who had met me at the coach-office, and I was glad to see him, because he was associated with my present happiness.

I scarcely knew him again, he was so uncommonly smart. He had an entirely new suit of glossy clothes on, a shining hat, lilac-kid gloves, a neckerchief of a variety of colours, a large hot-house flower in his button-hole, and a thick gold ring on his little finger. Besides which, he quite scented the dining-room with bear's-grease and other perfumery. He looked at me with an attention that quite confused me when I begged him to take a seat until the servant should return; and as he sat there crossing and uncrossing his legs in a corner, and I asked him if he had had a pleasant ride, and hoped that Mr. Kenge was well, I never looked at him, but I found him looking at me in the same scrutinizing and curious way.

When the request was brought to him that he would go upstairs to Mr. Boythorn's room, I mentioned that he would find lunch prepared for him when he came down, of which Mr. Jarndyce hoped he would partake. He said with some embarrassment, holding the handle of the door, "Shall I have the honour of finding you here, miss?" I replied yes, I should be there; and he went out with a bow and another look.

I thought him only awkward and shy, for he was evidently much embarrassed; and I fancied that the best thing I could do would be to wait until I saw that he had everything he wanted and then to leave him to himself. The lunch was soon brought, but it remained for some time on the table. The interview with Mr. Boythorn was a long one, and a stormy one too, I should think, for although his room was at some distance I heard his loud voice rising every now and then like a high wind, and evidently blowing perfect broadsides of denunciation.

At last Mr. Guppy came back, looking something the worse for the conference. "My eye, miss," he said in a low voice, "he's a Tartar!"

"Pray take some refreshment, sir," said I.

Mr. Guppy sat down at the table and began nervously sharpening the carving-knife on the carving-fork, still looking at me (as I felt quite sure without looking at him) in the same unusual manner. The sharpening lasted so long that at last I felt a kind of obligation on me to raise my eyes in order that I might break the spell under which he seemed to labour, of not being able to leave off.

He immediately looked at the dish and began to carve.

"What will you take yourself, miss? You'll take a morsel of something?"

"No, thank you," said I.

"Shan't I give you a piece of anything at all, miss?" said Mr. Guppy, hurriedly drinking off a glass of wine.

"Nothing, thank you," said I. "I have only waited to see that you have everything you want. Is there anything I can order for you?"

"No, I am much obliged to you, miss, I'm sure. I've everything that I can require to make me comfortable—at least I—not comfortable—I'm never that." He drank off two more glasses of wine, one after another.

I thought I had better go.

"I beg your pardon, miss!" said Mr. Guppy, rising when he saw me rise. "But would you allow me the favour of a minute's private conversation?"

Not knowing what to say, I sat down again.

"What follows is without prejudice, miss?" said Mr. Guppy, anxiously bringing a chair towards my table.

"I don't understand what you mean," said I, wondering.

"It's one of our law terms, miss. You won't make any use of it to my detriment at Kenge and Carboy's or elsewhere. If our conversation shouldn't lead to anything, I am to be as I was and am not to be prejudiced in my situation or worldly prospects. In short, it's in total confidence."

"I am at a loss, sir," said I, "to imagine what you can have to communicate in total confidence to me, whom you have never seen but once; but I should be very sorry to do you any injury."

"Thank you, miss. I'm sure of it—that's quite sufficient." All this time Mr. Guppy was either planing his forehead with his handkerchief or tightly rubbing the palm of his left hand with the palm of his right. "If you would excuse my taking another glass of wine, miss, I think it might assist me in getting on without a continual choke that cannot fail to be mutually unpleasant."

He did so, and came back again. I took the opportunity of moving well behind my table.

"You wouldn't allow me to offer you one, would you miss?" said Mr. Guppy, apparently refreshed.

"Not any," said I.

"Not half a glass?" said Mr. Guppy. "Quarter? No! Then, to proceed. My present salary, Miss Summerson, at Kenge and Carboy's, is two pound a week. When I first had the happiness of looking upon you, it was one fifteen, and had stood at that figure for a lengthened period. A rise of five has since taken place, and a further rise of five is guaranteed at the expiration of a term not exceeding twelve months from the present date. My mother has a little property, which takes the form of a small life annuity, upon which she lives in an independent though unassuming manner in the Old Street Road. She is eminently calculated for a mother-in-law. She never interferes, is all for peace, and her disposition easy. She has her failings—as who has not?—but I never knew her do it when company was present, at which time you may freely trust her with wines, spirits, or malt liquors. My own abode is lodgings at Penton Place, Pentonville. It is lowly, but airy, open at the back, and considered one of the 'ealthiest outlets. Miss Summerson! In the mildest language, I adore you. Would you be so kind as to allow me (as I may say) to file a declaration—to make an offer!"

Mr. Guppy went down on his knees. I was well behind my table and not much frightened. I said, "Get up from that ridiculous position immediately, sir, or you will oblige me to break my implied promise and ring the bell!"

"Hear me out, miss!" said Mr. Guppy, folding his hands.

"I cannot consent to hear another word, sir," I returned, "Unless you get up from the carpet directly and go and sit down at the table as you ought to do if you have any sense at all."

He looked piteously, but slowly rose and did so.

"Yet what a mockery it is, miss," he said with his hand upon his heart and shaking his head at me in a melancholy manner over the tray, "to be stationed behind food at such a moment. The soul recoils from food at such a moment, miss."

"I beg you to conclude," said I; "you have asked me to hear you out, and I beg you to conclude."

"I will, miss," said Mr. Guppy. "As I love and honour, so likewise I obey. Would that I could make thee the subject of that vow before the shrine!"

"That is quite impossible," said I, "and entirely out of the question."

"I am aware," said Mr. Guppy, leaning forward over the tray and regarding me, as I again strangely felt, though my eyes were not directed to him, with his late intent look, "I am aware that in a worldly point of view, according to all appearances, my offer is a poor one. But, Miss Summerson! Angel! No, don't ring—I have been brought up in a sharp school and am accustomed to a variety of general practice. Though a young man, I have ferreted out evidence, got up cases, and seen lots of life. Blest with your hand, what means might I not find of advancing your interests and pushing your fortunes! What might I not get to know, nearly concerning you? I know nothing now, certainly; but what MIGHT I not if I had your confidence, and you set me on?"

I told him that he addressed my interest or what he supposed to be my interest quite as unsuccessfully as he addressed my inclination, and he would now understand that I requested him, if he pleased, to go away immediately.

"Cruel miss," said Mr. Guppy, "hear but another word! I think you must have seen that I was struck with those charms on the day when I waited at the Whytorseller. I think you must have remarked that I could not forbear a tribute to those charms when I put up the steps of the 'ackney-coach. It was a feeble tribute to thee, but it was well meant. Thy image has ever since been fixed in my breast. I have walked up and down of an evening opposite Jellyby's house only to look upon the bricks that once contained thee. This out of to-day, quite an unnecessary out so far as the attendance, which was its pretended object, went, was planned by me alone for thee alone. If I speak of interest, it is only to recommend myself and my respectful wretchedness. Love was before it, and is before it."

"I should be pained, Mr. Guppy," said I, rising and putting my hand upon the bell-rope, "to do you or any one who was sincere the injustice of slighting any honest feeling, however disagreeably expressed. If you have really meant to give me a proof of your good opinion, though ill-timed and misplaced, I feel that I ought to thank you. I have very little reason to be proud, and I am not proud. I hope," I think I added, without very well knowing what I said, "that you will now go away as if you had never been so exceedingly foolish and attend to Messrs. Kenge and Carboy's business."

"Half a minute, miss!" cried Mr. Guppy, checking me as I was about to ring. "This has been without prejudice?"

"I will never mention it," said I, "unless you should give me future occasion to do so."

"A quarter of a minute, miss! In case you should think better at any time, however distant—THAT'S no consequence, for my feelings can never alter—of anything I have said, particularly what might I not do, Mr. William Guppy, eighty-seven, Penton Place, or if removed, or dead (of blighted hopes or anything of that sort), care of Mrs. Guppy, three hundred and two, Old Street Road, will be sufficient."

I rang the bell, the servant came, and Mr. Guppy, laying his written card upon the table and making a dejected bow, departed. Raising my eyes as he went out, I once more saw him looking at me after he had passed the door.

I sat there for another hour or more, finishing my books and payments and getting through plenty of business. Then I arranged my desk, and put everything away, and was so composed and cheerful that I thought I had quite dismissed this unexpected incident. But, when I went upstairs to my own room, I surprised myself by beginning to laugh about it and then surprised myself still more by beginning to cry about it. In short, I was in a flutter for a little while and felt as if an old chord had been more coarsely touched than it ever had been since the days of the dear old doll, long buried in the garden.

CHAPTER X
THE LAW-WRITER

On the eastern borders of Chancery Lane, that is to say, more particularly in Cook's Court, Cursitor Street, Mr. Snagsby, law-stationer, pursues his lawful calling. In the shade of Cook's Court, at most times a shady place, Mr. Snagsby has dealt in all sorts of blank forms of legal process; in skins and rolls of parchment; in paper—foolscap, brief, draft, brown, white, whitey-brown, and blotting; in stamps; in office-quills, pens, ink, India-rubber, pounce, pins, pencils, sealing-wax, and wafers; in red tape and green ferret; in pocket-books, almanacs, diaries, and law lists; in string boxes, rulers, inkstands—glass and leaden—pen-knives, scissors, bodkins, and other small office-cutlery; in short, in articles too numerous to mention, ever since he was out of his time and went into partnership with Peffer. On that occasion, Cook's Court was in a manner revolutionized by the new inscription in fresh paint, PEFFER AND SNAGSBY, displacing the time-honoured and not easily to be deciphered legend PEFFER only. For smoke, which is the London ivy, had so wreathed itself round Peffer's name and clung to his dwelling-place that the affectionate parasite quite overpowered the parent tree.

Peffer is never seen in Cook's Court now. He is not expected there, for he has been recumbent this quarter of a century in the churchyard of St. Andrews, Holborn, with the waggons and hackney-coaches roaring past him all the day and half the night like one great dragon. If he ever steal forth when the dragon is at rest to air himself again in Cook's Court until admonished to return by the crowing of the sanguine cock in the cellar at the little dairy in Cursitor Street, whose ideas of daylight it would be curious to ascertain, since he knows from his personal observation next to nothing about it—if Peffer ever do revisit the pale glimpses of Cook's Court, which no law-stationer in the trade can positively deny, he comes invisibly, and no one is the worse or wiser.

In his lifetime, and likewise in the period of Snagsby's "time" of seven long years, there dwelt with Peffer in the same law-stationering premises a niece—a short, shrewd niece, something too violently compressed about the waist, and with a sharp nose like a sharp autumn evening, inclining to be frosty towards the end. The Cook's Courtiers had a rumour flying among them that the mother of this niece did, in her daughter's childhood, moved by too jealous a solicitude that her figure should approach perfection, lace her up every morning with her maternal foot against the bed-post for a stronger hold and purchase; and further, that she exhibited internally pints of vinegar and lemon-juice, which acids, they held, had mounted to the nose and temper of the patient. With whichsoever of the many tongues of Rumour this frothy report originated, it either never reached or never influenced the ears of young Snagsby, who, having wooed and won its fair subject on his arrival at man's estate, entered into two partnerships at once. So now, in Cook's Court, Cursitor Street, Mr. Snagsby and the niece are one; and the niece still cherishes her figure, which, however tastes may differ, is unquestionably so far precious that there is mighty little of it.

Mr. and Mrs. Snagsby are not only one bone and one flesh, but, to the neighbours' thinking, one voice too. That voice, appearing to proceed from Mrs. Snagsby alone, is heard in Cook's Court very often. Mr. Snagsby, otherwise than as he finds expression through these dulcet tones, is rarely heard. He is a mild, bald, timid man with a shining head and a scrubby clump of black hair sticking out at the back. He tends to meekness and obesity. As he stands at his door in Cook's Court in his grey shop-coat and black calico sleeves, looking up at the clouds, or stands behind a desk in his dark shop with a heavy flat ruler, snipping and slicing at sheepskin in company with his two 'prentices, he is emphatically a retiring and unassuming man. From beneath his feet, at such times, as from a shrill ghost unquiet in its grave, there frequently arise complainings and lamentations in the voice already mentioned; and haply, on some occasions when these reach a sharper pitch than usual, Mr. Snagsby mentions to the 'prentices, "I think my little woman is a-giving it to Guster!"

This proper name, so used by Mr. Snagsby, has before now sharpened the wit of the Cook's Courtiers to remark that it ought to be the name of Mrs. Snagsby, seeing that she might with great force and expression be termed a Guster, in compliment to her stormy character. It is, however, the possession, and the only possession except fifty shillings per annum and a very small box indifferently filled with clothing, of a lean young woman from a workhouse (by some supposed to have been christened Augusta) who, although she was farmed or contracted for during her growing time by an amiable benefactor of his species resident at Tooting, and cannot fail to have been developed under the most favourable circumstances, "has fits," which the parish can't account for.

Guster, really aged three or four and twenty, but looking a round ten years older, goes cheap with this unaccountable drawback of fits, and is so apprehensive of being returned on the hands of her patron saint that except when she is found with her head in the pail, or the sink, or the copper, or the dinner, or anything else that happens to be near her at the time of her seizure, she is always at work. She is a satisfaction to the parents and guardians of the 'prentices, who feel that there is little danger of her inspiring tender emotions in the breast of youth; she is a satisfaction to Mrs. Snagsby, who can always find fault with her; she is a satisfaction to Mr. Snagsby, who thinks it a charity to keep her. The law-stationer's establishment is, in Guster's eyes, a temple of plenty and splendour. She believes the little drawing-room upstairs, always kept, as one may say, with its hair in papers and its pinafore on, to be the most elegant apartment in Christendom. The view it commands of Cook's Court at one end (not to mention a squint into Cursitor Street) and of Coavinses' the sheriff's officer's backyard at the other she regards as a prospect of unequalled beauty. The portraits it displays in oil—and plenty of it too—of Mr. Snagsby looking at Mrs. Snagsby and of Mrs. Snagsby looking at Mr. Snagsby are in her eyes as achievements of Raphael or Titian. Guster has some recompenses for her many privations.

Mr. Snagsby refers everything not in the practical mysteries of the business to Mrs. Snagsby. She manages the money, reproaches the tax-gatherers, appoints the times and places of devotion on Sundays, licenses Mr. Snagsby's entertainments, and acknowledges no responsibility as to what she thinks fit to provide for dinner, insomuch that she is the high standard of comparison among the neighbouring wives a long way down Chancery Lane on both sides, and even out in Holborn, who in any domestic passages of arms habitually call upon their husbands to look at the difference between their (the wives') position and Mrs. Snagsby's, and their (the husbands') behaviour and Mr. Snagsby's. Rumour, always flying bat-like about Cook's Court and skimming in and out at everybody's windows, does say that Mrs. Snagsby is jealous and inquisitive and that Mr. Snagsby is sometimes worried out of house and home, and that if he had the spirit of a mouse he wouldn't stand it. It is even observed that the wives who quote him to their self-willed husbands as a shining example in reality look down upon him and that nobody does so with greater superciliousness than one particular lady whose lord is more than suspected of laying his umbrella on her as an instrument of correction. But these vague whisperings may arise from Mr. Snagsby's being in his way rather a meditative and poetical man, loving to walk in Staple Inn in the summer-time and to observe how countrified the sparrows and the leaves are, also to lounge about the Rolls Yard of a Sunday afternoon and to remark (if in good spirits) that there were old times once and that you'd find a stone coffin or two now under that chapel, he'll be bound, if you was to dig for it. He solaces his imagination, too, by thinking of the many Chancellors and Vices, and Masters of the Rolls who are deceased; and he gets such a flavour of the country out of telling the two 'prentices how he HAS heard say that a brook "as clear as crystal" once ran right down the middle of Holborn, when Turnstile really was a turnstile, leading slap away into the meadows—gets such a flavour of the country out of this that he never wants to go there.

The day is closing in and the gas is lighted, but is not yet fully effective, for it is not quite dark. Mr. Snagsby standing at his shop-door looking up at the clouds sees a crow who is out late skim westward over the slice of sky belonging to Cook's Court. The crow flies straight across Chancery Lane and Lincoln's Inn Garden into Lincoln's Inn Fields.

Here, in a large house, formerly a house of state, lives Mr. Tulkinghorn.

It is let off in sets of chambers now, and in those shrunken fragments of its greatness, lawyers lie like maggots in nuts. But its roomy staircases, passages, and antechambers still remain; and even its painted ceilings, where Allegory, in Roman helmet and celestial linen, sprawls among balustrades and pillars, flowers, clouds, and big-legged boys, and makes the head ache—as would seem to be Allegory's object always, more or less. Here, among his many boxes labelled with transcendent names, lives Mr. Tulkinghorn, when not speechlessly at home in country-houses where the great ones of the earth are bored to death. Here he is to-day, quiet at his table. An oyster of the old school whom nobody can open.

Like as he is to look at, so is his apartment in the dusk of the present afternoon. Rusty, out of date, withdrawing from attention, able to afford it. Heavy, broad-backed, old-fashioned, mahogany-and-horsehair chairs, not easily lifted; obsolete tables with spindle-legs and dusty baize covers; presentation prints of the holders of great titles in the last generation or the last but one, environ him. A thick and dingy Turkey-carpet muffles the floor where he sits, attended by two candles in old-fashioned silver candlesticks that give a very insufficient light to his large room. The titles on the backs of his books have retired into the binding; everything that can have a lock has got one; no key is visible. Very few loose papers are about. He has some manuscript near him, but is not referring to it. With the round top of an inkstand and two broken bits of sealing-wax he is silently and slowly working out whatever train of indecision is in his mind. Now the inkstand top is in the middle, now the red bit of sealing-wax, now the black bit. That's not it. Mr. Tulkinghorn must gather them all up and begin again.

Here, beneath the painted ceiling, with foreshortened Allegory staring down at his intrusion as if it meant to swoop upon him, and he cutting it dead, Mr. Tulkinghorn has at once his house and office. He keeps no staff, only one middle-aged man, usually a little out at elbows, who sits in a high pew in the hall and is rarely overburdened with business. Mr. Tulkinghorn is not in a common way. He wants no clerks. He is a great reservoir of confidences, not to be so tapped. His clients want HIM; he is all in all. Drafts that he requires to be drawn are drawn by special-pleaders in the temple on mysterious instructions; fair copies that he requires to be made are made at the stationers', expense being no consideration. The middle-aged man in the pew knows scarcely more of the affairs of the peerage than any crossing-sweeper in Holborn.

The red bit, the black bit, the inkstand top, the other inkstand top, the little sand-box. So! You to the middle, you to the right, you to the left. This train of indecision must surely be worked out now or never. Now! Mr. Tulkinghorn gets up, adjusts his spectacles, puts on his hat, puts the manuscript in his pocket, goes out, tells the middle-aged man out at elbows, "I shall be back presently." Very rarely tells him anything more explicit.

Mr. Tulkinghorn goes, as the crow came—not quite so straight, but nearly—to Cook's Court, Cursitor Street. To Snagsby's, Law-Stationer's, Deeds engrossed and copied, Law-Writing executed in all its branches, &c., &c., &c.

It is somewhere about five or six o'clock in the afternoon, and a balmy fragrance of warm tea hovers in Cook's Court. It hovers about Snagsby's door. The hours are early there: dinner at half-past one and supper at half-past nine. Mr. Snagsby was about to descend into the subterranean regions to take tea when he looked out of his door just now and saw the crow who was out late.

"Master at home?"

Guster is minding the shop, for the 'prentices take tea in the kitchen with Mr. and Mrs. Snagsby; consequently, the robe-maker's two daughters, combing their curls at the two glasses in the two second-floor windows of the opposite house, are not driving the two 'prentices to distraction as they fondly suppose, but are merely awakening the unprofitable admiration of Guster, whose hair won't grow, and never would, and it is confidently thought, never will.

"Master at home?" says Mr. Tulkinghorn.

Master is at home, and Guster will fetch him. Guster disappears, glad to get out of the shop, which she regards with mingled dread and veneration as a storehouse of awful implements of the great torture of the law—a place not to be entered after the gas is turned off.

Mr. Snagsby appears, greasy, warm, herbaceous, and chewing. Bolts a bit of bread and butter. Says, "Bless my soul, sir! Mr. Tulkinghorn!"

"I want half a word with you, Snagsby."

"Certainly, sir! Dear me, sir, why didn't you send your young man round for me? Pray walk into the back shop, sir." Snagsby has brightened in a moment.

The confined room, strong of parchment-grease, is warehouse, counting-house, and copying-office. Mr. Tulkinghorn sits, facing round, on a stool at the desk.

"Jarndyce and Jarndyce, Snagsby."

"Yes, sir." Mr. Snagsby turns up the gas and coughs behind his hand, modestly anticipating profit. Mr. Snagsby, as a timid man, is accustomed to cough with a variety of expressions, and so to save words.

"You copied some affidavits in that cause for me lately."

"Yes, sir, we did."

"There was one of them," says Mr. Tulkinghorn, carelessly feeling—tight, unopenable oyster of the old school!—in the wrong coat-pocket, "the handwriting of which is peculiar, and I rather like. As I happened to be passing, and thought I had it about me, I looked in to ask you—but I haven't got it. No matter, any other time will do. Ah! here it is! I looked in to ask you who copied this."

"Who copied this, sir?" says Mr. Snagsby, taking it, laying it flat on the desk, and separating all the sheets at once with a twirl and a twist of the left hand peculiar to lawstationers. "We gave this out, sir. We were giving out rather a large quantity of work just at that time. I can tell you in a moment who copied it, sir, by referring to my book."

Mr. Snagsby takes his book down from the safe, makes another bolt of the bit of bread and butter which seemed to have stopped short, eyes the affidavit aside, and brings his right forefinger travelling down a page of the book, "Jewby—Packer—Jarndyce."

"Jarndyce! Here we are, sir," says Mr. Snagsby. "To be sure! I might have remembered it. This was given out, sir, to a writer who lodges just over on the opposite side of the lane."

Mr. Tulkinghorn has seen the entry, found it before the law-stationer, read it while the forefinger was coming down the hill.

"WHAT do you call him? Nemo?" says Mr. Tulkinghorn. "Nemo, sir. Here it is. Forty-two folio. Given out on the Wednesday night at eight o'clock, brought in on the Thursday morning at half after nine."

"Nemo!" repeats Mr. Tulkinghorn. "Nemo is Latin for no one."

"It must be English for some one, sir, I think," Mr. Snagsby submits with his deferential cough. "It is a person's name. Here it is, you see, sir! Forty-two folio. Given out Wednesday night, eight o'clock; brought in Thursday morning, half after nine."

The tail of Mr. Snagsby's eye becomes conscious of the head of Mrs. Snagsby looking in at the shop-door to know what he means by deserting his tea. Mr. Snagsby addresses an explanatory cough to Mrs. Snagsby, as who should say, "My dear, a customer!"

"Half after nine, sir," repeats Mr. Snagsby. "Our law-writers, who live by job-work, are a queer lot; and this may not be his name, but it's the name he goes by. I remember now, sir, that he gives it in a written advertisement he sticks up down at the Rule Office, and the King's Bench Office, and the Judges' Chambers, and so forth. You know the kind of document, sir—wanting employ?"

Mr. Tulkinghorn glances through the little window at the back of Coavinses', the sheriff's officer's, where lights shine in Coavinses' windows. Coavinses' coffee-room is at the back, and the shadows of several gentlemen under a cloud loom cloudily upon the blinds. Mr. Snagsby takes the opportunity of slightly turning his head to glance over his shoulder at his little woman and to make apologetic motions with his mouth to this effect: "Tul-king-horn—rich—in-flu-en-tial!"

"Have you given this man work before?" asks Mr. Tulkinghorn.

"Oh, dear, yes, sir! Work of yours."

"Thinking of more important matters, I forget where you said he lived?"

"Across the lane, sir. In fact, he lodges at a—" Mr. Snagsby makes another bolt, as if the bit of bread and butter were insurmountable "—at a rag and bottle shop."

"Can you show me the place as I go back?"

"With the greatest pleasure, sir!"

Mr. Snagsby pulls off his sleeves and his grey coat, pulls on his black coat, takes his hat from its peg. "Oh! Here is my little woman!" he says aloud. "My dear, will you be so kind as to tell one of the lads to look after the shop while I step across the lane with Mr. Tulkinghorn? Mrs. Snagsby, sir—I shan't be two minutes, my love!"

Mrs. Snagsby bends to the lawyer, retires behind the counter, peeps at them through the window-blind, goes softly into the back office, refers to the entries in the book still lying open. Is evidently curious.

"You will find that the place is rough, sir," says Mr. Snagsby, walking deferentially in the road and leaving the narrow pavement to the lawyer; "and the party is very rough. But they're a wild lot in general, sir. The advantage of this particular man is that he never wants sleep. He'll go at it right on end if you want him to, as long as ever you like."

It is quite dark now, and the gas-lamps have acquired their full effect. Jostling against clerks going to post the day's letters, and against counsel and attorneys going home to dinner, and against plaintiffs and defendants and suitors of all sorts, and against the general crowd, in whose way the forensic wisdom of ages has interposed a million of obstacles to the transaction of the commonest business of life; diving through law and equity, and through that kindred mystery, the street mud, which is made of nobody knows what and collects about us nobody knows whence or how—we only knowing in general that when there is too much of it we find it necessary to shovel it away—the lawyer and the law-stationer come to a rag and bottle shop and general emporium of much disregarded merchandise, lying and being in the shadow of the wall of Lincoln's Inn, and kept, as is announced in paint, to all whom it may concern, by one Krook.

"This is where he lives, sir," says the law-stationer.

"This is where he lives, is it?" says the lawyer unconcernedly. "Thank you."

"Are you not going in, sir?"

"No, thank you, no; I am going on to the Fields at present. Good evening. Thank you!" Mr. Snagsby lifts his hat and returns to his little woman and his tea.

But Mr. Tulkinghorn does not go on to the Fields at present. He goes a short way, turns back, comes again to the shop of Mr. Krook, and enters it straight. It is dim enough, with a blot-headed candle or so in the windows, and an old man and a cat sitting in the back part by a fire. The old man rises and comes forward, with another blot-headed candle in his hand.

"Pray is your lodger within?"

"Male or female, sir?" says Mr. Krook.

"Male. The person who does copying."

Mr. Krook has eyed his man narrowly. Knows him by sight. Has an indistinct impression of his aristocratic repute.

"Did you wish to see him, sir?"

"Yes."

"It's what I seldom do myself," says Mr. Krook with a grin. "Shall I call him down? But it's a weak chance if he'd come, sir!"

"I'll go up to him, then," says Mr. Tulkinghorn.

"Second floor, sir. Take the candle. Up there!" Mr. Krook, with his cat beside him, stands at the bottom of the staircase, looking after Mr. Tulkinghorn. "Hi-hi!" he says when Mr. Tulkinghorn has nearly disappeared. The lawyer looks down over the hand-rail. The cat expands her wicked mouth and snarls at him.

"Order, Lady Jane! Behave yourself to visitors, my lady! You know what they say of my lodger?" whispers Krook, going up a step or two.

"What do they say of him?"

"They say he has sold himself to the enemy, but you and I know better—he don't buy. I'll tell you what, though; my lodger is so black-humoured and gloomy that I believe he'd as soon make that bargain as any other. Don't put him out, sir. That's my advice!"

Mr. Tulkinghorn with a nod goes on his way. He comes to the dark door on the second floor. He knocks, receives no answer, opens it, and accidentally extinguishes his candle in doing so.

The air of the room is almost bad enough to have extinguished it if he had not. It is a small room, nearly black with soot, and grease, and dirt. In the rusty skeleton of a grate, pinched at the middle as if poverty had gripped it, a red coke fire burns low. In the corner by the chimney stand a deal table and a broken desk, a wilderness marked with a rain of ink. In another corner a ragged old portmanteau on one of the two chairs serves for cabinet or wardrobe; no larger one is needed, for it collapses like the cheeks of a starved man. The floor is bare, except that one old mat, trodden to shreds of rope-yarn, lies perishing upon the hearth. No curtain veils the darkness of the night, but the discoloured shutters are drawn together, and through the two gaunt holes pierced in them, famine might be staring in—the banshee of the man upon the bed.

For, on a low bed opposite the fire, a confusion of dirty patchwork, lean-ribbed ticking, and coarse sacking, the lawyer, hesitating just within the doorway, sees a man. He lies there, dressed in shirt and trousers, with bare feet. He has a yellow look in the spectral darkness of a candle that has guttered down until the whole length of its wick (still burning) has doubled over and left a tower of winding-sheet above it. His hair is ragged, mingling with his whiskers and his beard—the latter, ragged too, and grown, like the scum and mist around him, in neglect. Foul and filthy as the room is, foul and filthy as the air is, it is not easy to perceive what fumes those are which most oppress the senses in it; but through the general sickliness and faintness, and the odour of stale tobacco, there comes into the lawyer's mouth the bitter, vapid taste of opium.

"Hallo, my friend!" he cries, and strikes his iron candlestick against the door.

He thinks he has awakened his friend. He lies a little turned away, but his eyes are surely open.

"Hallo, my friend!" he cries again. "Hallo! Hallo!"

As he rattles on the door, the candle which has drooped so long goes out and leaves him in the dark, with the gaunt eyes in the shutters staring down upon the bed.

CHAPTER XI
OUR DEAR BROTHER

A touch on the lawyer's wrinkled hand as he stands in the dark room, irresolute, makes him start and say, "What's that?"

"It's me," returns the old man of the house, whose breath is in his ear. "Can't you wake him?"

"No."

"What have you done with your candle?"

"It's gone out. Here it is."

Krook takes it, goes to the fire, stoops over the red embers, and tries to get a light. The dying ashes have no light to spare, and his endeavours are vain. Muttering, after an ineffectual call to his lodger, that he will go downstairs and bring a lighted candle from the shop, the old man departs. Mr. Tulkinghorn, for some new reason that he has, does not await his return in the room, but on the stairs outside.

The welcome light soon shines upon the wall, as Krook comes slowly up with his green-eyed cat following at his heels. "Does the man generally sleep like this?" inquired the lawyer in a low voice. "Hi! I don't know," says Krook, shaking his head and lifting his eyebrows. "I know next to nothing of his habits except that he keeps himself very close."

Thus whispering, they both go in together. As the light goes in, the great eyes in the shutters, darkening, seem to close. Not so the eyes upon the bed.

"God save us!" exclaims Mr. Tulkinghorn. "He is dead!" Krook drops the heavy hand he has taken up so suddenly that the arm swings over the bedside.

They look at one another for a moment.

"Send for some doctor! Call for Miss Flite up the stairs, sir. Here's poison by the bed! Call out for Flite, will you?" says Krook, with his lean hands spread out above the body like a vampire's wings.

Mr. Tulkinghorn hurries to the landing and calls, "Miss Flite! Flite! Make haste, here, whoever you are! Flite!" Krook follows him with his eyes, and while he is calling, finds opportunity to steal to the old portmanteau and steal back again.

"Run, Flite, run! The nearest doctor! Run!" So Mr. Krook addresses a crazy little woman who is his female lodger, who appears and vanishes in a breath, who soon returns accompanied by a testy medical man brought from his dinner, with a broad, snuffy upper lip and a broad Scotch tongue.

"Ey! Bless the hearts o' ye," says the medical man, looking up at them after a moment's examination. "He's just as dead as Phairy!"

Mr. Tulkinghorn (standing by the old portmanteau) inquires if he has been dead any time.

"Any time, sir?" says the medical gentleman. "It's probable he wull have been dead aboot three hours."

"About that time, I should say," observes a dark young man on the other side of the bed.

"Air you in the maydickle prayfession yourself, sir?" inquires the first.

The dark young man says yes.

"Then I'll just tak' my depairture," replies the other, "for I'm nae gude here!" With which remark he finishes his brief attendance and returns to finish his dinner.

The dark young surgeon passes the candle across and across the face and carefully examines the law-writer, who has established his pretensions to his name by becoming indeed No one.

"I knew this person by sight very well," says he. "He has purchased opium of me for the last year and a half. Was anybody present related to him?" glancing round upon the three bystanders.

"I was his landlord," grimly answers Krook, taking the candle from the surgeon's outstretched hand. "He told me once I was the nearest relation he had."

"He has died," says the surgeon, "of an over-dose of opium, there is no doubt. The room is strongly flavoured with it. There is enough here now," taking an old tea-pot from Mr. Krook, "to kill a dozen people."

"Do you think he did it on purpose?" asks Krook.

"Took the over-dose?"

"Yes!" Krook almost smacks his lips with the unction of a horrible interest.

"I can't say. I should think it unlikely, as he has been in the habit of taking so much. But nobody can tell. He was very poor, I suppose?"

"I suppose he was. His room—don't look rich," says Krook, who might have changed eyes with his cat, as he casts his sharp glance around. "But I have never been in it since he had it, and he was too close to name his circumstances to me."

"Did he owe you any rent?"

"Six weeks."

"He will never pay it!" says the young man, resuming his examination. "It is beyond a doubt that he is indeed as dead as Pharaoh; and to judge from his appearance and condition, I should think it a happy release. Yet he must have been a good figure when a youth, and I dare say, good-looking." He says this, not unfeelingly, while sitting on the bedstead's edge with his face towards that other face and his hand upon the region of the heart. "I recollect once thinking there was something in his manner, uncouth as it was, that denoted a fall in life. Was that so?" he continues, looking round.

Krook replies, "You might as well ask me to describe the ladies whose heads of hair I have got in sacks downstairs. Than that he was my lodger for a year and a half and lived—or didn't live—by law-writing, I know no more of him."

During this dialogue Mr. Tulkinghorn has stood aloof by the old portmanteau, with his hands behind him, equally removed, to all appearance, from all three kinds of interest exhibited near the bed—from the young surgeon's professional interest in death, noticeable as being quite apart from his remarks on the deceased as an individual; from the old man's unction; and the little crazy woman's awe. His imperturbable face has been as inexpressive as his rusty clothes. One could not even say he has been thinking all this while. He has shown neither patience nor impatience, nor attention nor abstraction. He has shown nothing but his shell. As easily might the tone of a delicate musical instrument be inferred from its case, as the tone of Mr. Tulkinghorn from his case.

He now interposes, addressing the young surgeon in his unmoved, professional way.

"I looked in here," he observes, "just before you, with the intention of giving this deceased man, whom I never saw alive, some employment at his trade of copying. I had heard of him from my stationer—Snagsby of Cook's Court. Since no one here knows anything about him, it might be as well to send for Snagsby. Ah!" to the little crazy woman, who has often seen him in court, and whom he has often seen, and who proposes, in frightened dumb-show, to go for the law-stationer. "Suppose you do!"

While she is gone, the surgeon abandons his hopeless investigation and covers its subject with the patchwork counterpane. Mr. Krook and he interchange a word or two. Mr. Tulkinghorn says nothing, but stands, ever, near the old portmanteau.

Mr. Snagsby arrives hastily in his grey coat and his black sleeves. "Dear me, dear me," he says; "and it has come to this, has it! Bless my soul!"

"Can you give the person of the house any information about this unfortunate creature, Snagsby?" inquires Mr. Tulkinghorn. "He was in arrears with his rent, it seems. And he must be buried, you know."

"Well, sir," says Mr. Snagsby, coughing his apologetic cough behind his hand, "I really don't know what advice I could offer, except sending for the beadle."

"I don't speak of advice," returns Mr. Tulkinghorn. "I could advise—"

"No one better, sir, I am sure," says Mr. Snagsby, with his deferential cough.

"I speak of affording some clue to his connexions, or to where he came from, or to anything concerning him."

"I assure you, sir," says Mr. Snagsby after prefacing his reply with his cough of general propitiation, "that I no more know where he came from than I know—"

"Where he has gone to, perhaps," suggests the surgeon to help him out.

A pause. Mr. Tulkinghorn looking at the law-stationer. Mr. Krook, with his mouth open, looking for somebody to speak next.

"As to his connexions, sir," says Mr. Snagsby, "if a person was to say to me, 'Snagsby, here's twenty thousand pound down, ready for you in the Bank of

England if you'll only name one of 'em,' I couldn't do it, sir! About a year and a half ago—to the best of my belief, at the time when he first came to lodge at the present rag and bottle shop—"

"That was the time!" says Krook with a nod.

"About a year and a half ago," says Mr. Snagsby, strengthened, "he came into our place one morning after breakfast, and finding my little woman (which I name Mrs. Snagsby when I use that appellation) in our shop, produced a specimen of his handwriting and gave her to understand that he was in want of copying work to do and was, not to put too fine a point upon it," a favourite apology for plain speaking with Mr. Snagsby, which he always offers with a sort of argumentative frankness, "hard up! My little woman is not in general partial to strangers, particular—not to put too fine a point upon it—when they want anything. But she was rather took by something about this person, whether by his being unshaved, or by his hair being in want of attention, or by what other ladies' reasons, I leave you to judge; and she accepted of the specimen, and likewise of the address. My little woman hasn't a good ear for names," proceeds Mr. Snagsby after consulting his cough of consideration behind his hand, "and she considered Nemo equally the same as Nimrod. In consequence of which, she got into a habit of saying to me at meals, 'Mr. Snagsby, you haven't found Nimrod any work yet!' or 'Mr. Snagsby, why didn't you give that eight and thirty Chancery folio in Jarndyce to Nimrod?' or such like. And that is the way he gradually fell into job-work at our place; and that is the most I know of him except that he was a quick hand, and a hand not sparing of night-work, and that if you gave him out, say, five and forty folio on the Wednesday night, you would have it brought in on the Thursday morning. All of which—" Mr. Snagsby concludes by politely motioning with his hat towards the bed, as much as to add, "I have no doubt my honourable friend would confirm if he were in a condition to do it."

"Hadn't you better see," says Mr. Tulkinghorn to Krook, "whether he had any papers that may enlighten you? There will be an inquest, and you will be asked the question. You can read?"

"No, I can't," returns the old man with a sudden grin.

"Snagsby," says Mr. Tulkinghorn, "look over the room for him. He will get into some trouble or difficulty otherwise. Being here, I'll wait if you make haste, and then I can testify on his behalf, if it should ever be necessary, that all was fair and right. If you will hold the candle for Mr. Snagsby, my friend, he'll soon see whether there is anything to help you."

"In the first place, here's an old portmanteau, sir," says Snagsby.

Ah, to be sure, so there is! Mr. Tulkinghorn does not appear to have seen it before, though he is standing so close to it, and though there is very little else, heaven knows.

The marine-store merchant holds the light, and the law-stationer conducts the search. The surgeon leans against the corner of the chimney-piece; Miss

Flite peeps and trembles just within the door. The apt old scholar of the old school, with his dull black breeches tied with ribbons at the knees, his large black waistcoat, his long-sleeved black coat, and his wisp of limp white neckerchief tied in the bow the peerage knows so well, stands in exactly the same place and attitude.

There are some worthless articles of clothing in the old portmanteau; there is a bundle of pawnbrokers' duplicates, those turnpike tickets on the road of poverty; there is a crumpled paper, smelling of opium, on which are scrawled rough memoranda—as, took, such a day, so many grains; took, such another day, so many more—begun some time ago, as if with the intention of being regularly continued, but soon left off. There are a few dirty scraps of newspapers, all referring to coroners' inquests; there is nothing else. They search the cupboard and the drawer of the ink-splashed table. There is not a morsel of an old letter or of any other writing in either. The young surgeon examines the dress on the law-writer. A knife and some odd halfpence are all he finds. Mr. Snagsby's suggestion is the practical suggestion after all, and the beadle must be called in.

So the little crazy lodger goes for the beadle, and the rest come out of the room. "Don't leave the cat there!" says the surgeon; "that won't do!" Mr. Krook therefore drives her out before him, and she goes furtively downstairs, winding her lithe tail and licking her lips.

"Good night!" says Mr. Tulkinghorn, and goes home to Allegory and meditation.

By this time the news has got into the court. Groups of its inhabitants assemble to discuss the thing, and the outposts of the army of observation (principally boys) are pushed forward to Mr. Krook's window, which they closely invest. A policeman has already walked up to the room, and walked down again to the door, where he stands like a tower, only condescending to see the boys at his base occasionally; but whenever he does see them, they quail and fall back. Mrs. Perkins, who has not been for some weeks on speaking terms with Mrs. Piper in consequence for an unpleasantness originating in young Perkins' having "fetched" young Piper "a crack," renews her friendly intercourse on this auspicious occasion. The potboy at the corner, who is a privileged amateur, as possessing official knowledge of life and having to deal with drunken men occasionally, exchanges confidential communications with the policeman and has the appearance of an impregnable youth, unassailable by truncheons and unconfinable in station-houses. People talk across the court out of window, and bare-headed scouts come hurrying in from Chancery Lane to know what's the matter. The general feeling seems to be that it's a blessing Mr. Krook warn't made away with first, mingled with a little natural disappointment that he was not. In the midst of this sensation, the beadle arrives.

The beadle, though generally understood in the neighbourhood to be a ridiculous institution, is not without a certain popularity for the moment, if it were only as a man who is going to see the body. The policeman considers him an imbecile civilian, a remnant of the barbarous watchmen times, but gives him admission as something that must be borne with until government shall abolish him. The sensation is heightened as the tidings spread from mouth to mouth that the beadle is on the ground and has gone in.

By and by the beadle comes out, once more intensifying the sensation, which has rather languished in the interval. He is understood to be in want of witnesses for the inquest to-morrow who can tell the coroner and jury anything whatever respecting the deceased. Is immediately referred to innumerable people who can tell nothing whatever. Is made more imbecile by being constantly informed that Mrs. Green's son "was a law-writer his-self and knowed him better than anybody," which son of Mrs. Green's appears, on inquiry, to be at the present time aboard a vessel bound for China, three months out, but considered accessible by telegraph on application to the Lords of the Admiralty. Beadle goes into various shops and parlours, examining the inhabitants, always shutting the door first, and by exclusion, delay, and general idiotcy exasperating the public. Policeman seen to smile to potboy. Public loses interest and undergoes reaction. Taunts the beadle in shrill youthful voices with having boiled a boy, choruses fragments of a popular song to that effect and importing that the boy was made into soup for the workhouse. Policeman at last finds it necessary to support the law and seize a vocalist, who is released upon the flight of the rest on condition of his getting out of this then, come, and cutting it—a condition he immediately observes. So the sensation dies off for the time; and the unmoved policeman (to whom a little opium, more or less, is nothing), with his shining hat, stiff stock, inflexible great-coat, stout belt and bracelet, and all things fitting, pursues his lounging way with a heavy tread, beating the palms of his white gloves one against the other and stopping now and then at a street-corner to look casually about for anything between a lost child and a murder.

Under cover of the night, the feeble-minded beadle comes flitting about Chancery Lane with his summonses, in which every juror's name is wrongly spelt, and nothing rightly spelt but the beadle's own name, which nobody can read or wants to know. The summonses served and his witnesses forewarned, the beadle goes to Mr. Krook's to keep a small appointment he has made with certain paupers, who, presently arriving, are conducted upstairs, where they leave the great eyes in the shutter something new to stare at, in that last shape which earthly lodgings take for No one—and for Every one.

And all that night the coffin stands ready by the old portmanteau; and the lonely figure on the bed, whose path in life has lain through five and forty years, lies there with no more track behind him that any one can trace than a deserted infant.

Next day the court is all alive—is like a fair, as Mrs. Perkins, more than reconciled to Mrs. Piper, says in amicable conversation with that excellent woman. The coroner is to sit in the first-floor room at the Sol's Arms, where the Harmonic Meetings take place twice a week and where the chair is filled by a gentleman of professional celebrity, faced by Little Swills, the comic vocalist, who hopes (according to the bill in the window) that his friends will rally round him and support first-rate talent. The Sol's Arms does a brisk stroke of business all the morning. Even children so require sustaining under the general excitement that a pieman who has established himself for the occasion at the corner of the court says his brandy-balls go off like smoke. What time the beadle, hovering between the door of Mr. Krook's establishment and the door of the Sol's Arms, shows the curiosity in his keeping to a few discreet spirits and accepts the compliment of a glass of ale or so in return.

At the appointed hour arrives the coroner, for whom the jurymen are waiting and who is received with a salute of skittles from the good dry skittle-ground attached to the Sol's Arms. The coroner frequents more public-houses than any man alive. The smell of sawdust, beer, tobacco-smoke, and spirits is inseparable in his vocation from death in its most awful shapes. He is conducted by the beadle and the landlord to the Harmonic Meeting Room, where he puts his hat on the piano and takes a Windsor-chair at the head of a long table formed of several short tables put together and ornamented with glutinous rings in endless involutions, made by pots and glasses. As many of the jury as can crowd together at the table sit there. The rest get among the spittoons and pipes or lean against the piano. Over the coroner's head is a small iron garland, the pendant handle of a bell, which rather gives the majesty of the court the appearance of going to be hanged presently.

Call over and swear the jury! While the ceremony is in progress, sensation is created by the entrance of a chubby little man in a large shirt-collar, with a moist eye and an inflamed nose, who modestly takes a position near the door as one of the general public, but seems familiar with the room too. A whisper circulates that this is Little Swills. It is considered not unlikely that he will get up an imitation of the coroner and make it the principal feature of the Harmonic Meeting in the evening.

"Well, gentlemen—" the coroner begins.

"Silence there, will you!" says the beadle. Not to the coroner, though it might appear so.

"Well, gentlemen," resumes the coroner. "You are impanelled here to inquire into the death of a certain man. Evidence will be given before you as to the circumstances attending that death, and you will give your verdict according to the—skittles; they must be stopped, you know, beadle!—evidence, and not according to anything else. The first thing to be done is to view the body."

"Make way there!" cries the beadle.

So they go out in a loose procession, something after the manner of a straggling funeral, and make their inspection in Mr. Krook's back second floor, from which a few of the jurymen retire pale and precipitately. The beadle is very careful that two gentlemen not very neat about the cuffs and buttons (for whose accommodation he has provided a special little table near the coroner in the Harmonic Meeting Room) should see all that is to be seen. For they are the public chroniclers of such inquiries by the line; and he is not superior to the universal human infirmity, but hopes to read in print what "Mooney, the active and intelligent beadle of the district," said and did and even aspires to see the name of Mooney as familiarly and patronizingly mentioned as the name of the hangman is, according to the latest examples.

Little Swills is waiting for the coroner and jury on their return. Mr. Tulkinghorn, also. Mr. Tulkinghorn is received with distinction and seated near the coroner between that high judicial officer, a bagatelle-board, and the coal-box. The inquiry proceeds. The jury learn how the subject of their inquiry died, and learn no more about him. "A very eminent solicitor is in attendance, gentlemen," says the coroner, "who, I am informed, was accidentally present when discovery of the death was made, but he could only repeat the evidence you have already heard from the surgeon, the landlord, the lodger, and the law-stationer, and it is not necessary to trouble him. Is anybody in attendance who knows anything more?"

Mrs. Piper pushed forward by Mrs. Perkins. Mrs. Piper sworn.

Anastasia Piper, gentlemen. Married woman. Now, Mrs. Piper, what have you got to say about this?

Why, Mrs. Piper has a good deal to say, chiefly in parentheses and without punctuation, but not much to tell. Mrs. Piper lives in the court (which her husband is a cabinet-maker), and it has long been well beknown among the neighbours (counting from the day next but one before the half-baptizing of Alexander James Piper aged eighteen months and four days old on accounts of not being expected to live such was the sufferings gentlemen of that child in his gums) as the plaintive—so Mrs. Piper insists on calling the deceased—was reported to have sold himself. Thinks it was the plaintive's air in which that report originatinin. See the plaintive often and considered as his air was feariocious and not to be allowed to go about some children being timid (and if doubted hoping Mrs. Perkins may be brought forard for she is here and will do credit to her husband and herself and family). Has seen the plaintive wexed and worrited by the children (for children they will ever be and you cannot expect them specially if of playful dispositions to be Methoozellers which you was not yourself). On accounts of this and his dark looks has often dreamed as she see him take a pick-axe from his pocket and split Johnny's head (which the child knows not fear and has repeatually called after him close at his eels). Never however see the plaintive take a pick-axe or any other wepping far from it. Has seen him hurry away when run and called after as if not partial to children and never see him speak to neither child nor grown person at any time (excepting the boy that sweeps the crossing down the lane over the way round the corner which if he was here would tell you that he has been seen a-speaking to him frequent).

Says the coroner, is that boy here? Says the beadle, no, sir, he is not here. Says the coroner, go and fetch him then. In the absence of the active and intelligent, the coroner converses with Mr. Tulkinghorn.

Oh! Here's the boy, gentlemen!

Here he is, very muddy, very hoarse, very ragged. Now, boy! But stop a minute. Caution. This boy must be put through a few preliminary paces.

Name, Jo. Nothing else that he knows on. Don't know that everybody has two names. Never heerd of sich a think. Don't know that Jo is short for a longer name. Thinks it long enough for HIM. HE don't find no fault with it. Spell it? No. HE can't spell it. No father, no mother, no friends. Never been to school. What's home? Knows a broom's a broom, and knows it's wicked to tell a lie. Don't recollect who told him about the broom or about the lie, but knows both. Can't exactly say what'll be done to him arter he's dead if he tells a lie to the gentlemen here, but believes it'll be something wery bad to punish him, and serve him right—and so he'll tell the truth.

"This won't do, gentlemen!" says the coroner with a melancholy shake of the head.

"Don't you think you can receive his evidence, sir?" asks an attentive juryman.

"Out of the question," says the coroner. "You have heard the boy. 'Can't exactly say' won't do, you know. We can't take THAT in a court of justice, gentlemen. It's terrible depravity. Put the boy aside."

Boy put aside, to the great edification of the audience, especially of Little Swills, the comic vocalist.

Now. Is there any other witness? No other witness.

Very well, gentlemen! Here's a man unknown, proved to have been in the habit of taking opium in large quantities for a year and a half, found dead of too much opium. If you think you have any evidence to lead you to the conclusion that he committed suicide, you will come to that conclusion. If you think it is a case of accidental death, you will find a verdict accordingly.

Verdict accordingly. Accidental death. No doubt. Gentlemen, you are discharged. Good afternoon.

While the coroner buttons his great-coat, Mr. Tulkinghorn and he give private audience to the rejected witness in a corner.

That graceless creature only knows that the dead man (whom he recognized just now by his yellow face and black hair) was sometimes hooted and pursued about the streets. That one cold winter night when he, the boy, was shivering in a doorway near his crossing, the man turned to look at him, and came back, and having questioned him and found that he had not a friend in the world, said, "Neither have I. Not one!" and gave him the price of a supper and a night's lodging. That the man had often spoken to him since and asked him whether he slept sound at night, and how he bore cold and hunger, and whether he ever wished to die, and similar strange questions. That when the man had no money, he would say in passing, "I am as poor as you to-day, Jo," but that when he had any, he had always (as the boy most heartily believes) been glad to give him some.

"He was wery good to me," says the boy, wiping his eyes with his wretched sleeve. "Wen I see him a-layin' so stritched out just now, I wished he could have heerd me tell him so. He wos wery good to me, he wos!"

As he shuffles downstairs, Mr. Snagsby, lying in wait for him, puts a half-crown in his hand. "If you ever see me coming past your crossing with my little woman—I mean a lady—" says Mr. Snagsby with his finger on his nose, "don't allude to it!"

For some little time the jurymen hang about the Sol's Arms colloquially. In the sequel, half-a-dozen are caught up in a cloud of pipe-smoke that pervades the parlour of the Sol's Arms; two stroll to Hampstead; and four engage to go half-price to the play at night, and top up with oysters. Little Swills is treated on several hands. Being asked what he thinks of the proceedings, characterizes them (his strength lying in a slangular direction) as "a rummy start." The landlord of the Sol's Arms, finding Little Swills so popular, commends him highly to the jurymen and public, observing that for a song in character he don't know his equal and that that man's character-wardrobe would fill a cart.

Thus, gradually the Sol's Arms melts into the shadowy night and then flares out of it strong in gas. The Harmonic Meeting hour arriving, the gentleman of professional celebrity takes the chair, is faced (red-faced) by Little Swills; their friends rally round them and support first-rate talent. In the zenith of the evening, Little Swills says, "Gentlemen, if you'll permit me, I'll attempt a short description of a scene of real life that came off here to-day." Is much applauded and encouraged; goes out of the room as Swills; comes in as the coroner (not the least in the world like him); describes the inquest, with recreative intervals of piano-forte accompaniment, to the refrain: With his (the coroner's) tippy tol li doll, tippy tol lo doll, tippy tol li doll, Dee!

The jingling piano at last is silent, and the Harmonic friends rally round their pillows. Then there is rest around the lonely figure, now laid in its last earthly habitation; and it is watched by the gaunt eyes in the shutters through some quiet hours of night. If this forlorn man could have been prophetically seen lying here by the mother at whose breast he nestled, a little child, with eyes upraised to her loving face, and soft hand scarcely knowing how to close upon the neck to which it crept, what an impossibility the vision would have seemed! Oh, if in brighter days the now-extinguished fire within him ever burned for one woman who held him in her heart, where is she, while these ashes are above the ground!

It is anything but a night of rest at Mr. Snagsby's, in Cook's Court, where Guster murders sleep by going, as Mr. Snagsby himself allows—not to put too fine a point upon it—out of one fit into twenty. The occasion of this seizure is that Guster has a tender heart and a susceptible something that possibly might have been imagination, but for Tooting and her patron saint. Be it what it may, now, it was so direfully impressed at tea-time by Mr. Snagsby's account of the inquiry at which he had assisted that at supper-time she projected herself into the kitchen, preceded by a flying Dutch cheese, and fell into a fit of unusual duration, which she only came out of to go into another, and another, and so on through a chain of fits, with short intervals between, of which she has pathetically availed herself by consuming them in entreaties to Mrs. Snagsby not to give her warning "when she quite comes to," and also in appeals to the whole establishment to lay her down on the stones and go to bed. Hence, Mr. Snagsby, at last hearing the cock at the little dairy in Cursitor Street go into that disinterested ecstasy of his on the subject of daylight, says, drawing a long breath, though the most patient of men, "I thought you was dead, I am sure!"

What question this enthusiastic fowl supposes he settles when he strains himself to such an extent, or why he should thus crow (so men crow on various triumphant public occasions, however) about what cannot be of any moment to him, is his affair. It is enough that daylight comes, morning comes, noon comes.

Then the active and intelligent, who has got into the morning papers as such, comes with his pauper company to Mr. Krook's and bears off the body of our dear brother here departed to a hemmed-in churchyard, pestiferous and obscene, whence malignant diseases are communicated to the bodies of our dear brothers and sisters who have not departed, while our dear brothers and sisters who hang about official back-stairs—would to heaven they HAD departed!—are very complacent and agreeable. Into a beastly scrap of ground which a Turk would reject as a savage abomination and a Caffre would shudder at, they bring our dear brother here departed to receive Christian burial.

With houses looking on, on every side, save where a reeking little tunnel of a court gives access to the iron gate—with every villainy of life in action close on death, and every poisonous element of death in action close on life—here they lower our dear brother down a foot or two, here sow him in corruption, to be raised in corruption: an avenging ghost at many a sick-bedside, a shameful testimony to future ages how civilization and barbarism walked this boastful island together.

Come night, come darkness, for you cannot come too soon or stay too long by such a place as this! Come, straggling lights into the windows of the ugly houses; and you who do iniquity therein, do it at least with this dread scene shut out! Come, flame of gas, burning so sullenly above the iron gate, on which the poisoned air deposits its witch-ointment slimy to the touch! It is well that you should call to every passerby, "Look here!"

With the night comes a slouching figure through the tunnel-court to the outside of the iron gate. It holds the gate with its hands and looks in between the bars, stands looking in for a little while.

It then, with an old broom it carries, softly sweeps the step and makes the archway clean. It does so very busily and trimly, looks in again a little while, and so departs.

Jo, is it thou? Well, well! Though a rejected witness, who "can't exactly say" what will be done to him in greater hands than men's, thou art not quite in outer darkness. There is something like a distant ray of light in thy muttered reason for this: "He wos wery good to me, he wos!"

CHAPTER XII
ON THE WATCH

It has left off raining down in Lincolnshire at last, and Chesney Wold has taken heart. Mrs. Rouncewell is full of hospitable cares, for Sir Leicester and my Lady are coming home from Paris. The fashionable intelligence has found it out and communicates the glad tidings to benighted England. It has also found out that they will entertain a brilliant and distinguished circle of the ELITE of the BEAU MONDE (the fashionable intelligence is weak in English, but a giant refreshed in French) at the ancient and hospitable family seat in Lincolnshire.

For the greater honour of the brilliant and distinguished circle, and of Chesney Wold into the bargain, the broken arch of the bridge in the park is mended; and the water, now retired within its proper limits and again spanned gracefully, makes a figure in the prospect from the house. The clear, cold sunshine glances into the brittle woods and approvingly beholds the sharp wind scattering the leaves and drying the moss. It glides over the park after the moving shadows of the clouds, and chases them, and never catches them, all day. It looks in at the windows and touches the ancestral portraits with bars and patches of brightness never contemplated by the painters. Athwart the picture of my Lady, over the great chimney-piece, it throws a broad bend-sinister of light that strikes down crookedly into the hearth and seems to rend it.

Through the same cold sunshine and the same sharp wind, my Lady and Sir Leicester, in their travelling chariot (my Lady's woman and Sir Leicester's man affectionate in the rumble), start for home. With a considerable amount of jingling and whip-cracking, and many plunging demonstrations on the part of two bare-backed horses and two centaurs with glazed hats, jack-boots, and flowing manes and tails, they rattle out of the yard of the Hotel Bristol in the Place Vendome and canter between the sun-and-shadow-chequered colonnade of the Rue de Rivoli and the garden of the ill-fated palace of a headless king and queen, off by the Place of Concord, and the Elysian Fields, and the Gate of the Star, out of Paris.

Sooth to say, they cannot go away too fast, for even here my Lady Dedlock has been bored to death. Concert, assembly, opera, theatre, drive, nothing is new to my Lady under the worn-out heavens. Only last Sunday, when poor wretches were gay—within the walls playing with children among the clipped trees and the statues in the Palace Garden; walking, a score abreast, in the Elysian Fields, made more Elysian by performing dogs and wooden horses; between whiles filtering (a few) through the gloomy Cathedral of Our Lady to say a word or two at the base of a pillar within flare of a rusty little gridiron-full of gusty little tapers; without the walls encompassing Paris with dancing, love-making, wine-drinking, tobacco-smoking, tomb-visiting, billiard card and domino playing, quack-doctoring, and much murderous refuse, animate and inanimate—only last Sunday, my Lady, in the desolation of Boredom and the clutch of Giant Despair, almost hated her own maid for being in spirits.

She cannot, therefore, go too fast from Paris. Weariness of soul lies before her, as it lies behind—her Ariel has put a girdle of it round the whole earth, and it cannot be unclasped—but the imperfect remedy is always to fly from the last place where it has been experienced. Fling Paris back into the distance, then, exchanging it for endless avenues and cross-avenues of wintry trees! And, when next beheld, let it be some leagues away, with the Gate of the Star a white speck glittering in the sun, and the city a mere mound in a plain—two dark square towers rising out of it, and light and shadow descending on it aslant, like the angels in Jacob's dream!

Sir Leicester is generally in a complacent state, and rarely bored. When he has nothing else to do, he can always contemplate his own greatness. It is a considerable advantage to a man to have so inexhaustible a subject. After reading his letters, he leans back in his corner of the carriage and generally reviews his importance to society.

"You have an unusual amount of correspondence this morning?" says my Lady after a long time. She is fatigued with reading. Has almost read a page in twenty miles.

"Nothing in it, though. Nothing whatever."

"I saw one of Mr. Tulkinghorn's long effusions, I think?"

"You see everything," says Sir Leicester with admiration.

"Ha!" sighs my Lady. "He is the most tiresome of men!"

"He sends—I really beg your pardon—he sends," says Sir Leicester, selecting the letter and unfolding it, "a message to you. Our stopping to change horses as I came to his postscript drove it out of my memory. I beg you'll excuse me. He says—" Sir Leicester is so long in taking out his eye-glass and adjusting it that my Lady looks a little irritated. "He says 'In the matter of the right of way—' I beg your pardon, that's not the place. He says—yes! Here I have it! He says, 'I beg my respectful compliments to my Lady, who, I hope, has benefited by the change. Will you do me the favour to mention (as it may interest her) that I have something to tell her on her return in reference to the person who copied the affidavit in the Chancery suit, which so powerfully stimulated her curiosity. I have seen him.'"

My Lady, leaning forward, looks out of her window.

"That's the message," observes Sir Leicester.

"I should like to walk a little," says my Lady, still looking out of her window.

"Walk?" repeats Sir Leicester in a tone of surprise.

"I should like to walk a little," says my Lady with unmistakable distinctness.

"Please to stop the carriage."

The carriage is stopped, the affectionate man alights from the rumble, opens the door, and lets down the steps, obedient to an impatient motion of my Lady's hand. My Lady alights so quickly and walks away so quickly that Sir Leicester, for all his scrupulous politeness, is unable to assist her, and is left behind. A space of a minute or two has elapsed before he comes up with her. She smiles, looks very handsome, takes his arm, lounges with him for a quarter of a mile, is very much bored, and resumes her seat in the carriage.

The rattle and clatter continue through the greater part of three days, with more or less of bell-jingling and whip-cracking, and more or less plunging of centaurs and bare-backed horses. Their courtly politeness to each other at the hotels where they tarry is the theme of general admiration. Though my Lord IS a little aged for my Lady, says Madame, the hostess of the Golden Ape, and though he might be her amiable father, one can see at a glance that they love each other. One observes my Lord with his white hair, standing, hat in hand, to help my Lady to and from the carriage. One observes my Lady, how recognisant of my Lord's politeness, with an inclination of her gracious head and the concession of her so-genteel fingers! It is ravishing!

The sea has no appreciation of great men, but knocks them about like the small fry. It is habitually hard upon Sir Leicester, whose countenance it greenly mottles in the manner of sage-cheese and in whose aristocratic system it effects a dismal revolution. It is the Radical of Nature to him. Nevertheless, his dignity gets over it after stopping to refit, and he goes on with my Lady for Chesney Wold, lying only one night in London on the way to Lincolnshire.

Through the same cold sunlight, colder as the day declines, and through the same sharp wind, sharper as the separate shadows of bare trees gloom together in the woods, and as the Ghost's Walk, touched at the western corner by a pile of fire in the sky, resigns itself to coming night, they drive into the park. The rooks, swinging in their lofty houses in the elm-tree avenue, seem to discuss the question of the occupancy of the carriage as it passes underneath, some agreeing that Sir Leicester and my Lady are come down, some arguing with malcontents who won't admit it, now all consenting to consider the question disposed of, now all breaking out again in violent debate, incited by one obstinate and drowsy bird who will persist in putting in a last contradictory croak. Leaving them to swing and caw, the travelling chariot rolls on to the house, where fires gleam warmly through some of the windows, though not through so many as to give an inhabited expression to the darkening mass of front. But the brilliant and distinguished circle will soon do that.

Mrs. Rouncewell is in attendance and receives Sir Leicester's customary shake of the hand with a profound curtsy.

"How do you do, Mrs. Rouncewell? I am glad to see you."

"I hope I have the honour of welcoming you in good health, Sir Leicester?"

"In excellent health, Mrs. Rouncewell."

"My Lady is looking charmingly well," says Mrs. Rouncewell with another curtsy.

My Lady signifies, without profuse expenditure of words, that she is as wearily well as she can hope to be.

But Rosa is in the distance, behind the housekeeper; and my Lady, who has not subdued the quickness of her observation, whatever else she may have conquered, asks, "Who is that girl?"

"A young scholar of mine, my Lady. Rosa."

"Come here, Rosa!" Lady Dedlock beckons her, with even an appearance of interest. "Why, do you know how pretty you are, child?" she says, touching her shoulder with her two forefingers.

Rosa, very much abashed, says, "No, if you please, my Lady!" and glances up, and glances down, and don't know where to look, but looks all the prettier.

"How old are you?"

"Nineteen, my Lady."

"Nineteen," repeats my Lady thoughtfully. "Take care they don't spoil you by flattery."

"Yes, my Lady."

My Lady taps her dimpled cheek with the same delicate gloved fingers and goes on to the foot of the oak staircase, where Sir Leicester pauses for her as her knightly escort. A staring old Dedlock in a panel, as large as life and as dull, looks as if he didn't know what to make of it, which was probably his general state of mind in the days of Queen Elizabeth.

That evening, in the housekeeper's room, Rosa can do nothing but murmur Lady Dedlock's praises. She is so affable, so graceful, so beautiful, so elegant; has such a sweet voice and such a thrilling touch that Rosa can feel it yet! Mrs. Rouncewell confirms all this, not without personal pride, reserving only the one point of affability. Mrs. Rouncewell is not quite sure as to that. Heaven forbid that she should say a syllable in dispraise of any member of that excellent family, above all, of my Lady, whom the whole world admires; but if my Lady would only be "a little more free," not quite so cold and distant, Mrs. Rouncewell thinks she would be more affable.

"'Tis almost a pity," Mrs. Rouncewell adds—only "almost" because it borders on impiety to suppose that anything could be better than it is, in such an express dispensation as the Dedlock affairs—"that my Lady has no family. If she had had a daughter now, a grown young lady, to interest her, I think she would have had the only kind of excellence she wants."

"Might not that have made her still more proud, grandmother?" says Watt, who has been home and come back again, he is such a good grandson.

"More and most, my dear," returns the housekeeper with dignity, "are words it's not my place to use—nor so much as to hear—applied to any drawback on my Lady."

"I beg your pardon, grandmother. But she is proud, is she not?"

"If she is, she has reason to be. The Dedlock family have always reason to be."

"Well," says Watt, "it's to be hoped they line out of their prayer-books a certain passage for the common people about pride and vainglory. Forgive me, grandmother! Only a joke!"

"Sir Leicester and Lady Dedlock, my dear, are not fit subjects for joking."

"Sir Leicester is no joke by any means," says Watt, "and I humbly ask his pardon. I suppose, grandmother, that even with the family and their guests down here, there is no objection to my prolonging my stay at the Dedlock Arms for a day or two, as any other traveller might?"

"Surely, none in the world, child."

"I am glad of that," says Watt, "because I have an inexpressible desire to extend my knowledge of this beautiful neighbourhood."

He happens to glance at Rosa, who looks down and is very shy indeed. But according to the old superstition, it should be Rosa's ears that burn, and not her fresh bright cheeks, for my Lady's maid is holding forth about her at this moment with surpassing energy.

My Lady's maid is a Frenchwoman of two and thirty, from somewhere in the southern country about Avignon and Marseilles, a large-eyed brown woman with black hair who would be handsome but for a certain feline mouth and general uncomfortable tightness of face, rendering the jaws too eager and the skull too prominent. There is something indefinably keen and wan about her anatomy, and she has a watchful way of looking out of the corners of her eyes without turning her head which could be pleasantly dispensed with, especially when she is in an ill humour and near knives. Through all the good taste of her dress and little adornments, these objections so express themselves that she seems to go about like a very neat she-wolf imperfectly tamed. Besides being accomplished in all the knowledge appertaining to her post, she is almost an Englishwoman in her acquaintance with the language; consequently, she is in no want of words to shower upon Rosa for having attracted my Lady's attention, and she pours them out with such grim ridicule as she sits at dinner that her companion, the affectionate man, is rather relieved when she arrives at the spoon stage of that performance.

Ha, ha, ha! She, Hortense, been in my Lady's service since five years and always kept at the distance, and this doll, this puppet, caressed—absolutely caressed—by my Lady on the moment of her arriving at the house! Ha, ha, ha! "And do you know how pretty you are, child?" "No, my Lady." You are right there! "And how old are you, child! And take care they do not spoil you by flattery, child!" Oh, how droll! It is the BEST thing altogether.

In short, it is such an admirable thing that Mademoiselle Hortense can't forget it; but at meals for days afterwards, even among her countrywomen and others attached in like capacity to the troop of visitors, relapses into silent enjoyment of the joke—an enjoyment expressed, in her own convivial manner, by an additional tightness of face, thin elongation of compressed lips, and sidewise look, which intense appreciation of humour is frequently reflected in my Lady's mirrors when my Lady is not among them.

All the mirrors in the house are brought into action now, many of them after a long blank. They reflect handsome faces, simpering faces, youthful faces, faces of threescore and ten that will not submit to be old; the entire collection of faces that have come to pass a January week or two at Chesney Wold, and which the fashionable intelligence, a mighty hunter before the Lord, hunts with a keen scent, from their breaking cover at the Court of St. James's to their being run down to death. The place in Lincolnshire is all alive. By day guns and voices are heard ringing in the woods, horsemen and carriages enliven the park roads, servants and hangers-on pervade the village and the Dedlock Arms. Seen by night from distant openings in the trees, the row of windows in the long drawing-room, where my Lady's picture hangs over the great chimney-piece, is like a row of jewels set in a black frame. On Sunday the chill little church is almost warmed by so much gallant company, and the general flavour of the Dedlock dust is quenched in delicate perfumes.

The brilliant and distinguished circle comprehends within it no contracted amount of education, sense, courage, honour, beauty, and virtue. Yet there is something a little wrong about it in despite of its immense advantages. What can it be?

Dandyism? There is no King George the Fourth now (more the pity) to set the dandy fashion; there are no clear-starched jack-towel neckcloths, no short-waisted coats, no false calves, no stays. There are no caricatures, now, of effeminate exquisites so arrayed, swooning in opera boxes with excess of delight and being revived by other dainty creatures poking long-necked scent-bottles at their noses. There is no beau whom it takes four men at once to shake into his buckskins, or who goes to see all the executions, or who is troubled with the self-reproach of having once consumed a pea. But is there dandyism in the brilliant and distinguished circle notwithstanding, dandyism of a more mischievous sort, that has got below the surface and is doing less harmless things than jack-towelling itself and stopping its own digestion, to which no rational person need particularly object?

Why, yes. It cannot be disguised. There ARE at Chesney Wold this January week some ladies and gentlemen of the newest fashion, who have set up a dandyism—in religion, for instance. Who in mere lackadaisical want of an emotion have agreed upon a little dandy talk about the vulgar wanting faith in things in general, meaning in the things that have been tried and found wanting, as though a low fellow should unaccountably lose faith in a bad shilling after finding it out! Who would make the vulgar very picturesque and faithful by putting back the hands upon the clock of time and cancelling a few hundred years of history.

There are also ladies and gentlemen of another fashion, not so new, but very elegant, who have agreed to put a smooth glaze on the world and to keep down all its realities. For whom everything must be languid and pretty. Who have found out the perpetual stoppage. Who are to rejoice at nothing and be sorry for nothing. Who are not to be disturbed by ideas. On whom even the fine arts, attending in powder and walking backward like the Lord Chamberlain, must array themselves in the milliners' and tailors' patterns of past generations and be particularly careful not to be in earnest or to receive any impress from the moving age.

Then there is my Lord Boodle, of considerable reputation with his party, who has known what office is and who tells Sir Leicester Dedlock with much gravity, after dinner, that he really does not see to what the present age is tending. A debate is not what a debate used to be; the House is not what the House used to be; even a Cabinet is not what it formerly was. He perceives with astonishment that supposing the present government to be overthrown, the limited choice of the Crown, in the formation of a new ministry, would lie between Lord Coodle and Sir Thomas Doodle—supposing it to be impossible for the Duke of Foodle to act with Goodle, which may be assumed to be the case in consequence of the breach arising out of that affair with Hoodle. Then, giving the Home Department and the leadership of the House of Commons to Joodle, the Exchequer to Koodle, the Colonies to Loodle, and the Foreign Office to Moodle, what are you to do with Noodle? You can't offer him the Presidency of the Council; that is reserved for Poodle. You can't put him in the Woods and Forests; that is hardly good enough for Quoodle. What follows? That the country is shipwrecked, lost, and gone to pieces (as is made manifest to the patriotism of Sir Leicester Dedlock) because you can't provide for Noodle!

On the other hand, the Right Honourable William Buffy, M.P., contends across the table with some one else that the shipwreck of the country—about which there is no doubt; it is only the manner of it that is in question—is attributable to Cuffy. If you had done with Cuffy what you ought to have done when he first came into Parliament, and had prevented him from going over to Duffy, you would have got him into alliance with Fuffy, you would have had with you the weight attaching as a smart debater to Guffy, you would have brought to bear upon the elections the wealth of Huffy, you would have got in for three counties Juffy, Kuffy, and Luffy, and you would have strengthened your administration by the official knowledge and the business habits of Muffy. All this, instead of being as you now are, dependent on the mere caprice of Puffy!

As to this point, and as to some minor topics, there are differences of opinion; but it is perfectly clear to the brilliant and distinguished circle, all round, that nobody is in question but Boodle and his retinue, and Buffy and HIS retinue. These are the great actors for whom the stage is reserved. A People there are, no doubt—a certain large number of supernumeraries, who are to be occasionally addressed, and relied upon for shouts and choruses, as on the theatrical stage; but Boodle and Buffy, their followers and families, their heirs, executors, administrators, and assigns, are the born first-actors, managers, and leaders, and no others can appear upon the scene for ever and ever.

In this, too, there is perhaps more dandyism at Chesney Wold than the brilliant and distinguished circle will find good for itself in the long run. For it is, even with the stillest and politest circles, as with the circle the necromancer draws around him—very strange appearances may be seen in active motion outside. With this difference, that being realities and not phantoms, there is the greater danger of their breaking in.

Chesney Wold is quite full anyhow, so full that a burning sense of injury arises in the breasts of ill-lodged ladies'-maids, and is not to be extinguished. Only one room is empty. It is a turret chamber of the third order of merit, plainly but comfortably furnished and having an old-fashioned business air. It is Mr. Tulkinghorn's room, and is never bestowed on anybody else, for he may come at any time. He is not come yet. It is his quiet habit to walk across the park from the village in fine weather, to drop into this room as if he had never been out of it since he was last seen there, to request a servant to inform Sir Leicester that he is arrived in case he should be wanted, and to appear ten minutes before dinner in the shadow of the library-door. He sleeps in his turret with a complaining flag-staff over his head, and has some leads outside on which, any fine morning when he is down here, his black figure may be seen walking before breakfast like a larger species of rook.

Every day before dinner, my Lady looks for him in the dusk of the library, but he is not there. Every day at dinner, my Lady glances down the table for the vacant place that would be waiting to receive him if he had just arrived, but there is no vacant place. Every night my Lady casually asks her maid, "Is Mr. Tulkinghorn come?"

Every night the answer is, "No, my Lady, not yet."

One night, while having her hair undressed, my Lady loses herself in deep thought after this reply until she sees her own brooding face in the opposite glass, and a pair of black eyes curiously observing her.

"Be so good as to attend," says my Lady then, addressing the reflection of Hortense, "to your business. You can contemplate your beauty at another time."

"Pardon! It was your Ladyship's beauty."

"That," says my Lady, "you needn't contemplate at all."

At length, one afternoon a little before sunset, when the bright groups of figures which have for the last hour or two enlivened the Ghost's Walk are all dispersed and only Sir Leicester and my Lady remain upon the terrace, Mr. Tulkinghorn appears. He comes towards them at his usual methodical pace, which is never quickened, never slackened. He wears his usual expressionless mask—if it be a mask—and carries family secrets in every limb of his body and every crease of his dress. Whether his whole soul is devoted to the great or whether he yields them nothing beyond the services he sells is his personal secret. He keeps it, as he keeps the secrets of his clients; he is his own client in that matter, and will never betray himself.

"How do you do, Mr. Tulkinghorn?" says Sir Leicester, giving him his hand.

Mr. Tulkinghorn is quite well. Sir Leicester is quite well. My Lady is quite well. All highly satisfactory. The lawyer, with his hands behind him, walks at Sir Leicester's side along the terrace. My Lady walks upon the other side.

"We expected you before," says Sir Leicester. A gracious observation. As much as to say, "Mr. Tulkinghorn, we remember your existence when you are not here to remind us of it by your presence. We bestow a fragment of our minds upon you, sir, you see!"

Mr. Tulkinghorn, comprehending it, inclines his head and says he is much obliged.

"I should have come down sooner," he explains, "but that I have been much engaged with those matters in the several suits between yourself and Boythorn."

"A man of a very ill-regulated mind," observes Sir Leicester with severity. "An extremely dangerous person in any community. A man of a very low character of mind."

"He is obstinate," says Mr. Tulkinghorn.

"It is natural to such a man to be so," says Sir Leicester, looking most profoundly obstinate himself. "I am not at all surprised to hear it."

"The only question is," pursues the lawyer, "whether you will give up anything."

"No, sir," replies Sir Leicester. "Nothing. I give up?"

"I don't mean anything of importance. That, of course, I know you would not abandon. I mean any minor point."

"Mr. Tulkinghorn," returns Sir Leicester, "there can be no minor point between myself and Mr. Boythorn. If I go farther, and observe that I cannot readily conceive how ANY right of mine can be a minor point, I speak not so much in reference to myself as an individual as in reference to the family position I have it in charge to maintain."

Mr. Tulkinghorn inclines his head again. "I have now my instructions," he says. "Mr. Boythorn will give us a good deal of trouble—"

"It is the character of such a mind, Mr. Tulkinghorn," Sir Leicester interrupts him, "TO give trouble. An exceedingly ill-conditioned, levelling person. A person who, fifty years ago, would probably have been tried at the Old Bailey for some demagogue proceeding, and severely punished—if not," adds Sir Leicester after a moment's pause, "if not hanged, drawn, and quartered."

Sir Leicester appears to discharge his stately breast of a burden in passing this capital sentence, as if it were the next satisfactory thing to having the sentence executed.

"But night is coming on," says he, "and my Lady will take cold. My dear, let us go in."

As they turn towards the hall-door, Lady Dedlock addresses Mr. Tulkinghorn for the first time.

"You sent me a message respecting the person whose writing I happened to inquire about. It was like you to remember the circumstance; I had quite forgotten it. Your message reminded me of it again. I can't imagine what association I had with a hand like that, but I surely had some."

"You had some?" Mr. Tulkinghorn repeats.

"Oh, yes!" returns my Lady carelessly. "I think I must have had some. And did you really take the trouble to find out the writer of that actual thing—what is it!—affidavit?"

"Yes."

"How very odd!"

They pass into a sombre breakfast-room on the ground floor, lighted in the day by two deep windows. It is now twilight. The fire glows brightly on the panelled wall and palely on the window-glass, where, through the cold reflection of the blaze, the colder landscape shudders in the wind and a grey mist creeps along, the only traveller besides the waste of clouds.

My Lady lounges in a great chair in the chimney-corner, and Sir Leicester takes another great chair opposite. The lawyer stands before the fire with his hand out at arm's length, shading his face. He looks across his arm at my Lady.

"Yes," he says, "I inquired about the man, and found him. And, what is very strange, I found him—"

"Not to be any out-of-the-way person, I am afraid!" Lady Dedlock languidly anticipates.

"I found him dead."

"Oh, dear me!" remonstrated Sir Leicester. Not so much shocked by the fact as by the fact of the fact being mentioned.

"I was directed to his lodging—a miserable, poverty-stricken place—and I found him dead."

"You will excuse me, Mr. Tulkinghorn," observes Sir Leicester. "I think the less said—"

"Pray, Sir Leicester, let me hear the story out" (it is my Lady speaking). "It is quite a story for twilight. How very shocking! Dead?"

Mr. Tulkinghorn re-asserts it by another inclination of his head. "Whether by his own hand—"

"Upon my honour!" cries Sir Leicester. "Really!"

"Do let me hear the story!" says my Lady.

"Whatever you desire, my dear. But, I must say—"

"No, you mustn't say! Go on, Mr. Tulkinghorn."

Sir Leicester's gallantry concedes the point, though he still feels that to bring this sort of squalor among the upper classes is really—really—

"I was about to say," resumes the lawyer with undisturbed calmness, "that whether he had died by his own hand or not, it was beyond my power to tell you. I should amend that phrase, however, by saying that he had unquestionably died of his own act, though whether by his own deliberate intention or by mischance can never certainly be known. The coroner's jury found that he took the poison accidentally."

"And what kind of man," my Lady asks, "was this deplorable creature?"

"Very difficult to say," returns the lawyer, shaking his head. "He had lived so wretchedly and was so neglected, with his gipsy colour and his wild black hair and beard, that I should have considered him the commonest of the common. The surgeon had a notion that he had once been something better, both in appearance and condition."

"What did they call the wretched being?"

"They called him what he had called himself, but no one knew his name."

"Not even any one who had attended on him?"

"No one had attended on him. He was found dead. In fact, I found him."

"Without any clue to anything more?"

"Without any; there was," says the lawyer meditatively, "an old portmanteau, but—No, there were no papers."

During the utterance of every word of this short dialogue, Lady Dedlock and Mr. Tulkinghorn, without any other alteration in their customary deportment, have looked very steadily at one another—as was natural, perhaps, in the discussion of so unusual a subject. Sir Leicester has looked at the fire, with the general expression of the Dedlock on the staircase. The story being told, he renews his stately protest, saying that as it is quite clear that no association in my Lady's mind can possibly be traceable to this poor wretch (unless he was a begging-letter writer), he trusts to hear no more about a subject so far removed from my Lady's station.

"Certainly, a collection of horrors," says my Lady, gathering up her mantles and furs, "but they interest one for the moment! Have the kindness, Mr. Tulkinghorn, to open the door for me."

Mr. Tulkinghorn does so with deference and holds it open while she passes out. She passes close to him, with her usual fatigued manner and insolent grace. They meet again at dinner—again, next day—again, for many days in succession. Lady Dedlock is always the same exhausted deity, surrounded by worshippers, and terribly liable to be bored to death, even while presiding at her own shrine. Mr. Tulkinghorn is always the same speechless repository of noble confidences, so oddly out of place and yet so perfectly at home. They appear to take as little note of one another as any two people enclosed within the same walls could. But whether each evermore watches and suspects the other, evermore mistrustful of some great reservation; whether each is evermore prepared at all points for the other, and never to be taken unawares; what each would give to know how much the other knows—all this is hidden, for the time, in their own hearts.

CHAPTER XIII
ESTHER'S NARRATIVE

We held many consultations about what Richard was to be, first without Mr. Jarndyce, as he had requested, and afterwards with him, but it was a long time before we seemed to make progress. Richard said he was ready for anything. When Mr. Jarndyce doubted whether he might not already be too old to enter the Navy, Richard said he had thought of that, and perhaps he was. When Mr. Jarndyce asked him what he thought of the Army, Richard said he had thought of that, too, and it wasn't a bad idea. When Mr. Jarndyce advised him to try and decide within himself whether his old preference for the sea was an ordinary boyish inclination or a strong impulse, Richard answered, Well he really HAD tried very often, and he couldn't make out.

"How much of this indecision of character," Mr. Jarndyce said to me, "is chargeable on that incomprehensible heap of uncertainty and procrastination on which he has been thrown from his birth, I don't pretend to say; but that Chancery, among its other sins, is responsible for some of it, I can plainly see. It has engendered or confirmed in him a habit of putting off—and trusting to this, that, and the other chance, without knowing what chance—and dismissing everything as unsettled, uncertain, and confused. The character of much older and steadier people may be even changed by the circumstances surrounding them. It would be too much to expect that a boy's, in its formation, should be the subject of such influences and escape them."

I felt this to be true; though if I may venture to mention what I thought besides, I thought it much to be regretted that Richard's education had not counteracted those influences or directed his character. He had been eight years at a public school and had learnt, I understood, to make Latin verses of several sorts in the most admirable manner. But I never heard that it had been anybody's business to find out what his natural bent was, or where his failings lay, or to adapt any kind of knowledge to HIM. HE had been adapted to the verses and had learnt the art of making them to such perfection that if he had remained at school until he was of age, I suppose he could only have gone on making them over and over again unless he had enlarged his education by forgetting how to do it. Still, although I had no doubt that they were very beautiful, and very improving, and very sufficient for a great many purposes of life, and always remembered all through life, I did doubt whether Richard would not have profited by some one studying him a little, instead of his studying them quite so much.

To be sure, I knew nothing of the subject and do not even now know whether the young gentlemen of classic Rome or Greece made verses to the same extent—or whether the young gentlemen of any country ever did.

"I haven't the least idea," said Richard, musing, "what I had better be. Except that I am quite sure I don't want to go into the Church, it's a toss-up."

"You have no inclination in Mr. Kenge's way?" suggested Mr. Jarndyce.

"I don't know that, sir!" replied Richard. "I am fond of boating. Articled clerks go a good deal on the water. It's a capital profession!"

"Surgeon—" suggested Mr. Jarndyce.

"That's the thing, sir!" cried Richard.

I doubt if he had ever once thought of it before.

"That's the thing, sir," repeated Richard with the greatest enthusiasm. "We have got it at last. M.R.C.S.!"

He was not to be laughed out of it, though he laughed at it heartily. He said he had chosen his profession, and the more he thought of it, the more he felt that his destiny was clear; the art of healing was the art of all others for him. Mistrusting that he only came to this conclusion because, having never had much chance of finding out for himself what he was fitted for and having never been guided to the discovery, he was taken by the newest idea and was glad to get rid of the trouble of consideration, I wondered whether the Latin verses often ended in this or whether Richard's was a solitary case.

Mr. Jarndyce took great pains to talk with him seriously and to put it to his good sense not to deceive himself in so important a matter. Richard was a little grave after these interviews, but invariably told Ada and me that it was all right, and then began to talk about something else.

"By heaven!" cried Mr. Boythorn, who interested himself strongly in the subject—though I need not say that, for he could do nothing weakly; "I rejoice to find a young gentleman of spirit and gallantry devoting himself to that noble profession! The more spirit there is in it, the better for mankind and the worse for those mercenary task-masters and low tricksters who delight in putting that illustrious art at a disadvantage in the world. By all that is base and despicable," cried Mr. Boythorn, "the treatment of surgeons aboard ship is such that I would submit the legs—both legs—of every member of the Admiralty Board to a compound fracture and render it a transportable offence in any qualified practitioner to set them if the system were not wholly changed in eight and forty hours!"

"Wouldn't you give them a week?" asked Mr. Jarndyce.

"No!" cried Mr. Boythorn firmly. "Not on any consideration! Eight and forty hours! As to corporations, parishes, vestry-boards, and similar gatherings of jolter-headed clods who assemble to exchange such speeches that, by heaven, they ought to be worked in quicksilver mines for the short remainder of their miserable existence, if it were only to prevent their detestable English from contaminating a language spoken in the presence of the sun—as to those fellows, who meanly take advantage of the ardour of gentlemen in the pursuit of knowledge to recompense the inestimable services of the best years of their lives, their long study, and their expensive education with pittances too small for the acceptance of clerks, I would have the necks of every one of them wrung and their skulls arranged in Surgeons' Hall for the contemplation of the whole profession in order that its younger members might understand from actual measurement, in early life, HOW thick skulls may become!"

He wound up this vehement declaration by looking round upon us with a most agreeable smile and suddenly thundering, "Ha, ha, ha!" over and over again, until anybody else might have been expected to be quite subdued by the exertion.

As Richard still continued to say that he was fixed in his choice after repeated periods for consideration had been recommended by Mr. Jarndyce and had expired, and he still continued to assure Ada and me in the same final manner that it was "all right," it became advisable to take Mr. Kenge into council. Mr. Kenge, therefore, came down to dinner one day, and leaned back in his chair, and turned his eye-glasses over and over, and spoke in a sonorous voice, and did exactly what I remembered to have seen him do when I was a little girl.

"Ah!" said Mr. Kenge. "Yes. Well! A very good profession, Mr. Jarndyce, a very good profession."

"The course of study and preparation requires to be diligently pursued," observed my guardian with a glance at Richard.

"Oh, no doubt," said Mr. Kenge. "Diligently."

"But that being the case, more or less, with all pursuits that are worth much," said Mr. Jarndyce, "it is not a special consideration which another choice would be likely to escape."

"Truly," said Mr. Kenge. "And Mr. Richard Carstone, who has so meritoriously acquitted himself in the—shall I say the classic shades?—in which his youth had been passed, will, no doubt, apply the habits, if not the principles and practice, of versification in that tongue in which a poet was said (unless I mistake) to be born, not made, to the more eminently practical field of action on which he enters."

"You may rely upon it," said Richard in his off-hand manner, "that I shall go at it and do my best."

"Very well, Mr. Jarndyce!" said Mr. Kenge, gently nodding his head. "Really, when we are assured by Mr. Richard that he means to go at it and to do his best," nodding feelingly and smoothly over those expressions, "I would submit to you that we have only to inquire into the best mode of carrying out the object of his ambition. Now, with reference to placing Mr. Richard with some sufficiently eminent practitioner. Is there any one in view at present?"

"No one, Rick, I think?" said my guardian.

"No one, sir," said Richard.

"Quite so!" observed Mr. Kenge. "As to situation, now. Is there any particular feeling on that head?"

"N—no," said Richard.

"Quite so!" observed Mr. Kenge again.

"I should like a little variety," said Richard; "I mean a good range of experience."

"Very requisite, no doubt," returned Mr. Kenge. "I think this may be easily arranged, Mr. Jarndyce? We have only, in the first place, to discover a sufficiently eligible practitioner; and as soon as we make our want—and shall I add, our ability to pay a premium?—known, our only difficulty will be in the selection of one from a large number. We have only, in the second place, to observe those little formalities which are rendered necessary by our time of life and our being under the guardianship of the court. We shall soon be—shall I say, in Mr. Richard's own light-hearted manner, 'going at it'—to our heart's content. It is a coincidence," said Mr. Kenge with a tinge of melancholy in his smile, "one of those coincidences which may or may not require an explanation beyond our present limited faculties, that I have a cousin in the medical profession. He might be deemed eligible by you and might be disposed to respond to this proposal. I can answer for him as little as for you, but he MIGHT!"

As this was an opening in the prospect, it was arranged that Mr. Kenge should see his cousin. And as Mr. Jarndyce had before proposed to take us to London for a few weeks, it was settled next day that we should make our visit at once and combine Richard's business with it.

Mr. Boythorn leaving us within a week, we took up our abode at a cheerful lodging near Oxford Street over an upholsterer's shop. London was a great wonder to us, and we were out for hours and hours at a time, seeing the sights, which appeared to be less capable of exhaustion than we were. We made the round of the principal theatres, too, with great delight, and saw all the plays that were worth seeing. I mention this because it was at the theatre that I began to be made uncomfortable again by Mr. Guppy.

I was sitting in front of the box one night with Ada, and Richard was in the place he liked best, behind Ada's chair, when, happening to look down into the pit, I saw Mr. Guppy, with his hair flattened down upon his head and woe depicted in his face, looking up at me. I felt all through the performance that he never looked at the actors but constantly looked at me, and always with a carefully prepared expression of the deepest misery and the profoundest dejection.

It quite spoiled my pleasure for that night because it was so very embarrassing and so very ridiculous. But from that time forth, we never went to the play without my seeing Mr. Guppy in the pit, always with his hair straight and flat, his shirt-collar turned down, and a general feebleness about him. If he were not there when we went in, and I began to hope he would not come and yielded myself for a little while to the interest of the scene, I was certain to encounter his languishing eyes when I least expected it and, from that time, to be quite sure that they were fixed upon me all the evening.

I really cannot express how uneasy this made me. If he would only have brushed up his hair or turned up his collar, it would have been bad enough; but to know that that absurd figure was always gazing at me, and always in that demonstrative state of despondency, put such a constraint upon me that I did not like to laugh at the play, or to cry at it, or to move, or to speak. I seemed able to do nothing naturally. As to escaping Mr. Guppy by going to the back of the box, I could not bear to do that because I knew Richard and Ada relied on having me next them and that they could never have talked together so happily if anybody else had been in my place. So there I sat, not knowing where to look—for wherever I looked, I knew Mr. Guppy's eyes were following me—and thinking of the dreadful expense to which this young man was putting himself on my account.

Sometimes I thought of telling Mr. Jarndyce. Then I feared that the young man would lose his situation and that I might ruin him. Sometimes I thought of confiding in Richard, but was deterred by the possibility of his fighting Mr. Guppy and giving him black eyes. Sometimes I thought, should I frown at him or shake my head. Then I felt I could not do it. Sometimes I considered whether I should write to his mother, but that ended in my being convinced that to open a correspondence would be to make the matter worse. I always came to the conclusion, finally, that I could do nothing. Mr. Guppy's perseverance, all this time, not only produced him regularly at any theatre to which we went, but caused him to appear in the crowd as we were coming out, and even to get up behind our fly—where I am sure I saw him, two or three times, struggling among the most dreadful spikes. After we got home, he haunted a post opposite our house. The upholsterer's where we lodged being at the corner of two streets, and my bedroom window being opposite the post, I was afraid to go near the window when I went upstairs, lest I should see him (as I did one moonlight night) leaning against the post and evidently catching cold. If Mr. Guppy had not been, fortunately for me, engaged in the daytime, I really should have had no rest from him.

While we were making this round of gaieties, in which Mr. Guppy so extraordinarily participated, the business which had helped to bring us to town was not neglected. Mr. Kenge's cousin was a Mr. Bayham Badger, who had a good practice at Chelsea and attended a large public institution besides. He was quite willing to receive Richard into his house and to superintend his studies, and as it seemed that those could be pursued advantageously under Mr. Badger's roof, and Mr. Badger liked Richard, and as Richard said he liked Mr. Badger "well enough," an agreement was made, the Lord Chancellor's consent was obtained, and it was all settled.

On the day when matters were concluded between Richard and Mr. Badger, we were all under engagement to dine at Mr. Badger's house. We were to be "merely a family party," Mrs. Badger's note said; and we found no lady there but Mrs. Badger herself. She was surrounded in the drawing-room by various objects, indicative of her painting a little, playing the piano a little, playing the guitar a little, playing the harp a little, singing a little, working a little, reading a little, writing poetry a little, and botanizing a little. She was a lady of about fifty, I should think, youthfully dressed, and of a very fine complexion. If I add to the little list of her accomplishments that she rouged a little, I do not mean that there was any harm in it.

Mr. Bayham Badger himself was a pink, fresh-faced, crisp-looking gentleman with a weak voice, white teeth, light hair, and surprised eyes, some years younger, I should say, than Mrs. Bayham Badger. He admired her exceedingly, but principally, and to begin with, on the curious ground (as it seemed to us) of her having had three husbands. We had barely taken our seats when he said to Mr. Jarndyce quite triumphantly, "You would hardly suppose that I am Mrs. Bayham Badger's third!"

"Indeed?" said Mr. Jarndyce.

"Her third!" said Mr. Badger. "Mrs. Bayham Badger has not the appearance, Miss Summerson, of a lady who has had two former husbands?"

I said "Not at all!"

"And most remarkable men!" said Mr. Badger in a tone of confidence. "Captain Swosser of the Royal Navy, who was Mrs. Badger's first husband, was a very distinguished officer indeed. The name of Professor Dingo, my immediate predecessor, is one of European reputation."

Mrs. Badger overheard him and smiled.

"Yes, my dear!" Mr. Badger replied to the smile, "I was observing to Mr. Jarndyce and Miss Summerson that you had had two former husbands—both very distinguished men. And they found it, as people generally do, difficult to believe."

"I was barely twenty," said Mrs. Badger, "when I married Captain Swosser of the Royal Navy. I was in the Mediterranean with him; I am quite a sailor. On the twelfth anniversary of my wedding-day, I became the wife of Professor Dingo."

"Of European reputation," added Mr. Badger in an undertone.

"And when Mr. Badger and myself were married," pursued Mrs. Badger, "we were married on the same day of the year. I had become attached to the day."

"So that Mrs. Badger has been married to three husbands—two of them highly distinguished men," said Mr. Badger, summing up the facts, "and each time upon the twenty-first of March at eleven in the forenoon!"

We all expressed our admiration.

"But for Mr. Badger's modesty," said Mr. Jarndyce, "I would take leave to correct him and say three distinguished men."

"Thank you, Mr. Jarndyce! What I always tell him!" observed Mrs. Badger.

"And, my dear," said Mr. Badger, "what do I always tell you? That without any affectation of disparaging such professional distinction as I may have attained (which our friend Mr. Carstone will have many opportunities of estimating), I am not so weak—no, really," said Mr. Badger to us generally, "so unreasonable—as to put my reputation on the same footing with such first-rate men as Captain Swosser and Professor Dingo. Perhaps you may be interested, Mr. Jarndyce," continued Mr. Bayham Badger, leading the way into the next drawing-room, "in this portrait of Captain Swosser. It was taken on his return home from the African station, where he had suffered from the fever of the country. Mrs. Badger considers it too yellow. But it's a very fine head. A very fine head!"

We all echoed, "A very fine head!"

"I feel when I look at it," said Mr. Badger, "'That's a man I should like to have seen!' It strikingly bespeaks the first-class man that Captain Swosser pre-eminently was. On the other side, Professor Dingo. I knew him well—attended him in his last illness—a speaking likeness! Over the piano, Mrs. Bayham Badger when Mrs. Swosser. Over the sofa, Mrs. Bayham Badger when Mrs. Dingo. Of Mrs. Bayham Badger IN ESSE, I possess the original and have no copy."

Dinner was now announced, and we went downstairs. It was a very genteel entertainment, very handsomely served. But the captain and the professor still ran in Mr. Badger's head, and as Ada and I had the honour of being under his particular care, we had the full benefit of them.

"Water, Miss Summerson? Allow me! Not in that tumbler, pray. Bring me the professor's goblet, James!"

Ada very much admired some artificial flowers under a glass.

"Astonishing how they keep!" said Mr. Badger. "They were presented to Mrs. Bayham Badger when she was in the Mediterranean."

He invited Mr. Jarndyce to take a glass of claret.

"Not that claret!" he said. "Excuse me! This is an occasion, and ON an occasion I produce some very special claret I happen to have. (James, Captain Swosser's wine!) Mr. Jarndyce, this is a wine that was imported by the captain, we will not say how many years ago. You will find it very curious. My dear, I shall be happy to take some of this wine with you. (Captain Swosser's claret to your mistress, James!) My love, your health!"

After dinner, when we ladies retired, we took Mrs. Badger's first and second husband with us. Mrs. Badger gave us in the drawing-room a biographical sketch of the life and services of Captain Swosser before his marriage and a more minute account of him dating from the time when he fell in love with her at a ball on board the Crippler, given to the officers of that ship when she lay in Plymouth Harbour.

"The dear old Crippler!" said Mrs. Badger, shaking her head. "She was a noble vessel. Trim, ship-shape, all a taunto, as Captain Swosser used to say. You must excuse me if I occasionally introduce a nautical expression; I was quite a sailor once. Captain Swosser loved that craft for my sake. When she was no longer in commission, he frequently said that if he were rich enough to buy her old hulk, he would have an inscription let into the timbers of the quarter-deck where we stood as partners in the dance to mark the spot where he fell—raked fore and aft (Captain Swosser used to say) by the fire from my tops. It was his naval way of mentioning my eyes."

Mrs. Badger shook her head, sighed, and looked in the glass.

"It was a great change from Captain Swosser to Professor Dingo," she resumed with a plaintive smile. "I felt it a good deal at first. Such an entire revolution in my mode of life! But custom, combined with science—particularly science—inured me to it. Being the professor's sole companion in his botanical excursions, I almost forgot that I had ever been afloat, and became quite learned. It is singular that the professor was the antipodes of Captain Swosser and that Mr. Badger is not in the least like either!"

We then passed into a narrative of the deaths of Captain Swosser and Professor Dingo, both of whom seem to have had very bad complaints. In the course of it, Mrs. Badger signified to us that she had never madly loved but once and that the object of that wild affection, never to be recalled in its fresh enthusiasm, was Captain Swosser. The professor was yet dying by inches in the most dismal manner, and Mrs. Badger was giving us imitations of his way of saying, with great difficulty, "Where is Laura? Let Laura give me my toast and water!" when the entrance of the gentlemen consigned him to the tomb.

Now, I observed that evening, as I had observed for some days past, that Ada and Richard were more than ever attached to each other's society, which was but natural, seeing that they were going to be separated so soon. I was therefore not very much surprised when we got home, and Ada and I retired upstairs, to find Ada more silent than usual, though I was not quite prepared for her coming into my arms and beginning to speak to me, with her face hidden.

"My darling Esther!" murmured Ada. "I have a great secret to tell you!"

A mighty secret, my pretty one, no doubt!

"What is it, Ada?"

"Oh, Esther, you would never guess!"

"Shall I try to guess?" said I.

"Oh, no! Don't! Pray don't!" cried Ada, very much startled by the idea of my doing so.

"Now, I wonder who it can be about?" said I, pretending to consider.

"It's about—" said Ada in a whisper. "It's about—my cousin Richard!"

"Well, my own!" said I, kissing her bright hair, which was all I could see. "And what about him?"

"Oh, Esther, you would never guess!"

It was so pretty to have her clinging to me in that way, hiding her face, and to know that she was not crying in sorrow but in a little glow of joy, and pride, and hope, that I would not help her just yet.

"He says—I know it's very foolish, we are both so young—but he says," with a burst of tears, "that he loves me dearly, Esther."

"Does he indeed?" said I. "I never heard of such a thing! Why, my pet of pets, I could have told you that weeks and weeks ago!"

To see Ada lift up her flushed face in joyful surprise, and hold me round the neck, and laugh, and cry, and blush, was so pleasant!

"Why, my darling," said I, "what a goose you must take me for! Your cousin Richard has been loving you as plainly as he could for I don't know how long!"

"And yet you never said a word about it!" cried Ada, kissing me.

"No, my love," said I. "I waited to be told."

"But now I have told you, you don't think it wrong of me, do you?" returned Ada. She might have coaxed me to say no if I had been the hardest-hearted duenna in the world. Not being that yet, I said no very freely.

"And now," said I, "I know the worst of it."

"Oh, that's not quite the worst of it, Esther dear!" cried Ada, holding me tighter and laying down her face again upon my breast.

"No?" said I. "Not even that?"

"No, not even that!" said Ada, shaking her head.

"Why, you never mean to say—" I was beginning in joke.

But Ada, looking up and smiling through her tears, cried, "Yes, I do! You know, you know I do!" And then sobbed out, "With all my heart I do! With all my whole heart, Esther!"

I told her, laughing, why I had known that, too, just as well as I had known the other! And we sat before the fire, and I had all the talking to myself for a little while (though there was not much of it); and Ada was soon quiet and happy.

"Do you think my cousin John knows, dear Dame Durden?" she asked.

"Unless my cousin John is blind, my pet," said I, "I should think my cousin John knows pretty well as much as we know."

"We want to speak to him before Richard goes," said Ada timidly, "and we wanted you to advise us, and to tell him so. Perhaps you wouldn't mind Richard's coming in, Dame Durden?"

"Oh! Richard is outside, is he, my dear?" said I.

"I am not quite certain," returned Ada with a bashful simplicity that would have won my heart if she had not won it long before, "but I think he's waiting at the door."

There he was, of course. They brought a chair on either side of me, and put me between them, and really seemed to have fallen in love with me instead of one another, they were so confiding, and so trustful, and so fond of me. They went on in their own wild way for a little while—I never stopped them; I enjoyed it too much myself—and then we gradually fell to considering how young they were, and how there must be a lapse of several years before this early love could come to anything, and how it could come to happiness only if it were real and lasting and inspired them with a steady resolution to do their duty to each other, with constancy, fortitude, and perseverance, each always for the other's sake. Well! Richard said that he would work his fingers to the bone for Ada, and Ada said that she would work her fingers to the bone for Richard, and they called me all sorts of endearing and sensible names, and we sat there, advising and talking, half the night. Finally, before we parted, I gave them my promise to speak to their cousin John to-morrow.

So, when to-morrow came, I went to my guardian after breakfast, in the room that was our town-substitute for the growlery, and told him that I had it in trust to tell him something.

"Well, little woman," said he, shutting up his book, "if you have accepted the trust, there can be no harm in it."

"I hope not, guardian," said I. "I can guarantee that there is no secrecy in it. For it only happened yesterday."

"Aye? And what is it, Esther?"

"Guardian," said I, "you remember the happy night when first we came down to Bleak House? When Ada was singing in the dark room?"

I wished to call to his remembrance the look he had given me then. Unless I am much mistaken, I saw that I did so.

"Because—" said I with a little hesitation.

"Yes, my dear!" said he. "Don't hurry."

"Because," said I, "Ada and Richard have fallen in love. And have told each other so."

"Already!" cried my guardian, quite astonished.

"Yes!" said I. "And to tell you the truth, guardian, I rather expected it."

"The deuce you did!" said he.

He sat considering for a minute or two, with his smile, at once so handsome and so kind, upon his changing face, and then requested me to let them know that he wished to see them. When they came, he encircled Ada with one arm in his fatherly way and addressed himself to Richard with a cheerful gravity.

"Rick," said Mr. Jarndyce, "I am glad to have won your confidence. I hope to preserve it. When I contemplated these relations between us four which have so brightened my life and so invested it with new interests and pleasures, I certainly did contemplate, afar off, the possibility of you and your pretty cousin here (don't be shy, Ada, don't be shy, my dear!) being in a mind to go through life together. I saw, and do see, many reasons to make it desirable. But that was afar off, Rick, afar off!"

"We look afar off, sir," returned Richard.

"Well!" said Mr. Jarndyce. "That's rational. Now, hear me, my dears! I might tell you that you don't know your own minds yet, that a thousand things may happen to divert you from one another, that it is well this chain of flowers you have taken up is very easily broken, or it might become a chain of lead. But I will not do that. Such wisdom will come soon enough, I dare say, if it is to come at all. I will assume that a few years hence you will be in your hearts to one another what you are to-day. All I say before speaking to you according to that assumption is, if you DO change—if you DO come to find that you are more commonplace cousins to each other as man and woman than you were as boy and girl (your manhood will excuse me, Rick!)—don't be ashamed still to confide in me, for there will be nothing monstrous or uncommon in it. I am only your friend and distant kinsman. I have no power over you whatever. But I wish and hope to retain your confidence if I do nothing to forfeit it."

"I am very sure, sir," returned Richard, "that I speak for Ada too when I say that you have the strongest power over us both—rooted in respect, gratitude, and affection—strengthening every day."

"Dear cousin John," said Ada, on his shoulder, "my father's place can never be empty again. All the love and duty I could ever have rendered to him is transferred to you."

"Come!" said Mr. Jarndyce. "Now for our assumption. Now we lift our eyes up and look hopefully at the distance! Rick, the world is before you; and it is most probable that as you enter it, so it will receive you. Trust in nothing but in Providence and your own efforts. Never separate the two, like the heathen waggoner. Constancy in love is a good thing, but it means nothing, and is nothing, without constancy in every kind of effort. If you had the abilities of all the great men, past and present, you could do nothing well without sincerely meaning it and setting about it. If you entertain the supposition that any real success, in great things or in small, ever was or could be, ever will or can be, wrested from Fortune by fits and starts, leave that wrong idea here or leave your cousin Ada here."

"I will leave IT here, sir," replied Richard smiling, "if I brought it here just now (but I hope I did not), and will work my way on to my cousin Ada in the hopeful distance."

"Right!" said Mr. Jarndyce. "If you are not to make her happy, why should you pursue her?"

"I wouldn't make her unhappy—no, not even for her love," retorted Richard proudly.

"Well said!" cried Mr. Jarndyce. "That's well said! She remains here, in her home with me. Love her, Rick, in your active life, no less than in her home when you revisit it, and all will go well. Otherwise, all will go ill. That's the end of my preaching. I think you and Ada had better take a walk."

Ada tenderly embraced him, and Richard heartily shook hands with him, and then the cousins went out of the room, looking back again directly, though, to say that they would wait for me.

The door stood open, and we both followed them with our eyes as they passed down the adjoining room, on which the sun was shining, and out at its farther end. Richard with his head bent, and her hand drawn through his arm, was talking to her very earnestly; and she looked up in his face, listening, and seemed to see nothing else. So young, so beautiful, so full of hope and promise, they went on lightly through the sunlight as their own happy thoughts might then be traversing the years to come and making them all years of brightness. So they passed away into the shadow and were gone. It was only a burst of light that had been so radiant. The room darkened as they went out, and the sun was clouded over.

"Am I right, Esther?" said my guardian when they were gone.

He was so good and wise to ask ME whether he was right!

"Rick may gain, out of this, the quality he wants. Wants, at the core of so much that is good!" said Mr. Jarndyce, shaking his head. "I have said nothing to Ada, Esther. She has her friend and counsellor always near." And he laid his hand lovingly upon my head.

I could not help showing that I was a little moved, though I did all I could to conceal it.

"Tut tut!" said he. "But we must take care, too, that our little woman's life is not all consumed in care for others."

"Care? My dear guardian, I believe I am the happiest creature in the world!"

"I believe so, too," said he. "But some one may find out what Esther never will—that the little woman is to be held in remembrance above all other people!"

I have omitted to mention in its place that there was some one else at the family dinner party. It was not a lady. It was a gentleman. It was a gentleman of a dark complexion—a young surgeon. He was rather reserved, but I thought him very sensible and agreeable. At least, Ada asked me if I did not, and I said yes.

CHAPTER XIV
DEPORTMENT

Richard left us on the very next evening to begin his new career, and committed Ada to my charge with great love for her and great trust in me. It touched me then to reflect, and it touches me now, more nearly, to remember (having what I have to tell) how they both thought of me, even at that engrossing time. I was a part of all their plans, for the present and the future. I was to write Richard once a week, making my faithful report of Ada, who was to write to him every alternate day. I was to be informed, under his own hand, of all his labours and successes; I was to observe how resolute and persevering he would be; I was to be Ada's bridesmaid when they were married; I was to live with them afterwards; I was to keep all the keys of their house; I was to be made happy for ever and a day.

"And if the suit SHOULD make us rich, Esther—which it may, you know!" said Richard to crown all.

A shade crossed Ada's face.

"My dearest Ada," asked Richard, "why not?"

"It had better declare us poor at once," said Ada.

"Oh! I don't know about that," returned Richard, "but at all events, it won't declare anything at once. It hasn't declared anything in heaven knows how many years."

"Too true," said Ada.

"Yes, but," urged Richard, answering what her look suggested rather than her words, "the longer it goes on, dear cousin, the nearer it must be to a settlement one way or other. Now, is not that reasonable?"

"You know best, Richard. But I am afraid if we trust to it, it will make us unhappy."

"But, my Ada, we are not going to trust to it!" cried Richard gaily. "We know it better than to trust to it. We only say that if it SHOULD make us rich, we have no constitutional objection to being rich. The court is, by solemn settlement of law, our grim old guardian, and we are to suppose that what it gives us (when it gives us anything) is our right. It is not necessary to quarrel with our right."

"No," said Ada, "but it may be better to forget all about it."

"Well, well," cried Richard, "then we will forget all about it! We consign the whole thing to oblivion. Dame Durden puts on her approving face, and it's done!"

"Dame Durden's approving face," said I, looking out of the box in which I was packing his books, "was not very visible when you called it by that name; but it does approve, and she thinks you can't do better."

So, Richard said there was an end of it, and immediately began, on no other foundation, to build as many castles in the air as would man the Great Wall of China. He went away in high spirits. Ada and I, prepared to miss him very much, commenced our quieter career.

On our arrival in London, we had called with Mr. Jarndyce at Mrs. Jellyby's but had not been so fortunate as to find her at home. It appeared that she had gone somewhere to a tea-drinking and had taken Miss Jellyby with her. Besides the tea-drinking, there was to be some considerable speech-making and letter-writing on the general merits of the cultivation of coffee, conjointly with natives, at the Settlement of Borrioboola-Gha. All this involved, no doubt, sufficient active exercise of pen and ink to make her daughter's part in the proceedings anything but a holiday.

It being now beyond the time appointed for Mrs. Jellyby's return, we called again. She was in town, but not at home, having gone to Mile End directly after breakfast on some Borrioboolan business, arising out of a society called the East London Branch Aid Ramification. As I had not seen Peepy on the occasion of our last call (when he was not to be found anywhere, and when the cook rather thought he must have strolled away with the dustman's cart), I now inquired for him again. The oyster shells he had been building a house with were still in the passage, but he was nowhere discoverable, and the cook supposed that he had "gone after the sheep." When we repeated, with some surprise, "The sheep?" she said, Oh, yes, on market days he sometimes followed them quite out of town and came back in such a state as never was!

I was sitting at the window with my guardian on the following morning, and Ada was busy writing—of course to Richard—when Miss Jellyby was announced, and entered, leading the identical Peepy, whom she had made some endeavours to render presentable by wiping the dirt into corners of his face and hands and making his hair very wet and then violently frizzling it with her fingers. Everything the dear child wore was either too large for him or too small. Among his other contradictory decorations he had the hat of a bishop and the little gloves of a baby. His boots were, on a small scale, the boots of a ploughman, while his legs, so crossed and recrossed with scratches that they looked like maps, were bare below a very short pair of plaid drawers finished off with two frills of perfectly different patterns. The deficient buttons on his plaid frock had evidently been supplied from one of Mr. Jellyby's coats, they were so extremely brazen and so much too large. Most extraordinary specimens of needlework appeared on several parts of his dress, where it had been hastily mended, and I recognized the same hand on Miss Jellyby's. She was, however, unaccountably improved in her appearance and looked very pretty. She was conscious of poor little Peepy being but a failure after all her trouble, and she showed it as she came in by the way in which she glanced first at him and then at us.

"Oh, dear me!" said my guardian. "Due east!"

Ada and I gave her a cordial welcome and presented her to Mr. Jarndyce, to whom she said as she sat down, "Ma's compliments, and she hopes you'll excuse her, because she's correcting proofs of the plan. She's going to put out five thousand new circulars, and she knows you'll be interested to hear that. I have brought one of them with me. Ma's compliments." With which she presented it sulkily enough.

"Thank you," said my guardian. "I am much obliged to Mrs. Jellyby. Oh, dear me! This is a very trying wind!"

We were busy with Peepy, taking off his clerical hat, asking him if he remembered us, and so on. Peepy retired behind his elbow at first, but relented at the sight of sponge-cake and allowed me to take him on my lap, where he sat munching quietly. Mr. Jarndyce then withdrawing into the temporary growlery, Miss Jellyby opened a conversation with her usual abruptness.

"We are going on just as bad as ever in Thavies Inn," said she. "I have no peace of my life. Talk of Africa! I couldn't be worse off if I was a what's-his-name—man and a brother!"

I tried to say something soothing.

"Oh, it's of no use, Miss Summerson," exclaimed Miss Jellyby, "though I thank you for the kind intention all the same. I know how I am used, and I am not to be talked over. YOU wouldn't be talked over if you were used so. Peepy, go and play at Wild Beasts under the piano!"

"I shan't!" said Peepy.

"Very well, you ungrateful, naughty, hard-hearted boy!" returned Miss Jellyby with tears in her eyes. "I'll never take pains to dress you any more."

"Yes, I will go, Caddy!" cried Peepy, who was really a good child and who was so moved by his sister's vexation that he went at once.

"It seems a little thing to cry about," said poor Miss Jellyby apologetically, "but I am quite worn out. I was directing the new circulars till two this morning. I detest the whole thing so that that alone makes my head ache till I can't see out of my eyes. And look at that poor unfortunate child! Was there ever such a fright as he is!"

Peepy, happily unconscious of the defects in his appearance, sat on the carpet behind one of the legs of the piano, looking calmly out of his den at us while he ate his cake.

"I have sent him to the other end of the room," observed Miss Jellyby, drawing her chair nearer ours, "because I don't want him to hear the conversation. Those little things are so sharp! I was going to say, we really are going on worse than ever. Pa will be a bankrupt before long, and then I hope Ma will be satisfied. There'll he nobody but Ma to thank for it."

We said we hoped Mr. Jellyby's affairs were not in so bad a state as that.

"It's of no use hoping, though it's very kind of you," returned Miss Jellyby, shaking her head. "Pa told me only yesterday morning (and dreadfully unhappy he is) that he couldn't weather the storm. I should be surprised if he could. When all our tradesmen send into our house any stuff they like, and the servants do what they like with it, and I have no time to improve things if I knew how, and Ma don't care about anything, I should like to make out how Pa is to weather the storm. I declare if I was Pa, I'd run away."

"My dear!" said I, smiling. "Your papa, no doubt, considers his family."

"Oh, yes, his family is all very fine, Miss Summerson," replied Miss Jellyby; "but what comfort is his family to him? His family is nothing but bills, dirt, waste, noise, tumbles downstairs, confusion, and wretchedness. His scrambling home, from week's end to week's end, is like one great washing-day—only nothing's washed!"

Miss Jellyby tapped her foot upon the floor and wiped her eyes.

"I am sure I pity Pa to that degree," she said, "and am so angry with Ma that I can't find words to express myself! However, I am not going to bear it, I am determined. I won't be a slave all my life, and I won't submit to be proposed to by Mr. Quale. A pretty thing, indeed, to marry a philanthropist. As if I hadn't had enough of THAT!" said poor Miss Jellyby.

I must confess that I could not help feeling rather angry with Mrs. Jellyby myself, seeing and hearing this neglected girl and knowing how much of bitterly satirical truth there was in what she said.

"If it wasn't that we had been intimate when you stopped at our house," pursued Miss Jellyby, "I should have been ashamed to come here to-day, for I know what a figure I must seem to you two. But as it is, I made up my mind to call, especially as I am not likely to see you again the next time you come to town."

She said this with such great significance that Ada and I glanced at one another, foreseeing something more.

"No!" said Miss Jellyby, shaking her head. "Not at all likely! I know I may trust you two. I am sure you won't betray me. I am engaged."

"Without their knowledge at home?" said I.

"Why, good gracious me, Miss Summerson," she returned, justifying herself in a fretful but not angry manner, "how can it be otherwise? You know what Ma is—and I needn't make poor Pa more miserable by telling HIM."

"But would it not be adding to his unhappiness to marry without his knowledge or consent, my dear?" said I.

"No," said Miss Jellyby, softening. "I hope not. I should try to make him happy and comfortable when he came to see me, and Peepy and the others should take it in turns to come and stay with me, and they should have some care taken of them then."

There was a good deal of affection in poor Caddy. She softened more and more while saying this and cried so much over the unwonted little home-picture she had raised in her mind that Peepy, in his cave under the piano, was touched, and turned himself over on his back with loud lamentations. It was not until I had brought him to kiss his sister, and had restored him to his place on my lap, and had shown him that Caddy was laughing (she laughed expressly for the purpose), that we could recall his peace of mind; even then it was for some time conditional on his taking us in turns by the chin and smoothing our faces all over with his hand. At last, as his spirits were not equal to the piano, we put him on a chair to look out of window; and Miss Jellyby, holding him by one leg, resumed her confidence.

"It began in your coming to our house," she said.

We naturally asked how.

"I felt I was so awkward," she replied, "that I made up my mind to be improved in that respect at all events and to learn to dance. I told Ma I was ashamed of myself, and I must be taught to dance. Ma looked at me in that provoking way of hers as if I wasn't in sight, but I was quite determined to be taught to dance, and so I went to Mr. Turveydrop's Academy in Newman Street."

"And was it there, my dear—" I began.

"Yes, it was there," said Caddy, "and I am engaged to Mr. Turveydrop. There are two Mr. Turveydrops, father and son. My Mr. Turveydrop is the son, of course. I only wish I had been better brought up and was likely to make him a better wife, for I am very fond of him."

"I am sorry to hear this," said I, "I must confess."

"I don't know why you should be sorry," she retorted a little anxiously, "but I am engaged to Mr. Turveydrop, whether or no, and he is very fond of me. It's a secret as yet, even on his side, because old Mr. Turveydrop has a share in the connexion and it might break his heart or give him some other shock if he was told of it abruptly. Old Mr. Turveydrop is a very gentlemanly man indeed—very gentlemanly."

"Does his wife know of it?" asked Ada.

"Old Mr. Turveydrop's wife, Miss Clare?" returned Miss Jellyby, opening her eyes. "There's no such person. He is a widower."

We were here interrupted by Peepy, whose leg had undergone so much on account of his sister's unconsciously jerking it like a bell-rope whenever she was emphatic that the afflicted child now bemoaned his sufferings with a very low-spirited noise. As he appealed to me for compassion, and as I was only a listener, I undertook to hold him. Miss Jellyby proceeded, after begging Peepy's pardon with a kiss and assuring him that she hadn't meant to do it.

"That's the state of the case," said Caddy. "If I ever blame myself, I still think it's Ma's fault. We are to be married whenever we can, and then I shall go to Pa at the office and write to Ma. It won't much agitate Ma; I am only pen and ink to HER. One great comfort is," said Caddy with a sob, "that I shall never hear of Africa after I am married. Young Mr. Turveydrop hates it for my sake, and if old Mr. Turveydrop knows there is such a place, it's as much as he does."

"It was he who was very gentlemanly, I think!" said I.

"Very gentlemanly indeed," said Caddy. "He is celebrated almost everywhere for his deportment."

"Does he teach?" asked Ada.

"No, he don't teach anything in particular," replied Caddy. "But his deportment is beautiful."

Caddy went on to say with considerable hesitation and reluctance that there was one thing more she wished us to know, and felt we ought to know, and which she hoped would not offend us. It was that she had improved her acquaintance with Miss Flite, the little crazy old lady, and that she frequently went there early in the morning and met her lover for a few minutes before breakfast—only for a few minutes. "I go there at other times," said Caddy, "but Prince does not come then. Young Mr. Turveydrop's name is Prince; I wish it wasn't, because it sounds like a dog, but of course he didn't christen himself. Old Mr. Turveydrop had him christened Prince in remembrance of the Prince Regent. Old Mr. Turveydrop adored the Prince Regent on account of his deportment. I hope you won't think the worse of me for having made these little appointments at Miss Flite's, where I first went with you, because I like the poor thing for her own sake and I believe she likes me. If you could see young Mr. Turveydrop, I am sure you would think well of him—at least, I am sure you couldn't possibly think any ill of him. I am going there now for my lesson. I couldn't ask you to go with me, Miss Summerson; but if you would," said Caddy, who had said all this earnestly and tremblingly, "I should be very glad—very glad."

It happened that we had arranged with my guardian to go to Miss Flite's that day. We had told him of our former visit, and our account had interested him; but something had always happened to prevent our going there again. As I trusted that I might have sufficient influence with Miss Jellyby to prevent her taking any very rash step if I fully accepted the confidence she was so willing to place in me, poor girl, I proposed that she and I and Peepy should go to the academy and afterwards meet my guardian and Ada at Miss Flite's, whose name I now learnt for the first time. This was on condition that Miss Jellyby and Peepy should come back with us to dinner. The last article of the agreement being joyfully acceded to by both, we smartened Peepy up a little with the assistance of a few pins, some soap and water, and a hair-brush, and went out, bending our steps towards Newman Street, which was very near.

I found the academy established in a sufficiently dingy house at the corner of an archway, with busts in all the staircase windows. In the same house there were also established, as I gathered from the plates on the door, a drawing-master, a coal-merchant (there was, certainly, no room for his coals), and a lithographic artist. On the plate which, in size and situation, took precedence of all the rest, I read, MR. TURVEYDROP. The door was open, and the hall was blocked up by a grand piano, a harp, and several other musical instruments in cases, all in progress of removal, and all looking rakish in the daylight. Miss Jellyby informed me that the academy had been lent, last night, for a concert.

We went upstairs—it had been quite a fine house once, when it was anybody's business to keep it clean and fresh, and nobody's business to smoke in it all day—and into Mr. Turveydrop's great room, which was built out into a mews at the back and was lighted by a skylight. It was a bare, resounding room smelling of stables, with cane forms along the walls, and the walls ornamented at regular intervals with painted lyres and little cut-glass branches for candles, which seemed to be shedding their old-fashioned drops as other branches might shed autumn leaves. Several young lady pupils, ranging from thirteen or fourteen years of age to two or three and twenty, were assembled; and I was looking among them for their instructor when Caddy, pinching my arm, repeated the ceremony of introduction. "Miss Summerson, Mr. Prince Turveydrop!"

I curtsied to a little blue-eyed fair man of youthful appearance with flaxen hair parted in the middle and curling at the ends all round his head. He had a little fiddle, which we used to call at school a kit, under his left arm, and its little bow in the same hand. His little dancing-shoes were particularly diminutive, and he had a little innocent, feminine manner which not only appealed to me in an amiable way, but made this singular effect upon me, that I received the impression that he was like his mother and that his mother had not been much considered or well used.

"I am very happy to see Miss Jellyby's friend," he said, bowing low to me. "I began to fear," with timid tenderness, "as it was past the usual time, that Miss Jellyby was not coming."

"I beg you will have the goodness to attribute that to me, who have detained her, and to receive my excuses, sir," said I.

"Oh, dear!" said he.

"And pray," I entreated, "do not allow me to be the cause of any more delay."

With that apology I withdrew to a seat between Peepy (who, being well used to it, had already climbed into a corner place) and an old lady of a censorious countenance whose two nieces were in the class and who was very indignant with Peepy's boots. Prince Turveydrop then tinkled the strings of his kit with his fingers, and the young ladies stood up to dance. Just then there appeared from a side-door old Mr. Turveydrop, in the full lustre of his deportment.

He was a fat old gentleman with a false complexion, false teeth, false whiskers, and a wig. He had a fur collar, and he had a padded breast to his coat, which only wanted a star or a broad blue ribbon to be complete. He was pinched in, and swelled out, and got up, and strapped down, as much as he could possibly bear. He had such a neckcloth on (puffing his very eyes out of their natural shape), and his chin and even his ears so sunk into it, that it seemed as though he must inevitably double up if it were cast loose. He had under his arm a hat of great size and weight, shelving downward from the crown to the brim, and in his hand a pair of white gloves with which he flapped it as he stood poised on one leg in a high-shouldered, round-elbowed state of elegance not to be surpassed. He had a cane, he had an eye-glass, he had a snuff-box, he had rings, he had wristbands, he had everything but any touch of nature; he was not like youth, he was not like age, he was not like anything in the world but a model of deportment.

"Father! A visitor. Miss Jellyby's friend, Miss Summerson."

"Distinguished," said Mr. Turveydrop, "by Miss Summerson's presence." As he bowed to me in that tight state, I almost believe I saw creases come into the whites of his eyes.

"My father," said the son, aside, to me with quite an affecting belief in him, "is a celebrated character. My father is greatly admired."

"Go on, Prince! Go on!" said Mr. Turveydrop, standing with his back to the fire and waving his gloves condescendingly. "Go on, my son!"

At this command, or by this gracious permission, the lesson went on. Prince Turveydrop sometimes played the kit, dancing; sometimes played the piano, standing; sometimes hummed the tune with what little breath he could spare, while he set a pupil right; always conscientiously moved with the least proficient through every step and every part of the figure; and never rested for an instant. His distinguished father did nothing whatever but stand before the fire, a model of deportment.

"And he never does anything else," said the old lady of the censorious countenance. "Yet would you believe that it's HIS name on the door-plate?"

"His son's name is the same, you know," said I.

"He wouldn't let his son have any name if he could take it from him," returned the old lady. "Look at the son's dress!" It certainly was plain—threadbare—almost shabby. "Yet the father must be garnished and tricked out," said the old lady, "because of his deportment. I'd deport him! Transport him would be better!"

I felt curious to know more concerning this person. I asked, "Does he give lessons in deportment now?"

"Now!" returned the old lady shortly. "Never did."

After a moment's consideration, I suggested that perhaps fencing had been his accomplishment.

"I don't believe he can fence at all, ma'am," said the old lady.

I looked surprised and inquisitive. The old lady, becoming more and more incensed against the master of deportment as she dwelt upon the subject, gave me some particulars of his career, with strong assurances that they were mildly stated.

He had married a meek little dancing-mistress, with a tolerable connexion (having never in his life before done anything but deport himself), and had worked her to death, or had, at the best, suffered her to work herself to death, to maintain him in those expenses which were indispensable to his position.

At once to exhibit his deportment to the best models and to keep the best models constantly before himself, he had found it necessary to frequent all public places of fashionable and lounging resort, to be seen at Brighton and elsewhere at fashionable times, and to lead an idle life in the very best clothes. To enable him to do this, the affectionate little dancing-mistress had toiled and laboured and would have toiled and laboured to that hour if her strength had lasted so long. For the mainspring of the story was that in spite of the man's absorbing selfishness, his wife (overpowered by his deportment) had, to the last, believed in him and had, on her death-bed, in the most moving terms, confided him to their son as one who had an inextinguishable claim upon him and whom he could never regard with too much pride and deference. The son, inheriting his mother's belief, and having the deportment always before him, had lived and grown in the same faith, and now, at thirty years of age, worked for his father twelve hours a day and looked up to him with veneration on the old imaginary pinnacle.

"The airs the fellow gives himself!" said my informant, shaking her head at old Mr. Turveydrop with speechless indignation as he drew on his tight gloves, of course unconscious of the homage she was rendering. "He fully believes he is one of the aristocracy! And he is so condescending to the son he so egregiously deludes that you might suppose him the most virtuous of parents. Oh!" said the old lady, apostrophizing him with infinite vehemence. "I could bite you!"

I could not help being amused, though I heard the old lady out with feelings of real concern. It was difficult to doubt her with the father and son before me. What I might have thought of them without the old lady's account, or what I might have thought of the old lady's account without them, I cannot say. There was a fitness of things in the whole that carried conviction with it.

My eyes were yet wandering, from young Mr. Turveydrop working so hard, to old Mr. Turveydrop deporting himself so beautifully, when the latter came ambling up to me and entered into conversation.

He asked me, first of all, whether I conferred a charm and a distinction on London by residing in it? I did not think it necessary to reply that I was perfectly aware I should not do that, in any case, but merely told him where I did reside.

"A lady so graceful and accomplished," he said, kissing his right glove and afterwards extending it towards the pupils, "will look leniently on the deficiencies here. We do our best to polish—polish—polish!"

He sat down beside me, taking some pains to sit on the form, I thought, in imitation of the print of his illustrious model on the sofa. And really he did look very like it.

"To polish—polish—polish!" he repeated, taking a pinch of snuff and gently fluttering his fingers. "But we are not, if I may say so to one formed to be graceful both by Nature and Art—" with the high-shouldered bow, which it seemed impossible for him to make without lifting up his eyebrows and shutting his eyes "—we are not what we used to be in point of deportment."

"Are we not, sir?" said I.

"We have degenerated," he returned, shaking his head, which he could do to a very limited extent in his cravat. "A levelling age is not favourable to deportment. It develops vulgarity. Perhaps I speak with some little partiality. It may not be for me to say that I have been called, for some years now, Gentleman Turveydrop, or that his Royal Highness the Prince Regent did me the honour to inquire, on my removing my hat as he drove out of the Pavilion at Brighton (that fine building), 'Who is he? Who the devil is he? Why don't I know him? Why hasn't he thirty thousand a year?' But these are little matters of anecdote—the general property, ma'am—still repeated occasionally among the upper classes."

"Indeed?" said I.

He replied with the high-shouldered bow. "Where what is left among us of deportment," he added, "still lingers. England—alas, my country!—has degenerated very much, and is degenerating every day. She has not many gentlemen left. We are few. I see nothing to succeed us but a race of weavers."

"One might hope that the race of gentlemen would be perpetuated here," said I.

"You are very good." He smiled with a high-shouldered bow again. "You flatter me. But, no—no! I have never been able to imbue my poor boy with that part of his art. Heaven forbid that I should disparage my dear child, but he has—no deportment."

"He appears to be an excellent master," I observed.

"Understand me, my dear madam, he IS an excellent master. All that can be acquired, he has acquired. All that can be imparted, he can impart. But there ARE things—" He took another pinch of snuff and made the bow again, as if to add, "This kind of thing, for instance."

I glanced towards the centre of the room, where Miss Jellyby's lover, now engaged with single pupils, was undergoing greater drudgery than ever.

"My amiable child," murmured Mr. Turveydrop, adjusting his cravat.

"Your son is indefatigable," said I.

"It is my reward," said Mr. Turveydrop, "to hear you say so. In some respects, he treads in the footsteps of his sainted mother. She was a devoted creature. But wooman, lovely wooman," said Mr. Turveydrop with very disagreeable gallantry, "what a sex you are!"

I rose and joined Miss Jellyby, who was by this time putting on her bonnet. The time allotted to a lesson having fully elapsed, there was a general putting on of bonnets. When Miss Jellyby and the unfortunate Prince found an opportunity to become betrothed I don't know, but they certainly found none on this occasion to exchange a dozen words.

"My dear," said Mr. Turveydrop benignly to his son, "do you know the hour?"

"No, father." The son had no watch. The father had a handsome gold one, which he pulled out with an air that was an example to mankind.

"My son," said he, "it's two o'clock. Recollect your school at Kensington at three."

"That's time enough for me, father," said Prince. "I can take a morsel of dinner standing and be off."

"My dear boy," returned his father, "you must be very quick. You will find the cold mutton on the table."

"Thank you, father. Are YOU off now, father?"

"Yes, my dear. I suppose," said Mr. Turveydrop, shutting his eyes and lifting up his shoulders with modest consciousness, "that I must show myself, as usual, about town."

"You had better dine out comfortably somewhere," said his son.

"My dear child, I intend to. I shall take my little meal, I think, at the French house, in the Opera Colonnade."

"That's right. Good-bye, father!" said Prince, shaking hands.

"Good-bye, my son. Bless you!"

Mr. Turveydrop said this in quite a pious manner, and it seemed to do his son good, who, in parting from him, was so pleased with him, so dutiful to him, and so proud of him that I almost felt as if it were an unkindness to the younger man not to be able to believe implicitly in the elder. The few moments that were occupied by Prince in taking leave of us (and particularly of one of us, as I saw, being in the secret), enhanced my favourable impression of his almost childish character. I felt a liking for him and a compassion for him as he put his little kit in his pocket—and with it his desire to stay a little while with Caddy—and went away good-humouredly to his cold mutton and his school at Kensington, that made me scarcely less irate with his father than the censorious old lady.

The father opened the room door for us and bowed us out in a manner, I must acknowledge, worthy of his shining original. In the same style he presently passed us on the other side of the street, on his way to the aristocratic part of the town, where he was going to show himself among the few other gentlemen left. For some moments, I was so lost in reconsidering what I had heard and seen in Newman Street that I was quite unable to talk to Caddy or even to fix my attention on what she said to me, especially when I began to inquire in my mind whether there were, or ever had been, any other gentlemen, not in the dancing profession, who lived and founded a reputation entirely on their deportment. This became so bewildering and suggested the possibility of so many Mr. Turveydrops that I said, "Esther, you must make up your mind to abandon this subject altogether and attend to Caddy." I accordingly did so, and we chatted all the rest of the way to Lincoln's Inn.

Caddy told me that her lover's education had been so neglected that it was not always easy to read his notes. She said if he were not so anxious about his spelling and took less pains to make it clear, he would do better; but he put so many unnecessary letters into short words that they sometimes quite lost their English appearance. "He does it with the best intention," observed Caddy, "but it hasn't the effect he means, poor fellow!" Caddy then went on to reason, how could he be expected to be a scholar when he had passed his whole life in the dancing-school and had done nothing but teach and fag, fag and teach, morning, noon, and night! And what did it matter? She could write letters enough for both, as she knew to her cost, and it was far better for him to be amiable than learned. "Besides, it's not as if I was an accomplished girl who had any right to give herself airs," said Caddy. "I know little enough, I am sure, thanks to Ma!

"There's another thing I want to tell you, now we are alone," continued Caddy, "which I should not have liked to mention unless you had seen Prince, Miss Summerson. You know what a house ours is. It's of no use my trying to learn anything that it would be useful for Prince's wife to know in OUR house. We live in such a state of muddle that it's impossible, and I have only been more disheartened whenever I have tried. So I get a little practice with—who do you think? Poor Miss Flite! Early in the morning I help her to tidy her room and clean her birds, and I make her cup of coffee for her (of course she taught me), and I have learnt to make it so well that Prince says it's the very best coffee he ever tasted, and would quite delight old Mr. Turveydrop, who is very particular indeed about his coffee. I can make little puddings too; and I know how to buy neck of mutton, and tea, and sugar, and butter, and a good many housekeeping things. I am not clever at my needle, yet," said Caddy, glancing at the repairs on Peepy's frock, "but perhaps I shall improve, and since I have been engaged to Prince and have been doing all this, I have felt better-tempered, I hope, and more forgiving to Ma. It rather put me out at first this morning to see you and Miss Clare looking so neat and pretty and to feel ashamed of Peepy and myself too, but on the whole I hope I am better-tempered than I was and more forgiving to Ma."

The poor girl, trying so hard, said it from her heart, and touched mine. "Caddy, my love," I replied, "I begin to have a great affection for you, and I hope we shall become friends."

"Oh, do you?" cried Caddy. "How happy that would make me!"

"My dear Caddy," said I, "let us be friends from this time, and let us often have a chat about these matters and try to find the right way through them." Caddy was overjoyed. I said everything I could in my old-fashioned way to comfort and encourage her, and I would not have objected to old Mr. Turveydrop that day for any smaller consideration than a settlement on his daughter-in-law.

By this time we were come to Mr. Krook's, whose private door stood open.

There was a bill, pasted on the door-post, announcing a room to let on the second floor. It reminded Caddy to tell me as we proceeded upstairs that there had been a sudden death there and an inquest and that our little friend had been ill of the fright. The door and window of the vacant room being open, we looked in. It was the room with the dark door to which Miss Flite had secretly directed my attention when I was last in the house. A sad and desolate place it was, a gloomy, sorrowful place that gave me a strange sensation of mournfulness and even dread. "You look pale," said Caddy when we came out, "and cold!" I felt as if the room had chilled me.

We had walked slowly while we were talking, and my guardian and Ada were here before us. We found them in Miss Flite's garret. They were looking at the birds, while a medical gentleman who was so good as to attend Miss Flite with much solicitude and compassion spoke with her cheerfully by the fire.

"I have finished my professional visit," he said, coming forward. "Miss Flite is much better and may appear in court (as her mind is set upon it) to-morrow. She has been greatly missed there, I understand."

Miss Flite received the compliment with complacency and dropped a general curtsy to us.

"Honoured, indeed," said she, "by another visit from the wards in Jarndyce! Ve-ry happy to receive Jarndyce of Bleak House beneath my humble roof!" with a special curtsy. "Fitz-Jarndyce, my dear"—she had bestowed that name on Caddy, it appeared, and always called her by it—"a double welcome!"

"Has she been very ill?" asked Mr. Jarndyce of the gentleman whom we had found in attendance on her. She answered for herself directly, though he had put the question in a whisper.

"Oh, decidedly unwell! Oh, very unwell indeed," she said confidentially. "Not pain, you know—trouble. Not bodily so much as nervous, nervous! The truth is," in a subdued voice and trembling, "we have had death here. There was poison in the house. I am very susceptible to such horrid things. It frightened me. Only Mr. Woodcourt knows how much. My physician, Mr. Woodcourt!" with great stateliness. "The wards in Jarndyce—Jarndyce of Bleak House—Fitz-Jarndyce!"

"Miss Flite," said Mr. Woodcourt in a grave kind of voice, as if he were appealing to her while speaking to us, and laying his hand gently on her arm, "Miss Flite describes her illness with her usual accuracy. She was alarmed by an occurrence in the house which might have alarmed a stronger person, and was made ill by the distress and agitation. She brought me here in the first hurry of the discovery, though too late for me to be of any use to the unfortunate man. I have compensated myself for that disappointment by coming here since and being of some small use to her."

"The kindest physician in the college," whispered Miss Flite to me. "I expect a judgment. On the day of judgment. And shall then confer estates."

"She will be as well in a day or two," said Mr. Woodcourt, looking at her with an observant smile, "as she ever will be. In other words, quite well of course. Have you heard of her good fortune?"

"Most extraordinary!" said Miss Flite, smiling brightly. "You never heard of such a thing, my dear! Every Saturday, Conversation Kenge or Guppy (clerk to Conversation K.) places in my hand a paper of shillings. Shillings. I assure you! Always the same number in the paper. Always one for every day in the week. Now you know, really! So well-timed, is it not? Ye-es! From whence do these papers come, you say? That is the great question. Naturally. Shall I tell you what I think? I think," said Miss Flite, drawing herself back with a very shrewd look and shaking her right forefinger in a most significant manner, "that the Lord Chancellor, aware of the length of time during which the Great Seal has been open (for it has been open a long time!), forwards them. Until the judgment I expect is given. Now that's very creditable, you know. To confess in that way that he IS a little slow for human life. So delicate! Attending court the other day—I attend it regularly, with my documents—I taxed him with it, and he almost confessed. That is, I smiled at him from my bench, and HE smiled at me from his bench. But it's great good fortune, is it not? And Fitz-Jarndyce lays the money out for me to great advantage. Oh, I assure you to the greatest advantage!"

I congratulated her (as she addressed herself to me) upon this fortunate addition to her income and wished her a long continuance of it. I did not speculate upon the source from which it came or wonder whose humanity was so considerate. My guardian stood before me, contemplating the birds, and I had no need to look beyond him.

"And what do you call these little fellows, ma'am?" said he in his pleasant voice. "Have they any names?"

"I can answer for Miss Flite that they have," said I, "for she promised to tell us what they were. Ada remembers?"

Ada remembered very well.

"Did I?" said Miss Flite. "Who's that at my door? What are you listening at my door for, Krook?"

The old man of the house, pushing it open before him, appeared there with his fur cap in his hand and his cat at his heels.

"I warn't listening, Miss Flite," he said, "I was going to give a rap with my knuckles, only you're so quick!"

"Make your cat go down. Drive her away!" the old lady angrily exclaimed.

"Bah, bah! There ain't no danger, gentlefolks," said Mr. Krook, looking slowly and sharply from one to another until he had looked at all of us; "she'd never offer at the birds when I was here unless I told her to it."

"You will excuse my landlord," said the old lady with a dignified air. "M, quite M! What do you want, Krook, when I have company?"

"Hi!" said the old man. "You know I am the Chancellor."

"Well?" returned Miss Flite. "What of that?"

"For the Chancellor," said the old man with a chuckle, "not to be acquainted with a Jarndyce is queer, ain't it, Miss Flite? Mightn't I take the liberty? Your servant, sir. I know Jarndyce and Jarndyce a'most as well as you do, sir. I knowed old Squire Tom, sir. I never to my knowledge see you afore though, not even in court. Yet, I go there a mortal sight of times in the course of the year, taking one day with another."

"I never go there," said Mr. Jarndyce (which he never did on any consideration). "I would sooner go—somewhere else."

"Would you though?" returned Krook, grinning. "You're bearing hard upon my noble and learned brother in your meaning, sir, though perhaps it is but nat'ral in a Jarndyce. The burnt child, sir! What, you're looking at my lodger's birds, Mr. Jarndyce?" The old man had come by little and little into the room until he now touched my guardian with his elbow and looked close up into his face with his spectacled eyes. "It's one of her strange ways that she'll never tell the names of these birds if she can help it, though she named 'em all." This was in a whisper. "Shall I run 'em over, Flite?" he asked aloud, winking at us and pointing at her as she turned away, affecting to sweep the grate.

"If you like," she answered hurriedly.

The old man, looking up at the cages after another look at us, went through the list.

"Hope, Joy, Youth, Peace, Rest, Life, Dust, Ashes, Waste, Want, Ruin, Despair, Madness, Death, Cunning, Folly, Words, Wigs, Rags, Sheepskin, Plunder, Precedent, Jargon, Gammon, and Spinach. That's the whole collection," said the old man, "all cooped up together, by my noble and learned brother."

"This is a bitter wind!" muttered my guardian.

"When my noble and learned brother gives his judgment, they're to be let go free," said Krook, winking at us again. "And then," he added, whispering and grinning, "if that ever was to happen—which it won't—the birds that have never been caged would kill 'em."

"If ever the wind was in the east," said my guardian, pretending to look out of the window for a weathercock, "I think it's there to-day!"

We found it very difficult to get away from the house. It was not Miss Flite who detained us; she was as reasonable a little creature in consulting the convenience of others as there possibly could be. It was Mr. Krook. He seemed unable to detach himself from Mr. Jarndyce. If he had been linked to him, he could hardly have attended him more closely. He proposed to show us his Court of Chancery and all the strange medley it contained; during the whole of our inspection (prolonged by himself) he kept close to Mr. Jarndyce and sometimes detained him under one pretence or other until we had passed on, as if he were tormented by an inclination to enter upon some secret subject which he could not make up his mind to approach. I cannot imagine a countenance and manner more singularly expressive of caution and indecision, and a perpetual impulse to do something he could not resolve to venture on, than Mr. Krook's was that day. His watchfulness of my guardian was incessant. He rarely removed his eyes from his face. If he went on beside him, he observed him with the slyness of an old white fox. If he went before, he looked back. When we stood still, he got opposite to him, and drawing his hand across and across his open mouth with a curious expression of a sense of power, and turning up his eyes, and lowering his grey eyebrows until they appeared to be shut, seemed to scan every lineament of his face.

At last, having been (always attended by the cat) all over the house and having seen the whole stock of miscellaneous lumber, which was certainly curious, we came into the back part of the shop. Here on the head of an empty barrel stood on end were an ink-bottle, some old stumps of pens, and some dirty playbills; and against the wall were pasted several large printed alphabets in several plain hands.

"What are you doing here?" asked my guardian.

"Trying to learn myself to read and write," said Krook.

"And how do you get on?"

"Slow. Bad," returned the old man impatiently. "It's hard at my time of life."

"It would be easier to be taught by some one," said my guardian.

"Aye, but they might teach me wrong!" returned the old man with a wonderfully suspicious flash of his eye. "I don't know what I may have lost by not being learned afore. I wouldn't like to lose anything by being learned wrong now."

"Wrong?" said my guardian with his good-humoured smile. "Who do you suppose would teach you wrong?"

"I don't know, Mr. Jarndyce of Bleak House!" replied the old man, turning up his spectacles on his forehead and rubbing his hands. "I don't suppose as anybody would, but I'd rather trust my own self than another!"

These answers and his manner were strange enough to cause my guardian to inquire of Mr. Woodcourt, as we all walked across Lincoln's Inn together, whether Mr. Krook were really, as his lodger represented him, deranged. The young surgeon replied, no, he had seen no reason to think so. He was exceedingly distrustful, as ignorance usually was, and he was always more or less under the influence of raw gin, of which he drank great quantities and of which he and his back-shop, as we might have observed, smelt strongly; but he did not think him mad as yet.

On our way home, I so conciliated Peepy's affections by buying him a windmill and two flour-sacks that he would suffer nobody else to take off his hat and gloves and would sit nowhere at dinner but at my side. Caddy sat upon the other side of me, next to Ada, to whom we imparted the whole history of the engagement as soon as we got back. We made much of Caddy, and Peepy too; and Caddy brightened exceedingly; and my guardian was as merry as we were; and we were all very happy indeed until Caddy went home at night in a hackney-coach, with Peepy fast asleep, but holding tight to the windmill.

I have forgotten to mention—at least I have not mentioned—that Mr. Woodcourt was the same dark young surgeon whom we had met at Mr. Badger's. Or that Mr. Jarndyce invited him to dinner that day. Or that he came. Or that when they were all gone and I said to Ada, "Now, my darling, let us have a little talk about Richard!" Ada laughed and said—

But I don't think it matters what my darling said. She was always merry.

CHAPTER XV
BELL YARD

While we were in London Mr. Jarndyce was constantly beset by the crowd of excitable ladies and gentlemen whose proceedings had so much astonished us. Mr. Quale, who presented himself soon after our arrival, was in all such excitements. He seemed to project those two shining knobs of temples of his into everything that went on and to brush his hair farther and farther back, until the very roots were almost ready to fly out of his head in inappeasable philanthropy. All objects were alike to him, but he was always particularly ready for anything in the way of a testimonial to any one. His great power seemed to be his power of indiscriminate admiration. He would sit for any length of time, with the utmost enjoyment, bathing his temples in the light of any order of luminary. Having first seen him perfectly swallowed up in admiration of Mrs. Jellyby, I had supposed her to be the absorbing object of his devotion. I soon discovered my mistake and found him to be train-bearer and organ-blower to a whole procession of people.

Mrs. Pardiggle came one day for a subscription to something, and with her, Mr. Quale. Whatever Mrs. Pardiggle said, Mr. Quale repeated to us; and just as he had drawn Mrs. Jellyby out, he drew Mrs. Pardiggle out. Mrs. Pardiggle wrote a letter of introduction to my guardian in behalf of her eloquent friend Mr. Gusher. With Mr. Gusher appeared Mr. Quale again. Mr. Gusher, being a flabby gentleman with a moist surface and eyes so much too small for his moon of a face that they seemed to have been originally made for somebody else, was not at first sight prepossessing; yet he was scarcely seated before Mr. Quale asked Ada and me, not inaudibly, whether he was not a great creature—which he certainly was, flabbily speaking, though Mr. Quale meant in intellectual beauty—and whether we were not struck by his massive configuration of brow. In short, we heard of a great many missions of various sorts among this set of people, but nothing respecting them was half so clear to us as that it was Mr. Quale's mission to be in ecstasies with everybody else's mission and that it was the most popular mission of all.

Mr. Jarndyce had fallen into this company in the tenderness of his heart and his earnest desire to do all the good in his power; but that he felt it to be too often an unsatisfactory company, where benevolence took spasmodic forms, where charity was assumed as a regular uniform by loud professors and speculators in cheap notoriety, vehement in profession, restless and vain in action, servile in the last degree of meanness to the great, adulatory of one another, and intolerable to those who were anxious quietly to help the weak from failing rather than with a great deal of bluster and self-laudation to raise them up a little way when they were down, he plainly told us. When a testimonial was originated to Mr. Quale by Mr. Gusher (who had already got one, originated by Mr. Quale), and when Mr. Gusher spoke for an hour and a half on the subject to a meeting, including two charity schools of small boys and girls, who were specially reminded of the widow's mite, and requested to come forward with halfpence and be acceptable sacrifices, I think the wind was in the east for three whole weeks.

I mention this because I am coming to Mr. Skimpole again. It seemed to me that his off-hand professions of childishness and carelessness were a great relief to my guardian, by contrast with such things, and were the more readily believed in since to find one perfectly undesigning and candid man among many opposites could not fail to give him pleasure. I should be sorry to imply that Mr. Skimpole divined this and was politic; I really never understood him well enough to know. What he was to my guardian, he certainly was to the rest of the world.

He had not been very well; and thus, though he lived in London, we had seen nothing of him until now. He appeared one morning in his usual agreeable way and as full of pleasant spirits as ever.

Well, he said, here he was! He had been bilious, but rich men were often bilious, and therefore he had been persuading himself that he was a man of property. So he was, in a certain point of view—in his expansive intentions. He had been enriching his medical attendant in the most lavish manner. He had always doubled, and sometimes quadrupled, his fees. He had said to the doctor, "Now, my dear doctor, it is quite a delusion on your part to suppose that you attend me for nothing. I am overwhelming you with money—in my expansive intentions—if you only knew it!" And really (he said) he meant it to that degree that he thought it much the same as doing it. If he had had those bits of metal or thin paper to which mankind attached so much importance to put in the doctor's hand, he would have put them in the doctor's hand. Not having them, he substituted the will for the deed. Very well! If he really meant it—if his will were genuine and real, which it was—it appeared to him that it was the same as coin, and cancelled the obligation.

"It may be, partly, because I know nothing of the value of money," said Mr. Skimpole, "but I often feel this. It seems so reasonable! My butcher says to me he wants that little bill. It's a part of the pleasant unconscious poetry of the man's nature that he always calls it a 'little' bill—to make the payment appear easy to both of us. I reply to the butcher, 'My good friend, if you knew it, you are paid. You haven't had the trouble of coming to ask for the little bill. You are paid. I mean it.'"

"But, suppose," said my guardian, laughing, "he had meant the meat in the bill, instead of providing it?"

"My dear Jarndyce," he returned, "you surprise me. You take the butcher's position. A butcher I once dealt with occupied that very ground. Says he, 'Sir, why did you eat spring lamb at eighteen pence a pound?' 'Why did I eat spring lamb at eighteen pence a pound, my honest friend?' said I, naturally amazed by the question. 'I like spring lamb!' This was so far convincing. 'Well, sir,' says he, 'I wish I had meant the lamb as you mean the money!' 'My good fellow,' said I, 'pray let us reason like intellectual beings. How could that be? It was impossible. You HAD got the lamb, and I have NOT got the money. You couldn't really mean the lamb without sending it in, whereas I can, and do, really mean the money without paying it!' He had not a word. There was an end of the subject."

"Did he take no legal proceedings?" inquired my guardian.

"Yes, he took legal proceedings," said Mr. Skimpole. "But in that he was influenced by passion, not by reason. Passion reminds me of Boythorn. He writes me that you and the ladies have promised him a short visit at his bachelor-house in Lincolnshire."

"He is a great favourite with my girls," said Mr. Jarndyce, "and I have promised for them."

"Nature forgot to shade him off, I think," observed Mr. Skimpole to Ada and me. "A little too boisterous—like the sea. A little too vehement—like a bull who has made up his mind to consider every colour scarlet. But I grant a sledge-hammering sort of merit in him!"

I should have been surprised if those two could have thought very highly of one another, Mr. Boythorn attaching so much importance to many things and Mr. Skimpole caring so little for anything. Besides which, I had noticed Mr. Boythorn more than once on the point of breaking out into some strong opinion when Mr. Skimpole was referred to. Of course I merely joined Ada in saying that we had been greatly pleased with him.

"He has invited me," said Mr. Skimpole; "and if a child may trust himself in such hands—which the present child is encouraged to do, with the united tenderness of two angels to guard him—I shall go. He proposes to frank me down and back again. I suppose it will cost money? Shillings perhaps? Or pounds? Or something of that sort? By the by, Coavinses. You remember our friend Coavinses, Miss Summerson?"

He asked me as the subject arose in his mind, in his graceful, light-hearted manner and without the least embarrassment.

"Oh, yes!" said I.

"Coavinses has been arrested by the Great Bailiff," said Mr. Skimpole. "He will never do violence to the sunshine any more."

It quite shocked me to hear it, for I had already recalled with anything but a serious association the image of the man sitting on the sofa that night wiping his head.

"His successor informed me of it yesterday," said Mr. Skimpole. "His successor is in my house now—in possession, I think he calls it. He came yesterday, on my blue-eyed daughter's birthday. I put it to him, 'This is unreasonable and inconvenient. If you had a blue-eyed daughter you wouldn't like ME to come, uninvited, on HER birthday?' But he stayed."

Mr. Skimpole laughed at the pleasant absurdity and lightly touched the piano by which he was seated.

"And he told me," he said, playing little chords where I shall put full stops, "The Coavinses had left. Three children. No mother. And that Coavinses' profession. Being unpopular. The rising Coavinses. Were at a considerable disadvantage."

Mr. Jarndyce got up, rubbing his head, and began to walk about. Mr. Skimpole played the melody of one of Ada's favourite songs. Ada and I both looked at Mr. Jarndyce, thinking that we knew what was passing in his mind.

After walking and stopping, and several times leaving off rubbing his head, and beginning again, my guardian put his hand upon the keys and stopped Mr. Skimpole's playing. "I don't like this, Skimpole," he said thoughtfully.

Mr. Skimpole, who had quite forgotten the subject, looked up surprised.

"The man was necessary," pursued my guardian, walking backward and forward in the very short space between the piano and the end of the room and rubbing his hair up from the back of his head as if a high east wind had blown it into that form. "If we make such men necessary by our faults and follies, or by our want of worldly knowledge, or by our misfortunes, we must not revenge ourselves upon them. There was no harm in his trade. He maintained his children. One would like to know more about this."

"Oh! Coavinses?" cried Mr. Skimpole, at length perceiving what he meant. "Nothing easier. A walk to Coavinses' headquarters, and you can know what you will."

Mr. Jarndyce nodded to us, who were only waiting for the signal. "Come! We will walk that way, my dears. Why not that way as soon as another!" We were quickly ready and went out. Mr. Skimpole went with us and quite enjoyed the expedition. It was so new and so refreshing, he said, for him to want Coavinses instead of Coavinses wanting him!

He took us, first, to Cursitor Street, Chancery Lane, where there was a house with barred windows, which he called Coavinses' Castle. On our going into the entry and ringing a bell, a very hideous boy came out of a sort of office and looked at us over a spiked wicket.

"Who did you want?" said the boy, fitting two of the spikes into his chin.

"There was a follower, or an officer, or something, here," said Mr. Jarndyce, "who is dead."

"Yes?" said the boy. "Well?"

"I want to know his name, if you please?"

"Name of Neckett," said the boy.

"And his address?"

"Bell Yard," said the boy. "Chandler's shop, left hand side, name of Blinder."

"Was he—I don't know how to shape the question—" murmured my guardian, "industrious?"

"Was Neckett?" said the boy. "Yes, wery much so. He was never tired of watching. He'd set upon a post at a street corner eight or ten hours at a stretch if he undertook to do it."

"He might have done worse," I heard my guardian soliloquize. "He might have undertaken to do it and not done it. Thank you. That's all I want."

We left the boy, with his head on one side and his arms on the gate, fondling and sucking the spikes, and went back to Lincoln's Inn, where Mr. Skimpole, who had not cared to remain nearer Coavinses, awaited us. Then we all went to Bell Yard, a narrow alley at a very short distance. We soon found the chandler's shop. In it was a good-natured-looking old woman with a dropsy, or an asthma, or perhaps both.

"Neckett's children?" said she in reply to my inquiry. "Yes, Surely, miss. Three pair, if you please. Door right opposite the stairs." And she handed me the key across the counter.

I glanced at the key and glanced at her, but she took it for granted that I knew what to do with it. As it could only be intended for the children's door, I came out without asking any more questions and led the way up the dark stairs. We went as quietly as we could, but four of us made some noise on the aged boards, and when we came to the second story we found we had disturbed a man who was standing there looking out of his room.

"Is it Gridley that's wanted?" he said, fixing his eyes on me with an angry stare.

"No, sir," said I; "I am going higher up."

He looked at Ada, and at Mr. Jarndyce, and at Mr. Skimpole, fixing the same angry stare on each in succession as they passed and followed me. Mr. Jarndyce gave him good day. "Good day!" he said abruptly and fiercely. He was a tall, sallow man with a careworn head on which but little hair remained, a deeply lined face, and prominent eyes. He had a combative look and a chafing, irritable manner which, associated with his figure—still large and powerful, though evidently in its decline—rather alarmed me. He had a pen in his hand, and in the glimpse I caught of his room in passing, I saw that it was covered with a litter of papers.

Leaving him standing there, we went up to the top room. I tapped at the door, and a little shrill voice inside said, "We are locked in. Mrs. Blinder's got the key!"

I applied the key on hearing this and opened the door. In a poor room with a sloping ceiling and containing very little furniture was a mite of a boy, some five or six years old, nursing and hushing a heavy child of eighteen months. There was no fire, though the weather was cold; both children were wrapped in some poor shawls and tippets as a substitute. Their clothing was not so warm, however, but that their noses looked red and pinched and their small figures shrunken as the boy walked up and down nursing and hushing the child with its head on his shoulder.

"Who has locked you up here alone?" we naturally asked.

"Charley," said the boy, standing still to gaze at us.

"Is Charley your brother?"

"No. She's my sister, Charlotte. Father called her Charley."

"Are there any more of you besides Charley?"

"Me," said the boy, "and Emma," patting the limp bonnet of the child he was nursing. "And Charley."

"Where is Charley now?"

"Out a-washing," said the boy, beginning to walk up and down again and taking the nankeen bonnet much too near the bedstead by trying to gaze at us at the same time.

We were looking at one another and at these two children when there came into the room a very little girl, childish in figure but shrewd and older-looking in the face—pretty-faced too—wearing a womanly sort of bonnet much too large for her and drying her bare arms on a womanly sort of apron. Her fingers were white and wrinkled with washing, and the soap-suds were yet smoking which she wiped off her arms. But for this, she might have been a child playing at washing and imitating a poor working-woman with a quick observation of the truth.

She had come running from some place in the neighbourhood and had made all the haste she could. Consequently, though she was very light, she was out of breath and could not speak at first, as she stood panting, and wiping her arms, and looking quietly at us.

"Oh, here's Charley!" said the boy.

The child he was nursing stretched forth its arms and cried out to be taken by Charley. The little girl took it, in a womanly sort of manner belonging to the apron and the bonnet, and stood looking at us over the burden that clung to her most affectionately.

"Is it possible," whispered my guardian as we put a chair for the little creature and got her to sit down with her load, the boy keeping close to her, holding to her apron, "that this child works for the rest? Look at this! For God's sake, look at this!"

It was a thing to look at. The three children close together, and two of them relying solely on the third, and the third so young and yet with an air of age and steadiness that sat so strangely on the childish figure.

"Charley, Charley!" said my guardian. "How old are you?"

"Over thirteen, sir," replied the child.

"Oh! What a great age," said my guardian. "What a great age, Charley!"

I cannot describe the tenderness with which he spoke to her, half playfully yet all the more compassionately and mournfully.

"And do you live alone here with these babies, Charley?" said my guardian.

"Yes, sir," returned the child, looking up into his face with perfect confidence, "since father died."

"And how do you live, Charley? Oh! Charley," said my guardian, turning his face away for a moment, "how do you live?"

"Since father died, sir, I've gone out to work. I'm out washing to-day."

"God help you, Charley!" said my guardian. "You're not tall enough to reach the tub!"

"In pattens I am, sir," she said quickly. "I've got a high pair as belonged to mother."

"And when did mother die? Poor mother!"

"Mother died just after Emma was born," said the child, glancing at the face upon her bosom. "Then father said I was to be as good a mother to her as I could. And so I tried. And so I worked at home and did cleaning and nursing and washing for a long time before I began to go out. And that's how I know how; don't you see, sir?"

"And do you often go out?"

"As often as I can," said Charley, opening her eyes and smiling, "because of earning sixpences and shillings!"

"And do you always lock the babies up when you go out?"

"To keep 'em safe, sir, don't you see?" said Charley. "Mrs. Blinder comes up now and then, and Mr. Gridley comes up sometimes, and perhaps I can run in sometimes, and they can play you know, and Tom an't afraid of being locked up, are you, Tom?"

"No-o!" said Tom stoutly.

"When it comes on dark, the lamps are lighted down in the court, and they show up here quite bright—almost quite bright. Don't they, Tom?"

"Yes, Charley," said Tom, "almost quite bright."

"Then he's as good as gold," said the little creature—Oh, in such a motherly, womanly way! "And when Emma's tired, he puts her to bed. And when he's tired he goes to bed himself. And when I come home and light the candle and has a bit of supper, he sits up again and has it with me. Don't you, Tom?"

"Oh, yes, Charley!" said Tom. "That I do!" And either in this glimpse of the great pleasure of his life or in gratitude and love for Charley, who was all in all to him, he laid his face among the scanty folds of her frock and passed from laughing into crying.

It was the first time since our entry that a tear had been shed among these children. The little orphan girl had spoken of their father and their mother as if all that sorrow were subdued by the necessity of taking courage, and by her childish importance in being able to work, and by her bustling busy way. But now, when Tom cried, although she sat quite tranquil, looking quietly at us, and did not by any movement disturb a hair of the head of either of her little charges, I saw two silent tears fall down her face.

I stood at the window with Ada, pretending to look at the housetops, and the blackened stack of chimneys, and the poor plants, and the birds in little cages belonging to the neighbours, when I found that Mrs. Blinder, from the shop below, had come in (perhaps it had taken her all this time to get upstairs) and was talking to my guardian.

"It's not much to forgive 'em the rent, sir," she said; "who could take it from them!"

"Well, well!" said my guardian to us two. "It is enough that the time will come when this good woman will find that it WAS much, and that forasmuch as she did it unto the least of these—This child," he added after a few moments, "could she possibly continue this?"

"Really, sir, I think she might," said Mrs. Blinder, getting her heavy breath by painful degrees. "She's as handy as it's possible to be. Bless you, sir, the way she tended them two children after the mother died was the talk of the yard! And it was a wonder to see her with him after he was took ill, it really was! 'Mrs. Blinder,' he said to me the very last he spoke—he was lying there—'Mrs. Blinder, whatever my calling may have been, I see a angel sitting in this room last night along with my child, and I trust her to Our Father!'"

"He had no other calling?" said my guardian.

"No, sir," returned Mrs. Blinder, "he was nothing but a follerers. When he first came to lodge here, I didn't know what he was, and I confess that when I found out I gave him notice. It wasn't liked in the yard. It wasn't approved by the other lodgers. It is NOT a genteel calling," said Mrs. Blinder, "and most people do object to it. Mr. Gridley objected to it very strong, and he is a good lodger, though his temper has been hard tried."

"So you gave him notice?" said my guardian.

"So I gave him notice," said Mrs. Blinder. "But really when the time came, and I knew no other ill of him, I was in doubts. He was punctual and diligent; he did what he had to do, sir," said Mrs. Blinder, unconsciously fixing Mr. Skimpole with her eye, "and it's something in this world even to do that."

"So you kept him after all?"

"Why, I said that if he could arrange with Mr. Gridley, I could arrange it with the other lodgers and should not so much mind its being liked or disliked in the yard. Mr. Gridley gave his consent gruff—but gave it. He was always gruff with him, but he has been kind to the children since. A person is never known till a person is proved."

"Have many people been kind to the children?" asked Mr. Jarndyce.

"Upon the whole, not so bad, sir," said Mrs. Blinder; "but certainly not so many as would have been if their father's calling had been different. Mr. Coavins gave a guinea, and the follerers made up a little purse. Some neighbours in the yard that had always joked and tapped their shoulders when he went by came forward with a little subscription, and—in general—not so bad. Similarly with Charlotte. Some people won't employ her because she was a follerer's child; some people that do employ her cast it at her; some make a merit of having her to work for them, with that and all her draw-backs upon her, and perhaps pay her less and put upon her more. But she's patienter than others would be, and is clever too, and always willing, up to the full mark of her strength and over. So I should say, in general, not so bad, sir, but might be better."

Mrs. Blinder sat down to give herself a more favourable opportunity of recovering her breath, exhausted anew by so much talking before it was fully restored. Mr. Jarndyce was turning to speak to us when his attention was attracted by the abrupt entrance into the room of the Mr. Gridley who had been mentioned and whom we had seen on our way up.

"I don't know what you may be doing here, ladies and gentlemen," he said, as if he resented our presence, "but you'll excuse my coming in. I don't come in to stare about me. Well, Charley! Well, Tom! Well, little one! How is it with us all to-day?"

He bent over the group in a caressing way and clearly was regarded as a friend by the children, though his face retained its stern character and his manner to us was as rude as it could be. My guardian noticed it and respected it.

"No one, surely, would come here to stare about him," he said mildly.

"May be so, sir, may be so," returned the other, taking Tom upon his knee and waving him off impatiently. "I don't want to argue with ladies and gentlemen. I have had enough of arguing to last one man his life."

"You have sufficient reason, I dare say," said Mr. Jarndyce, "for being chafed and irritated—"

"There again!" exclaimed the man, becoming violently angry. "I am of a quarrelsome temper. I am irascible. I am not polite!"

"Not very, I think."

"Sir," said Gridley, putting down the child and going up to him as if he meant to strike him, "do you know anything of Courts of Equity?"

"Perhaps I do, to my sorrow."

"To your sorrow?" said the man, pausing in his wrath, "if so, I beg your pardon. I am not polite, I know. I beg your pardon! Sir," with renewed violence, "I have been dragged for five and twenty years over burning iron, and I have lost the habit of treading upon velvet. Go into the Court of Chancery yonder and ask what is one of the standing jokes that brighten up their business sometimes, and they will tell you that the best joke they have is the man from Shropshire. I," he said, beating one hand on the other passionately, "am the man from Shropshire."

"I believe I and my family have also had the honour of furnishing some entertainment in the same grave place," said my guardian composedly. "You may have heard my name—Jarndyce."

"Mr. Jarndyce," said Gridley with a rough sort of salutation, "you bear your wrongs more quietly than I can bear mine. More than that, I tell you—and I tell this gentleman, and these young ladies, if they are friends of yours—that if I took my wrongs in any other way, I should be driven mad! It is only by resenting them, and by revenging them in my mind, and by angrily demanding the justice I never get, that I am able to keep my wits together. It is only that!" he said, speaking in a homely, rustic way and with great vehemence. "You may tell me that I over-excite myself. I answer that it's in my nature to do it, under wrong, and I must do it. There's nothing between doing it, and sinking into the smiling state of the poor little mad woman that haunts the court. If I was once to sit down under it, I should become imbecile."

The passion and heat in which he was, and the manner in which his face worked, and the violent gestures with which he accompanied what he said, were most painful to see.

"Mr. Jarndyce," he said, "consider my case. As true as there is a heaven above us, this is my case. I am one of two brothers. My father (a farmer) made a will and left his farm and stock and so forth to my mother for her life. After my mother's death, all was to come to me except a legacy of three hundred pounds that I was then to pay my brother. My mother died. My brother some time afterwards claimed his legacy. I and some of my relations said that he had had a part of it already in board and lodging and some other things. Now mind! That was the question, and nothing else. No one disputed the will; no one disputed anything but whether part of that three hundred pounds had been already paid or not. To settle that question, my brother filing a bill, I was obliged to go into this accursed Chancery; I was forced there because the law forced me and would let me go nowhere else. Seventeen people were made defendants to that simple suit! It first came on after two years. It was then stopped for another two years while the master (may his head rot off!) inquired whether I was my father's son, about which there was no dispute at all with any mortal creature. He then found out that there were not defendants enough—remember, there were only seventeen as yet!—but that we must have another who had been left out and must begin all over again. The costs at that time—before the thing was begun!—were three times the legacy. My brother would have given up the legacy, and joyful, to escape more costs. My whole estate, left to me in that will of my father's, has gone in costs. The suit, still undecided, has fallen into rack, and ruin, and despair, with everything else—and here I stand, this day! Now, Mr. Jarndyce, in your suit there are thousands and thousands involved, where in mine there are hundreds. Is mine less hard to bear or is it harder to bear, when my whole living was in it and has been thus shamefully sucked away?"

Mr. Jarndyce said that he condoled with him with all his heart and that he set up no monopoly himself in being unjustly treated by this monstrous system.

"There again!" said Mr. Gridley with no diminution of his rage. "The system! I am told on all hands, it's the system. I mustn't look to individuals. It's the system. I mustn't go into court and say, 'My Lord, I beg to know this from you—is this right or wrong? Have you the face to tell me I have received justice and therefore am dismissed?' My Lord knows nothing of it. He sits there to administer the system. I mustn't go to Mr. Tulkinghorn, the solicitor in Lincoln's Inn Fields, and say to him when he makes me furious by being so cool and satisfied—as they all do, for I know they gain by it while I lose, don't I?—I mustn't say to him, 'I will have something out of some one for my ruin, by fair means or foul!' HE is not responsible. It's the system. But, if I do no violence to any of them, here—I may! I don't know what may happen if I am carried beyond myself at last! I will accuse the individual workers of that system against me, face to face, before the great eternal bar!"

His passion was fearful. I could not have believed in such rage without seeing it.

"I have done!" he said, sitting down and wiping his face. "Mr. Jarndyce, I have done! I am violent, I know. I ought to know it. I have been in prison for contempt of court. I have been in prison for threatening the solicitor. I have been in this trouble, and that trouble, and shall be again. I am the man from Shropshire, and I sometimes go beyond amusing them, though they have found it amusing, too, to see me committed into custody and brought up in custody and all that. It would be better for me, they tell me, if I restrained myself. I tell them that if I did restrain myself I should become imbecile. I was a good-enough-tempered man once, I believe. People in my part of the country say they remember me so, but now I must have this vent under my sense of injury or nothing could hold my wits together. It would be far better for you, Mr. Gridley,' the Lord Chancellor told me last week, 'not to waste your time here, and to stay, usefully employed, down in Shropshire.' 'My Lord, my Lord, I know it would,' said I to him, 'and it would have been far better for me never to have heard the name of your high office, but unhappily for me, I can't undo the past, and the past drives me here!' Besides," he added, breaking fiercely out, "I'll shame them. To the last, I'll show myself in that court to its shame. If I knew when I was going to die, and could be carried there, and had a voice to speak with, I would die there, saying, 'You have brought me here and sent me from here many and many a time. Now send me out feet foremost!'"

His countenance had, perhaps for years, become so set in its contentious expression that it did not soften, even now when he was quiet.

"I came to take these babies down to my room for an hour," he said, going to them again, "and let them play about. I didn't mean to say all this, but it don't much signify. You're not afraid of me, Tom, are you?"

"No!" said Tom. "You ain't angry with ME."

"You are right, my child. You're going back, Charley? Aye? Come then, little one!" He took the youngest child on his arm, where she was willing enough to be carried. "I shouldn't wonder if we found a ginger-bread soldier downstairs. Let's go and look for him!"

He made his former rough salutation, which was not deficient in a certain respect, to Mr. Jarndyce, and bowing slightly to us, went downstairs to his room.

Upon that, Mr. Skimpole began to talk, for the first time since our arrival, in his usual gay strain. He said, Well, it was really very pleasant to see how things lazily adapted themselves to purposes. Here was this Mr. Gridley, a man of a robust will and surprising energy—intellectually speaking, a sort of inharmonious blacksmith—and he could easily imagine that there Gridley was, years ago, wandering about in life for something to expend his superfluous combativeness upon—a sort of Young Love among the thorns—when the Court of Chancery came in his way and accommodated him with the exact thing he wanted. There they were, matched, ever afterwards! Otherwise he might have been a great general, blowing up all sorts of towns, or he might have been a great politician, dealing in all sorts of parliamentary rhetoric; but as it was, he and the Court of Chancery had fallen upon each other in the pleasantest way, and nobody was much the worse, and Gridley was, so to speak, from that hour provided for. Then look at Coavinses! How delightfully poor Coavinses (father of these charming children) illustrated the same principle! He, Mr. Skimpole, himself, had sometimes repined at the existence of Coavinses. He had found Coavinses in his way. He could had dispensed with Coavinses. There had been times when, if he had been a sultan, and his grand vizier had said one morning, "What does the Commander of the Faithful require at the hands of his slave?" he might have even gone so far as to reply, "The head of Coavinses!" But what turned out to be the case? That, all that time, he had been giving employment to a most deserving man, that he had been a benefactor to Coavinses, that he had actually been enabling Coavinses to bring up these charming children in this agreeable way, developing these social virtues! Insomuch that his heart had just now swelled and the tears had come into his eyes when he had looked round the room and thought, "I was the great patron of Coavinses, and his little comforts were MY work!"

There was something so captivating in his light way of touching these fantastic strings, and he was such a mirthful child by the side of the graver childhood we had seen, that he made my guardian smile even as he turned towards us from a little private talk with Mrs. Blinder. We kissed Charley, and took her downstairs with us, and stopped outside the house to see her run away to her work. I don't know where she was going, but we saw her run, such a little, little creature in her womanly bonnet and apron, through a covered way at the bottom of the court and melt into the city's strife and sound like a dewdrop in an ocean.

CHAPTER XVI
TOM-ALL-ALONE'S

My Lady Dedlock is restless, very restless. The astonished fashionable intelligence hardly knows where to have her. To-day she is at Chesney Wold; yesterday she was at her house in town; to-morrow she may be abroad, for anything the fashionable intelligence can with confidence predict. Even Sir Leicester's gallantry has some trouble to keep pace with her. It would have more but that his other faithful ally, for better and for worse—the gout—darts into the old oak bed-chamber at Chesney Wold and grips him by both legs.

Sir Leicester receives the gout as a troublesome demon, but still a demon of the patrician order. All the Dedlocks, in the direct male line, through a course of time during and beyond which the memory of man goeth not to the contrary, have had the gout. It can be proved, sir. Other men's fathers may have died of the rheumatism or may have taken base contagion from the tainted blood of the sick vulgar, but the Dedlock family have communicated something exclusive even to the levelling process of dying by dying of their own family gout. It has come down through the illustrious line like the plate, or the pictures, or the place in Lincolnshire. It is among their dignities. Sir Leicester is perhaps not wholly without an impression, though he has never resolved it into words, that the angel of death in the discharge of his necessary duties may observe to the shades of the aristocracy, "My lords and gentlemen, I have the honour to present to you another Dedlock certified to have arrived per the family gout."

Hence Sir Leicester yields up his family legs to the family disorder as if he held his name and fortune on that feudal tenure. He feels that for a Dedlock to be laid upon his back and spasmodically twitched and stabbed in his extremities is a liberty taken somewhere, but he thinks, "We have all yielded to this; it belongs to us; it has for some hundreds of years been understood that we are not to make the vaults in the park interesting on more ignoble terms; and I submit myself to the compromise."

And a goodly show he makes, lying in a flush of crimson and gold in the midst of the great drawing-room before his favourite picture of my Lady, with broad strips of sunlight shining in, down the long perspective, through the long line of windows, and alternating with soft reliefs of shadow. Outside, the stately oaks, rooted for ages in the green ground which has never known ploughshare, but was still a chase when kings rode to battle with sword and shield and rode a-hunting with bow and arrow, bear witness to his greatness. Inside, his forefathers, looking on him from the walls, say, "Each of us was a passing reality here and left this coloured shadow of himself and melted into remembrance as dreamy as the distant voices of the rooks now lulling you to rest," and hear their testimony to his greatness too. And he is very great this day. And woe to Boythorn or other daring wight who shall presumptuously contest an inch with him!

My Lady is at present represented, near Sir Leicester, by her portrait. She has flitted away to town, with no intention of remaining there, and will soon flit hither again, to the confusion of the fashionable intelligence. The house in town is not prepared for her reception. It is muffled and dreary. Only one Mercury in powder gapes disconsolate at the hall-window; and he mentioned last night to another Mercury of his acquaintance, also accustomed to good society, that if that sort of thing was to last—which it couldn't, for a man of his spirits couldn't bear it, and a man of his figure couldn't be expected to bear it—there would be no resource for him, upon his honour, but to cut his throat!

What connexion can there be between the place in Lincolnshire, the house in town, the Mercury in powder, and the whereabout of Jo the outlaw with the broom, who had that distant ray of light upon him when he swept the churchyard-step? What connexion can there have been between many people in the innumerable histories of this world who from opposite sides of great gulfs have, nevertheless, been very curiously brought together!

Jo sweeps his crossing all day long, unconscious of the link, if any link there be. He sums up his mental condition when asked a question by replying that he "don't know nothink." He knows that it's hard to keep the mud off the crossing in dirty weather, and harder still to live by doing it. Nobody taught him even that much; he found it out.

Jo lives—that is to say, Jo has not yet died—in a ruinous place known to the like of him by the name of Tom-all-Alone's. It is a black, dilapidated street, avoided by all decent people, where the crazy houses were seized upon, when their decay was far advanced, by some bold vagrants who after establishing their own possession took to letting them out in lodgings. Now, these tumbling tenements contain, by night, a swarm of misery. As on the ruined human wretch vermin parasites appear, so these ruined shelters have bred a crowd of foul existence that crawls in and out of gaps in walls and boards; and coils itself to sleep, in maggot numbers, where the rain drips in; and comes and goes, fetching and carrying fever and sowing more evil in its every footprint than Lord Coodle, and Sir Thomas Doodle, and the Duke of Foodle, and all the fine gentlemen in office, down to Zoodle, shall set right in five hundred years—though born expressly to do it.

Twice lately there has been a crash and a cloud of dust, like the springing of a mine, in Tom-all-Alone's; and each time a house has fallen. These accidents have made a paragraph in the newspapers and have filled a bed or two in the nearest hospital. The gaps remain, and there are not unpopular lodgings among the rubbish. As several more houses are nearly ready to go, the next crash in Tom-all-Alone's may be expected to be a good one.

This desirable property is in Chancery, of course. It would be an insult to the discernment of any man with half an eye to tell him so. Whether "Tom" is the popular representative of the original plaintiff or defendant in Jarndyce and Jarndyce, or whether Tom lived here when the suit had laid the street waste, all alone, until other settlers came to join him, or whether the traditional title is a comprehensive name for a retreat cut off from honest company and put out of the pale of hope, perhaps nobody knows. Certainly Jo don't know.

"For I don't," says Jo, "I don't know nothink."

It must be a strange state to be like Jo! To shuffle through the streets, unfamiliar with the shapes, and in utter darkness as to the meaning, of those mysterious symbols, so abundant over the shops, and at the corners of streets, and on the doors, and in the windows! To see people read, and to see people write, and to see the postmen deliver letters, and not to have the least idea of all that language—to be, to every scrap of it, stone blind and dumb! It must be very puzzling to see the good company going to the churches on Sundays, with their books in their hands, and to think (for perhaps Jo DOES think at odd times) what does it all mean, and if it means anything to anybody, how comes it that it means nothing to me? To be hustled, and jostled, and moved on; and really to feel that it would appear to be perfectly true that I have no business here, or there, or anywhere; and yet to be perplexed by the consideration that I AM here somehow, too, and everybody overlooked me until I became the creature that I am! It must be a strange state, not merely to be told that I am scarcely human (as in the case of my offering myself for a witness), but to feel it of my own knowledge all my life! To see the horses, dogs, and cattle go by me and to know that in ignorance I belong to them and not to the superior beings in my shape, whose delicacy I offend! Jo's ideas of a criminal trial, or a judge, or a bishop, or a government, or that inestimable jewel to him (if he only knew it) the Constitution, should be strange! His whole material and immaterial life is wonderfully strange; his death, the strangest thing of all.

Jo comes out of Tom-all-Alone's, meeting the tardy morning which is always late in getting down there, and munches his dirty bit of bread as he comes along. His way lying through many streets, and the houses not yet being open, he sits down to breakfast on the door-step of the Society for the Propagation of the Gospel in Foreign Parts and gives it a brush when he has finished as an acknowledgment of the accommodation. He admires the size of the edifice and wonders what it's all about. He has no idea, poor wretch, of the spiritual destitution of a coral reef in the Pacific or what it costs to look up the precious souls among the coco-nuts and bread-fruit.

He goes to his crossing and begins to lay it out for the day. The town awakes; the great tee-totum is set up for its daily spin and whirl; all that unaccountable reading and writing, which has been suspended for a few hours, recommences. Jo and the other lower animals get on in the unintelligible mess as they can. It is market-day. The blinded oxen, over-goaded, over-driven, never guided, run into wrong places and are beaten out, and plunge red-eyed and foaming at stone walls, and often sorely hurt the innocent, and often sorely hurt themselves. Very like Jo and his order; very, very like!

A band of music comes and plays. Jo listens to it. So does a dog—a drover's dog, waiting for his master outside a butcher's shop, and evidently thinking about those sheep he has had upon his mind for some hours and is happily rid of. He seems perplexed respecting three or four, can't remember where he left them, looks up and down the street as half expecting to see them astray, suddenly pricks up his ears and remembers all about it. A thoroughly vagabond dog, accustomed to low company and public-houses; a terrific dog to sheep, ready at a whistle to scamper over their backs and tear out mouthfuls of their wool; but an educated, improved, developed dog who has been taught his duties and knows how to discharge them. He and Jo listen to the music, probably with much the same amount of animal satisfaction; likewise as to awakened association, aspiration, or regret, melancholy or joyful reference to things beyond the senses, they are probably upon a par. But, otherwise, how far above the human listener is the brute!

Turn that dog's descendants wild, like Jo, and in a very few years they will so degenerate that they will lose even their bark—but not their bite.

The day changes as it wears itself away and becomes dark and drizzly. Jo fights it out at his crossing among the mud and wheels, the horses, whips, and umbrellas, and gets but a scanty sum to pay for the unsavoury shelter of Tom-all-Alone's. Twilight comes on; gas begins to start up in the shops; the lamplighter, with his ladder, runs along the margin of the pavement. A wretched evening is beginning to close in.

In his chambers Mr. Tulkinghorn sits meditating an application to the nearest magistrate to-morrow morning for a warrant. Gridley, a disappointed suitor, has been here to-day and has been alarming. We are not to be put in bodily fear, and that ill-conditioned fellow shall be held to bail again. From the ceiling, foreshortened Allegory, in the person of one impossible Roman upside down, points with the arm of Samson (out of joint, and an odd one) obtrusively toward the window. Why should Mr. Tulkinghorn, for such no reason, look out of window? Is the hand not always pointing there? So he does not look out of window.

And if he did, what would it be to see a woman going by? There are women enough in the world, Mr. Tulkinghorn thinks—too many; they are at the bottom of all that goes wrong in it, though, for the matter of that, they create business for lawyers. What would it be to see a woman going by, even though she were going secretly? They are all secret. Mr. Tulkinghorn knows that very well.

But they are not all like the woman who now leaves him and his house behind, between whose plain dress and her refined manner there is something exceedingly inconsistent. She should be an upper servant by her attire, yet in her air and step, though both are hurried and assumed—as far as she can assume in the muddy streets, which she treads with an unaccustomed foot—she is a lady. Her face is veiled, and still she sufficiently betrays herself to make more than one of those who pass her look round sharply.

She never turns her head. Lady or servant, she has a purpose in her and can follow it. She never turns her head until she comes to the crossing where Jo plies with his broom. He crosses with her and begs. Still, she does not turn her head until she has landed on the other side. Then she slightly beckons to him and says, "Come here!"

Jo follows her a pace or two into a quiet court.

"Are you the boy I've read of in the papers?" she asked behind her veil.

"I don't know," says Jo, staring moodily at the veil, "nothink about no papers. I don't know nothink about nothink at all."

"Were you examined at an inquest?"

"I don't know nothink about no—where I was took by the beadle, do you mean?" says Jo. "Was the boy's name at the inkwhich Jo?"

"Yes."

"That's me!" says Jo.

"Come farther up."

"You mean about the man?" says Jo, following. "Him as wos dead?"

"Hush! Speak in a whisper! Yes. Did he look, when he was living, so very ill and poor?"

"Oh, jist!" says Jo.

"Did he look like—not like YOU?" says the woman with abhorrence.

"Oh, not so bad as me," says Jo. "I'm a reg'lar one I am! You didn't know him, did you?"

"How dare you ask me if I knew him?"

"No offence, my lady," says Jo with much humility, for even he has got at the suspicion of her being a lady.

"I am not a lady. I am a servant."

"You are a jolly servant!" says Jo without the least idea of saying anything offensive, merely as a tribute of admiration.

"Listen and be silent. Don't talk to me, and stand farther from me! Can you show me all those places that were spoken of in the account I read? The place he wrote for, the place he died at, the place where you were taken to, and the place where he was buried? Do you know the place where he was buried?"

Jo answers with a nod, having also nodded as each other place was mentioned.

"Go before me and show me all those dreadful places. Stop opposite to each, and don't speak to me unless I speak to you. Don't look back. Do what I want, and I will pay you well."

Jo attends closely while the words are being spoken; tells them off on his broom-handle, finding them rather hard; pauses to consider their meaning; considers it satisfactory; and nods his ragged head.

"I'm fly," says Jo. "But fen larks, you know. Stow hooking it!"

"What does the horrible creature mean?" exclaims the servant, recoiling from him.

"Stow cutting away, you know!" says Jo.

"I don't understand you. Go on before! I will give you more money than you ever had in your life."

Jo screws up his mouth into a whistle, gives his ragged head a rub, takes his broom under his arm, and leads the way, passing deftly with his bare feet over the hard stones and through the mud and mire.

Cook's Court. Jo stops. A pause.

"Who lives here?"

"Him wot give him his writing and give me half a bull," says Jo in a whisper without looking over his shoulder.

"Go on to the next."

Krook's house. Jo stops again. A longer pause.

"Who lives here?"

"HE lived here," Jo answers as before.

After a silence he is asked, "In which room?"

"In the back room up there. You can see the winder from this corner. Up there! That's where I see him stritched out. This is the public-ouse where I was took to."

"Go on to the next!"

It is a longer walk to the next, but Jo, relieved of his first suspicions, sticks to the forms imposed upon him and does not look round. By many devious ways, reeking with offence of many kinds, they come to the little tunnel of a court, and to the gas-lamp (lighted now), and to the iron gate.

"He was put there," says Jo, holding to the bars and looking in.

"Where? Oh, what a scene of horror!"

"There!" says Jo, pointing. "Over yinder. Among them piles of bones, and close to that there kitchin winder! They put him wery nigh the top. They was obliged to stamp upon it to git it in. I could unkiver it for you with my broom if the gate was open. That's why they locks it, I s'pose," giving it a shake. "It's always locked. Look at the rat!" cries Jo, excited. "Hi! Look! There he goes! Ho! Into the ground!"

The servant shrinks into a corner, into a corner of that hideous archway, with its deadly stains contaminating her dress; and putting out her two hands and passionately telling him to keep away from her, for he is loathsome to her, so remains for some moments. Jo stands staring and is still staring when she recovers herself.

"Is this place of abomination consecrated ground?"

"I don't know nothink of consequential ground," says Jo, still staring.

"Is it blessed?"

"Which?" says Jo, in the last degree amazed.

"Is it blessed?"

"I'm blest if I know," says Jo, staring more than ever; "but I shouldn't think it warn't. Blest?" repeats Jo, something troubled in his mind. "It an't done it much good if it is. Blest? I should think it was t'othered myself. But I don't know nothink!"

The servant takes as little heed of what he says as she seems to take of what she has said herself. She draws off her glove to get some money from her purse. Jo silently notices how white and small her hand is and what a jolly servant she must be to wear such sparkling rings.

She drops a piece of money in his hand without touching it, and shuddering as their hands approach. "Now," she adds, "show me the spot again!"

Jo thrusts the handle of his broom between the bars of the gate, and with his utmost power of elaboration, points it out. At length, looking aside to see if he has made himself intelligible, he finds that he is alone.

His first proceeding is to hold the piece of money to the gas-light and to be overpowered at finding that it is yellow—gold. His next is to give it a one-sided bite at the edge as a test of its quality. His next, to put it in his mouth for safety and to sweep the step and passage with great care. His job done, he sets off for Tom-all-Alone's, stopping in the light of innumerable gas-lamps to produce the piece of gold and give it another one-sided bite as a reassurance of its being genuine.

The Mercury in powder is in no want of society to-night, for my Lady goes to a grand dinner and three or four balls. Sir Leicester is fidgety down at Chesney Wold, with no better company than the gout; he complains to Mrs. Rouncewell that the rain makes such a monotonous pattering on the terrace that he can't read the paper even by the fireside in his own snug dressing-room.

"Sir Leicester would have done better to try the other side of the house, my dear," says Mrs. Rouncewell to Rosa. "His dressing-room is on my Lady's side. And in all these years I never heard the step upon the Ghost's Walk more distinct than it is to-night!"

CHAPTER XVII
ESTHER'S NARRATIVE

Richard very often came to see us while we remained in London (though he soon failed in his letter-writing), and with his quick abilities, his good spirits, his good temper, his gaiety and freshness, was always delightful. But though I liked him more and more the better I knew him, I still felt more and more how much it was to be regretted that he had been educated in no habits of application and concentration. The system which had addressed him in exactly the same manner as it had addressed hundreds of other boys, all varying in character and capacity, had enabled him to dash through his tasks, always with fair credit and often with distinction, but in a fitful, dazzling way that had confirmed his reliance on those very qualities in himself which it had been most desirable to direct and train. They were good qualities, without which no high place can be meritoriously won, but like fire and water, though excellent servants, they were very bad masters. If they had been under Richard's direction, they would have been his friends; but Richard being under their direction, they became his enemies.

I write down these opinions not because I believe that this or any other thing was so because I thought so, but only because I did think so and I want to be quite candid about all I thought and did. These were my thoughts about Richard. I thought I often observed besides how right my guardian was in what he had said, and that the uncertainties and delays of the Chancery suit had imparted to his nature something of the careless spirit of a gamester who felt that he was part of a great gaming system.

Mr. and Mrs. Bayham Badger coming one afternoon when my guardian was not at home, in the course of conversation I naturally inquired after Richard.

"Why, Mr. Carstone," said Mrs. Badger, "is very well and is, I assure you, a great acquisition to our society. Captain Swosser used to say of me that I was always better than land a-head and a breeze a-starn to the midshipmen's mess when the purser's junk had become as tough as the fore-topsel weather earings. It was his naval way of mentioning generally that I was an acquisition to any society. I may render the same tribute, I am sure, to Mr. Carstone. But I—you won't think me premature if I mention it?"

I said no, as Mrs. Badger's insinuating tone seemed to require such an answer.

"Nor Miss Clare?" said Mrs. Bayham Badger sweetly.

Ada said no, too, and looked uneasy.

"Why, you see, my dears," said Mrs. Badger, "—you'll excuse me calling you my dears?"

We entreated Mrs. Badger not to mention it.

"Because you really are, if I may take the liberty of saying so," pursued Mrs. Badger, "so perfectly charming. You see, my dears, that although I am still young—or Mr. Bayham Badger pays me the compliment of saying so—"

"No," Mr. Badger called out like some one contradicting at a public meeting. "Not at all!"

"Very well," smiled Mrs. Badger, "we will say still young."

"Undoubtedly," said Mr. Badger.

"My dears, though still young, I have had many opportunities of observing young men. There were many such on board the dear old Crippler, I assure you. After that, when I was with Captain Swosser in the Mediterranean, I embraced every opportunity of knowing and befriending the midshipmen under Captain Swosser's command. YOU never heard them called the young gentlemen, my dears, and probably would not understand allusions to their pipe-claying their weekly accounts, but it is otherwise with me, for blue water has been a second home to me, and I have been quite a sailor. Again, with Professor Dingo."

"A man of European reputation," murmured Mr. Badger.

"When I lost my dear first and became the wife of my dear second," said Mrs. Badger, speaking of her former husbands as if they were parts of a charade, "I still enjoyed opportunities of observing youth. The class attendant on Professor Dingo's lectures was a large one, and it became my pride, as the wife of an eminent scientific man seeking herself in science the utmost consolation it could impart, to throw our house open to the students as a kind of Scientific Exchange. Every Tuesday evening there was lemonade and a mixed biscuit for all who chose to partake of those refreshments. And there was science to an unlimited extent."

"Remarkable assemblies those, Miss Summerson," said Mr. Badger reverentially. "There must have been great intellectual friction going on there under the auspices of such a man!"

"And now," pursued Mrs. Badger, "now that I am the wife of my dear third, Mr. Badger, I still pursue those habits of observation which were formed during the lifetime of Captain Swosser and adapted to new and unexpected purposes during the lifetime of Professor Dingo. I therefore have not come to the consideration of Mr. Carstone as a neophyte. And yet I am very much of the opinion, my dears, that he has not chosen his profession advisedly."

Ada looked so very anxious now that I asked Mrs. Badger on what she founded her supposition.

"My dear Miss Summerson," she replied, "on Mr. Carstone's character and conduct. He is of such a very easy disposition that probably he would never think it worth-while to mention how he really feels, but he feels languid about the profession. He has not that positive interest in it which makes it his vocation. If he has any decided impression in reference to it, I should say it was that it is a tiresome pursuit. Now, this is not promising. Young men like Mr. Allan Woodcourt who take it from a strong interest in all that it can do will find some reward in it through a great deal of work for a very little money and through years of considerable endurance and disappointment. But I am quite convinced that this would never be the case with Mr. Carstone."

"Does Mr. Badger think so too?" asked Ada timidly.

"Why," said Mr. Badger, "to tell the truth, Miss Clare, this view of the matter had not occurred to me until Mrs. Badger mentioned it. But when Mrs. Badger put it in that light, I naturally gave great consideration to it, knowing that Mrs. Badger's mind, in addition to its natural advantages, has had the rare advantage of being formed by two such very distinguished (I will even say illustrious) public men as Captain Swosser of the Royal Navy and Professor Dingo. The conclusion at which I have arrived is—in short, is Mrs. Badger's conclusion."

"It was a maxim of Captain Swosser's," said Mrs. Badger, "speaking in his figurative naval manner, that when you make pitch hot, you cannot make it too hot; and that if you only have to swab a plank, you should swab it as if Davy Jones were after you. It appears to me that this maxim is applicable to the medical as well as to the nautical profession.

"To all professions," observed Mr. Badger. "It was admirably said by Captain Swosser. Beautifully said."

"People objected to Professor Dingo when we were staying in the north of Devon after our marriage," said Mrs. Badger, "that he disfigured some of the houses and other buildings by chipping off fragments of those edifices with his little geological hammer. But the professor replied that he knew of no building save the Temple of Science. The principle is the same, I think?"

"Precisely the same," said Mr. Badger. "Finely expressed! The professor made the same remark, Miss Summerson, in his last illness, when (his mind wandering) he insisted on keeping his little hammer under the pillow and chipping at the countenances of the attendants. The ruling passion!"

Although we could have dispensed with the length at which Mr. and Mrs. Badger pursued the conversation, we both felt that it was disinterested in them to express the opinion they had communicated to us and that there was a great probability of its being sound. We agreed to say nothing to Mr. Jarndyce until we had spoken to Richard; and as he was coming next evening, we resolved to have a very serious talk with him.

So after he had been a little while with Ada, I went in and found my darling (as I knew she would be) prepared to consider him thoroughly right in whatever he said.

"And how do you get on, Richard?" said I. I always sat down on the other side of him. He made quite a sister of me.

"Oh! Well enough!" said Richard.

"He can't say better than that, Esther, can he?" cried my pet triumphantly.

I tried to look at my pet in the wisest manner, but of course I couldn't.

"Well enough?" I repeated.

"Yes," said Richard, "well enough. It's rather jog-trotty and humdrum. But it'll do as well as anything else!"

"Oh! My dear Richard!" I remonstrated.

"What's the matter?" said Richard.

"Do as well as anything else!"

"I don't think there's any harm in that, Dame Durden," said Ada, looking so confidingly at me across him; "because if it will do as well as anything else, it will do very well, I hope."

"Oh, yes, I hope so," returned Richard, carelessly tossing his hair from his forehead. "After all, it may be only a kind of probation till our suit is—I forgot though. I am not to mention the suit. Forbidden ground! Oh, yes, it's all right enough. Let us talk about something else."

Ada would have done so willingly, and with a full persuasion that we had brought the question to a most satisfactory state. But I thought it would be useless to stop there, so I began again.

"No, but Richard," said I, "and my dear Ada! Consider how important it is to you both, and what a point of honour it is towards your cousin, that you, Richard, should be quite in earnest without any reservation. I think we had better talk about this, really, Ada. It will be too late very soon."

"Oh, yes! We must talk about it!" said Ada. "But I think Richard is right."

What was the use of my trying to look wise when she was so pretty, and so engaging, and so fond of him!

"Mr. and Mrs. Badger were here yesterday, Richard," said I, "and they seemed disposed to think that you had no great liking for the profession."

"Did they though?" said Richard. "Oh! Well, that rather alters the case, because I had no idea that they thought so, and I should not have liked to disappoint or inconvenience them. The fact is, I don't care much about it. But, oh, it don't matter! It'll do as well as anything else!"

"You hear him, Ada!" said I.

"The fact is," Richard proceeded, half thoughtfully and half jocosely, "it is not quite in my way. I don't take to it. And I get too much of Mrs. Bayham Badger's first and second."

"I am sure THAT'S very natural!" cried Ada, quite delighted. "The very thing we both said yesterday, Esther!"

"Then," pursued Richard, "it's monotonous, and to-day is too like yesterday, and to-morrow is too like to-day."

"But I am afraid," said I, "this is an objection to all kinds of application—to life itself, except under some very uncommon circumstances."

"Do you think so?" returned Richard, still considering. "Perhaps! Ha! Why, then, you know," he added, suddenly becoming gay again, "we travel outside a circle to what I said just now. It'll do as well as anything else. Oh, it's all right enough! Let us talk about something else."

But even Ada, with her loving face—and if it had seemed innocent and trusting when I first saw it in that memorable November fog, how much more did it seem now when I knew her innocent and trusting heart—even Ada shook her head at this and looked serious. So I thought it a good opportunity to hint to Richard that if he were sometimes a little careless of himself, I was very sure he never meant to be careless of Ada, and that it was a part of his affectionate consideration for her not to slight the importance of a step that might influence both their lives. This made him almost grave.

"My dear Mother Hubbard," he said, "that's the very thing! I have thought of that several times and have been quite angry with myself for meaning to be so much in earnest and—somehow—not exactly being so. I don't know how it is; I seem to want something or other to stand by. Even you have no idea how fond I am of Ada (my darling cousin, I love you, so much!), but I don't settle down to constancy in other things. It's such uphill work, and it takes such a time!" said Richard with an air of vexation.

"That may be," I suggested, "because you don't like what you have chosen."

"Poor fellow!" said Ada. "I am sure I don't wonder at it!"

No. It was not of the least use my trying to look wise. I tried again, but how could I do it, or how could it have any effect if I could, while Ada rested her clasped hands upon his shoulder and while he looked at her tender blue eyes, and while they looked at him!

"You see, my precious girl," said Richard, passing her golden curls through and through his hand, "I was a little hasty perhaps; or I misunderstood my own inclinations perhaps. They don't seem to lie in that direction. I couldn't tell till I tried. Now the question is whether it's worth-while to undo all that has been done. It seems like making a great disturbance about nothing particular."

"My dear Richard," said I, "how CAN you say about nothing particular?"

"I don't mean absolutely that," he returned. "I mean that it MAY be nothing particular because I may never want it."

Both Ada and I urged, in reply, not only that it was decidedly worth-while to undo what had been done, but that it must be undone. I then asked Richard whether he had thought of any more congenial pursuit.

"There, my dear Mrs. Shipton," said Richard, "you touch me home. Yes, I have. I have been thinking that the law is the boy for me."

"The law!" repeated Ada as if she were afraid of the name.

"If I went into Kenge's office," said Richard, "and if I were placed under articles to Kenge, I should have my eye on the—hum!—the forbidden ground—and should be able to study it, and master it, and to satisfy myself that it was not neglected and was being properly conducted. I should be able to look after Ada's interests and my own interests (the same thing!); and I should peg away at Blackstone and all those fellows with the most tremendous ardour."

I was not by any means so sure of that, and I saw how his hankering after the vague things yet to come of those long-deferred hopes cast a shade on Ada's face. But I thought it best to encourage him in any project of continuous exertion, and only advised him to be quite sure that his mind was made up now.

"My dear Minerva," said Richard, "I am as steady as you are. I made a mistake; we are all liable to mistakes; I won't do so any more, and I'll become such a lawyer as is not often seen. That is, you know," said Richard, relapsing into doubt, "if it really is worth-while, after all, to make such a disturbance about nothing particular!"

This led to our saying again, with a great deal of gravity, all that we had said already and to our coming to much the same conclusion afterwards. But we so strongly advised Richard to be frank and open with Mr. Jarndyce, without a moment's delay, and his disposition was naturally so opposed to concealment that he sought him out at once (taking us with him) and made a full avowal. "Rick," said my guardian, after hearing him attentively, "we can retreat with honour, and we will. But we must be careful—for our cousin's sake, Rick, for our cousin's sake—that we make no more such mistakes. Therefore, in the matter of the law, we will have a good trial before we decide. We will look before we leap, and take plenty of time about it."

Richard's energy was of such an impatient and fitful kind that he would have liked nothing better than to have gone to Mr. Kenge's office in that hour and to have entered into articles with him on the spot. Submitting, however, with a good grace to the caution that we had shown to be so necessary, he contented himself with sitting down among us in his lightest spirits and talking as if his one unvarying purpose in life from childhood had been that one which now held possession of him. My guardian was very kind and cordial with him, but rather grave, enough so to cause Ada, when he had departed and we were going upstairs to bed, to say, "Cousin John, I hope you don't think the worse of Richard?"

"No, my love," said he.

"Because it was very natural that Richard should be mistaken in such a difficult case. It is not uncommon."

"No, no, my love," said he. "Don't look unhappy."

"Oh, I am not unhappy, cousin John!" said Ada, smiling cheerfully, with her hand upon his shoulder, where she had put it in bidding him good night. "But I should be a little so if you thought at all the worse of Richard."

"My dear," said Mr. Jarndyce, "I should think the worse of him only if you were ever in the least unhappy through his means. I should be more disposed to quarrel with myself even then, than with poor Rick, for I brought you together. But, tut, all this is nothing! He has time before him, and the race to run. I think the worse of him? Not I, my loving cousin! And not you, I swear!"

"No, indeed, cousin John," said Ada, "I am sure I could not—I am sure I would not—think any ill of Richard if the whole world did. I could, and I would, think better of him then than at any other time!"

So quietly and honestly she said it, with her hands upon his shoulders—both hands now—and looking up into his face, like the picture of truth!

"I think," said my guardian, thoughtfully regarding her, "I think it must be somewhere written that the virtues of the mothers shall occasionally be visited on the children, as well as the sins of the father. Good night, my rosebud. Good night, little woman. Pleasant slumbers! Happy dreams!"

This was the first time I ever saw him follow Ada with his eyes with something of a shadow on their benevolent expression. I well remembered the look with which he had contemplated her and Richard when she was singing in the firelight; it was but a very little while since he had watched them passing down the room in which the sun was shining, and away into the shade; but his glance was changed, and even the silent look of confidence in me which now followed it once more was not quite so hopeful and untroubled as it had originally been.

Ada praised Richard more to me that night than ever she had praised him yet. She went to sleep with a little bracelet he had given her clasped upon her arm. I fancied she was dreaming of him when I kissed her cheek after she had slept an hour and saw how tranquil and happy she looked.

For I was so little inclined to sleep myself that night that I sat up working. It would not be worth mentioning for its own sake, but I was wakeful and rather low-spirited. I don't know why. At least I don't think I know why. At least, perhaps I do, but I don't think it matters.

At any rate, I made up my mind to be so dreadfully industrious that I would leave myself not a moment's leisure to be low-spirited. For I naturally said, "Esther! You to be low-spirited. YOU!" And it really was time to say so, for I—yes, I really did see myself in the glass, almost crying. "As if you had anything to make you unhappy, instead of everything to make you happy, you ungrateful heart!" said I.

If I could have made myself go to sleep, I would have done it directly, but not being able to do that, I took out of my basket some ornamental work for our house (I mean Bleak House) that I was busy with at that time and sat down to it with great determination. It was necessary to count all the stitches in that work, and I resolved to go on with it until I couldn't keep my eyes open, and then to go to bed.

I soon found myself very busy. But I had left some silk downstairs in a work-table drawer in the temporary growlery, and coming to a stop for want of it, I took my candle and went softly down to get it. To my great surprise, on going in I found my guardian still there, and sitting looking at the ashes. He was lost in thought, his book lay unheeded by his side, his silvered iron-grey hair was scattered confusedly upon his forehead as though his hand had been wandering among it while his thoughts were elsewhere, and his face looked worn. Almost frightened by coming upon him so unexpectedly, I stood still for a moment and should have retired without speaking had he not, in again passing his hand abstractedly through his hair, seen me and started.

"Esther!"

I told him what I had come for.

"At work so late, my dear?"

"I am working late to-night," said I, "because I couldn't sleep and wished to tire myself. But, dear guardian, you are late too, and look weary. You have no trouble, I hope, to keep you waking?"

"None, little woman, that YOU would readily understand," said he.

He spoke in a regretful tone so new to me that I inwardly repeated, as if that would help me to his meaning, "That I could readily understand!"

"Remain a moment, Esther," said he, "You were in my thoughts."

"I hope I was not the trouble, guardian?"

He slightly waved his hand and fell into his usual manner. The change was so remarkable, and he appeared to make it by dint of so much self-command, that I found myself again inwardly repeating, "None that I could understand!"

"Little woman," said my guardian, "I was thinking—that is, I have been thinking since I have been sitting here—that you ought to know of your own history all I know. It is very little. Next to nothing."

"Dear guardian," I replied, "when you spoke to me before on that subject—"

"But since then," he gravely interposed, anticipating what I meant to say, "I have reflected that your having anything to ask me, and my having anything to tell you, are different considerations, Esther. It is perhaps my duty to impart to you the little I know."

"If you think so, guardian, it is right."

"I think so," he returned very gently, and kindly, and very distinctly. "My dear, I think so now. If any real disadvantage can attach to your position in the mind of any man or woman worth a thought, it is right that you at least of all the world should not magnify it to yourself by having vague impressions of its nature."

I sat down and said after a little effort to be as calm as I ought to be, "One of my earliest remembrances, guardian, is of these words: 'Your mother, Esther, is your disgrace, and you were hers. The time will come, and soon enough, when you will understand this better, and will feel it too, as no one save a woman can.'" I had covered my face with my hands in repeating the words, but I took them away now with a better kind of shame, I hope, and told him that to him I owed the blessing that I had from my childhood to that hour never, never, never felt it. He put up his hand as if to stop me. I well knew that he was never to be thanked, and said no more.

"Nine years, my dear," he said after thinking for a little while, "have passed since I received a letter from a lady living in seclusion, written with a stern passion and power that rendered it unlike all other letters I have ever read. It was written to me (as it told me in so many words), perhaps because it was the writer's idiosyncrasy to put that trust in me, perhaps because it was mine to justify it. It told me of a child, an orphan girl then twelve years old, in some such cruel words as those which live in your remembrance. It told me that the writer had bred her in secrecy from her birth, had blotted out all trace of her existence, and that if the writer were to die before the child became a woman, she would be left entirely friendless, nameless, and unknown. It asked me to consider if I would, in that case, finish what the writer had begun."

I listened in silence and looked attentively at him.

"Your early recollection, my dear, will supply the gloomy medium through which all this was seen and expressed by the writer, and the distorted religion which clouded her mind with impressions of the need there was for the child to expiate an offence of which she was quite innocent. I felt concerned for the little creature, in her darkened life, and replied to the letter."

I took his hand and kissed it.

"It laid the injunction on me that I should never propose to see the writer, who had long been estranged from all intercourse with the world, but who would see a confidential agent if I would appoint one. I accredited Mr. Kenge. The lady said, of her own accord and not of his seeking, that her name was an assumed one. That she was, if there were any ties of blood in such a case, the child's aunt. That more than this she would never (and he was well persuaded of the steadfastness of her resolution) for any human consideration disclose. My dear, I have told you all."

I held his hand for a little while in mine.

"I saw my ward oftener than she saw me," he added, cheerily making light of it, "and I always knew she was beloved, useful, and happy. She repays me twenty-thousandfold, and twenty more to that, every hour in every day!"

"And oftener still," said I, "she blesses the guardian who is a father to her!"

At the word father, I saw his former trouble come into his face. He subdued it as before, and it was gone in an instant; but it had been there and it had come so swiftly upon my words that I felt as if they had given him a shock. I again inwardly repeated, wondering, "That I could readily understand. None that I could readily understand!" No, it was true. I did not understand it. Not for many and many a day.

"Take a fatherly good night, my dear," said he, kissing me on the forehead, "and so to rest. These are late hours for working and thinking. You do that for all of us, all day long, little housekeeper!"

I neither worked nor thought any more that night. I opened my grateful heart to heaven in thankfulness for its providence to me and its care of me, and fell asleep.

We had a visitor next day. Mr. Allan Woodcourt came. He came to take leave of us; he had settled to do so beforehand. He was going to China and to India as a surgeon on board ship. He was to be away a long, long time.

I believe—at least I know—that he was not rich. All his widowed mother could spare had been spent in qualifying him for his profession. It was not lucrative to a young practitioner, with very little influence in London; and although he was, night and day, at the service of numbers of poor people and did wonders of gentleness and skill for them, he gained very little by it in money. He was seven years older than I. Not that I need mention it, for it hardly seems to belong to anything.

I think—I mean, he told us—that he had been in practice three or four years and that if he could have hoped to contend through three or four more, he would not have made the voyage on which he was bound. But he had no fortune or private means, and so he was going away. He had been to see us several times altogether. We thought it a pity he should go away. Because he was distinguished in his art among those who knew it best, and some of the greatest men belonging to it had a high opinion of him.

When he came to bid us good-bye, he brought his mother with him for the first time. She was a pretty old lady, with bright black eyes, but she seemed proud. She came from Wales and had had, a long time ago, an eminent person for an ancestor, of the name of Morgan ap-Kerrig—of some place that sounded like Gimlet—who was the most illustrious person that ever was known and all of whose relations were a sort of royal family. He appeared to have passed his life in always getting up into mountains and fighting somebody; and a bard whose name sounded like Crumlinwallinwer had sung his praises in a piece which was called, as nearly as I could catch it, Mewlinnwillinwodd.

Mrs. Woodcourt, after expatiating to us on the fame of her great kinsman, said that no doubt wherever her son Allan went he would remember his pedigree and would on no account form an alliance below it. She told him that there were many handsome English ladies in India who went out on speculation, and that there were some to be picked up with property, but that neither charms nor wealth would suffice for the descendant from such a line without birth, which must ever be the first consideration. She talked so much about birth that for a moment I half fancied, and with pain—But what an idle fancy to suppose that she could think or care what MINE was!

Mr. Woodcourt seemed a little distressed by her prolixity, but he was too considerate to let her see it and contrived delicately to bring the conversation round to making his acknowledgments to my guardian for his hospitality and for the very happy hours—he called them the very happy hours—he had passed with us. The recollection of them, he said, would go with him wherever he went and would be always treasured. And so we gave him our hands, one after another—at least, they did—and I did; and so he put his lips to Ada's hand—and to mine; and so he went away upon his long, long voyage!

I was very busy indeed all day and wrote directions home to the servants, and wrote notes for my guardian, and dusted his books and papers, and jingled my housekeeping keys a good deal, one way and another. I was still busy between the lights, singing and working by the window, when who should come in but Caddy, whom I had no expectation of seeing!

"Why, Caddy, my dear," said I, "what beautiful flowers!"

She had such an exquisite little nosegay in her hand.

"Indeed, I think so, Esther," replied Caddy. "They are the loveliest I ever saw."

"Prince, my dear?" said I in a whisper.

"No," answered Caddy, shaking her head and holding them to me to smell. "Not Prince."

"Well, to be sure, Caddy!" said I. "You must have two lovers!"

"What? Do they look like that sort of thing?" said Caddy.

"Do they look like that sort of thing?" I repeated, pinching her cheek.

Caddy only laughed in return, and telling me that she had come for half an hour, at the expiration of which time Prince would be waiting for her at the corner, sat chatting with me and Ada in the window, every now and then handing me the flowers again or trying how they looked against my hair. At last, when she was going, she took me into my room and put them in my dress.

"For me?" said I, surprised.

"For you," said Caddy with a kiss. "They were left behind by somebody."

"Left behind?"

"At poor Miss Flite's," said Caddy. "Somebody who has been very good to her was hurrying away an hour ago to join a ship and left these flowers behind. No, no! Don't take them out. Let the pretty little things lie here," said Caddy, adjusting them with a careful hand, "because I was present myself, and I shouldn't wonder if somebody left them on purpose!"

"Do they look like that sort of thing?" said Ada, coming laughingly behind me and clasping me merrily round the waist. "Oh, yes, indeed they do, Dame Durden! They look very, very like that sort of thing. Oh, very like it indeed, my dear!"

CHAPTER XVIII
LADY DEDLOCK

It was not so easy as it had appeared at first to arrange for Richard's making a trial of Mr. Kenge's office. Richard himself was the chief impediment. As soon as he had it in his power to leave Mr. Badger at any moment, he began to doubt whether he wanted to leave him at all. He didn't know, he said, really. It wasn't a bad profession; he couldn't assert that he disliked it; perhaps he liked it as well as he liked any other—suppose he gave it one more chance! Upon that, he shut himself up for a few weeks with some books and some bones and seemed to acquire a considerable fund of information with great rapidity. His fervour, after lasting about a month, began to cool, and when it was quite cooled, began to grow warm again. His vacillations between law and medicine lasted so long that midsummer arrived before he finally separated from Mr. Badger and entered on an experimental course of Messrs. Kenge and Carboy. For all his waywardness, he took great credit to himself as being determined to be in earnest "this time." And he was so good-natured throughout, and in such high spirits, and so fond of Ada, that it was very difficult indeed to be otherwise than pleased with him.

"As to Mr. Jarndyce," who, I may mention, found the wind much given, during this period, to stick in the east; "As to Mr. Jarndyce," Richard would say to me, "he is the finest fellow in the world, Esther! I must be particularly careful, if it were only for his satisfaction, to take myself well to task and have a regular wind-up of this business now."

The idea of his taking himself well to task, with that laughing face and heedless manner and with a fancy that everything could catch and nothing could hold, was ludicrously anomalous. However, he told us between-whiles that he was doing it to such an extent that he wondered his hair didn't turn grey. His regular wind-up of the business was (as I have said) that he went to Mr. Kenge's about midsummer to try how he liked it.

All this time he was, in money affairs, what I have described him in a former illustration—generous, profuse, wildly careless, but fully persuaded that he was rather calculating and prudent. I happened to say to Ada, in his presence, half jestingly, half seriously, about the time of his going to Mr. Kenge's, that he needed to have Fortunatus' purse, he made so light of money, which he answered in this way, "My jewel of a dear cousin, you hear this old woman! Why does she say that? Because I gave eight pounds odd (or whatever it was) for a certain neat waistcoat and buttons a few days ago. Now, if I had stayed at Badger's I should have been obliged to spend twelve pounds at a blow for some heart-breaking lecture-fees. So I make four pounds—in a lump—by the transaction!"

It was a question much discussed between him and my guardian what arrangements should be made for his living in London while he experimented on the law, for we had long since gone back to Bleak House, and it was too far off to admit of his coming there oftener than once a week. My guardian told me that if Richard were to settle down at Mr. Kenge's he would take some apartments or chambers where we too could occasionally stay for a few days at a time; "but, little woman," he added, rubbing his head very significantly, "he hasn't settled down there yet!" The discussions ended in our hiring for him, by the month, a neat little furnished lodging in a quiet old house near Queen Square. He immediately began to spend all the money he had in buying the oddest little ornaments and luxuries for this lodging; and so often as Ada and I dissuaded him from making any purchase that he had in contemplation which was particularly unnecessary and expensive, he took credit for what it would have cost and made out that to spend anything less on something else was to save the difference.

While these affairs were in abeyance, our visit to Mr. Boythorn's was postponed. At length, Richard having taken possession of his lodging, there was nothing to prevent our departure. He could have gone with us at that time of the year very well, but he was in the full novelty of his new position and was making most energetic attempts to unravel the mysteries of the fatal suit. Consequently we went without him, and my darling was delighted to praise him for being so busy.

We made a pleasant journey down into Lincolnshire by the coach and had an entertaining companion in Mr. Skimpole. His furniture had been all cleared off, it appeared, by the person who took possession of it on his blue-eyed daughter's birthday, but he seemed quite relieved to think that it was gone. Chairs and table, he said, were wearisome objects; they were monotonous ideas, they had no variety of expression, they looked you out of countenance, and you looked them out of countenance. How pleasant, then, to be bound to no particular chairs and tables, but to sport like a butterfly among all the furniture on hire, and to flit from rosewood to mahogany, and from mahogany to walnut, and from this shape to that, as the humour took one!

"The oddity of the thing is," said Mr. Skimpole with a quickened sense of the ludicrous, "that my chairs and tables were not paid for, and yet my landlord walks off with them as composedly as possible. Now, that seems droll! There is something grotesque in it. The chair and table merchant never engaged to pay my landlord my rent. Why should my landlord quarrel with HIM? If I have a pimple on my nose which is disagreeable to my landlord's peculiar ideas of beauty, my landlord has no business to scratch my chair and table merchant's nose, which has no pimple on it. His reasoning seems defective!"

"Well," said my guardian good-humouredly, "it's pretty clear that whoever became security for those chairs and tables will have to pay for them."

"Exactly!" returned Mr. Skimpole. "That's the crowning point of unreason in the business! I said to my landlord, 'My good man, you are not aware that my excellent friend Jarndyce will have to pay for those things that you are sweeping off in that indelicate manner. Have you no consideration for HIS property?' He hadn't the least."

"And refused all proposals," said my guardian.

"Refused all proposals," returned Mr. Skimpole. "I made him business proposals. I had him into my room. I said, 'You are a man of business, I believe?' He replied, 'I am,' 'Very well,' said I, 'now let us be business-like. Here is an inkstand, here are pens and paper, here are wafers. What do you want? I have occupied your house for a considerable period, I believe to our mutual satisfaction until this unpleasant misunderstanding arose; let us be at once friendly and business-like. What do you want?' In reply to this, he made use of the figurative expression—which has something Eastern about it—that he had never seen the colour of my money. 'My amiable friend,' said I, 'I never have any money. I never know anything about money.' 'Well, sir,' said he, 'what do you offer if I give you time?' 'My good fellow,' said I, 'I have no idea of time; but you say you are a man of business, and whatever you can suggest to be done in a business-like way with pen, and ink, and paper—and wafers—I am ready to do. Don't pay yourself at another man's expense (which is foolish), but be business-like!' However, he wouldn't be, and there was an end of it."

If these were some of the inconveniences of Mr. Skimpole's childhood, it assuredly possessed its advantages too. On the journey he had a very good appetite for such refreshment as came in our way (including a basket of choice hothouse peaches), but never thought of paying for anything. So when the coachman came round for his fee, he pleasantly asked him what he considered a very good fee indeed, now—a liberal one—and on his replying half a crown for a single passenger, said it was little enough too, all things considered, and left Mr. Jarndyce to give it him.

It was delightful weather. The green corn waved so beautifully, the larks sang so joyfully, the hedges were so full of wild flowers, the trees were so thickly out in leaf, the bean-fields, with a light wind blowing over them, filled the air with such a delicious fragrance! Late in the afternoon we came to the market-town where we were to alight from the coach—a dull little town with a church-spire, and a marketplace, and a market-cross, and one intensely sunny street, and a pond with an old horse cooling his legs in it, and a very few men sleepily lying and standing about in narrow little bits of shade. After the rustling of the leaves and the waving of the corn all along the road, it looked as still, as hot, as motionless a little town as England could produce.

At the inn we found Mr. Boythorn on horseback, waiting with an open carriage to take us to his house, which was a few miles off. He was overjoyed to see us and dismounted with great alacrity.

"By heaven!" said he after giving us a courteous greeting. "This a most infamous coach. It is the most flagrant example of an abominable public vehicle that ever encumbered the face of the earth. It is twenty-five minutes after its time this afternoon. The coachman ought to be put to death!"

"IS he after his time?" said Mr. Skimpole, to whom he happened to address himself. "You know my infirmity."

"Twenty-five minutes! Twenty-six minutes!" replied Mr. Boythorn, referring to his watch. "With two ladies in the coach, this scoundrel has deliberately delayed his arrival six and twenty minutes. Deliberately! It is impossible that it can be accidental! But his father—and his uncle—were the most profligate coachmen that ever sat upon a box."

While he said this in tones of the greatest indignation, he handed us into the little phaeton with the utmost gentleness and was all smiles and pleasure.

"I am sorry, ladies," he said, standing bare-headed at the carriage-door when all was ready, "that I am obliged to conduct you nearly two miles out of the way. But our direct road lies through Sir Leicester Dedlock's park, and in that fellow's property I have sworn never to set foot of mine, or horse's foot of mine, pending the present relations between us, while I breathe the breath of life!" And here, catching my guardian's eye, he broke into one of his tremendous laughs, which seemed to shake even the motionless little market-town.

"Are the Dedlocks down here, Lawrence?" said my guardian as we drove along and Mr. Boythorn trotted on the green turf by the roadside.

"Sir Arrogant Numskull is here," replied Mr. Boythorn. "Ha ha ha! Sir Arrogant is here, and I am glad to say, has been laid by the heels here. My Lady," in naming whom he always made a courtly gesture as if particularly to exclude her from any part in the quarrel, "is expected, I believe, daily. I am not in the least surprised that she postpones her appearance as long as possible. Whatever can have induced that transcendent woman to marry that effigy and figure-head of a baronet is one of the most impenetrable mysteries that ever baffled human inquiry. Ha ha ha ha!"

"I suppose," said my guardian, laughing, "WE may set foot in the park while we are here? The prohibition does not extend to us, does it?"

"I can lay no prohibition on my guests," he said, bending his head to Ada and me with the smiling politeness which sat so gracefully upon him, "except in the matter of their departure. I am only sorry that I cannot have the happiness of being their escort about Chesney Wold, which is a very fine place! But by the light of this summer day, Jarndyce, if you call upon the owner while you stay with me, you are likely to have but a cool reception. He carries himself like an eight-day clock at all times, like one of a race of eight-day clocks in gorgeous cases that never go and never went—Ha ha ha!—but he will have some extra stiffness, I can promise you, for the friends of his friend and neighbour Boythorn!"

"I shall not put him to the proof," said my guardian. "He is as indifferent to the honour of knowing me, I dare say, as I am to the honour of knowing him. The air of the grounds and perhaps such a view of the house as any other sightseer might get are quite enough for me."

"Well!" said Mr. Boythorn. "I am glad of it on the whole. It's in better keeping. I am looked upon about here as a second Ajax defying the lightning. Ha ha ha ha! When I go into our little church on a Sunday, a considerable part of the inconsiderable congregation expect to see me drop, scorched and withered, on the pavement under the Dedlock displeasure. Ha ha ha ha! I have no doubt he is surprised that I don't. For he is, by heaven, the most self-satisfied, and the shallowest, and the most coxcombical and utterly brainless ass!"

Our coming to the ridge of a hill we had been ascending enabled our friend to point out Chesney Wold itself to us and diverted his attention from its master.

It was a picturesque old house in a fine park richly wooded. Among the trees and not far from the residence he pointed out the spire of the little church of which he had spoken. Oh, the solemn woods over which the light and shadow travelled swiftly, as if heavenly wings were sweeping on benignant errands through the summer air; the smooth green slopes, the glittering water, the garden where the flowers were so symmetrically arranged in clusters of the richest colours, how beautiful they looked! The house, with gable and chimney, and tower, and turret, and dark doorway, and broad terrace-walk, twining among the balustrades of which, and lying heaped upon the vases, there was one great flush of roses, seemed scarcely real in its light solidity and in the serene and peaceful hush that rested on all around it. To Ada and to me, that above all appeared the pervading influence. On everything, house, garden, terrace, green slopes, water, old oaks, fern, moss, woods again, and far away across the openings in the prospect to the distance lying wide before us with a purple bloom upon it, there seemed to be such undisturbed repose.

When we came into the little village and passed a small inn with the sign of the Dedlock Arms swinging over the road in front, Mr. Boythorn interchanged greetings with a young gentleman sitting on a bench outside the inn-door who had some fishing-tackle lying beside him.

"That's the housekeeper's grandson, Mr. Rouncewell by name," said, he, "and he is in love with a pretty girl up at the house. Lady Dedlock has taken a fancy to the pretty girl and is going to keep her about her own fair person—an honour which my young friend himself does not at all appreciate. However, he can't marry just yet, even if his Rosebud were willing; so he is fain to make the best of it. In the meanwhile, he comes here pretty often for a day or two at a time to—fish. Ha ha ha ha!"

"Are he and the pretty girl engaged, Mr. Boythorn?" asked Ada.

"Why, my dear Miss Clare," he returned, "I think they may perhaps understand each other; but you will see them soon, I dare say, and I must learn from you on such a point—not you from me."

Ada blushed, and Mr. Boythorn, trotting forward on his comely grey horse, dismounted at his own door and stood ready with extended arm and uncovered head to welcome us when we arrived.

He lived in a pretty house, formerly the parsonage house, with a lawn in front, a bright flower-garden at the side, and a well-stocked orchard and kitchen-garden in the rear, enclosed with a venerable wall that had of itself a ripened ruddy look. But, indeed, everything about the place wore an aspect of maturity and abundance. The old lime-tree walk was like green cloisters, the very shadows of the cherry-trees and apple-trees were heavy with fruit, the gooseberry-bushes were so laden that their branches arched and rested on the earth, the strawberries and raspberries grew in like profusion, and the peaches basked by the hundred on the wall. Tumbled about among the spread nets and the glass frames sparkling and winking in the sun there were such heaps of drooping pods, and marrows, and cucumbers, that every foot of ground appeared a vegetable treasury, while the smell of sweet herbs and all kinds of wholesome growth (to say nothing of the neighbouring meadows where the hay was carrying) made the whole air a great nosegay. Such stillness and composure reigned within the orderly precincts of the old red wall that even the feathers hung in garlands to scare the birds hardly stirred; and the wall had such a ripening influence that where, here and there high up, a disused nail and scrap of list still clung to it, it was easy to fancy that they had mellowed with the changing seasons and that they had rusted and decayed according to the common fate.

The house, though a little disorderly in comparison with the garden, was a real old house with settles in the chimney of the brick-floored kitchen and great beams across the ceilings. On one side of it was the terrible piece of ground in dispute, where Mr. Boythorn maintained a sentry in a smock-frock day and night, whose duty was supposed to be, in cases of aggression, immediately to ring a large bell hung up there for the purpose, to unchain a great bull-dog established in a kennel as his ally, and generally to deal destruction on the enemy. Not content with these precautions, Mr. Boythorn had himself composed and posted there, on painted boards to which his name was attached in large letters, the following solemn warnings: "Beware of the bull-dog. He is most ferocious. Lawrence Boythorn." "The blunderbus is loaded with slugs. Lawrence Boythorn." "Man-traps and spring-guns are set here at all times of the day and night. Lawrence Boythorn." "Take notice. That any person or persons audaciously presuming to trespass on this property will be punished with the utmost severity of private chastisement and prosecuted with the utmost rigour of the law. Lawrence Boythorn." These he showed us from the drawing-room window, while his bird was hopping about his head, and he laughed, "Ha ha ha ha! Ha ha ha ha!" to that extent as he pointed them out that I really thought he would have hurt himself.

"But this is taking a good deal of trouble," said Mr. Skimpole in his light way, "when you are not in earnest after all."

"Not in earnest!" returned Mr. Boythorn with unspeakable warmth. "Not in earnest! If I could have hoped to train him, I would have bought a lion instead of that dog and would have turned him loose upon the first intolerable robber who should dare to make an encroachment on my rights. Let Sir Leicester Dedlock consent to come out and decide this question by single combat, and I will meet him with any weapon known to mankind in any age or country. I am that much in earnest. Not more!"

We arrived at his house on a Saturday. On the Sunday morning we all set forth to walk to the little church in the park. Entering the park, almost immediately by the disputed ground, we pursued a pleasant footpath winding among the verdant turf and the beautiful trees until it brought us to the church-porch.

The congregation was extremely small and quite a rustic one with the exception of a large muster of servants from the house, some of whom were already in their seats, while others were yet dropping in. There were some stately footmen, and there was a perfect picture of an old coachman, who looked as if he were the official representative of all the pomps and vanities that had ever been put into his coach. There was a very pretty show of young women, and above them, the handsome old face and fine responsible portly figure of the housekeeper towered pre-eminent. The pretty girl of whom Mr. Boythorn had told us was close by her. She was so very pretty that I might have known her by her beauty even if I had not seen how blushingly conscious she was of the eyes of the young fisherman, whom I discovered not far off. One face, and not an agreeable one, though it was handsome, seemed maliciously watchful of this pretty girl, and indeed of every one and everything there. It was a Frenchwoman's.

As the bell was yet ringing and the great people were not yet come, I had leisure to glance over the church, which smelt as earthy as a grave, and to think what a shady, ancient, solemn little church it was. The windows, heavily shaded by trees, admitted a subdued light that made the faces around me pale, and darkened the old brasses in the pavement and the time and damp-worn monuments, and rendered the sunshine in the little porch, where a monotonous ringer was working at the bell, inestimably bright. But a stir in that direction, a gathering of reverential awe in the rustic faces, and a blandly ferocious assumption on the part of Mr. Boythorn of being resolutely unconscious of somebody's existence forewarned me that the great people were come and that the service was going to begin.

"'Enter not into judgment with thy servant, O Lord, for in thy sight—'"

Shall I ever forget the rapid beating at my heart, occasioned by the look I met as I stood up! Shall I ever forget the manner in which those handsome proud eyes seemed to spring out of their languor and to hold mine! It was only a moment before I cast mine down—released again, if I may say so—on my book; but I knew the beautiful face quite well in that short space of time.

And, very strangely, there was something quickened within me, associated with the lonely days at my godmother's; yes, away even to the days when I had stood on tiptoe to dress myself at my little glass after dressing my doll. And this, although I had never seen this lady's face before in all my life—I was quite sure of it—absolutely certain.

It was easy to know that the ceremonious, gouty, grey-haired gentleman, the only other occupant of the great pew, was Sir Leicester Dedlock, and that the lady was Lady Dedlock. But why her face should be, in a confused way, like a broken glass to me, in which I saw scraps of old remembrances, and why I should be so fluttered and troubled (for I was still) by having casually met her eyes, I could not think.

I felt it to be an unmeaning weakness in me and tried to overcome it by attending to the words I heard. Then, very strangely, I seemed to hear them, not in the reader's voice, but in the well-remembered voice of my godmother. This made me think, did Lady Dedlock's face accidentally resemble my godmother's? It might be that it did, a little; but the expression was so different, and the stern decision which had worn into my godmother's face, like weather into rocks, was so completely wanting in the face before me that it could not be that resemblance which had struck me. Neither did I know the loftiness and haughtiness of Lady Dedlock's face, at all, in any one. And yet I—I, little Esther Summerson, the child who lived a life apart and on whose birthday there was no rejoicing—seemed to arise before my own eyes, evoked out of the past by some power in this fashionable lady, whom I not only entertained no fancy that I had ever seen, but whom I perfectly well knew I had never seen until that hour.

It made me tremble so to be thrown into this unaccountable agitation that I was conscious of being distressed even by the observation of the French maid, though I knew she had been looking watchfully here, and there, and everywhere, from the moment of her coming into the church. By degrees, though very slowly, I at last overcame my strange emotion. After a long time, I looked towards Lady Dedlock again. It was while they were preparing to sing, before the sermon. She took no heed of me, and the beating at my heart was gone. Neither did it revive for more than a few moments when she once or twice afterwards glanced at Ada or at me through her glass.

The service being concluded, Sir Leicester gave his arm with much taste and gallantry to Lady Dedlock—though he was obliged to walk by the help of a thick stick—and escorted her out of church to the pony carriage in which they had come. The servants then dispersed, and so did the congregation, whom Sir Leicester had contemplated all along (Mr. Skimpole said to Mr. Boythorn's infinite delight) as if he were a considerable landed proprietor in heaven.

"He believes he is!" said Mr. Boythorn. "He firmly believes it. So did his father, and his grandfather, and his great-grandfather!"

"Do you know," pursued Mr. Skimpole very unexpectedly to Mr. Boythorn, "it's agreeable to me to see a man of that sort."

"IS it!" said Mr. Boythorn.

"Say that he wants to patronize me," pursued Mr. Skimpole. "Very well! I don't object."

"I do," said Mr. Boythorn with great vigour.

"Do you really?" returned Mr. Skimpole in his easy light vein. "But that's taking trouble, surely. And why should you take trouble? Here am I, content to receive things childishly as they fall out, and I never take trouble! I come down here, for instance, and I find a mighty potentate exacting homage. Very well! I say 'Mighty potentate, here IS my homage! It's easier to give it than to withhold it. Here it is. If you have anything of an agreeable nature to show me, I shall be happy to see it; if you have anything of an agreeable nature to give me, I shall be happy to accept it.' Mighty potentate replies in effect, 'This is a sensible fellow. I find him accord with my digestion and my bilious system. He doesn't impose upon me the necessity of rolling myself up like a hedgehog with my points outward. I expand, I open, I turn my silver lining outward like Milton's cloud, and it's more agreeable to both of us.' That's my view of such things, speaking as a child!"

"But suppose you went down somewhere else to-morrow," said Mr. Boythorn, "where there was the opposite of that fellow—or of this fellow. How then?"

"How then?" said Mr. Skimpole with an appearance of the utmost simplicity and candour. "Just the same then! I should say, 'My esteemed Boythorn'—to make you the personification of our imaginary friend—'my esteemed Boythorn, you object to the mighty potentate? Very good. So do I. I take it that my business in the social system is to be agreeable; I take it that everybody's business in the social system is to be agreeable. It's a system of harmony, in short. Therefore if you object, I object. Now, excellent Boythorn, let us go to dinner!'"

"But excellent Boythorn might say," returned our host, swelling and growing very red, "I'll be—"

"I understand," said Mr. Skimpole. "Very likely he would."

"—if I WILL go to dinner!" cried Mr. Boythorn in a violent burst and stopping to strike his stick upon the ground. "And he would probably add, 'Is there such a thing as principle, Mr. Harold Skimpole?'"

"To which Harold Skimpole would reply, you know," he returned in his gayest manner and with his most ingenuous smile, "'Upon my life I have not the least idea! I don't know what it is you call by that name, or where it is, or who possesses it. If you possess it and find it comfortable, I am quite delighted and congratulate you heartily. But I know nothing about it, I assure you; for

I am a mere child, and I lay no claim to it, and I don't want it!' So, you see, excellent Boythorn and I would go to dinner after all!"

This was one of many little dialogues between them which I always expected to end, and which I dare say would have ended under other circumstances, in some violent explosion on the part of our host. But he had so high a sense of his hospitable and responsible position as our entertainer, and my guardian laughed so sincerely at and with Mr. Skimpole, as a child who blew bubbles and broke them all day long, that matters never went beyond this point. Mr. Skimpole, who always seemed quite unconscious of having been on delicate ground, then betook himself to beginning some sketch in the park which he never finished, or to playing fragments of airs on the piano, or to singing scraps of songs, or to lying down on his back under a tree and looking at the sky—which he couldn't help thinking, he said, was what he was meant for; it suited him so exactly.

"Enterprise and effort," he would say to us (on his back), "are delightful to me. I believe I am truly cosmopolitan. I have the deepest sympathy with them. I lie in a shady place like this and think of adventurous spirits going to the North Pole or penetrating to the heart of the Torrid Zone with admiration. Mercenary creatures ask, 'What is the use of a man's going to the North Pole? What good does it do?' I can't say; but, for anything I CAN say, he may go for the purpose—though he don't know it—of employing my thoughts as I lie here. Take an extreme case. Take the case of the slaves on American plantations. I dare say they are worked hard, I dare say they don't altogether like it. I dare say theirs is an unpleasant experience on the whole; but they people the landscape for me, they give it a poetry for me, and perhaps that is one of the pleasanter objects of their existence. I am very sensible of it, if it be, and I shouldn't wonder if it were!"

I always wondered on these occasions whether he ever thought of Mrs. Skimpole and the children, and in what point of view they presented themselves to his cosmopolitan mind. So far as I could understand, they rarely presented themselves at all.

The week had gone round to the Saturday following that beating of my heart in the church; and every day had been so bright and blue that to ramble in the woods, and to see the light striking down among the transparent leaves and sparkling in the beautiful interlacings of the shadows of the trees, while the birds poured out their songs and the air was drowsy with the hum of insects, had been most delightful. We had one favourite spot, deep in moss and last year's leaves, where there were some felled trees from which the bark was all stripped off. Seated among these, we looked through a green vista supported by thousands of natural columns, the whitened stems of trees, upon a distant prospect made so radiant by its contrast with the shade in which we sat and made so precious by the arched perspective through which we saw it that it was like a glimpse of the better land. Upon the Saturday we sat here,

Mr. Jarndyce, Ada, and I, until we heard thunder muttering in the distance and felt the large raindrops rattle through the leaves.

The weather had been all the week extremely sultry, but the storm broke so suddenly—upon us, at least, in that sheltered spot—that before we reached the outskirts of the wood the thunder and lightning were frequent and the rain came plunging through the leaves as if every drop were a great leaden bead. As it was not a time for standing among trees, we ran out of the wood, and up and down the moss-grown steps which crossed the plantation-fence like two broad-staved ladders placed back to back, and made for a keeper's lodge which was close at hand. We had often noticed the dark beauty of this lodge standing in a deep twilight of trees, and how the ivy clustered over it, and how there was a steep hollow near, where we had once seen the keeper's dog dive down into the fern as if it were water.

The lodge was so dark within, now the sky was overcast, that we only clearly saw the man who came to the door when we took shelter there and put two chairs for Ada and me. The lattice-windows were all thrown open, and we sat just within the doorway watching the storm. It was grand to see how the wind awoke, and bent the trees, and drove the rain before it like a cloud of smoke; and to hear the solemn thunder and to see the lightning; and while thinking with awe of the tremendous powers by which our little lives are encompassed, to consider how beneficent they are and how upon the smallest flower and leaf there was already a freshness poured from all this seeming rage which seemed to make creation new again.

"Is it not dangerous to sit in so exposed a place?"

"Oh, no, Esther dear!" said Ada quietly.

Ada said it to me, but I had not spoken.

The beating of my heart came back again. I had never heard the voice, as I had never seen the face, but it affected me in the same strange way. Again, in a moment, there arose before my mind innumerable pictures of myself.

Lady Dedlock had taken shelter in the lodge before our arrival there and had come out of the gloom within. She stood behind my chair with her hand upon it. I saw her with her hand close to my shoulder when I turned my head.

"I have frightened you?" she said.

No. It was not fright. Why should I be frightened!

"I believe," said Lady Dedlock to my guardian, "I have the pleasure of speaking to Mr. Jarndyce."

"Your remembrance does me more honour than I had supposed it would, Lady Dedlock," he returned.

"I recognized you in church on Sunday. I am sorry that any local disputes of Sir Leicester's—they are not of his seeking, however, I believe—should render it a matter of some absurd difficulty to show you any attention here."

"I am aware of the circumstances," returned my guardian with a smile, "and am sufficiently obliged."

She had given him her hand in an indifferent way that seemed habitual to her and spoke in a correspondingly indifferent manner, though in a very pleasant voice. She was as graceful as she was beautiful, perfectly self-possessed, and had the air, I thought, of being able to attract and interest any one if she had thought it worth her while. The keeper had brought her a chair on which she sat in the middle of the porch between us.

"Is the young gentleman disposed of whom you wrote to Sir Leicester about and whose wishes Sir Leicester was sorry not to have it in his power to advance in any way?" she said over her shoulder to my guardian.

"I hope so," said he.

She seemed to respect him and even to wish to conciliate him. There was something very winning in her haughty manner, and it became more familiar—I was going to say more easy, but that could hardly be—as she spoke to him over her shoulder.

"I presume this is your other ward, Miss Clare?"

He presented Ada, in form.

"You will lose the disinterested part of your Don Quixote character," said Lady Dedlock to Mr. Jarndyce over her shoulder again, "if you only redress the wrongs of beauty like this. But present me," and she turned full upon me, "to this young lady too!"

"Miss Summerson really is my ward," said Mr. Jarndyce. "I am responsible to no Lord Chancellor in her case."

"Has Miss Summerson lost both her parents?" said my Lady.

"Yes."

"She is very fortunate in her guardian."

Lady Dedlock looked at me, and I looked at her and said I was indeed. All at once she turned from me with a hasty air, almost expressive of displeasure or dislike, and spoke to him over her shoulder again.

"Ages have passed since we were in the habit of meeting, Mr. Jarndyce."

"A long time. At least I thought it was a long time, until I saw you last Sunday," he returned.

"What! Even you are a courtier, or think it necessary to become one to me!" she said with some disdain. "I have achieved that reputation, I suppose."

"You have achieved so much, Lady Dedlock," said my guardian, "that you pay some little penalty, I dare say. But none to me."

"So much!" she repeated, slightly laughing. "Yes!"

With her air of superiority, and power, and fascination, and I know not what, she seemed to regard Ada and me as little more than children. So, as she slightly laughed and afterwards sat looking at the rain, she was as self-possessed and as free to occupy herself with her own thoughts as if she had been alone.

"I think you knew my sister when we were abroad together better than you know me?" she said, looking at him again.

"Yes, we happened to meet oftener," he returned.

"We went our several ways," said Lady Dedlock, "and had little in common even before we agreed to differ. It is to be regretted, I suppose, but it could not be helped."

Lady Dedlock again sat looking at the rain. The storm soon began to pass upon its way. The shower greatly abated, the lightning ceased, the thunder rolled among the distant hills, and the sun began to glisten on the wet leaves and the falling rain. As we sat there, silently, we saw a little pony phaeton coming towards us at a merry pace.

"The messenger is coming back, my Lady," said the keeper, "with the carriage."

As it drove up, we saw that there were two people inside. There alighted from it, with some cloaks and wrappers, first the Frenchwoman whom I had seen in church, and secondly the pretty girl, the Frenchwoman with a defiant confidence, the pretty girl confused and hesitating.

"What now?" said Lady Dedlock. "Two!"

"I am your maid, my Lady, at the present," said the Frenchwoman. "The message was for the attendant."

"I was afraid you might mean me, my Lady," said the pretty girl.

"I did mean you, child," replied her mistress calmly. "Put that shawl on me."

She slightly stooped her shoulders to receive it, and the pretty girl lightly dropped it in its place. The Frenchwoman stood unnoticed, looking on with her lips very tightly set.

"I am sorry," said Lady Dedlock to Mr. Jarndyce, "that we are not likely to renew our former acquaintance. You will allow me to send the carriage back for your two wards. It shall be here directly."

But as he would on no account accept this offer, she took a graceful leave of Ada—none of me—and put her hand upon his proffered arm, and got into the carriage, which was a little, low, park carriage with a hood.

"Come in, child," she said to the pretty girl; "I shall want you. Go on!"

The carriage rolled away, and the Frenchwoman, with the wrappers she had brought hanging over her arm, remained standing where she had alighted.

I suppose there is nothing pride can so little bear with as pride itself, and that she was punished for her imperious manner. Her retaliation was the most singular I could have imagined. She remained perfectly still until the carriage had turned into the drive, and then, without the least discomposure of countenance, slipped off her shoes, left them on the ground, and walked deliberately in the same direction through the wettest of the wet grass.

"Is that young woman mad?" said my guardian.

"Oh, no, sir!" said the keeper, who, with his wife, was looking after her. "Hortense is not one of that sort. She has as good a head-piece as the best. But she's mortal high and passionate—powerful high and passionate; and what with having notice to leave, and having others put above her, she don't take kindly to it."

"But why should she walk shoeless through all that water?" said my guardian.

"Why, indeed, sir, unless it is to cool her down!" said the man.

"Or unless she fancies it's blood," said the woman. "She'd as soon walk through that as anything else, I think, when her own's up!"

We passed not far from the house a few minutes afterwards. Peaceful as it had looked when we first saw it, it looked even more so now, with a diamond spray glittering all about it, a light wind blowing, the birds no longer hushed but singing strongly, everything refreshed by the late rain, and the little carriage shining at the doorway like a fairy carriage made of silver. Still, very steadfastly and quietly walking towards it, a peaceful figure too in the landscape, went Mademoiselle Hortense, shoeless, through the wet grass.

CHAPTER XIX
MOVING ON

It is the long vacation in the regions of Chancery Lane. The good ships Law and Equity, those teak-built, copper-bottomed, iron-fastened, brazen-faced, and not by any means fast-sailing clippers are laid up in ordinary. The Flying Dutchman, with a crew of ghostly clients imploring all whom they may encounter to peruse their papers, has drifted, for the time being, heaven knows where. The courts are all shut up; the public offices lie in a hot sleep. Westminster Hall itself is a shady solitude where nightingales might sing, and a tenderer class of suitors than is usually found there, walk.

The Temple, Chancery Lane, Serjeants' Inn, and Lincoln's Inn even unto the Fields are like tidal harbours at low water, where stranded proceedings, offices at anchor, idle clerks lounging on lop-sided stools that will not recover their perpendicular until the current of Term sets in, lie high and dry upon the ooze of the long vacation. Outer doors of chambers are shut up by the score, messages and parcels are to be left at the Porter's Lodge by the bushel. A crop of grass would grow in the chinks of the stone pavement outside Lincoln's Inn Hall, but that the ticket-porters, who have nothing to do beyond sitting in the shade there, with their white aprons over their heads to keep the flies off, grub it up and eat it thoughtfully.

There is only one judge in town. Even he only comes twice a week to sit in chambers. If the country folks of those assize towns on his circuit could see him now! No full-bottomed wig, no red petticoats, no fur, no javelin-men, no white wands. Merely a close-shaved gentleman in white trousers and a white hat, with sea-bronze on the judicial countenance, and a strip of bark peeled by the solar rays from the judicial nose, who calls in at the shell-fish shop as he comes along and drinks iced ginger-beer!

The bar of England is scattered over the face of the earth. How England can get on through four long summer months without its bar—which is its acknowledged refuge in adversity and its only legitimate triumph in prosperity—is beside the question; assuredly that shield and buckler of Britannia are not in present wear. The learned gentleman who is always so tremendously indignant at the unprecedented outrage committed on the feelings of his client by the opposite party that he never seems likely to recover it is doing infinitely better than might be expected in Switzerland. The learned gentleman who does the withering business and who blights all opponents with his gloomy sarcasm is as merry as a grig at a French watering-place. The learned gentleman who weeps by the pint on the smallest provocation has not shed a tear these six weeks. The very learned gentleman who has cooled the natural heat of his gingery complexion in pools and fountains of law until he has become great in knotty arguments for term-time, when he poses the drowsy bench with legal "chaff," inexplicable to the uninitiated and to most of the initiated too, is roaming, with a characteristic delight in aridity and dust, about Constantinople. Other dispersed fragments of the same great palladium are to be found on the canals of Venice, at the second cataract of the Nile, in the baths of Germany, and sprinkled on the sea-sand all over the English coast. Scarcely one is to be encountered in the deserted region of Chancery Lane. If such a lonely member of the bar do flit across the waste and come upon a prowling suitor who is unable to leave off haunting the scenes of his anxiety, they frighten one another and retreat into opposite shades.

It is the hottest long vacation known for many years. All the young clerks are madly in love, and according to their various degrees, pine for bliss with the beloved object, at Margate, Ramsgate, or Gravesend. All the middle-aged clerks think their families too large. All the unowned dogs who stray into the Inns of Court and pant about staircases and other dry places seeking water give short howls of aggravation. All the blind men's dogs in the streets draw their masters against pumps or trip them over buckets. A shop with a sun-blind, and a watered pavement, and a bowl of gold and silver fish in the window, is a sanctuary. Temple Bar gets so hot that it is, to the adjacent Strand and Fleet Street, what a heater is in an urn, and keeps them simmering all night.

There are offices about the Inns of Court in which a man might be cool, if any coolness were worth purchasing at such a price in dullness; but the little thoroughfares immediately outside those retirements seem to blaze. In Mr. Krook's court, it is so hot that the people turn their houses inside out and sit in chairs upon the pavement—Mr. Krook included, who there pursues his studies, with his cat (who never is too hot) by his side. The Sol's Arms has discontinued the Harmonic Meetings for the season, and Little Swills is engaged at the Pastoral Gardens down the river, where he comes out in quite an innocent manner and sings comic ditties of a juvenile complexion calculated (as the bill says) not to wound the feelings of the most fastidious mind.

Over all the legal neighbourhood there hangs, like some great veil of rust or gigantic cobweb, the idleness and pensiveness of the long vacation. Mr. Snagsby, law-stationer of Cook's Court, Cursitor Street, is sensible of the influence not only in his mind as a sympathetic and contemplative man, but also in his business as a law-stationer aforesaid. He has more leisure for musing in Staple Inn and in the Rolls Yard during the long vacation than at other seasons, and he says to the two 'prentices, what a thing it is in such hot weather to think that you live in an island with the sea a-rolling and a-bowling right round you.

Guster is busy in the little drawing-room on this present afternoon in the long vacation, when Mr. and Mrs. Snagsby have it in contemplation to receive company. The expected guests are rather select than numerous, being Mr. and

Mrs. Chadband and no more. From Mr. Chadband's being much given to describe himself, both verbally and in writing, as a vessel, he is occasionally mistaken by strangers for a gentleman connected with navigation, but he is, as he expresses it, "in the ministry." Mr. Chadband is attached to no particular denomination and is considered by his persecutors to have nothing so very remarkable to say on the greatest of subjects as to render his volunteering, on his own account, at all incumbent on his conscience; but he has his followers, and Mrs. Snagsby is of the number. Mrs. Snagsby has but recently taken a passage upward by the vessel, Chadband; and her attention was attracted to that Bark A 1, when she was something flushed by the hot weather.

"My little woman," says Mr. Snagsby to the sparrows in Staple Inn, "likes to have her religion rather sharp, you see!"

So Guster, much impressed by regarding herself for the time as the handmaid of Chadband, whom she knows to be endowed with the gift of holding forth for four hours at a stretch, prepares the little drawing-room for tea. All the furniture is shaken and dusted, the portraits of Mr. and Mrs. Snagsby are touched up with a wet cloth, the best tea-service is set forth, and there is excellent provision made of dainty new bread, crusty twists, cool fresh butter, thin slices of ham, tongue, and German sausage, and delicate little rows of anchovies nestling in parsley, not to mention new-laid eggs, to be brought up warm in a napkin, and hot buttered toast. For Chadband is rather a consuming vessel—the persecutors say a gorging vessel—and can wield such weapons of the flesh as a knife and fork remarkably well.

Mr. Snagsby in his best coat, looking at all the preparations when they are completed and coughing his cough of deference behind his hand, says to Mrs. Snagsby, "At what time did you expect Mr. and Mrs. Chadband, my love?"

"At six," says Mrs. Snagsby.

Mr. Snagsby observes in a mild and casual way that "it's gone that."

"Perhaps you'd like to begin without them," is Mrs. Snagsby's reproachful remark.

Mr. Snagsby does look as if he would like it very much, but he says, with his cough of mildness, "No, my dear, no. I merely named the time."

"What's time," says Mrs. Snagsby, "to eternity?"

"Very true, my dear," says Mr. Snagsby. "Only when a person lays in victuals for tea, a person does it with a view—perhaps—more to time. And when a time is named for having tea, it's better to come up to it."

"To come up to it!" Mrs. Snagsby repeats with severity. "Up to it! As if Mr. Chadband was a fighter!"

"Not at all, my dear," says Mr. Snagsby.

Here, Guster, who had been looking out of the bedroom window, comes rustling and scratching down the little staircase like a popular ghost, and falling flushed into the drawing-room, announces that Mr. and Mrs. Chadband have appeared in the court. The bell at the inner door in the passage immediately thereafter tinkling, she is admonished by Mrs. Snagsby, on pain of instant reconsignment to her patron saint, not to omit the ceremony of announcement. Much discomposed in her nerves (which were previously in the best order) by this threat, she so fearfully mutilates that point of state as to announce "Mr. and Mrs. Cheeseming, least which, Imeantersay, whatsername!" and retires conscience-stricken from the presence.

Mr. Chadband is a large yellow man with a fat smile and a general appearance of having a good deal of train oil in his system. Mrs. Chadband is a stern, severe-looking, silent woman. Mr. Chadband moves softly and cumbrously, not unlike a bear who has been taught to walk upright. He is very much embarrassed about the arms, as if they were inconvenient to him and he wanted to grovel, is very much in a perspiration about the head, and never speaks without first putting up his great hand, as delivering a token to his hearers that he is going to edify them.

"My friends," says Mr. Chadband, "peace be on this house! On the master thereof, on the mistress thereof, on the young maidens, and on the young men! My friends, why do I wish for peace? What is peace? Is it war? No. Is it strife? No. Is it lovely, and gentle, and beautiful, and pleasant, and serene, and joyful? Oh, yes! Therefore, my friends, I wish for peace, upon you and upon yours."

In consequence of Mrs. Snagsby looking deeply edified, Mr. Snagsby thinks it expedient on the whole to say amen, which is well received.

"Now, my friends," proceeds Mr. Chadband, "since I am upon this theme—"

Guster presents herself. Mrs. Snagsby, in a spectral bass voice and without removing her eyes from Chadband, says with dreadful distinctness, "Go away!"

"Now, my friends," says Chadband, "since I am upon this theme, and in my lowly path improving it—"

Guster is heard unaccountably to murmur "one thousing seven hundred and eighty-two." The spectral voice repeats more solemnly, "Go away!"

"Now, my friends," says Mr. Chadband, "we will inquire in a spirit of love—"

Still Guster reiterates "one thousing seven hundred and eighty-two."

Mr. Chadband, pausing with the resignation of a man accustomed to be persecuted and languidly folding up his chin into his fat smile, says, "Let us hear the maiden! Speak, maiden!"

"One thousing seven hundred and eighty-two, if you please, sir. Which he wish to know what the shilling ware for," says Guster, breathless.

"For?" returns Mrs. Chadband. "For his fare!"

Guster replied that "he insistes on one and eightpence or on summonsizzing the party." Mrs. Snagsby and Mrs. Chadband are proceeding to grow shrill in indignation when Mr. Chadband quiets the tumult by lifting up his hand.

"My friends," says he, "I remember a duty unfulfilled yesterday. It is right that I should be chastened in some penalty. I ought not to murmur. Rachael, pay the eightpence!"

While Mrs. Snagsby, drawing her breath, looks hard at Mr. Snagsby, as who should say, "You hear this apostle!" and while Mr. Chadband glows with humility and train oil, Mrs. Chadband pays the money. It is Mr. Chadband's habit—it is the head and front of his pretensions indeed—to keep this sort of debtor and creditor account in the smallest items and to post it publicly on the most trivial occasions.

"My friends," says Chadband, "eightpence is not much; it might justly have been one and fourpence; it might justly have been half a crown. O let us be joyful, joyful! O let us be joyful!"

With which remark, which appears from its sound to be an extract in verse, Mr. Chadband stalks to the table, and before taking a chair, lifts up his admonitory hand.

"My friends," says he, "what is this which we now behold as being spread before us? Refreshment. Do we need refreshment then, my friends? We do. And why do we need refreshment, my friends? Because we are but mortal, because we are but sinful, because we are but of the earth, because we are not of the air. Can we fly, my friends? We cannot. Why can we not fly, my friends?"

Mr. Snagsby, presuming on the success of his last point, ventures to observe in a cheerful and rather knowing tone, "No wings." But is immediately frowned down by Mrs. Snagsby.

"I say, my friends," pursues Mr. Chadband, utterly rejecting and obliterating Mr. Snagsby's suggestion, "why can we not fly? Is it because we are calculated to walk? It is. Could we walk, my friends, without strength? We could not. What should we do without strength, my friends? Our legs would refuse to bear us, our knees would double up, our ankles would turn over, and we should come to the ground. Then from whence, my friends, in a human point of view, do we derive the strength that is necessary to our limbs? Is it," says Chadband, glancing over the table, "from bread in various forms, from butter which is churned from the milk which is yielded unto us by the cow, from the eggs which are laid by the fowl, from ham, from tongue, from sausage, and from such like? It is. Then let us partake of the good things which are set before us!"

The persecutors denied that there was any particular gift in Mr. Chadband's piling verbose flights of stairs, one upon another, after this fashion. But this can only be received as a proof of their determination to persecute, since it must be within everybody's experience that the Chadband style of oratory is widely received and much admired.

Mr. Chadband, however, having concluded for the present, sits down at Mr. Snagsby's table and lays about him prodigiously. The conversion of nutriment of any sort into oil of the quality already mentioned appears to be a process so inseparable from the constitution of this exemplary vessel that in beginning to eat and drink, he may be described as always becoming a kind of considerable oil mills or other large factory for the production of that article on a wholesale scale. On the present evening of the long vacation, in Cook's Court, Cursitor Street, he does such a powerful stroke of business that the warehouse appears to be quite full when the works cease.

At this period of the entertainment, Guster, who has never recovered her first failure, but has neglected no possible or impossible means of bringing the establishment and herself into contempt—among which may be briefly enumerated her unexpectedly performing clashing military music on Mr. Chadband's head with plates, and afterwards crowning that gentleman with muffins—at which period of the entertainment, Guster whispers Mr. Snagsby that he is wanted.

"And being wanted in the—not to put too fine a point upon it—in the shop," says Mr. Snagsby, rising, "perhaps this good company will excuse me for half a minute."

Mr. Snagsby descends and finds the two 'prentices intently contemplating a police constable, who holds a ragged boy by the arm.

"Why, bless my heart," says Mr. Snagsby, "what's the matter!"

"This boy," says the constable, "although he's repeatedly told to, won't move on—"

"I'm always a-moving on, sar," cries the boy, wiping away his grimy tears with his arm. "I've always been a-moving and a-moving on, ever since I was born. Where can I possibly move to, sir, more nor I do move!"

"He won't move on," says the constable calmly, with a slight professional hitch of his neck involving its better settlement in his stiff stock, "although he has been repeatedly cautioned, and therefore I am obliged to take him into custody. He's as obstinate a young gonoph as I know. He WON'T move on."

"Oh, my eye! Where can I move to!" cries the boy, clutching quite desperately at his hair and beating his bare feet upon the floor of Mr. Snagsby's passage.

"Don't you come none of that or I shall make blessed short work of you!" says the constable, giving him a passionless shake. "My instructions are that you are to move on. I have told you so five hundred times."

"But where?" cries the boy.

"Well! Really, constable, you know," says Mr. Snagsby wistfully, and coughing behind his hand his cough of great perplexity and doubt, "really, that does seem a question. Where, you know?"

"My instructions don't go to that," replies the constable. "My instructions are that this boy is to move on."

Do you hear, Jo? It is nothing to you or to any one else that the great lights of the parliamentary sky have failed for some few years in this business to set you the example of moving on. The one grand recipe remains for you—the profound philosophical prescription—the be-all and the end-all of your strange existence upon earth. Move on! You are by no means to move off, Jo, for the great lights can't at all agree about that. Move on!

Mr. Snagsby says nothing to this effect, says nothing at all indeed, but coughs his forlornest cough, expressive of no thoroughfare in any direction. By this time Mr. and Mrs. Chadband and Mrs. Snagsby, hearing the altercation, have appeared upon the stairs. Guster having never left the end of the passage, the whole household are assembled.

"The simple question is, sir," says the constable, "whether you know this boy. He says you do."

Mrs. Snagsby, from her elevation, instantly cries out, "No he don't!"

"My lit-tle woman!" says Mr. Snagsby, looking up the staircase. "My love, permit me! Pray have a moment's patience, my dear. I do know something of this lad, and in what I know of him, I can't say that there's any harm; perhaps on the contrary, constable." To whom the law-stationer relates his Joful and woeful experience, suppressing the half-crown fact.

"Well!" says the constable, "so far, it seems, he had grounds for what he said. When I took him into custody up in Holborn, he said you knew him. Upon that, a young man who was in the crowd said he was acquainted with you, and you were a respectable housekeeper, and if I'd call and make the inquiry, he'd appear. The young man don't seem inclined to keep his word, but—Oh! Here IS the young man!"

Enter Mr. Guppy, who nods to Mr. Snagsby and touches his hat with the chivalry of clerkship to the ladies on the stairs.

"I was strolling away from the office just now when I found this row going on," says Mr. Guppy to the law-stationer, "and as your name was mentioned, I thought it was right the thing should be looked into."

"It was very good-natured of you, sir," says Mr. Snagsby, "and I am obliged to you." And Mr. Snagsby again relates his experience, again suppressing the half-crown fact.

"Now, I know where you live," says the constable, then, to Jo. "You live down in Tom-all-Alone's. That's a nice innocent place to live in, ain't it?"

"I can't go and live in no nicer place, sir," replies Jo. "They wouldn't have nothink to say to me if I wos to go to a nice innocent place fur to live. Who ud go and let a nice innocent lodging to such a reg'lar one as me!"

"You are very poor, ain't you?" says the constable.

"Yes, I am indeed, sir, wery poor in gin'ral," replies Jo. "I leave you to judge now! I shook these two half-crowns out of him," says the constable, producing them to the company, "in only putting my hand upon him!"

"They're wot's left, Mr. Snagsby," says Jo, "out of a sov-ring as wos give me by a lady in a wale as sed she wos a servant and as come to my crossin one night and asked to be showd this 'ere ouse and the ouse wot him as you giv the writin to died at, and the berrin-ground wot he's berrid in. She ses to me she ses 'are you the boy at the inkwhich?' she ses. I ses 'yes' I ses. She ses to me she ses 'can you show me all them places?' I ses 'yes I can' I ses. And she ses to me 'do it' and I dun it and she giv me a sov'ring and hooked it. And I an't had much of the sov'ring neither," says Jo, with dirty tears, "fur I had to pay five bob, down in Tom-all-Alone's, afore they'd square it fur to give me change, and then a young man he thieved another five while I was asleep and another boy he thieved ninepence and the landlord he stood drains round with a lot more on it."

"You don't expect anybody to believe this, about the lady and the sovereign, do you?" says the constable, eyeing him aside with ineffable disdain.

"I don't know as I do, sir," replies Jo. "I don't expect nothink at all, sir, much, but that's the true hist'ry on it."

"You see what he is!" the constable observes to the audience. "Well, Mr. Snagsby, if I don't lock him up this time, will you engage for his moving on?"

"No!" cries Mrs. Snagsby from the stairs.

"My little woman!" pleads her husband. "Constable, I have no doubt he'll move on. You know you really must do it," says Mr. Snagsby.

"I'm everyways agreeable, sir," says the hapless Jo.

"Do it, then," observes the constable. "You know what you have got to do. Do it! And recollect you won't get off so easy next time. Catch hold of your money. Now, the sooner you're five mile off, the better for all parties."

With this farewell hint and pointing generally to the setting sun as a likely place to move on to, the constable bids his auditors good afternoon and makes the echoes of Cook's Court perform slow music for him as he walks away on the shady side, carrying his iron-bound hat in his hand for a little ventilation.

Now, Jo's improbable story concerning the lady and the sovereign has awakened more or less the curiosity of all the company. Mr. Guppy, who has an inquiring mind in matters of evidence and who has been suffering severely from the lassitude of the long vacation, takes that interest in the case that he enters on a regular cross-examination of the witness, which is found so interesting by the ladies that Mrs. Snagsby politely invites him to step upstairs and drink a cup of tea, if he will excuse the disarranged state of the tea-table, consequent on their previous exertions. Mr. Guppy yielding his assent to this proposal, Jo is requested to follow into the drawing-room doorway, where Mr. Guppy takes him in hand as a witness, patting him into this shape, that shape, and the other shape like a butterman dealing with so much butter, and worrying him according to the best models. Nor is the examination unlike many such model displays, both in respect of its eliciting nothing and of its being lengthy, for Mr. Guppy is sensible of his talent, and Mrs. Snagsby feels not only that it gratifies her inquisitive disposition, but that it lifts her husband's establishment higher up in the law. During the progress of this keen encounter, the vessel Chadband, being merely engaged in the oil trade, gets aground and waits to be floated off.

"Well!" says Mr. Guppy. "Either this boy sticks to it like cobbler's-wax or there is something out of the common here that beats anything that ever came into my way at Kenge and Carboy's."

Mrs. Chadband whispers Mrs. Snagsby, who exclaims, "You don't say so!"

"For years!" replied Mrs. Chadband.

"Has known Kenge and Carboy's office for years," Mrs. Snagsby triumphantly explains to Mr. Guppy. "Mrs. Chadband—this gentleman's wife—Reverend Mr. Chadband."

"Oh, indeed!" says Mr. Guppy.

"Before I married my present husband," says Mrs. Chadband.

"Was you a party in anything, ma'am?" says Mr. Guppy, transferring his cross-examination.

"No."

"NOT a party in anything, ma'am?" says Mr. Guppy.

Mrs. Chadband shakes her head.

"Perhaps you were acquainted with somebody who was a party in something, ma'am?" says Mr. Guppy, who likes nothing better than to model his conversation on forensic principles.

"Not exactly that, either," replies Mrs. Chadband, humouring the joke with a hard-favoured smile.

"Not exactly that, either!" repeats Mr. Guppy. "Very good. Pray, ma'am, was it a lady of your acquaintance who had some transactions (we will not at present say what transactions) with Kenge and Carboy's office, or was it a gentleman of your acquaintance? Take time, ma'am. We shall come to it presently. Man or woman, ma'am?"

"Neither," says Mrs. Chadband as before.

"Oh! A child!" says Mr. Guppy, throwing on the admiring Mrs. Snagsby the regular acute professional eye which is thrown on British jurymen. "Now, ma'am, perhaps you'll have the kindness to tell us WHAT child."

"You have got it at last, sir," says Mrs. Chadband with another hard-favoured smile. "Well, sir, it was before your time, most likely, judging from your appearance. I was left in charge of a child named Esther Summerson, who was put out in life by Messrs. Kenge and Carboy."

"Miss Summerson, ma'am!" cries Mr. Guppy, excited.

"I call her Esther Summerson," says Mrs. Chadband with austerity. "There was no Miss-ing of the girl in my time. It was Esther. 'Esther, do this! Esther, do that!' and she was made to do it."

"My dear ma'am," returns Mr. Guppy, moving across the small apartment, "the humble individual who now addresses you received that young lady in London when she first came here from the establishment to which you have alluded. Allow me to have the pleasure of taking you by the hand."

Mr. Chadband, at last seeing his opportunity, makes his accustomed signal and rises with a smoking head, which he dabs with his pocket-handkerchief. Mrs. Snagsby whispers "Hush!"

"My friends," says Chadband, "we have partaken in moderation" (which was certainly not the case so far as he was concerned) "of the comforts which have been provided for us. May this house live upon the fatness of the land; may corn and wine be plentiful therein; may it grow, may it thrive, may it prosper, may it advance, may it proceed, may it press forward! But, my friends, have we partaken of anything else? We have. My friends, of what else have we partaken? Of spiritual profit? Yes. From whence have we derived that spiritual profit? My young friend, stand forth!"

Jo, thus apostrophized, gives a slouch backward, and another slouch forward, and another slouch to each side, and confronts the eloquent Chadband with evident doubts of his intentions.

"My young friend," says Chadband, "you are to us a pearl, you are to us a diamond, you are to us a gem, you are to us a jewel. And why, my young friend?"

"I don't know," replies Jo. "I don't know nothink."

"My young friend," says Chadband, "it is because you know nothing that you are to us a gem and jewel. For what are you, my young friend? Are you a beast of the field? No. A bird of the air? No. A fish of the sea or river? No. You are a human boy, my young friend. A human boy. O glorious to be a human boy! And why glorious, my young friend? Because you are capable of receiving the lessons of wisdom, because you are capable of profiting by this discourse which I now deliver for your good, because you are not a stick, or a staff, or a stock, or a stone, or a post, or a pillar.

O running stream of sparkling joy
To be a soaring human boy!

And do you cool yourself in that stream now, my young friend? No. Why do you not cool yourself in that stream now? Because you are in a state of darkness, because you are in a state of obscurity, because you are in a state of sinfulness, because you are in a state of bondage. My young friend, what is bondage? Let us, in a spirit of love, inquire."

At this threatening stage of the discourse, Jo, who seems to have been gradually going out of his mind, smears his right arm over his face and gives a terrible yawn. Mrs. Snagsby indignantly expresses her belief that he is a limb of the arch-fiend.

"My friends," says Mr. Chadband with his persecuted chin folding itself into its fat smile again as he looks round, "it is right that I should be humbled, it is right that I should be tried, it is right that I should be mortified, it is right that I should be corrected. I stumbled, on Sabbath last, when I thought with pride of my three hours' improving. The account is now favourably balanced: my creditor has accepted a composition. O let us be joyful, joyful! O let us be joyful!"

Great sensation on the part of Mrs. Snagsby.

"My friends," says Chadband, looking round him in conclusion, "I will not proceed with my young friend now. Will you come to-morrow, my young friend, and inquire of this good lady where I am to be found to deliver a discourse unto you, and will you come like the thirsty swallow upon the next day, and upon the day after that, and upon the day after that, and upon many pleasant days, to hear discourses?" (This with a cow-like lightness.)

Jo, whose immediate object seems to be to get away on any terms, gives a shuffling nod. Mr. Guppy then throws him a penny, and Mrs. Snagsby calls to Guster to see him safely out of the house. But before he goes downstairs, Mr. Snagsby loads him with some broken meats from the table, which he carries away, hugging in his arms.

So, Mr. Chadband—of whom the persecutors say that it is no wonder he should go on for any length of time uttering such abominable nonsense, but that the wonder rather is that he should ever leave off, having once the audacity to begin—retires into private life until he invests a little capital of supper in the oil-trade. Jo moves on, through the long vacation, down to Blackfriars Bridge, where he finds a baking stony corner wherein to settle to his repast.

And there he sits, munching and gnawing, and looking up at the great cross on the summit of St. Paul's Cathedral, glittering above a red-and-violet-tinted cloud of smoke. From the boy's face one might suppose that sacred emblem to be, in his eyes, the crowning confusion of the great, confused city—so golden, so high up, so far out of his reach. There he sits, the sun going down, the river running fast, the crowd flowing by him in two streams—everything moving on to some purpose and to one end—until he is stirred up and told to "move on" too.

CHAPTER XX
A NEW LODGER

The long vacation saunters on towards term-time like an idle river very leisurely strolling down a flat country to the sea. Mr. Guppy saunters along with it congenially. He has blunted the blade of his penknife and broken the point off by sticking that instrument into his desk in every direction. Not that he bears the desk any ill will, but he must do something, and it must be something of an unexciting nature, which will lay neither his physical nor his intellectual energies under too heavy contribution. He finds that nothing agrees with him so well as to make little gyrations on one leg of his stool, and stab his desk, and gape.

Kenge and Carboy are out of town, and the articled clerk has taken out a shooting license and gone down to his father's, and Mr. Guppy's two fellow-stipendiaries are away on leave. Mr. Guppy and Mr. Richard Carstone divide the dignity of the office. But Mr. Carstone is for the time being established in Kenge's room, whereat Mr. Guppy chafes. So exceedingly that he with biting sarcasm informs his mother, in the confidential moments when he sups with her off a lobster and lettuce in the Old Street Road, that he is afraid the office is hardly good enough for swells, and that if he had known there was a swell coming, he would have got it painted.

Mr. Guppy suspects everybody who enters on the occupation of a stool in Kenge and Carboy's office of entertaining, as a matter of course, sinister designs upon him. He is clear that every such person wants to depose him. If he be ever asked how, why, when, or wherefore, he shuts up one eye and shakes his head. On the strength of these profound views, he in the most ingenious manner takes infinite pains to counterplot when there is no plot, and plays the deepest games of chess without any adversary.

It is a source of much gratification to Mr. Guppy, therefore, to find the new-comer constantly poring over the papers in Jarndyce and Jarndyce, for he well knows that nothing but confusion and failure can come of that. His satisfaction communicates itself to a third saunterer through the long vacation in Kenge and Carboy's office, to wit, Young Smallweed.

Whether Young Smallweed (metaphorically called Small and eke Chick Weed, as it were jocularly to express a fledgling) was ever a boy is much doubted in Lincoln's Inn. He is now something under fifteen and an old limb of the law. He is facetiously understood to entertain a passion for a lady at a cigar-shop in the neighbourhood of Chancery Lane and for her sake to have broken off a contract with another lady, to whom he had been engaged some years. He is a town-made article, of small stature and weazen features, but may be perceived from a considerable distance by means of his very tall hat.

To become a Guppy is the object of his ambition. He dresses at that gentleman (by whom he is patronized), talks at him, walks at him, founds himself entirely on him. He is honoured with Mr. Guppy's particular confidence and occasionally advises him, from the deep wells of his experience, on difficult points in private life.

Mr. Guppy has been lolling out of window all the morning after trying all the stools in succession and finding none of them easy, and after several times putting his head into the iron safe with a notion of cooling it. Mr. Smallweed has been twice dispatched for effervescent drinks, and has twice mixed them in the two official tumblers and stirred them up with the ruler. Mr. Guppy propounds for Mr. Smallweed's consideration the paradox that the more you drink the thirstier you are and reclines his head upon the window-sill in a state of hopeless languor.

While thus looking out into the shade of Old Square, Lincoln's Inn, surveying the intolerable bricks and mortar, Mr. Guppy becomes conscious of a manly whisker emerging from the cloistered walk below and turning itself up in the direction of his face. At the same time, a low whistle is wafted through the Inn and a suppressed voice cries, "Hip! Gup-py!"

"Why, you don't mean it!" says Mr. Guppy, aroused. "Small! Here's Jobling!" Small's head looks out of window too and nods to Jobling.

"Where have you sprung up from?" inquires Mr. Guppy.

"From the market-gardens down by Deptford. I can't stand it any longer. I must enlist. I say! I wish you'd lend me half a crown. Upon my soul, I'm hungry."

Jobling looks hungry and also has the appearance of having run to seed in the market-gardens down by Deptford.

"I say! Just throw out half a crown if you have got one to spare. I want to get some dinner."

"Will you come and dine with me?" says Mr. Guppy, throwing out the coin, which Mr. Jobling catches neatly.

"How long should I have to hold out?" says Jobling.

"Not half an hour. I am only waiting here till the enemy goes, returns Mr. Guppy, butting inward with his head.

"What enemy?"

"A new one. Going to be articled. Will you wait?"

"Can you give a fellow anything to read in the meantime?" says Mr. Jobling.

Smallweed suggests the law list. But Mr. Jobling declares with much earnestness that he "can't stand it."

"You shall have the paper," says Mr. Guppy. "He shall bring it down. But you had better not be seen about here. Sit on our staircase and read. It's a quiet place."

Jobling nods intelligence and acquiescence. The sagacious Smallweed supplies him with the newspaper and occasionally drops his eye upon him from the landing as a precaution against his becoming disgusted with waiting and making an untimely departure. At last the enemy retreats, and then Smallweed fetches Mr. Jobling up.

"Well, and how are you?" says Mr. Guppy, shaking hands with him.

"So, so. How are you?"

Mr. Guppy replying that he is not much to boast of, Mr. Jobling ventures on the question, "How is SHE?" This Mr. Guppy resents as a liberty, retorting, "Jobling, there ARE chords in the human mind—" Jobling begs pardon.

"Any subject but that!" says Mr. Guppy with a gloomy enjoyment of his injury. "For there ARE chords, Jobling—"

Mr. Jobling begs pardon again.

During this short colloquy, the active Smallweed, who is of the dinner party, has written in legal characters on a slip of paper, "Return immediately." This notification to all whom it may concern, he inserts in the letter-box, and then putting on the tall hat at the angle of inclination at which Mr. Guppy wears his, informs his patron that they may now make themselves scarce.

Accordingly they betake themselves to a neighbouring dining-house, of the class known among its frequenters by the denomination slap-bang, where the waitress, a bouncing young female of forty, is supposed to have made some impression on the susceptible Smallweed, of whom it may be remarked that he is a weird changeling to whom years are nothing. He stands precociously possessed of centuries of owlish wisdom. If he ever lay in a cradle, it seems as if he must have lain there in a tail-coat. He has an old, old eye, has Smallweed; and he drinks and smokes in a monkeyish way; and his neck is stiff in his collar; and he is never to be taken in; and he knows all about it, whatever it is. In short, in his bringing up he has been so nursed by Law and Equity that he has become a kind of fossil imp, to account for whose terrestrial existence it is reported at the public offices that his father was John Doe and his mother the only female member of the Roe family, also that his first long-clothes were made from a blue bag.

Into the dining-house, unaffected by the seductive show in the window of artificially whitened cauliflowers and poultry, verdant baskets of peas, coolly blooming cucumbers, and joints ready for the spit, Mr. Smallweed leads the way. They know him there and defer to him. He has his favourite box, he bespeaks all the papers, he is down upon bald patriarchs, who keep them more than ten minutes afterwards. It is of no use trying him with anything less than a full-sized "bread" or proposing to him any joint in cut unless it is in the very best cut. In the matter of gravy he is adamant.

Conscious of his elfin power and submitting to his dread experience, Mr. Guppy consults him in the choice of that day's banquet, turning an appealing look towards him as the waitress repeats the catalogue of viands and saying "What do YOU take, Chick?" Chick, out of the profundity of his artfulness, preferring "veal and ham and French beans—and don't you forget the stuffing, Polly" (with an unearthly cock of his venerable eye), Mr. Guppy and Mr. Jobling give the like order. Three pint pots of half-and-half are superadded. Quickly the waitress returns bearing what is apparently a model of the Tower of Babel but what is really a pile of plates and flat tin dish-covers. Mr. Smallweed, approving of what is set before him, conveys intelligent benignity into his ancient eye and winks upon her. Then, amid a constant coming in, and going out, and running about, and a clatter of crockery, and a rumbling up and down of the machine which brings the nice cuts from the kitchen, and a shrill crying for more nice cuts down the speaking-pipe, and a shrill reckoning of the cost of nice cuts that have been disposed of, and a general flush and steam of hot joints, cut and uncut, and a considerably heated atmosphere in which the soiled knives and tablecloths seem to break out spontaneously into eruptions of grease and blotches of beer, the legal triumvirate appease their appetites.

Mr. Jobling is buttoned up closer than mere adornment might require. His hat presents at the rims a peculiar appearance of a glistening nature, as if it had been a favourite snail-promenade. The same phenomenon is visible on some parts of his coat, and particularly at the seams. He has the faded appearance of a gentleman in embarrassed circumstances; even his light whiskers droop with something of a shabby air.

His appetite is so vigorous that it suggests spare living for some little time back. He makes such a speedy end of his plate of veal and ham, bringing it to a close while his companions are yet midway in theirs, that Mr. Guppy proposes another. "Thank you, Guppy," says Mr. Jobling, "I really don't know but what I WILL take another."

Another being brought, he falls to with great goodwill.

Mr. Guppy takes silent notice of him at intervals until he is half way through this second plate and stops to take an enjoying pull at his pint pot of half-and-half (also renewed) and stretches out his legs and rubs his hands. Beholding him in which glow of contentment, Mr. Guppy says, "You are a man again, Tony!"

"Well, not quite yet," says Mr. Jobling. "Say, just born."

"Will you take any other vegetables? Grass? Peas? Summer cabbage?"

"Thank you, Guppy," says Mr. Jobling. "I really don't know but what I WILL take summer cabbage."

Order given; with the sarcastic addition (from Mr. Smallweed) of "Without slugs, Polly!" And cabbage produced.

"I am growing up, Guppy," says Mr. Jobling, plying his knife and fork with a relishing steadiness.

"Glad to hear it."

"In fact, I have just turned into my teens," says Mr. Jobling.

He says no more until he has performed his task, which he achieves as Messrs. Guppy and Smallweed finish theirs, thus getting over the ground in excellent style and beating those two gentlemen easily by a veal and ham and a cabbage.

"Now, Small," says Mr. Guppy, "what would you recommend about pastry?"

"Marrow puddings," says Mr. Smallweed instantly.

"Aye, aye!" cries Mr. Jobling with an arch look. "You're there, are you? Thank you, Mr. Guppy, I don't know but what I WILL take a marrow pudding."

Three marrow puddings being produced, Mr. Jobling adds in a pleasant humour that he is coming of age fast. To these succeed, by command of Mr. Smallweed, "three Cheshires," and to those "three small rums." This apex of the entertainment happily reached, Mr. Jobling puts up his legs on the carpeted seat (having his own side of the box to himself), leans against the wall, and says, "I am grown up now, Guppy. I have arrived at maturity."

"What do you think, now," says Mr. Guppy, "about—you don't mind Smallweed?"

"Not the least in the world. I have the pleasure of drinking his good health."

"Sir, to you!" says Mr. Smallweed.

"I was saying, what do you think NOW," pursues Mr. Guppy, "of enlisting?"

"Why, what I may think after dinner," returns Mr. Jobling, "is one thing, my dear Guppy, and what I may think before dinner is another thing. Still, even after dinner, I ask myself the question, What am I to do? How am I to live? Ill fo manger, you know," says Mr. Jobling, pronouncing that word as if he meant a necessary fixture in an English stable. "Ill fo manger. That's the French saying, and mangering is as necessary to me as it is to a Frenchman. Or more so."

Mr. Smallweed is decidedly of opinion "much more so."

"If any man had told me," pursues Jobling, "even so lately as when you and I had the frisk down in Lincolnshire, Guppy, and drove over to see that house at Castle Wold—"

Mr. Smallweed corrects him—Chesney Wold.

"Chesney Wold. (I thank my honourable friend for that cheer.) If any man had told me then that I should be as hard up at the present time as I literally find myself, I should have—well, I should have pitched into him," says Mr. Jobling, taking a little rum-and-water with an air of desperate resignation; "I should have let fly at his head."

"Still, Tony, you were on the wrong side of the post then," remonstrates Mr. Guppy. "You were talking about nothing else in the gig."

"Guppy," says Mr. Jobling, "I will not deny it. I was on the wrong side of the post. But I trusted to things coming round."

That very popular trust in flat things coming round! Not in their being beaten round, or worked round, but in their "coming" round! As though a lunatic should trust in the world's "coming" triangular!

"I had confident expectations that things would come round and be all square," says Mr. Jobling with some vagueness of expression and perhaps of meaning too. "But I was disappointed. They never did. And when it came to creditors making rows at the office and to people that the office dealt with making complaints about dirty trifles of borrowed money, why there was an end of that connexion. And of any new professional connexion too, for if I was to give a reference to-morrow, it would be mentioned and would sew me up. Then what's a fellow to do? I have been keeping out of the way and living cheap down about the market-gardens, but what's the use of living cheap when you have got no money? You might as well live dear."

"Better," Mr. Smallweed thinks.

"Certainly. It's the fashionable way; and fashion and whiskers have been my weaknesses, and I don't care who knows it," says Mr. Jobling. "They are great weaknesses—Damme, sir, they are great. Well," proceeds Mr. Jobling after a defiant visit to his rum-and-water, "what can a fellow do, I ask you, BUT enlist?"

Mr. Guppy comes more fully into the conversation to state what, in his opinion, a fellow can do. His manner is the gravely impressive manner of a man who has not committed himself in life otherwise than as he has become the victim of a tender sorrow of the heart.

"Jobling," says Mr. Guppy, "myself and our mutual friend Smallweed—"

Mr. Smallweed modestly observes, "Gentlemen both!" and drinks.

"—Have had a little conversation on this matter more than once since you—"

"Say, got the sack!" cries Mr. Jobling bitterly. "Say it, Guppy. You mean it."

"No-o-o! Left the Inn," Mr. Smallweed delicately suggests.

"Since you left the Inn, Jobling," says Mr. Guppy; "and I have mentioned to our mutual friend Smallweed a plan I have lately thought of proposing. You know Snagsby the stationer?"

"I know there is such a stationer," returns Mr. Jobling. "He was not ours, and I am not acquainted with him."

"He IS ours, Jobling, and I AM acquainted with him," Mr. Guppy retorts. "Well, sir! I have lately become better acquainted with him through some accidental circumstances that have made me a visitor of his in private life. Those circumstances it is not necessary to offer in argument. They may—or they may not—have some reference to a subject which may—or may not—have cast its shadow on my existence."

As it is Mr. Guppy's perplexing way with boastful misery to tempt his particular friends into this subject, and the moment they touch it, to turn on them with that trenchant severity about the chords in the human mind, both Mr. Jobling and Mr. Smallweed decline the pitfall by remaining silent.

"Such things may be," repeats Mr. Guppy, "or they may not be. They are no part of the case. It is enough to mention that both Mr. and Mrs. Snagsby are very willing to oblige me and that Snagsby has, in busy times, a good deal of copying work to give out. He has all Tulkinghorn's, and an excellent business besides. I believe if our mutual friend Smallweed were put into the box, he could prove this?"

Mr. Smallweed nods and appears greedy to be sworn.

"Now, gentlemen of the jury," says Mr. Guppy, "—I mean, now, Jobling—you may say this is a poor prospect of a living. Granted. But it's better than nothing, and better than enlistment. You want time. There must be time for these late affairs to blow over. You might live through it on much worse terms than by writing for Snagsby."

Mr. Jobling is about to interrupt when the sagacious Smallweed checks him with a dry cough and the words, "Hem! Shakspeare!"

"There are two branches to this subject, Jobling," says Mr. Guppy. "That is the first. I come to the second. You know Krook, the Chancellor, across the lane. Come, Jobling," says Mr. Guppy in his encouraging cross-examination-tone, "I think you know Krook, the Chancellor, across the lane?"

"I know him by sight," says Mr. Jobling.

"You know him by sight. Very well. And you know little Flite?"

"Everybody knows her," says Mr. Jobling.

"Everybody knows her. VERY well. Now it has been one of my duties of late to pay Flite a certain weekly allowance, deducting from it the amount of her weekly rent, which I have paid (in consequence of instructions I have received) to Krook himself, regularly in her presence. This has brought me into communication with Krook and into a knowledge of his house and his habits. I know he has a room to let. You may live there at a very low charge under any name you like, as quietly as if you were a hundred miles off. He'll ask no questions and would accept you as a tenant at a word from me—before the clock strikes, if you chose. And I tell you another thing, Jobling," says Mr. Guppy, who has suddenly lowered his voice and become familiar again, "he's an extraordinary old chap—always rummaging among a litter of papers and grubbing away at teaching himself to read and write, without getting on a bit, as it seems to me. He is a most extraordinary old chap, sir. I don't know but what it might be worth a fellow's while to look him up a bit."

"You don't mean—" Mr. Jobling begins.

"I mean," returns Mr. Guppy, shrugging his shoulders with becoming modesty, "that I can't make him out. I appeal to our mutual friend Smallweed whether he has or has not heard me remark that I can't make him out."

Mr. Smallweed bears the concise testimony, "A few!"

"I have seen something of the profession and something of life, Tony," says Mr. Guppy, "and it's seldom I can't make a man out, more or less. But such an old card as this, so deep, so sly, and secret (though I don't believe he is ever sober), I never came across. Now, he must be precious old, you know, and he has not a soul about him, and he is reported to be immensely rich; and whether he is a smuggler, or a receiver, or an unlicensed pawnbroker, or a money-lender—all of which I have thought likely at different times—it might pay you to knock up a sort of knowledge of him. I don't see why you shouldn't go in for it, when everything else suits."

Mr. Jobling, Mr. Guppy, and Mr. Smallweed all lean their elbows on the table and their chins upon their hands, and look at the ceiling. After a time, they all drink, slowly lean back, put their hands in their pockets, and look at one another.

"If I had the energy I once possessed, Tony!" says Mr. Guppy with a sigh. "But there are chords in the human mind—"

Expressing the remainder of the desolate sentiment in rum-and-water, Mr. Guppy concludes by resigning the adventure to Tony Jobling and informing him that during the vacation and while things are slack, his purse, "as far as three or four or even five pound goes," will be at his disposal. "For never shall it be said," Mr. Guppy adds with emphasis, "that William Guppy turned his back upon his friend!"

The latter part of the proposal is so directly to the purpose that Mr. Jobling says with emotion, "Guppy, my trump, your fist!" Mr. Guppy presents it, saying, "Jobling, my boy, there it is!" Mr. Jobling returns, "Guppy, we have been pals now for some years!" Mr. Guppy replies, "Jobling, we have."

They then shake hands, and Mr. Jobling adds in a feeling manner, "Thank you, Guppy, I don't know but what I WILL take another glass for old acquaintance sake."

"Krook's last lodger died there," observes Mr. Guppy in an incidental way.

"Did he though!" says Mr. Jobling.

"There was a verdict. Accidental death. You don't mind that?"

"No," says Mr. Jobling, "I don't mind it; but he might as well have died somewhere else. It's devilish odd that he need go and die at MY place!" Mr. Jobling quite resents this liberty, several times returning to it with such remarks as, "There are places enough to die in, I should think!" or, "He wouldn't have liked my dying at HIS place, I dare say!"

However, the compact being virtually made, Mr. Guppy proposes to dispatch the trusty Smallweed to ascertain if Mr. Krook is at home, as in that case they may complete the negotiation without delay. Mr. Jobling approving, Smallweed puts himself under the tall hat and conveys it out of the dining-rooms in the Guppy manner. He soon returns with the intelligence that Mr. Krook is at home and that he has seen him through the shop-door, sitting in the back premises, sleeping "like one o'clock."

"Then I'll pay," says Mr. Guppy, "and we'll go and see him. Small, what will it be?"

Mr. Smallweed, compelling the attendance of the waitress with one hitch of his eyelash, instantly replies as follows: "Four veals and hams is three, and four potatoes is three and four, and one summer cabbage is three and six, and three marrows is four and six, and six breads is five, and three Cheshires is five and three, and four half-pints of half-and-half is six and three, and four small rums is eight and three, and three Pollys is eight and six. Eight and six in half a sovereign, Polly, and eighteenpence out!"

Not at all excited by these stupendous calculations, Smallweed dismisses his friends with a cool nod and remains behind to take a little admiring notice of Polly, as opportunity may serve, and to read the daily papers, which are so very large in proportion to himself, shorn of his hat, that when he holds up the Times to run his eye over the columns, he seems to have retired for the night and to have disappeared under the bedclothes.

Mr. Guppy and Mr. Jobling repair to the rag and bottle shop, where they find Krook still sleeping like one o'clock, that is to say, breathing stertorously with his chin upon his breast and quite insensible to any external sounds or even to gentle shaking. On the table beside him, among the usual lumber, stand an empty gin-bottle and a glass. The unwholesome air is so stained with this liquor that even the green eyes of the cat upon her shelf, as they open and shut and glimmer on the visitors, look drunk.

"Hold up here!" says Mr. Guppy, giving the relaxed figure of the old man another shake. "Mr. Krook! Halloa, sir!"

But it would seem as easy to wake a bundle of old clothes with a spirituous heat smouldering in it. "Did you ever see such a stupor as he falls into, between drink and sleep?" says Mr. Guppy.

"If this is his regular sleep," returns Jobling, rather alarmed, "it'll last a long time one of these days, I am thinking."

"It's always more like a fit than a nap," says Mr. Guppy, shaking him again. "Halloa, your lordship! Why, he might be robbed fifty times over! Open your eyes!"

After much ado, he opens them, but without appearing to see his visitors or any other objects. Though he crosses one leg on another, and folds his hands, and several times closes and opens his parched lips, he seems to all intents and purposes as insensible as before.

"He is alive, at any rate," says Mr. Guppy. "How are you, my Lord Chancellor. I have brought a friend of mine, sir, on a little matter of business."

The old man still sits, often smacking his dry lips without the least consciousness. After some minutes he makes an attempt to rise. They help him up, and he staggers against the wall and stares at them.

"How do you do, Mr. Krook?" says Mr. Guppy in some discomfiture. "How do you do, sir? You are looking charming, Mr. Krook. I hope you are pretty well?"

The old man, in aiming a purposeless blow at Mr. Guppy, or at nothing, feebly swings himself round and comes with his face against the wall. So he remains for a minute or two, heaped up against it, and then staggers down the shop to the front door. The air, the movement in the court, the lapse of time, or the combination of these things recovers him. He comes back pretty steadily, adjusting his fur cap on his head and looking keenly at them.

"Your servant, gentlemen; I've been dozing. Hi! I am hard to wake, odd times."

"Rather so, indeed, sir," responds Mr. Guppy.

"What? You've been a-trying to do it, have you?" says the suspicious Krook.

"Only a little," Mr. Guppy explains.

The old man's eye resting on the empty bottle, he takes it up, examines it, and slowly tilts it upside down.

"I say!" he cries like the hobgoblin in the story. "Somebody's been making free here!"

"I assure you we found it so," says Mr. Guppy. "Would you allow me to get it filled for you?"

"Yes, certainly I would!" cries Krook in high glee. "Certainly I would! Don't mention it! Get it filled next door—Sol's Arms—the Lord Chancellor's fourteenpenny. Bless you, they know ME!"

He so presses the empty bottle upon Mr. Guppy that that gentleman, with a nod to his friend, accepts the trust and hurries out and hurries in again with the bottle filled. The old man receives it in his arms like a beloved grandchild and pats it tenderly.

"But, I say," he whispers, with his eyes screwed up, after tasting it, "this ain't the Lord Chancellor's fourteenpenny. This is eighteenpenny!"

"I thought you might like that better," says Mr. Guppy.

"You're a nobleman, sir," returns Krook with another taste, and his hot breath seems to come towards them like a flame. "You're a baron of the land."

Taking advantage of this auspicious moment, Mr. Guppy presents his friend under the impromptu name of Mr. Weevle and states the object of their visit. Krook, with his bottle under his arm (he never gets beyond a certain point of either drunkenness or sobriety), takes time to survey his proposed lodger and seems to approve of him. "You'd like to see the room, young man?" he says. "Ah! It's a good room! Been whitewashed. Been cleaned down with soft soap and soda. Hi! It's worth twice the rent, letting alone my company when you want it and such a cat to keep the mice away."

Commending the room after this manner, the old man takes them upstairs, where indeed they do find it cleaner than it used to be and also containing some old articles of furniture which he has dug up from his inexhaustible stores. The terms are easily concluded—for the Lord Chancellor cannot be hard on Mr. Guppy, associated as he is with Kenge and Carboy, Jarndyce and Jarndyce, and other famous claims on his professional consideration—and it is agreed that Mr. Weevle shall take possession on the morrow. Mr. Weevle and Mr. Guppy then repair to Cook's Court, Cursitor Street, where the personal introduction of the former to Mr. Snagsby is effected and (more important) the vote and interest of Mrs. Snagsby are secured. They then report progress to the eminent Smallweed, waiting at the office in his tall hat for that purpose, and separate, Mr. Guppy explaining that he would terminate his little entertainment by standing treat at the play but that there are chords in the human mind which would render it a hollow mockery.

On the morrow, in the dusk of evening, Mr. Weevle modestly appears at Krook's, by no means incommoded with luggage, and establishes himself in his new lodging, where the two eyes in the shutters stare at him in his sleep, as if they were full of wonder. On the following day Mr. Weevle, who is a handy good-for-nothing kind of young fellow, borrows a needle and thread of Miss Flite and a hammer of his landlord and goes to work devising apologies for window-curtains, and knocking up apologies for shelves, and hanging up his two teacups, milkpot, and crockery sundries on a pennyworth of little hooks, like a shipwrecked sailor making the best of it.

But what Mr. Weevle prizes most of all his few possessions (next after his light whiskers, for which he has an attachment that only whiskers can awaken in the breast of man) is a choice collection of copper-plate impressions from that truly national work The Divinities of Albion, or Galaxy Gallery of British Beauty, representing ladies of title and fashion in every variety of smirk that art, combined with capital, is capable of producing. With these magnificent portraits, unworthily confined in a band-box during his seclusion among the market-gardens, he decorates his apartment; and as the Galaxy Gallery of British Beauty wears every variety of fancy dress, plays every variety of musical instrument, fondles every variety of dog, ogles every variety of prospect, and is backed up by every variety of flower-pot and balustrade, the result is very imposing.

But fashion is Mr. Weevle's, as it was Tony Jobling's, weakness. To borrow yesterday's paper from the Sol's Arms of an evening and read about the brilliant and distinguished meteors that are shooting across the fashionable sky in every direction is unspeakable consolation to him. To know what member of what brilliant and distinguished circle accomplished the brilliant and distinguished feat of joining it yesterday or contemplates the no less brilliant and distinguished feat of leaving it to-morrow gives him a thrill of joy. To be informed what the Galaxy Gallery of British Beauty is about, and means to be about, and what Galaxy marriages are on the tapis, and what Galaxy rumours are in circulation, is to become acquainted with the most glorious destinies of mankind. Mr. Weevle reverts from this intelligence to the Galaxy portraits implicated, and seems to know the originals, and to be known of them.

For the rest he is a quiet lodger, full of handy shifts and devices as before mentioned, able to cook and clean for himself as well as to carpenter, and developing social inclinations after the shades of evening have fallen on the court. At those times, when he is not visited by Mr. Guppy or by a small light in his likeness quenched in a dark hat, he comes out of his dull room—where he has inherited the deal wilderness of desk bespattered with a rain of ink—and talks to Krook or is "very free," as they call it in the court, commendingly, with any one disposed for conversation. Wherefore, Mrs. Piper, who leads the court, is impelled to offer two remarks to Mrs. Perkins: firstly, that if her Johnny was to have whiskers, she could wish 'em to be identically like that young man's; and secondly, "Mark my words, Mrs. Perkins, ma'am, and don't you be surprised, Lord bless you, if that young man comes in at last for old Krook's money!"

CHAPTER XXI
THE SMALLWEED FAMILY

In a rather ill-favoured and ill-savoured neighbourhood, though one of its rising grounds bears the name of Mount Pleasant, the Elfin Smallweed, christened Bartholomew and known on the domestic hearth as Bart, passes that limited portion of his time on which the office and its contingencies have no claim. He dwells in a little narrow street, always solitary, shady, and sad, closely bricked in on all sides like a tomb, but where there yet lingers the stump of an old forest tree whose flavour is about as fresh and natural as the Smallweed smack of youth.

There has been only one child in the Smallweed family for several generations. Little old men and women there have been, but no child, until Mr. Smallweed's grandmother, now living, became weak in her intellect and fell (for the first time) into a childish state. With such infantine graces as a total want of observation, memory, understanding, and interest, and an eternal disposition to fall asleep over the fire and into it, Mr. Smallweed's grandmother has undoubtedly brightened the family.

Mr. Smallweed's grandfather is likewise of the party. He is in a helpless condition as to his lower, and nearly so as to his upper, limbs, but his mind is unimpaired. It holds, as well as it ever held, the first four rules of arithmetic and a certain small collection of the hardest facts. In respect of ideality, reverence, wonder, and other such phrenological attributes, it is no worse off than it used to be. Everything that Mr. Smallweed's grandfather ever put away in his mind was a grub at first, and is a grub at last. In all his life he has never bred a single butterfly.

The father of this pleasant grandfather, of the neighbourhood of Mount Pleasant, was a horny-skinned, two-legged, money-getting species of spider who spun webs to catch unwary flies and retired into holes until they were entrapped. The name of this old pagan's god was Compound Interest. He lived for it, married it, died of it. Meeting with a heavy loss in an honest little enterprise in which all the loss was intended to have been on the other side, he broke something—something necessary to his existence, therefore it couldn't have been his heart—and made an end of his career. As his character was not good, and he had been bred at a charity school in a complete course, according to question and answer, of those ancient people the Amorites and Hittites, he was frequently quoted as an example of the failure of education.

His spirit shone through his son, to whom he had always preached of "going out" early in life and whom he made a clerk in a sharp scrivener's office at twelve years old. There the young gentleman improved his mind, which was of a lean and anxious character, and developing the family gifts, gradually elevated himself into the discounting profession. Going out early in life and marrying late, as his father had done before him, he too begat a lean and anxious-minded son, who in his turn, going out early in life and marrying late, became the father of Bartholomew and Judith Smallweed, twins. During the whole time consumed in the slow growth of this family tree, the house of Smallweed, always early to go out and late to marry, has strengthened itself in its practical character, has discarded all amusements, discountenanced all story-books, fairy-tales, fictions, and fables, and banished all levities whatsoever. Hence the gratifying fact that it has had no child born to it and that the complete little men and women whom it has produced have been observed to bear a likeness to old monkeys with something depressing on their minds.

At the present time, in the dark little parlour certain feet below the level of the street—a grim, hard, uncouth parlour, only ornamented with the coarsest of baize table-covers, and the hardest of sheet-iron tea-trays, and offering in its decorative character no bad allegorical representation of Grandfather Smallweed's mind—seated in two black horsehair porter's chairs, one on each side of the fire-place, the superannuated Mr. and Mrs. Smallweed while away the rosy hours. On the stove are a couple of trivets for the pots and kettles which it is Grandfather Smallweed's usual occupation to watch, and projecting from the chimney-piece between them is a sort of brass gallows for roasting, which he also superintends when it is in action. Under the venerable Mr. Smallweed's seat and guarded by his spindle legs is a drawer in his chair, reported to contain property to a fabulous amount. Beside him is a spare cushion with which he is always provided in order that he may have something to throw at the venerable partner of his respected age whenever she makes an allusion to money—a subject on which he is particularly sensitive.

"And where's Bart?" Grandfather Smallweed inquires of Judy, Bart's twin sister.

"He an't come in yet," says Judy.

"It's his tea-time, isn't it?"

"No."

"How much do you mean to say it wants then?"

"Ten minutes."

"Hey?"

"Ten minutes." (Loud on the part of Judy.)

"Ho!" says Grandfather Smallweed. "Ten minutes."

Grandmother Smallweed, who has been mumbling and shaking her head at the trivets, hearing figures mentioned, connects them with money and screeches like a horrible old parrot without any plumage, "Ten ten-pound notes!"

Grandfather Smallweed immediately throws the cushion at her.

"Drat you, be quiet!" says the good old man.

The effect of this act of jaculation is twofold. It not only doubles up Mrs.

Smallweed's head against the side of her porter's chair and causes her to present, when extricated by her granddaughter, a highly unbecoming state of cap, but the necessary exertion recoils on Mr. Smallweed himself, whom it throws back into HIS porter's chair like a broken puppet. The excellent old gentleman being at these times a mere clothes-bag with a black skull-cap on the top of it, does not present a very animated appearance until he has undergone the two operations at the hands of his granddaughter of being shaken up like a great bottle and poked and punched like a great bolster. Some indication of a neck being developed in him by these means, he and the sharer of his life's evening again fronting one another in their two porter's chairs, like a couple of sentinels long forgotten on their post by the Black Serjeant, Death.

Judy the twin is worthy company for these associates. She is so indubitably sister to Mr. Smallweed the younger that the two kneaded into one would hardly make a young person of average proportions, while she so happily exemplifies the before-mentioned family likeness to the monkey tribe that attired in a spangled robe and cap she might walk about the table-land on the top of a barrel-organ without exciting much remark as an unusual specimen. Under existing circumstances, however, she is dressed in a plain, spare gown of brown stuff.

Judy never owned a doll, never heard of Cinderella, never played at any game. She once or twice fell into children's company when she was about ten years old, but the children couldn't get on with Judy, and Judy couldn't get on with them. She seemed like an animal of another species, and there was instinctive repugnance on both sides. It is very doubtful whether Judy knows how to laugh. She has so rarely seen the thing done that the probabilities are strong the other way. Of anything like a youthful laugh, she certainly can have no conception. If she were to try one, she would find her teeth in her way, modelling that action of her face, as she has unconsciously modelled all its other expressions, on her pattern of sordid age. Such is Judy.

And her twin brother couldn't wind up a top for his life. He knows no more of Jack the Giant Killer or of Sinbad the Sailor than he knows of the people in the stars. He could as soon play at leap-frog or at cricket as change into a cricket or a frog himself. But he is so much the better off than his sister that on his narrow world of fact an opening has dawned into such broader regions as lie within the ken of Mr. Guppy. Hence his admiration and his emulation of that shining enchanter.

Judy, with a gong-like clash and clatter, sets one of the sheet-iron tea-trays on the table and arranges cups and saucers. The bread she puts on in an iron basket, and the butter (and not much of it) in a small pewter plate. Grandfather Smallweed looks hard after the tea as it is served out and asks Judy where the girl is.

"Charley, do you mean?" says Judy.

"Hey?" from Grandfather Smallweed.

"Charley, do you mean?"

This touches a spring in Grandmother Smallweed, who, chuckling as usual at the trivets, cries, "Over the water! Charley over the water, Charley over the water, over the water to Charley, Charley over the water, over the water to Charley!" and becomes quite energetic about it. Grandfather looks at the cushion but has not sufficiently recovered his late exertion.

"Ha!" he says when there is silence. "If that's her name. She eats a deal. It would be better to allow her for her keep."

Judy, with her brother's wink, shakes her head and purses up her mouth into no without saying it.

"No?" returns the old man. "Why not?"

"She'd want sixpence a day, and we can do it for less," says Judy.

"Sure?"

Judy answers with a nod of deepest meaning and calls, as she scrapes the butter on the loaf with every precaution against waste and cuts it into slices, "You, Charley, where are you?" Timidly obedient to the summons, a little girl in a rough apron and a large bonnet, with her hands covered with soap and water and a scrubbing brush in one of them, appears, and curtsys.

"What work are you about now?" says Judy, making an ancient snap at her like a very sharp old beldame.

"I'm a-cleaning the upstairs back room, miss," replies Charley.

"Mind you do it thoroughly, and don't loiter. Shirking won't do for me. Make haste! Go along!" cries Judy with a stamp upon the ground. "You girls are more trouble than you're worth, by half."

On this severe matron, as she returns to her task of scraping the butter and cutting the bread, falls the shadow of her brother, looking in at the window. For whom, knife and loaf in hand, she opens the street-door.

"Aye, aye, Bart!" says Grandfather Smallweed. "Here you are, hey?"

"Here I am," says Bart.

"Been along with your friend again, Bart?"

Small nods.

"Dining at his expense, Bart?"

Small nods again.

"That's right. Live at his expense as much as you can, and take warning by his foolish example. That's the use of such a friend. The only use you can put him to," says the venerable sage.

His grandson, without receiving this good counsel as dutifully as he might, honours it with all such acceptance as may lie in a slight wink and a nod and takes a chair at the tea-table. The four old faces then hover over teacups like a company of ghastly cherubim, Mrs. Smallweed perpetually twitching her head and chattering at the trivets and Mr. Smallweed requiring to be repeatedly shaken up like a large black draught.

"Yes, yes," says the good old gentleman, reverting to his lesson of wisdom.

"That's such advice as your father would have given you, Bart. You never saw your father. More's the pity. He was my true son." Whether it is intended to be conveyed that he was particularly pleasant to look at, on that account, does not appear.

"He was my true son," repeats the old gentleman, folding his bread and butter on his knee, "a good accountant, and died fifteen years ago."

Mrs. Smallweed, following her usual instinct, breaks out with "Fifteen hundred pound. Fifteen hundred pound in a black box, fifteen hundred pound locked up, fifteen hundred pound put away and hid!" Her worthy husband, setting aside his bread and butter, immediately discharges the cushion at her, crushes her against the side of her chair, and falls back in his own, overpowered. His appearance, after visiting Mrs. Smallweed with one of these admonitions, is particularly impressive and not wholly prepossessing, firstly because the exertion generally twists his black skull-cap over one eye and gives him an air of goblin rakishness, secondly because he mutters violent imprecations against Mrs. Smallweed, and thirdly because the contrast between those powerful expressions and his powerless figure is suggestive of a baleful old malignant who would be very wicked if he could. All this, however, is so common in the Smallweed family circle that it produces no impression. The old gentleman is merely shaken and has his internal feathers beaten up, the cushion is restored to its usual place beside him, and the old lady, perhaps with her cap adjusted and perhaps not, is planted in her chair again, ready to be bowled down like a ninepin.

Some time elapses in the present instance before the old gentleman is sufficiently cool to resume his discourse, and even then he mixes it up with several edifying expletives addressed to the unconscious partner of his bosom, who holds communication with nothing on earth but the trivets. As thus: "If your father, Bart, had lived longer, he might have been worth a deal of money—you brimstone chatterer!—but just as he was beginning to build up the house that he had been making the foundations for, through many a year—you jade of a magpie, jackdaw, and poll-parrot, what do you mean!—he took ill and died of a low fever, always being a sparing and a spare man, full of business care—I should like to throw a cat at you instead of a cushion, and I will too if you make such a confounded fool of yourself!—and your mother, who was a prudent woman as dry as a chip, just dwindled away like touchwood after you and Judy were born—you are an old pig. You are a brimstone pig. You're a head of swine!"

Judy, not interested in what she has often heard, begins to collect in a basin various tributary streams of tea, from the bottoms of cups and saucers and from the bottom of the tea-pot for the little charwoman's evening meal. In like manner she gets together, in the iron bread-basket, as many outside fragments and worn-down heels of loaves as the rigid economy of the house has left in existence.

"But your father and me were partners, Bart," says the old gentleman, "and when I am gone, you and Judy will have all there is. It's rare for you both that you went out early in life—Judy to the flower business, and you to the law. You won't want to spend it. You'll get your living without it, and put more to it. When I am gone, Judy will go back to the flower business and you'll still stick to the law."

One might infer from Judy's appearance that her business rather lay with the thorns than the flowers, but she has in her time been apprenticed to the art and mystery of artificial flower-making. A close observer might perhaps detect both in her eye and her brother's, when their venerable grandsire anticipates his being gone, some little impatience to know when he may be going, and some resentful opinion that it is time he went.

"Now, if everybody has done," says Judy, completing her preparations, "I'll have that girl in to her tea. She would never leave off if she took it by herself in the kitchen."

Charley is accordingly introduced, and under a heavy fire of eyes, sits down to her basin and a Druidical ruin of bread and butter. In the active superintendence of this young person, Judy Smallweed appears to attain a perfectly geological age and to date from the remotest periods. Her systematic manner of flying at her and pouncing on her, with or without pretence, whether or no, is wonderful, evincing an accomplishment in the art of girl-driving seldom reached by the oldest practitioners.

"Now, don't stare about you all the afternoon," cries Judy, shaking her head and stamping her foot as she happens to catch the glance which has been previously sounding the basin of tea, "but take your victuals and get back to your work."

"Yes, miss," says Charley.

"Don't say yes," returns Miss Smallweed, "for I know what you girls are. Do it without saying it, and then I may begin to believe you."

Charley swallows a great gulp of tea in token of submission and so disperses the Druidical ruins that Miss Smallweed charges her not to gormandize, which "in you girls," she observes, is disgusting. Charley might find some more difficulty in meeting her views on the general subject of girls but for a knock at the door.

"See who it is, and don't chew when you open it!" cries Judy.

The object of her attentions withdrawing for the purpose, Miss Smallweed takes that opportunity of jumbling the remainder of the bread and butter together and launching two or three dirty tea-cups into the ebb-tide of the basin of tea as a hint that she considers the eating and drinking terminated.

"Now! Who is it, and what's wanted?" says the snappish Judy.

It is one Mr. George, it appears. Without other announcement or ceremony, Mr. George walks in.

"Whew!" says Mr. George. "You are hot here. Always a fire, eh? Well! Perhaps you do right to get used to one." Mr. George makes the latter remark to himself as he nods to Grandfather Smallweed.

"Ho! It's you!" cries the old gentleman. "How de do? How de do?"

"Middling," replies Mr. George, taking a chair. "Your granddaughter I have had the honour of seeing before; my service to you, miss."

"This is my grandson," says Grandfather Smallweed. "You ha'n't seen him before. He is in the law and not much at home."

"My service to him, too! He is like his sister. He is very like his sister. He is devilish like his sister," says Mr. George, laying a great and not altogether complimentary stress on his last adjective.

"And how does the world use you, Mr. George?" Grandfather Smallweed inquires, slowly rubbing his legs.

"Pretty much as usual. Like a football."

He is a swarthy brown man of fifty, well made, and good looking, with crisp dark hair, bright eyes, and a broad chest. His sinewy and powerful hands, as sunburnt as his face, have evidently been used to a pretty rough life. What is curious about him is that he sits forward on his chair as if he were, from long habit, allowing space for some dress or accoutrements that he has altogether laid aside. His step too is measured and heavy and would go well with a weighty clash and jingle of spurs. He is close-shaved now, but his mouth is set as if his upper lip had been for years familiar with a great moustache; and his manner of occasionally laying the open palm of his broad brown hand upon it is to the same effect. Altogether one might guess Mr. George to have been a trooper once upon a time.

A special contrast Mr. George makes to the Smallweed family. Trooper was never yet billeted upon a household more unlike him. It is a broadsword to an oyster-knife. His developed figure and their stunted forms, his large manner filling any amount of room and their little narrow pinched ways, his sounding voice and their sharp spare tones, are in the strongest and the strangest opposition. As he sits in the middle of the grim parlour, leaning a little forward, with his hands upon his thighs and his elbows squared, he looks as though, if he remained there long, he would absorb into himself the whole family and the whole four-roomed house, extra little back-kitchen and all.

"Do you rub your legs to rub life into 'em?" he asks of Grandfather Smallweed after looking round the room.

"Why, it's partly a habit, Mr. George, and—yes—it partly helps the circulation," he replies.

"The cir-cu-la-tion!" repeats Mr. George, folding his arms upon his chest and seeming to become two sizes larger. "Not much of that, I should think."

"Truly I'm old, Mr. George," says Grandfather Smallweed. "But I can carry my years. I'm older than HER," nodding at his wife, "and see what she is? You're a brimstone chatterer!" with a sudden revival of his late hostility.

"Unlucky old soul!" says Mr. George, turning his head in that direction.

"Don't scold the old lady. Look at her here, with her poor cap half off her head and her poor hair all in a muddle. Hold up, ma'am. That's better. There we are! Think of your mother, Mr. Smallweed," says Mr. George, coming back to his seat from assisting her, "if your wife an't enough."

"I suppose you were an excellent son, Mr. George?" the old man hints with a leer.

The colour of Mr. George's face rather deepens as he replies, "Why no. I wasn't."

"I am astonished at it."

"So am I. I ought to have been a good son, and I think I meant to have been one. But I wasn't. I was a thundering bad son, that's the long and the short of it, and never was a credit to anybody."

"Surprising!" cries the old man.

"However," Mr. George resumes, "the less said about it, the better now. Come! You know the agreement. Always a pipe out of the two months' interest! (Bosh! It's all correct. You needn't be afraid to order the pipe. Here's the new bill, and here's the two months' interest-money, and a devil-and-all of a scrape it is to get it together in my business.)"

Mr. George sits, with his arms folded, consuming the family and the parlour while Grandfather Smallweed is assisted by Judy to two black leathern cases out of a locked bureau, in one of which he secures the document he has just received, and from the other takes another similar document which he hands to Mr. George, who twists it up for a pipelight. As the old man inspects, through his glasses, every up-stroke and down-stroke of both documents before he releases them from their leathern prison, and as he counts the money three times over and requires Judy to say every word she utters at least twice, and is as tremulously slow of speech and action as it is possible to be, this business is a long time in progress. When it is quite concluded, and not before, he disengages his ravenous eyes and fingers from it and answers Mr. George's last remark by saying, "Afraid to order the pipe? We are not so mercenary as that, sir. Judy, see directly to the pipe and the glass of cold brandy-and-water for Mr. George."

The sportive twins, who have been looking straight before them all this time except when they have been engrossed by the black leathern cases, retire together, generally disdainful of the visitor, but leaving him to the old man as two young cubs might leave a traveller to the parental bear.

"And there you sit, I suppose, all the day long, eh?" says Mr. George with folded arms.

"Just so, just so," the old man nods.

"And don't you occupy yourself at all?"

"I watch the fire—and the boiling and the roasting—"

"When there is any," says Mr. George with great expression.

"Just so. When there is any."

"Don't you read or get read to?"

The old man shakes his head with sharp sly triumph. "No, no. We have never been readers in our family. It don't pay. Stuff. Idleness. Folly. No, no!"

"There's not much to choose between your two states," says the visitor in a key too low for the old man's dull hearing as he looks from him to the old woman and back again. "I say!" in a louder voice.

"I hear you."

"You'll sell me up at last, I suppose, when I am a day in arrear."

"My dear friend!" cries Grandfather Smallweed, stretching out both hands to embrace him. "Never! Never, my dear friend! But my friend in the city that I got to lend you the money—HE might!"

"Oh! You can't answer for him?" says Mr. George, finishing the inquiry in his lower key with the words "You lying old rascal!"

"My dear friend, he is not to be depended on. I wouldn't trust him. He will have his bond, my dear friend."

"Devil doubt him," says Mr. George. Charley appearing with a tray, on which are the pipe, a small paper of tobacco, and the brandy-and-water, he asks her, "How do you come here! You haven't got the family face."

"I goes out to work, sir," returns Charley.

The trooper (if trooper he be or have been) takes her bonnet off, with a light touch for so strong a hand, and pats her on the head. "You give the house almost a wholesome look. It wants a bit of youth as much as it wants fresh air." Then he dismisses her, lights his pipe, and drinks to Mr. Smallweed's friend in the city—the one solitary flight of that esteemed old gentleman's imagination.

"So you think he might be hard upon me, eh?"

"I think he might—I am afraid he would. I have known him do it," says Grandfather Smallweed incautiously, "twenty times."

Incautiously, because his stricken better-half, who has been dozing over the fire for some time, is instantly aroused and jabbers "Twenty thousand pounds, twenty twenty-pound notes in a money-box, twenty guineas, twenty million twenty per cent, twenty—" and is then cut short by the flying cushion, which the visitor, to whom this singular experiment appears to be a novelty, snatches from her face as it crushes her in the usual manner.

"You're a brimstone idiot. You're a scorpion—a brimstone scorpion! You're a sweltering toad. You're a chattering clattering broomstick witch that ought to be burnt!" gasps the old man, prostrate in his chair. "My dear friend, will you shake me up a little?"

Mr. George, who has been looking first at one of them and then at the other, as if he were demented, takes his venerable acquaintance by the throat on receiving this request, and dragging him upright in his chair as easily as if he were a doll, appears in two minds whether or no to shake all future power of cushioning out of him and shake him into his grave. Resisting the temptation, but agitating him violently enough to make his head roll like a harlequin's, he puts him smartly down in his chair again and adjusts his skull-cap with such a rub that the old man winks with both eyes for a minute afterwards.

"O Lord!" gasps Mr. Smallweed. "That'll do. Thank you, my dear friend, that'll do. Oh, dear me, I'm out of breath. O Lord!" And Mr. Smallweed says it not without evident apprehensions of his dear friend, who still stands over him looming larger than ever.

The alarming presence, however, gradually subsides into its chair and falls to smoking in long puffs, consoling itself with the philosophical reflection, "The name of your friend in the city begins with a D, comrade, and you're about right respecting the bond."

"Did you speak, Mr. George?" inquires the old man.

The trooper shakes his head, and leaning forward with his right elbow on his right knee and his pipe supported in that hand, while his other hand, resting on his left leg, squares his left elbow in a martial manner, continues to smoke. Meanwhile he looks at Mr. Smallweed with grave attention and now and then fans the cloud of smoke away in order that he may see him the more clearly.

"I take it," he says, making just as much and as little change in his position as will enable him to reach the glass to his lips with a round, full action, "that I am the only man alive (or dead either) that gets the value of a pipe out of YOU?"

"Well," returns the old man, "it's true that I don't see company, Mr. George, and that I don't treat. I can't afford to it. But as you, in your pleasant way, made your pipe a condition—"

"Why, it's not for the value of it; that's no great thing. It was a fancy to get it out of you. To have something in for my money."

"Ha! You're prudent, prudent, sir!" cries Grandfather Smallweed, rubbing his legs.

"Very. I always was." Puff. "It's a sure sign of my prudence that I ever found the way here." Puff. "Also, that I am what I am." Puff. "I am well known to be prudent," says Mr. George, composedly smoking. "I rose in life that way."

"Don't be down-hearted, sir. You may rise yet."

Mr. George laughs and drinks.

"Ha'n't you no relations, now," asks Grandfather Smallweed with a twinkle in his eyes, "who would pay off this little principal or who would lend you a good name or two that I could persuade my friend in the city to make you a further advance upon? Two good names would be sufficient for my friend in the city. Ha'n't you no such relations, Mr. George?"

Mr. George, still composedly smoking, replies, "If I had, I shouldn't trouble them. I have been trouble enough to my belongings in my day. It MAY be a very good sort of penitence in a vagabond, who has wasted the best time of his life, to go back then to decent people that he never was a credit to and live upon them, but it's not my sort. The best kind of amends then for having gone away is to keep away, in my opinion."

"But natural affection, Mr. George," hints Grandfather Smallweed.

"For two good names, hey?" says Mr. George, shaking his head and still composedly smoking. "No. That's not my sort either."

Grandfather Smallweed has been gradually sliding down in his chair since his last adjustment and is now a bundle of clothes with a voice in it calling for Judy. That houri, appearing, shakes him up in the usual manner and is charged by the old gentleman to remain near him. For he seems chary of putting his visitor to the trouble of repeating his late attentions.

"Ha!" he observes when he is in trim again. "If you could have traced out the captain, Mr. George, it would have been the making of you. If when you first came here, in consequence of our advertisement in the newspapers—when I say 'our,' I'm alluding to the advertisements of my friend in the city, and one or two others who embark their capital in the same way, and are so friendly towards me as sometimes to give me a lift with my little pittance—if at that time you could have helped us, Mr. George, it would have been the making of you."

"I was willing enough to be 'made,' as you call it," says Mr. George, smoking not quite so placidly as before, for since the entrance of Judy he has been in some measure disturbed by a fascination, not of the admiring kind, which obliges him to look at her as she stands by her grandfather's chair, "but on the whole, I am glad I wasn't now."

"Why, Mr. George? In the name of—of brimstone, why?" says Grandfather Smallweed with a plain appearance of exasperation. (Brimstone apparently suggested by his eye lighting on Mrs. Smallweed in her slumber.)

"For two reasons, comrade."

"And what two reasons, Mr. George? In the name of the—"

"Of our friend in the city?" suggests Mr. George, composedly drinking.

"Aye, if you like. What two reasons?"

"In the first place," returns Mr. George, but still looking at Judy as if she being so old and so like her grandfather it is indifferent which of the two he addresses, "you gentlemen took me in. You advertised that Mr. Hawdon (Captain Hawdon, if you hold to the saying 'Once a captain, always a captain') was to hear of something to his advantage."

"Well?" returns the old man shrilly and sharply.

"Well!" says Mr. George, smoking on. "It wouldn't have been much to his advantage to have been clapped into prison by the whole bill and judgment trade of London."

"How do you know that? Some of his rich relations might have paid his debts or compounded for 'em. Besides, he had taken US in. He owed us immense sums all round. I would sooner have strangled him than had no return. If I sit here thinking of him," snarls the old man, holding up his impotent ten fingers, "I want to strangle him now." And in a sudden access of fury, he throws the cushion at the unoffending Mrs. Smallweed, but it passes harmlessly on one side of her chair.

"I don't need to be told," returns the trooper, taking his pipe from his lips for a moment and carrying his eyes back from following the progress of the cushion to the pipe-bowl which is burning low, "that he carried on heavily and went to ruin. I have been at his right hand many a day when he was charging upon ruin full-gallop. I was with him when he was sick and well, rich and poor. I laid this hand upon him after he had run through everything and broken down everything beneath him—when he held a pistol to his head."

"I wish he had let it off," says the benevolent old man, "and blown his head into as many pieces as he owed pounds!"

"That would have been a smash indeed," returns the trooper coolly; "any way, he had been young, hopeful, and handsome in the days gone by, and I am glad I never found him, when he was neither, to lead to a result so much to his advantage. That's reason number one."

"I hope number two's as good?" snarls the old man.

"Why, no. It's more of a selfish reason. If I had found him, I must have gone to the other world to look. He was there."

"How do you know he was there?"

"He wasn't here."

"How do you know he wasn't here?"

"Don't lose your temper as well as your money," says Mr. George, calmly knocking the ashes out of his pipe. "He was drowned long before. I am convinced of it. He went over a ship's side. Whether intentionally or accidentally, I don't know. Perhaps your friend in the city does. Do you know what that tune is, Mr. Smallweed?" he adds after breaking off to whistle one, accompanied on the table with the empty pipe.

"Tune!" replied the old man. "No. We never have tunes here."

"That's the Dead March in Saul. They bury soldiers to it, so it's the natural end of the subject. Now, if your pretty granddaughter—excuse me, miss—will condescend to take care of this pipe for two months, we shall save the cost of one next time. Good evening, Mr. Smallweed!"

"My dear friend!" the old man gives him both his hands.

"So you think your friend in the city will be hard upon me if I fall in a payment?" says the trooper, looking down upon him like a giant.

"My dear friend, I am afraid he will," returns the old man, looking up at him like a pygmy.

Mr. George laughs, and with a glance at Mr. Smallweed and a parting salutation to the scornful Judy, strides out of the parlour, clashing imaginary sabres and other metallic appurtenances as he goes.

"You're a damned rogue," says the old gentleman, making a hideous grimace at the door as he shuts it. "But I'll lime you, you dog, I'll lime you!"

After this amiable remark, his spirit soars into those enchanting regions of reflection which its education and pursuits have opened to it, and again he and Mrs. Smallweed while away the rosy hours, two unrelieved sentinels forgotten as aforesaid by the Black Serjeant.

While the twain are faithful to their post, Mr. George strides through the streets with a massive kind of swagger and a grave-enough face. It is eight o'clock now, and the day is fast drawing in. He stops hard by Waterloo Bridge and reads a playbill, decides to go to Astley's Theatre. Being there, is much delighted with the horses and the feats of strength; looks at the weapons with a critical eye; disapproves of the combats as giving evidences of unskilful swordsmanship; but is touched home by the sentiments. In the last scene, when the Emperor of Tartary gets up into a cart and condescends to bless the united lovers by hovering over them with the Union Jack, his eyelashes are moistened with emotion.

The theatre over, Mr. George comes across the water again and makes his way to that curious region lying about the Haymarket and Leicester Square which is a centre of attraction to indifferent foreign hotels and indifferent foreigners, racket-courts, fighting-men, swordsmen, footguards, old china, gaming-houses, exhibitions, and a large medley of shabbiness and shrinking out of sight. Penetrating to the heart of this region, he arrives by a court and a long whitewashed passage at a great brick building composed of bare walls, floors, roof-rafters, and skylights, on the front of which, if it can be said to have any front, is painted GEORGE'S SHOOTING GALLERY, &c.

Into George's Shooting Gallery, &c., he goes; and in it there are gaslights (partly turned off now), and two whitened targets for rifle-shooting, and archery accommodation, and fencing appliances, and all necessaries for the British art of boxing. None of these sports or exercises being pursued in George's Shooting Gallery to-night, which is so devoid of company that a little grotesque man with a large head has it all to himself and lies asleep upon the floor.

The little man is dressed something like a gunsmith, in a green-baize apron and cap; and his face and hands are dirty with gunpowder and begrimed with the loading of guns. As he lies in the light before a glaring white target, the black upon him shines again. Not far off is the strong, rough, primitive table with a vice upon it at which he has been working. He is a little man with a face all crushed together, who appears, from a certain blue and speckled appearance that one of his cheeks presents, to have been blown up, in the way of business, at some odd time or times.

"Phil!" says the trooper in a quiet voice.

"All right!" cries Phil, scrambling to his feet.

"Anything been doing?"

"Flat as ever so much swipes," says Phil. "Five dozen rifle and a dozen pistol. As to aim!" Phil gives a howl at the recollection.

"Shut up shop, Phil!"

As Phil moves about to execute this order, it appears that he is lame, though able to move very quickly. On the speckled side of his face he has no eyebrow, and on the other side he has a bushy black one, which want of uniformity gives him a very singular and rather sinister appearance. Everything seems to have happened to his hands that could possibly take place consistently with the retention of all the fingers, for they are notched, and seamed, and crumpled all over. He appears to be very strong and lifts heavy benches about as if he had no idea what weight was. He has a curious way of limping round the gallery with his shoulder against the wall and tacking off at objects he wants to lay hold of instead of going straight to them, which has left a smear all round the four walls, conventionally called "Phil's mark."

This custodian of George's Gallery in George's absence concludes his proceedings, when he has locked the great doors and turned out all the lights but one, which he leaves to glimmer, by dragging out from a wooden cabin in a corner two mattresses and bedding. These being drawn to opposite ends of the gallery, the trooper makes his own bed and Phil makes his.

"Phil!" says the master, walking towards him without his coat and waistcoat, and looking more soldierly than ever in his braces. "You were found in a doorway, weren't you?"

"Gutter," says Phil. "Watchman tumbled over me."

"Then vagabondizing came natural to YOU from the beginning."

"As nat'ral as possible," says Phil.

"Good night!"

"Good night, guv'ner."

Phil cannot even go straight to bed, but finds it necessary to shoulder round two sides of the gallery and then tack off at his mattress. The trooper, after taking a turn or two in the rifle-distance and looking up at the moon now shining through the skylights, strides to his own mattress by a shorter route and goes to bed too.

CHAPTER XXII
MR. BUCKET

Allegory looks pretty cool in Lincoln's Inn Fields, though the evening is hot, for both Mr. Tulkinghorn's windows are wide open, and the room is lofty, gusty, and gloomy. These may not be desirable characteristics when November comes with fog and sleet or January with ice and snow, but they have their merits in the sultry long vacation weather. They enable Allegory, though it has cheeks like peaches, and knees like bunches of blossoms, and rosy swellings for calves to its legs and muscles to its arms, to look tolerably cool to-night.

Plenty of dust comes in at Mr. Tulkinghorn's windows, and plenty more has generated among his furniture and papers. It lies thick everywhere. When a breeze from the country that has lost its way takes fright and makes a blind hurry to rush out again, it flings as much dust in the eyes of Allegory as the law—or Mr. Tulkinghorn, one of its trustiest representatives—may scatter, on occasion, in the eyes of the laity.

In his lowering magazine of dust, the universal article into which his papers and himself, and all his clients, and all things of earth, animate and inanimate, are resolving, Mr. Tulkinghorn sits at one of the open windows enjoying a bottle of old port. Though a hard-grained man, close, dry, and silent, he can enjoy old wine with the best. He has a priceless bin of port in some artful cellar under the Fields, which is one of his many secrets. When he dines alone in chambers, as he has dined to-day, and has his bit of fish and his steak or chicken brought in from the coffee-house, he descends with a candle to the echoing regions below the deserted mansion, and heralded by a remote reverberation of thundering doors, comes gravely back encircled by an earthy atmosphere and carrying a bottle from which he pours a radiant nectar, two score and ten years old, that blushes in the glass to find itself so famous and fills the whole room with the fragrance of southern grapes.

Mr. Tulkinghorn, sitting in the twilight by the open window, enjoys his wine. As if it whispered to him of its fifty years of silence and seclusion, it shuts him up the closer. More impenetrable than ever, he sits, and drinks, and mellows as it were in secrecy, pondering at that twilight hour on all the mysteries he knows, associated with darkening woods in the country, and vast blank shut-up houses in town, and perhaps sparing a thought or two for himself, and his family history, and his money, and his will—all a mystery to every one—and that one bachelor friend of his, a man of the same mould and a lawyer too, who lived the same kind of life until he was seventy-five years old, and then suddenly conceiving (as it is supposed) an impression that it was too monotonous, gave his gold watch to his hair-dresser one summer evening and walked leisurely home to the Temple and hanged himself.

But Mr. Tulkinghorn is not alone to-night to ponder at his usual length. Seated at the same table, though with his chair modestly and uncomfortably drawn a little way from it, sits a bald, mild, shining man who coughs respectfully behind his hand when the lawyer bids him fill his glass.

"Now, Snagsby," says Mr. Tulkinghorn, "to go over this odd story again."

"If you please, sir."

"You told me when you were so good as to step round here last night—"

"For which I must ask you to excuse me if it was a liberty, sir; but I remember that you had taken a sort of an interest in that person, and I thought it possible that you might—just—wish—to—"

Mr. Tulkinghorn is not the man to help him to any conclusion or to admit anything as to any possibility concerning himself. So Mr. Snagsby trails off into saying, with an awkward cough, "I must ask you to excuse the liberty, sir, I am sure."

"Not at all," says Mr. Tulkinghorn. "You told me, Snagsby, that you put on your hat and came round without mentioning your intention to your wife. That was prudent I think, because it's not a matter of such importance that it requires to be mentioned."

"Well, sir," returns Mr. Snagsby, "you see, my little woman is—not to put too fine a point upon it—inquisitive. She's inquisitive. Poor little thing, she's liable to spasms, and it's good for her to have her mind employed. In consequence of which she employs it—I should say upon every individual thing she can lay hold of, whether it concerns her or not—especially not. My little woman has a very active mind, sir."

Mr. Snagsby drinks and murmurs with an admiring cough behind his hand, "Dear me, very fine wine indeed!"

"Therefore you kept your visit to yourself last night?" says Mr. Tulkinghorn. "And to-night too?"

"Yes, sir, and to-night, too. My little woman is at present in—not to put too fine a point on it—in a pious state, or in what she considers such, and attends the Evening Exertions (which is the name they go by) of a reverend party of the name of Chadband. He has a great deal of eloquence at his command, undoubtedly, but I am not quite favourable to his style myself. That's neither here nor there. My little woman being engaged in that way made it easier for me to step round in a quiet manner."

Mr. Tulkinghorn assents. "Fill your glass, Snagsby."

"Thank you, sir, I am sure," returns the stationer with his cough of deference. "This is wonderfully fine wine, sir!"

"It is a rare wine now," says Mr. Tulkinghorn. "It is fifty years old."

"Is it indeed, sir? But I am not surprised to hear it, I am sure. It might be—any age almost." After rendering this general tribute to the port, Mr. Snagsby in his modesty coughs an apology behind his hand for drinking anything so precious.

"Will you run over, once again, what the boy said?" asks Mr. Tulkinghorn, putting his hands into the pockets of his rusty smallclothes and leaning quietly back in his chair.

"With pleasure, sir."

Then, with fidelity, though with some prolixity, the law-stationer repeats Jo's statement made to the assembled guests at his house. On coming to the end of his narrative, he gives a great start and breaks off with, "Dear me, sir, I wasn't aware there was any other gentleman present!"

Mr. Snagsby is dismayed to see, standing with an attentive face between himself and the lawyer at a little distance from the table, a person with a hat and stick in his hand who was not there when he himself came in and has not since entered by the door or by either of the windows. There is a press in the room, but its hinges have not creaked, nor has a step been audible upon the floor. Yet this third person stands there with his attentive face, and his hat and stick in his hands, and his hands behind him, a composed and quiet listener. He is a stoutly built, steady-looking, sharp-eyed man in black, of about the middle-age. Except that he looks at Mr. Snagsby as if he were going to take his portrait, there is nothing remarkable about him at first sight but his ghostly manner of appearing.

"Don't mind this gentleman," says Mr. Tulkinghorn in his quiet way. "This is only Mr. Bucket."

"Oh, indeed, sir?" returns the stationer, expressing by a cough that he is quite in the dark as to who Mr. Bucket may be.

"I wanted him to hear this story," says the lawyer, "because I have half a mind (for a reason) to know more of it, and he is very intelligent in such things. What do you say to this, Bucket?"

"It's very plain, sir. Since our people have moved this boy on, and he's not to be found on his old lay, if Mr. Snagsby don't object to go down with me to Tom-all-Alone's and point him out, we can have him here in less than a couple of hours' time. I can do it without Mr. Snagsby, of course, but this is the shortest way."

"Mr. Bucket is a detective officer, Snagsby," says the lawyer in explanation.

"Is he indeed, sir?" says Mr. Snagsby with a strong tendency in his clump of hair to stand on end.

"And if you have no real objection to accompany Mr. Bucket to the place in question," pursues the lawyer, "I shall feel obliged to you if you will do so."

In a moment's hesitation on the part of Mr. Snagsby, Bucket dips down to the bottom of his mind.

"Don't you be afraid of hurting the boy," he says. "You won't do that. It's all right as far as the boy's concerned. We shall only bring him here to ask him a question or so I want to put to him, and he'll be paid for his trouble and sent away again. It'll be a good job for him. I promise you, as a man, that you shall see the boy sent away all right. Don't you be afraid of hurting him; you an't going to do that."

"Very well, Mr. Tulkinghorn!" cries Mr. Snagsby cheerfully. And reassured, "Since that's the case—"

"Yes! And lookee here, Mr. Snagsby," resumes Bucket, taking him aside by the arm, tapping him familiarly on the breast, and speaking in a confidential tone. "You're a man of the world, you know, and a man of business, and a man of sense. That's what YOU are."

"I am sure I am much obliged to you for your good opinion," returns the stationer with his cough of modesty, "but—"

"That's what YOU are, you know," says Bucket. "Now, it an't necessary to say to a man like you, engaged in your business, which is a business of trust and requires a person to be wide awake and have his senses about him and his head screwed on tight (I had an uncle in your business once)—it an't necessary to say to a man like you that it's the best and wisest way to keep little matters like this quiet. Don't you see? Quiet!"

"Certainly, certainly," returns the other.

"I don't mind telling YOU," says Bucket with an engaging appearance of frankness, "that as far as I can understand it, there seems to be a doubt whether this dead person wasn't entitled to a little property, and whether this female hasn't been up to some games respecting that property, don't you see?"

"Oh!" says Mr. Snagsby, but not appearing to see quite distinctly.

"Now, what YOU want," pursues Bucket, again tapping Mr. Snagsby on the breast in a comfortable and soothing manner, "is that every person should have their rights according to justice. That's what YOU want."

"To be sure," returns Mr. Snagsby with a nod.

"On account of which, and at the same time to oblige a—do you call it, in your business, customer or client? I forget how my uncle used to call it."

"Why, I generally say customer myself," replies Mr. Snagsby.

"You're right!" returns Mr. Bucket, shaking hands with him quite affectionately. "—On account of which, and at the same time to oblige a real good customer, you mean to go down with me, in confidence, to Tom-all-Alone's and to keep the whole thing quiet ever afterwards and never mention it to any one. That's about your intentions, if I understand you?"

"You are right, sir. You are right," says Mr. Snagsby.

"Then here's your hat," returns his new friend, quite as intimate with it as if he had made it; "and if you're ready, I am."

They leave Mr. Tulkinghorn, without a ruffle on the surface of his unfathomable depths, drinking his old wine, and go down into the streets.

"You don't happen to know a very good sort of person of the name of Gridley, do you?" says Bucket in friendly converse as they descend the stairs.

"No," says Mr. Snagsby, considering, "I don't know anybody of that name. Why?"

"Nothing particular," says Bucket; "only having allowed his temper to get a little the better of him and having been threatening some respectable people, he is keeping out of the way of a warrant I have got against him—which it's a pity that a man of sense should do."

As they walk along, Mr. Snagsby observes, as a novelty, that however quick their pace may be, his companion still seems in some undefinable manner to lurk and lounge; also, that whenever he is going to turn to the right or left, he pretends to have a fixed purpose in his mind of going straight ahead, and wheels off, sharply, at the very last moment. Now and then, when they pass a police-constable on his beat, Mr. Snagsby notices that both the constable and his guide fall into a deep abstraction as they come towards each other, and appear entirely to overlook each other, and to gaze into space. In a few instances, Mr. Bucket, coming behind some under-sized young man with a shining hat on, and his sleek hair twisted into one flat curl on each side of his head, almost without glancing at him touches him with his stick, upon which the young man, looking round, instantly evaporates. For the most part Mr. Bucket notices things in general, with a face as unchanging as the great mourning ring on his little finger or the brooch, composed of not much diamond and a good deal of setting, which he wears in his shirt.

When they come at last to Tom-all-Alone's, Mr. Bucket stops for a moment at the corner and takes a lighted bull's-eye from the constable on duty there, who then accompanies him with his own particular bull's-eye at his waist. Between his two conductors, Mr. Snagsby passes along the middle of a villainous street, undrained, unventilated, deep in black mud and corrupt water—though the roads are dry elsewhere—and reeking with such smells and sights that he, who has lived in London all his life, can scarce believe his senses. Branching from this street and its heaps of ruins are other streets and courts so infamous that Mr. Snagsby sickens in body and mind and feels as if he were going every moment deeper down into the infernal gulf.

"Draw off a bit here, Mr. Snagsby," says Bucket as a kind of shabby palanquin is borne towards them, surrounded by a noisy crowd. "Here's the fever coming up the street!"

As the unseen wretch goes by, the crowd, leaving that object of attraction, hovers round the three visitors like a dream of horrible faces and fades away up alleys and into ruins and behind walls, and with occasional cries and shrill whistles of warning, thenceforth flits about them until they leave the place.

"Are those the fever-houses, Darby?" Mr. Bucket coolly asks as he turns his bull's-eye on a line of stinking ruins.

Darby replies that "all them are," and further that in all, for months and months, the people "have been down by dozens" and have been carried out dead and dying "like sheep with the rot." Bucket observing to Mr. Snagsby as they go on again that he looks a little poorly, Mr. Snagsby answers that he feels as if he couldn't breathe the dreadful air.

There is inquiry made at various houses for a boy named Jo. As few people are known in Tom-all-Alone's by any Christian sign, there is much reference to Mr. Snagsby whether he means Carrots, or the Colonel, or Gallows, or Young Chisel, or Terrier Tip, or Lanky, or the Brick. Mr. Snagsby describes over and over again. There are conflicting opinions respecting the original of his picture. Some think it must be Carrots, some say the Brick. The Colonel is produced, but is not at all near the thing. Whenever Mr. Snagsby and his conductors are stationary, the crowd flows round, and from its squalid depths obsequious advice heaves up to Mr. Bucket. Whenever they move, and the angry bull's-eyes glare, it fades away and flits about them up the alleys, and in the ruins, and behind the walls, as before.

At last there is a lair found out where Toughy, or the Tough Subject, lays him down at night; and it is thought that the Tough Subject may be Jo. Comparison of notes between Mr. Snagsby and the proprietress of the house—a drunken face tied up in a black bundle, and flaring out of a heap of rags on the floor of a dog-hutch which is her private apartment—leads to the establishment of this conclusion. Toughy has gone to the doctor's to get a bottle of stuff for a sick woman but will be here anon.

"And who have we got here to-night?" says Mr. Bucket, opening another door and glaring in with his bull's-eye. "Two drunken men, eh? And two women? The men are sound enough," turning back each sleeper's arm from his face to look at him. "Are these your good men, my dears?"

"Yes, sir," returns one of the women. "They are our husbands."

"Brickmakers, eh?"

"Yes, sir."

"What are you doing here? You don't belong to London."

"No, sir. We belong to Hertfordshire."

"Whereabouts in Hertfordshire?"

"Saint Albans."

"Come up on the tramp?"

"We walked up yesterday. There's no work down with us at present, but we have done no good by coming here, and shall do none, I expect."

"That's not the way to do much good," says Mr. Bucket, turning his head in the direction of the unconscious figures on the ground.

"It an't indeed," replies the woman with a sigh. "Jenny and me knows it full well."

The room, though two or three feet higher than the door, is so low that the head of the tallest of the visitors would touch the blackened ceiling if he stood upright. It is offensive to every sense; even the gross candle burns pale and sickly in the polluted air. There are a couple of benches and a higher bench by way of table. The men lie asleep where they stumbled down, but the women sit by the candle. Lying in the arms of the woman who has spoken is a very young child.

"Why, what age do you call that little creature?" says Bucket. "It looks as if it was born yesterday." He is not at all rough about it; and as he turns his light gently on the infant, Mr. Snagsby is strangely reminded of another infant, encircled with light, that he has seen in pictures.

"He is not three weeks old yet, sir," says the woman.

"Is he your child?"

"Mine."

The other woman, who was bending over it when they came in, stoops down again and kisses it as it lies asleep.

"You seem as fond of it as if you were the mother yourself," says Mr. Bucket.

"I was the mother of one like it, master, and it died."

"Ah, Jenny, Jenny!" says the other woman to her. "Better so. Much better to think of dead than alive, Jenny! Much better!"

"Why, you an't such an unnatural woman, I hope," returns Bucket sternly, "as to wish your own child dead?"

"God knows you are right, master," she returns. "I am not. I'd stand between it and death with my own life if I could, as true as any pretty lady."

"Then don't talk in that wrong manner," says Mr. Bucket, mollified again. "Why do you do it?"

"It's brought into my head, master," returns the woman, her eyes filling with tears, "when I look down at the child lying so. If it was never to wake no more, you'd think me mad, I should take on so. I know that very well. I was with Jenny when she lost hers—warn't I, Jenny?—and I know how she grieved. But look around you at this place. Look at them," glancing at the sleepers on the ground. "Look at the boy you're waiting for, who's gone out to do me a good turn. Think of the children that your business lays with often and often, and that YOU see grow up!"

"Well, well," says Mr. Bucket, "you train him respectable, and he'll be a comfort to you, and look after you in your old age, you know."

"I mean to try hard," she answers, wiping her eyes. "But I have been a-thinking, being over-tired to-night and not well with the ague, of all the many things that'll come in his way. My master will be against it, and he'll be beat, and see me beat, and made to fear his home, and perhaps to stray wild. If I work for him ever so much, and ever so hard, there's no one to help me; and if he should be turned bad 'spite of all I could do, and the time should come when I should sit by him in his sleep, made hard and changed, an't it likely I should think of him as he lies in my lap now and wish he had died as Jenny's child died!"

"There, there!" says Jenny. "Liz, you're tired and ill. Let me take him."

In doing so, she displaces the mother's dress, but quickly readjusts it over the wounded and bruised bosom where the baby has been lying.

"It's my dead child," says Jenny, walking up and down as she nurses, "that makes me love this child so dear, and it's my dead child that makes her love it so dear too, as even to think of its being taken away from her now. While she thinks that, I think what fortune would I give to have my darling back. But we mean the same thing, if we knew how to say it, us two mothers does in our poor hearts!"

As Mr. Snagsby blows his nose and coughs his cough of sympathy, a step is heard without. Mr. Bucket throws his light into the doorway and says to Mr. Snagsby, "Now, what do you say to Toughy? Will HE do?"

"That's Jo," says Mr. Snagsby.

Jo stands amazed in the disk of light, like a ragged figure in a magic-lantern, trembling to think that he has offended against the law in not having moved on far enough. Mr. Snagsby, however, giving him the consolatory assurance, "It's only a job you will be paid for, Jo," he recovers; and on being taken outside by Mr. Bucket for a little private confabulation, tells his tale satisfactorily, though out of breath.

"I have squared it with the lad," says Mr. Bucket, returning, "and it's all right. Now, Mr. Snagsby, we're ready for you."

First, Jo has to complete his errand of good nature by handing over the physic he has been to get, which he delivers with the laconic verbal direction that "it's to be all took d'rectly." Secondly, Mr. Snagsby has to lay upon the table half a crown, his usual panacea for an immense variety of afflictions. Thirdly, Mr. Bucket has to take Jo by the arm a little above the elbow and walk him on before him, without which observance neither the Tough Subject nor any other Subject could be professionally conducted to Lincoln's Inn Fields. These arrangements completed, they give the women good night and come out once more into black and foul Tom-all-Alone's.

By the noisome ways through which they descended into that pit, they gradually emerge from it, the crowd flitting, and whistling, and skulking about them until they come to the verge, where restoration of the bull's-eyes is made to Darby. Here the crowd, like a concourse of imprisoned demons, turns back, yelling, and is seen no more. Through the clearer and fresher streets, never so clear and fresh to Mr. Snagsby's mind as now, they walk and ride until they come to Mr. Tulkinghorn's gate.

As they ascend the dim stairs (Mr. Tulkinghorn's chambers being on the first floor), Mr. Bucket mentions that he has the key of the outer door in his pocket and that there is no need to ring. For a man so expert in most things of that kind, Bucket takes time to open the door and makes some noise too. It may be that he sounds a note of preparation.

Howbeit, they come at last into the hall, where a lamp is burning, and so into Mr. Tulkinghorn's usual room—the room where he drank his old wine to-night. He is not there, but his two old-fashioned candlesticks are, and the room is tolerably light.

Mr. Bucket, still having his professional hold of Jo and appearing to Mr. Snagsby to possess an unlimited number of eyes, makes a little way into this room, when Jo starts and stops.

"What's the matter?" says Bucket in a whisper.

"There she is!" cries Jo.

"Who!"

"The lady!"

A female figure, closely veiled, stands in the middle of the room, where the light falls upon it. It is quite still and silent. The front of the figure is towards them, but it takes no notice of their entrance and remains like a statue.

"Now, tell me," says Bucket aloud, "how you know that to be the lady."

"I know the wale," replies Jo, staring, "and the bonnet, and the gownd."

"Be quite sure of what you say, Tough," returns Bucket, narrowly observant of him. "Look again."

"I am a-looking as hard as ever I can look," says Jo with starting eyes, "and that there's the wale, the bonnet, and the gownd."

"What about those rings you told me of?" asks Bucket.

"A-sparkling all over here," says Jo, rubbing the fingers of his left hand on the knuckles of his right without taking his eyes from the figure.

The figure removes the right-hand glove and shows the hand.

"Now, what do you say to that?" asks Bucket.

Jo shakes his head. "Not rings a bit like them. Not a hand like that."

"What are you talking of?" says Bucket, evidently pleased though, and well pleased too.

"Hand was a deal whiter, a deal delicater, and a deal smaller," returns Jo.

"Why, you'll tell me I'm my own mother next," says Mr. Bucket. "Do you recollect the lady's voice?"

"I think I does," says Jo.

The figure speaks. "Was it at all like this? I will speak as long as you like if you are not sure. Was it this voice, or at all like this voice?"

Jo looks aghast at Mr. Bucket. "Not a bit!"

"Then, what," retorts that worthy, pointing to the figure, "did you say it was the lady for?"

"Cos," says Jo with a perplexed stare but without being at all shaken in his certainty, "cos that there's the wale, the bonnet, and the gownd. It is her and it an't her. It an't her hand, nor yet her rings, nor yet her woice. But that there's the wale, the bonnet, and the gownd, and they're wore the same way wot she wore 'em, and it's her height wot she wos, and she giv me a sov'ring and hooked it."

"Well!" says Mr. Bucket slightly, "we haven't got much good out of YOU. But, however, here's five shillings for you. Take care how you spend it, and don't get yourself into trouble." Bucket stealthily tells the coins from one hand into the other like counters—which is a way he has, his principal use of them being in these games of skill—and then puts them, in a little pile, into the boy's hand and takes him out to the door, leaving Mr. Snagsby, not by any means comfortable under these mysterious circumstances, alone with the veiled figure. But on Mr. Tulkinghorn's coming into the room, the veil is raised and a sufficiently good-looking Frenchwoman is revealed, though her expression is something of the intensest.

"Thank you, Mademoiselle Hortense," says Mr. Tulkinghorn with his usual equanimity. "I will give you no further trouble about this little wager."

"You will do me the kindness to remember, sir, that I am not at present placed?" says mademoiselle.

"Certainly, certainly!"

"And to confer upon me the favour of your distinguished recommendation?"

"By all means, Mademoiselle Hortense."

"A word from Mr. Tulkinghorn is so powerful."

"It shall not be wanting, mademoiselle."

"Receive the assurance of my devoted gratitude, dear sir."

"Good night."

Mademoiselle goes out with an air of native gentility; and Mr. Bucket, to whom it is, on an emergency, as natural to be groom of the ceremonies as it is to be anything else, shows her downstairs, not without gallantry.

"Well, Bucket?" quoth Mr. Tulkinghorn on his return.

"It's all squared, you see, as I squared it myself, sir. There an't a doubt that it was the other one with this one's dress on. The boy was exact respecting colours and everything. Mr. Snagsby, I promised you as a man that he should be sent away all right. Don't say it wasn't done!"

"You have kept your word, sir," returns the stationer; "and if I can be of no further use, Mr. Tulkinghorn, I think, as my little woman will be getting anxious—"

"Thank you, Snagsby, no further use," says Mr. Tulkinghorn. "I am quite indebted to you for the trouble you have taken already."

"Not at all, sir. I wish you good night."

"You see, Mr. Snagsby," says Mr. Bucket, accompanying him to the door and shaking hands with him over and over again, "what I like in you is that you're a man it's of no use pumping; that's what YOU are. When you know you have done a right thing, you put it away, and it's done with and gone, and there's an end of it. That's what YOU do."

"That is certainly what I endeavour to do, sir," returns Mr. Snagsby.

"No, you don't do yourself justice. It an't what you endeavour to do," says Mr. Bucket, shaking hands with him and blessing him in the tenderest manner, "it's what you DO. That's what I estimate in a man in your way of business."

Mr. Snagsby makes a suitable response and goes homeward so confused by the events of the evening that he is doubtful of his being awake and out—doubtful of the reality of the streets through which he goes—doubtful of the reality of the moon that shines above him. He is presently reassured on these subjects by the unchallengeable reality of Mrs. Snagsby, sitting up with her head in a perfect beehive of curl-papers and night-cap, who has dispatched Guster to the police-station with official intelligence of her husband's being made away with, and who within the last two hours has passed through every stage of swooning with the greatest decorum. But as the little woman feelingly says, many thanks she gets for it!

CHAPTER XXIII
ESTHER'S NARRATIVE

We came home from Mr. Boythorn's after six pleasant weeks. We were often in the park and in the woods and seldom passed the lodge where we had taken shelter without looking in to speak to the keeper's wife; but we saw no more of Lady Dedlock, except at church on Sundays. There was company at Chesney Wold; and although several beautiful faces surrounded her, her face retained the same influence on me as at first. I do not quite know even now whether it was painful or pleasurable, whether it drew me towards her or made me shrink from her. I think I admired her with a kind of fear, and I know that in her presence my thoughts always wandered back, as they had done at first, to that old time of my life.

I had a fancy, on more than one of these Sundays, that what this lady so curiously was to me, I was to her—I mean that I disturbed her thoughts as she influenced mine, though in some different way. But when I stole a glance at her and saw her so composed and distant and unapproachable, I felt this to be a foolish weakness. Indeed, I felt the whole state of my mind in reference to her to be weak and unreasonable, and I remonstrated with myself about it as much as I could.

One incident that occurred before we quitted Mr. Boythorn's house, I had better mention in this place.

I was walking in the garden with Ada when I was told that some one wished to see me. Going into the breakfast-room where this person was waiting, I found it to be the French maid who had cast off her shoes and walked through the wet grass on the day when it thundered and lightened.

"Mademoiselle," she began, looking fixedly at me with her too-eager eyes, though otherwise presenting an agreeable appearance and speaking neither with boldness nor servility, "I have taken a great liberty in coming here, but you know how to excuse it, being so amiable, mademoiselle."

"No excuse is necessary," I returned, "if you wish to speak to me."

"That is my desire, mademoiselle. A thousand thanks for the permission. I have your leave to speak. Is it not?" she said in a quick, natural way.

"Certainly," said I.

"Mademoiselle, you are so amiable! Listen then, if you please. I have left my Lady. We could not agree. My Lady is so high, so very high. Pardon! Mademoiselle, you are right!" Her quickness anticipated what I might have said presently but as yet had only thought. "It is not for me to come here to complain of my Lady. But I say she is so high, so very high. I will not say a word more. All the world knows that."

"Go on, if you please," said I.

"Assuredly; mademoiselle, I am thankful for your politeness. Mademoiselle, I have an inexpressible desire to find service with a young lady who is good, accomplished, beautiful. You are good, accomplished, and beautiful as an angel. Ah, could I have the honour of being your domestic!"

"I am sorry—" I began.

"Do not dismiss me so soon, mademoiselle!" she said with an involuntary contraction of her fine black eyebrows. "Let me hope a moment! Mademoiselle, I know this service would be more retired than that which I have quitted. Well! I wish that. I know this service would be less distinguished than that which I have quitted. Well! I wish that, I know that I should win less, as to wages here. Good. I am content."

"I assure you," said I, quite embarrassed by the mere idea of having such an attendant, "that I keep no maid—"

"Ah, mademoiselle, but why not? Why not, when you can have one so devoted to you! Who would be enchanted to serve you; who would be so true, so zealous, and so faithful every day! Mademoiselle, I wish with all my heart to serve you. Do not speak of money at present. Take me as I am. For nothing!"

She was so singularly earnest that I drew back, almost afraid of her. Without appearing to notice it, in her ardour she still pressed herself upon me, speaking in a rapid subdued voice, though always with a certain grace and propriety.

"Mademoiselle, I come from the South country where we are quick and where we like and dislike very strong. My Lady was too high for me; I was too high for her. It is done—past—finished! Receive me as your domestic, and I will serve you well. I will do more for you than you figure to yourself now. Chut! Mademoiselle, I will—no matter, I will do my utmost possible in all things. If you accept my service, you will not repent it. Mademoiselle, you will not repent it, and I will serve you well. You don't know how well!"

There was a lowering energy in her face as she stood looking at me while I explained the impossibility of my engaging her (without thinking it necessary to say how very little I desired to do so), which seemed to bring visibly before me some woman from the streets of Paris in the reign of terror.

She heard me out without interruption and then said with her pretty accent and in her mildest voice, "Hey, mademoiselle, I have received my answer! I am sorry of it. But I must go elsewhere and seek what I have not found here. Will you graciously let me kiss your hand?"

She looked at me more intently as she took it, and seemed to take note, with her momentary touch, of every vein in it. "I fear I surprised you, mademoiselle, on the day of the storm?" she said with a parting curtsy.

I confessed that she had surprised us all.

"I took an oath, mademoiselle," she said, smiling, "and I wanted to stamp it on my mind so that I might keep it faithfully. And I will! Adieu, mademoiselle!"

So ended our conference, which I was very glad to bring to a close. I supposed she went away from the village, for I saw her no more; and nothing else occurred to disturb our tranquil summer pleasures until six weeks were out and we returned home as I began just now by saying.

At that time, and for a good many weeks after that time, Richard was constant in his visits. Besides coming every Saturday or Sunday and remaining with us until Monday morning, he sometimes rode out on horseback unexpectedly and passed the evening with us and rode back again early next day. He was as vivacious as ever and told us he was very industrious, but I was not easy in my mind about him. It appeared to me that his industry was all misdirected. I could not find that it led to anything but the formation of delusive hopes in connexion with the suit already the pernicious cause of so much sorrow and ruin. He had got at the core of that mystery now, he told us, and nothing could be plainer than that the will under which he and Ada were to take I don't know how many thousands of pounds must be finally established if there were any sense or justice in the Court of Chancery—but oh, what a great IF that sounded in my ears—and that this happy conclusion could not be much longer delayed. He proved this to himself by all the weary arguments on that side he had read, and every one of them sunk him deeper in the infatuation. He had even begun to haunt the court. He told us how he saw Miss Flite there daily, how they talked together, and how he did her little kindnesses, and how, while he laughed at her, he pitied her from his heart. But he never thought—never, my poor, dear, sanguine Richard, capable of so much happiness then, and with such better things before him—what a fatal link was riveting between his fresh youth and her faded age, between his free hopes and her caged birds, and her hungry garret, and her wandering mind.

Ada loved him too well to mistrust him much in anything he said or did, and my guardian, though he frequently complained of the east wind and read more than usual in the growlery, preserved a strict silence on the subject. So I thought one day when I went to London to meet Caddy Jellyby, at her solicitation, I would ask Richard to be in waiting for me at the coach-office, that we might have a little talk together. I found him there when I arrived, and we walked away arm in arm.

"Well, Richard," said I as soon as I could begin to be grave with him, "are you beginning to feel more settled now?"

"Oh, yes, my dear!" returned Richard. "I'm all right enough."

"But settled?" said I.

"How do you mean, settled?" returned Richard with his gay laugh.

"Settled in the law," said I.

"Oh, aye," replied Richard, "I'm all right enough."

"You said that before, my dear Richard."

"And you don't think it's an answer, eh? Well! Perhaps it's not. Settled? You mean, do I feel as if I were settling down?"

"Yes."

"Why, no, I can't say I am settling down," said Richard, strongly emphasizing "down," as if that expressed the difficulty, "because one can't settle down while this business remains in such an unsettled state. When I say this business, of course I mean the—forbidden subject."

"Do you think it will ever be in a settled state?" said I.

"Not the least doubt of it," answered Richard.

We walked a little way without speaking, and presently Richard addressed me in his frankest and most feeling manner, thus: "My dear Esther, I understand you, and I wish to heaven I were a more constant sort of fellow. I don't mean constant to Ada, for I love her dearly—better and better every day—but constant to myself. (Somehow, I mean something that I can't very well express, but you'll make it out.) If I were a more constant sort of fellow, I should have held on either to Badger or to Kenge and Carboy like grim death, and should have begun to be steady and systematic by this time, and shouldn't be in debt, and—"

"ARE you in debt, Richard?"

"Yes," said Richard, "I am a little so, my dear. Also, I have taken rather too much to billiards and that sort of thing. Now the murder's out; you despise me, Esther, don't you?"

"You know I don't," said I.

"You are kinder to me than I often am to myself," he returned. "My dear Esther, I am a very unfortunate dog not to be more settled, but how CAN I be more settled? If you lived in an unfinished house, you couldn't settle down in it; if you were condemned to leave everything you undertook unfinished, you would find it hard to apply yourself to anything; and yet that's my unhappy case. I was born into this unfinished contention with all its chances and changes, and it began to unsettle me before I quite knew the difference between a suit at law and a suit of clothes; and it has gone on unsettling me ever since; and here I am now, conscious sometimes that I am but a worthless fellow to love my confiding cousin Ada."

We were in a solitary place, and he put his hands before his eyes and sobbed as he said the words.

"Oh, Richard!" said I. "Do not be so moved. You have a noble nature, and Ada's love may make you worthier every day."

"I know, my dear," he replied, pressing my arm, "I know all that. You mustn't mind my being a little soft now, for I have had all this upon my mind for a long time, and have often meant to speak to you, and have sometimes wanted opportunity and sometimes courage. I know what the thought of Ada ought to do for me, but it doesn't do it. I am too unsettled even for that. I love her most devotedly, and yet I do her wrong, in doing myself wrong, every day and hour. But it can't last for ever. We shall come on for a final hearing and get judgment in our favour, and then you and Ada shall see what I can really be!"

It had given me a pang to hear him sob and see the tears start out between his fingers, but that was infinitely less affecting to me than the hopeful animation with which he said these words.

"I have looked well into the papers, Esther. I have been deep in them for months," he continued, recovering his cheerfulness in a moment, "and you may rely upon it that we shall come out triumphant. As to years of delay, there has been no want of them, heaven knows! And there is the greater probability of our bringing the matter to a speedy close; in fact, it's on the paper now. It will be all right at last, and then you shall see!"

Recalling how he had just now placed Messrs. Kenge and Carboy in the same category with Mr. Badger, I asked him when he intended to be articled in Lincoln's Inn.

"There again! I think not at all, Esther," he returned with an effort. "I fancy I have had enough of it. Having worked at Jarndyce and Jarndyce like a galley slave, I have slaked my thirst for the law and satisfied myself that I shouldn't like it. Besides, I find it unsettles me more and more to be so constantly upon the scene of action. So what," continued Richard, confident again by this time, "do I naturally turn my thoughts to?"

"I can't imagine," said I.

"Don't look so serious," returned Richard, "because it's the best thing I can do, my dear Esther, I am certain. It's not as if I wanted a profession for life. These proceedings will come to a termination, and then I am provided for. No. I look upon it as a pursuit which is in its nature more or less unsettled, and therefore suited to my temporary condition—I may say, precisely suited. What is it that I naturally turn my thoughts to?"

I looked at him and shook my head.

"What," said Richard, in a tone of perfect conviction, "but the army!"

"The army?" said I.

"The army, of course. What I have to do is to get a commission; and—there I am, you know!" said Richard.

And then he showed me, proved by elaborate calculations in his pocket-book, that supposing he had contracted, say, two hundred pounds of debt in six months out of the army; and that he contracted no debt at all within a corresponding period in the army—as to which he had quite made up his mind; this step must involve a saving of four hundred pounds in a year, or two thousand pounds in five years, which was a considerable sum. And then he spoke so ingenuously and sincerely of the sacrifice he made in withdrawing himself for a time from Ada, and of the earnestness with which he aspired—as in thought he always did, I know full well—to repay her love, and to ensure her happiness, and to conquer what was amiss in himself, and to acquire the very soul of decision, that he made my heart ache keenly, sorely. For, I thought, how would this end, how could this end, when so soon and so surely all his manly qualities were touched by the fatal blight that ruined everything it rested on!

I spoke to Richard with all the earnestness I felt, and all the hope I could not quite feel then, and implored him for Ada's sake not to put any trust in Chancery. To all I said, Richard readily assented, riding over the court and everything else in his easy way and drawing the brightest pictures of the character he was to settle into—alas, when the grievous suit should loose its hold upon him! We had a long talk, but it always came back to that, in substance.

At last we came to Soho Square, where Caddy Jellyby had appointed to wait for me, as a quiet place in the neighbourhood of Newman Street. Caddy was in the garden in the centre and hurried out as soon as I appeared. After a few cheerful words, Richard left us together.

"Prince has a pupil over the way, Esther," said Caddy, "and got the key for us. So if you will walk round and round here with me, we can lock ourselves in and I can tell you comfortably what I wanted to see your dear good face about."

"Very well, my dear," said I. "Nothing could be better." So Caddy, after affectionately squeezing the dear good face as she called it, locked the gate, and took my arm, and we began to walk round the garden very cosily.

"You see, Esther," said Caddy, who thoroughly enjoyed a little confidence, "after you spoke to me about its being wrong to marry without Ma's knowledge, or even to keep Ma long in the dark respecting our engagement—though I don't believe Ma cares much for me, I must say—I thought it right to mention your opinions to Prince. In the first place because I want to profit by everything you tell me, and in the second place because I have no secrets from Prince."

"I hope he approved, Caddy?"

"Oh, my dear! I assure you he would approve of anything you could say. You have no idea what an opinion he has of you!"

"Indeed!"

"Esther, it's enough to make anybody but me jealous," said Caddy, laughing and shaking her head; "but it only makes me joyful, for you are the first friend I ever had, and the best friend I ever can have, and nobody can respect and love you too much to please me."

"Upon my word, Caddy," said I, "you are in the general conspiracy to keep me in a good humour. Well, my dear?"

"Well! I am going to tell you," replied Caddy, crossing her hands confidentially upon my arm. "So we talked a good deal about it, and so I said to Prince, 'Prince, as Miss Summerson—'"

"I hope you didn't say 'Miss Summerson'?"

"No. I didn't!" cried Caddy, greatly pleased and with the brightest of faces. "I said, 'Esther.' I said to Prince, 'As Esther is decidedly of that opinion, Prince, and has expressed it to me, and always hints it when she writes those kind notes, which you are so fond of hearing me read to you, I am prepared to disclose the truth to Ma whenever you think proper. And I think, Prince,' said I, 'that Esther thinks that I should be in a better, and truer, and more honourable position altogether if you did the same to your papa.'"

"Yes, my dear," said I. "Esther certainly does think so."

"So I was right, you see!" exclaimed Caddy. "Well! This troubled Prince a good deal, not because he had the least doubt about it, but because he is so considerate of the feelings of old Mr. Turveydrop; and he had his apprehensions that old Mr. Turveydrop might break his heart, or faint away, or be very much overcome in some affecting manner or other if he made such an announcement. He feared old Mr. Turveydrop might consider it undutiful and might receive too great a shock. For old Mr. Turveydrop's deportment is very beautiful, you know, Esther," said Caddy, "and his feelings are extremely sensitive."

"Are they, my dear?"

"Oh, extremely sensitive. Prince says so. Now, this has caused my darling child—I didn't mean to use the expression to you, Esther," Caddy apologized, her face suffused with blushes, "but I generally call Prince my darling child."

I laughed; and Caddy laughed and blushed, and went on.

"This has caused him, Esther—"

"Caused whom, my dear?"

"Oh, you tiresome thing!" said Caddy, laughing, with her pretty face on fire. "My darling child, if you insist upon it! This has caused him weeks of uneasiness and has made him delay, from day to day, in a very anxious manner. At last he said to me, 'Caddy, if Miss Summerson, who is a great favourite with my father, could be prevailed upon to be present when I broke the subject, I think I could do it.' So I promised I would ask you. And I made up my mind, besides," said Caddy, looking at me hopefully but timidly, "that if you consented, I would ask you afterwards to come with me to Ma. This is what I meant when I said in my note that I had a great favour and a great assistance to beg of you. And if you thought you could grant it, Esther, we should both be very grateful."

"Let me see, Caddy," said I, pretending to consider. "Really, I think I could do a greater thing than that if the need were pressing. I am at your service and the darling child's, my dear, whenever you like."

Caddy was quite transported by this reply of mine, being, I believe, as susceptible to the least kindness or encouragement as any tender heart that ever beat in this world; and after another turn or two round the garden, during which she put on an entirely new pair of gloves and made herself as resplendent as possible that she might do no avoidable discredit to the Master of Deportment, we went to Newman Street direct.

Prince was teaching, of course. We found him engaged with a not very hopeful pupil—a stubborn little girl with a sulky forehead, a deep voice, and an inanimate, dissatisfied mama—whose case was certainly not rendered more hopeful by the confusion into which we threw her preceptor. The lesson at last came to an end, after proceeding as discordantly as possible; and when the little girl had changed her shoes and had had her white muslin extinguished in shawls, she was taken away. After a few words of preparation, we then went in search of Mr. Turveydrop, whom we found, grouped with his hat and gloves, as a model of deportment, on the sofa in his private apartment—the only comfortable room in the house. He appeared to have dressed at his leisure in the intervals of a light collation, and his dressing-case, brushes, and so forth, all of quite an elegant kind, lay about.

"Father, Miss Summerson; Miss Jellyby."

"Charmed! Enchanted!" said Mr. Turveydrop, rising with his high-shouldered bow. "Permit me!" Handing chairs. "Be seated!" Kissing the tips of his left fingers. "Overjoyed!" Shutting his eyes and rolling. "My little retreat is made a paradise." Recomposing himself on the sofa like the second gentleman in Europe.

"Again you find us, Miss Summerson," said he, "using our little arts to polish, polish! Again the sex stimulates us and rewards us by the condescension of its lovely presence. It is much in these times (and we have made an awfully degenerating business of it since the days of his Royal Highness the Prince Regent—my patron, if I may presume to say so) to experience that deportment is not wholly trodden under foot by mechanics. That it can yet bask in the smile of beauty, my dear madam."

I said nothing, which I thought a suitable reply; and he took a pinch of snuff.

"My dear son," said Mr. Turveydrop, "you have four schools this afternoon. I would recommend a hasty sandwich."

"Thank you, father," returned Prince, "I will be sure to be punctual. My dear father, may I beg you to prepare your mind for what I am going to say?"

"Good heaven!" exclaimed the model, pale and aghast as Prince and Caddy, hand in hand, bent down before him. "What is this? Is this lunacy! Or what is this?"

"Father," returned Prince with great submission, "I love this young lady, and we are engaged."

"Engaged!" cried Mr. Turveydrop, reclining on the sofa and shutting out the sight with his hand. "An arrow launched at my brain by my own child!"

"We have been engaged for some time, father," faltered Prince, "and Miss Summerson, hearing of it, advised that we should declare the fact to you and was so very kind as to attend on the present occasion. Miss Jellyby is a young lady who deeply respects you, father."

Mr. Turveydrop uttered a groan.

"No, pray don't! Pray don't, father," urged his son. "Miss Jellyby is a young lady who deeply respects you, and our first desire is to consider your comfort."

Mr. Turveydrop sobbed.

"No, pray don't, father!" cried his son.

"Boy," said Mr. Turveydrop, "it is well that your sainted mother is spared this pang. Strike deep, and spare not. Strike home, sir, strike home!"

"Pray don't say so, father," implored Prince, in tears. "It goes to my heart. I do assure you, father, that our first wish and intention is to consider your comfort. Caroline and I do not forget our duty—what is my duty is Caroline's, as we have often said together—and with your approval and consent, father, we will devote ourselves to making your life agreeable."

"Strike home," murmured Mr. Turveydrop. "Strike home!" But he seemed to listen, I thought, too.

"My dear father," returned Prince, "we well know what little comforts you are accustomed to and have a right to, and it will always be our study and our pride to provide those before anything. If you will bless us with your approval and consent, father, we shall not think of being married until it is quite agreeable to you; and when we ARE married, we shall always make you—of course—our first consideration. You must ever be the head and master here, father; and we feel how truly unnatural it would be in us if we failed to know it or if we failed to exert ourselves in every possible way to please you."

Mr. Turveydrop underwent a severe internal struggle and came upright on the sofa again with his cheeks puffing over his stiff cravat, a perfect model of parental deportment.

"My son!" said Mr. Turveydrop. "My children! I cannot resist your prayer. Be happy!"

His benignity as he raised his future daughter-in-law and stretched out his hand to his son (who kissed it with affectionate respect and gratitude) was the most confusing sight I ever saw.

"My children," said Mr. Turveydrop, paternally encircling Caddy with his left arm as she sat beside him, and putting his right hand gracefully on his hip. "My son and daughter, your happiness shall be my care. I will watch over you. You shall always live with me"—meaning, of course, I will always live with you—"this house is henceforth as much yours as mine; consider it your home. May you long live to share it with me!"

The power of his deportment was such that they really were as much overcome with thankfulness as if, instead of quartering himself upon them for the rest of his life, he were making some munificent sacrifice in their favour.

"For myself, my children," said Mr. Turveydrop, "I am falling into the sear and yellow leaf, and it is impossible to say how long the last feeble traces of gentlemanly deportment may linger in this weaving and spinning age. But, so long, I will do my duty to society and will show myself, as usual, about town. My wants are few and simple. My little apartment here, my few essentials for the toilet, my frugal morning meal, and my little dinner will suffice. I charge your dutiful affection with the supply of these requirements, and I charge myself with all the rest."

They were overpowered afresh by his uncommon generosity.

"My son," said Mr. Turveydrop, "for those little points in which you are deficient—points of deportment, which are born with a man, which may be improved by cultivation, but can never be originated—you may still rely on me. I have been faithful to my post since the days of his Royal Highness the Prince Regent, and I will not desert it now. No, my son. If you have ever contemplated your father's poor position with a feeling of pride, you may rest assured that he will do nothing to tarnish it. For yourself, Prince, whose character is different (we cannot be all alike, nor is it advisable that we should), work, be industrious, earn money, and extend the connexion as much as possible."

"That you may depend I will do, dear father, with all my heart," replied Prince.

"I have no doubt of it," said Mr. Turveydrop. "Your qualities are not shining, my dear child, but they are steady and useful. And to both of you, my children, I would merely observe, in the spirit of a sainted wooman on whose path I had the happiness of casting, I believe, SOME ray of light, take care of the establishment, take care of my simple wants, and bless you both!"

Old Mr. Turveydrop then became so very gallant, in honour of the occasion, that I told Caddy we must really go to Thavies Inn at once if we were to go at all that day. So we took our departure after a very loving farewell between Caddy and her betrothed, and during our walk she was so happy and so full of old Mr. Turveydrop's praises that I would not have said a word in his disparagement for any consideration.

The house in Thavies Inn had bills in the windows announcing that it was to let, and it looked dirtier and gloomier and ghastlier than ever. The name of poor Mr. Jellyby had appeared in the list of bankrupts but a day or two before, and he was shut up in the dining-room with two gentlemen and a heap of blue bags, account-books, and papers, making the most desperate endeavours to understand his affairs. They appeared to me to be quite beyond his comprehension, for when Caddy took me into the dining-room by mistake and we came upon Mr. Jellyby in his spectacles, forlornly fenced into a corner by the great dining-table and the two gentlemen, he seemed to have given up the whole thing and to be speechless and insensible.

Going upstairs to Mrs. Jellyby's room (the children were all screaming in the kitchen, and there was no servant to be seen), we found that lady in the midst of a voluminous correspondence, opening, reading, and sorting letters, with a great accumulation of torn covers on the floor. She was so preoccupied that at first she did not know me, though she sat looking at me with that curious, bright-eyed, far-off look of hers.

"Ah! Miss Summerson!" she said at last. "I was thinking of something so different! I hope you are well. I am happy to see you. Mr. Jarndyce and Miss

Clare quite well?"

I hoped in return that Mr. Jellyby was quite well.

"Why, not quite, my dear," said Mrs. Jellyby in the calmest manner. "He has been unfortunate in his affairs and is a little out of spirits. Happily for me, I am so much engaged that I have no time to think about it. We have, at the present moment, one hundred and seventy families, Miss Summerson, averaging five persons in each, either gone or going to the left bank of the Niger."

I thought of the one family so near us who were neither gone nor going to the left bank of the Niger, and wondered how she could be so placid.

"You have brought Caddy back, I see," observed Mrs. Jellyby with a glance at her daughter. "It has become quite a novelty to see her here. She has almost deserted her old employment and in fact obliges me to employ a boy."

"I am sure, Ma—" began Caddy.

"Now you know, Caddy," her mother mildly interposed, "that I DO employ a boy, who is now at his dinner. What is the use of your contradicting?"

"I was not going to contradict, Ma," returned Caddy. "I was only going to say that surely you wouldn't have me be a mere drudge all my life."

"I believe, my dear," said Mrs. Jellyby, still opening her letters, casting her bright eyes smilingly over them, and sorting them as she spoke, "that you have a business example before you in your mother. Besides. A mere drudge? If you had any sympathy with the destinies of the human race, it would raise you high above any such idea. But you have none. I have often told you, Caddy, you have no such sympathy."

"Not if it's Africa, Ma, I have not."

"Of course you have not. Now, if I were not happily so much engaged, Miss Summerson," said Mrs. Jellyby, sweetly casting her eyes for a moment on me and considering where to put the particular letter she had just opened, "this would distress and disappoint me. But I have so much to think of, in connexion with Borrioboola-Gha and it is so necessary I should concentrate myself that there is my remedy, you see."

As Caddy gave me a glance of entreaty, and as Mrs. Jellyby was looking far away into Africa straight through my bonnet and head, I thought it a good opportunity to come to the subject of my visit and to attract Mrs. Jellyby's attention.

"Perhaps," I began, "you will wonder what has brought me here to interrupt you."

"I am always delighted to see Miss Summerson," said Mrs. Jellyby, pursuing her employment with a placid smile. "Though I wish," and she shook her head, "she was more interested in the Borrioboolan project."

"I have come with Caddy," said I, "because Caddy justly thinks she ought not to have a secret from her mother and fancies I shall encourage and aid her (though I am sure I don't know how) in imparting one."

"Caddy," said Mrs. Jellyby, pausing for a moment in her occupation and then serenely pursuing it after shaking her head, "you are going to tell me some nonsense."

Caddy untied the strings of her bonnet, took her bonnet off, and letting it dangle on the floor by the strings, and crying heartily, said, "Ma, I am engaged."

"Oh, you ridiculous child!" observed Mrs. Jellyby with an abstracted air as she looked over the dispatch last opened; "what a goose you are!"

"I am engaged, Ma," sobbed Caddy, "to young Mr. Turveydrop, at the academy; and old Mr. Turveydrop (who is a very gentlemanly man indeed) has given his consent, and I beg and pray you'll give us yours, Ma, because I never could be happy without it. I never, never could!" sobbed Caddy, quite forgetful of her general complainings and of everything but her natural affection.

"You see again, Miss Summerson," observed Mrs. Jellyby serenely, "what a happiness it is to be so much occupied as I am and to have this necessity for self-concentration that I have. Here is Caddy engaged to a dancing-master's son—mixed up with people who have no more sympathy with the destinies of the human race than she has herself! This, too, when Mr. Quale, one of the first philanthropists of our time, has mentioned to me that he was really disposed to be interested in her!"

"Ma, I always hated and detested Mr. Quale!" sobbed Caddy.

"Caddy, Caddy!" returned Mrs. Jellyby, opening another letter with the greatest complacency. "I have no doubt you did. How could you do otherwise, being totally destitute of the sympathies with which he overflows! Now, if my public duties were not a favourite child to me, if I were not occupied with large measures on a vast scale, these petty details might grieve me very much, Miss Summerson. But can I permit the film of a silly proceeding on the part of Caddy (from whom I expect nothing else) to interpose between me and the great African continent? No. No," repeated Mrs. Jellyby in a calm clear voice, and with an agreeable smile, as she opened more letters and sorted them. "No, indeed."

I was so unprepared for the perfect coolness of this reception, though I might have expected it, that I did not know what to say. Caddy seemed equally at a loss. Mrs. Jellyby continued to open and sort letters and to repeat occasionally in quite a charming tone of voice and with a smile of perfect composure, "No, indeed."

"I hope, Ma," sobbed poor Caddy at last, "you are not angry?"

"Oh, Caddy, you really are an absurd girl," returned Mrs. Jellyby, "to ask such questions after what I have said of the preoccupation of my mind."

"And I hope, Ma, you give us your consent and wish us well?" said Caddy.

"You are a nonsensical child to have done anything of this kind," said Mrs. Jellyby; "and a degenerate child, when you might have devoted yourself to the great public measure. But the step is taken, and I have engaged a boy, and there is no more to be said. Now, pray, Caddy," said Mrs. Jellyby, for Caddy was kissing her, "don't delay me in my work, but let me clear off this heavy batch of papers before the afternoon post comes in!"

I thought I could not do better than take my leave; I was detained for a moment by Caddy's saying, "You won't object to my bringing him to see you, Ma?"

"Oh, dear me, Caddy," cried Mrs. Jellyby, who had relapsed into that distant contemplation, "have you begun again? Bring whom?"

"Him, Ma."

"Caddy, Caddy!" said Mrs. Jellyby, quite weary of such little matters. "Then you must bring him some evening which is not a Parent Society night, or a Branch night, or a Ramification night. You must accommodate the visit to the demands upon my time. My dear Miss Summerson, it was very kind of you to come here to help out this silly chit. Good-bye! When I tell you that I have fifty-eight new letters from manufacturing families anxious to understand the details of the native and coffee-cultivation question this morning, I need not apologize for having very little leisure."

I was not surprised by Caddy's being in low spirits when we went downstairs, or by her sobbing afresh on my neck, or by her saying she would far rather have been scolded than treated with such indifference, or by her confiding to me that she was so poor in clothes that how she was ever to be married creditably she didn't know. I gradually cheered her up by dwelling on the many things she would do for her unfortunate father and for Peepy when she had a home of her own; and finally we went downstairs into the damp dark kitchen, where Peepy and his little brothers and sisters were grovelling on the stone floor and where we had such a game of play with them that to prevent myself from being quite torn to pieces I was obliged to fall back on my fairy-tales. From time to time I heard loud voices in the parlour overhead, and occasionally a violent tumbling about of the furniture. The last effect I am afraid was caused by poor Mr. Jellyby's breaking away from the dining-table and making rushes at the window with the intention of throwing himself into the area whenever he made any new attempt to understand his affairs.

As I rode quietly home at night after the day's bustle, I thought a good deal of Caddy's engagement and felt confirmed in my hopes (in spite of the elder Mr. Turveydrop) that she would be the happier and better for it. And if there seemed to be but a slender chance of her and her husband ever finding out what the model of deportment really was, why that was all for the best too, and who would wish them to be wiser? I did not wish them to be any wiser and indeed was half ashamed of not entirely believing in him myself. And I looked up at the stars, and thought about travellers in distant countries and the stars THEY saw, and hoped I might always be so blest and happy as to be useful to some one in my small way.

They were so glad to see me when I got home, as they always were, that I could have sat down and cried for joy if that had not been a method of making myself disagreeable. Everybody in the house, from the lowest to the highest, showed me such a bright face of welcome, and spoke so cheerily, and was so happy to do anything for me, that I suppose there never was such a fortunate little creature in the world.

We got into such a chatty state that night, through Ada and my guardian drawing me out to tell them all about Caddy, that I went on prose, prose, prosing for a length of time. At last I got up to my own room, quite red to think how I had been holding forth, and then I heard a soft tap at my door. So I said, "Come in!" and there came in a pretty little girl, neatly dressed in mourning, who dropped a curtsy.

"If you please, miss," said the little girl in a soft voice, "I am Charley."

"Why, so you are," said I, stooping down in astonishment and giving her a kiss. "How glad am I to see you, Charley!"

"If you please, miss," pursued Charley in the same soft voice, "I'm your maid."

"Charley?"

"If you please, miss, I'm a present to you, with Mr. Jarndyce's love."

I sat down with my hand on Charley's neck and looked at Charley.

"And oh, miss," says Charley, clapping her hands, with the tears starting down her dimpled cheeks, "Tom's at school, if you please, and learning so good! And little Emma, she's with Mrs. Blinder, miss, a-being took such care of! And Tom, he would have been at school—and Emma, she would have been left with Mrs. Blinder—and me, I should have been here—all a deal sooner, miss; only Mr. Jarndyce thought that Tom and Emma and me had better get a little used to parting first, we was so small. Don't cry, if you please, miss!"

"I can't help it, Charley."

"No, miss, nor I can't help it," says Charley. "And if you please, miss, Mr. Jarndyce's love, and he thinks you'll like to teach me now and then. And if you please, Tom and Emma and me is to see each other once a month. And I'm so happy and so thankful, miss," cried Charley with a heaving heart, "and I'll try to be such a good maid!"

"Oh, Charley dear, never forget who did all this!"

"No, miss, I never will. Nor Tom won't. Nor yet Emma. It was all you, miss."

"I have known nothing of it. It was Mr. Jarndyce, Charley."

"Yes, miss, but it was all done for the love of you and that you might be my mistress. If you please, miss, I am a little present with his love, and it was all done for the love of you. Me and Tom was to be sure to remember it."

Charley dried her eyes and entered on her functions, going in her matronly little way about and about the room and folding up everything she could lay her hands upon. Presently Charley came creeping back to my side and said, "Oh, don't cry, if you please, miss."

And I said again, "I can't help it, Charley."

And Charley said again, "No, miss, nor I can't help it." And so, after all, I did cry for joy indeed, and so did she.

CHAPTER XXIX
AN APPEAL CASE

As soon as Richard and I had held the conversation of which I have given an account, Richard communicated the state of his mind to Mr. Jarndyce. I doubt if my guardian were altogether taken by surprise when he received the representation, though it caused him much uneasiness and disappointment. He and Richard were often closeted together, late at night and early in the morning, and passed whole days in London, and had innumerable appointments with Mr. Kenge, and laboured through a quantity of disagreeable business. While they were thus employed, my guardian, though he underwent considerable inconvenience from the state of the wind and rubbed his head so constantly that not a single hair upon it ever rested in its right place, was as genial with Ada and me as at any other time, but maintained a steady reserve on these matters. And as our utmost endeavours could only elicit from Richard himself sweeping assurances that everything was going on capitally and that it really was all right at last, our anxiety was not much relieved by him.

We learnt, however, as the time went on, that a new application was made to the Lord Chancellor on Richard's behalf as an infant and a ward, and I don't know what, and that there was a quantity of talking, and that the Lord Chancellor described him in open court as a vexatious and capricious infant, and that the matter was adjourned and readjourned, and referred, and reported on, and petitioned about until Richard began to doubt (as he told us) whether, if he entered the army at all, it would not be as a veteran of seventy or eighty years of age. At last an appointment was made for him to see the Lord Chancellor again in his private room, and there the Lord Chancellor very seriously reproved him for trifling with time and not knowing his mind—"a pretty good joke, I think," said Richard, "from that quarter!"—and at last it was settled that his application should be granted. His name was entered at the Horse Guards as an applicant for an ensign's commission; the purchase-money was deposited at an agent's; and Richard, in his usual characteristic way, plunged into a violent course of military study and got up at five o'clock every morning to practise the broadsword exercise.

Thus, vacation succeeded term, and term succeeded vacation. We sometimes heard of Jarndyce and Jarndyce as being in the paper or out of the paper, or as being to be mentioned, or as being to be spoken to; and it came on, and it went off. Richard, who was now in a professor's house in London, was able to be with us less frequently than before; my guardian still maintained the same reserve; and so time passed until the commission was obtained and Richard received directions with it to join a regiment in Ireland.

He arrived post-haste with the intelligence one evening, and had a long conference with my guardian. Upwards of an hour elapsed before my guardian put his head into the room where Ada and I were sitting and said, "Come in, my dears!" We went in and found Richard, whom we had last seen in high spirits, leaning on the chimney-piece looking mortified and angry.

"Rick and I, Ada," said Mr. Jarndyce, "are not quite of one mind. Come, come, Rick, put a brighter face upon it!"

"You are very hard with me, sir," said Richard. "The harder because you have been so considerate to me in all other respects and have done me kindnesses that I can never acknowledge. I never could have been set right without you, sir."

"Well, well!" said Mr. Jarndyce. "I want to set you more right yet. I want to set you more right with yourself."

"I hope you will excuse my saying, sir," returned Richard in a fiery way, but yet respectfully, "that I think I am the best judge about myself."

"I hope you will excuse my saying, my dear Rick," observed Mr. Jarndyce with the sweetest cheerfulness and good humour, "that it's quite natural in you to think so, but I don't think so. I must do my duty, Rick, or you could never care for me in cool blood; and I hope you will always care for me, cool and hot."

Ada had turned so pale that he made her sit down in his reading-chair and sat beside her.

"It's nothing, my dear," he said, "it's nothing. Rick and I have only had a friendly difference, which we must state to you, for you are the theme. Now you are afraid of what's coming."

"I am not indeed, cousin John," replied Ada with a smile, "if it is to come from you."

"Thank you, my dear. Do you give me a minute's calm attention, without looking at Rick. And, little woman, do you likewise. My dear girl," putting his hand on hers as it lay on the side of the easy-chair, "you recollect the talk we had, we four when the little woman told me of a little love affair?"

"It is not likely that either Richard or I can ever forget your kindness that day, cousin John."

"I can never forget it," said Richard.

"And I can never forget it," said Ada.

"So much the easier what I have to say, and so much the easier for us to agree," returned my guardian, his face irradiated by the gentleness and honour of his heart. "Ada, my bird, you should know that Rick has now chosen his profession for the last time. All that he has of certainty will be expended when he is fully equipped. He has exhausted his resources and is bound henceforward to the tree he has planted."

"Quite true that I have exhausted my present resources, and I am quite content to know it. But what I have of certainty, sir," said Richard, "is not all I have."

"Rick, Rick!" cried my guardian with a sudden terror in his manner, and in an altered voice, and putting up his hands as if he would have stopped his ears. "For the love of God, don't found a hope or expectation on the family curse! Whatever you do on this side the grave, never give one lingering glance towards the horrible phantom that has haunted us so many years. Better to borrow, better to beg, better to die!"

We were all startled by the fervour of this warning. Richard bit his lip and held his breath, and glanced at me as if he felt, and knew that I felt too, how much he needed it.

"Ada, my dear," said Mr. Jarndyce, recovering his cheerfulness, "these are strong words of advice, but I live in Bleak House and have seen a sight here. Enough of that. All Richard had to start him in the race of life is ventured. I recommend to him and you, for his sake and your own, that he should depart from us with the understanding that there is no sort of contract between you. I must go further. I will be plain with you both. You were to confide freely in me, and I will confide freely in you. I ask you wholly to relinquish, for the present, any tie but your relationship."

"Better to say at once, sir," returned Richard, "that you renounce all confidence in me and that you advise Ada to do the same."

"Better to say nothing of the sort, Rick, because I don't mean it."

"You think I have begun ill, sir," retorted Richard. "I HAVE, I know."

"How I hoped you would begin, and how go on, I told you when we spoke of these things last," said Mr. Jarndyce in a cordial and encouraging manner. "You have not made that beginning yet, but there is a time for all things, and yours is not gone by; rather, it is just now fully come. Make a clear beginning altogether. You two (very young, my dears) are cousins. As yet, you are nothing more. What more may come must come of being worked out, Rick, and no sooner."

"You are very hard with me, sir," said Richard. "Harder than I could have supposed you would be."

"My dear boy," said Mr. Jarndyce, "I am harder with myself when I do anything that gives you pain. You have your remedy in your own hands. Ada, it is better for him that he should be free and that there should be no youthful engagement between you. Rick, it is better for her, much better; you owe it to her. Come! Each of you will do what is best for the other, if not what is best for yourselves."

"Why is it best, sir?" returned Richard hastily. "It was not when we opened our hearts to you. You did not say so then."

"I have had experience since. I don't blame you, Rick, but I have had experience since."

"You mean of me, sir."

"Well! Yes, of both of you," said Mr. Jarndyce kindly. "The time is not come for your standing pledged to one another. It is not right, and I must not recognize it. Come, come, my young cousins, begin afresh! Bygones shall be bygones, and a new page turned for you to write your lives in."

Richard gave an anxious glance at Ada but said nothing.

"I have avoided saying one word to either of you or to Esther," said Mr. Jarndyce, "until now, in order that we might be open as the day, and all on equal terms. I now affectionately advise, I now most earnestly entreat, you two to part as you came here. Leave all else to time, truth, and steadfastness. If you do otherwise, you will do wrong, and you will have made me do wrong in ever bringing you together."

A long silence succeeded.

"Cousin Richard," said Ada then, raising her blue eyes tenderly to his face, "after what our cousin John has said, I think no choice is left us. Your mind may be quite at ease about me, for you will leave me here under his care and will be sure that I can have nothing to wish for—quite sure if I guide myself by his advice. I—I don't doubt, cousin Richard," said Ada, a little confused, "that you are very fond of me, and I—I don't think you will fall in love with anybody else. But I should like you to consider well about it too, as I should like you to be in all things very happy. You may trust in me, cousin Richard. I am not at all changeable; but I am not unreasonable, and should never blame you. Even cousins may be sorry to part; and in truth I am very, very sorry, Richard, though I know it's for your welfare. I shall always think of you affectionately, and often talk of you with Esther, and—and perhaps you will sometimes think a little of me, cousin Richard. So now," said Ada, going up to him and giving him her trembling hand, "we are only cousins again, Richard—for the time perhaps—and I pray for a blessing on my dear cousin, wherever he goes!"

It was strange to me that Richard should not be able to forgive my guardian for entertaining the very same opinion of him which he himself had expressed of himself in much stronger terms to me. But it was certainly the case. I observed with great regret that from this hour he never was as free and open with Mr. Jarndyce as he had been before. He had every reason given him to be so, but he was not; and solely on his side, an estrangement began to arise between them.

In the business of preparation and equipment he soon lost himself, and even his grief at parting from Ada, who remained in Hertfordshire while he, Mr. Jarndyce, and I went up to London for a week. He remembered her by fits and starts, even with bursts of tears, and at such times would confide to me the heaviest self-reproaches. But in a few minutes he would recklessly conjure up some undefinable means by which they were both to be made rich and happy for ever, and would become as gay as possible.

It was a busy time, and I trotted about with him all day long, buying a variety of things of which he stood in need. Of the things he would have bought if he had been left to his own ways I say nothing. He was perfectly confidential with me, and often talked so sensibly and feelingly about his faults and his vigorous resolutions, and dwelt so much upon the encouragement he derived from these conversations that I could never have been tired if I had tried.

There used, in that week, to come backward and forward to our lodging to fence with Richard a person who had formerly been a cavalry soldier; he was a fine bluff-looking man, of a frank free bearing, with whom Richard had practised for some months. I heard so much about him, not only from Richard, but from my guardian too, that I was purposely in the room with my work one morning after breakfast when he came.

"Good morning, Mr. George," said my guardian, who happened to be alone with me. "Mr. Carstone will be here directly. Meanwhile, Miss Summerson is very happy to see you, I know. Sit down."

He sat down, a little disconcerted by my presence, I thought, and without looking at me, drew his heavy sunburnt hand across and across his upper lip.

"You are as punctual as the sun," said Mr. Jarndyce.

"Military time, sir," he replied. "Force of habit. A mere habit in me, sir. I am not at all business-like."

"Yet you have a large establishment, too, I am told?" said Mr. Jarndyce.

"Not much of a one, sir. I keep a shooting gallery, but not much of a one."

"And what kind of a shot and what kind of a swordsman do you make of Mr. Carstone?" said my guardian.

"Pretty good, sir," he replied, folding his arms upon his broad chest and looking very large. "If Mr. Carstone was to give his full mind to it, he would come out very good."

"But he don't, I suppose?" said my guardian.

"He did at first, sir, but not afterwards. Not his full mind. Perhaps he has something else upon it—some young lady, perhaps." His bright dark eyes glanced at me for the first time.

"He has not me upon his mind, I assure you, Mr. George," said I, laughing, "though you seem to suspect me."

He reddened a little through his brown and made me a trooper's bow. "No offence, I hope, miss. I am one of the roughs."

"Not at all," said I. "I take it as a compliment."

If he had not looked at me before, he looked at me now in three or four quick successive glances. "I beg your pardon, sir," he said to my guardian with a manly kind of diffidence, "but you did me the honour to mention the young lady's name—"

"Miss Summerson."

"Miss Summerson," he repeated, and looked at me again.

"Do you know the name?" I asked.

"No, miss. To my knowledge I never heard it. I thought I had seen you somewhere."

"I think not," I returned, raising my head from my work to look at him; and there was something so genuine in his speech and manner that I was glad of the opportunity. "I remember faces very well."

"So do I, miss!" he returned, meeting my look with the fullness of his dark eyes and broad forehead. "Humph! What set me off, now, upon that!"

His once more reddening through his brown and being disconcerted by his efforts to remember the association brought my guardian to his relief.

"Have you many pupils, Mr. George?"

"They vary in their number, sir. Mostly they're but a small lot to live by."

"And what classes of chance people come to practise at your gallery?"

"All sorts, sir. Natives and foreigners. From gentlemen to 'prentices. I have had Frenchwomen come, before now, and show themselves dabs at pistol-shooting. Mad people out of number, of course, but THEY go everywhere where the doors stand open."

"People don't come with grudges and schemes of finishing their practice with live targets, I hope?" said my guardian, smiling.

"Not much of that, sir, though that HAS happened. Mostly they come for skill—or idleness. Six of one, and half-a-dozen of the other. I beg your pardon," said Mr. George, sitting stiffly upright and squaring an elbow on each knee, "but I believe you're a Chancery suitor, if I have heard correct?"

"I am sorry to say I am."

"I have had one of YOUR compatriots in my time, sir."

"A Chancery suitor?" returned my guardian. "How was that?"

"Why, the man was so badgered and worried and tortured by being knocked about from post to pillar, and from pillar to post," said Mr. George, "that he got out of sorts. I don't believe he had any idea of taking aim at anybody, but he was in that condition of resentment and violence that he would come and pay for fifty shots and fire away till he was red hot. One day I said to him when there was nobody by and he had been talking to me angrily about his wrongs, 'If this practice is a safety-valve, comrade, well and good; but I don't altogether like your being so bent upon it in your present state of mind; I'd rather you took to something else.' I was on my guard for a blow, he was that passionate; but he received it in very good part and left off directly. We shook hands and struck up a sort of friendship."

"What was that man?" asked my guardian in a new tone of interest.

"Why, he began by being a small Shropshire farmer before they made a baited bull of him," said Mr. George.

"Was his name Gridley?"

"It was, sir."

Mr. George directed another succession of quick bright glances at me as my guardian and I exchanged a word or two of surprise at the coincidence, and I therefore explained to him how we knew the name. He made me another of his soldierly bows in acknowledgment of what he called my condescension.

"I don't know," he said as he looked at me, "what it is that sets me off again—but—bosh! What's my head running against!" He passed one of his heavy hands over his crisp dark hair as if to sweep the broken thoughts out of his mind and sat a little forward, with one arm akimbo and the other resting on his leg, looking in a brown study at the ground.

"I am sorry to learn that the same state of mind has got this Gridley into new troubles and that he is in hiding," said my guardian.

"So I am told, sir," returned Mr. George, still musing and looking on the ground. "So I am told."

"You don't know where?"

"No, sir," returned the trooper, lifting up his eyes and coming out of his reverie. "I can't say anything about him. He will be worn out soon, I expect. You may file a strong man's heart away for a good many years, but it will tell all of a sudden at last."

Richard's entrance stopped the conversation. Mr. George rose, made me another of his soldierly bows, wished my guardian a good day, and strode heavily out of the room.

This was the morning of the day appointed for Richard's departure. We had no more purchases to make now; I had completed all his packing early in the afternoon; and our time was disengaged until night, when he was to go to Liverpool for Holyhead. Jarndyce and Jarndyce being again expected to come on that day, Richard proposed to me that we should go down to the court and hear what passed. As it was his last day, and he was eager to go, and I had never been there, I gave my consent and we walked down to Westminster, where the court was then sitting. We beguiled the way with arrangements concerning the letters that Richard was to write to me and the letters that I was to write to him and with a great many hopeful projects. My guardian knew where we were going and therefore was not with us.

When we came to the court, there was the Lord Chancellor—the same whom I had seen in his private room in Lincoln's Inn—sitting in great state and gravity on the bench, with the mace and seals on a red table below him and an immense flat nosegay, like a little garden, which scented the whole court. Below the table, again, was a long row of solicitors, with bundles of papers on the matting at their feet; and then there were the gentlemen of the bar in wigs and gowns—some awake and some asleep, and one talking, and nobody paying much attention to what he said. The Lord Chancellor leaned back in his very easy chair with his elbow on the cushioned arm and his forehead resting on his hand; some of those who were present dozed; some read the newspapers; some walked about or whispered in groups: all seemed perfectly at their ease, by no means in a hurry, very unconcerned, and extremely comfortable.

To see everything going on so smoothly and to think of the roughness of the suitors' lives and deaths; to see all that full dress and ceremony and to think of the waste, and want, and beggared misery it represented; to consider that while the sickness of hope deferred was raging in so many hearts this polite show went calmly on from day to day, and year to year, in such good order and composure; to behold the Lord Chancellor and the whole array of practitioners under him looking at one another and at the spectators as if nobody had ever heard that all over England the name in which they were assembled was a bitter jest, was held in universal horror, contempt, and indignation, was known for something so flagrant and bad that little short of a miracle could bring any good out of it to any one—this was so curious and self-contradictory to me, who had no experience of it, that it was at first incredible, and I could not comprehend it. I sat where Richard put me, and tried to listen, and looked about me; but there seemed to be no reality in the whole scene except poor little Miss Flite, the madwoman, standing on a bench and nodding at it.

Miss Flite soon espied us and came to where we sat. She gave me a gracious welcome to her domain and indicated, with much gratification and pride, its principal attractions. Mr. Kenge also came to speak to us and did the honours of the place in much the same way, with the bland modesty of a proprietor. It was not a very good day for a visit, he said; he would have preferred the first day of term; but it was imposing, it was imposing.

When we had been there half an hour or so, the case in progress—if I may use a phrase so ridiculous in such a connexion—seemed to die out of its own vapidity, without coming, or being by anybody expected to come, to any result. The Lord Chancellor then threw down a bundle of papers from his desk to the gentlemen below him, and somebody said, "Jarndyce and Jarndyce." Upon this there was a buzz, and a laugh, and a general withdrawal of the bystanders, and a bringing in of great heaps, and piles, and bags and bags full of papers.

I think it came on "for further directions"—about some bill of costs, to the best of my understanding, which was confused enough. But I counted twenty-three gentlemen in wigs who said they were "in it," and none of them appeared to understand it much better than I. They chatted about it with the Lord Chancellor, and contradicted and explained among themselves, and some of them said it was this way, and some of them said it was that way, and some of them jocosely proposed to read huge volumes of affidavits, and there was more buzzing and laughing, and everybody concerned was in a state of idle entertainment, and nothing could be made of it by anybody. After an hour or so of this, and a good many speeches being begun and cut short, it was "referred back for the present," as Mr. Kenge said, and the papers were bundled up again before the clerks had finished bringing them in.

I glanced at Richard on the termination of these hopeless proceedings and was shocked to see the worn look of his handsome young face. "It can't last for ever, Dame Durden. Better luck next time!" was all he said.

I had seen Mr. Guppy bringing in papers and arranging them for Mr.

Kenge; and he had seen me and made me a forlorn bow, which rendered me desirous to get out of the court. Richard had given me his arm and was taking me away when Mr. Guppy came up.

"I beg your pardon, Mr. Carstone," said he in a whisper, "and Miss Summerson's also, but there's a lady here, a friend of mine, who knows her and wishes to have the pleasure of shaking hands." As he spoke, I saw before me, as if she had started into bodily shape from my remembrance, Mrs. Rachael of my godmother's house.

"How do you do, Esther?" said she. "Do you recollect me?"

I gave her my hand and told her yes and that she was very little altered.

"I wonder you remember those times, Esther," she returned with her old asperity. "They are changed now. Well! I am glad to see you, and glad you are not too proud to know me." But indeed she seemed disappointed that I was not.

"Proud, Mrs. Rachael!" I remonstrated.

"I am married, Esther," she returned, coldly correcting me, "and am Mrs. Chadband. Well! I wish you good day, and I hope you'll do well."

Mr. Guppy, who had been attentive to this short dialogue, heaved a sigh in my ear and elbowed his own and Mrs. Rachael's way through the confused little crowd of people coming in and going out, which we were in the midst of and which the change in the business had brought together. Richard and I were making our way through it, and I was yet in the first chill of the late unexpected recognition when I saw, coming towards us, but not seeing us, no less a person than Mr. George. He made nothing of the people about him as he tramped on, staring over their heads into the body of the court.

"George!" said Richard as I called his attention to him.

"You are well met, sir," he returned. "And you, miss. Could you point a person out for me, I want? I don't understand these places."

Turning as he spoke and making an easy way for us, he stopped when we were out of the press in a corner behind a great red curtain.

"There's a little cracked old woman," he began, "that—"

I put up my finger, for Miss Flite was close by me, having kept beside me all the time and having called the attention of several of her legal acquaintance to me (as I had overheard to my confusion) by whispering in their ears, "Hush! Fitz Jarndyce on my left!"

"Hem!" said Mr. George. "You remember, miss, that we passed some conversation on a certain man this morning? Gridley," in a low whisper behind his hand.

"Yes," said I.

"He is hiding at my place. I couldn't mention it. Hadn't his authority. He is on his last march, miss, and has a whim to see her. He says they can feel for one another, and she has been almost as good as a friend to him here. I came down to look for her, for when I sat by Gridley this afternoon, I seemed to hear the roll of the muffled drums."

"Shall I tell her?" said I.

"Would you be so good?" he returned with a glance of something like apprehension at Miss Flite. "It's a providence I met you, miss; I doubt if I should have known how to get on with that lady." And he put one hand in his breast and stood upright in a martial attitude as I informed little Miss Flite, in her ear, of the purport of his kind errand.

"My angry friend from Shropshire! Almost as celebrated as myself!" she exclaimed. "Now really! My dear, I will wait upon him with the greatest pleasure."

"He is living concealed at Mr. George's," said I. "Hush! This is Mr. George."

"In—deed!" returned Miss Flite. "Very proud to have the honour! A military man, my dear. You know, a perfect general!" she whispered to me.

Poor Miss Flite deemed it necessary to be so courtly and polite, as a mark of her respect for the army, and to curtsy so very often that it was no easy matter to get her out of the court. When this was at last done, and addressing Mr. George as "General," she gave him her arm, to the great entertainment of some idlers who were looking on, he was so discomposed and begged me so respectfully "not to desert him" that I could not make up my mind to do it, especially as Miss Flite was always tractable with me and as she too said, "Fitz Jarndyce, my dear, you will accompany us, of course." As Richard seemed quite willing, and even anxious, that we should see them safely to their destination, we agreed to do so. And as Mr. George informed us that Gridley's mind had run on Mr. Jarndyce all the afternoon after hearing of their interview in the morning, I wrote a hasty note in pencil to my guardian to say where we were gone and why. Mr. George sealed it at a coffee-house, that it might lead to no discovery, and we sent it off by a ticket-porter.

We then took a hackney-coach and drove away to the neighbourhood of Leicester Square. We walked through some narrow courts, for which Mr. George apologized, and soon came to the shooting gallery, the door of which was closed. As he pulled a bell-handle which hung by a chain to the doorpost, a very respectable old gentleman with grey hair, wearing spectacles, and dressed in a black spencer and gaiters and a broad-brimmed hat, and carrying a large gold-beaded cane, addressed him.

"I ask your pardon, my good friend," said he, "but is this George's Shooting Gallery?"

"It is, sir," returned Mr. George, glancing up at the great letters in which that inscription was painted on the whitewashed wall.

"Oh! To be sure!" said the old gentleman, following his eyes. "Thank you. Have you rung the bell?"

"My name is George, sir, and I have rung the bell."

"Oh, indeed?" said the old gentleman. "Your name is George? Then I am here as soon as you, you see. You came for me, no doubt?"

"No, sir. You have the advantage of me."

"Oh, indeed?" said the old gentleman. "Then it was your young man who came for me. I am a physician and was requested—five minutes ago—to come and visit a sick man at George's Shooting Gallery."

"The muffled drums," said Mr. George, turning to Richard and me and gravely shaking his head. "It's quite correct, sir. Will you please to walk in."

The door being at that moment opened by a very singular-looking little man in a green-baize cap and apron, whose face and hands and dress were blackened all over, we passed along a dreary passage into a large building with bare brick walls where there were targets, and guns, and swords, and other things of that kind. When we had all arrived here, the physician stopped, and taking off his hat, appeared to vanish by magic and to leave another and quite a different man in his place.

"Now lookee here, George," said the man, turning quickly round upon him and tapping him on the breast with a large forefinger. "You know me, and I know you. You're a man of the world, and I'm a man of the world. My name's Bucket, as you are aware, and I have got a peace-warrant against Gridley. You have kept him out of the way a long time, and you have been artful in it, and it does you credit."

Mr. George, looking hard at him, bit his lip and shook his head.

"Now, George," said the other, keeping close to him, "you're a sensible man and a well-conducted man; that's what YOU are, beyond a doubt. And mind you, I don't talk to you as a common character, because you have served your country and you know that when duty calls we must obey. Consequently you're very far from wanting to give trouble. If I required assistance, you'd assist me; that's what YOU'D do. Phil Squod, don't you go a-sidling round the gallery like that"—the dirty little man was shuffling about with his shoulder against the wall, and his eyes on the intruder, in a manner that looked threatening—"because I know you and won't have it."

"Phil!" said Mr. George.

"Yes, guv'ner."

"Be quiet."

The little man, with a low growl, stood still.

"Ladies and gentlemen," said Mr. Bucket, "you'll excuse anything that may appear to be disagreeable in this, for my name's Inspector Bucket of the Detective, and I have a duty to perform. George, I know where my man is because I was on the roof last night and saw him through the skylight, and you along with him. He is in there, you know," pointing; "that's where HE is—on a sofy. Now I must see my man, and I must tell my man to consider himself in custody; but you know me, and you know I don't want to take any uncomfortable measures. You give me your word, as from one man to another (and an old soldier, mind you, likewise), that it's honourable between us two, and I'll accommodate you to the utmost of my power."

"I give it," was the reply. "But it wasn't handsome in you, Mr. Bucket."

"Gammon, George! Not handsome?" said Mr. Bucket, tapping him on his broad breast again and shaking hands with him. "I don't say it wasn't handsome in you to keep my man so close, do I? Be equally good-tempered to me, old boy! Old William Tell, Old Shaw, the Life Guardsman! Why, he's a model of the whole British army in himself, ladies and gentlemen. I'd give a fifty-pun' note to be such a figure of a man!"

The affair being brought to this head, Mr. George, after a little consideration, proposed to go in first to his comrade (as he called him), taking Miss Flite with him. Mr. Bucket agreeing, they went away to the further end of the gallery, leaving us sitting and standing by a table covered with guns. Mr. Bucket took this opportunity of entering into a little light conversation, asking me if I were afraid of fire-arms, as most young ladies were; asking Richard if he were a good shot; asking Phil Squod which he considered the best of those rifles and what it might be worth first-hand, telling him in return that it was a pity he ever gave way to his temper, for he was naturally so amiable that he might have been a young woman, and making himself generally agreeable.

After a time he followed us to the further end of the gallery, and Richard and I were going quietly away when Mr. George came after us. He said that if we had no objection to see his comrade, he would take a visit from us very kindly. The words had hardly passed his lips when the bell was rung and my guardian appeared, "on the chance," he slightly observed, "of being able to do any little thing for a poor fellow involved in the same misfortune as himself." We all four went back together and went into the place where Gridley was.

It was a bare room, partitioned off from the gallery with unpainted wood. As the screening was not more than eight or ten feet high and only enclosed the sides, not the top, the rafters of the high gallery roof were overhead, and the skylight through which Mr. Bucket had looked down. The sun was low—near setting—and its light came redly in above, without descending to the ground. Upon a plain canvas-covered sofa lay the man from Shropshire, dressed much as we had seen him last, but so changed that at first I recognized no likeness in his colourless face to what I recollected.

He had been still writing in his hiding-place, and still dwelling on his grievances, hour after hour. A table and some shelves were covered with manuscript papers and with worn pens and a medley of such tokens. Touchingly and awfully drawn together, he and the little mad woman were side by side and, as it were, alone. She sat on a chair holding his hand, and none of us went close to them.

His voice had faded, with the old expression of his face, with his strength, with his anger, with his resistance to the wrongs that had at last subdued him. The faintest shadow of an object full of form and colour is such a picture of it as he was of the man from Shropshire whom we had spoken with before.

He inclined his head to Richard and me and spoke to my guardian.

"Mr. Jarndyce, it is very kind of you to come to see me. I am not long to be seen, I think. I am very glad to take your hand, sir. You are a good man, superior to injustice, and God knows I honour you."

They shook hands earnestly, and my guardian said some words of comfort to him.

"It may seem strange to you, sir," returned Gridley; "I should not have liked to see you if this had been the first time of our meeting. But you know I made a fight for it, you know I stood up with my single hand against them all, you know I told them the truth to the last, and told them what they were, and what they had done to me; so I don't mind your seeing me, this wreck."

"You have been courageous with them many and many a time," returned my guardian.

"Sir, I have been," with a faint smile. "I told you what would come of it when I ceased to be so, and see here! Look at us—look at us!" He drew the hand Miss Flite held through her arm and brought her something nearer to him.

"This ends it. Of all my old associations, of all my old pursuits and hopes, of all the living and the dead world, this one poor soul alone comes natural to me, and I am fit for. There is a tie of many suffering years between us two, and it is the only tie I ever had on earth that Chancery has not broken."

"Accept my blessing, Gridley," said Miss Flite in tears. "Accept my blessing!"

"I thought, boastfully, that they never could break my heart, Mr. Jarndyce. I was resolved that they should not. I did believe that I could, and would, charge them with being the mockery they were until I died of some bodily disorder. But I am worn out. How long I have been wearing out, I don't know; I seemed to break down in an hour. I hope they may never come to hear of it. I hope everybody here will lead them to believe that I died defying them, consistently and perseveringly, as I did through so many years."

Here Mr. Bucket, who was sitting in a corner by the door, good-naturedly offered such consolation as he could administer.

"Come, come!" he said from his corner. "Don't go on in that way, Mr. Gridley. You are only a little low. We are all of us a little low sometimes. I am. Hold up, hold up! You'll lose your temper with the whole round of 'em, again and again; and I shall take you on a score of warrants yet, if I have luck."

He only shook his head.

"Don't shake your head," said Mr. Bucket. "Nod it; that's what I want to see you do. Why, Lord bless your soul, what times we have had together! Haven't I seen you in the Fleet over and over again for contempt? Haven't I come into court, twenty afternoons for no other purpose than to see you pin the Chancellor like a bull-dog? Don't you remember when you first began to threaten the lawyers, and the peace was sworn against you two or three times a week? Ask the little old lady there; she has been always present. Hold up, Mr. Gridley, hold up, sir!"

"What are you going to do about him?" asked George in a low voice.

"I don't know yet," said Bucket in the same tone. Then resuming his encouragement, he pursued aloud: "Worn out, Mr. Gridley? After dodging me for all these weeks and forcing me to climb the roof here like a tom cat and to come to see you as a doctor? That ain't like being worn out. I should think not! Now I tell you what you want. You want excitement, you know, to keep YOU up; that's what YOU want. You're used to it, and you can't do without it. I couldn't myself. Very well, then; here's this warrant got by Mr. Tulkinghorn of Lincoln's Inn Fields, and backed into half-a-dozen counties since. What do you say to coming along with me, upon this warrant, and having a good angry argument before the magistrates? It'll do you good; it'll freshen you up and get you into training for another turn at the Chancellor. Give in? Why, I am surprised to hear a man of your energy talk of giving in. You mustn't do that. You're half the fun of the fair in the Court of Chancery. George, you lend Mr. Gridley a hand, and let's see now whether he won't be better up than down."

"He is very weak," said the trooper in a low voice.

"Is he?" returned Bucket anxiously. "I only want to rouse him. I don't like to see an old acquaintance giving in like this. It would cheer him up more than anything if I could make him a little waxy with me. He's welcome to drop into me, right and left, if he likes. I shall never take advantage of it."

The roof rang with a scream from Miss Flite, which still rings in my ears.

"Oh, no, Gridley!" she cried as he fell heavily and calmly back from before her. "Not without my blessing. After so many years!"

The sun was down, the light had gradually stolen from the roof, and the shadow had crept upward. But to me the shadow of that pair, one living and one dead, fell heavier on Richard's departure than the darkness of the darkest night. And through Richard's farewell words I heard it echoed: "Of all my old associations, of all my old pursuits and hopes, of all the living and the dead world, this one poor soul alone comes natural to me, and I am fit for. There is a tie of many suffering years between us two, and it is the only tie I ever had on earth that Chancery has not broken!"

CHAPTER XXV
MRS. SNAGSBY SEES IT ALL

There is disquietude in Cook's Court, Cursitor Street. Black suspicion hides in that peaceful region. The mass of Cook's Courtiers are in their usual state of mind, no better and no worse; but Mr. Snagsby is changed, and his little woman knows it.

For Tom-all-Alone's and Lincoln's Inn Fields persist in harnessing themselves, a pair of ungovernable coursers, to the chariot of Mr. Snagsby's imagination; and Mr. Bucket drives; and the passengers are Jo and Mr. Tulkinghorn; and the complete equipage whirls though the law-stationery business at wild speed all round the clock. Even in the little front kitchen where the family meals are taken, it rattles away at a smoking pace from the dinner-table, when Mr. Snagsby pauses in carving the first slice of the leg of mutton baked with potatoes and stares at the kitchen wall.

Mr. Snagsby cannot make out what it is that he has had to do with. Something is wrong somewhere, but what something, what may come of it, to whom, when, and from which unthought of and unheard of quarter is the puzzle of his life. His remote impressions of the robes and coronets, the stars and garters, that sparkle through the surface-dust of Mr. Tulkinghorn's chambers; his veneration for the mysteries presided over by that best and closest of his customers, whom all the Inns of Court, all Chancery Lane, and all the legal neighbourhood agree to hold in awe; his remembrance of Detective Mr. Bucket with his forefinger and his confidential manner, impossible to be evaded or declined, persuade him that he is a party to some dangerous secret without knowing what it is. And it is the fearful peculiarity of this condition that, at any hour of his daily life, at any opening of the shop-door, at any pull of the bell, at any entrance of a messenger, or any delivery of a letter, the secret may take air and fire, explode, and blow up—Mr. Bucket only knows whom.

For which reason, whenever a man unknown comes into the shop (as many men unknown do) and says, "Is Mr. Snagsby in?" or words to that innocent effect, Mr. Snagsby's heart knocks hard at his guilty breast. He undergoes so much from such inquiries that when they are made by boys he revenges himself by flipping at their ears over the counter and asking the young dogs what they mean by it and why they can't speak out at once? More impracticable men and boys persist in walking into Mr. Snagsby's sleep and terrifying him with unaccountable questions, so that often when the cock at the little dairy in Cursitor Street breaks out in his usual absurd way about the morning, Mr. Snagsby finds himself in a crisis of nightmare, with his little woman shaking him and saying "What's the matter with the man!"

The little woman herself is not the least item in his difficulty. To know that he is always keeping a secret from her, that he has under all circumstances to conceal and hold fast a tender double tooth, which her sharpness is ever ready to twist out of his head, gives Mr. Snagsby, in her dentistical presence, much of the air of a dog who has a reservation from his master and will look anywhere rather than meet his eye.

These various signs and tokens, marked by the little woman, are not lost upon her. They impel her to say, "Snagsby has something on his mind!" And thus suspicion gets into Cook's Court, Cursitor Street. From suspicion to jealousy, Mrs. Snagsby finds the road as natural and short as from Cook's Court to Chancery Lane. And thus jealousy gets into Cook's Court, Cursitor Street. Once there (and it was always lurking thereabout), it is very active and nimble in Mrs. Snagsby's breast, prompting her to nocturnal examinations of Mr. Snagsby's pockets; to secret perusals of Mr. Snagsby's letters; to private researches in the day book and ledger, till, cash-box, and iron safe; to watchings at windows, listenings behind doors, and a general putting of this and that together by the wrong end.

Mrs. Snagsby is so perpetually on the alert that the house becomes ghostly with creaking boards and rustling garments. The 'prentices think somebody may have been murdered there in bygone times. Guster holds certain loose atoms of an idea (picked up at Tooting, where they were found floating among the orphans) that there is buried money underneath the cellar, guarded by an old man with a white beard, who cannot get out for seven thousand years because he said the Lord's Prayer backwards.

"Who was Nimrod?" Mrs. Snagsby repeatedly inquires of herself. "Who was that lady—that creature? And who is that boy?" Now, Nimrod being as dead as the mighty hunter whose name Mrs. Snagsby has appropriated, and the lady being unproducible, she directs her mental eye, for the present, with redoubled vigilance to the boy. "And who," quoth Mrs. Snagsby for the thousand and first time, "is that boy? Who is that—!" And there Mrs. Snagsby is seized with an inspiration.

He has no respect for Mr. Chadband. No, to be sure, and he wouldn't have, of course. Naturally he wouldn't, under those contagious circumstances. He was invited and appointed by Mr. Chadband—why, Mrs. Snagsby heard it herself with her own ears!—to come back, and be told where he was to go, to be addressed by Mr. Chadband; and he never came! Why did he never come? Because he was told not to come. Who told him not to come? Who? Ha, ha! Mrs. Snagsby sees it all.

But happily (and Mrs. Snagsby tightly shakes her head and tightly smiles) that boy was met by Mr. Chadband yesterday in the streets; and that boy, as affording a subject which Mr. Chadband desires to improve for the spiritual delight of a select congregation, was seized by Mr. Chadband and threatened with being delivered over to the police unless he showed the reverend gentleman where he lived and unless he entered into, and fulfilled, an undertaking to appear in Cook's Court to-morrow night, "to—mor—row—night," Mrs. Snagsby repeats for mere emphasis with another tight smile and another tight shake of her head; and to-morrow night that boy will be here, and to-morrow night Mrs. Snagsby will have her eye upon him and upon some one else; and oh, you may walk a long while in your secret ways (says Mrs. Snagsby with haughtiness and scorn), but you can't blind ME!

Mrs. Snagsby sounds no timbrel in anybody's ears, but holds her purpose quietly, and keeps her counsel. To-morrow comes, the savoury preparations for the Oil Trade come, the evening comes. Comes Mr. Snagsby in his black coat; come the Chadbands; come (when the gorging vessel is replete) the 'prentices and Guster, to be edified; comes at last, with his slouching head, and his shuffle backward, and his shuffle forward, and his shuffle to the right, and his shuffle to the left, and his bit of fur cap in his muddy hand, which he picks as if it were some mangy bird he had caught and was plucking before eating raw, Jo, the very, very tough subject Mr. Chadband is to improve.

Mrs. Snagsby screws a watchful glance on Jo as he is brought into the little drawing-room by Guster. He looks at Mr. Snagsby the moment he comes in. Aha! Why does he look at Mr. Snagsby? Mr. Snagsby looks at him. Why should he do that, but that Mrs. Snagsby sees it all? Why else should that look pass between them, why else should Mr. Snagsby be confused and cough a signal cough behind his hand? It is as clear as crystal that Mr. Snagsby is that boy's father.

"Peace, my friends," says Chadband, rising and wiping the oily exudations from his reverend visage. "Peace be with us! My friends, why with us? Because," with his fat smile, "it cannot be against us, because it must be for us; because it is not hardening, because it is softening; because it does not make war like the hawk, but comes home unto us like the dove. Therefore, my friends, peace be with us! My human boy, come forward!"

Stretching forth his flabby paw, Mr. Chadband lays the same on Jo's arm and considers where to station him. Jo, very doubtful of his reverend friend's intentions and not at all clear but that something practical and painful is going to be done to him, mutters, "You let me alone. I never said nothink to you. You let me alone."

"No, my young friend," says Chadband smoothly, "I will not let you alone. And why? Because I am a harvest-labourer, because I am a toiler and a moiler, because you are delivered over unto me and are become as a precious instrument in my hands. My friends, may I so employ this instrument as to use it to your advantage, to your profit, to your gain, to your welfare, to your enrichment! My young friend, sit upon this stool."

Jo, apparently possessed by an impression that the reverend gentleman wants to cut his hair, shields his head with both arms and is got into the required position with great difficulty and every possible manifestation of reluctance.

When he is at last adjusted like a lay-figure, Mr. Chadband, retiring behind the table, holds up his bear's-paw and says, "My friends!" This is the signal for a general settlement of the audience. The 'prentices giggle internally and nudge each other. Guster falls into a staring and vacant state, compounded of a stunned admiration of Mr. Chadband and pity for the friendless outcast whose condition touches her nearly. Mrs. Snagsby silently lays trains of gunpowder. Mrs. Chadband composes herself grimly by the fire and warms her knees, finding that sensation favourable to the reception of eloquence.

It happens that Mr. Chadband has a pulpit habit of fixing some member of his congregation with his eye and fatly arguing his points with that particular person, who is understood to be expected to be moved to an occasional grunt, groan, gasp, or other audible expression of inward working, which expression of inward working, being echoed by some elderly lady in the next pew and so communicated like a game of forfeits through a circle of the more fermentable sinners present, serves the purpose of parliamentary cheering and gets Mr. Chadband's steam up. From mere force of habit, Mr. Chadband in saying "My friends!" has rested his eye on Mr. Snagsby and proceeds to make that ill-starred stationer, already sufficiently confused, the immediate recipient of his discourse.

"We have here among us, my friends," says Chadband, "a Gentile and a heathen, a dweller in the tents of Tom-all-Alone's and a mover-on upon the surface of the earth. We have here among us, my friends," and Mr. Chadband, untwisting the point with his dirty thumb-nail, bestows an oily smile on Mr. Snagsby, signifying that he will throw him an argumentative back-fall presently if he be not already down, "a brother and a boy. Devoid of parents, devoid of relations, devoid of flocks and herds, devoid of gold and silver and of precious stones. Now, my friends, why do I say he is devoid of these possessions? Why? Why is he?" Mr. Chadband states the question as if he were propounding an entirely new riddle of much ingenuity and merit to Mr. Snagsby and entreating him not to give it up.

Mr. Snagsby, greatly perplexed by the mysterious look he received just now from his little woman—at about the period when Mr. Chadband mentioned the word parents—is tempted into modestly remarking, "I don't know, I'm sure, sir." On which interruption Mrs. Chadband glares and Mrs. Snagsby says, "For shame!"

"I hear a voice," says Chadband; "is it a still small voice, my friends? I fear not, though I fain would hope so—"

"Ah—h!" from Mrs. Snagsby.

"Which says, 'I don't know.' Then I will tell you why. I say this brother present here among us is devoid of parents, devoid of relations, devoid of flocks and herds, devoid of gold, of silver, and of precious stones because he is devoid of the light that shines in upon some of us. What is that light? What is it? I ask you, what is that light?"

Mr. Chadband draws back his head and pauses, but Mr. Snagsby is not to be lured on to his destruction again. Mr. Chadband, leaning forward over the table, pierces what he has got to follow directly into Mr. Snagsby with the thumb-nail already mentioned.

"It is," says Chadband, "the ray of rays, the sun of suns, the moon of moons, the star of stars. It is the light of Terewth."

Mr. Chadband draws himself up again and looks triumphantly at Mr. Snagsby as if he would be glad to know how he feels after that.

"Of Terewth," says Mr. Chadband, hitting him again. "Say not to me that it is NOT the lamp of lamps. I say to you it is. I say to you, a million of times over, it is. It is! I say to you that I will proclaim it to you, whether you like it or not; nay, that the less you like it, the more I will proclaim it to you. With a speaking-trumpet! I say to you that if you rear yourself against it, you shall fall, you shall be bruised, you shall be battered, you shall be flawed, you shall be smashed."

The present effect of this flight of oratory—much admired for its general power by Mr. Chadband's followers—being not only to make Mr. Chadband unpleasantly warm, but to represent the innocent Mr. Snagsby in the light of a determined enemy to virtue, with a forehead of brass and a heart of adamant, that unfortunate tradesman becomes yet more disconcerted and is in a very advanced state of low spirits and false position when Mr. Chadband accidentally finishes him.

"My friends," he resumes after dabbing his fat head for some time—and it smokes to such an extent that he seems to light his pocket-handkerchief at it, which smokes, too, after every dab—"to pursue the subject we are endeavouring with our lowly gifts to improve, let us in a spirit of love inquire what is that Terewth to which I have alluded. For, my young friends," suddenly addressing the 'prentices and Guster, to their consternation, "if I am told by the doctor that calomel or castor-oil is good for me, I may naturally ask what is calomel, and what is castor-oil. I may wish to be informed of that before I dose myself with either or with both. Now, my young friends, what is this Terewth then? Firstly (in a spirit of love), what is the common sort of Terewth—the working clothes—the every-day wear, my young friends? Is it deception?"

"Ah—h!" from Mrs. Snagsby.

"Is it suppression?"

A shiver in the negative from Mrs. Snagsby.

"Is it reservation?"

A shake of the head from Mrs. Snagsby—very long and very tight.

"No, my friends, it is neither of these. Neither of these names belongs to it. When this young heathen now among us—who is now, my friends, asleep, the seal of indifference and perdition being set upon his eyelids; but do not wake him, for it is right that I should have to wrestle, and to combat and to struggle, and to conquer, for his sake—when this young hardened heathen told us a story of a cock, and of a bull, and of a lady, and of a sovereign, was THAT the Terewth? No. Or if it was partly, was it wholly and entirely? No, my friends, no!"

If Mr. Snagsby could withstand his little woman's look as it enters at his eyes, the windows of his soul, and searches the whole tenement, he were other than the man he is. He cowers and droops.

"Or, my juvenile friends," says Chadband, descending to the level of their comprehension with a very obtrusive demonstration in his greasily meek smile of coming a long way downstairs for the purpose, "if the master of this house was to go forth into the city and there see an eel, and was to come back, and was to call unto him the mistress of this house, and was to say, 'Sarah, rejoice with me, for I have seen an elephant!' would THAT be Terewth?"

Mrs. Snagsby in tears.

"Or put it, my juvenile friends, that he saw an elephant, and returning said 'Lo, the city is barren, I have seen but an eel,' would THAT be Terewth?"

Mrs. Snagsby sobbing loudly.

"Or put it, my juvenile friends," said Chadband, stimulated by the sound, "that the unnatural parents of this slumbering heathen—for parents he had, my juvenile friends, beyond a doubt—after casting him forth to the wolves and the vultures, and the wild dogs and the young gazelles, and the serpents, went back to their dwellings and had their pipes, and their pots, and their flutings and their dancings, and their malt liquors, and their butcher's meat and poultry, would THAT be Terewth?"

Mrs. Snagsby replies by delivering herself a prey to spasms, not an unresisting prey, but a crying and a tearing one, so that Cook's Court re-echoes with her shrieks. Finally, becoming cataleptic, she has to be carried up the narrow staircase like a grand piano. After unspeakable suffering, productive of the utmost consternation, she is pronounced, by expresses from the bedroom, free from pain, though much exhausted, in which state of affairs Mr. Snagsby, trampled and crushed in the piano-forte removal, and extremely timid and feeble, ventures to come out from behind the door in the drawing-room.

All this time Jo has been standing on the spot where he woke up, ever picking his cap and putting bits of fur in his mouth. He spits them out with a remorseful air, for he feels that it is in his nature to be an unimprovable reprobate and that it's no good HIS trying to keep awake, for HE won't never know nothink. Though it may be, Jo, that there is a history so interesting and affecting even to minds as near the brutes as thine, recording deeds done on this earth for common men, that if the Chadbands, removing their own persons from the light, would but show it thee in simple reverence, would but leave it unimproved, would but regard it as being eloquent enough without their modest aid—it might hold thee awake, and thou might learn from it yet!

Jo never heard of any such book. Its compilers and the Reverend Chadband are all one to him, except that he knows the Reverend Chadband and would rather run away from him for an hour than hear him talk for five minutes. "It an't no good my waiting here no longer," thinks Jo. "Mr. Snagsby an't a-going to say nothink to me to-night." And downstairs he shuffles.

But downstairs is the charitable Guster, holding by the handrail of the kitchen stairs and warding off a fit, as yet doubtfully, the same having been induced by Mrs. Snagsby's screaming. She has her own supper of bread and cheese to hand to Jo, with whom she ventures to interchange a word or so for the first time.

"Here's something to eat, poor boy," says Guster.

"Thankee, mum," says Jo.

"Are you hungry?"

"Jist!" says Jo.

"What's gone of your father and your mother, eh?"

Jo stops in the middle of a bite and looks petrified. For this orphan charge of the Christian saint whose shrine was at Tooting has patted him on the shoulder, and it is the first time in his life that any decent hand has been so laid upon him.

"I never know'd nothink about 'em," says Jo.

"No more didn't I of mine," cries Guster. She is repressing symptoms favourable to the fit when she seems to take alarm at something and vanishes down the stairs.

"Jo," whispers the law-stationer softly as the boy lingers on the step.

"Here I am, Mr. Snagsby!"

"I didn't know you were gone—there's another half-crown, Jo. It was quite right of you to say nothing about the lady the other night when we were out together. It would breed trouble. You can't be too quiet, Jo."

"I am fly, master!"

And so, good night.

A ghostly shade, frilled and night-capped, follows the law-stationer to the room he came from and glides higher up. And henceforth he begins, go where he will, to be attended by another shadow than his own, hardly less constant than his own, hardly less quiet than his own. And into whatsoever atmosphere of secrecy his own shadow may pass, let all concerned in the secrecy beware! For the watchful Mrs. Snagsby is there too—bone of his bone, flesh of his flesh, shadow of his shadow.

CHAPTER XXVI
SHARPSHOOTERS

Wintry morning, looking with dull eyes and sallow face upon the neighbourhood of Leicester Square, finds its inhabitants unwilling to get out of bed. Many of them are not early risers at the brightest of times, being birds of night who roost when the sun is high and are wide awake and keen for prey when the stars shine out. Behind dingy blind and curtain, in upper story and garret, skulking more or less under false names, false hair, false titles, false jewellery, and false histories, a colony of brigands lie in their first sleep. Gentlemen of the green-baize road who could discourse from personal experience of foreign galleys and home treadmills; spies of strong governments that eternally quake with weakness and miserable fear, broken traitors, cowards, bullies, gamesters, shufflers, swindlers, and false witnesses; some not unmarked by the branding-iron beneath their dirty braid; all with more cruelty in them than was in Nero, and more crime than is in Newgate. For howsoever bad the devil can be in fustian or smock-frock (and he can be very bad in both), he is a more designing, callous, and intolerable devil when he sticks a pin in his shirt-front, calls himself a gentleman, backs a card or colour, plays a game or so of billiards, and knows a little about bills and promissory notes than in any other form he wears. And in such form Mr. Bucket shall find him, when he will, still pervading the tributary channels of Leicester Square.

But the wintry morning wants him not and wakes him not. It wakes Mr. George of the shooting gallery and his familiar. They arise, roll up and stow away their mattresses. Mr. George, having shaved himself before a looking-glass of minute proportions, then marches out, bare-headed and bare-chested, to the pump in the little yard and anon comes back shining with yellow soap, friction, drifting rain, and exceedingly cold water. As he rubs himself upon a large jack-towel, blowing like a military sort of diver just come up, his hair curling tighter and tighter on his sunburnt temples the more he rubs it so that it looks as if it never could be loosened by any less coercive instrument than an iron rake or a curry-comb—as he rubs, and puffs, and polishes, and blows, turning his head from side to side the more conveniently to excoriate his throat, and standing with his body well bent forward to keep the wet from his martial legs, Phil, on his knees lighting a fire, looks round as if it were enough washing for him to see all that done, and sufficient renovation for one day to take in the superfluous health his master throws off.

When Mr. George is dry, he goes to work to brush his head with two hard brushes at once, to that unmerciful degree that Phil, shouldering his way round the gallery in the act of sweeping it, winks with sympathy. This chafing over, the ornamental part of Mr. George's toilet is soon performed. He fills his pipe, lights it, and marches up and down smoking, as his custom is, while Phil, raising a powerful odour of hot rolls and coffee, prepares breakfast. He smokes gravely and marches in slow time. Perhaps this morning's pipe is devoted to the memory of Gridley in his grave.

"And so, Phil," says George of the shooting gallery after several turns in silence, "you were dreaming of the country last night?"

Phil, by the by, said as much in a tone of surprise as he scrambled out of bed.

"Yes, guv'ner."

"What was it like?"

"I hardly know what it was like, guv'ner," said Phil, considering.

"How did you know it was the country?"

"On account of the grass, I think. And the swans upon it," says Phil after further consideration.

"What were the swans doing on the grass?"

"They was a-eating of it, I expect," says Phil.

The master resumes his march, and the man resumes his preparation of breakfast. It is not necessarily a lengthened preparation, being limited to the setting forth of very simple breakfast requisites for two and the broiling of a rasher of bacon at the fire in the rusty grate; but as Phil has to sidle round a considerable part of the gallery for every object he wants, and never brings two objects at once, it takes time under the circumstances. At length the breakfast is ready. Phil announcing it, Mr. George knocks the ashes out of his pipe on the hob, stands his pipe itself in the chimney corner, and sits down to the meal. When he has helped himself, Phil follows suit, sitting at the extreme end of the little oblong table and taking his plate on his knees. Either in humility, or to hide his blackened hands, or because it is his natural manner of eating.

"The country," says Mr. George, plying his knife and fork; "why, I suppose you never clapped your eyes on the country, Phil?"

"I see the marshes once," says Phil, contentedly eating his breakfast.

"What marshes?"

"THE marshes, commander," returns Phil.

"Where are they?"

"I don't know where they are," says Phil; "but I see 'em, guv'ner. They was flat. And miste."

Governor and commander are interchangeable terms with Phil, expressive of the same respect and deference and applicable to nobody but Mr. George.

"I was born in the country, Phil."

"Was you indeed, commander?"

"Yes. And bred there."

Phil elevates his one eyebrow, and after respectfully staring at his master to express interest, swallows a great gulp of coffee, still staring at him.

"There's not a bird's note that I don't know," says Mr. George. "Not many an English leaf or berry that I couldn't name. Not many a tree that I couldn't climb yet if I was put to it. I was a real country boy, once. My good mother lived in the country."

"She must have been a fine old lady, guv'ner," Phil observes.

"Aye! And not so old either, five and thirty years ago," says Mr. George. "But I'll wager that at ninety she would be near as upright as me, and near as broad across the shoulders."

"Did she die at ninety, guv'ner?" inquires Phil.

"No. Bosh! Let her rest in peace, God bless her!" says the trooper. "What set me on about country boys, and runaways, and good-for-nothings? You, to be sure! So you never clapped your eyes upon the country—marshes and dreams excepted. Eh?"

Phil shakes his head.

"Do you want to see it?"

"N-no, I don't know as I do, particular," says Phil.

"The town's enough for you, eh?"

"Why, you see, commander," says Phil, "I ain't acquainted with anythink else, and I doubt if I ain't a-getting too old to take to novelties."

"How old ARE you, Phil?" asks the trooper, pausing as he conveys his smoking saucer to his lips.

"I'm something with a eight in it," says Phil. "It can't be eighty. Nor yet eighteen. It's betwixt 'em, somewheres."

Mr. George, slowly putting down his saucer without tasting its contents, is laughingly beginning, "Why, what the deuce, Phil—" when he stops, seeing that Phil is counting on his dirty fingers.

"I was just eight," says Phil, "agreeable to the parish calculation, when I went with the tinker. I was sent on a errand, and I see him a-sittin under a old buildin with a fire all to himself wery comfortable, and he says, 'Would you like to come along a me, my man?' I says 'Yes,' and him and me and the fire goes home to Clerkenwell together. That was April Fool Day. I was able to count up to ten; and when April Fool Day come round again, I says to myself, 'Now, old chap, you're one and a eight in it.' April Fool Day after that, I says, 'Now, old chap, you're two and a eight in it.' In course of time, I come to ten and a eight in it; two tens and a eight in it. When it got so high, it got the upper hand of me, but this is how I always know there's a eight in it."

"Ah!" says Mr. George, resuming his breakfast. "And where's the tinker?"

"Drink put him in the hospital, guv'ner, and the hospital put him—in a glass-case, I HAVE heerd," Phil replies mysteriously.

"By that means you got promotion? Took the business, Phil?"

"Yes, commander, I took the business. Such as it was. It wasn't much of a beat—round Saffron Hill, Hatton Garden, Clerkenwell, Smiffeld, and there—poor neighbourhood, where they uses up the kettles till they're past mending.

Most of the tramping tinkers used to come and lodge at our place; that was the best part of my master's earnings. But they didn't come to me. I warn't like him. He could sing 'em a good song. I couldn't! He could play 'em a tune on any sort of pot you please, so as it was iron or block tin. I never could do nothing with a pot but mend it or bile it—never had a note of music in me. Besides, I was too ill-looking, and their wives complained of me."

"They were mighty particular. You would pass muster in a crowd, Phil!" says the trooper with a pleasant smile.

"No, guv'ner," returns Phil, shaking his head. "No, I shouldn't. I was passable enough when I went with the tinker, though nothing to boast of then; but what with blowing the fire with my mouth when I was young, and spileing my complexion, and singeing my hair off, and swallering the smoke, and what with being nat'rally unfort'nate in the way of running against hot metal and marking myself by sich means, and what with having turn-ups with the tinker as I got older, almost whenever he was too far gone in drink—which was almost always—my beauty was queer, wery queer, even at that time. As to since, what with a dozen years in a dark forge where the men was given to larking, and what with being scorched in a accident at a gas-works, and what with being blowed out of winder case-filling at the firework business, I am ugly enough to be made a show on!"

Resigning himself to which condition with a perfectly satisfied manner, Phil begs the favour of another cup of coffee. While drinking it, he says, "It was after the case-filling blow-up when I first see you, commander. You remember?"

"I remember, Phil. You were walking along in the sun."

"Crawling, guv'ner, again a wall—"

"True, Phil—shouldering your way on—"

"In a night-cap!" exclaims Phil, excited.

"In a night-cap—"

"And hobbling with a couple of sticks!" cries Phil, still more excited.

"With a couple of sticks. When—"

"When you stops, you know," cries Phil, putting down his cup and saucer and hastily removing his plate from his knees, "and says to me, 'What, comrade! You have been in the wars!' I didn't say much to you, commander, then, for I was took by surprise that a person so strong and healthy and bold as you was should stop to speak to such a limping bag of bones as I was. But you says to me, says you, delivering it out of your chest as hearty as possible, so that it was like a glass of something hot, 'What accident have you met with? You have been badly hurt. What's amiss, old boy? Cheer up, and tell us about it!' Cheer up! I was cheered already! I says as much to you, you says more to me, I says more to you, you says more to me, and here I am, commander! Here I am, commander!" cries Phil, who has started from his chair and unaccountably begun to sidle away. "If a mark's wanted, or if it will improve the business, let the customers take aim at me. They can't spoil MY beauty. I'M all right. Come on! If they want a man to box at, let 'em box at me. Let 'em knock me well about the head. I don't mind. If they want a light-weight to be throwed for practice, Cornwall, Devonshire, or Lancashire, let 'em throw me. They won't hurt ME. I have been throwed, all sorts of styles, all my life!"

With this unexpected speech, energetically delivered and accompanied by action illustrative of the various exercises referred to, Phil Squod shoulders his way round three sides of the gallery, and abruptly tacking off at his commander, makes a butt at him with his head, intended to express devotion to his service. He then begins to clear away the breakfast.

Mr. George, after laughing cheerfully and clapping him on the shoulder, assists in these arrangements and helps to get the gallery into business order. That done, he takes a turn at the dumb-bells, and afterwards weighing himself and opining that he is getting "too fleshy," engages with great gravity in solitary broadsword practice. Meanwhile Phil has fallen to work at his usual table, where he screws and unscrews, and cleans, and files, and whistles into small apertures, and blackens himself more and more, and seems to do and undo everything that can be done and undone about a gun.

Master and man are at length disturbed by footsteps in the passage, where they make an unusual sound, denoting the arrival of unusual company. These steps, advancing nearer and nearer to the gallery, bring into it a group at first sight scarcely reconcilable with any day in the year but the fifth of November.

It consists of a limp and ugly figure carried in a chair by two bearers and attended by a lean female with a face like a pinched mask, who might be expected immediately to recite the popular verses commemorative of the time when they did contrive to blow Old England up alive but for her keeping her lips tightly and defiantly closed as the chair is put down. At which point the figure in it gasping, "O Lord! Oh, dear me! I am shaken!" adds, "How de do, my dear friend, how de do?" Mr. George then descries, in the procession, the venerable Mr. Smallweed out for an airing, attended by his granddaughter Judy as body-guard.

"Mr. George, my dear friend," says Grandfather Smallweed, removing his right arm from the neck of one of his bearers, whom he has nearly throttled coming along, "how de do? You're surprised to see me, my dear friend."

"I should hardly have been more surprised to have seen your friend in the city," returns Mr. George.

"I am very seldom out," pants Mr. Smallweed. "I haven't been out for many months. It's inconvenient—and it comes expensive. But I longed so much to see you, my dear Mr. George. How de do, sir?"

"I am well enough," says Mr. George. "I hope you are the same."

"You can't be too well, my dear friend." Mr. Smallweed takes him by both hands. "I have brought my granddaughter Judy. I couldn't keep her away. She longed so much to see you."

"Hum! She bears it calmly!" mutters Mr. George.

"So we got a hackney-cab, and put a chair in it, and just round the corner they lifted me out of the cab and into the chair, and carried me here that I might see my dear friend in his own establishment! This," says Grandfather Smallweed, alluding to the bearer, who has been in danger of strangulation and who withdraws adjusting his windpipe, "is the driver of the cab. He has nothing extra. It is by agreement included in his fare. This person," the other bearer, "we engaged in the street outside for a pint of beer. Which is twopence. Judy, give the person twopence. I was not sure you had a workman of your own here, my dear friend, or we needn't have employed this person."

Grandfather Smallweed refers to Phil with a glance of considerable terror and a half-subdued "O Lord! Oh, dear me!" Nor in his apprehension, on the surface of things, without some reason, for Phil, who has never beheld the apparition in the black-velvet cap before, has stopped short with a gun in his hand with much of the air of a dead shot intent on picking Mr. Smallweed off as an ugly old bird of the crow species.

"Judy, my child," says Grandfather Smallweed, "give the person his twopence. It's a great deal for what he has done."

The person, who is one of those extraordinary specimens of human fungus that spring up spontaneously in the western streets of London, ready dressed in an old red jacket, with a "mission" for holding horses and calling coaches, received his twopence with anything but transport, tosses the money into the air, catches it over-handed, and retires.

"My dear Mr. George," says Grandfather Smallweed, "would you be so kind as help to carry me to the fire? I am accustomed to a fire, and I am an old man, and I soon chill. Oh, dear me!"

His closing exclamation is jerked out of the venerable gentleman by the suddenness with which Mr. Squod, like a genie, catches him up, chair and all, and deposits him on the hearth-stone.

"O Lord!" says Mr. Smallweed, panting. "Oh, dear me! Oh, my stars! My dear friend, your workman is very strong—and very prompt. O Lord, he is very prompt! Judy, draw me back a little. I'm being scorched in the legs," which indeed is testified to the noses of all present by the smell of his worsted stockings.

The gentle Judy, having backed her grandfather a little way from the fire, and having shaken him up as usual, and having released his overshadowed eye from its black-velvet extinguisher, Mr. Smallweed again says, "Oh, dear me! O Lord!" and looking about and meeting Mr. George's glance, again stretches out both hands.

"My dear friend! So happy in this meeting! And this is your establishment? It's a delightful place. It's a picture! You never find that anything goes off here accidentally, do you, my dear friend?" adds Grandfather Smallweed, very ill at ease.

"No, no. No fear of that."

"And your workman. He—Oh, dear me!—he never lets anything off without meaning it, does he, my dear friend?"

"He has never hurt anybody but himself," says Mr. George, smiling.

"But he might, you know. He seems to have hurt himself a good deal, and he might hurt somebody else," the old gentleman returns. "He mightn't mean it—or he even might. Mr. George, will you order him to leave his infernal fire-arms alone and go away?"

Obedient to a nod from the trooper, Phil retires, empty-handed, to the other end of the gallery. Mr. Smallweed, reassured, falls to rubbing his legs.

"And you're doing well, Mr. George?" he says to the trooper, squarely standing faced about towards him with his broadsword in his hand. "You are prospering, please the Powers?"

Mr. George answers with a cool nod, adding, "Go on. You have not come to say that, I know."

"You are so sprightly, Mr. George," returns the venerable grandfather. "You are such good company."

"Ha ha! Go on!" says Mr. George.

"My dear friend! But that sword looks awful gleaming and sharp. It might cut somebody, by accident. It makes me shiver, Mr. George. Curse him!" says the excellent old gentleman apart to Judy as the trooper takes a step or two away to lay it aside. "He owes me money, and might think of paying off old scores in this murdering place. I wish your brimstone grandmother was here, and he'd shave her head off."

Mr. George, returning, folds his arms, and looking down at the old man, sliding every moment lower and lower in his chair, says quietly, "Now for it!"

"Ho!" cries Mr. Smallweed, rubbing his hands with an artful chuckle. "Yes. Now for it. Now for what, my dear friend?"

"For a pipe," says Mr. George, who with great composure sets his chair in the chimney-corner, takes his pipe from the grate, fills it and lights it, and falls to smoking peacefully.

This tends to the discomfiture of Mr. Smallweed, who finds it so difficult to resume his object, whatever it may be, that he becomes exasperated and secretly claws the air with an impotent vindictiveness expressive of an intense desire to tear and rend the visage of Mr. George. As the excellent old gentleman's nails are long and leaden, and his hands lean and veinous, and his eyes green and watery; and, over and above this, as he continues, while he claws, to slide down in his chair and to collapse into a shapeless bundle, he becomes such a ghastly spectacle, even in the accustomed eyes of Judy, that that young virgin pounces at him with something more than the ardour of affection and so shakes him up and pats and pokes him in divers parts of his body, but particularly in that part which the science of self-defence would call his wind, that in his grievous distress he utters enforced sounds like a paviour's rammer.

When Judy has by these means set him up again in his chair, with a white face and a frosty nose (but still clawing), she stretches out her weazen forefinger and gives Mr. George one poke in the back. The trooper raising his head, she makes another poke at her esteemed grandfather, and having thus brought them together, stares rigidly at the fire.

"Aye, aye! Ho, ho! U—u—u—ugh!" chatters Grandfather Smallweed, swallowing his rage. "My dear friend!" (still clawing).

"I tell you what," says Mr. George. "If you want to converse with me, you must speak out. I am one of the roughs, and I can't go about and about. I haven't the art to do it. I am not clever enough. It don't suit me. When you go winding round and round me," says the trooper, putting his pipe between his lips again, "damme, if I don't feel as if I was being smothered!"

And he inflates his broad chest to its utmost extent as if to assure himself that he is not smothered yet.

"If you have come to give me a friendly call," continues Mr. George, "I am obliged to you; how are you? If you have come to see whether there's any property on the premises, look about you; you are welcome. If you want to out with something, out with it!"

The blooming Judy, without removing her gaze from the fire, gives her grandfather one ghostly poke.

"You see! It's her opinion too. And why the devil that young woman won't sit down like a Christian," says Mr. George with his eyes musingly fixed on Judy, "I can't comprehend."

"She keeps at my side to attend to me, sir," says Grandfather Smallweed. "I am an old man, my dear Mr. George, and I need some attention. I can carry my years; I am not a brimstone poll-parrot" (snarling and looking unconsciously for the cushion), "but I need attention, my dear friend."

"Well!" returns the trooper, wheeling his chair to face the old man. "Now then?"

"My friend in the city, Mr. George, has done a little business with a pupil of yours."

"Has he?" says Mr. George. "I am sorry to hear it."

"Yes, sir." Grandfather Smallweed rubs his legs. "He is a fine young soldier now, Mr. George, by the name of Carstone. Friends came forward and paid it all up, honourable."

"Did they?" returns Mr. George. "Do you think your friend in the city would like a piece of advice?"

"I think he would, my dear friend. From you."

"I advise him, then, to do no more business in that quarter. There's no more to be got by it. The young gentleman, to my knowledge, is brought to a dead halt."

"No, no, my dear friend. No, no, Mr. George. No, no, no, sir," remonstrates

Grandfather Smallweed, cunningly rubbing his spare legs. "Not quite a dead halt, I think. He has good friends, and he is good for his pay, and he is good for the selling price of his commission, and he is good for his chance in a lawsuit, and he is good for his chance in a wife, and—oh, do you know, Mr. George, I think my friend would consider the young gentleman good for something yet?" says Grandfather Smallweed, turning up his velvet cap and scratching his ear like a monkey.

Mr. George, who has put aside his pipe and sits with an arm on his chair-back, beats a tattoo on the ground with his right foot as if he were not particularly pleased with the turn the conversation has taken.

"But to pass from one subject to another," resumes Mr. Smallweed. "'To promote the conversation,' as a joker might say. To pass, Mr. George, from the ensign to the captain."

"What are you up to, now?" asks Mr. George, pausing with a frown in stroking the recollection of his moustache. "What captain?"

"Our captain. The captain we know of. Captain Hawdon."

"Oh! That's it, is it?" says Mr. George with a low whistle as he sees both grandfather and granddaughter looking hard at him. "You are there! Well? What about it? Come, I won't be smothered any more. Speak!"

"My dear friend," returns the old man, "I was applied—Judy, shake me up a little!—I was applied to yesterday about the captain, and my opinion still is that the captain is not dead."

"Bosh!" observes Mr. George.

"What was your remark, my dear friend?" inquires the old man with his hand to his ear.

"Bosh!"

"Ho!" says Grandfather Smallweed. "Mr. George, of my opinion you can judge for yourself according to the questions asked of me and the reasons given for asking 'em. Now, what do you think the lawyer making the inquiries wants?"

"A job," says Mr. George.

"Nothing of the kind!"

"Can't be a lawyer, then," says Mr. George, folding his arms with an air of confirmed resolution.

"My dear friend, he is a lawyer, and a famous one. He wants to see some fragment in Captain Hawdon's writing. He don't want to keep it. He only wants to see it and compare it with a writing in his possession."

"Well?"

"Well, Mr. George. Happening to remember the advertisement concerning Captain Hawdon and any information that could be given respecting him, he looked it up and came to me—just as you did, my dear friend. WILL you shake hands? So glad you came that day! I should have missed forming such a friendship if you hadn't come!"

"Well, Mr. Smallweed?" says Mr. George again after going through the ceremony with some stiffness.

"I had no such thing. I have nothing but his signature. Plague pestilence and famine, battle murder and sudden death upon him," says the old man, making a curse out of one of his few remembrances of a prayer and squeezing up his velvet cap between his angry hands, "I have half a million of his signatures, I think! But you," breathlessly recovering his mildness of speech as Judy re-adjusts the cap on his skittle-ball of a head, "you, my dear Mr. George, are likely to have some letter or paper that would suit the purpose. Anything would suit the purpose, written in the hand."

"Some writing in that hand," says the trooper, pondering; "may be, I have."

"My dearest friend!"

"May be, I have not."

"Ho!" says Grandfather Smallweed, crest-fallen.

"But if I had bushels of it, I would not show as much as would make a cartridge without knowing why."

"Sir, I have told you why. My dear Mr. George, I have told you why."

"Not enough," says the trooper, shaking his head. "I must know more, and approve it."

"Then, will you come to the lawyer? My dear friend, will you come and see the gentleman?" urges Grandfather Smallweed, pulling out a lean old silver watch with hands like the leg of a skeleton. "I told him it was probable I might call upon him between ten and eleven this forenoon, and it's now half after ten. Will you come and see the gentleman, Mr. George?"

"Hum!" says he gravely. "I don't mind that. Though why this should concern you so much, I don't know."

"Everything concerns me that has a chance in it of bringing anything to light about him. Didn't he take us all in? Didn't he owe us immense sums, all round? Concern me? Who can anything about him concern more than me? Not, my dear friend," says Grandfather Smallweed, lowering his tone, "that I want YOU to betray anything. Far from it. Are you ready to come, my dear friend?"

"Aye! I'll come in a moment. I promise nothing, you know."

"No, my dear Mr. George; no."

"And you mean to say you're going to give me a lift to this place, wherever it is, without charging for it?" Mr. George inquires, getting his hat and thick wash-leather gloves.

This pleasantry so tickles Mr. Smallweed that he laughs, long and low, before the fire. But ever while he laughs, he glances over his paralytic shoulder at Mr. George and eagerly watches him as he unlocks the padlock of a homely cupboard at the distant end of the gallery, looks here and there upon the higher shelves, and ultimately takes something out with a rustling of paper, folds it, and puts it in his breast. Then Judy pokes Mr. Smallweed once, and

Mr. Smallweed pokes Judy once.

"I am ready," says the trooper, coming back. "Phil, you can carry this old gentleman to his coach, and make nothing of him."

"Oh, dear me! O Lord! Stop a moment!" says Mr. Smallweed. "He's so very prompt! Are you sure you can do it carefully, my worthy man?"

Phil makes no reply, but seizing the chair and its load, sidles away, tightly hugged by the now speechless Mr. Smallweed, and bolts along the passage as if he had an acceptable commission to carry the old gentleman to the nearest volcano. His shorter trust, however, terminating at the cab, he deposits him there; and the fair Judy takes her place beside him, and the chair embellishes the roof, and Mr. George takes the vacant place upon the box.

Mr. George is quite confounded by the spectacle he beholds from time to time as he peeps into the cab through the window behind him, where the grim Judy is always motionless, and the old gentleman with his cap over one eye is always sliding off the seat into the straw and looking upward at him out of his other eye with a helpless expression of being jolted in the back.

CHAPTER XXVII
MORE OLD SOLDIERS THAN ONE

Mr. George has not far to ride with folded arms upon the box, for their destination is Lincoln's Inn Fields. When the driver stops his horses, Mr. George alights, and looking in at the window, says, "What, Mr. Tulkinghorn's your man, is he?"

"Yes, my dear friend. Do you know him, Mr. George?"

"Why, I have heard of him—seen him too, I think. But I don't know him, and he don't know me."

There ensues the carrying of Mr. Smallweed upstairs, which is done to perfection with the trooper's help. He is borne into Mr. Tulkinghorn's great room and deposited on the Turkey rug before the fire. Mr. Tulkinghorn is not within at the present moment but will be back directly. The occupant of the pew in the hall, having said thus much, stirs the fire and leaves the triumvirate to warm themselves.

Mr. George is mightily curious in respect of the room. He looks up at the painted ceiling, looks round at the old law-books, contemplates the portraits of the great clients, reads aloud the names on the boxes.

"'Sir Leicester Dedlock, Baronet,'" Mr. George reads thoughtfully. "Ha! 'Manor of Chesney Wold.' Humph!" Mr. George stands looking at these boxes a long while—as if they were pictures—and comes back to the fire repeating, "Sir Leicester Dedlock, Baronet, and Manor of Chesney Wold, hey?"

"Worth a mint of money, Mr. George!" whispers Grandfather Smallweed, rubbing his legs. "Powerfully rich!"

"Who do you mean? This old gentleman, or the Baronet?"

"This gentleman, this gentleman."

"So I have heard; and knows a thing or two, I'll hold a wager. Not bad quarters, either," says Mr. George, looking round again. "See the strong-box yonder!"

This reply is cut short by Mr. Tulkinghorn's arrival. There is no change in him, of course. Rustily drest, with his spectacles in his hand, and their very case worn threadbare. In manner, close and dry. In voice, husky and low. In face, watchful behind a blind; habitually not uncensorious and contemptuous perhaps. The peerage may have warmer worshippers and faithfuller believers than Mr. Tulkinghorn, after all, if everything were known.

"Good morning, Mr. Smallweed, good morning!" he says as he comes in. "You have brought the sergeant, I see. Sit down, sergeant."

As Mr. Tulkinghorn takes off his gloves and puts them in his hat, he looks with half-closed eyes across the room to where the trooper stands and says within himself perchance, "You'll do, my friend!"

"Sit down, sergeant," he repeats as he comes to his table, which is set on one side of the fire, and takes his easy-chair. "Cold and raw this morning, cold and raw!" Mr. Tulkinghorn warms before the bars, alternately, the palms and knuckles of his hands and looks (from behind that blind which is always down) at the trio sitting in a little semicircle before him.

"Now, I can feel what I am about" (as perhaps he can in two senses), "Mr. Smallweed." The old gentleman is newly shaken up by Judy to bear his part in the conversation. "You have brought our good friend the sergeant, I see."

"Yes, sir," returns Mr. Smallweed, very servile to the lawyer's wealth and influence.

"And what does the sergeant say about this business?"

"Mr. George," says Grandfather Smallweed with a tremulous wave of his shrivelled hand, "this is the gentleman, sir."

Mr. George salutes the gentleman but otherwise sits bolt upright and profoundly silent—very forward in his chair, as if the full complement of regulation appendages for a field-day hung about him.

Mr. Tulkinghorn proceeds, "Well, George—I believe your name is George?"

"It is so, Sir."

"What do you say, George?"

"I ask your pardon, sir," returns the trooper, "but I should wish to know what YOU say?"

"Do you mean in point of reward?"

"I mean in point of everything, sir."

This is so very trying to Mr. Smallweed's temper that he suddenly breaks out with "You're a brimstone beast!" and as suddenly asks pardon of Mr. Tulkinghorn, excusing himself for this slip of the tongue by saying to Judy, "I was thinking of your grandmother, my dear."

"I supposed, sergeant," Mr. Tulkinghorn resumes as he leans on one side of his chair and crosses his legs, "that Mr. Smallweed might have sufficiently explained the matter. It lies in the smallest compass, however. You served under Captain Hawdon at one time, and were his attendant in illness, and rendered him many little services, and were rather in his confidence, I am told. That is so, is it not?"

"Yes, sir, that is so," says Mr. George with military brevity.

"Therefore you may happen to have in your possession something—anything, no matter what; accounts, instructions, orders, a letter, anything—in Captain Hawdon's writing. I wish to compare his writing with some that I have. If you can give me the opportunity, you shall be rewarded for your trouble. Three, four, five, guineas, you would consider handsome, I dare say."

"Noble, my dear friend!" cries Grandfather Smallweed, screwing up his eyes.

"If not, say how much more, in your conscience as a soldier, you can demand. There is no need for you to part with the writing, against your inclination—though I should prefer to have it."

Mr. George sits squared in exactly the same attitude, looks at the painted ceiling, and says never a word. The irascible Mr. Smallweed scratches the air.

"The question is," says Mr. Tulkinghorn in his methodical, subdued, uninterested way, "first, whether you have any of Captain Hawdon's writing?"

"First, whether I have any of Captain Hawdon's writing, sir," repeats Mr. George.

"Secondly, what will satisfy you for the trouble of producing it?"

"Secondly, what will satisfy me for the trouble of producing it, sir," repeats Mr. George.

"Thirdly, you can judge for yourself whether it is at all like that," says Mr. Tulkinghorn, suddenly handing him some sheets of written paper tied together.

"Whether it is at all like that, sir. Just so," repeats Mr. George.

All three repetitions Mr. George pronounces in a mechanical manner, looking straight at Mr. Tulkinghorn; nor does he so much as glance at the affidavit in Jarndyce and Jarndyce, that has been given to him for his inspection (though he still holds it in his hand), but continues to look at the lawyer with an air of troubled meditation.

"Well?" says Mr. Tulkinghorn. "What do you say?"

"Well, sir," replies Mr. George, rising erect and looking immense, "I would rather, if you'll excuse me, have nothing to do with this."

Mr. Tulkinghorn, outwardly quite undisturbed, demands, "Why not?"

"Why, sir," returns the trooper. "Except on military compulsion, I am not a man of business. Among civilians I am what they call in Scotland a ne'er-do-weel. I have no head for papers, sir. I can stand any fire better than a fire of cross questions. I mentioned to Mr. Smallweed, only an hour or so ago, that when I come into things of this kind I feel as if I was being smothered. And that is my sensation," says Mr. George, looking round upon the company, "at the present moment."

With that, he takes three strides forward to replace the papers on the lawyer's table and three strides backward to resume his former station, where he stands perfectly upright, now looking at the ground and now at the painted ceiling, with his hands behind him as if to prevent himself from accepting any other document whatever.

Under this provocation, Mr. Smallweed's favourite adjective of disparagement is so close to his tongue that he begins the words "my dear friend" with the monosyllable "brim," thus converting the possessive pronoun into brimmy and appearing to have an impediment in his speech. Once past this difficulty, however, he exhorts his dear friend in the tenderest manner not to be rash, but to do what so eminent a gentleman requires, and to do it with a good grace, confident that it must be unobjectionable as well as profitable. Mr. Tulkinghorn merely utters an occasional sentence, as, "You are the best judge of your own interest, sergeant." "Take care you do no harm by this." "Please yourself, please yourself." "If you know what you mean, that's quite enough." These he utters with an appearance of perfect indifference as he looks over the papers on his table and prepares to write a letter.

Mr. George looks distrustfully from the painted ceiling to the ground, from the ground to Mr. Smallweed, from Mr. Smallweed to Mr. Tulkinghorn, and from Mr. Tulkinghorn to the painted ceiling again, often in his perplexity changing the leg on which he rests.

"I do assure you, sir," says Mr. George, "not to say it offensively, that between you and Mr. Smallweed here, I really am being smothered fifty times over. I really am, sir. I am not a match for you gentlemen. Will you allow me to ask why you want to see the captain's hand, in the case that I could find any specimen of it?"

Mr. Tulkinghorn quietly shakes his head. "No. If you were a man of business, sergeant, you would not need to be informed that there are confidential reasons, very harmless in themselves, for many such wants in the profession to which I belong. But if you are afraid of doing any injury to Captain Hawdon, you may set your mind at rest about that."

"Aye! He is dead, sir."

"IS he?" Mr. Tulkinghorn quietly sits down to write.

"Well, sir," says the trooper, looking into his hat after another disconcerted pause, "I am sorry not to have given you more satisfaction. If it would be any satisfaction to any one that I should be confirmed in my judgment that I would rather have nothing to do with this by a friend of mine who has a better head for business than I have, and who is an old soldier, I am willing to consult with him. I—I really am so completely smothered myself at present," says Mr. George, passing his hand hopelessly across his brow, "that I don't know but what it might be a satisfaction to me."

Mr. Smallweed, hearing that this authority is an old soldier, so strongly inculcates the expediency of the trooper's taking counsel with him, and particularly informing him of its being a question of five guineas or more, that Mr. George engages to go and see him. Mr. Tulkinghorn says nothing either way.

"I'll consult my friend, then, by your leave, sir," says the trooper, "and I'll take the liberty of looking in again with the final answer in the course of the day. Mr. Smallweed, if you wish to be carried downstairs—"

"In a moment, my dear friend, in a moment. Will you first let me speak half a word with this gentleman in private?"

"Certainly, sir. Don't hurry yourself on my account." The trooper retires to a distant part of the room and resumes his curious inspection of the boxes, strong and otherwise.

"If I wasn't as weak as a brimstone baby, sir," whispers Grandfather Smallweed, drawing the lawyer down to his level by the lapel of his coat and flashing some half-quenched green fire out of his angry eyes, "I'd tear the writing away from him. He's got it buttoned in his breast. I saw him put it there. Judy saw him put it there. Speak up, you crabbed image for the sign of a walking-stick shop, and say you saw him put it there!"

This vehement conjuration the old gentleman accompanies with such a thrust at his granddaughter that it is too much for his strength, and he slips away out of his chair, drawing Mr. Tulkinghorn with him, until he is arrested by Judy, and well shaken.

"Violence will not do for me, my friend," Mr. Tulkinghorn then remarks coolly.

"No, no, I know, I know, sir. But it's chafing and galling—it's—it's worse than your smattering chattering magpie of a grandmother," to the imperturbable Judy, who only looks at the fire, "to know he has got what's wanted and won't give it up. He, not to give it up! HE! A vagabond! But never mind, sir, never mind. At the most, he has only his own way for a little while. I have him periodically in a vice. I'll twist him, sir. I'll screw him, sir. If he won't do it with a good grace, I'll make him do it with a bad one, sir! Now, my dear Mr. George," says Grandfather Smallweed, winking at the lawyer hideously as he releases him, "I am ready for your kind assistance, my excellent friend!"

Mr. Tulkinghorn, with some shadowy sign of amusement manifesting itself through his self-possession, stands on the hearth-rug with his back to the fire, watching the disappearance of Mr. Smallweed and acknowledging the trooper's parting salute with one slight nod.

It is more difficult to get rid of the old gentleman, Mr. George finds, than to bear a hand in carrying him downstairs, for when he is replaced in his conveyance, he is so loquacious on the subject of the guineas and retains such an affectionate hold of his button—having, in truth, a secret longing to rip his coat open and rob him—that some degree of force is necessary on the trooper's part to effect a separation. It is accomplished at last, and he proceeds alone in quest of his adviser.

By the cloisterly Temple, and by Whitefriars (there, not without a glance at Hanging-Sword Alley, which would seem to be something in his way), and by Blackfriars Bridge, and Blackfriars Road, Mr. George sedately marches to a street of little shops lying somewhere in that ganglion of roads from Kent and Surrey, and of streets from the bridges of London, centring in the far-famed elephant who has lost his castle formed of a thousand four-horse coaches to a stronger iron monster than he, ready to chop him into mince-meat any day he dares. To one of the little shops in this street, which is a musician's shop, having a few fiddles in the window, and some Pan's pipes and a tambourine, and a triangle, and certain elongated scraps of music, Mr. George directs his massive tread. And halting at a few paces from it, as he sees a soldierly looking woman, with her outer skirts tucked up, come forth with a small wooden tub, and in that tub commence a-whisking and a-splashing on the margin of the pavement, Mr. George says to himself, "She's as usual, washing greens. I never saw her, except upon a baggage-waggon, when she wasn't washing greens!"

The subject of this reflection is at all events so occupied in washing greens at present that she remains unsuspicious of Mr. George's approach until, lifting up herself and her tub together when she has poured the water off into the gutter, she finds him standing near her. Her reception of him is not flattering.

"George, I never see you but I wish you was a hundred mile away!"

The trooper, without remarking on this welcome, follows into the musical-instrument shop, where the lady places her tub of greens upon the counter, and having shaken hands with him, rests her arms upon it.

"I never," she says, "George, consider Matthew Bagnet safe a minute when you're near him. You are that restless and that roving—"

"Yes! I know I am, Mrs. Bagnet. I know I am."

"You know you are!" says Mrs. Bagnet. "What's the use of that? WHY are you?"

"The nature of the animal, I suppose," returns the trooper good-humouredly.

"Ah!" cries Mrs. Bagnet, something shrilly. "But what satisfaction will the nature of the animal be to me when the animal shall have tempted my Mat away from the musical business to New Zealand or Australey?"

Mrs. Bagnet is not at all an ill-looking woman. Rather large-boned, a little coarse in the grain, and freckled by the sun and wind which have tanned her hair upon the forehead, but healthy, wholesome, and bright-eyed. A strong, busy, active, honest-faced woman of from forty-five to fifty. Clean, hardy, and so economically dressed (though substantially) that the only article of ornament of which she stands possessed appear's to be her wedding-ring, around which her finger has grown to be so large since it was put on that it will never come off again until it shall mingle with Mrs. Bagnet's dust.

"Mrs. Bagnet," says the trooper, "I am on my parole with you. Mat will get no harm from me. You may trust me so far."

"Well, I think I may. But the very looks of you are unsettling," Mrs. Bagnet rejoins. "Ah, George, George! If you had only settled down and married Joe Pouch's widow when he died in North America, SHE'D have combed your hair for you."

"It was a chance for me, certainly," returns the trooper half laughingly, half seriously, "but I shall never settle down into a respectable man now. Joe Pouch's widow might have done me good—there was something in her, and something of her—but I couldn't make up my mind to it. If I had had the luck to meet with such a wife as Mat found!"

Mrs. Bagnet, who seems in a virtuous way to be under little reserve with a good sort of fellow, but to be another good sort of fellow herself for that matter, receives this compliment by flicking Mr. George in the face with a head of greens and taking her tub into the little room behind the shop.

"Why, Quebec, my poppet," says George, following, on invitation, into that department. "And little Malta, too! Come and kiss your Bluffy!"

These young ladies—not supposed to have been actually christened by the names applied to them, though always so called in the family from the places of their birth in barracks—are respectively employed on three-legged stools, the younger (some five or six years old) in learning her letters out of a penny primer, the elder (eight or nine perhaps) in teaching her and sewing with great assiduity. Both hail Mr. George with acclamations as an old friend and after some kissing and romping plant their stools beside him.

"And how's young Woolwich?" says Mr. George.

"Ah! There now!" cries Mrs. Bagnet, turning about from her saucepans (for she is cooking dinner) with a bright flush on her face. "Would you believe it? Got an engagement at the theayter, with his father, to play the fife in a military piece."

"Well done, my godson!" cries Mr. George, slapping his thigh.

"I believe you!" says Mrs. Bagnet. "He's a Briton. That's what Woolwich is. A Briton!"

"And Mat blows away at his bassoon, and you're respectable civilians one and all," says Mr. George. "Family people. Children growing up. Mat's old mother in Scotland, and your old father somewhere else, corresponded with, and helped a little, and—well, well! To be sure, I don't know why I shouldn't be wished a hundred mile away, for I have not much to do with all this!"

Mr. George is becoming thoughtful, sitting before the fire in the white-washed room, which has a sanded floor and a barrack smell and contains nothing superfluous and has not a visible speck of dirt or dust in it, from the faces of Quebec and Malta to the bright tin pots and pannikins upon the dresser shelves—Mr. George is becoming thoughtful, sitting here while Mrs. Bagnet is busy, when Mr. Bagnet and young Woolwich opportunely come home. Mr. Bagnet is an ex-artilleryman, tall and upright, with shaggy eyebrows and whiskers like the fibres of a coco-nut, not a hair upon his head, and a torrid complexion. His voice, short, deep, and resonant, is not at all unlike the tones of the instrument to which he is devoted. Indeed there may be generally observed in him an unbending, unyielding, brass-bound air, as if he were himself the bassoon of the human orchestra. Young Woolwich is the type and model of a young drummer.

Both father and son salute the trooper heartily. He saying, in due season, that he has come to advise with Mr. Bagnet, Mr. Bagnet hospitably declares that he will hear of no business until after dinner and that his friend shall not partake of his counsel without first partaking of boiled pork and greens. The trooper yielding to this invitation, he and Mr. Bagnet, not to embarrass the domestic preparations, go forth to take a turn up and down the little street, which they promenade with measured tread and folded arms, as if it were a rampart.

"George," says Mr. Bagnet. "You know me. It's my old girl that advises. She has the head. But I never own to it before her. Discipline must be maintained. Wait till the greens is off her mind. Then we'll consult. Whatever the old girl says, do—do it!"

"I intend to, Mat," replies the other. "I would sooner take her opinion than that of a college."

"College," returns Mr. Bagnet in short sentences, bassoon-like. "What college could you leave—in another quarter of the world—with nothing but a grey cloak and an umbrella—to make its way home to Europe? The old girl would do it to-morrow. Did it once!"

"You are right," says Mr. George.

"What college," pursues Bagnet, "could you set up in life—with two penn'orth of white lime—a penn'orth of fuller's earth—a ha'porth of sand—and the rest of the change out of sixpence in money? That's what the old girl started on. In the present business."

"I am rejoiced to hear it's thriving, Mat."

"The old girl," says Mr. Bagnet, acquiescing, "saves. Has a stocking somewhere. With money in it. I never saw it. But I know she's got it. Wait till the greens is off her mind. Then she'll set you up."

"She is a treasure!" exclaims Mr. George.

"She's more. But I never own to it before her. Discipline must be maintained. It was the old girl that brought out my musical abilities. I should have been in the artillery now but for the old girl. Six years I hammered at the fiddle. Ten at the flute. The old girl said it wouldn't do; intention good, but want of flexibility; try the bassoon. The old girl borrowed a bassoon from the bandmaster of the Rifle Regiment. I practised in the trenches. Got on, got another, get a living by it!"

George remarks that she looks as fresh as a rose and as sound as an apple.

"The old girl," says Mr. Bagnet in reply, "is a thoroughly fine woman. Consequently she is like a thoroughly fine day. Gets finer as she gets on. I never saw the old girl's equal. But I never own to it before her. Discipline must be maintained!"

Proceeding to converse on indifferent matters, they walk up and down the little street, keeping step and time, until summoned by Quebec and Malta to do justice to the pork and greens, over which Mrs. Bagnet, like a military chaplain, says a short grace. In the distribution of these comestibles, as in every other household duty, Mrs. Bagnet developes an exact system, sitting with every dish before her, allotting to every portion of pork its own portion of pot-liquor, greens, potatoes, and even mustard, and serving it out complete. Having likewise served out the beer from a can and thus supplied the mess with all things necessary, Mrs. Bagnet proceeds to satisfy her own hunger, which is in a healthy state. The kit of the mess, if the table furniture may be so denominated, is chiefly composed of utensils of horn and tin that have done duty in several parts of the world. Young Woolwich's knife, in particular, which is of the oyster kind, with the additional feature of a strong shutting-up movement which frequently balks the appetite of that young musician, is mentioned as having gone in various hands the complete round of foreign service.

The dinner done, Mrs. Bagnet, assisted by the younger branches (who polish their own cups and platters, knives and forks), makes all the dinner garniture shine as brightly as before and puts it all away, first sweeping the hearth, to the end that Mr. Bagnet and the visitor may not be retarded in the smoking of their pipes. These household cares involve much pattening and counter-pattening in the backyard and considerable use of a pail, which is finally so happy as to assist in the ablutions of Mrs. Bagnet herself. That old girl reappearing by and by, quite fresh, and sitting down to her needlework, then and only then—the greens being only then to be considered as entirely off her mind—Mr. Bagnet requests the trooper to state his case.

This Mr. George does with great discretion, appearing to address himself to Mr. Bagnet, but having an eye solely on the old girl all the time, as Bagnet has himself. She, equally discreet, busies herself with her needlework. The case fully stated, Mr. Bagnet resorts to his standard artifice for the maintenance of discipline.

"That's the whole of it, is it, George?" says he.

"That's the whole of it."

"You act according to my opinion?"

"I shall be guided," replies George, "entirely by it."

"Old girl," says Mr. Bagnet, "give him my opinion. You know it. Tell him what it is."

It is that he cannot have too little to do with people who are too deep for him and cannot be too careful of interference with matters he does not understand—that the plain rule is to do nothing in the dark, to be a party to nothing underhanded or mysterious, and never to put his foot where he cannot see the ground. This, in effect, is Mr. Bagnet's opinion, as delivered through the old girl, and it so relieves Mr. George's mind by confirming his own opinion and banishing his doubts that he composes himself to smoke another pipe on that exceptional occasion and to have a talk over old times with the whole Bagnet family, according to their various ranges of experience.

Through these means it comes to pass that Mr. George does not again rise to his full height in that parlour until the time is drawing on when the bassoon and fife are expected by a British public at the theatre; and as it takes time even then for Mr. George, in his domestic character of Bluffy, to take leave of Quebec and Malta and insinuate a sponsorial shilling into the pocket of his godson with felicitations on his success in life, it is dark when Mr. George again turns his face towards Lincoln's Inn Fields.

"A family home," he ruminates as he marches along, "however small it is, makes a man like me look lonely. But it's well I never made that evolution of matrimony. I shouldn't have been fit for it. I am such a vagabond still, even at my present time of life, that I couldn't hold to the gallery a month together if it was a regular pursuit or if I didn't camp there, gipsy fashion. Come! I disgrace nobody and cumber nobody; that's something. I have not done that for many a long year!"

So he whistles it off and marches on.

Arrived in Lincoln's Inn Fields and mounting Mr. Tulkinghorn's stair, he finds the outer door closed and the chambers shut, but the trooper not knowing much about outer doors, and the staircase being dark besides, he is yet fumbling and groping about, hoping to discover a bell-handle or to open the door for himself, when Mr. Tulkinghorn comes up the stairs (quietly, of course) and angrily asks, "Who is that? What are you doing there?"

"I ask your pardon, sir. It's George. The sergeant."

"And couldn't George, the sergeant, see that my door was locked?"

"Why, no, sir, I couldn't. At any rate, I didn't," says the trooper, rather nettled.

"Have you changed your mind? Or are you in the same mind?" Mr. Tulkinghorn demands. But he knows well enough at a glance.

"In the same mind, sir."

"I thought so. That's sufficient. You can go. So you are the man," says Mr. Tulkinghorn, opening his door with the key, "in whose hiding-place Mr. Gridley was found?"

"Yes, I AM the man," says the trooper, stopping two or three stairs down. "What then, sir?"

"What then? I don't like your associates. You should not have seen the inside of my door this morning if I had thought of your being that man. Gridley? A threatening, murderous, dangerous fellow."

With these words, spoken in an unusually high tone for him, the lawyer goes into his rooms and shuts the door with a thundering noise.

Mr. George takes his dismissal in great dudgeon, the greater because a clerk coming up the stairs has heard the last words of all and evidently applies them to him. "A pretty character to bear," the trooper growls with a hasty oath as he strides downstairs. "A threatening, murderous, dangerous fellow!" And looking up, he sees the clerk looking down at him and marking him as he passes a lamp. This so intensifies his dudgeon that for five minutes he is in an ill humour. But he whistles that off like the rest of it and marches home to the shooting gallery.

CHAPTER XXVIII
THE IRONMASTER

Sir Leicester Dedlock has got the better, for the time being, of the family gout and is once more, in a literal no less than in a figurative point of view, upon his legs. He is at his place in Lincolnshire; but the waters are out again on the low-lying grounds, and the cold and damp steal into Chesney Wold, though well defended, and eke into Sir Leicester's bones. The blazing fires of faggot and coal—Dedlock timber and antediluvian forest—that blaze upon the broad wide hearths and wink in the twilight on the frowning woods, sullen to see how trees are sacrificed, do not exclude the enemy. The hot-water pipes that trail themselves all over the house, the cushioned doors and windows, and the screens and curtains fail to supply the fires' deficiencies and to satisfy Sir Leicester's need. Hence the fashionable intelligence proclaims one morning to the listening earth that Lady Dedlock is expected shortly to return to town for a few weeks.

It is a melancholy truth that even great men have their poor relations. Indeed great men have often more than their fair share of poor relations, inasmuch as very red blood of the superior quality, like inferior blood unlawfully shed, WILL cry aloud and WILL be heard. Sir Leicester's cousins, in the remotest degree, are so many murders in the respect that they "will out." Among whom there are cousins who are so poor that one might almost dare to think it would have been the happier for them never to have been plated links upon the Dedlock chain of gold, but to have been made of common iron at first and done base service.

Service, however (with a few limited reservations, genteel but not profitable), they may not do, being of the Dedlock dignity. So they visit their richer cousins, and get into debt when they can, and live but shabbily when they can't, and find—the women no husbands, and the men no wives—and ride in borrowed carriages, and sit at feasts that are never of their own making, and so go through high life. The rich family sum has been divided by so many figures, and they are the something over that nobody knows what to do with.

Everybody on Sir Leicester Dedlock's side of the question and of his way of thinking would appear to be his cousin more or less. From my Lord Boodle, through the Duke of Foodle, down to Noodle, Sir Leicester, like a glorious spider, stretches his threads of relationship. But while he is stately in the cousinship of the Everybodys, he is a kind and generous man, according to his dignified way, in the cousinship of the Nobodys; and at the present time, in despite of the damp, he stays out the visit of several such cousins at Chesney Wold with the constancy of a martyr.

Of these, foremost in the front rank stands Volumnia Dedlock, a young lady (of sixty) who is doubly highly related, having the honour to be a poor relation, by the mother's side, to another great family. Miss Volumnia, displaying in early life a pretty talent for cutting ornaments out of coloured paper, and also for singing to the guitar in the Spanish tongue, and propounding French conundrums in country houses, passed the twenty years of her existence between twenty and forty in a sufficiently agreeable manner. Lapsing then out of date and being considered to bore mankind by her vocal performances in the Spanish language, she retired to Bath, where she lives slenderly on an annual present from Sir Leicester and whence she makes occasional resurrections in the country houses of her cousins. She has an extensive acquaintance at Bath among appalling old gentlemen with thin legs and nankeen trousers, and is of high standing in that dreary city. But she is a little dreaded elsewhere in consequence of an indiscreet profusion in the article of rouge and persistency in an obsolete pearl necklace like a rosary of little bird's-eggs.

In any country in a wholesome state, Volumnia would be a clear case for the pension list. Efforts have been made to get her on it, and when William Buffy came in, it was fully expected that her name would be put down for a couple of hundred a year. But William Buffy somehow discovered, contrary to all expectation, that these were not the times when it could be done, and this was the first clear indication Sir Leicester Dedlock had conveyed to him that the country was going to pieces.

There is likewise the Honourable Bob Stables, who can make warm mashes with the skill of a veterinary surgeon and is a better shot than most gamekeepers. He has been for some time particularly desirous to serve his country in a post of good emoluments, unaccompanied by any trouble or responsibility. In a well-regulated body politic this natural desire on the part of a spirited young gentleman so highly connected would be speedily recognized, but somehow William Buffy found when he came in that these were not times in which he could manage that little matter either, and this was the second indication Sir Leicester Dedlock had conveyed to him that the country was going to pieces.

The rest of the cousins are ladies and gentlemen of various ages and capacities, the major part amiable and sensible and likely to have done well enough in life if they could have overcome their cousinship; as it is, they are almost all a little worsted by it, and lounge in purposeless and listless paths, and seem to be quite as much at a loss how to dispose of themselves as anybody else can be how to dispose of them.

In this society, and where not, my Lady Dedlock reigns supreme. Beautiful, elegant, accomplished, and powerful in her little world (for the world of fashion does not stretch ALL the way from pole to pole), her influence in Sir Leicester's house, however haughty and indifferent her manner, is greatly to improve it and refine it. The cousins, even those older cousins who were paralysed when Sir Leicester married her, do her feudal homage; and the Honourable Bob Stables daily repeats to some chosen person between breakfast and lunch his favourite original remark, that she is the best-groomed woman in the whole stud.

Such the guests in the long drawing-room at Chesney Wold this dismal night when the step on the Ghost's Walk (inaudible here, however) might be the step of a deceased cousin shut out in the cold. It is near bed-time. Bedroom fires blaze brightly all over the house, raising ghosts of grim furniture on wall and ceiling. Bedroom candlesticks bristle on the distant table by the door, and cousins yawn on ottomans. Cousins at the piano, cousins at the soda-water tray, cousins rising from the card-table, cousins gathered round the fire. Standing on one side of his own peculiar fire (for there are two), Sir Leicester. On the opposite side of the broad hearth, my Lady at her table. Volumnia, as one of the more privileged cousins, in a luxurious chair between them. Sir Leicester glancing, with magnificent displeasure, at the rouge and the pearl necklace.

"I occasionally meet on my staircase here," drawls Volumnia, whose thoughts perhaps are already hopping up it to bed, after a long evening of very desultory talk, "one of the prettiest girls, I think, that I ever saw in my life."

"A PROTEGEE of my Lady's," observes Sir Leicester.

"I thought so. I felt sure that some uncommon eye must have picked that girl out. She really is a marvel. A dolly sort of beauty perhaps," says Miss Volumnia, reserving her own sort, "but in its way, perfect; such bloom I never saw!"

Sir Leicester, with his magnificent glance of displeasure at the rouge, appears to say so too.

"Indeed," remarks my Lady languidly, "if there is any uncommon eye in the case, it is Mrs. Rouncewell's, and not mine. Rosa is her discovery."

"Your maid, I suppose?"

"No. My anything; pet—secretary—messenger—I don't know what."

"You like to have her about you, as you would like to have a flower, or a bird, or a picture, or a poodle—no, not a poodle, though—or anything else that was equally pretty?" says Volumnia, sympathizing. "Yes, how charming now! And how well that delightful old soul Mrs. Rouncewell is looking. She must be an immense age, and yet she is as active and handsome! She is the dearest friend I have, positively!"

Sir Leicester feels it to be right and fitting that the housekeeper of Chesney Wold should be a remarkable person. Apart from that, he has a real regard for Mrs. Rouncewell and likes to hear her praised. So he says, "You are right, Volumnia," which Volumnia is extremely glad to hear.

"She has no daughter of her own, has she?"

"Mrs. Rouncewell? No, Volumnia. She has a son. Indeed, she had two."

My Lady, whose chronic malady of boredom has been sadly aggravated by

Volumnia this evening, glances wearily towards the candlesticks and heaves a noiseless sigh.

"And it is a remarkable example of the confusion into which the present age has fallen; of the obliteration of landmarks, the opening of floodgates, and the uprooting of distinctions," says Sir Leicester with stately gloom, "that I have been informed by Mr. Tulkinghorn that Mrs. Rouncewell's son has been invited to go into Parliament."

Miss Volumnia utters a little sharp scream.

"Yes, indeed," repeats Sir Leicester. "Into Parliament."

"I never heard of such a thing! Good gracious, what is the man?" exclaims Volumnia.

"He is called, I believe—an—ironmaster." Sir Leicester says it slowly and with gravity and doubt, as not being sure but that he is called a lead-mistress or that the right word may be some other word expressive of some other relationship to some other metal.

Volumnia utters another little scream.

"He has declined the proposal, if my information from Mr. Tulkinghorn be correct, as I have no doubt it is. Mr. Tulkinghorn being always correct and exact; still that does not," says Sir Leicester, "that does not lessen the anomaly, which is fraught with strange considerations—startling considerations, as it appears to me."

Miss Volumnia rising with a look candlestick-wards, Sir Leicester politely performs the grand tour of the drawing-room, brings one, and lights it at my Lady's shaded lamp.

"I must beg you, my Lady," he says while doing so, "to remain a few moments, for this individual of whom I speak arrived this evening shortly before dinner and requested in a very becoming note"—Sir Leicester, with his habitual regard to truth, dwells upon it—"I am bound to say, in a very becoming and well-expressed note, the favour of a short interview with yourself and MYself on the subject of this young girl. As it appeared that he wished to depart to-night, I replied that we would see him before retiring."

Miss Volumnia with a third little scream takes flight, wishing her hosts—O Lud!—well rid of the—what is it?—ironmaster!

The other cousins soon disperse, to the last cousin there. Sir Leicester rings the bell, "Make my compliments to Mr. Rouncewell, in the housekeeper's apartments, and say I can receive him now."

My Lady, who has heard all this with slight attention outwardly, looks towards Mr. Rouncewell as he comes in. He is a little over fifty perhaps, of a good figure, like his mother, and has a clear voice, a broad forehead from which his dark hair has retired, and a shrewd though open face. He is a responsible-looking gentleman dressed in black, portly enough, but strong and active. Has a perfectly natural and easy air and is not in the least embarrassed by the great presence into which he comes.

"Sir Leicester and Lady Dedlock, as I have already apologized for intruding on you, I cannot do better than be very brief. I thank you, Sir Leicester."

The head of the Dedlocks has motioned towards a sofa between himself and my Lady. Mr. Rouncewell quietly takes his seat there.

"In these busy times, when so many great undertakings are in progress, people like myself have so many workmen in so many places that we are always on the flight."

Sir Leicester is content enough that the ironmaster should feel that there is no hurry there; there, in that ancient house, rooted in that quiet park, where the ivy and the moss have had time to mature, and the gnarled and warted elms and the umbrageous oaks stand deep in the fern and leaves of a hundred years; and where the sun-dial on the terrace has dumbly recorded for centuries that time which was as much the property of every Dedlock—while he lasted—as the house and lands. Sir Leicester sits down in an easy-chair, opposing his repose and that of Chesney Wold to the restless flights of ironmasters.

"Lady Dedlock has been so kind," proceeds Mr. Rouncewell with a respectful glance and a bow that way, "as to place near her a young beauty of the name of Rosa. Now, my son has fallen in love with Rosa and has asked my consent to his proposing marriage to her and to their becoming engaged if she will take him—which I suppose she will. I have never seen Rosa until to-day, but I have some confidence in my son's good sense—even in love. I find her what he represents her, to the best of my judgment; and my mother speaks of her with great commendation."

"She in all respects deserves it," says my Lady.

"I am happy, Lady Dedlock, that you say so, and I need not comment on the value to me of your kind opinion of her."

"That," observes Sir Leicester with unspeakable grandeur, for he thinks the ironmaster a little too glib, "must be quite unnecessary."

"Quite unnecessary, Sir Leicester. Now, my son is a very young man, and Rosa is a very young woman. As I made my way, so my son must make his; and his being married at present is out of the question. But supposing I gave my consent to his engaging himself to this pretty girl, if this pretty girl will engage herself to him, I think it a piece of candour to say at once—I am sure, Sir Leicester and Lady Dedlock, you will understand and excuse me—I should make it a condition that she did not remain at Chesney Wold. Therefore, before communicating further with my son, I take the liberty of saying that if her removal would be in any way inconvenient or objectionable, I will hold the matter over with him for any reasonable time and leave it precisely where it is."

Not remain at Chesney Wold! Make it a condition! All Sir Leicester's old misgivings relative to Wat Tyler and the people in the iron districts who do nothing but turn out by torchlight come in a shower upon his head, the fine grey hair of which, as well as of his whiskers, actually stirs with indignation.

"Am I to understand, sir," says Sir Leicester, "and is my Lady to understand"—he brings her in thus specially, first as a point of gallantry, and next as a point of prudence, having great reliance on her sense—"am I to understand, Mr. Rouncewell, and is my Lady to understand, sir, that you consider this young woman too good for Chesney Wold or likely to be injured by remaining here?"

"Certainly not, Sir Leicester,"

"I am glad to hear it." Sir Leicester very lofty indeed.

"Pray, Mr. Rouncewell," says my Lady, warning Sir Leicester off with the slightest gesture of her pretty hand, as if he were a fly, "explain to me what you mean."

"Willingly, Lady Dedlock. There is nothing I could desire more."

Addressing her composed face, whose intelligence, however, is too quick and active to be concealed by any studied impassiveness, however habitual, to the strong Saxon face of the visitor, a picture of resolution and perseverance, my Lady listens with attention, occasionally slightly bending her head.

"I am the son of your housekeeper, Lady Dedlock, and passed my childhood about this house. My mother has lived here half a century and will die here I have no doubt. She is one of those examples—perhaps as good a one as there is—of love, and attachment, and fidelity in such a nation, which England may well be proud of, but of which no order can appropriate the whole pride or the whole merit, because such an instance bespeaks high worth on two sides—on the great side assuredly, on the small one no less assuredly."

Sir Leicester snorts a little to hear the law laid down in this way, but in his honour and his love of truth, he freely, though silently, admits the justice of the ironmaster's proposition.

"Pardon me for saying what is so obvious, but I wouldn't have it hastily supposed," with the least turn of his eyes towards Sir Leicester, "that I am ashamed of my mother's position here, or wanting in all just respect for Chesney Wold and the family. I certainly may have desired—I certainly have desired, Lady Dedlock—that my mother should retire after so many years and end her days with me. But as I have found that to sever this strong bond would be to break her heart, I have long abandoned that idea."

Sir Leicester very magnificent again at the notion of Mrs. Rouncewell being spirited off from her natural home to end her days with an ironmaster.

"I have been," proceeds the visitor in a modest, clear way, "an apprentice and a workman. I have lived on workman's wages, years and years, and beyond a certain point have had to educate myself. My wife was a foreman's daughter, and plainly brought up. We have three daughters besides this son of whom I have spoken, and being fortunately able to give them greater advantages than we have had ourselves, we have educated them well, very well. It has been one of our great cares and pleasures to make them worthy of any station."

A little boastfulness in his fatherly tone here, as if he added in his heart, "even of the Chesney Wold station." Not a little more magnificence, therefore, on the part of Sir Leicester.

"All this is so frequent, Lady Dedlock, where I live, and among the class to which I belong, that what would be generally called unequal marriages are not of such rare occurrence with us as elsewhere. A son will sometimes make it known to his father that he has fallen in love, say, with a young woman in the factory. The father, who once worked in a factory himself, will be a little disappointed at first very possibly. It may be that he had other views for his son. However, the chances are that having ascertained the young woman to be of unblemished character, he will say to his son, 'I must be quite sure you are in earnest here. This is a serious matter for both of you. Therefore I shall have this girl educated for two years,' or it may be, 'I shall place this girl at the same school with your sisters for such a time, during which you will give me your word and honour to see her only so often. If at the expiration of that time, when she has so far profited by her advantages as that you may be upon a fair equality, you are both in the same mind, I will do my part to make you happy.' I know of several cases such as I describe, my Lady, and I think they indicate to me my own course now."

Sir Leicester's magnificence explodes. Calmly, but terribly.

"Mr. Rouncewell," says Sir Leicester with his right hand in the breast of his blue coat, the attitude of state in which he is painted in the gallery, "do you draw a parallel between Chesney Wold and a—" Here he resists a disposition to choke, "a factory?"

"I need not reply, Sir Leicester, that the two places are very different; but for the purposes of this case, I think a parallel may be justly drawn between them."

Sir Leicester directs his majestic glance down one side of the long drawing-room and up the other before he can believe that he is awake.

"Are you aware, sir, that this young woman whom my Lady—my Lady—has placed near her person was brought up at the village school outside the gates?"

"Sir Leicester, I am quite aware of it. A very good school it is, and handsomely supported by this family."

"Then, Mr. Rouncewell," returns Sir Leicester, "the application of what you have said is, to me, incomprehensible."

"Will it be more comprehensible, Sir Leicester, if I say," the ironmaster is reddening a little, "that I do not regard the village school as teaching everything desirable to be known by my son's wife?"

From the village school of Chesney Wold, intact as it is this minute, to the whole framework of society; from the whole framework of society, to the aforesaid framework receiving tremendous cracks in consequence of people (iron-masters, lead-mistresses, and what not) not minding their catechism, and getting out of the station unto which they are called—necessarily and for ever, according to Sir Leicester's rapid logic, the first station in which they happen to find themselves; and from that, to their educating other people out of THEIR stations, and so obliterating the landmarks, and opening the floodgates, and all the rest of it; this is the swift progress of the Dedlock mind.

"My Lady, I beg your pardon. Permit me, for one moment!" She has given a faint indication of intending to speak. "Mr. Rouncewell, our views of duty, and our views of station, and our views of education, and our views of—in short, ALL our views—are so diametrically opposed, that to prolong this discussion must be repellent to your feelings and repellent to my own. This young woman is honoured with my Lady's notice and favour. If she wishes to withdraw herself from that notice and favour or if she chooses to place herself under the influence of any one who may in his peculiar opinions—you will allow me to say, in his peculiar opinions, though I readily admit that he is not accountable for them to me—who may, in his peculiar opinions, withdraw her from that notice and favour, she is at any time at liberty to do so. We are obliged to you for the plainness with which you have spoken. It will have no effect of itself, one way or other, on the young woman's position here. Beyond this, we can make no terms; and here we beg—if you will be so good—to leave the subject."

The visitor pauses a moment to give my Lady an opportunity, but she says nothing. He then rises and replies, "Sir Leicester and Lady Dedlock, allow me to thank you for your attention and only to observe that I shall very seriously recommend my son to conquer his present inclinations. Good night!"

"Mr. Rouncewell," says Sir Leicester with all the nature of a gentleman shining in him, "it is late, and the roads are dark. I hope your time is not so precious but that you will allow my Lady and myself to offer you the hospitality of Chesney Wold, for to-night at least."

"I hope so," adds my Lady.

"I am much obliged to you, but I have to travel all night in order to reach a distant part of the country punctually at an appointed time in the morning."

Therewith the ironmaster takes his departure, Sir Leicester ringing the bell and my Lady rising as he leaves the room.

When my Lady goes to her boudoir, she sits down thoughtfully by the fire, and inattentive to the Ghost's Walk, looks at Rosa, writing in an inner room. Presently my Lady calls her.

"Come to me, child. Tell me the truth. Are you in love?"

"Oh! My Lady!"

My Lady, looking at the downcast and blushing face, says smiling, "Who is it? Is it Mrs. Rouncewell's grandson?"

"Yes, if you please, my Lady. But I don't know that I am in love with him—yet."

"Yet, you silly little thing! Do you know that he loves YOU, yet?"

"I think he likes me a little, my Lady." And Rosa bursts into tears.

Is this Lady Dedlock standing beside the village beauty, smoothing her dark hair with that motherly touch, and watching her with eyes so full of musing interest? Aye, indeed it is!

"Listen to me, child. You are young and true, and I believe you are attached to me."

"Indeed I am, my Lady. Indeed there is nothing in the world I wouldn't do to show how much."

"And I don't think you would wish to leave me just yet, Rosa, even for a lover?"

"No, my Lady! Oh, no!" Rosa looks up for the first time, quite frightened at the thought.

"Confide in me, my child. Don't fear me. I wish you to be happy, and will make you so—if I can make anybody happy on this earth."

Rosa, with fresh tears, kneels at her feet and kisses her hand. My Lady takes the hand with which she has caught it, and standing with her eyes fixed on the fire, puts it about and about between her own two hands, and gradually lets it fall. Seeing her so absorbed, Rosa softly withdraws; but still my Lady's eyes are on the fire.

In search of what? Of any hand that is no more, of any hand that never was, of any touch that might have magically changed her life? Or does she listen to the Ghost's Walk and think what step does it most resemble? A man's? A woman's? The pattering of a little child's feet, ever coming on—on—on? Some melancholy influence is upon her, or why should so proud a lady close the doors and sit alone upon the hearth so desolate?

Volumnia is away next day, and all the cousins are scattered before dinner. Not a cousin of the batch but is amazed to hear from Sir Leicester at breakfast-time of the obliteration of landmarks, and opening of floodgates, and cracking of the framework of society, manifested through Mrs. Rouncewell's son. Not a cousin of the batch but is really indignant, and connects it with the feebleness of William Buffy when in office, and really does feel deprived of a stake in the country—or the pension list—or something—by fraud and wrong. As to Volumnia, she is handed down the great staircase by Sir Leicester, as eloquent upon the theme as if there were a general rising in the north of England to obtain her rouge-pot and pearl necklace. And thus, with a clatter of maids and valets—for it is one appurtenance of their cousinship that however difficult they may find it to keep themselves, they MUST keep maids and valets—the cousins disperse to the four winds of heaven; and the one wintry wind that blows to-day shakes a shower from the trees near the deserted house, as if all the cousins had been changed into leaves.

CHAPTER XXIX
THE YOUNG MAN

Chesney Wold is shut up, carpets are rolled into great scrolls in corners of comfortless rooms, bright damask does penance in brown holland, carving and gilding puts on mortification, and the Dedlock ancestors retire from the light of day again. Around and around the house the leaves fall thick, but never fast, for they come circling down with a dead lightness that is sombre and slow. Let the gardener sweep and sweep the turf as he will, and press the leaves into full barrows, and wheel them off, still they lie ankle-deep. Howls the shrill wind round Chesney Wold; the sharp rain beats, the windows rattle, and the chimneys growl. Mists hide in the avenues, veil the points of view, and move in funeral-wise across the rising grounds. On all the house there is a cold, blank smell like the smell of a little church, though something dryer, suggesting that the dead and buried Dedlocks walk there in the long nights and leave the flavour of their graves behind them.

But the house in town, which is rarely in the same mind as Chesney Wold at the same time, seldom rejoicing when it rejoices or mourning when it mourns, excepting when a Dedlock dies—the house in town shines out awakened. As warm and bright as so much state may be, as delicately redolent of pleasant scents that bear no trace of winter as hothouse flowers can make it, soft and hushed so that the ticking of the clocks and the crisp burning of the fires alone disturb the stillness in the rooms, it seems to wrap those chilled bones of Sir Leicester's in rainbow-coloured wool. And Sir Leicester is glad to repose in dignified contentment before the great fire in the library, condescendingly perusing the backs of his books or honouring the fine arts with a glance of approbation. For he has his pictures, ancient and modern. Some of the Fancy Ball School in which art occasionally condescends to become a master, which would be best catalogued like the miscellaneous articles in a sale. As "Three high-backed chairs, a table and cover, long-necked bottle (containing wine), one flask, one Spanish female's costume, three-quarter face portrait of Miss Jogg the model, and a suit of armour containing Don Quixote." Or "One stone terrace (cracked), one gondola in distance, one Venetian senator's dress complete, richly embroidered white satin costume with profile portrait of Miss Jogg the model, one Scimitar superbly mounted in gold with jewelled handle, elaborate Moorish dress (very rare), and Othello."

Mr. Tulkinghorn comes and goes pretty often, there being estate business to do, leases to be renewed, and so on. He sees my Lady pretty often, too; and he and she are as composed, and as indifferent, and take as little heed of one another, as ever. Yet it may be that my Lady fears this Mr. Tulkinghorn and that he knows it. It may be that he pursues her doggedly and steadily, with no touch of compunction, remorse, or pity. It may be that her beauty and all the state and brilliancy surrounding her only gives him the greater zest for what he is set upon and makes him the more inflexible in it. Whether he be cold and cruel, whether immovable in what he has made his duty, whether absorbed in love of power, whether determined to have nothing hidden from him in ground where he has burrowed among secrets all his life, whether he in his heart despises the splendour of which he is a distant beam, whether he is always treasuring up slights and offences in the affability of his gorgeous clients—whether he be any of this, or all of this, it may be that my Lady had better have five thousand pairs of fashionable eyes upon her, in distrustful vigilance, than the two eyes of this rusty lawyer with his wisp of neckcloth and his dull black breeches tied with ribbons at the knees.

Sir Leicester sits in my Lady's room—that room in which Mr. Tulkinghorn read the affidavit in Jarndyce and Jarndyce—particularly complacent. My Lady, as on that day, sits before the fire with her screen in her hand. Sir Leicester is particularly complacent because he has found in his newspaper some congenial remarks bearing directly on the floodgates and the framework of society. They apply so happily to the late case that Sir Leicester has come from the library to my Lady's room expressly to read them aloud. "The man who wrote this article," he observes by way of preface, nodding at the fire as if he were nodding down at the man from a mount, "has a well-balanced mind."

The man's mind is not so well balanced but that he bores my Lady, who, after a languid effort to listen, or rather a languid resignation of herself to a show of listening, becomes distraught and falls into a contemplation of the fire as if it were her fire at Chesney Wold, and she had never left it. Sir Leicester, quite unconscious, reads on through his double eye-glass, occasionally stopping to remove his glass and express approval, as "Very true indeed," "Very properly put," "I have frequently made the same remark myself," invariably losing his place after each observation, and going up and down the column to find it again.

Sir Leicester is reading with infinite gravity and state when the door opens, and the Mercury in powder makes this strange announcement, "The young man, my Lady, of the name of Guppy."

Sir Leicester pauses, stares, repeats in a killing voice, "The young man of the name of Guppy?"

Looking round, he beholds the young man of the name of Guppy, much discomfited and not presenting a very impressive letter of introduction in his manner and appearance.

"Pray," says Sir Leicester to Mercury, "what do you mean by announcing with this abruptness a young man of the name of Guppy?"

"I beg your pardon, Sir Leicester, but my Lady said she would see the young man whenever he called. I was not aware that you were here, Sir Leicester."

With this apology, Mercury directs a scornful and indignant look at the young man of the name of Guppy which plainly says, "What do you come calling here for and getting ME into a row?"

"It's quite right. I gave him those directions," says my Lady. "Let the young man wait."

"By no means, my Lady. Since he has your orders to come, I will not interrupt you." Sir Leicester in his gallantry retires, rather declining to accept a bow from the young man as he goes out and majestically supposing him to be some shoemaker of intrusive appearance.

Lady Dedlock looks imperiously at her visitor when the servant has left the room, casting her eyes over him from head to foot. She suffers him to stand by the door and asks him what he wants.

"That your ladyship would have the kindness to oblige me with a little conversation," returns Mr. Guppy, embarrassed.

"You are, of course, the person who has written me so many letters?"

"Several, your ladyship. Several before your ladyship condescended to favour me with an answer."

"And could you not take the same means of rendering a Conversation unnecessary? Can you not still?"

Mr. Guppy screws his mouth into a silent "No!" and shakes his head.

"You have been strangely importunate. If it should appear, after all, that what you have to say does not concern me—and I don't know how it can, and don't expect that it will—you will allow me to cut you short with but little ceremony. Say what you have to say, if you please."

My Lady, with a careless toss of her screen, turns herself towards the fire again, sitting almost with her back to the young man of the name of Guppy.

"With your ladyship's permission, then," says the young man, "I will now enter on my business. Hem! I am, as I told your ladyship in my first letter, in the law. Being in the law, I have learnt the habit of not committing myself in writing, and therefore I did not mention to your ladyship the name of the firm with which I am connected and in which my standing—and I may add income—is tolerably good. I may now state to your ladyship, in confidence, that the name of that firm is Kenge and Carboy, of Lincoln's Inn, which may not be altogether unknown to your ladyship in connexion with the case in Chancery of Jarndyce and Jarndyce."

My Lady's figure begins to be expressive of some attention. She has ceased to toss the screen and holds it as if she were listening.

"Now, I may say to your ladyship at once," says Mr. Guppy, a little emboldened, "it is no matter arising out of Jarndyce and Jarndyce that made me so desirous to speak to your ladyship, which conduct I have no doubt did appear, and does appear, obtrusive—in fact, almost blackguardly."

After waiting for a moment to receive some assurance to the contrary, and not receiving any, Mr. Guppy proceeds, "If it had been Jarndyce and Jarndyce, I should have gone at once to your ladyship's solicitor, Mr. Tulkinghorn, of the Fields. I have the pleasure of being acquainted with Mr. Tulkinghorn—at least we move when we meet one another—and if it had been any business of that sort, I should have gone to him."

My Lady turns a little round and says, "You had better sit down."

"Thank your ladyship." Mr. Guppy does so. "Now, your ladyship"—Mr. Guppy refers to a little slip of paper on which he has made small notes of his line of argument and which seems to involve him in the densest obscurity whenever he looks at it—"I—Oh, yes!—I place myself entirely in your ladyship's hands. If your ladyship was to make any complaint to Kenge and Carboy or to Mr. Tulkinghorn of the present visit, I should be placed in a very disagreeable situation. That, I openly admit. Consequently, I rely upon your ladyship's honour."

My Lady, with a disdainful gesture of the hand that holds the screen, assures him of his being worth no complaint from her.

"Thank your ladyship," says Mr. Guppy; "quite satisfactory. Now—I—dash it!—The fact is that I put down a head or two here of the order of the points I thought of touching upon, and they're written short, and I can't quite make out what they mean. If your ladyship will excuse me taking it to the window half a moment, I—"

Mr. Guppy, going to the window, tumbles into a pair of love-birds, to whom he says in his confusion, "I beg your pardon, I am sure." This does not tend to the greater legibility of his notes. He murmurs, growing warm and red and holding the slip of paper now close to his eyes, now a long way off, "C.S. What's C.S. for? Oh! C.S.! Oh, I know! Yes, to be sure!" And comes back enlightened.

"I am not aware," says Mr. Guppy, standing midway between my Lady and his chair, "whether your ladyship ever happened to hear of, or to see, a young lady of the name of Miss Esther Summerson."

My Lady's eyes look at him full. "I saw a young lady of that name not long ago. This past autumn."

"Now, did it strike your ladyship that she was like anybody?" asks Mr. Guppy, crossing his arms, holding his head on one side, and scratching the corner of his mouth with his memoranda.

My Lady removes her eyes from him no more.

"No."

"Not like your ladyship's family?"

"No."

"I think your ladyship," says Mr. Guppy, "can hardly remember Miss Summerson's face?"

"I remember the young lady very well. What has this to do with me?"

"Your ladyship, I do assure you that having Miss Summerson's image imprinted on my 'eart—which I mention in confidence—I found, when I had the honour of going over your ladyship's mansion of Chesney Wold while on a short out in the county of Lincolnshire with a friend, such a resemblance between Miss Esther Summerson and your ladyship's own portrait that it completely knocked me over, so much so that I didn't at the moment even know what it WAS that knocked me over. And now I have the honour of beholding your ladyship near (I have often, since that, taken the liberty of looking at your ladyship in your carriage in the park, when I dare say you was not aware of me, but I never saw your ladyship so near), it's really more surprising than I thought it."

Young man of the name of Guppy! There have been times, when ladies lived in strongholds and had unscrupulous attendants within call, when that poor life of yours would NOT have been worth a minute's purchase, with those beautiful eyes looking at you as they look at this moment.

My Lady, slowly using her little hand-screen as a fan, asks him again what he supposes that his taste for likenesses has to do with her.

"Your ladyship," replies Mr. Guppy, again referring to his paper, "I am coming to that. Dash these notes! Oh! 'Mrs. Chadband.' Yes." Mr. Guppy draws his chair a little forward and seats himself again. My Lady reclines in her chair composedly, though with a trifle less of graceful ease than usual perhaps, and never falters in her steady gaze. "A—stop a minute, though!" Mr. Guppy refers again. "E.S. twice? Oh, yes! Yes, I see my way now, right on."

Rolling up the slip of paper as an instrument to point his speech with, Mr. Guppy proceeds.

"Your ladyship, there is a mystery about Miss Esther Summerson's birth and bringing up. I am informed of that fact because—which I mention in confidence—I know it in the way of my profession at Kenge and Carboy's. Now, as I have already mentioned to your ladyship, Miss Summerson's image is imprinted on my 'eart. If I could clear this mystery for her, or prove her to be well related, or find that having the honour to be a remote branch of your ladyship's family she had a right to be made a party in Jarndyce and Jarndyce, why, I might make a sort of a claim upon Miss Summerson to look with an eye of more dedicated favour on my proposals than she has exactly done as yet. In fact, as yet she hasn't favoured them at all."

A kind of angry smile just dawns upon my Lady's face.

"Now, it's a very singular circumstance, your ladyship," says Mr. Guppy, "though one of those circumstances that do fall in the way of us professional men—which I may call myself, for though not admitted, yet I have had a present of my articles made to me by Kenge and Carboy, on my mother's advancing from the principal of her little income the money for the stamp, which comes heavy—that I have encountered the person who lived as servant with the lady who brought Miss Summerson up before Mr. Jarndyce took charge of her. That lady was a Miss Barbary, your ladyship."

Is the dead colour on my Lady's face reflected from the screen which has a green silk ground and which she holds in her raised hand as if she had forgotten it, or is it a dreadful paleness that has fallen on her?

"Did your ladyship," says Mr. Guppy, "ever happen to hear of Miss Barbary?"

"I don't know. I think so. Yes."

"Was Miss Barbary at all connected with your ladyship's family?"

My Lady's lips move, but they utter nothing. She shakes her head.

"NOT connected?" says Mr. Guppy. "Oh! Not to your ladyship's knowledge, perhaps? Ah! But might be? Yes." After each of these interrogatories, she has inclined her head. "Very good! Now, this Miss Barbary was extremely close—seems to have been extraordinarily close for a female, females being generally (in common life at least) rather given to conversation—and my witness never had an idea whether she possessed a single relative. On one occasion, and only one, she seems to have been confidential to my witness on a single point, and she then told her that the little girl's real name was not Esther Summerson, but Esther Hawdon."

"My God!"

Mr. Guppy stares. Lady Dedlock sits before him looking him through, with the same dark shade upon her face, in the same attitude even to the holding of the screen, with her lips a little apart, her brow a little contracted, but for the moment dead. He sees her consciousness return, sees a tremor pass across her frame like a ripple over water, sees her lips shake, sees her compose them by a great effort, sees her force herself back to the knowledge of his presence and of what he has said. All this, so quickly, that her exclamation and her dead condition seem to have passed away like the features of those long-preserved dead bodies sometimes opened up in tombs, which, struck by the air like lightning, vanish in a breath.

"Your ladyship is acquainted with the name of Hawdon?"

"I have heard it before."

"Name of any collateral or remote branch of your ladyship's family?"

"No."

"Now, your ladyship," says Mr. Guppy, "I come to the last point of the case, so far as I have got it up. It's going on, and I shall gather it up closer and closer as it goes on. Your ladyship must know—if your ladyship don't happen, by any chance, to know already—that there was found dead at the house of a person named Krook, near Chancery Lane, some time ago, a law-writer in great distress. Upon which law-writer there was an inquest, and which law-writer was an anonymous character, his name being unknown. But, your ladyship, I have discovered very lately that that law-writer's name was Hawdon."

"And what is THAT to me?"

"Aye, your ladyship, that's the question! Now, your ladyship, a queer thing happened after that man's death. A lady started up, a disguised lady, your ladyship, who went to look at the scene of action and went to look at his grave. She hired a crossing-sweeping boy to show it her. If your ladyship would wish to have the boy produced in corroboration of this statement, I can lay my hand upon him at any time."

The wretched boy is nothing to my Lady, and she does NOT wish to have him produced.

"Oh, I assure your ladyship it's a very queer start indeed," says Mr. Guppy. "If you was to hear him tell about the rings that sparkled on her fingers when she took her glove off, you'd think it quite romantic."

There are diamonds glittering on the hand that holds the screen. My Lady trifles with the screen and makes them glitter more, again with that expression which in other times might have been so dangerous to the young man of the name of Guppy.

"It was supposed, your ladyship, that he left no rag or scrap behind him by which he could be possibly identified. But he did. He left a bundle of old letters."

The screen still goes, as before. All this time her eyes never once release him.

"They were taken and secreted. And to-morrow night, your ladyship, they will come into my possession."

"Still I ask you, what is this to me?"

"Your ladyship, I conclude with that." Mr. Guppy rises. "If you think there's enough in this chain of circumstances put together—in the undoubted strong likeness of this young lady to your ladyship, which is a positive fact for a jury; in her having been brought up by Miss Barbary; in Miss Barbary stating Miss Summerson's real name to be Hawdon; in your ladyship's knowing both these names VERY WELL; and in Hawdon's dying as he did—to give your ladyship a family interest in going further into the case, I will bring these papers here. I don't know what they are, except that they are old letters: I have never had them in my possession yet. I will bring those papers here as soon as I get them and go over them for the first time with your ladyship. I have told your ladyship my object. I have told your ladyship that I should be placed in a very disagreeable situation if any complaint was made, and all is in strict confidence."

Is this the full purpose of the young man of the name of Guppy, or has he any other? Do his words disclose the length, breadth, depth, of his object and suspicion in coming here; or if not, what do they hide? He is a match for my Lady there. She may look at him, but he can look at the table and keep that witness-box face of his from telling anything.

"You may bring the letters," says my Lady, "if you choose."

"Your ladyship is not very encouraging, upon my word and honour," says Mr. Guppy, a little injured.

"You may bring the letters," she repeats in the same tone, "if you—please."

"It shall be done. I wish your ladyship good day."

On a table near her is a rich bauble of a casket, barred and clasped like an old strong-chest. She, looking at him still, takes it to her and unlocks it.

"Oh! I assure your ladyship I am not actuated by any motives of that sort," says Mr. Guppy, "and I couldn't accept anything of the kind. I wish your ladyship good day, and am much obliged to you all the same."

So the young man makes his bow and goes downstairs, where the supercilious Mercury does not consider himself called upon to leave his Olympus by the hall-fire to let the young man out.

As Sir Leicester basks in his library and dozes over his newspaper, is there no influence in the house to startle him, not to say to make the very trees at Chesney Wold fling up their knotted arms, the very portraits frown, the very armour stir?

No. Words, sobs, and cries are but air, and air is so shut in and shut out throughout the house in town that sounds need be uttered trumpet-tongued indeed by my Lady in her chamber to carry any faint vibration to Sir Leicester's ears; and yet this cry is in the house, going upward from a wild figure on its knees.

"O my child, my child! Not dead in the first hours of her life, as my cruel sister told me, but sternly nurtured by her, after she had renounced me and my name! O my child, O my child!"

CHAPTER XXX
ESTHER'S NARRATIVE

Richard had been gone away some time when a visitor came to pass a few days with us. It was an elderly lady. It was Mrs. Woodcourt, who, having come from Wales to stay with Mrs. Bayham Badger and having written to my guardian, "by her son Allan's desire," to report that she had heard from him and that he was well "and sent his kind remembrances to all of us," had been invited by my guardian to make a visit to Bleak House. She stayed with us nearly three weeks. She took very kindly to me and was extremely confidential, so much so that sometimes she almost made me uncomfortable. I had no right, I knew very well, to be uncomfortable because she confided in me, and I felt it was unreasonable; still, with all I could do, I could not quite help it.

She was such a sharp little lady and used to sit with her hands folded in each other looking so very watchful while she talked to me that perhaps I found that rather irksome. Or perhaps it was her being so upright and trim, though I don't think it was that, because I thought that quaintly pleasant. Nor can it have been the general expression of her face, which was very sparkling and pretty for an old lady. I don't know what it was. Or at least if I do now, I thought I did not then. Or at least—but it don't matter.

Of a night when I was going upstairs to bed, she would invite me into her room, where she sat before the fire in a great chair; and, dear me, she would tell me about Morgan ap-Kerrig until I was quite low-spirited! Sometimes she recited a few verses from Crumlinwallinwer and the Mewlinnwillinwodd (if those are the right names, which I dare say they are not), and would become quite fiery with the sentiments they expressed. Though I never knew what they were (being in Welsh), further than that they were highly eulogistic of the lineage of Morgan ap-Kerrig.

"So, Miss Summerson," she would say to me with stately triumph, "this, you see, is the fortune inherited by my son. Wherever my son goes, he can claim kindred with Ap-Kerrig. He may not have money, but he always has what is much better—family, my dear."

I had my doubts of their caring so very much for Morgan ap-Kerrig in India and China, but of course I never expressed them. I used to say it was a great thing to be so highly connected.

"It IS, my dear, a great thing," Mrs. Woodcourt would reply. "It has its disadvantages; my son's choice of a wife, for instance, is limited by it, but the matrimonial choice of the royal family is limited in much the same manner."

Then she would pat me on the arm and smooth my dress, as much as to assure me that she had a good opinion of me, the distance between us notwithstanding.

"Poor Mr. Woodcourt, my dear," she would say, and always with some emotion, for with her lofty pedigree she had a very affectionate heart, "was descended from a great Highland family, the MacCoorts of MacCoort. He served his king and country as an officer in the Royal Highlanders, and he died on the field. My son is one of the last representatives of two old families. With the blessing of heaven he will set them up again and unite them with another old family."

It was in vain for me to try to change the subject, as I used to try, only for the sake of novelty or perhaps because—but I need not be so particular. Mrs. Woodcourt never would let me change it.

"My dear," she said one night, "you have so much sense and you look at the world in a quiet manner so superior to your time of life that it is a comfort to me to talk to you about these family matters of mine. You don't know much of my son, my dear; but you know enough of him, I dare say, to recollect him?"

"Yes, ma'am. I recollect him."

"Yes, my dear. Now, my dear, I think you are a judge of character, and I should like to have your opinion of him."

"Oh, Mrs. Woodcourt," said I, "that is so difficult!"

"Why is it so difficult, my dear?" she returned. "I don't see it myself."

"To give an opinion—"

"On so slight an acquaintance, my dear. THAT'S true."

I didn't mean that, because Mr. Woodcourt had been at our house a good deal altogether and had become quite intimate with my guardian. I said so, and added that he seemed to be very clever in his profession—we thought—and that his kindness and gentleness to Miss Flite were above all praise.

"You do him justice!" said Mrs. Woodcourt, pressing my hand. "You define him exactly. Allan is a dear fellow, and in his profession faultless. I say it, though I am his mother. Still, I must confess he is not without faults, love."

"None of us are," said I.

"Ah! But his really are faults that he might correct, and ought to correct," returned the sharp old lady, sharply shaking her head. "I am so much attached to you that I may confide in you, my dear, as a third party wholly disinterested, that he is fickleness itself."

I said I should have thought it hardly possible that he could have been otherwise than constant to his profession and zealous in the pursuit of it, judging from the reputation he had earned.

"You are right again, my dear," the old lady retorted, "but I don't refer to his profession, look you."

"Oh!" said I.

"No," said she. "I refer, my dear, to his social conduct. He is always paying trivial attentions to young ladies, and always has been, ever since he was eighteen. Now, my dear, he has never really cared for any one of them and has never meant in doing this to do any harm or to express anything but politeness and good nature. Still, it's not right, you know; is it?"

"No," said I, as she seemed to wait for me.

"And it might lead to mistaken notions, you see, my dear."

I supposed it might.

"Therefore, I have told him many times that he really should be more careful, both in justice to himself and in justice to others. And he has always said, 'Mother, I will be; but you know me better than anybody else does, and you know I mean no harm—in short, mean nothing.' All of which is very true, my dear, but is no justification. However, as he is now gone so far away and for an indefinite time, and as he will have good opportunities and introductions, we may consider this past and gone. And you, my dear," said the old lady, who was now all nods and smiles, "regarding your dear self, my love?"

"Me, Mrs. Woodcourt?"

"Not to be always selfish, talking of my son, who has gone to seek his fortune and to find a wife—when do you mean to seek YOUR fortune and to find a husband, Miss Summerson? Hey, look you! Now you blush!"

I don't think I did blush—at all events, it was not important if I did—and I said my present fortune perfectly contented me and I had no wish to change it.

"Shall I tell you what I always think of you and the fortune yet to come for you, my love?" said Mrs. Woodcourt.

"If you believe you are a good prophet," said I.

"Why, then, it is that you will marry some one very rich and very worthy, much older—five and twenty years, perhaps—than yourself. And you will be an excellent wife, and much beloved, and very happy."

"That is a good fortune," said I. "But why is it to be mine?"

"My dear," she returned, "there's suitability in it—you are so busy, and so neat, and so peculiarly situated altogether that there's suitability in it, and it will come to pass. And nobody, my love, will congratulate you more sincerely on such a marriage than I shall."

It was curious that this should make me uncomfortable, but I think it did. I know it did. It made me for some part of that night uncomfortable. I was so ashamed of my folly that I did not like to confess it even to Ada, and that made me more uncomfortable still. I would have given anything not to have been so much in the bright old lady's confidence if I could have possibly declined it. It gave me the most inconsistent opinions of her. At one time I thought she was a story-teller, and at another time that she was the pink of truth. Now I suspected that she was very cunning, next moment I believed her honest Welsh heart to be perfectly innocent and simple. And after all, what did it matter to me, and why did it matter to me? Why could not I, going up to bed with my basket of keys, stop to sit down by her fire and accommodate myself for a little while to her, at least as well as to anybody else, and not trouble myself about the harmless things she said to me? Impelled towards her, as I certainly was, for I was very anxious that she should like me and was very glad indeed that she did, why should I harp afterwards, with actual distress and pain, on every word she said and weigh it over and over again in twenty scales? Why was it so worrying to me to have her in our house, and confidential to me every night, when I yet felt that it was better and safer somehow that she should be there than anywhere else? These were perplexities and contradictions that I could not account for. At least, if I could—but I shall come to all that by and by, and it is mere idleness to go on about it now.

So when Mrs. Woodcourt went away, I was sorry to lose her but was relieved too. And then Caddy Jellyby came down, and Caddy brought such a packet of domestic news that it gave us abundant occupation.

First Caddy declared (and would at first declare nothing else) that I was the best adviser that ever was known. This, my pet said, was no news at all; and this, I said, of course, was nonsense. Then Caddy told us that she was going to be married in a month and that if Ada and I would be her bridesmaids, she was the happiest girl in the world. To be sure, this was news indeed; and I thought we never should have done talking about it, we had so much to say to Caddy, and Caddy had so much to say to us.

It seemed that Caddy's unfortunate papa had got over his bankruptcy—"gone through the Gazette," was the expression Caddy used, as if it were a tunnel—with the general clemency and commiseration of his creditors, and had got rid of his affairs in some blessed manner without succeeding in understanding them, and had given up everything he possessed (which was not worth much, I should think, to judge from the state of the furniture), and had satisfied every one concerned that he could do no more, poor man. So, he had been honourably dismissed to "the office" to begin the world again. What he did at the office, I never knew; Caddy said he was a "custom-house and general agent," and the only thing I ever understood about that business was that when he wanted money more than usual he went to the docks to look for it, and hardly ever found it.

As soon as her papa had tranquillized his mind by becoming this shorn lamb, and they had removed to a furnished lodging in Hatton Garden (where I found the children, when I afterwards went there, cutting the horse hair out of the seats of the chairs and choking themselves with it), Caddy had brought about a meeting between him and old Mr. Turveydrop; and poor Mr. Jellyby, being very humble and meek, had deferred to Mr. Turveydrop's deportment so submissively that they had become excellent friends. By degrees, old Mr. Turveydrop, thus familiarized with the idea of his son's marriage, had worked up his parental feelings to the height of contemplating that event as being near at hand and had given his gracious consent to the young couple commencing housekeeping at the academy in Newman Street when they would.

"And your papa, Caddy. What did he say?"

"Oh! Poor Pa," said Caddy, "only cried and said he hoped we might get on better than he and Ma had got on. He didn't say so before Prince, he only said so to me. And he said, 'My poor girl, you have not been very well taught how to make a home for your husband, but unless you mean with all your heart to strive to do it, you had better murder him than marry him—if you really love him.'"

"And how did you reassure him, Caddy?"

"Why, it was very distressing, you know, to see poor Pa so low and hear him say such terrible things, and I couldn't help crying myself. But I told him that I DID mean it with all my heart and that I hoped our house would be a place for him to come and find some comfort in of an evening and that I hoped and thought I could be a better daughter to him there than at home. Then I mentioned Peepy's coming to stay with me, and then Pa began to cry again and said the children were Indians."

"Indians, Caddy?"

"Yes," said Caddy, "wild Indians. And Pa said"—here she began to sob, poor girl, not at all like the happiest girl in the world—"that he was sensible the best thing that could happen to them was their being all tomahawked together."

Ada suggested that it was comfortable to know that Mr. Jellyby did not mean these destructive sentiments.

"No, of course I know Pa wouldn't like his family to be weltering in their blood," said Caddy, "but he means that they are very unfortunate in being Ma's children and that he is very unfortunate in being Ma's husband; and I am sure that's true, though it seems unnatural to say so."

I asked Caddy if Mrs. Jellyby knew that her wedding-day was fixed.

"Oh! You know what Ma is, Esther," she returned. "It's impossible to say whether she knows it or not. She has been told it often enough; and when she IS told it, she only gives me a placid look, as if I was I don't know what—a steeple in the distance," said Caddy with a sudden idea; "and then she shakes her head and says 'Oh, Caddy, Caddy, what a tease you are!' and goes on with the Borrioboola letters."

"And about your wardrobe, Caddy?" said I. For she was under no restraint with us.

"Well, my dear Esther," she returned, drying her eyes, "I must do the best I can and trust to my dear Prince never to have an unkind remembrance of my coming so shabbily to him. If the question concerned an outfit for Borrioboola, Ma would know all about it and would be quite excited. Being what it is, she neither knows nor cares."

Caddy was not at all deficient in natural affection for her mother, but mentioned this with tears as an undeniable fact, which I am afraid it was. We were sorry for the poor dear girl and found so much to admire in the good disposition which had survived under such discouragement that we both at once (I mean Ada and I) proposed a little scheme that made her perfectly joyful. This was her staying with us for three weeks, my staying with her for one, and our all three contriving and cutting out, and repairing, and sewing, and saving, and doing the very best we could think of to make the most of her stock. My guardian being as pleased with the idea as Caddy was, we took her home next day to arrange the matter and brought her out again in triumph with her boxes and all the purchases that could be squeezed out of a ten-pound note, which Mr. Jellyby had found in the docks I suppose, but which he at all events gave her. What my guardian would not have given her if we had encouraged him, it would be difficult to say, but we thought it right to compound for no more than her wedding-dress and bonnet. He agreed to this compromise, and if Caddy had ever been happy in her life, she was happy when we sat down to work.

She was clumsy enough with her needle, poor girl, and pricked her fingers as much as she had been used to ink them. She could not help reddening a little now and then, partly with the smart and partly with vexation at being able to do no better, but she soon got over that and began to improve rapidly. So day after day she, and my darling, and my little maid Charley, and a milliner out of the town, and I, sat hard at work, as pleasantly as possible.

Over and above this, Caddy was very anxious "to learn housekeeping," as she said. Now, mercy upon us! The idea of her learning housekeeping of a person of my vast experience was such a joke that I laughed, and coloured up, and fell into a comical confusion when she proposed it. However, I said, "Caddy, I am sure you are very welcome to learn anything that you can learn of ME, my dear," and I showed her all my books and methods and all my fidgety ways. You would have supposed that I was showing her some wonderful inventions, by her study of them; and if you had seen her, whenever I jingled my housekeeping keys, get up and attend me, certainly you might have thought that there never was a greater imposter than I with a blinder follower than Caddy Jellyby.

So what with working and housekeeping, and lessons to Charley, and backgammon in the evening with my guardian, and duets with Ada, the three weeks slipped fast away. Then I went home with Caddy to see what could be done there, and Ada and Charley remained behind to take care of my guardian.

When I say I went home with Caddy, I mean to the furnished lodging in Hatton Garden. We went to Newman Street two or three times, where preparations were in progress too—a good many, I observed, for enhancing the comforts of old Mr. Turveydrop, and a few for putting the newly married couple away cheaply at the top of the house—but our great point was to make the furnished lodging decent for the wedding-breakfast and to imbue Mrs. Jellyby beforehand with some faint sense of the occasion.

The latter was the more difficult thing of the two because Mrs. Jellyby and an unwholesome boy occupied the front sitting-room (the back one was a mere closet), and it was littered down with waste-paper and Borrioboolan documents, as an untidy stable might be littered with straw. Mrs. Jellyby sat there all day drinking strong coffee, dictating, and holding Borrioboolan interviews by appointment. The unwholesome boy, who seemed to me to be going into a decline, took his meals out of the house. When Mr. Jellyby came home, he usually groaned and went down into the kitchen. There he got something to eat if the servant would give him anything, and then, feeling that he was in the way, went out and walked about Hatton Garden in the wet. The poor children scrambled up and tumbled down the house as they had always been accustomed to do.

The production of these devoted little sacrifices in any presentable condition being quite out of the question at a week's notice, I proposed to Caddy that we should make them as happy as we could on her marriage morning in the attic where they all slept, and should confine our greatest efforts to her mama and her mama's room, and a clean breakfast. In truth Mrs. Jellyby required a good deal of attention, the lattice-work up her back having widened considerably since I first knew her and her hair looking like the mane of a dustman's horse.

Thinking that the display of Caddy's wardrobe would be the best means of approaching the subject, I invited Mrs. Jellyby to come and look at it spread out on Caddy's bed in the evening after the unwholesome boy was gone.

"My dear Miss Summerson," said she, rising from her desk with her usual sweetness of temper, "these are really ridiculous preparations, though your assisting them is a proof of your kindness. There is something so inexpressibly absurd to me in the idea of Caddy being married! Oh, Caddy, you silly, silly, silly puss!"

She came upstairs with us notwithstanding and looked at the clothes in her customary far-off manner. They suggested one distinct idea to her, for she said with her placid smile, and shaking her head, "My good Miss Summerson, at half the cost, this weak child might have been equipped for Africa!"

On our going downstairs again, Mrs. Jellyby asked me whether this troublesome business was really to take place next Wednesday. And on my replying yes, she said, "Will my room be required, my dear Miss Summerson? For it's quite impossible that I can put my papers away."

I took the liberty of saying that the room would certainly be wanted and that I thought we must put the papers away somewhere. "Well, my dear Miss Summerson," said Mrs. Jellyby, "you know best, I dare say. But by obliging me to employ a boy, Caddy has embarrassed me to that extent, overwhelmed as I am with public business, that I don't know which way to turn. We have a Ramification meeting, too, on Wednesday afternoon, and the inconvenience is very serious."

"It is not likely to occur again," said I, smiling. "Caddy will be married but once, probably."

"That's true," Mrs. Jellyby replied; "that's true, my dear. I suppose we must make the best of it!"

The next question was how Mrs. Jellyby should be dressed on the occasion. I thought it very curious to see her looking on serenely from her writing-table while Caddy and I discussed it, occasionally shaking her head at us with a half-reproachful smile like a superior spirit who could just bear with our trifling.

The state in which her dresses were, and the extraordinary confusion in which she kept them, added not a little to our difficulty; but at length we devised something not very unlike what a common-place mother might wear on such an occasion. The abstracted manner in which Mrs. Jellyby would deliver herself up to having this attire tried on by the dressmaker, and the sweetness with which she would then observe to me how sorry she was that I had not turned my thoughts to Africa, were consistent with the rest of her behaviour.

The lodging was rather confined as to space, but I fancied that if Mrs. Jellyby's household had been the only lodgers in Saint Paul's or Saint Peter's, the sole advantage they would have found in the size of the building would have been its affording a great deal of room to be dirty in. I believe that nothing belonging to the family which it had been possible to break was unbroken at the time of those preparations for Caddy's marriage, that nothing which it had been possible to spoil in any way was unspoilt, and that no domestic object which was capable of collecting dirt, from a dear child's knee to the door-plate, was without as much dirt as could well accumulate upon it.

Poor Mr. Jellyby, who very seldom spoke and almost always sat when he was at home with his head against the wall, became interested when he saw that Caddy and I were attempting to establish some order among all this waste and ruin and took off his coat to help. But such wonderful things came tumbling out of the closets when they were opened—bits of mouldy pie, sour bottles, Mrs. Jellyby's caps, letters, tea, forks, odd boots and shoes of children, firewood, wafers, saucepan-lids, damp sugar in odds and ends of paper bags, footstools, blacklead brushes, bread, Mrs. Jellyby's bonnets, books with butter sticking to the binding, guttered candle ends put out by being turned upside down in broken candlesticks, nutshells, heads and tails of shrimps, dinner-mats, gloves, coffee-grounds, umbrellas—that he looked frightened, and left off again. But he came regularly every evening and sat without his coat, with his head against the wall, as though he would have helped us if he had known how.

"Poor Pa!" said Caddy to me on the night before the great day, when we really had got things a little to rights. "It seems unkind to leave him, Esther. But what could I do if I stayed! Since I first knew you, I have tidied and tidied over and over again, but it's useless. Ma and Africa, together, upset the whole house directly. We never have a servant who don't drink. Ma's ruinous to everything."

Mr. Jellyby could not hear what she said, but he seemed very low indeed and shed tears, I thought.

"My heart aches for him; that it does!" sobbed Caddy. "I can't help thinking to-night, Esther, how dearly I hope to be happy with Prince, and how dearly Pa hoped, I dare say, to be happy with Ma. What a disappointed life!"

"My dear Caddy!" said Mr. Jellyby, looking slowly round from the wail. It was the first time, I think, I ever heard him say three words together.

"Yes, Pa!" cried Caddy, going to him and embracing him affectionately.

"My dear Caddy," said Mr. Jellyby. "Never have—"

"Not Prince, Pa?" faltered Caddy. "Not have Prince?"

"Yes, my dear," said Mr. Jellyby. "Have him, certainly. But, never have—"

I mentioned in my account of our first visit in Thavies Inn that Richard described Mr. Jellyby as frequently opening his mouth after dinner without saying anything. It was a habit of his. He opened his mouth now a great many times and shook his head in a melancholy manner.

"What do you wish me not to have? Don't have what, dear Pa?" asked Caddy, coaxing him, with her arms round his neck.

"Never have a mission, my dear child."

Mr. Jellyby groaned and laid his head against the wall again, and this was the only time I ever heard him make any approach to expressing his sentiments on the Borrioboolan question. I suppose he had been more talkative and lively once, but he seemed to have been completely exhausted long before I knew him.

I thought Mrs. Jellyby never would have left off serenely looking over her papers and drinking coffee that night. It was twelve o'clock before we could obtain possession of the room, and the clearance it required then was so discouraging that Caddy, who was almost tired out, sat down in the middle of the dust and cried. But she soon cheered up, and we did wonders with it before we went to bed.

In the morning it looked, by the aid of a few flowers and a quantity of soap and water and a little arrangement, quite gay. The plain breakfast made a cheerful show, and Caddy was perfectly charming. But when my darling came, I thought—and I think now—that I never had seen such a dear face as my beautiful pet's.

We made a little feast for the children upstairs, and we put Peepy at the head of the table, and we showed them Caddy in her bridal dress, and they clapped their hands and hurrahed, and Caddy cried to think that she was going away from them and hugged them over and over again until we brought Prince up to fetch her away—when, I am sorry to say, Peepy bit him. Then there was old Mr. Turveydrop downstairs, in a state of deportment not to be expressed, benignly blessing Caddy and giving my guardian to understand that his son's happiness was his own parental work and that he sacrificed personal considerations to ensure it. "My dear sir," said Mr. Turveydrop, "these young people will live with me; my house is large enough for their accommodation, and they shall not want the shelter of my roof. I could have wished—you will understand the allusion, Mr. Jarndyce, for you remember my illustrious patron the Prince Regent—I could have wished that my son had married into a family where there was more deportment, but the will of heaven be done!"

Mr. and Mrs. Pardiggle were of the party—Mr. Pardiggle, an obstinate-looking man with a large waistcoat and stubbly hair, who was always talking in a loud bass voice about his mite, or Mrs. Pardiggle's mite, or their five boys' mites. Mr. Quale, with his hair brushed back as usual and his knobs of temples shining very much, was also there, not in the character of a disappointed lover, but as the accepted of a young—at least, an unmarried—lady, a Miss Wisk, who was also there. Miss Wisk's mission, my guardian said, was to show the world that woman's mission was man's mission and that the only genuine mission of both man and woman was to be always moving declaratory resolutions about things in general at public meetings. The guests were few, but were, as one might expect at Mrs. Jellyby's, all devoted to public objects only. Besides those I have mentioned, there was an extremely dirty lady with her bonnet all awry and the ticketed price of her dress still sticking on it, whose neglected home, Caddy told me, was like a filthy wilderness, but whose church was like a fancy fair. A very contentious gentleman, who said it was his mission to be everybody's brother but who appeared to be on terms of coolness with the whole of his large family, completed the party.

A party, having less in common with such an occasion, could hardly have been got together by any ingenuity. Such a mean mission as the domestic mission was the very last thing to be endured among them; indeed, Miss Wisk informed us, with great indignation, before we sat down to breakfast, that the idea of woman's mission lying chiefly in the narrow sphere of home was an outrageous slander on the part of her tyrant, man. One other singularity was that nobody with a mission—except Mr. Quale, whose mission, as I think I have formerly said, was to be in ecstasies with everybody's mission—cared at all for anybody's mission. Mrs. Pardiggle being as clear that the only one infallible course was her course of pouncing upon the poor and applying benevolence to them like a strait-waistcoat; as Miss Wisk was that the only practical thing for the world was the emancipation of woman from the thraldom of her tyrant, man. Mrs. Jellyby, all the while, sat smiling at the limited vision that could see anything but Borrioboola-Gha.

But I am anticipating now the purport of our conversation on the ride home instead of first marrying Caddy. We all went to church, and Mr. Jellyby gave her away. Of the air with which old Mr. Turveydrop, with his hat under his left arm (the inside presented at the clergyman like a cannon) and his eyes creasing themselves up into his wig, stood stiff and high-shouldered behind us bridesmaids during the ceremony, and afterwards saluted us, I could never say enough to do it justice. Miss Wisk, whom I cannot report as prepossessing in appearance, and whose manner was grim, listened to the proceedings, as part of woman's wrongs, with a disdainful face. Mrs. Jellyby, with her calm smile and her bright eyes, looked the least concerned of all the company.

We duly came back to breakfast, and Mrs. Jellyby sat at the head of the table and Mr. Jellyby at the foot. Caddy had previously stolen upstairs to hug the children again and tell them that her name was Turveydrop. But this piece of information, instead of being an agreeable surprise to Peepy, threw him on his back in such transports of kicking grief that I could do nothing on being sent for but accede to the proposal that he should be admitted to the breakfast table. So he came down and sat in my lap; and Mrs. Jellyby, after saying, in reference to the state of his pinafore, "Oh, you naughty Peepy, what a shocking little pig you are!" was not at all discomposed. He was very good except that he brought down Noah with him (out of an ark I had given him before we went to church) and WOULD dip him head first into the wine-glasses and then put him in his mouth.

My guardian, with his sweet temper and his quick perception and his amiable face, made something agreeable even out of the ungenial company. None of them seemed able to talk about anything but his, or her, own one subject, and none of them seemed able to talk about even that as part of a world in which there was anything else; but my guardian turned it all to the merry encouragement of Caddy and the honour of the occasion, and brought us through the breakfast nobly. What we should have done without him, I am afraid to think, for all the company despising the bride and bridegroom and old Mr. Turveydrop—and old Mr. Thurveydrop, in virtue of his deportment, considering himself vastly superior to all the company—it was a very unpromising case.

At last the time came when poor Caddy was to go and when all her property was packed on the hired coach and pair that was to take her and her husband to Gravesend. It affected us to see Caddy clinging, then, to her deplorable home and hanging on her mother's neck with the greatest tenderness.

"I am very sorry I couldn't go on writing from dictation, Ma," sobbed Caddy. "I hope you forgive me now."

"Oh, Caddy, Caddy!" said Mrs. Jellyby. "I have told you over and over again that I have engaged a boy, and there's an end of it."

"You are sure you are not the least angry with me, Ma? Say you are sure before I go away, Ma?"

"You foolish Caddy," returned Mrs. Jellyby, "do I look angry, or have I inclination to be angry, or time to be angry? How CAN you?"

"Take a little care of Pa while I am gone, Mama!"

Mrs. Jellyby positively laughed at the fancy. "You romantic child," said she, lightly patting Caddy's back. "Go along. I am excellent friends with you. Now, good-bye, Caddy, and be very happy!"

Then Caddy hung upon her father and nursed his cheek against hers as if he were some poor dull child in pain. All this took place in the hall. Her father released her, took out his pocket handkerchief, and sat down on the stairs with his head against the wall. I hope he found some consolation in walls. I almost think he did.

And then Prince took her arm in his and turned with great emotion and respect to his father, whose deportment at that moment was overwhelming.

"Thank you over and over again, father!" said Prince, kissing his hand. "I am very grateful for all your kindness and consideration regarding our marriage, and so, I can assure you, is Caddy."

"Very," sobbed Caddy. "Ve-ry!"

"My dear son," said Mr. Turveydrop, "and dear daughter, I have done my duty. If the spirit of a sainted wooman hovers above us and looks down on the occasion, that, and your constant affection, will be my recompense. You will not fail in YOUR duty, my son and daughter, I believe?"

"Dear father, never!" cried Prince.

"Never, never, dear Mr. Turveydrop!" said Caddy.

"This," returned Mr. Turveydrop, "is as it should be. My children, my home is yours, my heart is yours, my all is yours. I will never leave you; nothing but death shall part us. My dear son, you contemplate an absence of a week, I think?"

"A week, dear father. We shall return home this day week."

"My dear child," said Mr. Turveydrop, "let me, even under the present exceptional circumstances, recommend strict punctuality. It is highly important to keep the connexion together; and schools, if at all neglected, are apt to take offence."

"This day week, father, we shall be sure to be home to dinner."

"Good!" said Mr. Turveydrop. "You will find fires, my dear Caroline, in your own room, and dinner prepared in my apartment. Yes, yes, Prince!" anticipating some self-denying objection on his son's part with a great air. "You and our Caroline will be strange in the upper part of the premises and will, therefore, dine that day in my apartment. Now, bless ye!"

They drove away, and whether I wondered most at Mrs. Jellyby or at Mr. Turveydrop, I did not know. Ada and my guardian were in the same condition when we came to talk it over. But before we drove away too, I received a most unexpected and eloquent compliment from Mr. Jellyby. He came up to me in the hall, took both my hands, pressed them earnestly, and opened his mouth twice. I was so sure of his meaning that I said, quite flurried, "You are very welcome, sir. Pray don't mention it!"

"I hope this marriage is for the best, guardian," said I when we three were on our road home.

"I hope it is, little woman. Patience. We shall see."

"Is the wind in the east to-day?" I ventured to ask him.

He laughed heartily and answered, "No."

"But it must have been this morning, I think," said I.

He answered "No" again, and this time my dear girl confidently answered "No" too and shook the lovely head which, with its blooming flowers against the golden hair, was like the very spring. "Much YOU know of east winds, my ugly darling," said I, kissing her in my admiration—I couldn't help it.

Well! It was only their love for me, I know very well, and it is a long time ago. I must write it even if I rub it out again, because it gives me so much pleasure. They said there could be no east wind where Somebody was; they said that wherever Dame Durden went, there was sunshine and summer air.

CHAPTER XXXI
NURSE AND PATIENT

I had not been at home again many days when one evening I went upstairs into my own room to take a peep over Charley's shoulder and see how she was getting on with her copy-book. Writing was a trying business to Charley, who seemed to have no natural power over a pen, but in whose hand every pen appeared to become perversely animated, and to go wrong and crooked, and to stop, and splash, and sidle into corners like a saddle-donkey. It was very odd to see what old letters Charley's young hand had made, they so wrinkled, and shrivelled, and tottering, it so plump and round. Yet Charley was uncommonly expert at other things and had as nimble little fingers as I ever watched.

"Well, Charley," said I, looking over a copy of the letter O in which it was represented as square, triangular, pear-shaped, and collapsed in all kinds of ways, "we are improving. If we only get to make it round, we shall be perfect, Charley."

Then I made one, and Charley made one, and the pen wouldn't join Charley's neatly, but twisted it up into a knot.

"Never mind, Charley. We shall do it in time."

Charley laid down her pen, the copy being finished, opened and shut her cramped little hand, looked gravely at the page, half in pride and half in doubt, and got up, and dropped me a curtsy.

"Thank you, miss. If you please, miss, did you know a poor person of the name of Jenny?"

"A brickmaker's wife, Charley? Yes."

"She came and spoke to me when I was out a little while ago, and said you knew her, miss. She asked me if I wasn't the young lady's little maid—meaning you for the young lady, miss—and I said yes, miss."

"I thought she had left this neighbourhood altogether, Charley."

"So she had, miss, but she's come back again to where she used to live—she and Liz. Did you know another poor person of the name of Liz, miss?"

"I think I do, Charley, though not by name."

"That's what she said!" returned Charley. "They have both come back, miss, and have been tramping high and low."

"Tramping high and low, have they, Charley?"

"Yes, miss." If Charley could only have made the letters in her copy as round as the eyes with which she looked into my face, they would have been excellent. "And this poor person came about the house three or four days, hoping to get a glimpse of you, miss—all she wanted, she said—but you were away. That was when she saw me. She saw me a-going about, miss," said Charley with a short laugh of the greatest delight and pride, "and she thought I looked like your maid!"

"Did she though, really, Charley?"

"Yes, miss!" said Charley. "Really and truly." And Charley, with another short laugh of the purest glee, made her eyes very round again and looked as serious as became my maid. I was never tired of seeing Charley in the full enjoyment of that great dignity, standing before me with her youthful face and figure, and her steady manner, and her childish exultation breaking through it now and then in the pleasantest way.

"And where did you see her, Charley?" said I.

My little maid's countenance fell as she replied, "By the doctor's shop, miss." For Charley wore her black frock yet.

I asked if the brickmaker's wife were ill, but Charley said no. It was some one else. Some one in her cottage who had tramped down to Saint Albans and was tramping he didn't know where. A poor boy, Charley said. No father, no mother, no any one. "Like as Tom might have been, miss, if Emma and me had died after father," said Charley, her round eyes filling with tears.

"And she was getting medicine for him, Charley?"

"She said, miss," returned Charley, "how that he had once done as much for her."

My little maid's face was so eager and her quiet hands were folded so closely in one another as she stood looking at me that I had no great difficulty in reading her thoughts. "Well, Charley," said I, "it appears to me that you and I can do no better than go round to Jenny's and see what's the matter."

The alacrity with which Charley brought my bonnet and veil, and having dressed me, quaintly pinned herself into her warm shawl and made herself look like a little old woman, sufficiently expressed her readiness. So Charley and I, without saying anything to any one, went out.

It was a cold, wild night, and the trees shuddered in the wind. The rain had been thick and heavy all day, and with little intermission for many days. None was falling just then, however. The sky had partly cleared, but was very gloomy—even above us, where a few stars were shining. In the north and north-west, where the sun had set three hours before, there was a pale dead light both beautiful and awful; and into it long sullen lines of cloud waved up like a sea stricken immovable as it was heaving. Towards London a lurid glare overhung the whole dark waste, and the contrast between these two lights, and the fancy which the redder light engendered of an unearthly fire, gleaming on all the unseen buildings of the city and on all the faces of its many thousands of wondering inhabitants, was as solemn as might be.

I had no thought that night—none, I am quite sure—of what was soon to happen to me. But I have always remembered since that when we had stopped at the garden-gate to look up at the sky, and when we went upon our way, I had for a moment an undefinable impression of myself as being something different from what I then was. I know it was then and there that I had it. I have ever since connected the feeling with that spot and time and with everything associated with that spot and time, to the distant voices in the town, the barking of a dog, and the sound of wheels coming down the miry hill.

It was Saturday night, and most of the people belonging to the place where we were going were drinking elsewhere. We found it quieter than I had previously seen it, though quite as miserable. The kilns were burning, and a stifling vapour set towards us with a pale-blue glare.

We came to the cottage, where there was a feeble candle in the patched window. We tapped at the door and went in. The mother of the little child who had died was sitting in a chair on one side of the poor fire by the bed; and opposite to her, a wretched boy, supported by the chimney-piece, was cowering on the floor. He held under his arm, like a little bundle, a fragment of a fur cap; and as he tried to warm himself, he shook until the crazy door and window shook. The place was closer than before and had an unhealthy and a very peculiar smell.

I had not lifted my veil when I first spoke to the woman, which was at the moment of our going in. The boy staggered up instantly and stared at me with a remarkable expression of surprise and terror.

His action was so quick and my being the cause of it was so evident that I stood still instead of advancing nearer.

"I won't go no more to the berryin ground," muttered the boy; "I ain't a-going there, so I tell you!"

I lifted my veil and spoke to the woman. She said to me in a low voice, "Don't mind him, ma'am. He'll soon come back to his head," and said to him, "Jo, Jo, what's the matter?"

"I know wot she's come for!" cried the boy.

"Who?"

"The lady there. She's come to get me to go along with her to the berryin ground. I won't go to the berryin ground. I don't like the name on it. She might go a-berryin ME." His shivering came on again, and as he leaned against the wall, he shook the hovel.

"He has been talking off and on about such like all day, ma'am," said Jenny softly. "Why, how you stare! This is MY lady, Jo."

"Is it?" returned the boy doubtfully, and surveying me with his arm held out above his burning eyes. "She looks to me the t'other one. It ain't the bonnet, nor yet it ain't the gownd, but she looks to me the t'other one."

My little Charley, with her premature experience of illness and trouble, had pulled off her bonnet and shawl and now went quietly up to him with a chair and sat him down in it like an old sick nurse. Except that no such attendant could have shown him Charley's youthful face, which seemed to engage his confidence.

"I say!" said the boy. "YOU tell me. Ain't the lady the t'other lady?"

Charley shook her head as she methodically drew his rags about him and made him as warm as she could.

"Oh!" the boy muttered. "Then I s'pose she ain't."

"I came to see if I could do you any good," said I. "What is the matter with you?"

"I'm a-being froze," returned the boy hoarsely, with his haggard gaze wandering about me, "and then burnt up, and then froze, and then burnt up, ever so many times in a hour. And my head's all sleepy, and all a-going mad-like—and I'm so dry—and my bones isn't half so much bones as pain.

"When did he come here?" I asked the woman.

"This morning, ma'am, I found him at the corner of the town. I had known him up in London yonder. Hadn't I, Jo?"

"Tom-all-Alone's," the boy replied.

Whenever he fixed his attention or his eyes, it was only for a very little while. He soon began to droop his head again, and roll it heavily, and speak as if he were half awake.

"When did he come from London?" I asked.

"I come from London yes'day," said the boy himself, now flushed and hot. "I'm a-going somewheres."

"Where is he going?" I asked.

"Somewheres," repeated the boy in a louder tone. "I have been moved on, and moved on, more nor ever I was afore, since the t'other one give me the sov'ring. Mrs. Snagsby, she's always a-watching, and a-driving of me—what have I done to her?—and they're all a-watching and a-driving of me. Every one of 'em's doing of it, from the time when I don't get up, to the time when I don't go to bed. And I'm a-going somewheres. That's where I'm a-going. She told me, down in Tom-all-Alone's, as she came from Stolbuns, and so I took the Stolbuns Road. It's as good as another."

He always concluded by addressing Charley.

"What is to be done with him?" said I, taking the woman aside. "He could not travel in this state even if he had a purpose and knew where he was going!"

"I know no more, ma'am, than the dead," she replied, glancing compassionately at him. "Perhaps the dead know better, if they could only tell us. I've kept him here all day for pity's sake, and I've given him broth and physic, and Liz has gone to try if any one will take him in (here's my pretty in the bed—her child, but I call it mine); but I can't keep him long, for if my husband was to come home and find him here, he'd be rough in putting him out and might do him a hurt. Hark! Here comes Liz back!"

The other woman came hurriedly in as she spoke, and the boy got up with a half-obscured sense that he was expected to be going. When the little child awoke, and when and how Charley got at it, took it out of bed, and began to walk about hushing it, I don't know. There she was, doing all this in a quiet motherly manner as if she were living in Mrs. Blinder's attic with Tom and Emma again.

The friend had been here and there, and had been played about from hand to hand, and had come back as she went. At first it was too early for the boy to be received into the proper refuge, and at last it was too late. One official sent her to another, and the other sent her back again to the first, and so backward and forward, until it appeared to me as if both must have been appointed for their skill in evading their duties instead of performing them. And now, after all, she said, breathing quickly, for she had been running and was frightened too, "Jenny, your master's on the road home, and mine's not far behind, and the Lord help the boy, for we can do no more for him!" They put a few halfpence together and hurried them into his hand, and so, in an oblivious, half-thankful, half-insensible way, he shuffled out of the house.

"Give me the child, my dear," said its mother to Charley, "and thank you kindly too! Jenny, woman dear, good night! Young lady, if my master don't fall out with me, I'll look down by the kiln by and by, where the boy will be most like, and again in the morning!" She hurried off, and presently we passed her hushing and singing to her child at her own door and looking anxiously along the road for her drunken husband.

I was afraid of staying then to speak to either woman, lest I should bring her into trouble. But I said to Charley that we must not leave the boy to die. Charley, who knew what to do much better than I did, and whose quickness equalled her presence of mind, glided on before me, and presently we came up with Jo, just short of the brick-kiln.

I think he must have begun his journey with some small bundle under his arm and must have had it stolen or lost it. For he still carried his wretched fragment of fur cap like a bundle, though he went bare-headed through the rain, which now fell fast. He stopped when we called to him and again showed a dread of me when I came up, standing with his lustrous eyes fixed upon me, and even arrested in his shivering fit.

I asked him to come with us, and we would take care that he had some shelter for the night.

"I don't want no shelter," he said; "I can lay amongst the warm bricks."

"But don't you know that people die there?" replied Charley.

"They dies everywheres," said the boy. "They dies in their lodgings—she knows where; I showed her—and they dies down in Tom-all-Alone's in heaps. They dies more than they lives, according to what I see." Then he hoarsely whispered Charley, "If she ain't the t'other one, she ain't the forrenner. Is there THREE of 'em then?"

Charley looked at me a little frightened. I felt half frightened at myself when the boy glared on me so.

But he turned and followed when I beckoned to him, and finding that he acknowledged that influence in me, I led the way straight home. It was not far, only at the summit of the hill. We passed but one man. I doubted if we should have got home without assistance, the boy's steps were so uncertain and tremulous. He made no complaint, however, and was strangely unconcerned about himself, if I may say so strange a thing.

Leaving him in the hall for a moment, shrunk into the corner of the window-seat and staring with an indifference that scarcely could be called wonder at the comfort and brightness about him, I went into the drawing-room to speak to my guardian. There I found Mr. Skimpole, who had come down by the coach, as he frequently did without notice, and never bringing any clothes with him, but always borrowing everything he wanted.

They came out with me directly to look at the boy. The servants had gathered in the hall too, and he shivered in the window-seat with Charley standing by him, like some wounded animal that had been found in a ditch.

"This is a sorrowful case," said my guardian after asking him a question or two and touching him and examining his eyes. "What do you say, Harold?"

"You had better turn him out," said Mr. Skimpole.

"What do you mean?" inquired my guardian, almost sternly.

"My dear Jarndyce," said Mr. Skimpole, "you know what I am: I am a child. Be cross to me if I deserve it. But I have a constitutional objection to this sort of thing. I always had, when I was a medical man. He's not safe, you know. There's a very bad sort of fever about him."

Mr. Skimpole had retreated from the hall to the drawing-room again and said this in his airy way, seated on the music-stool as we stood by.

"You'll say it's childish," observed Mr. Skimpole, looking gaily at us. "Well, I dare say it may be; but I AM a child, and I never pretend to be anything else. If you put him out in the road, you only put him where he was before. He will be no worse off than he was, you know. Even make him better off, if you like. Give him sixpence, or five shillings, or five pound ten—you are arithmeticians, and I am not—and get rid of him!"

"And what is he to do then?" asked my guardian.

"Upon my life," said Mr. Skimpole, shrugging his shoulders with his engaging smile, "I have not the least idea what he is to do then. But I have no doubt he'll do it."

"Now, is it not a horrible reflection," said my guardian, to whom I had hastily explained the unavailing efforts of the two women, "is it not a horrible reflection," walking up and down and rumpling his hair, "that if this wretched creature were a convicted prisoner, his hospital would be wide open to him, and he would be as well taken care of as any sick boy in the kingdom?"

"My dear Jarndyce," returned Mr. Skimpole, "you'll pardon the simplicity of the question, coming as it does from a creature who is perfectly simple in worldly matters, but why ISN'T he a prisoner then?"

My guardian stopped and looked at him with a whimsical mixture of amusement and indignation in his face.

"Our young friend is not to be suspected of any delicacy, I should imagine," said Mr. Skimpole, unabashed and candid. "It seems to me that it would be wiser, as well as in a certain kind of way more respectable, if he showed some misdirected energy that got him into prison. There would be more of an adventurous spirit in it, and consequently more of a certain sort of poetry."

"I believe," returned my guardian, resuming his uneasy walk, "that there is not such another child on earth as yourself."

"Do you really?" said Mr. Skimpole. "I dare say! But I confess I don't see why our young friend, in his degree, should not seek to invest himself with such poetry as is open to him. He is no doubt born with an appetite—probably, when he is in a safer state of health, he has an excellent appetite. Very well. At our young friend's natural dinner hour, most likely about noon, our young friend says in effect to society, 'I am hungry; will you have the goodness to produce your spoon and feed me?' Society, which has taken upon itself the general arrangement of the whole system of spoons and professes to have a spoon for our young friend, does NOT produce that spoon; and our young friend, therefore, says 'You really must excuse me if I seize it.' Now, this appears to me a case of misdirected energy, which has a certain amount of reason in it and a certain amount of romance; and I don't know but what I should be more interested in our young friend, as an illustration of such a case, than merely as a poor vagabond—which any one can be."

"In the meantime," I ventured to observe, "he is getting worse."

"In the meantime," said Mr. Skimpole cheerfully, "as Miss Summerson, with her practical good sense, observes, he is getting worse. Therefore I recommend your turning him out before he gets still worse."

The amiable face with which he said it, I think I shall never forget.

"Of course, little woman," observed my guardian, turning to me, "I can ensure his admission into the proper place by merely going there to enforce it, though it's a bad state of things when, in his condition, that is necessary. But it's growing late, and is a very bad night, and the boy is worn out already. There is a bed in the wholesome loft-room by the stable; we had better keep him there till morning, when he can be wrapped up and removed. We'll do that."

"Oh!" said Mr. Skimpole, with his hands upon the keys of the piano as we moved away. "Are you going back to our young friend?"

"Yes," said my guardian.

"How I envy you your constitution, Jarndyce!" returned Mr. Skimpole with playful admiration. "You don't mind these things; neither does Miss Summerson. You are ready at all times to go anywhere, and do anything. Such is will! I have no will at all—and no won't—simply can't."

"You can't recommend anything for the boy, I suppose?" said my guardian, looking back over his shoulder half angrily; only half angrily, for he never seemed to consider Mr. Skimpole an accountable being.

"My dear Jarndyce, I observed a bottle of cooling medicine in his pocket, and it's impossible for him to do better than take it. You can tell them to sprinkle a little vinegar about the place where he sleeps and to keep it moderately cool and him moderately warm. But it is mere impertinence in me to offer any recommendation. Miss Summerson has such a knowledge of detail and such a capacity for the administration of detail that she knows all about it."

We went back into the hall and explained to Jo what we proposed to do, which Charley explained to him again and which he received with the languid unconcern I had already noticed, wearily looking on at what was done as if it were for somebody else. The servants compassionating his miserable state and being very anxious to help, we soon got the loft-room ready; and some of the men about the house carried him across the wet yard, well wrapped up. It was pleasant to observe how kind they were to him and how there appeared to be a general impression among them that frequently calling him "Old Chap" was likely to revive his spirits. Charley directed the operations and went to and fro between the loft-room and the house with such little stimulants and comforts as we thought it safe to give him. My guardian himself saw him before he was left for the night and reported to me when he returned to the growlery to write a letter on the boy's behalf, which a messenger was charged to deliver at day-light in the morning, that he seemed easier and inclined to sleep. They had fastened his door on the outside, he said, in case of his being delirious, but had so arranged that he could not make any noise without being heard.

Ada being in our room with a cold, Mr. Skimpole was left alone all this time and entertained himself by playing snatches of pathetic airs and sometimes singing to them (as we heard at a distance) with great expression and feeling. When we rejoined him in the drawing-room he said he would give us a little ballad which had come into his head "apropos of our young friend," and he sang one about a peasant boy,

"Thrown on the wide world, doomed to wander and roam,
Bereft of his parents, bereft of a home."

quite exquisitely. It was a song that always made him cry, he told us.

He was extremely gay all the rest of the evening, for he absolutely chirped—those were his delighted words—when he thought by what a happy talent for business he was surrounded. He gave us, in his glass of negus, "Better health to our young friend!" and supposed and gaily pursued the case of his being reserved like Whittington to become Lord Mayor of London. In that event, no doubt, he would establish the Jarndyce Institution and the Summerson Almshouses, and a little annual Corporation Pilgrimage to St. Albans. He had no doubt, he said, that our young friend was an excellent boy in his way, but his way was not the Harold Skimpole way; what Harold Skimpole was, Harold Skimpole had found himself, to his considerable surprise, when he first made his own acquaintance; he had accepted himself with all his failings and had thought it sound philosophy to make the best of the bargain; and he hoped we would do the same.

Charley's last report was that the boy was quiet. I could see, from my window, the lantern they had left him burning quietly; and I went to bed very happy to think that he was sheltered.

There was more movement and more talking than usual a little before daybreak, and it awoke me. As I was dressing, I looked out of my window and asked one of our men who had been among the active sympathizers last night whether there was anything wrong about the house. The lantern was still burning in the loft-window.

"It's the boy, miss," said he.

"Is he worse?" I inquired.

"Gone, miss.

"Dead!"

"Dead, miss? No. Gone clean off."

At what time of the night he had gone, or how, or why, it seemed hopeless ever to divine. The door remaining as it had been left, and the lantern standing in the window, it could only be supposed that he had got out by a trap in the floor which communicated with an empty cart-house below. But he had shut it down again, if that were so; and it looked as if it had not been raised. Nothing of any kind was missing. On this fact being clearly ascertained, we all yielded to the painful belief that delirium had come upon him in the night and that, allured by some imaginary object or pursued by some imaginary horror, he had strayed away in that worse than helpless state; all of us, that is to say, but Mr. Skimpole, who repeatedly suggested, in his usual easy light style, that it had occurred to our young friend that he was not a safe inmate, having a bad kind of fever upon him, and that he had with great natural politeness taken himself off.

Every possible inquiry was made, and every place was searched. The brick-kilns were examined, the cottages were visited, the two women were particularly questioned, but they knew nothing of him, and nobody could doubt that their wonder was genuine. The weather had for some time been too wet and the night itself had been too wet to admit of any tracing by footsteps. Hedge and ditch, and wall, and rick and stack, were examined by our men for a long distance round, lest the boy should be lying in such a place insensible or dead; but nothing was seen to indicate that he had ever been near. From the time when he was left in the loft-room, he vanished.

The search continued for five days. I do not mean that it ceased even then, but that my attention was then diverted into a current very memorable to me.

As Charley was at her writing again in my room in the evening, and as I sat opposite to her at work, I felt the table tremble. Looking up, I saw my little maid shivering from head to foot.

"Charley," said I, "are you so cold?"

"I think I am, miss," she replied. "I don't know what it is. I can't hold myself still. I felt so yesterday at about this same time, miss. Don't be uneasy, I think I'm ill."

I heard Ada's voice outside, and I hurried to the door of communication between my room and our pretty sitting-room, and locked it. Just in time, for she tapped at it while my hand was yet upon the key.

Ada called to me to let her in, but I said, "Not now, my dearest. Go away. There's nothing the matter; I will come to you presently." Ah! It was a long, long time before my darling girl and I were companions again.

Charley fell ill. In twelve hours she was very ill. I moved her to my room, and laid her in my bed, and sat down quietly to nurse her. I told my guardian all about it, and why I felt it was necessary that I should seclude myself, and my reason for not seeing my darling above all. At first she came very often to the door, and called to me, and even reproached me with sobs and tears; but I wrote her a long letter saying that she made me anxious and unhappy and imploring her, as she loved me and wished my mind to be at peace, to come no nearer than the garden. After that she came beneath the window even oftener than she had come to the door, and if I had learnt to love her dear sweet voice before when we were hardly ever apart, how did I learn to love it then, when I stood behind the window-curtain listening and replying, but not so much as looking out! How did I learn to love it afterwards, when the harder time came!

They put a bed for me in our sitting-room; and by keeping the door wide open, I turned the two rooms into one, now that Ada had vacated that part of the house, and kept them always fresh and airy. There was not a servant in or about the house but was so good that they would all most gladly have come to me at any hour of the day or night without the least fear or unwillingness, but I thought it best to choose one worthy woman who was never to see Ada and whom I could trust to come and go with all precaution. Through her means I got out to take the air with my guardian when there was no fear of meeting Ada, and wanted for nothing in the way of attendance, any more than in any other respect.

And thus poor Charley sickened and grew worse, and fell into heavy danger of death, and lay severely ill for many a long round of day and night. So patient she was, so uncomplaining, and inspired by such a gentle fortitude that very often as I sat by Charley holding her head in my arms—repose would come to her, so, when it would come to her in no other attitude—I silently prayed to our Father in heaven that I might not forget the lesson which this little sister taught me.

I was very sorrowful to think that Charley's pretty looks would change and be disfigured, even if she recovered—she was such a child with her dimpled face—but that thought was, for the greater part, lost in her greater peril. When she was at the worst, and her mind rambled again to the cares of her father's sick bed and the little children, she still knew me so far as that she would be quiet in my arms when she could lie quiet nowhere else, and murmur out the wanderings of her mind less restlessly. At those times I used to think, how should I ever tell the two remaining babies that the baby who had learned of her faithful heart to be a mother to them in their need was dead!

There were other times when Charley knew me well and talked to me, telling me that she sent her love to Tom and Emma and that she was sure Tom would grow up to be a good man. At those times Charley would speak to me of what she had read to her father as well as she could to comfort him, of that young man carried out to be buried who was the only son of his mother and she was a widow, of the ruler's daughter raised up by the gracious hand upon her bed of death. And Charley told me that when her father died she had kneeled down and prayed in her first sorrow that he likewise might be raised up and given back to his poor children, and that if she should never get better and should die too, she thought it likely that it might come into Tom's mind to offer the same prayer for her. Then would I show Tom how these people of old days had been brought back to life on earth, only that we might know our hope to be restored to heaven!

But of all the various times there were in Charley's illness, there was not one when she lost the gentle qualities I have spoken of. And there were many, many when I thought in the night of the last high belief in the watching angel, and the last higher trust in God, on the part of her poor despised father.

And Charley did not die. She flutteringly and slowly turned the dangerous point, after long lingering there, and then began to mend. The hope that never had been given, from the first, of Charley being in outward appearance Charley any more soon began to be encouraged; and even that prospered, and I saw her growing into her old childish likeness again.

It was a great morning when I could tell Ada all this as she stood out in the garden; and it was a great evening when Charley and I at last took tea together in the next room. But on that same evening, I felt that I was stricken cold.

Happily for both of us, it was not until Charley was safe in bed again and placidly asleep that I began to think the contagion of her illness was upon me. I had been able easily to hide what I felt at tea-time, but I was past that already now, and I knew that I was rapidly following in Charley's steps.

I was well enough, however, to be up early in the morning, and to return my darling's cheerful blessing from the garden, and to talk with her as long as usual. But I was not free from an impression that I had been walking about the two rooms in the night, a little beside myself, though knowing where I was; and I felt confused at times—with a curious sense of fullness, as if I were becoming too large altogether.

In the evening I was so much worse that I resolved to prepare Charley, with which view I said, "You're getting quite strong, Charley, are you not?'

"Oh, quite!" said Charley.

"Strong enough to be told a secret, I think, Charley?"

"Quite strong enough for that, miss!" cried Charley. But Charley's face fell in the height of her delight, for she saw the secret in MY face; and she came out of the great chair, and fell upon my bosom, and said "Oh, miss, it's my doing! It's my doing!" and a great deal more out of the fullness of her grateful heart.

"Now, Charley," said I after letting her go on for a little while, "if I am to be ill, my great trust, humanly speaking, is in you. And unless you are as quiet and composed for me as you always were for yourself, you can never fulfil it, Charley."

"If you'll let me cry a little longer, miss," said Charley. "Oh, my dear, my dear! If you'll only let me cry a little longer. Oh, my dear!"—how affectionately and devotedly she poured this out as she clung to my neck, I never can remember without tears—"I'll be good."

So I let Charley cry a little longer, and it did us both good.

"Trust in me now, if you please, miss," said Charley quietly. "I am listening to everything you say."

"It's very little at present, Charley. I shall tell your doctor to-night that I don't think I am well and that you are going to nurse me."

For that the poor child thanked me with her whole heart. "And in the morning, when you hear Miss Ada in the garden, if I should not be quite able to go to the window-curtain as usual, do you go, Charley, and say I am asleep—that I have rather tired myself, and am asleep. At all times keep the room as I have kept it, Charley, and let no one come."

Charley promised, and I lay down, for I was very heavy. I saw the doctor that night and asked the favour of him that I wished to ask relative to his saying nothing of my illness in the house as yet. I have a very indistinct remembrance of that night melting into day, and of day melting into night again; but I was just able on the first morning to get to the window and speak to my darling.

On the second morning I heard her dear voice—Oh, how dear now!—outside; and I asked Charley, with some difficulty (speech being painful to me), to go and say I was asleep. I heard her answer softly, "Don't disturb her, Charley, for the world!"

"How does my own Pride look, Charley?" I inquired.

"Disappointed, miss," said Charley, peeping through the curtain.

"But I know she is very beautiful this morning."

"She is indeed, miss," answered Charley, peeping. "Still looking up at the window."

With her blue clear eyes, God bless them, always loveliest when raised like that!

I called Charley to me and gave her her last charge.

"Now, Charley, when she knows I am ill, she will try to make her way into the room. Keep her out, Charley, if you love me truly, to the last! Charley, if you let her in but once, only to look upon me for one moment as I lie here, I shall die."

"I never will! I never will!" she promised me.

"I believe it, my dear Charley. And now come and sit beside me for a little while, and touch me with your hand. For I cannot see you, Charley; I am blind."

CHAPTER XXXII
THE APPOINTED TIME

It is night in Lincoln's Inn—perplexed and troublous valley of the shadow of the law, where suitors generally find but little day—and fat candles are snuffed out in offices, and clerks have rattled down the crazy wooden stairs and dispersed. The bell that rings at nine o'clock has ceased its doleful clangour about nothing; the gates are shut; and the night-porter, a solemn warder with a mighty power of sleep, keeps guard in his lodge. From tiers of staircase windows clogged lamps like the eyes of Equity, bleared Argus with a fathomless pocket for every eye and an eye upon it, dimly blink at the stars. In dirty upper casements, here and there, hazy little patches of candle-light reveal where some wise draughtsman and conveyancer yet toils for the entanglement of real estate in meshes of sheep-skin, in the average ratio of about a dozen of sheep to an acre of land. Over which bee-like industry these benefactors of their species linger yet, though office-hours be past, that they may give, for every day, some good account at last.

In the neighbouring court, where the Lord Chancellor of the rag and bottle shop dwells, there is a general tendency towards beer and supper. Mrs. Piper and Mrs. Perkins, whose respective sons, engaged with a circle of acquaintance in the game of hide and seek, have been lying in ambush about the by-ways of Chancery Lane for some hours and scouring the plain of the same thoroughfare to the confusion of passengers—Mrs. Piper and Mrs. Perkins have but now exchanged congratulations on the children being abed, and they still linger on a door-step over a few parting words. Mr. Krook and his lodger, and the fact of Mr. Krook's being "continually in liquor," and the testamentary prospects of the young man are, as usual, the staple of their conversation. But they have something to say, likewise, of the Harmonic Meeting at the Sol's Arms, where the sound of the piano through the partly opened windows jingles out into the court, and where Little Swills, after keeping the lovers of harmony in a roar like a very Yorick, may now be heard taking the gruff line in a concerted piece and sentimentally adjuring his friends and patrons to "Listen, listen, listen, tew the wa-ter fall!" Mrs. Perkins and Mrs. Piper compare opinions on the subject of the young lady of professional celebrity who assists at the Harmonic Meetings and who has a space to herself in the manuscript announcement in the window, Mrs. Perkins possessing information that she has been married a year and a half, though announced as Miss M. Melvilleson, the noted siren, and that her baby is clandestinely conveyed to the Sol's Arms every night to receive its natural nourishment during the entertainments. "Sooner than which, myself," says Mrs. Perkins, "I would get my living by selling lucifers." Mrs. Piper, as in duty bound, is of the same opinion, holding that a private station is better than public applause, and thanking heaven for her own (and, by implication, Mrs. Perkins') respectability. By this time the pot-boy of the Sol's Arms appearing with her supper-pint well frothed, Mrs. Piper accepts that tankard and retires indoors, first giving a fair good night to Mrs. Perkins, who has had her own pint in her hand ever since it was fetched from the same hostelry by young Perkins before he was sent to bed. Now there is a sound of putting up shop-shutters in the court and a smell as of the smoking of pipes; and shooting stars are seen in upper windows, further indicating retirement to rest. Now, too, the policeman begins to push at doors; to try fastenings; to be suspicious of bundles; and to administer his beat, on the hypothesis that every one is either robbing or being robbed.

It is a close night, though the damp cold is searching too, and there is a laggard mist a little way up in the air. It is a fine steaming night to turn the slaughter-houses, the unwholesome trades, the sewerage, bad water, and burial-grounds to account, and give the registrar of deaths some extra business. It may be something in the air—there is plenty in it—or it may be something in himself that is in fault; but Mr. Weevle, otherwise Jobling, is very ill at ease. He comes and goes between his own room and the open street door twenty times an hour. He has been doing so ever since it fell dark. Since the Chancellor shut up his shop, which he did very early to-night, Mr. Weevle has been down and up, and down and up (with a cheap tight velvet skull-cap on his head, making his whiskers look out of all proportion), oftener than before.

It is no phenomenon that Mr. Snagsby should be ill at ease too, for he always is so, more or less, under the oppressive influence of the secret that is upon him. Impelled by the mystery of which he is a partaker and yet in which he is not a sharer, Mr. Snagsby haunts what seems to be its fountain-head—the rag and bottle shop in the court. It has an irresistible attraction for him. Even now, coming round by the Sol's Arms with the intention of passing down the court, and out at the Chancery Lane end, and so terminating his unpremeditated after-supper stroll of ten minutes' long from his own door and back again, Mr. Snagsby approaches.

"What, Mr. Weevle?" says the stationer, stopping to speak. "Are YOU there?"

"Aye!" says Weevle, "Here I am, Mr. Snagsby."

"Airing yourself, as I am doing, before you go to bed?" the stationer inquires.

"Why, there's not much air to be got here; and what there is, is not very freshening," Weevle answers, glancing up and down the court.

"Very true, sir. Don't you observe," says Mr. Snagsby, pausing to sniff and taste the air a little, "don't you observe, Mr. Weevle, that you're—not to put too fine a point upon it—that you're rather greasy here, sir?"

"Why, I have noticed myself that there is a queer kind of flavour in the place to-night," Mr. Weevle rejoins. "I suppose it's chops at the Sol's Arms."

"Chops, do you think? Oh! Chops, eh?" Mr. Snagsby sniffs and tastes again. "Well, sir, I suppose it is. But I should say their cook at the Sol wanted a little looking after. She has been burning 'em, sir! And I don't think"—Mr. Snagsby sniffs and tastes again and then spits and wipes his mouth—"I don't think—not to put too fine a point upon it—that they were quite fresh when they were shown the gridiron."

"That's very likely. It's a tainting sort of weather."

"It IS a tainting sort of weather," says Mr. Snagsby, "and I find it sinking to the spirits."

"By George! I find it gives me the horrors," returns Mr. Weevle.

"Then, you see, you live in a lonesome way, and in a lonesome room, with a black circumstance hanging over it," says Mr. Snagsby, looking in past the other's shoulder along the dark passage and then falling back a step to look up at the house. "I couldn't live in that room alone, as you do, sir. I should get so fidgety and worried of an evening, sometimes, that I should be driven to come to the door and stand here sooner than sit there. But then it's very true that you didn't see, in your room, what I saw there. That makes a difference."

"I know quite enough about it," returns Tony.

"It's not agreeable, is it?" pursues Mr. Snagsby, coughing his cough of mild persuasion behind his hand. "Mr. Krook ought to consider it in the rent. I hope he does, I am sure."

"I hope he does," says Tony. "But I doubt it."

"You find the rent too high, do you, sir?" returns the stationer. "Rents ARE high about here. I don't know how it is exactly, but the law seems to put things up in price. Not," adds Mr. Snagsby with his apologetic cough, "that I mean to say a word against the profession I get my living by."

Mr. Weevle again glances up and down the court and then looks at the stationer. Mr. Snagsby, blankly catching his eye, looks upward for a star or so and coughs a cough expressive of not exactly seeing his way out of this conversation.

"It's a curious fact, sir," he observes, slowly rubbing his hands, "that he should have been—"

"Who's he?" interrupts Mr. Weevle.

"The deceased, you know," says Mr. Snagsby, twitching his head and right eyebrow towards the staircase and tapping his acquaintance on the button.

"Ah, to be sure!" returns the other as if he were not over-fond of the subject. "I thought we had done with him."

"I was only going to say it's a curious fact, sir, that he should have come and lived here, and been one of my writers, and then that you should come and live here, and be one of my writers too. Which there is nothing derogatory, but far from it in the appellation," says Mr. Snagsby, breaking off with a mistrust that he may have unpolitely asserted a kind of proprietorship in Mr.

Weevle, "because I have known writers that have gone into brewers' houses and done really very respectable indeed. Eminently respectable, sir," adds Mr. Snagsby with a misgiving that he has not improved the matter.

"It's a curious coincidence, as you say," answers Weevle, once more glancing up and down the court.

"Seems a fate in it, don't there?" suggests the stationer.

"There does."

"Just so," observes the stationer with his confirmatory cough. "Quite a fate in it. Quite a fate. Well, Mr. Weevle, I am afraid I must bid you good night"—Mr. Snagsby speaks as if it made him desolate to go, though he has been casting about for any means of escape ever since he stopped to speak—"my little woman will be looking for me else. Good night, sir!"

If Mr. Snagsby hastens home to save his little woman the trouble of looking for him, he might set his mind at rest on that score. His little woman has had her eye upon him round the Sol's Arms all this time and now glides after him with a pocket handkerchief wrapped over her head, honouring Mr. Weevle and his doorway with a searching glance as she goes past.

"You'll know me again, ma'am, at all events," says Mr. Weevle to himself; "and I can't compliment you on your appearance, whoever you are, with your head tied up in a bundle. Is this fellow NEVER coming!"

This fellow approaches as he speaks. Mr. Weevle softly holds up his finger, and draws him into the passage, and closes the street door. Then they go upstairs, Mr. Weevle heavily, and Mr. Guppy (for it is he) very lightly indeed. When they are shut into the back room, they speak low.

"I thought you had gone to Jericho at least instead of coming here," says Tony.

"Why, I said about ten."

"You said about ten," Tony repeats. "Yes, so you did say about ten. But according to my count, it's ten times ten—it's a hundred o'clock. I never had such a night in my life!"

"What has been the matter?"

"That's it!" says Tony. "Nothing has been the matter. But here have I been stewing and fuming in this jolly old crib till I have had the horrors falling on me as thick as hail. THERE'S a blessed-looking candle!" says Tony, pointing to the heavily burning taper on his table with a great cabbage head and a long winding-sheet.

"That's easily improved," Mr. Guppy observes as he takes the snuffers in hand.

"IS it?" returns his friend. "Not so easily as you think. It has been smouldering like that ever since it was lighted."

"Why, what's the matter with you, Tony?" inquires Mr. Guppy, looking at him, snuffers in hand, as he sits down with his elbow on the table.

"William Guppy," replies the other, "I am in the downs. It's this unbearably dull, suicidal room—and old Boguey downstairs, I suppose." Mr. Weevle moodily pushes the snuffers-tray from him with his elbow, leans his head on his hand, puts his feet on the fender, and looks at the fire. Mr. Guppy, observing him, slightly tosses his head and sits down on the other side of the table in an easy attitude.

"Wasn't that Snagsby talking to you, Tony?"

"Yes, and he—yes, it was Snagsby," said Mr. Weevle, altering the construction of his sentence.

"On business?"

"No. No business. He was only sauntering by and stopped to prose."

"I thought it was Snagsby," says Mr. Guppy, "and thought it as well that he shouldn't see me, so I waited till he was gone."

"There we go again, William G.!" cried Tony, looking up for an instant. "So mysterious and secret! By George, if we were going to commit a murder, we couldn't have more mystery about it!"

Mr. Guppy affects to smile, and with the view of changing the conversation, looks with an admiration, real or pretended, round the room at the Galaxy Gallery of British Beauty, terminating his survey with the portrait of Lady Dedlock over the mantelshelf, in which she is represented on a terrace, with a pedestal upon the terrace, and a vase upon the pedestal, and her shawl upon the vase, and a prodigious piece of fur upon the shawl, and her arm on the prodigious piece of fur, and a bracelet on her arm.

"That's very like Lady Dedlock," says Mr. Guppy. "It's a speaking likeness."

"I wish it was," growls Tony, without changing his position. "I should have some fashionable conversation, here, then."

Finding by this time that his friend is not to be wheedled into a more sociable humour, Mr. Guppy puts about upon the ill-used tack and remonstrates with him.

"Tony," says he, "I can make allowances for lowness of spirits, for no man knows what it is when it does come upon a man better than I do, and no man perhaps has a better right to know it than a man who has an unrequited image imprinted on his 'eart. But there are bounds to these things when an unoffending party is in question, and I will acknowledge to you, Tony, that I don't think your manner on the present occasion is hospitable or quite gentlemanly."

"This is strong language, William Guppy," returns Mr. Weevle.

"Sir, it may be," retorts Mr. William Guppy, "but I feel strongly when I use it."

Mr. Weevle admits that he has been wrong and begs Mr. William Guppy to think no more about it. Mr. William Guppy, however, having got the advantage, cannot quite release it without a little more injured remonstrance.

"No! Dash it, Tony," says that gentleman, "you really ought to be careful how you wound the feelings of a man who has an unrequited image imprinted on his 'eart and who is NOT altogether happy in those chords which vibrate to the tenderest emotions. You, Tony, possess in yourself all that is calculated to charm the eye and allure the taste. It is not—happily for you, perhaps, and I may wish that I could say the same—it is not your character to hover around one flower. The ole garden is open to you, and your airy pinions carry you through it. Still, Tony, far be it from me, I am sure, to wound even your feelings without a cause!"

Tony again entreats that the subject may be no longer pursued, saying emphatically, "William Guppy, drop it!" Mr. Guppy acquiesces, with the reply, "I never should have taken it up, Tony, of my own accord."

"And now," says Tony, stirring the fire, "touching this same bundle of letters. Isn't it an extraordinary thing of Krook to have appointed twelve o'clock to-night to hand 'em over to me?"

"Very. What did he do it for?"

"What does he do anything for? HE don't know. Said to-day was his birthday and he'd hand 'em over to-night at twelve o'clock. He'll have drunk himself blind by that time. He has been at it all day."

"He hasn't forgotten the appointment, I hope?"

"Forgotten? Trust him for that. He never forgets anything. I saw him to-night, about eight—helped him to shut up his shop—and he had got the letters then in his hairy cap. He pulled it off and showed 'em me. When the shop was closed, he took them out of his cap, hung his cap on the chair-back, and stood turning them over before the fire. I heard him a little while afterwards, through the floor here, humming like the wind, the only song he knows—about Bibo, and old Charon, and Bibo being drunk when he died, or something or other. He has been as quiet since as an old rat asleep in his hole."

"And you are to go down at twelve?"

"At twelve. And as I tell you, when you came it seemed to me a hundred."

"Tony," says Mr. Guppy after considering a little with his legs crossed, "he can't read yet, can he?"

"Read! He'll never read. He can make all the letters separately, and he knows most of them separately when he sees them; he has got on that much, under me; but he can't put them together. He's too old to acquire the knack of it now—and too drunk."

"Tony," says Mr. Guppy, uncrossing and recrossing his legs, "how do you suppose he spelt out that name of Hawdon?"

"He never spelt it out. You know what a curious power of eye he has and how he has been used to employ himself in copying things by eye alone. He imitated it, evidently from the direction of a letter, and asked me what it meant."

"Tony," says Mr. Guppy, uncrossing and recrossing his legs again, "should you say that the original was a man's writing or a woman's?"

"A woman's. Fifty to one a lady's—slopes a good deal, and the end of the letter 'n,' long and hasty."

Mr. Guppy has been biting his thumb-nail during this dialogue, generally changing the thumb when he has changed the cross leg. As he is going to do so again, he happens to look at his coat-sleeve. It takes his attention. He stares at it, aghast.

"Why, Tony, what on earth is going on in this house to-night? Is there a chimney on fire?"

"Chimney on fire!"

"Ah!" returns Mr. Guppy. "See how the soot's falling. See here, on my arm! See again, on the table here! Confound the stuff, it won't blow off—smears like black fat!"

They look at one another, and Tony goes listening to the door, and a little way upstairs, and a little way downstairs. Comes back and says it's all right and all quiet, and quotes the remark he lately made to Mr. Snagsby about their cooking chops at the Sol's Arms.

"And it was then," resumes Mr. Guppy, still glancing with remarkable aversion at the coat-sleeve, as they pursue their conversation before the fire, leaning on opposite sides of the table, with their heads very near together, "that he told you of his having taken the bundle of letters from his lodger's portmanteau?"

"That was the time, sir," answers Tony, faintly adjusting his whiskers. "Whereupon I wrote a line to my dear boy, the Honourable William Guppy, informing him of the appointment for to-night and advising him not to call before, Boguey being a slyboots."

The light vivacious tone of fashionable life which is usually assumed by Mr. Weevle sits so ill upon him to-night that he abandons that and his whiskers together, and after looking over his shoulder, appears to yield himself up a prey to the horrors again.

"You are to bring the letters to your room to read and compare, and to get yourself into a position to tell him all about them. That's the arrangement, isn't it, Tony?" asks Mr. Guppy, anxiously biting his thumb-nail.

"You can't speak too low. Yes. That's what he and I agreed."

"I tell you what, Tony—"

"You can't speak too low," says Tony once more. Mr. Guppy nods his sagacious head, advances it yet closer, and drops into a whisper.

"I tell you what. The first thing to be done is to make another packet like the real one so that if he should ask to see the real one while it's in my possession, you can show him the dummy."

"And suppose he detects the dummy as soon as he sees it, which with his biting screw of an eye is about five hundred times more likely than not," suggests Tony.

"Then we'll face it out. They don't belong to him, and they never did. You found that, and you placed them in my hands—a legal friend of yours—for security. If he forces us to it, they'll be producible, won't they?"

"Ye-es," is Mr. Weevle's reluctant admission.

"Why, Tony," remonstrates his friend, "how you look! You don't doubt William Guppy? You don't suspect any harm?"

"I don't suspect anything more than I know, William," returns the other gravely.

"And what do you know?" urges Mr. Guppy, raising his voice a little; but on his friend's once more warning him, "I tell you, you can't speak too low," he repeats his question without any sound at all, forming with his lips only the words, "What do you know?"

"I know three things. First, I know that here we are whispering in secrecy, a pair of conspirators."

"Well!" says Mr. Guppy. "And we had better be that than a pair of noodles, which we should be if we were doing anything else, for it's the only way of doing what we want to do. Secondly?"

"Secondly, it's not made out to me how it's likely to be profitable, after all."

Mr. Guppy casts up his eyes at the portrait of Lady Dedlock over the mantelshelf and replies, "Tony, you are asked to leave that to the honour of your friend. Besides its being calculated to serve that friend in those chords of the human mind which—which need not be called into agonizing vibration on the present occasion—your friend is no fool. What's that?"

"It's eleven o'clock striking by the bell of Saint Paul's. Listen and you'll hear all the bells in the city jangling."

Both sit silent, listening to the metal voices, near and distant, resounding from towers of various heights, in tones more various than their situations. When these at length cease, all seems more mysterious and quiet than before. One disagreeable result of whispering is that it seems to evoke an atmosphere of silence, haunted by the ghosts of sound—strange cracks and tickings, the rustling of garments that have no substance in them, and the tread of dreadful feet that would leave no mark on the sea-sand or the winter snow. So sensitive the two friends happen to be that the air is full of these phantoms, and the two look over their shoulders by one consent to see that the door is shut.

"Yes, Tony?" says Mr. Guppy, drawing nearer to the fire and biting his unsteady thumb-nail. "You were going to say, thirdly?"

"It's far from a pleasant thing to be plotting about a dead man in the room where he died, especially when you happen to live in it."

"But we are plotting nothing against him, Tony."

"May be not, still I don't like it. Live here by yourself and see how YOU like it."

"As to dead men, Tony," proceeds Mr. Guppy, evading this proposal, "there have been dead men in most rooms."

"I know there have, but in most rooms you let them alone, and—and they let you alone," Tony answers.

The two look at each other again. Mr. Guppy makes a hurried remark to the effect that they may be doing the deceased a service, that he hopes so. There is an oppressive blank until Mr. Weevle, by stirring the fire suddenly, makes Mr. Guppy start as if his heart had been stirred instead.

"Fah! Here's more of this hateful soot hanging about," says he. "Let us open the window a bit and get a mouthful of air. It's too close."

He raises the sash, and they both rest on the window-sill, half in and half out of the room. The neighbouring houses are too near to admit of their seeing any sky without craning their necks and looking up, but lights in frowsy windows here and there, and the rolling of distant carriages, and the new expression that there is of the stir of men, they find to be comfortable. Mr. Guppy, noiselessly tapping on the window-sill, resumes his whispering in quite a light-comedy tone.

"By the by, Tony, don't forget old Smallweed," meaning the younger of that name. "I have not let him into this, you know. That grandfather of his is too keen by half. It runs in the family."

"I remember," says Tony. "I am up to all that."

"And as to Krook," resumes Mr. Guppy. "Now, do you suppose he really has got hold of any other papers of importance, as he has boasted to you, since you have been such allies?"

Tony shakes his head. "I don't know. Can't Imagine. If we get through this business without rousing his suspicions, I shall be better informed, no doubt. How can I know without seeing them, when he don't know himself? He is always spelling out words from them, and chalking them over the table and the shop-wall, and asking what this is and what that is; but his whole stock from beginning to end may easily be the waste-paper he bought it as, for anything I can say. It's a monomania with him to think he is possessed of documents. He has been going to learn to read them this last quarter of a century, I should judge, from what he tells me."

"How did he first come by that idea, though? That's the question," Mr. Guppy suggests with one eye shut, after a little forensic meditation. "He may have found papers in something he bought, where papers were not supposed to be, and may have got it into his shrewd head from the manner and place of their concealment that they are worth something."

"Or he may have been taken in, in some pretended bargain. Or he may have been muddled altogether by long staring at whatever he HAS got, and by drink, and by hanging about the Lord Chancellor's Court and hearing of documents for ever," returns Mr. Weevle.

Mr. Guppy sitting on the window-sill, nodding his head and balancing all these possibilities in his mind, continues thoughtfully to tap it, and clasp it, and measure it with his hand, until he hastily draws his hand away.

"What, in the devil's name," he says, "is this! Look at my fingers!"

A thick, yellow liquor defiles them, which is offensive to the touch and sight and more offensive to the smell. A stagnant, sickening oil with some natural repulsion in it that makes them both shudder.

"What have you been doing here? What have you been pouring out of window?"

"I pouring out of window! Nothing, I swear! Never, since I have been here!" cries the lodger.

And yet look here—and look here! When he brings the candle here, from the corner of the window-sill, it slowly drips and creeps away down the bricks, here lies in a little thick nauseous pool.

"This is a horrible house," says Mr. Guppy, shutting down the window. "Give me some water or I shall cut my hand off."

He so washes, and rubs, and scrubs, and smells, and washes, that he has not long restored himself with a glass of brandy and stood silently before the fire when Saint Paul's bell strikes twelve and all those other bells strike twelve from their towers of various heights in the dark air, and in their many tones. When all is quiet again, the lodger says, "It's the appointed time at last. Shall I go?"

Mr. Guppy nods and gives him a "lucky touch" on the back, but not with the washed hand, though it is his right hand.

He goes downstairs, and Mr. Guppy tries to compose himself before the fire for waiting a long time. But in no more than a minute or two the stairs creak and Tony comes swiftly back.

"Have you got them?"

"Got them! No. The old man's not there."

He has been so horribly frightened in the short interval that his terror seizes the other, who makes a rush at him and asks loudly, "What's the matter?"

"I couldn't make him hear, and I softly opened the door and looked in. And the burning smell is there—and the soot is there, and the oil is there—and he is not there!" Tony ends this with a groan.

Mr. Guppy takes the light. They go down, more dead than alive, and holding one another, push open the door of the back shop. The cat has retreated close to it and stands snarling, not at them, at something on the ground before the fire. There is a very little fire left in the grate, but there is a smouldering, suffocating vapour in the room and a dark, greasy coating on the walls and ceiling. The chairs and table, and the bottle so rarely absent from the table, all stand as usual. On one chair-back hang the old man's hairy cap and coat.

"Look!" whispers the lodger, pointing his friend's attention to these objects with a trembling finger. "I told you so. When I saw him last, he took his cap off, took out the little bundle of old letters, hung his cap on the back of the chair—his coat was there already, for he had pulled that off before he went to put the shutters up—and I left him turning the letters over in his hand, standing just where that crumbled black thing is upon the floor."

Is he hanging somewhere? They look up. No.

"See!" whispers Tony. "At the foot of the same chair there lies a dirty bit of thin red cord that they tie up pens with. That went round the letters. He undid it slowly, leering and laughing at me, before he began to turn them over, and threw it there. I saw it fall."

"What's the matter with the cat?" says Mr. Guppy. "Look at her!"

"Mad, I think. And no wonder in this evil place."

They advance slowly, looking at all these things. The cat remains where they found her, still snarling at the something on the ground before the fire and between the two chairs. What is it? Hold up the light.

Here is a small burnt patch of flooring; here is the tinder from a little bundle of burnt paper, but not so light as usual, seeming to be steeped in something; and here is—is it the cinder of a small charred and broken log of wood sprinkled with white ashes, or is it coal? Oh, horror, he IS here! And this from which we run away, striking out the light and overturning one another into the street, is all that represents him.

Help, help, help! Come into this house for heaven's sake! Plenty will come in, but none can help. The Lord Chancellor of that court, true to his title in his last act, has died the death of all lord chancellors in all courts and of all authorities in all places under all names soever, where false pretences are made, and where injustice is done. Call the death by any name your Highness will, attribute it to whom you will, or say it might have been prevented how you will, it is the same death eternally—inborn, inbred, engendered in the corrupted humours of the vicious body itself, and that only—spontaneous combustion, and none other of all the deaths that can be died.

CHAPTER XXXIII
INTERLOPERS

Now do those two gentlemen not very neat about the cuffs and buttons who attended the last coroner's inquest at the Sol's Arms reappear in the precincts with surprising swiftness (being, in fact, breathlessly fetched by the active and intelligent beadle), and institute perquisitions through the court, and dive into the Sol's parlour, and write with ravenous little pens on tissue-paper. Now do they note down, in the watches of the night, how the neighbourhood of Chancery Lane was yesterday, at about midnight, thrown into a state of the most intense agitation and excitement by the following alarming and horrible discovery. Now do they set forth how it will doubtless be remembered that some time back a painful sensation was created in the public mind by a case of mysterious death from opium occurring in the first floor of the house occupied as a rag, bottle, and general marine store shop, by an eccentric individual of intemperate habits, far advanced in life, named Krook; and how, by a remarkable coincidence, Krook was examined at the inquest, which it may be recollected was held on that occasion at the Sol's Arms, a well-conducted tavern immediately adjoining the premises in question on the west side and licensed to a highly respectable landlord, Mr. James George Bogsby. Now do they show (in as many words as possible) how during some hours of yesterday evening a very peculiar smell was observed by the inhabitants of the court, in which the tragical occurrence which forms the subject of that present account transpired; and which odour was at one time so powerful that Mr. Swills, a comic vocalist professionally engaged by Mr. J. G. Bogsby, has himself stated to our reporter that he mentioned to Miss M. Melvilleson, a lady of some pretensions to musical ability, likewise engaged by Mr. J. G. Bogsby to sing at a series of concerts called Harmonic Assemblies, or Meetings, which it would appear are held at the Sol's Arms under Mr. Bogsby's direction pursuant to the Act of George the Second, that he (Mr. Swills) found his voice seriously affected by the impure state of the atmosphere, his jocose expression at the time being that he was like an empty post-office, for he hadn't a single note in him. How this account of Mr. Swills is entirely corroborated by two intelligent married females residing in the same court and known respectively by the names of Mrs. Piper and Mrs. Perkins, both of whom observed the foetid effluvia and regarded them as being emitted from the premises in the occupation of Krook, the unfortunate deceased. All this and a great deal more the two gentlemen who have formed an amicable partnership in the melancholy catastrophe write down on the spot; and the boy population of the court (out of bed in a moment) swarm up the shutters of the Sol's Arms parlour, to behold the tops of their heads while they are about it.

The whole court, adult as well as boy, is sleepless for that night, and can do nothing but wrap up its many heads, and talk of the ill-fated house, and look at it. Miss Flite has been bravely rescued from her chamber, as if it were in flames, and accommodated with a bed at the Sol's Arms. The Sol neither turns off its gas nor shuts its door all night, for any kind of public excitement makes good for the Sol and causes the court to stand in need of comfort. The house has not done so much in the stomachic article of cloves or in brandy-and-water warm since the inquest. The moment the pot-boy heard what had happened, he rolled up his shirt-sleeves tight to his shoulders and said, "There'll be a run upon us!" In the first outcry, young Piper dashed off for the fire-engines and returned in triumph at a jolting gallop perched up aloft on the Phoenix and holding on to that fabulous creature with all his might in the midst of helmets and torches. One helmet remains behind after careful investigation of all chinks and crannies and slowly paces up and down before the house in company with one of the two policemen who have likewise been left in charge thereof. To this trio everybody in the court possessed of sixpence has an insatiate desire to exhibit hospitality in a liquid form.

Mr. Weevle and his friend Mr. Guppy are within the bar at the Sol and are worth anything to the Sol that the bar contains if they will only stay there. "This is not a time," says Mr. Bogsby, "to haggle about money," though he looks something sharply after it, over the counter; "give your orders, you two gentlemen, and you're welcome to whatever you put a name to."

Thus entreated, the two gentlemen (Mr. Weevle especially) put names to so many things that in course of time they find it difficult to put a name to anything quite distinctly, though they still relate to all new-comers some version of the night they have had of it, and of what they said, and what they thought, and what they saw. Meanwhile, one or other of the policemen often flits about the door, and pushing it open a little way at the full length of his arm, looks in from outer gloom. Not that he has any suspicions, but that he may as well know what they are up to in there.

Thus night pursues its leaden course, finding the court still out of bed through the unwonted hours, still treating and being treated, still conducting itself similarly to a court that has had a little money left it unexpectedly. Thus night at length with slow-retreating steps departs, and the lamp-lighter going his rounds, like an executioner to a despotic king, strikes off the little heads of fire that have aspired to lessen the darkness. Thus the day cometh, whether or no.

And the day may discern, even with its dim London eye, that the court has been up all night. Over and above the faces that have fallen drowsily on tables and the heels that lie prone on hard floors instead of beds, the brick and mortar physiognomy of the very court itself looks worn and jaded. And now the neighbourhood, waking up and beginning to hear of what has happened, comes streaming in, half dressed, to ask questions; and the two policemen and the helmet (who are far less impressible externally than the court) have enough to do to keep the door.

"Good gracious, gentlemen!" says Mr. Snagsby, coming up. "What's this I hear!"

"Why, it's true," returns one of the policemen. "That's what it is. Now move on here, come!"

"Why, good gracious, gentlemen," says Mr. Snagsby, somewhat promptly backed away, "I was at this door last night betwixt ten and eleven o'clock in conversation with the young man who lodges here."

"Indeed?" returns the policeman. "You will find the young man next door then. Now move on here, some of you."

"Not hurt, I hope?" says Mr. Snagsby.

"Hurt? No. What's to hurt him!"

Mr. Snagsby, wholly unable to answer this or any question in his troubled mind, repairs to the Sol's Arms and finds Mr. Weevle languishing over tea and toast with a considerable expression on him of exhausted excitement and exhausted tobacco-smoke.

"And Mr. Guppy likewise!" quoth Mr. Snagsby. "Dear, dear, dear! What a fate there seems in all this! And my lit—"

Mr. Snagsby's power of speech deserts him in the formation of the words "my little woman." For to see that injured female walk into the Sol's Arms at that hour of the morning and stand before the beer-engine, with her eyes fixed upon him like an accusing spirit, strikes him dumb.

"My dear," says Mr. Snagsby when his tongue is loosened, "will you take anything? A little—not to put too fine a point upon it—drop of shrub?"

"No," says Mrs. Snagsby.

"My love, you know these two gentlemen?"

"Yes!" says Mrs. Snagsby, and in a rigid manner acknowledges their presence, still fixing Mr. Snagsby with her eye.

The devoted Mr. Snagsby cannot bear this treatment. He takes Mrs. Snagsby by the hand and leads her aside to an adjacent cask.

"My little woman, why do you look at me in that way? Pray don't do it."

"I can't help my looks," says Mrs. Snagsby, "and if I could I wouldn't."

Mr. Snagsby, with his cough of meekness, rejoins, "Wouldn't you really, my dear?" and meditates. Then coughs his cough of trouble and says, "This is a dreadful mystery, my love!" still fearfully disconcerted by Mrs. Snagsby's eye.

"It IS," returns Mrs. Snagsby, shaking her head, "a dreadful mystery."

"My little woman," urges Mr. Snagsby in a piteous manner, "don't for goodness' sake speak to me with that bitter expression and look at me in that searching way! I beg and entreat of you not to do it. Good Lord, you don't suppose that I would go spontaneously combusting any person, my dear?"

"I can't say," returns Mrs. Snagsby.

On a hasty review of his unfortunate position, Mr. Snagsby "can't say" either. He is not prepared positively to deny that he may have had something to do with it. He has had something—he don't know what—to do with so much in this connexion that is mysterious that it is possible he may even be implicated, without knowing it, in the present transaction. He faintly wipes his forehead with his handkerchief and gasps.

"My life," says the unhappy stationer, "would you have any objections to mention why, being in general so delicately circumspect in your conduct, you come into a wine-vaults before breakfast?"

"Why do YOU come here?" inquires Mrs. Snagsby.

"My dear, merely to know the rights of the fatal accident which has happened to the venerable party who has been—combusted." Mr. Snagsby has made a pause to suppress a groan. "I should then have related them to you, my love, over your French roll."

"I dare say you would! You relate everything to me, Mr. Snagsby."

"Every—my lit—"

"I should be glad," says Mrs. Snagsby after contemplating his increased confusion with a severe and sinister smile, "if you would come home with me; I think you may be safer there, Mr. Snagsby, than anywhere else."

"My love, I don't know but what I may be, I am sure. I am ready to go."

Mr. Snagsby casts his eye forlornly round the bar, gives Messrs. Weevle and Guppy good morning, assures them of the satisfaction with which he sees them uninjured, and accompanies Mrs. Snagsby from the Sol's Arms. Before night his doubt whether he may not be responsible for some inconceivable part in the catastrophe which is the talk of the whole neighbourhood is almost resolved into certainty by Mrs. Snagsby's pertinacity in that fixed gaze. His mental sufferings are so great that he entertains wandering ideas of delivering himself up to justice and requiring to be cleared if innocent and punished with the utmost rigour of the law if guilty.

Mr. Weevle and Mr. Guppy, having taken their breakfast, step into Lincoln's Inn to take a little walk about the square and clear as many of the dark cobwebs out of their brains as a little walk may.

"There can be no more favourable time than the present, Tony," says Mr. Guppy after they have broodingly made out the four sides of the square, "for a word or two between us upon a point on which we must, with very little delay, come to an understanding."

"Now, I tell you what, William G.!" returns the other, eyeing his companion with a bloodshot eye. "If it's a point of conspiracy, you needn't take the trouble to mention it. I have had enough of that, and I ain't going to have any more. We shall have YOU taking fire next or blowing up with a bang."

This supposititious phenomenon is so very disagreeable to Mr. Guppy that his voice quakes as he says in a moral way, "Tony, I should have thought that what we went through last night would have been a lesson to you never to be personal any more as long as you lived." To which Mr. Weevle returns, "William, I should have thought it would have been a lesson to YOU never to conspire any more as long as you lived." To which Mr. Guppy says, "Who's conspiring?" To which Mr. Jobling replies, "Why, YOU are!" To which Mr. Guppy retorts, "No, I am not." To which Mr. Jobling retorts again, "Yes, you are!" To which Mr. Guppy retorts, "Who says so?" To which Mr. Jobling retorts, "I say so!" To which Mr. Guppy retorts, "Oh, indeed?" To which Mr. Jobling retorts, "Yes, indeed!" And both being now in a heated state, they walk on silently for a while to cool down again.

"Tony," says Mr. Guppy then, "if you heard your friend out instead of flying at him, you wouldn't fall into mistakes. But your temper is hasty and you are not considerate. Possessing in yourself, Tony, all that is calculated to charm the eye—"

"Oh! Blow the eye!" cries Mr. Weevle, cutting him short. "Say what you have got to say!"

Finding his friend in this morose and material condition, Mr. Guppy only expresses the finer feelings of his soul through the tone of injury in which he recommences, "Tony, when I say there is a point on which we must come to an understanding pretty soon, I say so quite apart from any kind of conspiring, however innocent. You know it is professionally arranged beforehand in all cases that are tried what facts the witnesses are to prove. Is it or is it not desirable that we should know what facts we are to prove on the inquiry into the death of this unfortunate old mo—gentleman?" (Mr. Guppy was going to say "mogul," but thinks "gentleman" better suited to the circumstances.)

"What facts? THE facts."

"The facts bearing on that inquiry. Those are"—Mr. Guppy tells them off on his fingers—"what we knew of his habits, when you saw him last, what his condition was then, the discovery that we made, and how we made it."

"Yes," says Mr. Weevle. "Those are about the facts."

"We made the discovery in consequence of his having, in his eccentric way, an appointment with you at twelve o'clock at night, when you were to explain some writing to him as you had often done before on account of his not being able to read. I, spending the evening with you, was called down—and so forth. The inquiry being only into the circumstances touching the death of the deceased, it's not necessary to go beyond these facts, I suppose you'll agree?"

"No!" returns Mr. Weevle. "I suppose not."

"And this is not a conspiracy, perhaps?" says the injured Guppy.

"No," returns his friend; "if it's nothing worse than this, I withdraw the observation."

"Now, Tony," says Mr. Guppy, taking his arm again and walking him slowly on, "I should like to know, in a friendly way, whether you have yet thought over the many advantages of your continuing to live at that place?"

"What do you mean?" says Tony, stopping.

"Whether you have yet thought over the many advantages of your continuing to live at that place?" repeats Mr. Guppy, walking him on again.

"At what place? THAT place?" pointing in the direction of the rag and bottle shop.

Mr. Guppy nods.

"Why, I wouldn't pass another night there for any consideration that you could offer me," says Mr. Weevle, haggardly staring.

"Do you mean it though, Tony?"

"Mean it! Do I look as if I mean it? I feel as if I do; I know that," says Mr. Weevle with a very genuine shudder.

"Then the possibility or probability—for such it must be considered—of your never being disturbed in possession of those effects lately belonging to a lone old man who seemed to have no relation in the world, and the certainty of your being able to find out what he really had got stored up there, don't weigh with you at all against last night, Tony, if I understand you?" says Mr. Guppy, biting his thumb with the appetite of vexation.

"Certainly not. Talk in that cool way of a fellow's living there?" cries Mr. Weevle indignantly. "Go and live there yourself."

"Oh! I, Tony!" says Mr. Guppy, soothing him. "I have never lived there and couldn't get a lodging there now, whereas you have got one."

"You are welcome to it," rejoins his friend, "and—ugh!—you may make yourself at home in it."

"Then you really and truly at this point," says Mr. Guppy, "give up the whole thing, if I understand you, Tony?"

"You never," returns Tony with a most convincing steadfastness, "said a truer word in all your life. I do!"

While they are so conversing, a hackney-coach drives into the square, on the box of which vehicle a very tall hat makes itself manifest to the public. Inside the coach, and consequently not so manifest to the multitude, though sufficiently so to the two friends, for the coach stops almost at their feet, are the venerable Mr. Smallweed and Mrs. Smallweed, accompanied by their granddaughter Judy.

An air of haste and excitement pervades the party, and as the tall hat (surmounting Mr. Smallweed the younger) alights, Mr. Smallweed the elder pokes his head out of window and bawls to Mr. Guppy, "How de do, sir! How de do!"

"What do Chick and his family want here at this time of the morning, I wonder!" says Mr. Guppy, nodding to his familiar.

"My dear sir," cries Grandfather Smallweed, "would you do me a favour? Would you and your friend be so very obleeging as to carry me into the public-house in the court, while Bart and his sister bring their grandmother along? Would you do an old man that good turn, sir?"

Mr. Guppy looks at his friend, repeating inquiringly, "The public-house in the court?" And they prepare to bear the venerable burden to the Sol's Arms.

"There's your fare!" says the patriarch to the coachman with a fierce grin and shaking his incapable fist at him. "Ask me for a penny more, and I'll have my lawful revenge upon you. My dear young men, be easy with me, if you please. Allow me to catch you round the neck. I won't squeeze you tighter than I can help. Oh, Lord! Oh, dear me! Oh, my bones!"

It is well that the Sol is not far off, for Mr. Weevle presents an apoplectic appearance before half the distance is accomplished. With no worse aggravation of his symptoms, however, than the utterance of divers croaking sounds expressive of obstructed respiration, he fulfils his share of the porterage and the benevolent old gentleman is deposited by his own desire in the parlour of the Sol's Arms.

"Oh, Lord!" gasps Mr. Smallweed, looking about him, breathless, from an arm-chair. "Oh, dear me! Oh, my bones and back! Oh, my aches and pains! Sit down, you dancing, prancing, shambling, scrambling poll-parrot! Sit down!"

This little apostrophe to Mrs. Smallweed is occasioned by a propensity on the part of that unlucky old lady whenever she finds herself on her feet to amble about and "set" to inanimate objects, accompanying herself with a chattering noise, as in a witch dance. A nervous affection has probably as much to do with these demonstrations as any imbecile intention in the poor old woman, but on the present occasion they are so particularly lively in connexion with the Windsor arm-chair, fellow to that in which Mr. Smallweed is seated, that she only quite desists when her grandchildren have held her down in it, her lord in the meanwhile bestowing upon her, with great volubility, the endearing epithet of "a pig-headed jackdaw," repeated a surprising number of times.

"My dear sir," Grandfather Smallweed then proceeds, addressing Mr. Guppy, "there has been a calamity here. Have you heard of it, either of you?"

"Heard of it, sir! Why, we discovered it."

"You discovered it. You two discovered it! Bart, THEY discovered it!"

The two discoverers stare at the Smallweeds, who return the compliment.

"My dear friends," whines Grandfather Smallweed, putting out both his hands, "I owe you a thousand thanks for discharging the melancholy office of discovering the ashes of Mrs. Smallweed's brother."

"Eh?" says Mr. Guppy.

"Mrs. Smallweed's brother, my dear friend—her only relation. We were not on terms, which is to be deplored now, but he never WOULD be on terms. He was not fond of us. He was eccentric—he was very eccentric. Unless he has left a will (which is not at all likely) I shall take out letters of administration. I have come down to look after the property; it must be sealed up, it must be protected. I have come down," repeats Grandfather Smallweed, hooking the air towards him with all his ten fingers at once, "to look after the property."

"I think, Small," says the disconsolate Mr. Guppy, "you might have mentioned that the old man was your uncle."

"You two were so close about him that I thought you would like me to be the same," returns that old bird with a secretly glistening eye. "Besides, I wasn't proud of him."

"Besides which, it was nothing to you, you know, whether he was or not," says Judy. Also with a secretly glistening eye.

"He never saw me in his life to know me," observed Small; "I don't know why I should introduce HIM, I am sure!"

"No, he never communicated with us, which is to be deplored," the old gentleman strikes in, "but I have come to look after the property—to look over the papers, and to look after the property. We shall make good our title. It is in the hands of my solicitor. Mr. Tulkinghorn, of Lincoln's Inn Fields, over the way there, is so good as to act as my solicitor; and grass don't grow under HIS feet, I can tell ye. Krook was Mrs. Smallweed's only brother; she had no relation but Krook, and Krook had no relation but Mrs. Smallweed. I am speaking of your brother, you brimstone black-beetle, that was seventy-six years of age."

Mrs. Smallweed instantly begins to shake her head and pipe up, "Seventy-six pound seven and sevenpence! Seventy-six thousand bags of money! Seventy-six hundred thousand million of parcels of bank-notes!"

"Will somebody give me a quart pot?" exclaims her exasperated husband, looking helplessly about him and finding no missile within his reach. "Will somebody obleege me with a spittoon? Will somebody hand me anything hard and bruising to pelt at her? You hag, you cat, you dog, you brimstone barker!" Here Mr. Smallweed, wrought up to the highest pitch by his own eloquence, actually throws Judy at her grandmother in default of anything else, by butting that young virgin at the old lady with such force as he can muster and then dropping into his chair in a heap.

"Shake me up, somebody, if you'll be so good," says the voice from within the faintly struggling bundle into which he has collapsed. "I have come to look after the property. Shake me up, and call in the police on duty at the next house to be explained to about the property. My solicitor will be here presently to protect the property. Transportation or the gallows for anybody who shall touch the property!" As his dutiful grandchildren set him up, panting, and putting him through the usual restorative process of shaking and punching, he still repeats like an echo, "The—the property! The property! Property!"

Mr. Weevle and Mr. Guppy look at each other, the former as having relinquished the whole affair, the latter with a discomfited countenance as having entertained some lingering expectations yet. But there is nothing to be done in opposition to the Smallweed interest. Mr. Tulkinghorn's clerk comes down from his official pew in the chambers to mention to the police that Mr. Tulkinghorn is answerable for its being all correct about the next of kin and that the papers and effects will be formally taken possession of in due time and course. Mr. Smallweed is at once permitted so far to assert his supremacy as to be carried on a visit of sentiment into the next house and upstairs into Miss Flite's deserted room, where he looks like a hideous bird of prey newly added to her aviary.

The arrival of this unexpected heir soon taking wind in the court still makes good for the Sol and keeps the court upon its mettle. Mrs. Piper and Mrs. Perkins think it hard upon the young man if there really is no will, and consider that a handsome present ought to be made him out of the estate. Young Piper and young Perkins, as members of that restless juvenile circle which is the terror of the foot-passengers in Chancery Lane, crumble into ashes behind the pump and under the archway all day long, where wild yells and hootings take place over their remains. Little Swills and Miss M. Melvilleson enter into affable conversation with their patrons, feeling that these unusual occurrences level the barriers between professionals and non-professionals. Mr. Bogsby puts up "The popular song of King Death, with chorus by the whole strength of the company," as the great Harmonic feature of the week and announces in the bill that "J. G. B. is induced to do so at a considerable extra expense in consequence of a wish which has been very generally expressed at the bar by a large body of respectable individuals and in homage to a late melancholy event which has aroused so much sensation." There is one point connected with the deceased upon which the court is particularly anxious, namely, that the fiction of a full-sized coffin should be preserved, though there is so little to put in it. Upon the undertaker's stating in the Sol's bar in the course of the day that he has received orders to construct "a six-footer," the general solicitude is much relieved, and it is considered that Mr. Smallweed's conduct does him great honour.

Out of the court, and a long way out of it, there is considerable excitement too, for men of science and philosophy come to look, and carriages set down doctors at the corner who arrive with the same intent, and there is more learned talk about inflammable gases and phosphuretted hydrogen than the court has ever imagined. Some of these authorities (of course the wisest) hold with indignation that the deceased had no business to die in the alleged manner; and being reminded by other authorities of a certain inquiry into the evidence for such deaths reprinted in the sixth volume of the Philosophical Transactions; and also of a book not quite unknown on English medical jurisprudence; and likewise of the Italian case of the Countess Cornelia Baudi as set forth in detail by one Bianchini, prebendary of Verona, who wrote a scholarly work or so and was occasionally heard of in his time as having gleams of reason in him; and also of the testimony of Messrs. Fodere and Mere, two pestilent Frenchmen who WOULD investigate the subject; and further, of the corroborative testimony of Monsieur Le Cat, a rather celebrated French surgeon once upon a time, who had the unpoliteness to live in a house where such a case occurred and even to write an account of it—still they regard the late Mr. Krook's obstinacy in going out of the world by any such by-way as wholly unjustifiable and personally offensive. The less the court understands of all this, the more the court likes it, and the greater enjoyment it has in the stock in trade of the Sol's Arms. Then there comes the artist of a picture newspaper, with a foreground and figures ready drawn for anything from a wreck on the Cornish coast to a review in Hyde Park or a meeting in Manchester, and in Mrs. Perkins' own room, memorable evermore, he then and there throws in upon the block Mr. Krook's house, as large as life; in fact, considerably larger, making a very temple of it. Similarly, being permitted to look in at the door of the fatal chamber, he depicts that apartment as three-quarters of a mile long by fifty yards high, at which the court is particularly charmed. All this time the two gentlemen before mentioned pop in and out of every house and assist at the philosophical disputations—go everywhere and listen to everybody—and yet are always diving into the Sol's parlour and writing with the ravenous little pens on the tissue-paper.

At last come the coroner and his inquiry, like as before, except that the coroner cherishes this case as being out of the common way and tells the gentlemen of the jury, in his private capacity, that "that would seem to be an unlucky house next door, gentlemen, a destined house; but so we sometimes find it, and these are mysteries we can't account for!" After which the six-footer comes into action and is much admired.

In all these proceedings Mr. Guppy has so slight a part, except when he gives his evidence, that he is moved on like a private individual and can only haunt the secret house on the outside, where he has the mortification of seeing Mr. Smallweed padlocking the door, and of bitterly knowing himself to be shut out. But before these proceedings draw to a close, that is to say, on the night next after the catastrophe, Mr. Guppy has a thing to say that must be said to Lady Dedlock.

For which reason, with a sinking heart and with that hang-dog sense of guilt upon him which dread and watching enfolded in the Sol's Arms have produced, the young man of the name of Guppy presents himself at the town mansion at about seven o'clock in the evening and requests to see her ladyship. Mercury replies that she is going out to dinner; don't he see the carriage at the door? Yes, he does see the carriage at the door; but he wants to see my Lady too.

Mercury is disposed, as he will presently declare to a fellow-gentleman in waiting, "to pitch into the young man"; but his instructions are positive. Therefore he sulkily supposes that the young man must come up into the library. There he leaves the young man in a large room, not over-light, while he makes report of him.

Mr. Guppy looks into the shade in all directions, discovering everywhere a certain charred and whitened little heap of coal or wood. Presently he hears a rustling. Is it—? No, it's no ghost, but fair flesh and blood, most brilliantly dressed.

"I have to beg your ladyship's pardon," Mr. Guppy stammers, very downcast. "This is an inconvenient time—"

"I told you, you could come at any time." She takes a chair, looking straight at him as on the last occasion.

"Thank your ladyship. Your ladyship is very affable."

"You can sit down." There is not much affability in her tone.

"I don't know, your ladyship, that it's worth while my sitting down and detaining you, for I—I have not got the letters that I mentioned when I had the honour of waiting on your ladyship."

"Have you come merely to say so?"

"Merely to say so, your ladyship." Mr. Guppy besides being depressed, disappointed, and uneasy, is put at a further disadvantage by the splendour and beauty of her appearance.

She knows its influence perfectly, has studied it too well to miss a grain of its effect on any one. As she looks at him so steadily and coldly, he not only feels conscious that he has no guide in the least perception of what is really the complexion of her thoughts, but also that he is being every moment, as it were, removed further and further from her.

She will not speak, it is plain. So he must.

"In short, your ladyship," says Mr. Guppy like a meanly penitent thief, "the person I was to have had the letters of, has come to a sudden end, and—" He stops. Lady Dedlock calmly finishes the sentence.

"And the letters are destroyed with the person?"

Mr. Guppy would say no if he could—as he is unable to hide.

"I believe so, your ladyship."

If he could see the least sparkle of relief in her face now? No, he could see no such thing, even if that brave outside did not utterly put him away, and he were not looking beyond it and about it.

He falters an awkward excuse or two for his failure.

"Is this all you have to say?" inquires Lady Dedlock, having heard him out—or as nearly out as he can stumble.

Mr. Guppy thinks that's all.

"You had better be sure that you wish to say nothing more to me, this being the last time you will have the opportunity."

Mr. Guppy is quite sure. And indeed he has no such wish at present, by any means.

"That is enough. I will dispense with excuses. Good evening to you!" And she rings for Mercury to show the young man of the name of Guppy out.

But in that house, in that same moment, there happens to be an old man of the name of Tulkinghorn. And that old man, coming with his quiet footstep to the library, has his hand at that moment on the handle of the door—comes in—and comes face to face with the young man as he is leaving the room.

One glance between the old man and the lady, and for an instant the blind that is always down flies up. Suspicion, eager and sharp, looks out. Another instant, close again.

"I beg your pardon, Lady Dedlock. I beg your pardon a thousand times. It is so very unusual to find you here at this hour. I supposed the room was empty. I beg your pardon!"

"Stay!" She negligently calls him back. "Remain here, I beg. I am going out to dinner. I have nothing more to say to this young man!"

The disconcerted young man bows, as he goes out, and cringingly hopes that Mr. Tulkinghorn of the Fields is well.

"Aye, aye?" says the lawyer, looking at him from under his bent brows, though he has no need to look again—not he. "From Kenge and Carboy's, surely?"

"Kenge and Carboy's, Mr. Tulkinghorn. Name of Guppy, sir."

"To be sure. Why, thank you, Mr. Guppy, I am very well!"

"Happy to hear it, sir. You can't be too well, sir, for the credit of the profession."

"Thank you, Mr. Guppy!"

Mr. Guppy sneaks away. Mr. Tulkinghorn, such a foil in his old-fashioned rusty black to Lady Dedlock's brightness, hands her down the staircase to her carriage. He returns rubbing his chin, and rubs it a good deal in the course of the evening.

CHAPTER XXXIV
A TURN OF THE SCREW

"Now, what," says Mr. George, "may this be? Is it blank cartridge or ball? A flash in the pan or a shot?"

An open letter is the subject of the trooper's speculations, and it seems to perplex him mightily. He looks at it at arm's length, brings it close to him, holds it in his right hand, holds it in his left hand, reads it with his head on this side, with his head on that side, contracts his eyebrows, elevates them, still cannot satisfy himself. He smooths it out upon the table with his heavy palm, and thoughtfully walking up and down the gallery, makes a halt before it every now and then to come upon it with a fresh eye. Even that won't do. "Is it," Mr. George still muses, "blank cartridge or ball?"

Phil Squod, with the aid of a brush and paint-pot, is employed in the distance whitening the targets, softly whistling in quick-march time and in drum-and-fife manner that he must and will go back again to the girl he left behind him.

"Phil!" The trooper beckons as he calls him.

Phil approaches in his usual way, sidling off at first as if he were going anywhere else and then bearing down upon his commander like a bayonet-charge. Certain splashes of white show in high relief upon his dirty face, and he scrapes his one eyebrow with the handle of the brush.

"Attention, Phil! Listen to this."

"Steady, commander, steady."

"'Sir. Allow me to remind you (though there is no legal necessity for my doing so, as you are aware) that the bill at two months' date drawn on yourself by Mr. Matthew Bagnet, and by you accepted, for the sum of ninety-seven pounds four shillings and ninepence, will become due to-morrow, when you will please be prepared to take up the same on presentation. Yours, Joshua Smallweed.' What do you make of that, Phil?"

"Mischief, guv'ner."

"Why?"

"I think," replies Phil after pensively tracing out a cross-wrinkle in his forehead with the brush-handle, "that mischeevious consequences is always meant when money's asked for."

"Lookye, Phil," says the trooper, sitting on the table. "First and last, I have paid, I may say, half as much again as this principal in interest and one thing and another."

Phil intimates by sidling back a pace or two, with a very unaccountable wrench of his wry face, that he does not regard the transaction as being made more promising by this incident.

"And lookye further, Phil," says the trooper, staying his premature conclusions with a wave of his hand. "There has always been an understanding that this bill was to be what they call renewed. And it has been renewed no end of times. What do you say now?"

"I say that I think the times is come to a end at last."

"You do? Humph! I am much of the same mind myself."

"Joshua Smallweed is him that was brought here in a chair?"

"The same."

"Guv'ner," says Phil with exceeding gravity, "he's a leech in his dispositions, he's a screw and a wice in his actions, a snake in his twistings, and a lobster in his claws."

Having thus expressively uttered his sentiments, Mr. Squod, after waiting a little to ascertain if any further remark be expected of him, gets back by his usual series of movements to the target he has in hand and vigorously signifies through his former musical medium that he must and he will return to that ideal young lady. George, having folded the letter, walks in that direction.

"There IS a way, commander," says Phil, looking cunningly at him, "of settling this."

"Paying the money, I suppose? I wish I could."

Phil shakes his head. "No, guv'ner, no; not so bad as that. There IS a way," says Phil with a highly artistic turn of his brush; "what I'm a-doing at present."

"Whitewashing."

Phil nods.

"A pretty way that would be! Do you know what would become of the Bagnets in that case? Do you know they would be ruined to pay off my old scores? YOU'RE a moral character," says the trooper, eyeing him in his large way with no small indignation; "upon my life you are, Phil!"

Phil, on one knee at the target, is in course of protesting earnestly, though not without many allegorical scoops of his brush and smoothings of the white surface round the rim with his thumb, that he had forgotten the Bagnet responsibility and would not so much as injure a hair of the head of any member of that worthy family when steps are audible in the long passage without, and a cheerful voice is heard to wonder whether George is at home. Phil, with a look at his master, hobbles up, saying, "Here's the guv'ner, Mrs. Bagnet! Here he is!" and the old girl herself, accompanied by Mr. Bagnet, appears.

The old girl never appears in walking trim, in any season of the year, without a grey cloth cloak, coarse and much worn but very clean, which is, undoubtedly, the identical garment rendered so interesting to Mr. Bagnet by having made its way home to Europe from another quarter of the globe in company with Mrs. Bagnet and an umbrella. The latter faithful appendage is also invariably a part of the old girl's presence out of doors. It is of no colour known in this life and has a corrugated wooden crook for a handle, with a metallic object let into its prow, or beak, resembling a little model of a fanlight over a street door or one of the oval glasses out of a pair of spectacles, which ornamental object has not that tenacious capacity of sticking to its post that might be desired in an article long associated with the British army. The old girl's umbrella is of a flabby habit of waist and seems to be in need of stays—an appearance that is possibly referable to its having served through a series of years at home as a cupboard and on journeys as a carpet bag. She never puts it up, having the greatest reliance on her well-proved cloak with its capacious hood, but generally uses the instrument as a wand with which to point out joints of meat or bunches of greens in marketing or to arrest the attention of tradesmen by a friendly poke. Without her market-basket, which is a sort of wicker well with two flapping lids, she never stirs abroad. Attended by these her trusty companions, therefore, her honest sunburnt face looking cheerily out of a rough straw bonnet, Mrs. Bagnet now arrives, fresh-coloured and bright, in George's Shooting Gallery.

"Well, George, old fellow," says she, "and how do YOU do, this sunshiny morning?"

Giving him a friendly shake of the hand, Mrs. Bagnet draws a long breath after her walk and sits down to enjoy a rest. Having a faculty, matured on the tops of baggage-waggons and in other such positions, of resting easily anywhere, she perches on a rough bench, unties her bonnet-strings, pushes back her bonnet, crosses her arms, and looks perfectly comfortable.

Mr. Bagnet in the meantime has shaken hands with his old comrade and with Phil, on whom Mrs. Bagnet likewise bestows a good-humoured nod and smile.

"Now, George," said Mrs. Bagnet briskly, "here we are, Lignum and myself"—she often speaks of her husband by this appellation, on account, as it is supposed, of Lignum Vitae having been his old regimental nickname when they first became acquainted, in compliment to the extreme hardness and toughness of his physiognomy—"just looked in, we have, to make it all correct as usual about that security. Give him the new bill to sign, George, and he'll sign it like a man."

"I was coming to you this morning," observes the trooper reluctantly.

"Yes, we thought you'd come to us this morning, but we turned out early and left Woolwich, the best of boys, to mind his sisters and came to you instead—as you see! For Lignum, he's tied so close now, and gets so little exercise, that a walk does him good. But what's the matter, George?" asks Mrs. Bagnet, stopping in her cheerful talk. "You don't look yourself."

"I am not quite myself," returns the trooper; "I have been a little put out, Mrs. Bagnet."

Her bright quick eye catches the truth directly. "George!" holding up her forefinger. "Don't tell me there's anything wrong about that security of Lignum's! Don't do it, George, on account of the children!"

The trooper looks at her with a troubled visage.

"George," says Mrs. Bagnet, using both her arms for emphasis and occasionally bringing down her open hands upon her knees. "If you have allowed anything wrong to come to that security of Lignum's, and if you have let him in for it, and if you have put us in danger of being sold up—and I see sold up in your face, George, as plain as print—you have done a shameful action and have deceived us cruelly. I tell you, cruelly, George. There!"

Mr. Bagnet, otherwise as immovable as a pump or a lamp-post, puts his large right hand on the top of his bald head as if to defend it from a shower-bath and looks with great uneasiness at Mrs. Bagnet.

"George," says that old girl, "I wonder at you! George, I am ashamed of you! George, I couldn't have believed you would have done it! I always knew you to be a rolling stone that gathered no moss, but I never thought you would have taken away what little moss there was for Bagnet and the children to lie upon. You know what a hard-working, steady-going chap he is. You know what Quebec and Malta and Woolwich are, and I never did think you would, or could, have had the heart to serve us so. Oh, George!" Mrs. Bagnet gathers up her cloak to wipe her eyes on in a very genuine manner, "How could you do it?"

Mrs. Bagnet ceasing, Mr. Bagnet removes his hand from his head as if the shower-bath were over and looks disconsolately at Mr. George, who has turned quite white and looks distressfully at the grey cloak and straw bonnet.

"Mat," says the trooper in a subdued voice, addressing him but still looking at his wife, "I am sorry you take it so much to heart, because I do hope it's not so bad as that comes to. I certainly have, this morning, received this letter"—which he reads aloud—"but I hope it may be set right yet. As to a rolling stone, why, what you say is true. I AM a rolling stone, and I never rolled in anybody's way, I fully believe, that I rolled the least good to. But it's impossible for an old vagabond comrade to like your wife and family better than I like 'em, Mat, and I trust you'll look upon me as forgivingly as you can. Don't think I've kept anything from you. I haven't had the letter more than a quarter of an hour."

"Old girl," murmurs Mr. Bagnet after a short silence, "will you tell him my opinion?"

"Oh! Why didn't he marry," Mrs. Bagnet answers, half laughing and half crying, "Joe Pouch's widder in North America? Then he wouldn't have got himself into these troubles."

"The old girl," says Mr. Bagnet, "puts it correct—why didn't you?"

"Well, she has a better husband by this time, I hope," returns the trooper. "Anyhow, here I stand, this present day, NOT married to Joe Pouch's widder. What shall I do? You see all I have got about me. It's not mine; it's yours. Give the word, and I'll sell off every morsel. If I could have hoped it would have brought in nearly the sum wanted, I'd have sold all long ago. Don't believe that I'll leave you or yours in the lurch, Mat. I'd sell myself first. I only wish," says the trooper, giving himself a disparaging blow in the chest, "that I knew of any one who'd buy such a second-hand piece of old stores."

"Old girl," murmurs Mr. Bagnet, "give him another bit of my mind."

"George," says the old girl, "you are not so much to be blamed, on full consideration, except for ever taking this business without the means."

"And that was like me!" observes the penitent trooper, shaking his head. "Like me, I know."

"Silence! The old girl," says Mr. Bagnet, "is correct—in her way of giving my opinions—hear me out!"

"That was when you never ought to have asked for the security, George, and when you never ought to have got it, all things considered. But what's done can't be undone. You are always an honourable and straightforward fellow, as far as lays in your power, though a little flighty. On the other hand, you can't admit but what it's natural in us to be anxious with such a thing hanging over our heads. So forget and forgive all round, George. Come! Forget and forgive all round!"

Mrs. Bagnet, giving him one of her honest hands and giving her husband the other, Mr. George gives each of them one of his and holds them while he speaks.

"I do assure you both, there's nothing I wouldn't do to discharge this obligation. But whatever I have been able to scrape together has gone every two months in keeping it up. We have lived plainly enough here, Phil and I. But the gallery don't quite do what was expected of it, and it's not—in short, it's not the mint. It was wrong in me to take it? Well, so it was. But I was in a manner drawn into that step, and I thought it might steady me, and set me up, and you'll try to overlook my having such expectations, and upon my soul, I am very much obliged to you, and very much ashamed of myself." With these concluding words, Mr. George gives a shake to each of the hands he holds, and relinquishing them, backs a pace or two in a broad-chested, upright attitude, as if he had made a final confession and were immediately going to be shot with all military honours.

"George, hear me out!" says Mr. Bagnet, glancing at his wife. "Old girl, go on!"

Mr. Bagnet, being in this singular manner heard out, has merely to observe that the letter must be attended to without any delay, that it is advisable that George and he should immediately wait on Mr. Smallweed in person, and that the primary object is to save and hold harmless Mr. Bagnet, who had none of the money. Mr. George, entirely assenting, puts on his hat and prepares to march with Mr. Bagnet to the enemy's camp.

"Don't you mind a woman's hasty word, George," says Mrs. Bagnet, patting him on the shoulder. "I trust my old Lignum to you, and I am sure you'll bring him through it."

The trooper returns that this is kindly said and that he WILL bring Lignum through it somehow. Upon which Mrs. Bagnet, with her cloak, basket, and umbrella, goes home, bright-eyed again, to the rest of her family, and the comrades sally forth on the hopeful errand of mollifying Mr. Smallweed.

Whether there are two people in England less likely to come satisfactorily out of any negotiation with Mr. Smallweed than Mr. George and Mr. Matthew Bagnet may be very reasonably questioned. Also, notwithstanding their martial appearance, broad square shoulders, and heavy tread, whether there are within the same limits two more simple and unaccustomed children in all the Smallweedy affairs of life. As they proceed with great gravity through the streets towards the region of Mount Pleasant, Mr. Bagnet, observing his companion to be thoughtful, considers it a friendly part to refer to Mrs. Bagnet's late sally.

"George, you know the old girl—she's as sweet and as mild as milk. But touch her on the children—or myself—and she's off like gunpowder."

"It does her credit, Mat!"

"George," says Mr. Bagnet, looking straight before him, "the old girl—can't do anything—that don't do her credit. More or less. I never say so. Discipline must be maintained."

"She's worth her weight in gold," says the trooper.

"In gold?" says Mr. Bagnet. "I'll tell you what. The old girl's weight—is twelve stone six. Would I take that weight—in any metal—for the old girl? No. Why not? Because the old girl's metal is far more precious—than the preciousest metal. And she's ALL metal!"

"You are right, Mat!"

"When she took me—and accepted of the ring—she 'listed under me and the children—heart and head, for life. She's that earnest," says Mr. Bagnet, "and true to her colours—that, touch us with a finger—and she turns out—and stands to her arms. If the old girl fires wide—once in a way—at the call of duty—look over it, George. For she's loyal!"

"Why, bless her, Mat," returns the trooper, "I think the higher of her for it!"

"You are right!" says Mr. Bagnet with the warmest enthusiasm, though without relaxing the rigidity of a single muscle. "Think as high of the old girl—as the rock of Gibraltar—and still you'll be thinking low—of such merits. But I never own to it before her. Discipline must be maintained."

These encomiums bring them to Mount Pleasant and to Grandfather Smallweed's house. The door is opened by the perennial Judy, who, having surveyed them from top to toe with no particular favour, but indeed with a malignant sneer, leaves them standing there while she consults the oracle as to their admission. The oracle may be inferred to give consent from the circumstance of her returning with the words on her honey lips that they can come in if they want to it. Thus privileged, they come in and find Mr. Smallweed with his feet in the drawer of his chair as if it were a paper foot-bath and Mrs. Smallweed obscured with the cushion like a bird that is not to sing.

"My dear friend," says Grandfather Smallweed with those two lean affectionate arms of his stretched forth. "How de do? How de do? Who is our friend, my dear friend?"

"Why this," returns George, not able to be very conciliatory at first, "is Matthew Bagnet, who has obliged me in that matter of ours, you know."

"Oh! Mr. Bagnet? Surely!" The old man looks at him under his hand.

"Hope you're well, Mr. Bagnet? Fine man, Mr. George! Military air, sir!"

No chairs being offered, Mr. George brings one forward for Bagnet and one for himself. They sit down, Mr. Bagnet as if he had no power of bending himself, except at the hips, for that purpose.

"Judy," says Mr. Smallweed, "bring the pipe."

"Why, I don't know," Mr. George interposes, "that the young woman need give herself that trouble, for to tell you the truth, I am not inclined to smoke it to-day."

"Ain't you?" returns the old man. "Judy, bring the pipe."

"The fact is, Mr. Smallweed," proceeds George, "that I find myself in rather an unpleasant state of mind. It appears to me, sir, that your friend in the city has been playing tricks."

"Oh, dear no!" says Grandfather Smallweed. "He never does that!"

"Don't he? Well, I am glad to hear it, because I thought it might be HIS doing. This, you know, I am speaking of. This letter."

Grandfather Smallweed smiles in a very ugly way in recognition of the letter.

"What does it mean?" asks Mr. George.

"Judy," says the old man. "Have you got the pipe? Give it to me. Did you say what does it mean, my good friend?"

"Aye! Now, come, come, you know, Mr. Smallweed," urges the trooper, constraining himself to speak as smoothly and confidentially as he can, holding the open letter in one hand and resting the broad knuckles of the other on his thigh, "a good lot of money has passed between us, and we are face to face at the present moment, and are both well aware of the understanding there has always been. I am prepared to do the usual thing which I have done regularly and to keep this matter going. I never got a letter like this from you before, and I have been a little put about by it this morning, because here's my friend Matthew Bagnet, who, you know, had none of the money—"

"I DON'T know it, you know," says the old man quietly.

"Why, con-found you—it, I mean—I tell you so, don't I?"

"Oh, yes, you tell me so," returns Grandfather Smallweed. "But I don't know it."

"Well!" says the trooper, swallowing his fire. "I know it."

Mr. Smallweed replies with excellent temper, "Ah! That's quite another thing!" And adds, "But it don't matter. Mr. Bagnet's situation is all one, whether or no."

The unfortunate George makes a great effort to arrange the affair comfortably and to propitiate Mr. Smallweed by taking him upon his own terms.

"That's just what I mean. As you say, Mr. Smallweed, here's Matthew Bagnet liable to be fixed whether or no. Now, you see, that makes his good lady very uneasy in her mind, and me too, for whereas I'm a harum-scarum sort of a good-for-nought that more kicks than halfpence come natural to, why he's a steady family man, don't you see? Now, Mr. Smallweed," says the trooper, gaining confidence as he proceeds in his soldierly mode of doing business, "although you and I are good friends enough in a certain sort of a way, I am well aware that I can't ask you to let my friend Bagnet off entirely."

"Oh, dear, you are too modest. You can ASK me anything, Mr. George." (There is an ogreish kind of jocularity in Grandfather Smallweed to-day.)

"And you can refuse, you mean, eh? Or not you so much, perhaps, as your friend in the city? Ha ha ha!"

"Ha ha ha!" echoes Grandfather Smallweed. In such a very hard manner and with eyes so particularly green that Mr. Bagnet's natural gravity is much deepened by the contemplation of that venerable man.

"Come!" says the sanguine George. "I am glad to find we can be pleasant, because I want to arrange this pleasantly. Here's my friend Bagnet, and here am I. We'll settle the matter on the spot, if you please, Mr. Smallweed, in the usual way. And you'll ease my friend Bagnet's mind, and his family's mind, a good deal if you'll just mention to him what our understanding is."

Here some shrill spectre cries out in a mocking manner, "Oh, good gracious! Oh!" Unless, indeed, it be the sportive Judy, who is found to be silent when the startled visitors look round, but whose chin has received a recent toss, expressive of derision and contempt. Mr. Bagnet's gravity becomes yet more profound.

"But I think you asked me, Mr. George"—old Smallweed, who all this time has had the pipe in his hand, is the speaker now—"I think you asked me, what did the letter mean?"

"Why, yes, I did," returns the trooper in his off-hand way, "but I don't care to know particularly, if it's all correct and pleasant."

Mr. Smallweed, purposely balking himself in an aim at the trooper's head, throws the pipe on the ground and breaks it to pieces.

"That's what it means, my dear friend. I'll smash you. I'll crumble you. I'll powder you. Go to the devil!"

The two friends rise and look at one another. Mr. Bagnet's gravity has now attained its profoundest point.

"Go to the devil!" repeats the old man. "I'll have no more of your pipe-smokings and swaggerings. What? You're an independent dragoon, too! Go to my lawyer (you remember where; you have been there before) and show your independence now, will you? Come, my dear friend, there's a chance for you. Open the street door, Judy; put these blusterers out! Call in help if they don't go. Put 'em out!"

He vociferates this so loudly that Mr. Bagnet, laying his hands on the shoulders of his comrade before the latter can recover from his amazement, gets him on the outside of the street door, which is instantly slammed by the triumphant Judy. Utterly confounded, Mr. George awhile stands looking at the knocker. Mr. Bagnet, in a perfect abyss of gravity, walks up and down before the little parlour window like a sentry and looks in every time he passes, apparently revolving something in his mind.

"Come, Mat," says Mr. George when he has recovered himself, "we must try the lawyer. Now, what do you think of this rascal?"

Mr. Bagnet, stopping to take a farewell look into the parlour, replies with one shake of his head directed at the interior, "If my old girl had been here—I'd have told him!" Having so discharged himself of the subject of his cogitations, he falls into step and marches off with the trooper, shoulder to shoulder.

When they present themselves in Lincoln's Inn Fields, Mr. Tulkinghorn is engaged and not to be seen. He is not at all willing to see them, for when they have waited a full hour, and the clerk, on his bell being rung, takes the opportunity of mentioning as much, he brings forth no more encouraging message than that Mr. Tulkinghorn has nothing to say to them and they had better not wait. They do wait, however, with the perseverance of military tactics, and at last the bell rings again and the client in possession comes out of Mr. Tulkinghorn's room.

The client is a handsome old lady, no other than Mrs. Rouncewell, housekeeper at Chesney Wold. She comes out of the sanctuary with a fair old-fashioned curtsy and softly shuts the door. She is treated with some distinction there, for the clerk steps out of his pew to show her through the outer office and to let her out. The old lady is thanking him for his attention when she observes the comrades in waiting.

"I beg your pardon, sir, but I think those gentlemen are military?"

The clerk referring the question to them with his eye, and Mr. George not turning round from the almanac over the fire-place. Mr. Bagnet takes upon himself to reply, "Yes, ma'am. Formerly."

"I thought so. I was sure of it. My heart warms, gentlemen, at the sight of you. It always does at the sight of such. God bless you, gentlemen! You'll excuse an old woman, but I had a son once who went for a soldier. A fine handsome youth he was, and good in his bold way, though some people did disparage him to his poor mother. I ask your pardon for troubling you, sir. God bless you, gentlemen!"

"Same to you, ma'am!" returns Mr. Bagnet with right good will.

There is something very touching in the earnestness of the old lady's voice and in the tremble that goes through her quaint old figure. But Mr. George is so occupied with the almanac over the fire-place (calculating the coming months by it perhaps) that he does not look round until she has gone away and the door is closed upon her.

"George," Mr. Bagnet gruffly whispers when he does turn from the almanac at last. "Don't be cast down! 'Why, soldiers, why—should we be melancholy, boys?' Cheer up, my hearty!"

The clerk having now again gone in to say that they are still there and Mr. Tulkinghorn being heard to return with some irascibility, "Let 'em come in then!" they pass into the great room with the painted ceiling and find him standing before the fire.

"Now, you men, what do you want? Sergeant, I told you the last time I saw you that I don't desire your company here."

Sergeant replies—dashed within the last few minutes as to his usual manner of speech, and even as to his usual carriage—that he has received this letter, has been to Mr. Smallweed about it, and has been referred there.

"I have nothing to say to you," rejoins Mr. Tulkinghorn. "If you get into debt, you must pay your debts or take the consequences. You have no occasion to come here to learn that, I suppose?"

Sergeant is sorry to say that he is not prepared with the money.

"Very well! Then the other man—this man, if this is he—must pay it for you."

Sergeant is sorry to add that the other man is not prepared with the money either.

"Very well! Then you must pay it between you or you must both be sued for it and both suffer. You have had the money and must refund it. You are not to pocket other people's pounds, shillings, and pence and escape scot-free."

The lawyer sits down in his easy-chair and stirs the fire. Mr. George hopes he will have the goodness to—"I tell you, sergeant, I have nothing to say to you. I don't like your associates and don't want you here. This matter is not at all in my course of practice and is not in my office. Mr. Smallweed is good enough to offer these affairs to me, but they are not in my way. You must go to Melchisedech's in Clifford's Inn."

"I must make an apology to you, sir," says Mr. George, "for pressing myself upon you with so little encouragement—which is almost as unpleasant to me as it can be to you—but would you let me say a private word to you?"

Mr. Tulkinghorn rises with his hands in his pockets and walks into one of the window recesses. "Now! I have no time to waste." In the midst of his perfect assumption of indifference, he directs a sharp look at the trooper, taking care to stand with his own back to the light and to have the other with his face towards it.

"Well, sir," says Mr. George, "this man with me is the other party implicated in this unfortunate affair—nominally, only nominally—and my sole object is to prevent his getting into trouble on my account. He is a most respectable man with a wife and family, formerly in the Royal Artillery—"

"My friend, I don't care a pinch of snuff for the whole Royal Artillery establishment—officers, men, tumbrils, waggons, horses, guns, and ammunition."

"'Tis likely, sir. But I care a good deal for Bagnet and his wife and family being injured on my account. And if I could bring them through this matter, I should have no help for it but to give up without any other consideration what you wanted of me the other day."

"Have you got it here?"

"I have got it here, sir."

"Sergeant," the lawyer proceeds in his dry passionless manner, far more hopeless in the dealing with than any amount of vehemence, "make up your mind while I speak to you, for this is final. After I have finished speaking I have closed the subject, and I won't re-open it. Understand that. You can leave here, for a few days, what you say you have brought here if you choose; you can take it away at once if you choose. In case you choose to leave it here, I can do this for you—I can replace this matter on its old footing, and I can go so far besides as to give you a written undertaking that this man Bagnet shall never be troubled in any way until you have been proceeded against to the utmost, that your means shall be exhausted before the creditor looks to his. This is in fact all but freeing him. Have you decided?"

The trooper puts his hand into his breast and answers with a long breath, "I must do it, sir."

So Mr. Tulkinghorn, putting on his spectacles, sits down and writes the undertaking, which he slowly reads and explains to Bagnet, who has all this time been staring at the ceiling and who puts his hand on his bald head again, under this new verbal shower-bath, and seems exceedingly in need of the old girl through whom to express his sentiments. The trooper then takes from his breast-pocket a folded paper, which he lays with an unwilling hand at the lawyer's elbow. "'Tis only a letter of instructions, sir. The last I ever had from him."

Look at a millstone, Mr. George, for some change in its expression, and you will find it quite as soon as in the face of Mr. Tulkinghorn when he opens and reads the letter! He refolds it and lays it in his desk with a countenance as unperturbable as death.

Nor has he anything more to say or do but to nod once in the same frigid and discourteous manner and to say briefly, "You can go. Show these men out, there!" Being shown out, they repair to Mr. Bagnet's residence to dine.

Boiled beef and greens constitute the day's variety on the former repast of boiled pork and greens, and Mrs. Bagnet serves out the meal in the same way and seasons it with the best of temper, being that rare sort of old girl that she receives Good to her arms without a hint that it might be Better and catches light from any little spot of darkness near her. The spot on this occasion is the darkened brow of Mr. George; he is unusually thoughtful and depressed. At first Mrs. Bagnet trusts to the combined endearments of Quebec and Malta to restore him, but finding those young ladies sensible that their existing Bluffy is not the Bluffy of their usual frolicsome acquaintance, she winks off the light infantry and leaves him to deploy at leisure on the open ground of the domestic hearth.

But he does not. He remains in close order, clouded and depressed. During the lengthy cleaning up and pattening process, when he and Mr. Bagnet are supplied with their pipes, he is no better than he was at dinner. He forgets to smoke, looks at the fire and ponders, lets his pipe out, fills the breast of Mr. Bagnet with perturbation and dismay by showing that he has no enjoyment of tobacco.

Therefore when Mrs. Bagnet at last appears, rosy from the invigorating pail, and sits down to her work, Mr. Bagnet growls, "Old girl!" and winks monitions to her to find out what's the matter.

"Why, George!" says Mrs. Bagnet, quietly threading her needle. "How low you are!"

"Am I? Not good company? Well, I am afraid I am not."

"He ain't at all like Bluffy, mother!" cries little Malta.

"Because he ain't well, I think, mother," adds Quebec.

"Sure that's a bad sign not to be like Bluffy, too!" returns the trooper, kissing the young damsels. "But it's true," with a sigh, "true, I am afraid. These little ones are always right!"

"George," says Mrs. Bagnet, working busily, "if I thought you cross enough to think of anything that a shrill old soldier's wife—who could have bitten her tongue off afterwards and ought to have done it almost—said this morning, I don't know what I shouldn't say to you now."

"My kind soul of a darling," returns the trooper. "Not a morsel of it."

"Because really and truly, George, what I said and meant to say was that I trusted Lignum to you and was sure you'd bring him through it. And you HAVE brought him through it, noble!"

"Thankee, my dear!" says George. "I am glad of your good opinion."

In giving Mrs. Bagnet's hand, with her work in it, a friendly shake—for she took her seat beside him—the trooper's attention is attracted to her face. After looking at it for a little while as she plies her needle, he looks to young Woolwich, sitting on his stool in the corner, and beckons that fifer to him.

"See there, my boy," says George, very gently smoothing the mother's hair with his hand, "there's a good loving forehead for you! All bright with love of you, my boy. A little touched by the sun and the weather through following your father about and taking care of you, but as fresh and wholesome as a ripe apple on a tree."

Mr. Bagnet's face expresses, so far as in its wooden material lies, the highest approbation and acquiescence.

"The time will come, my boy," pursues the trooper, "when this hair of your mother's will be grey, and this forehead all crossed and re-crossed with wrinkles, and a fine old lady she'll be then. Take care, while you are young, that you can think in those days, 'I never whitened a hair of her dear head—I never marked a sorrowful line in her face!' For of all the many things that you can think of when you are a man, you had better have THAT by you, Woolwich!"

Mr. George concludes by rising from his chair, seating the boy beside his mother in it, and saying, with something of a hurry about him, that he'll smoke his pipe in the street a bit.

CHAPTER XXXV
ESTHER'S NARRATIVE

I lay ill through several weeks, and the usual tenor of my life became like an old remembrance. But this was not the effect of time so much as of the change in all my habits made by the helplessness and inaction of a sick-room. Before I had been confined to it many days, everything else seemed to have retired into a remote distance where there was little or no separation between the various stages of my life which had been really divided by years. In falling ill, I seemed to have crossed a dark lake and to have left all my experiences, mingled together by the great distance, on the healthy shore.

My housekeeping duties, though at first it caused me great anxiety to think that they were unperformed, were soon as far off as the oldest of the old duties at Greenleaf or the summer afternoons when I went home from school with my portfolio under my arm, and my childish shadow at my side, to my godmother's house. I had never known before how short life really was and into how small a space the mind could put it.

While I was very ill, the way in which these divisions of time became confused with one another distressed my mind exceedingly. At once a child, an elder girl, and the little woman I had been so happy as, I was not only oppressed by cares and difficulties adapted to each station, but by the great perplexity of endlessly trying to reconcile them. I suppose that few who have not been in such a condition can quite understand what I mean or what painful unrest arose from this source.

For the same reason I am almost afraid to hint at that time in my disorder—it seemed one long night, but I believe there were both nights and days in it—when I laboured up colossal staircases, ever striving to reach the top, and ever turned, as I have seen a worm in a garden path, by some obstruction, and labouring again. I knew perfectly at intervals, and I think vaguely at most times, that I was in my bed; and I talked with Charley, and felt her touch, and knew her very well; yet I would find myself complaining, "Oh, more of these never-ending stairs, Charley—more and more—piled up to the sky', I think!" and labouring on again.

Dare I hint at that worse time when, strung together somewhere in great black space, there was a flaming necklace, or ring, or starry circle of some kind, of which I was one of the beads! And when my only prayer was to be taken off from the rest and when it was such inexplicable agony and misery to be a part of the dreadful thing?

Perhaps the less I say of these sick experiences, the less tedious and the more intelligible I shall be. I do not recall them to make others unhappy or because I am now the least unhappy in remembering them. It may be that if we knew more of such strange afflictions we might be the better able to alleviate their intensity.

The repose that succeeded, the long delicious sleep, the blissful rest, when in my weakness I was too calm to have any care for myself and could have heard (or so I think now) that I was dying, with no other emotion than with a pitying love for those I left behind—this state can be perhaps more widely understood. I was in this state when I first shrunk from the light as it twinkled on me once more, and knew with a boundless joy for which no words are rapturous enough that I should see again.

I had heard my Ada crying at the door, day and night; I had heard her calling to me that I was cruel and did not love her; I had heard her praying and imploring to be let in to nurse and comfort me and to leave my bedside no more; but I had only said, when I could speak, "Never, my sweet girl, never!" and I had over and over again reminded Charley that she was to keep my darling from the room whether I lived or died. Charley had been true to me in that time of need, and with her little hand and her great heart had kept the door fast.

But now, my sight strengthening and the glorious light coming every day more fully and brightly on me, I could read the letters that my dear wrote to me every morning and evening and could put them to my lips and lay my cheek upon them with no fear of hurting her. I could see my little maid, so tender and so careful, going about the two rooms setting everything in order and speaking cheerfully to Ada from the open window again. I could understand the stillness in the house and the thoughtfulness it expressed on the part of all those who had always been so good to me. I could weep in the exquisite felicity of my heart and be as happy in my weakness as ever I had been in my strength.

By and by my strength began to be restored. Instead of lying, with so strange a calmness, watching what was done for me, as if it were done for some one else whom I was quietly sorry for, I helped it a little, and so on to a little more and much more, until I became useful to myself, and interested, and attached to life again.

How well I remember the pleasant afternoon when I was raised in bed with pillows for the first time to enjoy a great tea-drinking with Charley! The little creature—sent into the world, surely, to minister to the weak and sick—was so happy, and so busy, and stopped so often in her preparations to lay her head upon my bosom, and fondle me, and cry with joyful tears she was so glad, she was so glad, that I was obliged to say, "Charley, if you go on in this way, I must lie down again, my darling, for I am weaker than I thought I was!" So Charley became as quiet as a mouse and took her bright face here and there across and across the two rooms, out of the shade into the divine sunshine, and out of the sunshine into the shade, while I watched her peacefully. When all her preparations were concluded and the pretty tea-table with its little delicacies to tempt me, and its white cloth, and its flowers, and everything so lovingly and beautifully arranged for me by Ada downstairs, was ready at the bedside, I felt sure I was steady enough to say something to Charley that was not new to my thoughts.

First I complimented Charley on the room, and indeed it was so fresh and airy, so spotless and neat, that I could scarce believe I had been lying there so long. This delighted Charley, and her face was brighter than before.

"Yet, Charley," said I, looking round, "I miss something, surely, that I am accustomed to?"

Poor little Charley looked round too and pretended to shake her head as if there were nothing absent.

"Are the pictures all as they used to be?" I asked her.

"Every one of them, miss," said Charley.

"And the furniture, Charley?"

"Except where I have moved it about to make more room, miss."

"And yet," said I, "I miss some familiar object. Ah, I know what it is, Charley! It's the looking-glass."

Charley got up from the table, making as if she had forgotten something, and went into the next room; and I heard her sob there.

I had thought of this very often. I was now certain of it. I could thank God that it was not a shock to me now. I called Charley back, and when she came—at first pretending to smile, but as she drew nearer to me, looking grieved—I took her in my arms and said, "It matters very little, Charley. I hope I can do without my old face very well."

I was presently so far advanced as to be able to sit up in a great chair and even giddily to walk into the adjoining room, leaning on Charley. The mirror was gone from its usual place in that room too, but what I had to bear was none the harder to bear for that.

My guardian had throughout been earnest to visit me, and there was now no good reason why I should deny myself that happiness. He came one morning, and when he first came in, could only hold me in his embrace and say, "My dear, dear girl!" I had long known—who could know better?—what a deep fountain of affection and generosity his heart was; and was it not worth my trivial suffering and change to fill such a place in it? "Oh, yes!" I thought. "He has seen me, and he loves me better than he did; he has seen me and is even fonder of me than he was before; and what have I to mourn for!"

He sat down by me on the sofa, supporting me with his arm. For a little while he sat with his hand over his face, but when he removed it, fell into his usual manner. There never can have been, there never can be, a pleasanter manner.

"My little woman," said he, "what a sad time this has been. Such an inflexible little woman, too, through all!"

"Only for the best, guardian," said I.

"For the best?" he repeated tenderly. "Of course, for the best. But here have Ada and I been perfectly forlorn and miserable; here has your friend Caddy been coming and going late and early; here has every one about the house been utterly lost and dejected; here has even poor Rick been writing—to ME too—in his anxiety for you!"

I had read of Caddy in Ada's letters, but not of Richard. I told him so.

"Why, no, my dear," he replied. "I have thought it better not to mention it to her."

"And you speak of his writing to YOU," said I, repeating his emphasis. "As if it were not natural for him to do so, guardian; as if he could write to a better friend!"

"He thinks he could, my love," returned my guardian, "and to many a better. The truth is, he wrote to me under a sort of protest while unable to write to you with any hope of an answer—wrote coldly, haughtily, distantly, resentfully. Well, dearest little woman, we must look forbearingly on it. He is not to blame. Jarndyce and Jarndyce has warped him out of himself and perverted me in his eyes. I have known it do as bad deeds, and worse, many a time. If two angels could be concerned in it, I believe it would change their nature."

"It has not changed yours, guardian."

"Oh, yes, it has, my dear," he said laughingly. "It has made the south wind easterly, I don't know how often. Rick mistrusts and suspects me—goes to lawyers, and is taught to mistrust and suspect me. Hears I have conflicting interests, claims clashing against his and what not. Whereas, heaven knows that if I could get out of the mountains of wiglomeration on which my unfortunate name has been so long bestowed (which I can't) or could level them by the extinction of my own original right (which I can't either, and no human power ever can, anyhow, I believe, to such a pass have we got), I would do it this hour. I would rather restore to poor Rick his proper nature than be endowed with all the money that dead suitors, broken, heart and soul, upon the wheel of Chancery, have left unclaimed with the Accountant-General—and that's money enough, my dear, to be cast into a pyramid, in memory of Chancery's transcendent wickedness."

"IS it possible, guardian," I asked, amazed, "that Richard can be suspicious of you?"

"Ah, my love, my love," he said, "it is in the subtle poison of such abuses to breed such diseases. His blood is infected, and objects lose their natural aspects in his sight. It is not HIS fault."

"But it is a terrible misfortune, guardian."

"It is a terrible misfortune, little woman, to be ever drawn within the influences of Jarndyce and Jarndyce. I know none greater. By little and little he has been induced to trust in that rotten reed, and it communicates some portion of its rottenness to everything around him. But again I say with all my soul, we must be patient with poor Rick and not blame him. What a troop of fine fresh hearts like his have I seen in my time turned by the same means!"

I could not help expressing something of my wonder and regret that his benevolent, disinterested intentions had prospered so little.

"We must not say so, Dame Durden," he cheerfully replied; "Ada is the happier, I hope, and that is much. I did think that I and both these young creatures might be friends instead of distrustful foes and that we might so far counter-act the suit and prove too strong for it. But it was too much to expect. Jarndyce and Jarndyce was the curtain of Rick's cradle."

"But, guardian, may we not hope that a little experience will teach him what a false and wretched thing it is?"

"We WILL hope so, my Esther," said Mr. Jarndyce, "and that it may not teach him so too late. In any case we must not be hard on him. There are not many grown and matured men living while we speak, good men too, who if they were thrown into this same court as suitors would not be vitally changed and depreciated within three years—within two—within one. How can we stand amazed at poor Rick? A young man so unfortunate," here he fell into a lower tone, as if he were thinking aloud, "cannot at first believe (who could?) that Chancery is what it is. He looks to it, flushed and fitfully, to do something with his interests and bring them to some settlement. It procrastinates, disappoints, tries, tortures him; wears out his sanguine hopes and patience, thread by thread; but he still looks to it, and hankers after it, and finds his whole world treacherous and hollow. Well, well, well! Enough of this, my dear!"

He had supported me, as at first, all this time, and his tenderness was so precious to me that I leaned my head upon his shoulder and loved him as if he had been my father. I resolved in my own mind in this little pause, by some means, to see Richard when I grew strong and try to set him right.

"There are better subjects than these," said my guardian, "for such a joyful time as the time of our dear girl's recovery. And I had a commission to broach one of them as soon as I should begin to talk. When shall Ada come to see you, my love?"

I had been thinking of that too. A little in connexion with the absent mirrors, but not much, for I knew my loving girl would be changed by no change in my looks.

"Dear guardian," said I, "as I have shut her out so long—though indeed, indeed, she is like the light to me—"

"I know it well, Dame Durden, well."

He was so good, his touch expressed such endearing compassion and affection, and the tone of his voice carried such comfort into my heart that I stopped for a little while, quite unable to go on. "Yes, yes, you are tired," said he. "Rest a little."

"As I have kept Ada out so long," I began afresh after a short while, "I think I should like to have my own way a little longer, guardian. It would be best to be away from here before I see her. If Charley and I were to go to some country lodging as soon as I can move, and if I had a week there in which to grow stronger and to be revived by the sweet air and to look forward to the happiness of having Ada with me again, I think it would be better for us."

I hope it was not a poor thing in me to wish to be a little more used to my altered self before I met the eyes of the dear girl I longed so ardently to see, but it is the truth. I did. He understood me, I was sure; but I was not afraid of that. If it were a poor thing, I knew he would pass it over.

"Our spoilt little woman," said my guardian, "shall have her own way even in her inflexibility, though at the price, I know, of tears downstairs. And see here! Here is Boythorn, heart of chivalry, breathing such ferocious vows as never were breathed on paper before, that if you don't go and occupy his whole house, he having already turned out of it expressly for that purpose, by heaven and by earth he'll pull it down and not leave one brick standing on another!"

And my guardian put a letter in my hand, without any ordinary beginning such as "My dear Jarndyce," but rushing at once into the words, "I swear if Miss Summerson do not come down and take possession of my house, which I vacate for her this day at one o'clock, P.M.," and then with the utmost seriousness, and in the most emphatic terms, going on to make the extraordinary declaration he had quoted. We did not appreciate the writer the less for laughing heartily over it, and we settled that I should send him a letter of thanks on the morrow and accept his offer. It was a most agreeable one to me, for all the places I could have thought of, I should have liked to go to none so well as Chesney Wold.

"Now, little housewife," said my guardian, looking at his watch, "I was strictly timed before I came upstairs, for you must not be tired too soon; and my time has waned away to the last minute. I have one other petition. Little Miss Flite, hearing a rumour that you were ill, made nothing of walking down here—twenty miles, poor soul, in a pair of dancing shoes—to inquire. It was heaven's mercy we were at home, or she would have walked back again."

The old conspiracy to make me happy! Everybody seemed to be in it!

"Now, pet," said my guardian, "if it would not be irksome to you to admit the harmless little creature one afternoon before you save Boythorn's otherwise devoted house from demolition, I believe you would make her prouder and better pleased with herself than I—though my eminent name is Jarndyce—could do in a lifetime."

I have no doubt he knew there would be something in the simple image of the poor afflicted creature that would fall like a gentle lesson on my mind at that time. I felt it as he spoke to me. I could not tell him heartily enough how ready I was to receive her. I had always pitied her, never so much as now. I had always been glad of my little power to soothe her under her calamity, but never, never, half so glad before.

We arranged a time for Miss Flite to come out by the coach and share my early dinner. When my guardian left me, I turned my face away upon my couch and prayed to be forgiven if I, surrounded by such blessings, had magnified to myself the little trial that I had to undergo. The childish prayer of that old birthday when I had aspired to be industrious, contented, and true-hearted and to do good to some one and win some love to myself if I could came back into my mind with a reproachful sense of all the happiness I had since enjoyed and all the affectionate hearts that had been turned towards me. If I were weak now, what had I profited by those mercies? I repeated the old childish prayer in its old childish words and found that its old peace had not departed from it.

My guardian now came every day. In a week or so more I could walk about our rooms and hold long talks with Ada from behind the window-curtain. Yet I never saw her, for I had not as yet the courage to look at the dear face, though I could have done so easily without her seeing me.

On the appointed day Miss Flite arrived. The poor little creature ran into my room quite forgetful of her usual dignity, and crying from her very heart of hearts, "My dear Fitz Jarndyce!" fell upon my neck and kissed me twenty times.

"Dear me!" said she, putting her hand into her reticule, "I have nothing here but documents, my dear Fitz Jarndyce; I must borrow a pocket handkerchief."

Charley gave her one, and the good creature certainly made use of it, for she held it to her eyes with both hands and sat so, shedding tears for the next ten minutes.

"With pleasure, my dear Fitz Jarndyce," she was careful to explain. "Not the least pain. Pleasure to see you well again. Pleasure at having the honour of being admitted to see you. I am so much fonder of you, my love, than of the Chancellor. Though I DO attend court regularly. By the by, my dear, mentioning pocket handkerchiefs—"

Miss Flite here looked at Charley, who had been to meet her at the place where the coach stopped. Charley glanced at me and looked unwilling to pursue the suggestion.

"Ve-ry right!" said Miss Flite, "Ve-ry correct. Truly! Highly indiscreet of me to mention it; but my dear Miss Fitz Jarndyce, I am afraid I am at times (between ourselves, you wouldn't think it) a little—rambling you know," said Miss Flite, touching her forehead. "Nothing more."

"What were you going to tell me?" said I, smiling, for I saw she wanted to go on. "You have roused my curiosity, and now you must gratify it."

Miss Flite looked at Charley for advice in this important crisis, who said, "If you please, ma'am, you had better tell then," and therein gratified Miss Flite beyond measure.

"So sagacious, our young friend," said she to me in her mysterious way. "Diminutive. But ve-ry sagacious! Well, my dear, it's a pretty anecdote. Nothing more. Still I think it charming. Who should follow us down the road from the coach, my dear, but a poor person in a very ungenteel bonnet—"

"Jenny, if you please, miss," said Charley.

"Just so!" Miss Flite acquiesced with the greatest suavity. "Jenny. Ye-es! And what does she tell our young friend but that there has been a lady with a veil inquiring at her cottage after my dear Fitz Jarndyce's health and taking a handkerchief away with her as a little keepsake merely because it was my amiable Fitz Jarndyce's! Now, you know, so very prepossessing in the lady with the veil!"

"If you please, miss," said Charley, to whom I looked in some astonishment, "Jenny says that when her baby died, you left a handkerchief there, and that she put it away and kept it with the baby's little things. I think, if you please, partly because it was yours, miss, and partly because it had covered the baby."

"Diminutive," whispered Miss Flite, making a variety of motions about her own forehead to express intellect in Charley. "But exceedingly sagacious! And so dear! My love, she's clearer than any counsel I ever heard!"

"Yes, Charley," I returned. "I remember it. Well?"

"Well, miss," said Charley, "and that's the handkerchief the lady took. And Jenny wants you to know that she wouldn't have made away with it herself for a heap of money but that the lady took it and left some money instead. Jenny don't know her at all, if you please, miss!"

"Why, who can she be?" said I.

"My love," Miss Flite suggested, advancing her lips to my ear with her most mysterious look, "in MY opinion—don't mention this to our diminutive friend—she's the Lord Chancellor's wife. He's married, you know. And I understand she leads him a terrible life. Throws his lordship's papers into the fire, my dear, if he won't pay the jeweller!"

I did not think very much about this lady then, for I had an impression that it might be Caddy. Besides, my attention was diverted by my visitor, who was cold after her ride and looked hungry and who, our dinner being brought in, required some little assistance in arraying herself with great satisfaction in a pitiable old scarf and a much-worn and often-mended pair of gloves, which she had brought down in a paper parcel. I had to preside, too, over the entertainment, consisting of a dish of fish, a roast fowl, a sweetbread, vegetables, pudding, and Madeira; and it was so pleasant to see how she enjoyed it, and with what state and ceremony she did honour to it, that I was soon thinking of nothing else.

When we had finished and had our little dessert before us, embellished by the hands of my dear, who would yield the superintendence of everything prepared for me to no one, Miss Flite was so very chatty and happy that I thought I would lead her to her own history, as she was always pleased to talk about herself. I began by saying "You have attended on the Lord Chancellor many years, Miss Flite?"

"Oh, many, many, many years, my dear. But I expect a judgment. Shortly."

There was an anxiety even in her hopefulness that made me doubtful if I had done right in approaching the subject. I thought I would say no more about it.

"My father expected a judgment," said Miss Flite. "My brother. My sister. They all expected a judgment. The same that I expect."

"They are all—"

"Ye-es. Dead of course, my dear," said she.

As I saw she would go on, I thought it best to try to be serviceable to her by meeting the theme rather than avoiding it.

"Would it not be wiser," said I, "to expect this judgment no more?"

"Why, my dear," she answered promptly, "of course it would!"

"And to attend the court no more?"

"Equally of course," said she. "Very wearing to be always in expectation of what never comes, my dear Fitz Jarndyce! Wearing, I assure you, to the bone!"

She slightly showed me her arm, and it was fearfully thin indeed.

"But, my dear," she went on in her mysterious way, "there's a dreadful attraction in the place. Hush! Don't mention it to our diminutive friend when she comes in. Or it may frighten her. With good reason. There's a cruel attraction in the place. You CAN'T leave it. And you MUST expect."

I tried to assure her that this was not so. She heard me patiently and smilingly, but was ready with her own answer.

"Aye, aye, aye! You think so because I am a little rambling. Ve-ry absurd, to be a little rambling, is it not? Ve-ry confusing, too. To the head. I find it so. But, my dear, I have been there many years, and I have noticed. It's the mace and seal upon the table."

What could they do, did she think? I mildly asked her.

"Draw," returned Miss Flite. "Draw people on, my dear. Draw peace out of them. Sense out of them. Good looks out of them. Good qualities out of them. I have felt them even drawing my rest away in the night. Cold and glittering devils!"

She tapped me several times upon the arm and nodded good-humouredly as if she were anxious I should understand that I had no cause to fear her, though she spoke so gloomily, and confided these awful secrets to me.

"Let me see," said she. "I'll tell you my own case. Before they ever drew me—before I had ever seen them—what was it I used to do? Tambourine playing? No. Tambour work. I and my sister worked at tambour work. Our father and our brother had a builder's business. We all lived together. Ve-ry respectably, my dear! First, our father was drawn—slowly. Home was drawn with him. In a few years he was a fierce, sour, angry bankrupt without a kind word or a kind look for any one. He had been so different, Fitz Jarndyce. He was drawn to a debtors' prison. There he died. Then our brother was drawn—swiftly—to drunkenness. And rags. And death. Then my sister was drawn. Hush! Never ask to what! Then I was ill and in misery, and heard, as I had often heard before, that this was all the work of Chancery. When I got better, I went to look at the monster. And then I found out how it was, and I was drawn to stay there."

Having got over her own short narrative, in the delivery of which she had spoken in a low, strained voice, as if the shock were fresh upon her, she gradually resumed her usual air of amiable importance.

"You don't quite credit me, my dear! Well, well! You will, some day. I am a little rambling. But I have noticed. I have seen many new faces come, unsuspicious, within the influence of the mace and seal in these many years. As my father's came there. As my brother's. As my sister's. As my own. I hear Conversation Kenge and the rest of them say to the new faces, 'Here's little Miss Flite. Oh, you are new here; and you must come and be presented to little Miss Flite!' Ve-ry good. Proud I am sure to have the honour! And we all laugh. But, Fitz Jarndyce, I know what will happen. I know, far better than they do, when the attraction has begun. I know the signs, my dear. I saw them begin in Gridley. And I saw them end. Fitz Jarndyce, my love," speaking low again, "I saw them beginning in our friend the ward in Jarndyce. Let some one hold him back. Or he'll be drawn to ruin."

She looked at me in silence for some moments, with her face gradually softening into a smile. Seeming to fear that she had been too gloomy, and seeming also to lose the connexion in her mind, she said politely as she sipped her glass of wine, "Yes, my dear, as I was saying, I expect a judgment shortly. Then I shall release my birds, you know, and confer estates."

I was much impressed by her allusion to Richard and by the sad meaning, so sadly illustrated in her poor pinched form, that made its way through all her incoherence. But happily for her, she was quite complacent again now and beamed with nods and smiles.

"But, my dear," she said, gaily, reaching another hand to put it upon mine. "You have not congratulated me on my physician. Positively not once, yet!"

I was obliged to confess that I did not quite know what she meant.

"My physician, Mr. Woodcourt, my dear, who was so exceedingly attentive to me. Though his services were rendered quite gratuitously. Until the Day of Judgment. I mean THE judgment that will dissolve the spell upon me of the mace and seal."

"Mr. Woodcourt is so far away, now," said I, "that I thought the time for such congratulation was past, Miss Flite."

"But, my child," she returned, "is it possible that you don't know what has happened?"

"No," said I.

"Not what everybody has been talking of, my beloved Fitz Jarndyce!"

"No," said I. "You forget how long I have been here."

"True! My dear, for the moment—true. I blame myself. But my memory has been drawn out of me, with everything else, by what I mentioned. Ve-ry strong influence, is it not? Well, my dear, there has been a terrible shipwreck over in those East Indian seas."

"Mr. Woodcourt shipwrecked!"

"Don't be agitated, my dear. He is safe. An awful scene. Death in all shapes. Hundreds of dead and dying. Fire, storm, and darkness. Numbers of the drowning thrown upon a rock. There, and through it all, my dear physician was a hero. Calm and brave through everything. Saved many lives, never complained in hunger and thirst, wrapped naked people in his spare clothes, took the lead, showed them what to do, governed them, tended the sick, buried the dead, and brought the poor survivors safely off at last! My dear, the poor emaciated creatures all but worshipped him. They fell down at his feet when they got to the land and blessed him. The whole country rings with it. Stay! Where's my bag of documents? I have got it there, and you shall read it, you shall read it!"

And I DID read all the noble history, though very slowly and imperfectly then, for my eyes were so dimmed that I could not see the words, and I cried so much that I was many times obliged to lay down the long account she had cut out of the newspaper. I felt so triumphant ever to have known the man who had done such generous and gallant deeds, I felt such glowing exultation in his renown, I so admired and loved what he had done, that I envied the storm-worn people who had fallen at his feet and blessed him as their preserver. I could myself have kneeled down then, so far away, and blessed him in my rapture that he should be so truly good and brave. I felt that no one—mother, sister, wife—could honour him more than I. I did, indeed!

My poor little visitor made me a present of the account, and when as the evening began to close in she rose to take her leave, lest she should miss the coach by which she was to return, she was still full of the shipwreck, which I had not yet sufficiently composed myself to understand in all its details.

"My dear," said she as she carefully folded up her scarf and gloves, "my brave physician ought to have a title bestowed upon him. And no doubt he will. You are of that opinion?"

That he well deserved one, yes. That he would ever have one, no.

"Why not, Fitz Jarndyce?" she asked rather sharply.

I said it was not the custom in England to confer titles on men distinguished by peaceful services, however good and great, unless occasionally when they consisted of the accumulation of some very large amount of money.

"Why, good gracious," said Miss Flite, "how can you say that? Surely you know, my dear, that all the greatest ornaments of England in knowledge, imagination, active humanity, and improvement of every sort are added to its nobility! Look round you, my dear, and consider. YOU must be rambling a little now, I think, if you don't know that this is the great reason why titles will always last in the land!"

I am afraid she believed what she said, for there were moments when she was very mad indeed.

And now I must part with the little secret I have thus far tried to keep. I had thought, sometimes, that Mr. Woodcourt loved me and that if he had been richer he would perhaps have told me that he loved me before he went away. I had thought, sometimes, that if he had done so, I should have been glad of it. But how much better it was now that this had never happened! What should I have suffered if I had had to write to him and tell him that the poor face he had known as mine was quite gone from me and that I freely released him from his bondage to one whom he had never seen!

Oh, it was so much better as it was! With a great pang mercifully spared me, I could take back to my heart my childish prayer to be all he had so brightly shown himself; and there was nothing to be undone: no chain for me to break or for him to drag; and I could go, please God, my lowly way along the path of duty, and he could go his nobler way upon its broader road; and though we were apart upon the journey, I might aspire to meet him, unselfishly, innocently, better far than he had thought me when I found some favour in his eyes, at the journey's end.

CHAPTER XXXVI
CHESNEY WOLD

Charley and I did not set off alone upon our expedition into Lincolnshire. My guardian had made up his mind not to lose sight of me until I was safe in Mr. Boythorn's house, so he accompanied us, and we were two days upon the road. I found every breath of air, and every scent, and every flower and leaf and blade of grass, and every passing cloud, and everything in nature, more beautiful and wonderful to me than I had ever found it yet. This was my first gain from my illness. How little I had lost, when the wide world was so full of delight for me.

My guardian intending to go back immediately, we appointed, on our way down, a day when my dear girl should come. I wrote her a letter, of which he took charge, and he left us within half an hour of our arrival at our destination, on a delightful evening in the early summer-time.

If a good fairy had built the house for me with a wave of her wand, and I had been a princess and her favoured god-child, I could not have been more considered in it. So many preparations were made for me and such an endearing remembrance was shown of all my little tastes and likings that I could have sat down, overcome, a dozen times before I had revisited half the rooms. I did better than that, however, by showing them all to Charley instead. Charley's delight calmed mine; and after we had had a walk in the garden, and Charley had exhausted her whole vocabulary of admiring expressions, I was as tranquilly happy as I ought to have been. It was a great comfort to be able to say to myself after tea, "Esther, my dear, I think you are quite sensible enough to sit down now and write a note of thanks to your host." He had left a note of welcome for me, as sunny as his own face, and had confided his bird to my care, which I knew to be his highest mark of confidence. Accordingly I wrote a little note to him in London, telling him how all his favourite plants and trees were looking, and how the most astonishing of birds had chirped the honours of the house to me in the most hospitable manner, and how, after singing on my shoulder, to the inconceivable rapture of my little maid, he was then at roost in the usual corner of his cage, but whether dreaming or no I could not report. My note finished and sent off to the post, I made myself very busy in unpacking and arranging; and I sent Charley to bed in good time and told her I should want her no more that night.

For I had not yet looked in the glass and had never asked to have my own restored to me. I knew this to be a weakness which must be overcome, but I had always said to myself that I would begin afresh when I got to where I now was. Therefore I had wanted to be alone, and therefore I said, now alone, in my own room, "Esther, if you are to be happy, if you are to have any right to pray to be true-hearted, you must keep your word, my dear." I was quite resolved to keep it, but I sat down for a little while first to reflect upon all my blessings. And then I said my prayers and thought a little more.

My hair had not been cut off, though it had been in danger more than once. It was long and thick. I let it down, and shook it out, and went up to the glass upon the dressing-table. There was a little muslin curtain drawn across it. I drew it back and stood for a moment looking through such a veil of my own hair that I could see nothing else. Then I put my hair aside and looked at the reflection in the mirror, encouraged by seeing how placidly it looked at me. I was very much changed—oh, very, very much. At first my face was so strange to me that I think I should have put my hands before it and started back but for the encouragement I have mentioned. Very soon it became more familiar, and then I knew the extent of the alteration in it better than I had done at first. It was not like what I had expected, but I had expected nothing definite, and I dare say anything definite would have surprised me.

I had never been a beauty and had never thought myself one, but I had been very different from this. It was all gone now. Heaven was so good to me that I could let it go with a few not bitter tears and could stand there arranging my hair for the night quite thankfully.

One thing troubled me, and I considered it for a long time before I went to sleep. I had kept Mr. Woodcourt's flowers. When they were withered I had dried them and put them in a book that I was fond of. Nobody knew this, not even Ada. I was doubtful whether I had a right to preserve what he had sent to one so different—whether it was generous towards him to do it. I wished to be generous to him, even in the secret depths of my heart, which he would never know, because I could have loved him—could have been devoted to him. At last I came to the conclusion that I might keep them if I treasured them only as a remembrance of what was irrevocably past and gone, never to be looked back on any more, in any other light. I hope this may not seem trivial. I was very much in earnest.

I took care to be up early in the morning and to be before the glass when Charley came in on tiptoe.

"Dear, dear, miss!" cried Charley, starting. "Is that you?"

"Yes, Charley," said I, quietly putting up my hair. "And I am very well indeed, and very happy."

I saw it was a weight off Charley's mind, but it was a greater weight off mine. I knew the worst now and was composed to it. I shall not conceal, as I go on, the weaknesses I could not quite conquer, but they always passed from me soon and the happier frame of mind stayed by me faithfully.

Wishing to be fully re-established in my strength and my good spirits before Ada came, I now laid down a little series of plans with Charley for being in the fresh air all day long. We were to be out before breakfast, and were to dine early, and were to be out again before and after dinner, and were to talk in the garden after tea, and were to go to rest betimes, and were to climb every hill and explore every road, lane, and field in the neighbourhood. As to restoratives and strengthening delicacies, Mr. Boythorn's good housekeeper was for ever trotting about with something to eat or drink in her hand; I could not even be heard of as resting in the park but she would come trotting after me with a basket, her cheerful face shining with a lecture on the importance of frequent nourishment. Then there was a pony expressly for my riding, a chubby pony with a short neck and a mane all over his eyes who could canter—when he would—so easily and quietly that he was a treasure. In a very few days he would come to me in the paddock when I called him, and eat out of my hand, and follow me about. We arrived at such a capital understanding that when he was jogging with me lazily, and rather obstinately, down some shady lane, if I patted his neck and said, "Stubbs, I am surprised you don't canter when you know how much I like it; and I think you might oblige me, for you are only getting stupid and going to sleep," he would give his head a comical shake or two and set off directly, while Charley would stand still and laugh with such enjoyment that her laughter was like music. I don't know who had given Stubbs his name, but it seemed to belong to him as naturally as his rough coat. Once we put him in a little chaise and drove him triumphantly through the green lanes for five miles; but all at once, as we were extolling him to the skies, he seemed to take it ill that he should have been accompanied so far by the circle of tantalizing little gnats that had been hovering round and round his ears the whole way without appearing to advance an inch, and stopped to think about it. I suppose he came to the decision that it was not to be borne, for he steadily refused to move until I gave the reins to Charley and got out and walked, when he followed me with a sturdy sort of good humour, putting his head under my arm and rubbing his ear against my sleeve. It was in vain for me to say, "Now, Stubbs, I feel quite sure from what I know of you that you will go on if I ride a little while," for the moment I left him, he stood stock still again. Consequently I was obliged to lead the way, as before; and in this order we returned home, to the great delight of the village.

Charley and I had reason to call it the most friendly of villages, I am sure, for in a week's time the people were so glad to see us go by, though ever so frequently in the course of a day, that there were faces of greeting in every cottage. I had known many of the grown people before and almost all the children, but now the very steeple began to wear a familiar and affectionate look. Among my new friends was an old old woman who lived in such a little thatched and whitewashed dwelling that when the outside shutter was turned up on its hinges, it shut up the whole house-front. This old lady had a grandson who was a sailor, and I wrote a letter to him for her and drew at the top of it the chimney-corner in which she had brought him up and where his old stool yet occupied its old place. This was considered by the whole village the most wonderful achievement in the world, but when an answer came back all the way from Plymouth, in which he mentioned that he was going to take the picture all the way to America, and from America would write again, I got all the credit that ought to have been given to the post-office and was invested with the merit of the whole system.

Thus, what with being so much in the air, playing with so many children, gossiping with so many people, sitting on invitation in so many cottages, going on with Charley's education, and writing long letters to Ada every day, I had scarcely any time to think about that little loss of mine and was almost always cheerful. If I did think of it at odd moments now and then, I had only to be busy and forget it. I felt it more than I had hoped I should once when a child said, "Mother, why is the lady not a pretty lady now like she used to be?" But when I found the child was not less fond of me, and drew its soft hand over my face with a kind of pitying protection in its touch, that soon set me up again. There were many little occurrences which suggested to me, with great consolation, how natural it is to gentle hearts to be considerate and delicate towards any inferiority. One of these particularly touched me. I happened to stroll into the little church when a marriage was just concluded, and the young couple had to sign the register.

The bridegroom, to whom the pen was handed first, made a rude cross for his mark; the bride, who came next, did the same. Now, I had known the bride when I was last there, not only as the prettiest girl in the place, but as having quite distinguished herself in the school, and I could not help looking at her with some surprise. She came aside and whispered to me, while tears of honest love and admiration stood in her bright eyes, "He's a dear good fellow, miss; but he can't write yet—he's going to learn of me—and I wouldn't shame him for the world!" Why, what had I to fear, I thought, when there was this nobility in the soul of a labouring man's daughter!

The air blew as freshly and revivingly upon me as it had ever blown, and the healthy colour came into my new face as it had come into my old one. Charley was wonderful to see, she was so radiant and so rosy; and we both enjoyed the whole day and slept soundly the whole night.

There was a favourite spot of mine in the park-woods of Chesney Wold where a seat had been erected commanding a lovely view. The wood had been cleared and opened to improve this point of sight, and the bright sunny landscape beyond was so beautiful that I rested there at least once every day. A picturesque part of the Hall, called the Ghost's Walk, was seen to advantage from this higher ground; and the startling name, and the old legend in the Dedlock family which I had heard from Mr. Boythorn accounting for it, mingled with the view and gave it something of a mysterious interest in addition to its real charms. There was a bank here, too, which was a famous one for violets; and as it was a daily delight of Charley's to gather wild flowers, she took as much to the spot as I did.

It would be idle to inquire now why I never went close to the house or never went inside it. The family were not there, I had heard on my arrival, and were not expected. I was far from being incurious or uninterested about the building; on the contrary, I often sat in this place wondering how the rooms ranged and whether any echo like a footstep really did resound at times, as the story said, upon the lonely Ghost's Walk. The indefinable feeling with which Lady Dedlock had impressed me may have had some influence in keeping me from the house even when she was absent. I am not sure. Her face and figure were associated with it, naturally; but I cannot say that they repelled me from it, though something did. For whatever reason or no reason, I had never once gone near it, down to the day at which my story now arrives.

I was resting at my favourite point after a long ramble, and Charley was gathering violets at a little distance from me. I had been looking at the Ghost's Walk lying in a deep shade of masonry afar off and picturing to myself the female shape that was said to haunt it when I became aware of a figure approaching through the wood. The perspective was so long and so darkened by leaves, and the shadows of the branches on the ground made it so much more intricate to the eye, that at first I could not discern what figure it was. By little and little it revealed itself to be a woman's—a lady's—Lady Dedlock's. She was alone and coming to where I sat with a much quicker step, I observed to my surprise, than was usual with her.

I was fluttered by her being unexpectedly so near (she was almost within speaking distance before I knew her) and would have risen to continue my walk. But I could not. I was rendered motionless. Not so much by her hurried gesture of entreaty, not so much by her quick advance and outstretched hands, not so much by the great change in her manner and the absence of her haughty self-restraint, as by a something in her face that I had pined for and dreamed of when I was a little child, something I had never seen in any face, something I had never seen in hers before.

A dread and faintness fell upon me, and I called to Charley. Lady Dedlock stopped upon the instant and changed back almost to what I had known her.

"Miss Summerson, I am afraid I have startled you," she said, now advancing slowly. "You can scarcely be strong yet. You have been very ill, I know. I have been much concerned to hear it."

I could no more have removed my eyes from her pale face than I could have stirred from the bench on which I sat. She gave me her hand, and its deadly coldness, so at variance with the enforced composure of her features, deepened the fascination that overpowered me. I cannot say what was in my whirling thoughts.

"You are recovering again?" she asked kindly.

"I was quite well but a moment ago, Lady Dedlock."

"Is this your young attendant?"

"Yes."

"Will you send her on before and walk towards your house with me?"

"Charley," said I, "take your flowers home, and I will follow you directly."

Charley, with her best curtsy, blushingly tied on her bonnet and went her way. When she was gone, Lady Dedlock sat down on the seat beside me.

I cannot tell in any words what the state of my mind was when I saw in her hand my handkerchief with which I had covered the dead baby.

I looked at her, but I could not see her, I could not hear her, I could not draw my breath. The beating of my heart was so violent and wild that I felt as if my life were breaking from me. But when she caught me to her breast, kissed me, wept over me, compassionated me, and called me back to myself; when she fell down on her knees and cried to me, "Oh, my child, my child, I am your wicked and unhappy mother! Oh, try to forgive me!"—when I saw her at my feet on the bare earth in her great agony of mind, I felt, through all my tumult of emotion, a burst of gratitude to the providence of God that I was so changed as that I never could disgrace her by any trace of likeness, as that nobody could ever now look at me and look at her and remotely think of any near tie between us.

I raised my mother up, praying and beseeching her not to stoop before me in such affliction and humiliation. I did so in broken, incoherent words, for besides the trouble I was in, it frightened me to see her at MY feet. I told her—or I tried to tell her—that if it were for me, her child, under any circumstances to take upon me to forgive her, I did it, and had done it, many, many years. I told her that my heart overflowed with love for her, that it was natural love which nothing in the past had changed or could change. That it was not for me, then resting for the first time on my mother's bosom, to take her to account for having given me life, but that my duty was to bless her and receive her, though the whole world turned from her, and that I only asked her leave to do it. I held my mother in my embrace, and she held me in hers, and among the still woods in the silence of the summer day there seemed to be nothing but our two troubled minds that was not at peace.

"To bless and receive me," groaned my mother, "it is far too late. I must travel my dark road alone, and it will lead me where it will. From day to day, sometimes from hour to hour, I do not see the way before my guilty feet. This is the earthly punishment I have brought upon myself. I bear it, and I hide it."

Even in the thinking of her endurance, she drew her habitual air of proud indifference about her like a veil, though she soon cast it off again.

"I must keep this secret, if by any means it can be kept, not wholly for myself. I have a husband, wretched and dishonouring creature that I am!"

These words she uttered with a suppressed cry of despair, more terrible in its sound than any shriek. Covering her face with her hands, she shrank down in my embrace as if she were unwilling that I should touch her; nor could I, by my utmost persuasions or by any endearments I could use, prevail upon her to rise. She said, no, no, no, she could only speak to me so; she must be proud and disdainful everywhere else; she would be humbled and ashamed there, in the only natural moments of her life.

My unhappy mother told me that in my illness she had been nearly frantic. She had but then known that her child was living. She could not have suspected me to be that child before. She had followed me down here to speak to me but once in all her life. We never could associate, never could communicate, never probably from that time forth could interchange another word on earth. She put into my hands a letter she had written for my reading only and said when I had read it and destroyed it—but not so much for her sake, since she asked nothing, as for her husband's and my own—I must evermore consider her as dead. If I could believe that she loved me, in this agony in which I saw her, with a mother's love, she asked me to do that, for then I might think of her with a greater pity, imagining what she suffered. She had put herself beyond all hope and beyond all help. Whether she preserved her secret until death or it came to be discovered and she brought dishonour and disgrace upon the name she had taken, it was her solitary struggle always; and no affection could come near her, and no human creature could render her any aid.

"But is the secret safe so far?" I asked. "Is it safe now, dearest mother?"

"No," replied my mother. "It has been very near discovery. It was saved by an accident. It may be lost by another accident—to-morrow, any day."

"Do you dread a particular person?"

"Hush! Do not tremble and cry so much for me. I am not worthy of these tears," said my mother, kissing my hands. "I dread one person very much."

"An enemy?"

"Not a friend. One who is too passionless to be either. He is Sir Leicester Dedlock's lawyer, mechanically faithful without attachment, and very jealous of the profit, privilege, and reputation of being master of the mysteries of great houses."

"Has he any suspicions?"

"Many."

"Not of you?" I said alarmed.

"Yes! He is always vigilant and always near me. I may keep him at a standstill, but I can never shake him off."

"Has he so little pity or compunction?"

"He has none, and no anger. He is indifferent to everything but his calling. His calling is the acquisition of secrets and the holding possession of such power as they give him, with no sharer or opponent in it."

"Could you trust in him?"

"I shall never try. The dark road I have trodden for so many years will end where it will. I follow it alone to the end, whatever the end be. It may be near, it may be distant; while the road lasts, nothing turns me."

"Dear mother, are you so resolved?"

"I AM resolved. I have long outbidden folly with folly, pride with pride, scorn with scorn, insolence with insolence, and have outlived many vanities with many more. I will outlive this danger, and outdie it, if I can. It has closed around me almost as awfully as if these woods of Chesney Wold had closed around the house, but my course through it is the same. I have but one; I can have but one."

"Mr. Jarndyce—" I was beginning when my mother hurriedly inquired, "Does HE suspect?"

"No," said I. "No, indeed! Be assured that he does not!" And I told her what he had related to me as his knowledge of my story. "But he is so good and sensible," said I, "that perhaps if he knew—"

My mother, who until this time had made no change in her position, raised her hand up to my lips and stopped me.

"Confide fully in him," she said after a little while. "You have my free consent—a small gift from such a mother to her injured child!—but do not tell me of it. Some pride is left in me even yet."

I explained, as nearly as I could then, or can recall now—for my agitation and distress throughout were so great that I scarcely understood myself, though every word that was uttered in the mother's voice, so unfamiliar and so melancholy to me, which in my childhood I had never learned to love and recognize, had never been sung to sleep with, had never heard a blessing from, had never had a hope inspired by, made an enduring impression on my memory—I say I explained, or tried to do it, how I had only hoped that Mr. Jarndyce, who had been the best of fathers to me, might be able to afford some counsel and support to her. But my mother answered no, it was impossible; no one could help her. Through the desert that lay before her, she must go alone.

"My child, my child!" she said. "For the last time! These kisses for the last time! These arms upon my neck for the last time! We shall meet no more. To hope to do what I seek to do, I must be what I have been so long. Such is my reward and doom. If you hear of Lady Dedlock, brilliant, prosperous, and flattered, think of your wretched mother, conscience-stricken, underneath that mask! Think that the reality is in her suffering, in her useless remorse, in her murdering within her breast the only love and truth of which it is capable! And then forgive her if you can, and cry to heaven to forgive her, which it never can!"

We held one another for a little space yet, but she was so firm that she took my hands away, and put them back against my breast, and with a last kiss as she held them there, released them, and went from me into the wood. I was alone, and calm and quiet below me in the sun and shade lay the old house, with its terraces and turrets, on which there had seemed to me to be such complete repose when I first saw it, but which now looked like the obdurate and unpitying watcher of my mother's misery.

Stunned as I was, as weak and helpless at first as I had ever been in my sick chamber, the necessity of guarding against the danger of discovery, or even of the remotest suspicion, did me service. I took such precautions as I could to hide from Charley that I had been crying, and I constrained myself to think of every sacred obligation that there was upon me to be careful and collected. It was not a little while before I could succeed or could even restrain bursts of grief, but after an hour or so I was better and felt that I might return. I went home very slowly and told Charley, whom I found at the gate looking for me, that I had been tempted to extend my walk after Lady Dedlock had left me and that I was over-tired and would lie down. Safe in my own room, I read the letter. I clearly derived from it—and that was much then—that I had not been abandoned by my mother. Her elder and only sister, the godmother of my childhood, discovering signs of life in me when I had been laid aside as dead, had in her stern sense of duty, with no desire or willingness that I should live, reared me in rigid secrecy and had never again beheld my mother's face from within a few hours of my birth. So strangely did I hold my place in this world that until within a short time back I had never, to my own mother's knowledge, breathed—had been buried—had never been endowed with life—had never borne a name. When she had first seen me in the church she had been startled and had thought of what would have been like me if it had ever lived, and had lived on, but that was all then.

What more the letter told me needs not to be repeated here. It has its own times and places in my story.

My first care was to burn what my mother had written and to consume even its ashes. I hope it may not appear very unnatural or bad in me that I then became heavily sorrowful to think I had ever been reared. That I felt as if I knew it would have been better and happier for many people if indeed I had never breathed. That I had a terror of myself as the danger and the possible disgrace of my own mother and of a proud family name. That I was so confused and shaken as to be possessed by a belief that it was right and had been intended that I should die in my birth, and that it was wrong and not intended that I should be then alive.

These are the real feelings that I had. I fell asleep worn out, and when I awoke I cried afresh to think that I was back in the world with my load of trouble for others. I was more than ever frightened of myself, thinking anew of her against whom I was a witness, of the owner of Chesney Wold, of the new and terrible meaning of the old words now moaning in my ear like a surge upon the shore, "Your mother, Esther, was your disgrace, and you are hers. The time will come—and soon enough—when you will understand this better, and will feel it too, as no one save a woman can." With them, those other words returned, "Pray daily that the sins of others be not visited upon your head." I could not disentangle all that was about me, and I felt as if the blame and the shame were all in me, and the visitation had come down.

The day waned into a gloomy evening, overcast and sad, and I still contended with the same distress. I went out alone, and after walking a little in the park, watching the dark shades falling on the trees and the fitful flight of the bats, which sometimes almost touched me, was attracted to the house for the first time. Perhaps I might not have gone near it if I had been in a stronger frame of mind. As it was, I took the path that led close by it.

I did not dare to linger or to look up, but I passed before the terrace garden with its fragrant odours, and its broad walks, and its well-kept beds and smooth turf; and I saw how beautiful and grave it was, and how the old stone balustrades and parapets, and wide flights of shallow steps, were seamed by time and weather; and how the trained moss and ivy grew about them, and around the old stone pedestal of the sun-dial; and I heard the fountain falling. Then the way went by long lines of dark windows diversified by turreted towers and porches of eccentric shapes, where old stone lions and grotesque monsters bristled outside dens of shadow and snarled at the evening gloom over the escutcheons they held in their grip. Thence the path wound underneath a gateway, and through a court-yard where the principal entrance was (I hurried quickly on), and by the stables where none but deep voices seemed to be, whether in the murmuring of the wind through the strong mass of ivy holding to a high red wall, or in the low complaining of the weathercock, or in the barking of the dogs, or in the slow striking of a clock. So, encountering presently a sweet smell of limes, whose rustling I could hear, I turned with the turning of the path to the south front, and there above me were the balustrades of the Ghost's Walk and one lighted window that might be my mother's.

The way was paved here, like the terrace overhead, and my footsteps from being noiseless made an echoing sound upon the flags. Stopping to look at nothing, but seeing all I did see as I went, I was passing quickly on, and in a few moments should have passed the lighted window, when my echoing footsteps brought it suddenly into my mind that there was a dreadful truth in the legend of the Ghost's Walk, that it was I who was to bring calamity upon the stately house and that my warning feet were haunting it even then. Seized with an augmented terror of myself which turned me cold, I ran from myself and everything, retraced the way by which I had come, and never paused until I had gained the lodge-gate, and the park lay sullen and black behind me.

Not before I was alone in my own room for the night and had again been dejected and unhappy there did I begin to know how wrong and thankless this state was. But from my darling who was coming on the morrow, I found a joyful letter, full of such loving anticipation that I must have been of marble if it had not moved me; from my guardian, too, I found another letter, asking me to tell Dame Durden, if I should see that little woman anywhere, that they had moped most pitiably without her, that the housekeeping was going to rack and ruin, that nobody else could manage the keys, and that everybody in and about the house declared it was not the same house and was becoming rebellious for her return. Two such letters together made me think how far beyond my deserts I was beloved and how happy I ought to be. That made me think of all my past life; and that brought me, as it ought to have done before, into a better condition.

For I saw very well that I could not have been intended to die, or I should never have lived; not to say should never have been reserved for such a happy life. I saw very well how many things had worked together for my welfare, and that if the sins of the fathers were sometimes visited upon the children, the phrase did not mean what I had in the morning feared it meant. I knew I was as innocent of my birth as a queen of hers and that before my Heavenly Father I should not be punished for birth nor a queen rewarded for it. I had had experience, in the shock of that very day, that I could, even thus soon, find comforting reconcilements to the change that had fallen on me. I renewed my resolutions and prayed to be strengthened in them, pouring out my heart for myself and for my unhappy mother and feeling that the darkness of the morning was passing away. It was not upon my sleep; and when the next day's light awoke me, it was gone.

My dear girl was to arrive at five o'clock in the afternoon. How to help myself through the intermediate time better than by taking a long walk along the road by which she was to come, I did not know; so Charley and I and Stubbs—Stubbs saddled, for we never drove him after the one great occasion—made a long expedition along that road and back. On our return, we held a great review of the house and garden and saw that everything was in its prettiest condition, and had the bird out ready as an important part of the establishment.

There were more than two full hours yet to elapse before she could come, and in that interval, which seemed a long one, I must confess I was nervously anxious about my altered looks. I loved my darling so well that I was more concerned for their effect on her than on any one. I was not in this slight distress because I at all repined—I am quite certain I did not, that day—but, I thought, would she be wholly prepared? When she first saw me, might she not be a little shocked and disappointed? Might it not prove a little worse than she expected? Might she not look for her old Esther and not find her? Might she not have to grow used to me and to begin all over again?

I knew the various expressions of my sweet girl's face so well, and it was such an honest face in its loveliness, that I was sure beforehand she could not hide that first look from me. And I considered whether, if it should signify any one of these meanings, which was so very likely, could I quite answer for myself?

Well, I thought I could. After last night, I thought I could. But to wait and wait, and expect and expect, and think and think, was such bad preparation that I resolved to go along the road again and meet her.

So I said to Charley, "Charley, I will go by myself and walk along the road until she comes." Charley highly approving of anything that pleased me, I went and left her at home.

But before I got to the second milestone, I had been in so many palpitations from seeing dust in the distance (though I knew it was not, and could not, be the coach yet) that I resolved to turn back and go home again. And when I had turned, I was in such fear of the coach coming up behind me (though I still knew that it neither would, nor could, do any such thing) that I ran the greater part of the way to avoid being overtaken.

Then, I considered, when I had got safe back again, this was a nice thing to have done! Now I was hot and had made the worst of it instead of the best.

At last, when I believed there was at least a quarter of an hour more yet, Charley all at once cried out to me as I was trembling in the garden, "Here she comes, miss! Here she is!"

I did not mean to do it, but I ran upstairs into my room and hid myself behind the door. There I stood trembling, even when I heard my darling calling as she came upstairs, "Esther, my dear, my love, where are you? Little woman, dear Dame Durden!"

She ran in, and was running out again when she saw me. Ah, my angel girl! The old dear look, all love, all fondness, all affection. Nothing else in it—no, nothing, nothing!

Oh, how happy I was, down upon the floor, with my sweet beautiful girl down upon the floor too, holding my scarred face to her lovely cheek, bathing it with tears and kisses, rocking me to and fro like a child, calling me by every tender name that she could think of, and pressing me to her faithful heart.

CHAPTER XXXVII
JARNDYCE AND JARNDYCE

If the secret I had to keep had been mine, I must have confided it to Ada before we had been long together. But it was not mine, and I did not feel that I had a right to tell it, even to my guardian, unless some great emergency arose. It was a weight to bear alone; still my present duty appeared to be plain, and blest in the attachment of my dear, I did not want an impulse and encouragement to do it. Though often when she was asleep and all was quiet, the remembrance of my mother kept me waking and made the night sorrowful, I did not yield to it at another time; and Ada found me what I used to be—except, of course, in that particular of which I have said enough and which I have no intention of mentioning any more just now, if I can help it.

The difficulty that I felt in being quite composed that first evening when Ada asked me, over our work, if the family were at the house, and when I was obliged to answer yes, I believed so, for Lady Dedlock had spoken to me in the woods the day before yesterday, was great. Greater still when Ada asked me what she had said, and when I replied that she had been kind and interested, and when Ada, while admitting her beauty and elegance, remarked upon her proud manner and her imperious chilling air. But Charley helped me through, unconsciously, by telling us that Lady Dedlock had only stayed at the house two nights on her way from London to visit at some other great house in the next county and that she had left early on the morning after we had seen her at our view, as we called it. Charley verified the adage about little pitchers, I am sure, for she heard of more sayings and doings in a day than would have come to my ears in a month.

We were to stay a month at Mr. Boythorn's. My pet had scarcely been there a bright week, as I recollect the time, when one evening after we had finished helping the gardener in watering his flowers, and just as the candles were lighted, Charley, appearing with a very important air behind Ada's chair, beckoned me mysteriously out of the room.

"Oh! If you please, miss," said Charley in a whisper, with her eyes at their roundest and largest. "You're wanted at the Dedlock Arms."

"Why, Charley," said I, "who can possibly want me at the public-house?"

"I don't know, miss," returned Charley, putting her head forward and folding her hands tight upon the band of her little apron, which she always did in the enjoyment of anything mysterious or confidential, "but it's a gentleman, miss, and his compliments, and will you please to come without saying anything about it."

"Whose compliments, Charley?"

"His'n, miss," returned Charley, whose grammatical education was advancing, but not very rapidly.

"And how do you come to be the messenger, Charley?"

"I am not the messenger, if you please, miss," returned my little maid. "It was W. Grubble, miss."

"And who is W. Grubble, Charley?"

"Mister Grubble, miss," returned Charley. "Don't you know, miss? The Dedlock Arms, by W. Grubble," which Charley delivered as if she were slowly spelling out the sign.

"Aye? The landlord, Charley?"

"Yes, miss. If you please, miss, his wife is a beautiful woman, but she broke her ankle, and it never joined. And her brother's the sawyer that was put in the cage, miss, and they expect he'll drink himself to death entirely on beer," said Charley.

Not knowing what might be the matter, and being easily apprehensive now, I thought it best to go to this place by myself. I bade Charley be quick with my bonnet and veil and my shawl, and having put them on, went away down the little hilly street, where I was as much at home as in Mr. Boythorn's garden.

Mr. Grubble was standing in his shirt-sleeves at the door of his very clean little tavern waiting for me. He lifted off his hat with both hands when he saw me coming, and carrying it so, as if it were an iron vessel (it looked as heavy), preceded me along the sanded passage to his best parlour, a neat carpeted room with more plants in it than were quite convenient, a coloured print of Queen Caroline, several shells, a good many tea-trays, two stuffed and dried fish in glass cases, and either a curious egg or a curious pumpkin (but I don't know which, and I doubt if many people did) hanging from his ceiling. I knew Mr. Grubble very well by sight, from his often standing at his door. A pleasant-looking, stoutish, middle-aged man who never seemed to consider himself cozily dressed for his own fire-side without his hat and top-boots, but who never wore a coat except at church.

He snuffed the candle, and backing away a little to see how it looked, backed out of the room—unexpectedly to me, for I was going to ask him by whom he had been sent. The door of the opposite parlour being then opened, I heard some voices, familiar in my ears I thought, which stopped. A quick light step approached the room in which I was, and who should stand before me but Richard!

"My dear Esther!" he said. "My best friend!" And he really was so warm-hearted and earnest that in the first surprise and pleasure of his brotherly greeting I could scarcely find breath to tell him that Ada was well.

"Answering my very thoughts—always the same dear girl!" said Richard, leading me to a chair and seating himself beside me.

I put my veil up, but not quite.

"Always the same dear girl!" said Richard just as heartily as before.

I put up my veil altogether, and laying my hand on Richard's sleeve and looking in his face, told him how much I thanked him for his kind welcome and how greatly I rejoiced to see him, the more so because of the determination I had made in my illness, which I now conveyed to him.

"My love," said Richard, "there is no one with whom I have a greater wish to talk than you, for I want you to understand me."

"And I want you, Richard," said I, shaking my head, "to understand some one else."

"Since you refer so immediately to John Jarndyce," said Richard, "—I suppose you mean him?"

"Of course I do."

"Then I may say at once that I am glad of it, because it is on that subject that I am anxious to be understood. By you, mind—you, my dear! I am not accountable to Mr. Jarndyce or Mr. Anybody."

I was pained to find him taking this tone, and he observed it.

"Well, well, my dear," said Richard, "we won't go into that now. I want to appear quietly in your country-house here, with you under my arm, and give my charming cousin a surprise. I suppose your loyalty to John Jarndyce will allow that?"

"My dear Richard," I returned, "you know you would be heartily welcome at his house—your home, if you will but consider it so; and you are as heartily welcome here!"

"Spoken like the best of little women!" cried Richard gaily.

I asked him how he liked his profession.

"Oh, I like it well enough!" said Richard. "It's all right. It does as well as anything else, for a time. I don't know that I shall care about it when I come to be settled, but I can sell out then and—however, never mind all that botheration at present."

So young and handsome, and in all respects so perfectly the opposite of Miss Flite! And yet, in the clouded, eager, seeking look that passed over him, so dreadfully like her!

"I am in town on leave just now," said Richard.

"Indeed?"

"Yes. I have run over to look after my—my Chancery interests before the long vacation," said Richard, forcing a careless laugh. "We are beginning to spin along with that old suit at last, I promise you."

No wonder that I shook my head!

"As you say, it's not a pleasant subject." Richard spoke with the same shade crossing his face as before. "Let it go to the four winds for to-night. Puff! Gone! Who do you suppose is with me?"

"Was it Mr. Skimpole's voice I heard?"

"That's the man! He does me more good than anybody. What a fascinating child it is!"

I asked Richard if any one knew of their coming down together. He answered, no, nobody. He had been to call upon the dear old infant—so he called Mr. Skimpole—and the dear old infant had told him where we were, and he had told the dear old infant he was bent on coming to see us, and the dear old infant had directly wanted to come too; and so he had brought him. "And he is worth—not to say his sordid expenses—but thrice his weight in gold," said Richard. "He is such a cheery fellow. No worldliness about him. Fresh and green-hearted!"

I certainly did not see the proof of Mr. Skimpole's worldliness in his having his expenses paid by Richard, but I made no remark about that. Indeed, he came in and turned our conversation. He was charmed to see me, said he had been shedding delicious tears of joy and sympathy at intervals for six weeks on my account, had never been so happy as in hearing of my progress, began to understand the mixture of good and evil in the world now, felt that he appreciated health the more when somebody else was ill, didn't know but what it might be in the scheme of things that A should squint to make B happier in looking straight or that C should carry a wooden leg to make D better satisfied with his flesh and blood in a silk stocking.

"My dear Miss Summerson, here is our friend Richard," said Mr. Skimpole, "full of the brightest visions of the future, which he evokes out of the darkness of Chancery. Now that's delightful, that's inspiriting, that's full of poetry! In old times the woods and solitudes were made joyous to the shepherd by the imaginary piping and dancing of Pan and the nymphs. This present shepherd, our pastoral Richard, brightens the dull Inns of Court by making Fortune and her train sport through them to the melodious notes of a judgment from the bench. That's very pleasant, you know! Some ill-conditioned growling fellow may say to me, 'What's the use of these legal and equitable abuses? How do you defend them?' I reply, 'My growling friend, I DON'T defend them, but they are very agreeable to me. There is a shepherd—youth, a friend of mine, who transmutes them into something highly fascinating to my simplicity. I don't say it is for this that they exist—for I am a child among you worldly grumblers, and not called upon to account to you or myself for anything—but it may be so.'"

I began seriously to think that Richard could scarcely have found a worse friend than this. It made me uneasy that at such a time when he most required some right principle and purpose he should have this captivating looseness and putting-off of everything, this airy dispensing with all principle and purpose, at his elbow. I thought I could understand how such a nature as my guardian's, experienced in the world and forced to contemplate the miserable evasions and contentions of the family misfortune, found an immense relief in Mr. Skimpole's avowal of his weaknesses and display of guileless candour; but I could not satisfy myself that it was as artless as it seemed or that it did not serve Mr. Skimpole's idle turn quite as well as any other part, and with less trouble.

They both walked back with me, and Mr. Skimpole leaving us at the gate, I walked softly in with Richard and said, "Ada, my love, I have brought a gentleman to visit you." It was not difficult to read the blushing, startled face. She loved him dearly, and he knew it, and I knew it. It was a very transparent business, that meeting as cousins only.

I almost mistrusted myself as growing quite wicked in my suspicions, but I was not so sure that Richard loved her dearly. He admired her very much—any one must have done that—and I dare say would have renewed their youthful engagement with great pride and ardour but that he knew how she would respect her promise to my guardian. Still I had a tormenting idea that the influence upon him extended even here, that he was postponing his best truth and earnestness in this as in all things until Jarndyce and Jarndyce should be off his mind. Ah me! What Richard would have been without that blight, I never shall know now!

He told Ada, in his most ingenuous way, that he had not come to make any secret inroad on the terms she had accepted (rather too implicitly and confidingly, he thought) from Mr. Jarndyce, that he had come openly to see her and to see me and to justify himself for the present terms on which he stood with Mr. Jarndyce. As the dear old infant would be with us directly, he begged that I would make an appointment for the morning, when he might set himself right through the means of an unreserved conversation with me. I proposed to walk with him in the park at seven o'clock, and this was arranged. Mr. Skimpole soon afterwards appeared and made us merry for an hour. He particularly requested to see little Coavinses (meaning Charley) and told her, with a patriarchal air, that he had given her late father all the business in his power and that if one of her little brothers would make haste to get set up in the same profession, he hoped he should still be able to put a good deal of employment in his way.

"For I am constantly being taken in these nets," said Mr. Skimpole, looking beamingly at us over a glass of wine-and-water, "and am constantly being bailed out—like a boat. Or paid off—like a ship's company. Somebody always does it for me. I can't do it, you know, for I never have any money. But somebody does it. I get out by somebody's means; I am not like the starling; I get out. If you were to ask me who somebody is, upon my word I couldn't tell you. Let us drink to somebody. God bless him!"

Richard was a little late in the morning, but I had not to wait for him long, and we turned into the park. The air was bright and dewy and the sky without a cloud. The birds sang delightfully; the sparkles in the fern, the grass, and trees, were exquisite to see; the richness of the woods seemed to have increased twenty-fold since yesterday, as if, in the still night when they had looked so massively hushed in sleep, Nature, through all the minute details of every wonderful leaf, had been more wakeful than usual for the glory of that day.

"This is a lovely place," said Richard, looking round. "None of the jar and discord of law-suits here!"

But there was other trouble.

"I tell you what, my dear girl," said Richard, "when I get affairs in general settled, I shall come down here, I think, and rest."

"Would it not be better to rest now?" I asked.

"Oh, as to resting NOW," said Richard, "or as to doing anything very definite NOW, that's not easy. In short, it can't be done; I can't do it at least."

"Why not?" said I.

"You know why not, Esther. If you were living in an unfinished house, liable to have the roof put on or taken off—to be from top to bottom pulled down or built up—to-morrow, next day, next week, next month, next year—you would find it hard to rest or settle. So do I. Now? There's no now for us suitors."

I could almost have believed in the attraction on which my poor little wandering friend had expatiated when I saw again the darkened look of last night. Terrible to think it had in it also a shade of that unfortunate man who had died.

"My dear Richard," said I, "this is a bad beginning of our conversation."

"I knew you would tell me so, Dame Durden."

"And not I alone, dear Richard. It was not I who cautioned you once never to found a hope or expectation on the family curse."

"There you come back to John Jarndyce!" said Richard impatiently. "Well! We must approach him sooner or later, for he is the staple of what I have to say, and it's as well at once. My dear Esther, how can you be so blind? Don't you see that he is an interested party and that it may be very well for him to wish me to know nothing of the suit, and care nothing about it, but that it may not be quite so well for me?"

"Oh, Richard," I remonstrated, "is it possible that you can ever have seen him and heard him, that you can ever have lived under his roof and known him, and can yet breathe, even to me in this solitary place where there is no one to hear us, such unworthy suspicions?"

He reddened deeply, as if his natural generosity felt a pang of reproach. He was silent for a little while before he replied in a subdued voice, "Esther, I am sure you know that I am not a mean fellow and that I have some sense of suspicion and distrust being poor qualities in one of my years."

"I know it very well," said I. "I am not more sure of anything."

"That's a dear girl," retorted Richard, "and like you, because it gives me comfort. I had need to get some scrap of comfort out of all this business, for it's a bad one at the best, as I have no occasion to tell you."

"I know perfectly," said I. "I know as well, Richard—what shall I say? as well as you do—that such misconstructions are foreign to your nature. And I know, as well as you know, what so changes it."

"Come, sister, come," said Richard a little more gaily, "you will be fair with me at all events. If I have the misfortune to be under that influence, so has he. If it has a little twisted me, it may have a little twisted him too. I don't say that he is not an honourable man, out of all this complication and uncertainty; I am sure he is. But it taints everybody. You know it taints everybody. You have heard him say so fifty times. Then why should HE escape?"

"Because," said I, "his is an uncommon character, and he has resolutely kept himself outside the circle, Richard."

"Oh, because and because!" replied Richard in his vivacious way. "I am not sure, my dear girl, but that it may be wise and specious to preserve that outward indifference. It may cause other parties interested to become lax about their interests; and people may die off, and points may drag themselves out of memory, and many things may smoothly happen that are convenient enough."

I was so touched with pity for Richard that I could not reproach him any more, even by a look. I remembered my guardian's gentleness towards his errors and with what perfect freedom from resentment he had spoken of them.

"Esther," Richard resumed, "you are not to suppose that I have come here to make underhanded charges against John Jarndyce. I have only come to justify myself. What I say is, it was all very well and we got on very well while I was a boy, utterly regardless of this same suit; but as soon as I began to take an interest in it and to look into it, then it was quite another thing. Then John Jarndyce discovers that Ada and I must break off and that if I don't amend that very objectionable course, I am not fit for her. Now, Esther, I don't mean to amend that very objectionable course: I will not hold John Jarndyce's favour on those unfair terms of compromise, which he has no right to dictate. Whether it pleases him or displeases him, I must maintain my rights and Ada's. I have been thinking about it a good deal, and this is the conclusion I have come to."

Poor dear Richard! He had indeed been thinking about it a good deal. His face, his voice, his manner, all showed that too plainly.

"So I tell him honourably (you are to know I have written to him about all this) that we are at issue and that we had better be at issue openly than covertly. I thank him for his goodwill and his protection, and he goes his road, and I go mine. The fact is, our roads are not the same. Under one of the wills in dispute, I should take much more than he. I don't mean to say that it is the one to be established, but there it is, and it has its chance."

"I have not to learn from you, my dear Richard," said I, "of your letter. I had heard of it already without an offended or angry word."

"Indeed?" replied Richard, softening. "I am glad I said he was an honourable man, out of all this wretched affair. But I always say that and have never doubted it. Now, my dear Esther, I know these views of mine appear extremely harsh to you, and will to Ada when you tell her what has passed between us. But if you had gone into the case as I have, if you had only applied yourself to the papers as I did when I was at Kenge's, if you only knew what an accumulation of charges and counter-charges, and suspicions and cross-suspicions, they involve, you would think me moderate in comparison."

"Perhaps so," said I. "But do you think that, among those many papers, there is much truth and justice, Richard?"

"There is truth and justice somewhere in the case, Esther—"

"Or was once, long ago," said I.

"Is—is—must be somewhere," pursued Richard impetuously, "and must be brought out. To allow Ada to be made a bribe and hush-money of is not the way to bring it out. You say the suit is changing me; John Jarndyce says it changes, has changed, and will change everybody who has any share in it. Then the greater right I have on my side when I resolve to do all I can to bring it to an end."

"All you can, Richard! Do you think that in these many years no others have done all they could? Has the difficulty grown easier because of so many failures?"

"It can't last for ever," returned Richard with a fierceness kindling in him which again presented to me that last sad reminder. "I am young and earnest, and energy and determination have done wonders many a time. Others have only half thrown themselves into it. I devote myself to it. I make it the object of my life."

"Oh, Richard, my dear, so much the worse, so much the worse!"

"No, no, no, don't you be afraid for me," he returned affectionately. "You're a dear, good, wise, quiet, blessed girl; but you have your prepossessions. So I come round to John Jarndyce. I tell you, my good Esther, when he and I were on those terms which he found so convenient, we were not on natural terms."

"Are division and animosity your natural terms, Richard?"

"No, I don't say that. I mean that all this business puts us on unnatural terms, with which natural relations are incompatible. See another reason for urging it on! I may find out when it's over that I have been mistaken in John Jarndyce. My head may be clearer when I am free of it, and I may then agree with what you say to-day. Very well. Then I shall acknowledge it and make him reparation."

Everything postponed to that imaginary time! Everything held in confusion and indecision until then!

"Now, my best of confidantes," said Richard, "I want my cousin Ada to understand that I am not captious, fickle, and wilful about John Jarndyce, but that I have this purpose and reason at my back. I wish to represent myself to her through you, because she has a great esteem and respect for her cousin John; and I know you will soften the course I take, even though you disapprove of it; and—and in short," said Richard, who had been hesitating through these words, "I—I don't like to represent myself in this litigious, contentious, doubting character to a confiding girl like Ada."

I told him that he was more like himself in those latter words than in anything he had said yet.

"Why," acknowledged Richard, "that may be true enough, my love. I rather feel it to be so. But I shall be able to give myself fair-play by and by. I shall come all right again, then, don't you be afraid."

I asked him if this were all he wished me to tell Ada.

"Not quite," said Richard. "I am bound not to withhold from her that John Jarndyce answered my letter in his usual manner, addressing me as 'My dear Rick,' trying to argue me out of my opinions, and telling me that they should make no difference in him. (All very well of course, but not altering the case.) I also want Ada to know that if I see her seldom just now, I am looking after her interests as well as my own—we two being in the same boat exactly—and that I hope she will not suppose from any flying rumours she may hear that I am at all light-headed or imprudent; on the contrary, I am always looking forward to the termination of the suit, and always planning in that direction. Being of age now and having taken the step I have taken, I consider myself free from any accountability to John Jarndyce; but Ada being still a ward of the court, I don't yet ask her to renew our engagement. When she is free to act for herself, I shall be myself once more and we shall both be in very different worldly circumstances, I believe. If you tell her all this with the advantage of your considerate way, you will do me a very great and a very kind service, my dear Esther; and I shall knock Jarndyce and Jarndyce on the head with greater vigour. Of course I ask for no secrecy at Bleak House."

"Richard," said I, "you place great confidence in me, but I fear you will not take advice from me?"

"It's impossible that I can on this subject, my dear girl. On any other, readily."

As if there were any other in his life! As if his whole career and character were not being dyed one colour!

"But I may ask you a question, Richard?"

"I think so," said he, laughing. "I don't know who may not, if you may not."

"You say, yourself, you are not leading a very settled life."

"How can I, my dear Esther, with nothing settled!"

"Are you in debt again?"

"Why, of course I am," said Richard, astonished at my simplicity.

"Is it of course?"

"My dear child, certainly. I can't throw myself into an object so completely without expense. You forget, or perhaps you don't know, that under either of the wills Ada and I take something. It's only a question between the larger sum and the smaller. I shall be within the mark any way. Bless your heart, my excellent girl," said Richard, quite amused with me, "I shall be all right! I shall pull through, my dear!"

I felt so deeply sensible of the danger in which he stood that I tried, in Ada's name, in my guardian's, in my own, by every fervent means that I could think of, to warn him of it and to show him some of his mistakes. He received everything I said with patience and gentleness, but it all rebounded from him without taking the least effect. I could not wonder at this after the reception his preoccupied mind had given to my guardian's letter, but I determined to try Ada's influence yet.

So when our walk brought us round to the village again, and I went home to breakfast, I prepared Ada for the account I was going to give her and told her exactly what reason we had to dread that Richard was losing himself and scattering his whole life to the winds. It made her very unhappy, of course, though she had a far, far greater reliance on his correcting his errors than I could have—which was so natural and loving in my dear!—and she presently wrote him this little letter:

My dearest cousin,

Esther has told me all you said to her this morning. I write this to repeat most earnestly for myself all that she said to you and to let you know how sure I am that you will sooner or later find our cousin John a pattern of truth, sincerity, and goodness, when you will deeply, deeply grieve to have done him (without intending it) so much wrong.

I do not quite know how to write what I wish to say next, but I trust you will understand it as I mean it. I have some fears, my dearest cousin, that it may be partly for my sake you are now laying up so much unhappiness for yourself—and if for yourself, for me. In case this should be so, or in case you should entertain much thought of me in what you are doing, I most earnestly entreat and beg you to desist. You can do nothing for my sake that will make me half so happy as for ever turning your back upon the shadow in which we both were born. Do not be angry with me for saying this. Pray, pray, dear Richard, for my sake, and for your own, and in a natural repugnance for that source of trouble which had its share in making us both orphans when we were very young, pray, pray, let it go for ever. We have reason to know by this time that there is no good in it and no hope, that there is nothing to be got from it but sorrow.

My dearest cousin, it is needless for me to say that you are quite free and that it is very likely you may find some one whom you will love much better than your first fancy. I am quite sure, if you will let me say so, that the object of your choice would greatly prefer to follow your fortunes far and wide, however moderate or poor, and see you happy, doing your duty and pursuing your chosen way, than to have the hope of being, or even to be, very rich with you (if such a thing were possible) at the cost of dragging years of procrastination and anxiety and of your indifference to other aims. You may wonder at my saying this so confidently with so little knowledge or experience, but I know it for a certainty from my own heart.

Ever, my dearest cousin, your most affectionate
Ada

This note brought Richard to us very soon, but it made little change in him if any. We would fairly try, he said, who was right and who was wrong—he would show us—we should see! He was animated and glowing, as if Ada's tenderness had gratified him; but I could only hope, with a sigh, that the letter might have some stronger effect upon his mind on re-perusal than it assuredly had then.

As they were to remain with us that day and had taken their places to return by the coach next morning, I sought an opportunity of speaking to Mr. Skimpole. Our out-of-door life easily threw one in my way, and I delicately said that there was a responsibility in encouraging Richard.

"Responsibility, my dear Miss Summerson?" he repeated, catching at the word with the pleasantest smile. "I am the last man in the world for such a thing. I never was responsible in my life—I can't be."

"I am afraid everybody is obliged to be," said I timidly enough, he being so much older and more clever than I.

"No, really?" said Mr. Skimpole, receiving this new light with a most agreeable jocularity of surprise. "But every man's not obliged to be solvent? I am not. I never was. See, my dear Miss Summerson," he took a handful of loose silver and halfpence from his pocket, "there's so much money. I have not an idea how much. I have not the power of counting. Call it four and ninepence—call it four pound nine. They tell me I owe more than that. I dare say I do. I dare say I owe as much as good-natured people will let me owe. If they don't stop, why should I? There you have Harold Skimpole in little. If that's responsibility, I am responsible."

The perfect ease of manner with which he put the money up again and looked at me with a smile on his refined face, as if he had been mentioning a curious little fact about somebody else, almost made me feel as if he really had nothing to do with it.

"Now, when you mention responsibility," he resumed, "I am disposed to say that I never had the happiness of knowing any one whom I should consider so refreshingly responsible as yourself. You appear to me to be the very touchstone of responsibility. When I see you, my dear Miss Summerson, intent upon the perfect working of the whole little orderly system of which you are the centre, I feel inclined to say to myself—in fact I do say to myself very often—THAT'S responsibility!"

It was difficult, after this, to explain what I meant; but I persisted so far as to say that we all hoped he would check and not confirm Richard in the sanguine views he entertained just then.

"Most willingly," he retorted, "if I could. But, my dear Miss Summerson, I have no art, no disguise. If he takes me by the hand and leads me through

Westminster Hall in an airy procession after fortune, I must go. If he says, 'Skimpole, join the dance!' I must join it. Common sense wouldn't, I know, but I have NO common sense."

It was very unfortunate for Richard, I said.

"Do you think so!" returned Mr. Skimpole. "Don't say that, don't say that. Let us suppose him keeping company with Common Sense—an excellent man—a good deal wrinkled—dreadfully practical—change for a ten-pound note in every pocket—ruled account-book in his hand—say, upon the whole, resembling a tax-gatherer. Our dear Richard, sanguine, ardent, overleaping obstacles, bursting with poetry like a young bud, says to this highly respectable companion, 'I see a golden prospect before me; it's very bright, it's very beautiful, it's very joyous; here I go, bounding over the landscape to come at it!' The respectable companion instantly knocks him down with the ruled account-book; tells him in a literal, prosaic way that he sees no such thing; shows him it's nothing but fees, fraud, horsehair wigs, and black gowns. Now you know that's a painful change—sensible in the last degree, I have no doubt, but disagreeable. I can't do it. I haven't got the ruled account-book, I have none of the tax-gathering elements in my composition, I am not at all respectable, and I don't want to be. Odd perhaps, but so it is!"

It was idle to say more, so I proposed that we should join Ada and Richard, who were a little in advance, and I gave up Mr. Skimpole in despair. He had been over the Hall in the course of the morning and whimsically described the family pictures as we walked. There were such portentous shepherdesses among the Ladies Dedlock dead and gone, he told us, that peaceful crooks became weapons of assault in their hands. They tended their flocks severely in buckram and powder and put their sticking-plaster patches on to terrify commoners as the chiefs of some other tribes put on their war-paint. There was a Sir Somebody Dedlock, with a battle, a sprung-mine, volumes of smoke, flashes of lightning, a town on fire, and a stormed fort, all in full action between his horse's two hind legs, showing, he supposed, how little a Dedlock made of such trifles. The whole race he represented as having evidently been, in life, what he called "stuffed people"—a large collection, glassy eyed, set up in the most approved manner on their various twigs and perches, very correct, perfectly free from animation, and always in glass cases.

I was not so easy now during any reference to the name but that I felt it a relief when Richard, with an exclamation of surprise, hurried away to meet a stranger whom he first descried coming slowly towards us.

"Dear me!" said Mr. Skimpole. "Vholes!"

We asked if that were a friend of Richard's.

"Friend and legal adviser," said Mr. Skimpole. "Now, my dear Miss Summerson, if you want common sense, responsibility, and respectability, all united—if you want an exemplary man—Vholes is THE man."

We had not known, we said, that Richard was assisted by any gentleman of that name.

"When he emerged from legal infancy," returned Mr. Skimpole, "he parted from our conversational friend Kenge and took up, I believe, with Vholes. Indeed, I know he did, because I introduced him to Vholes."

"Had you known him long?" asked Ada.

"Vholes? My dear Miss Clare, I had had that kind of acquaintance with him which I have had with several gentlemen of his profession. He had done something or other in a very agreeable, civil manner—taken proceedings, I think, is the expression—which ended in the proceeding of his taking ME. Somebody was so good as to step in and pay the money—something and fourpence was the amount; I forget the pounds and shillings, but I know it ended with fourpence, because it struck me at the time as being so odd that I could owe anybody fourpence—and after that I brought them together. Vholes asked me for the introduction, and I gave it. Now I come to think of it," he looked inquiringly at us with his frankest smile as he made the discovery, "Vholes bribed me, perhaps? He gave me something and called it commission. Was it a five-pound note? Do you know, I think it MUST have been a five-pound note!"

His further consideration of the point was prevented by Richard's coming back to us in an excited state and hastily representing Mr. Vholes—a sallow man with pinched lips that looked as if they were cold, a red eruption here and there upon his face, tall and thin, about fifty years of age, high-shouldered, and stooping. Dressed in black, black-gloved, and buttoned to the chin, there was nothing so remarkable in him as a lifeless manner and a slow, fixed way he had of looking at Richard.

"I hope I don't disturb you, ladies," said Mr. Vholes, and now I observed that he was further remarkable for an inward manner of speaking. "I arranged with Mr. Carstone that he should always know when his cause was in the Chancellor's paper, and being informed by one of my clerks last night after post time that it stood, rather unexpectedly, in the paper for to-morrow, I put myself into the coach early this morning and came down to confer with him."

"Yes," said Richard, flushed, and looking triumphantly at Ada and me, "we don't do these things in the old slow way now. We spin along now! Mr. Vholes, we must hire something to get over to the post town in, and catch the mail to-night, and go up by it!"

"Anything you please, sir," returned Mr. Vholes. "I am quite at your service."

"Let me see," said Richard, looking at his watch. "If I run down to the Dedlock, and get my portmanteau fastened up, and order a gig, or a chaise, or whatever's to be got, we shall have an hour then before starting. I'll come back to tea. Cousin Ada, will you and Esther take care of Mr. Vholes when I am gone?"

He was away directly, in his heat and hurry, and was soon lost in the dusk of evening. We who were left walked on towards the house.

"Is Mr. Carstone's presence necessary to-morrow, Sir?" said I. "Can it do any good?"

"No, miss," Mr. Vholes replied. "I am not aware that it can."

Both Ada and I expressed our regret that he should go, then, only to be disappointed.

"Mr. Carstone has laid down the principle of watching his own interests," said Mr. Vholes, "and when a client lays down his own principle, and it is not immoral, it devolves upon me to carry it out. I wish in business to be exact and open. I am a widower with three daughters—Emma, Jane, and Caroline—and my desire is so to discharge the duties of life as to leave them a good name. This appears to be a pleasant spot, miss."

The remark being made to me in consequence of my being next him as we walked, I assented and enumerated its chief attractions.

"Indeed?" said Mr. Vholes. "I have the privilege of supporting an aged father in the Vale of Taunton—his native place—and I admire that country very much. I had no idea there was anything so attractive here."

To keep up the conversation, I asked Mr. Vholes if he would like to live altogether in the country.

"There, miss," said he, "you touch me on a tender string. My health is not good (my digestion being much impaired), and if I had only myself to consider, I should take refuge in rural habits, especially as the cares of business have prevented me from ever coming much into contact with general society, and particularly with ladies' society, which I have most wished to mix in. But with my three daughters, Emma, Jane, and Caroline—and my aged father—I cannot afford to be selfish. It is true I have no longer to maintain a dear grandmother who died in her hundred and second year, but enough remains to render it indispensable that the mill should be always going."

It required some attention to hear him on account of his inward speaking and his lifeless manner.

"You will excuse my having mentioned my daughters," he said. "They are my weak point. I wish to leave the poor girls some little independence, as well as a good name."

We now arrived at Mr. Boythorn's house, where the tea-table, all prepared, was awaiting us. Richard came in restless and hurried shortly afterwards, and leaning over Mr. Vholes's chair, whispered something in his ear. Mr. Vholes replied aloud—or as nearly aloud I suppose as he had ever replied to anything—"You will drive me, will you, sir? It is all the same to me, sir. Anything you please. I am quite at your service."

We understood from what followed that Mr. Skimpole was to be left until the morning to occupy the two places which had been already paid for. As Ada and I were both in low spirits concerning Richard and very sorry so to part with him, we made it as plain as we politely could that we should leave Mr. Skimpole to the Dedlock Arms and retire when the night-travellers were gone.

Richard's high spirits carrying everything before them, we all went out together to the top of the hill above the village, where he had ordered a gig to wait and where we found a man with a lantern standing at the head of the gaunt pale horse that had been harnessed to it.

I never shall forget those two seated side by side in the lantern's light, Richard all flush and fire and laughter, with the reins in his hand; Mr. Vholes quite still, black-gloved, and buttoned up, looking at him as if he were looking at his prey and charming it. I have before me the whole picture of the warm dark night, the summer lightning, the dusty track of road closed in by hedgerows and high trees, the gaunt pale horse with his ears pricked up, and the driving away at speed to Jarndyce and Jarndyce.

My dear girl told me that night how Richard's being thereafter prosperous or ruined, befriended or deserted, could only make this difference to her, that the more he needed love from one unchanging heart, the more love that unchanging heart would have to give him; how he thought of her through his present errors, and she would think of him at all times—never of herself if she could devote herself to him, never of her own delights if she could minister to his.

And she kept her word?

I look along the road before me, where the distance already shortens and the journey's end is growing visible; and true and good above the dead sea of the Chancery suit and all the ashy fruit it cast ashore, I think I see my darling.

CHAPTER XXXVIII
A STRUGGLE

When our time came for returning to Bleak House again, we were punctual to the day and were received with an overpowering welcome. I was perfectly restored to health and strength, and finding my housekeeping keys laid ready for me in my room, rang myself in as if I had been a new year, with a merry little peal. "Once more, duty, duty, Esther," said I; "and if you are not overjoyed to do it, more than cheerfully and contentedly, through anything and everything, you ought to be. That's all I have to say to you, my dear!"

The first few mornings were mornings of so much bustle and business, devoted to such settlements of accounts, such repeated journeys to and fro between the growlery and all other parts of the house, so many rearrangements of drawers and presses, and such a general new beginning altogether, that I had not a moment's leisure. But when these arrangements were completed and everything was in order, I paid a visit of a few hours to London, which something in the letter I had destroyed at Chesney Wold had induced me to decide upon in my own mind.

I made Caddy Jellyby—her maiden name was so natural to me that I always called her by it—the pretext for this visit and wrote her a note previously asking the favour of her company on a little business expedition. Leaving home very early in the morning, I got to London by stage-coach in such good time that I got to Newman Street with the day before me.

Caddy, who had not seen me since her wedding-day, was so glad and so affectionate that I was half inclined to fear I should make her husband jealous. But he was, in his way, just as bad—I mean as good; and in short it was the old story, and nobody would leave me any possibility of doing anything meritorious.

The elder Mr. Turveydrop was in bed, I found, and Caddy was milling his chocolate, which a melancholy little boy who was an apprentice—it seemed such a curious thing to be apprenticed to the trade of dancing—was waiting to carry upstairs. Her father-in-law was extremely kind and considerate, Caddy told me, and they lived most happily together. (When she spoke of their living together, she meant that the old gentleman had all the good things and all the good lodging, while she and her husband had what they could get, and were poked into two corner rooms over the Mews.)

"And how is your mama, Caddy?" said I.

"Why, I hear of her, Esther," replied Caddy, "through Pa, but I see very little of her. We are good friends, I am glad to say, but Ma thinks there is something absurd in my having married a dancing-master, and she is rather afraid of its extending to her."

It struck me that if Mrs. Jellyby had discharged her own natural duties and obligations before she swept the horizon with a telescope in search of others, she would have taken the best precautions against becoming absurd, but I need scarcely observe that I kept this to myself.

"And your papa, Caddy?"

"He comes here every evening," returned Caddy, "and is so fond of sitting in the corner there that it's a treat to see him."

Looking at the corner, I plainly perceived the mark of Mr. Jellyby's head against the wall. It was consolatory to know that he had found such a resting-place for it.

"And you, Caddy," said I, "you are always busy, I'll be bound?"

"Well, my dear," returned Caddy, "I am indeed, for to tell you a grand secret, I am qualifying myself to give lessons. Prince's health is not strong, and I want to be able to assist him. What with schools, and classes here, and private pupils, AND the apprentices, he really has too much to do, poor fellow!"

The notion of the apprentices was still so odd to me that I asked Caddy if there were many of them.

"Four," said Caddy. "One in-door, and three out. They are very good children; only when they get together they WILL play—children-like—instead of attending to their work. So the little boy you saw just now waltzes by himself in the empty kitchen, and we distribute the others over the house as well as we can."

"That is only for their steps, of course?" said I.

"Only for their steps," said Caddy. "In that way they practise, so many hours at a time, whatever steps they happen to be upon. They dance in the academy, and at this time of year we do figures at five every morning."

"Why, what a laborious life!" I exclaimed.

"I assure you, my dear," returned Caddy, smiling, "when the out-door apprentices ring us up in the morning (the bell rings into our room, not to disturb old Mr. Turveydrop), and when I put up the window and see them standing on the door-step with their little pumps under their arms, I am actually reminded of the Sweeps."

All this presented the art to me in a singular light, to be sure. Caddy enjoyed the effect of her communication and cheerfully recounted the particulars of her own studies.

"You see, my dear, to save expense I ought to know something of the piano, and I ought to know something of the kit too, and consequently I have to practise those two instruments as well as the details of our profession. If Ma had been like anybody else, I might have had some little musical knowledge to begin upon. However, I hadn't any; and that part of the work is, at first, a little discouraging, I must allow. But I have a very good ear, and I am used to drudgery—I have to thank Ma for that, at all events—and where there's a will there's a way, you know, Esther, the world over." Saying these words,

Caddy laughingly sat down at a little jingling square piano and really rattled off a quadrille with great spirit. Then she good-humouredly and blushingly got up again, and while she still laughed herself, said, "Don't laugh at me, please; that's a dear girl!"

I would sooner have cried, but I did neither. I encouraged her and praised her with all my heart. For I conscientiously believed, dancing-master's wife though she was, and dancing-mistress though in her limited ambition she aspired to be, she had struck out a natural, wholesome, loving course of industry and perseverance that was quite as good as a mission.

"My dear," said Caddy, delighted, "you can't think how you cheer me. I shall owe you, you don't know how much. What changes, Esther, even in my small world! You recollect that first night, when I was so unpolite and inky? Who would have thought, then, of my ever teaching people to dance, of all other possibilities and impossibilities!"

Her husband, who had left us while we had this chat, now coming back, preparatory to exercising the apprentices in the ball-room, Caddy informed me she was quite at my disposal. But it was not my time yet, I was glad to tell her, for I should have been vexed to take her away then. Therefore we three adjourned to the apprentices together, and I made one in the dance.

The apprentices were the queerest little people. Besides the melancholy boy, who, I hoped, had not been made so by waltzing alone in the empty kitchen, there were two other boys and one dirty little limp girl in a gauzy dress. Such a precocious little girl, with such a dowdy bonnet on (that, too, of a gauzy texture), who brought her sandalled shoes in an old threadbare velvet reticule. Such mean little boys, when they were not dancing, with string, and marbles, and cramp-bones in their pockets, and the most untidy legs and feet—and heels particularly.

I asked Caddy what had made their parents choose this profession for them. Caddy said she didn't know; perhaps they were designed for teachers, perhaps for the stage. They were all people in humble circumstances, and the melancholy boy's mother kept a ginger-beer shop.

We danced for an hour with great gravity, the melancholy child doing wonders with his lower extremities, in which there appeared to be some sense of enjoyment though it never rose above his waist. Caddy, while she was observant of her husband and was evidently founded upon him, had acquired a grace and self-possession of her own, which, united to her pretty face and figure, was uncommonly agreeable. She already relieved him of much of the instruction of these young people, and he seldom interfered except to walk his part in the figure if he had anything to do in it. He always played the tune. The affectation of the gauzy child, and her condescension to the boys, was a sight. And thus we danced an hour by the clock.

When the practice was concluded, Caddy's husband made himself ready to go out of town to a school, and Caddy ran away to get ready to go out with me. I sat in the ball-room in the interval, contemplating the apprentices. The two out-door boys went upon the staircase to put on their half-boots and pull the in-door boy's hair, as I judged from the nature of his objections. Returning with their jackets buttoned and their pumps stuck in them, they then produced packets of cold bread and meat and bivouacked under a painted lyre on the wall. The little gauzy child, having whisked her sandals into the reticule and put on a trodden-down pair of shoes, shook her head into the dowdy bonnet at one shake, and answering my inquiry whether she liked dancing by replying, "Not with boys," tied it across her chin, and went home contemptuous.

"Old Mr. Turveydrop is so sorry," said Caddy, "that he has not finished dressing yet and cannot have the pleasure of seeing you before you go. You are such a favourite of his, Esther."

I expressed myself much obliged to him, but did not think it necessary to add that I readily dispensed with this attention.

"It takes him a long time to dress," said Caddy, "because he is very much looked up to in such things, you know, and has a reputation to support. You can't think how kind he is to Pa. He talks to Pa of an evening about the Prince Regent, and I never saw Pa so interested."

There was something in the picture of Mr. Turveydrop bestowing his deportment on Mr. Jellyby that quite took my fancy. I asked Caddy if he brought her papa out much.

"No," said Caddy, "I don't know that he does that, but he talks to Pa, and Pa greatly admires him, and listens, and likes it. Of course I am aware that Pa has hardly any claims to deportment, but they get on together delightfully. You can't think what good companions they make. I never saw Pa take snuff before in my life, but he takes one pinch out of Mr. Turveydrop's box regularly and keeps putting it to his nose and taking it away again all the evening."

That old Mr. Turveydrop should ever, in the chances and changes of life, have come to the rescue of Mr. Jellyby from Borrioboola-Gha appeared to me to be one of the pleasantest of oddities.

"As to Peepy," said Caddy with a little hesitation, "whom I was most afraid of—next to having any family of my own, Esther—as an inconvenience to Mr. Turveydrop, the kindness of the old gentleman to that child is beyond everything. He asks to see him, my dear! He lets him take the newspaper up to him in bed; he gives him the crusts of his toast to eat; he sends him on little errands about the house; he tells him to come to me for sixpences. In short," said Caddy cheerily, "and not to prose, I am a very fortunate girl and ought to be very grateful. Where are we going, Esther?"

"To the Old Street Road," said I, "where I have a few words to say to the solicitor's clerk who was sent to meet me at the coach-office on the very day when I came to London and first saw you, my dear. Now I think of it, the gentleman who brought us to your house."

"Then, indeed, I seem to be naturally the person to go with you," returned Caddy.

To the Old Street Road we went and there inquired at Mrs. Guppy's residence for Mrs. Guppy. Mrs. Guppy, occupying the parlours and having indeed been visibly in danger of cracking herself like a nut in the front-parlour door by peeping out before she was asked for, immediately presented herself and requested us to walk in. She was an old lady in a large cap, with rather a red nose and rather an unsteady eye, but smiling all over. Her close little sitting-room was prepared for a visit, and there was a portrait of her son in it which, I had almost written here, was more like than life: it insisted upon him with such obstinacy, and was so determined not to let him off.

Not only was the portrait there, but we found the original there too. He was dressed in a great many colours and was discovered at a table reading law-papers with his forefinger to his forehead.

"Miss Summerson," said Mr. Guppy, rising, "this is indeed an oasis. Mother, will you be so good as to put a chair for the other lady and get out of the gangway."

Mrs. Guppy, whose incessant smiling gave her quite a waggish appearance, did as her son requested and then sat down in a corner, holding her pocket handkerchief to her chest, like a fomentation, with both hands.

I presented Caddy, and Mr. Guppy said that any friend of mine was more than welcome. I then proceeded to the object of my visit.

"I took the liberty of sending you a note, sir," said I.

Mr. Guppy acknowledged the receipt by taking it out of his breast-pocket, putting it to his lips, and returning it to his pocket with a bow. Mr. Guppy's mother was so diverted that she rolled her head as she smiled and made a silent appeal to Caddy with her elbow.

"Could I speak to you alone for a moment?" said I.

Anything like the jocoseness of Mr. Guppy's mother just now, I think I never saw. She made no sound of laughter, but she rolled her head, and shook it, and put her handkerchief to her mouth, and appealed to Caddy with her elbow, and her hand, and her shoulder, and was so unspeakably entertained altogether that it was with some difficulty she could marshal Caddy through the little folding-door into her bedroom adjoining.

"Miss Summerson," said Mr. Guppy, "you will excuse the waywardness of a parent ever mindful of a son's appiness. My mother, though highly exasperating to the feelings, is actuated by maternal dictates."

I could hardly have believed that anybody could in a moment have turned so red or changed so much as Mr. Guppy did when I now put up my veil.

"I asked the favour of seeing you for a few moments here," said I, "in preference to calling at Mr. Kenge's because, remembering what you said on an occasion when you spoke to me in confidence, I feared I might otherwise cause you some embarrassment, Mr. Guppy."

I caused him embarrassment enough as it was, I am sure. I never saw such faltering, such confusion, such amazement and apprehension.

"Miss Summerson," stammered Mr. Guppy, "I—I—beg your pardon, but in our profession—we—we—find it necessary to be explicit. You have referred to an occasion, miss, when I—when I did myself the honour of making a declaration which—"

Something seemed to rise in his throat that he could not possibly swallow. He put his hand there, coughed, made faces, tried again to swallow it, coughed again, made faces again, looked all round the room, and fluttered his papers.

"A kind of giddy sensation has come upon me, miss," he explained, "which rather knocks me over. I—er—a little subject to this sort of thing—er—by George!"

I gave him a little time to recover. He consumed it in putting his hand to his forehead and taking it away again, and in backing his chair into the corner behind him.

"My intention was to remark, miss," said Mr. Guppy, "dear me—something bronchial, I think—hem!—to remark that you was so good on that occasion as to repel and repudiate that declaration. You—you wouldn't perhaps object to admit that? Though no witnesses are present, it might be a satisfaction to—to your mind—if you was to put in that admission."

"There can be no doubt," said I, "that I declined your proposal without any reservation or qualification whatever, Mr. Guppy."

"Thank you, miss," he returned, measuring the table with his troubled hands. "So far that's satisfactory, and it does you credit. Er—this is certainly bronchial!—must be in the tubes—er—you wouldn't perhaps be offended if I was to mention—not that it's necessary, for your own good sense or any person's sense must show 'em that—if I was to mention that such declaration on my part was final, and there terminated?"

"I quite understand that," said I.

"Perhaps—er—it may not be worth the form, but it might be a satisfaction to your mind—perhaps you wouldn't object to admit that, miss?" said Mr. Guppy.

"I admit it most fully and freely," said I.

"Thank you," returned Mr. Guppy. "Very honourable, I am sure. I regret that my arrangements in life, combined with circumstances over which I have no control, will put it out of my power ever to fall back upon that offer or to renew it in any shape or form whatever, but it will ever be a retrospect entwined—er—with friendship's bowers." Mr. Guppy's bronchitis came to his relief and stopped his measurement of the table.

"I may now perhaps mention what I wished to say to you?" I began.

"I shall be honoured, I am sure," said Mr. Guppy. "I am so persuaded that your own good sense and right feeling, miss, will—will keep you as square as possible—that I can have nothing but pleasure, I am sure, in hearing any observations you may wish to offer."

"You were so good as to imply, on that occasion—"

"Excuse me, miss," said Mr. Guppy, "but we had better not travel out of the record into implication. I cannot admit that I implied anything."

"You said on that occasion," I recommenced, "that you might possibly have the means of advancing my interests and promoting my fortunes by making discoveries of which I should be the subject. I presume that you founded that belief upon your general knowledge of my being an orphan girl, indebted for everything to the benevolence of Mr. Jarndyce. Now, the beginning and the end of what I have come to beg of you is, Mr. Guppy, that you will have the kindness to relinquish all idea of so serving me. I have thought of this sometimes, and I have thought of it most lately—since I have been ill. At length I have decided, in case you should at any time recall that purpose and act upon it in any way, to come to you and assure you that you are altogether mistaken. You could make no discovery in reference to me that would do me the least service or give me the least pleasure. I am acquainted with my personal history, and I have it in my power to assure you that you never can advance my welfare by such means. You may, perhaps, have abandoned this project a long time. If so, excuse my giving you unnecessary trouble. If not, I entreat you, on the assurance I have given you, henceforth to lay it aside. I beg you to do this, for my peace."

"I am bound to confess," said Mr. Guppy, "that you express yourself, miss, with that good sense and right feeling for which I gave you credit. Nothing can be more satisfactory than such right feeling, and if I mistook any intentions on your part just now, I am prepared to tender a full apology. I should wish to be understood, miss, as hereby offering that apology—limiting it, as your own good sense and right feeling will point out the necessity of, to the present proceedings."

I must say for Mr. Guppy that the snuffling manner he had had upon him improved very much. He seemed truly glad to be able to do something I asked, and he looked ashamed.

"If you will allow me to finish what I have to say at once so that I may have no occasion to resume," I went on, seeing him about to speak, "you will do me a kindness, sir. I come to you as privately as possible because you announced this impression of yours to me in a confidence which I have really wished to respect—and which I always have respected, as you remember. I have mentioned my illness. There really is no reason why I should hesitate to say that I know very well that any little delicacy I might have had in making a request to you is quite removed. Therefore I make the entreaty I have now preferred, and I hope you will have sufficient consideration for me to accede to it."

I must do Mr. Guppy the further justice of saying that he had looked more and more ashamed and that he looked most ashamed and very earnest when he now replied with a burning face, "Upon my word and honour, upon my life, upon my soul, Miss Summerson, as I am a living man, I'll act according to your wish! I'll never go another step in opposition to it. I'll take my oath to it if it will be any satisfaction to you. In what I promise at this present time touching the matters now in question," continued Mr. Guppy rapidly, as if he were repeating a familiar form of words, "I speak the truth, the whole truth, and nothing but the truth, so—"

"I am quite satisfied," said I, rising at this point, "and I thank you very much. Caddy, my dear, I am ready!"

Mr. Guppy's mother returned with Caddy (now making me the recipient of her silent laughter and her nudges), and we took our leave. Mr. Guppy saw us to the door with the air of one who was either imperfectly awake or walking in his sleep; and we left him there, staring.

But in a minute he came after us down the street without any hat, and with his long hair all blown about, and stopped us, saying fervently, "Miss Summerson, upon my honour and soul, you may depend upon me!"

"I do," said I, "quite confidently."

"I beg your pardon, miss," said Mr. Guppy, going with one leg and staying with the other, "but this lady being present—your own witness—it might be a satisfaction to your mind (which I should wish to set at rest) if you was to repeat those admissions."

"Well, Caddy," said I, turning to her, "perhaps you will not be surprised when I tell you, my dear, that there never has been any engagement—"

"No proposal or promise of marriage whatsoever," suggested Mr. Guppy.

"No proposal or promise of marriage whatsoever," said I, "between this gentleman—"

"William Guppy, of Penton Place, Pentonville, in the county of Middlesex," he murmured.

"Between this gentleman, Mr. William Guppy, of Penton Place, Pentonville, in the county of Middlesex, and myself."

"Thank you, miss," said Mr. Guppy. "Very full—er—excuse me—lady's name, Christian and surname both?"

I gave them.

"Married woman, I believe?" said Mr. Guppy. "Married woman. Thank you. Formerly Caroline Jellyby, spinster, then of Thavies Inn, within the city of London, but extra-parochial; now of Newman Street, Oxford Street. Much obliged."

He ran home and came running back again.

"Touching that matter, you know, I really and truly am very sorry that my arrangements in life, combined with circumstances over which I have no control, should prevent a renewal of what was wholly terminated some time back," said Mr. Guppy to me forlornly and despondently, "but it couldn't be. Now COULD it, you know! I only put it to you."

I replied it certainly could not. The subject did not admit of a doubt. He thanked me and ran to his mother's again—and back again.

"It's very honourable of you, miss, I am sure," said Mr. Guppy. "If an altar could be erected in the bowers of friendship—but, upon my soul, you may rely upon me in every respect save and except the tender passion only!"

The struggle in Mr. Guppy's breast and the numerous oscillations it occasioned him between his mother's door and us were sufficiently conspicuous in the windy street (particularly as his hair wanted cutting) to make us hurry away. I did so with a lightened heart; but when we last looked back, Mr. Guppy was still oscillating in the same troubled state of mind.

CHAPTER XXXIX
ATTORNEY AND CLIENT

The name of Mr. Vholes, preceded by the legend Ground-Floor, is inscribed upon a door-post in Symond's Inn, Chancery Lane—a little, pale, wall-eyed, woebegone inn like a large dust-binn of two compartments and a sifter. It looks as if Symond were a sparing man in his way and constructed his inn of old building materials which took kindly to the dry rot and to dirt and all things decaying and dismal, and perpetuated Symond's memory with congenial shabbiness. Quartered in this dingy hatchment commemorative of Symond are the legal bearings of Mr. Vholes.

Mr. Vholes's office, in disposition retiring and in situation retired, is squeezed up in a corner and blinks at a dead wall. Three feet of knotty-floored dark passage bring the client to Mr. Vholes's jet-black door, in an angle profoundly dark on the brightest midsummer morning and encumbered by a black bulk-head of cellarage staircase against which belated civilians generally strike their brows. Mr. Vholes's chambers are on so small a scale that one clerk can open the door without getting off his stool, while the other who elbows him at the same desk has equal facilities for poking the fire. A smell as of unwholesome sheep blending with the smell of must and dust is referable to the nightly (and often daily) consumption of mutton fat in candles and to the fretting of parchment forms and skins in greasy drawers. The atmosphere is otherwise stale and close. The place was last painted or whitewashed beyond the memory of man, and the two chimneys smoke, and there is a loose outer surface of soot everywhere, and the dull cracked windows in their heavy frames have but one piece of character in them, which is a determination to be always dirty and always shut unless coerced. This accounts for the phenomenon of the weaker of the two usually having a bundle of firewood thrust between its jaws in hot weather.

Mr. Vholes is a very respectable man. He has not a large business, but he is a very respectable man. He is allowed by the greater attorneys who have made good fortunes or are making them to be a most respectable man. He never misses a chance in his practice, which is a mark of respectability. He never takes any pleasure, which is another mark of respectability. He is reserved and serious, which is another mark of respectability. His digestion is impaired, which is highly respectable. And he is making hay of the grass which is flesh, for his three daughters. And his father is dependent on him in the Vale of Taunton.

The one great principle of the English law is to make business for itself. There is no other principle distinctly, certainly, and consistently maintained through all its narrow turnings. Viewed by this light it becomes a coherent scheme and not the monstrous maze the laity are apt to think it. Let them but once clearly perceive that its grand principle is to make business for itself at their expense, and surely they will cease to grumble.

But not perceiving this quite plainly—only seeing it by halves in a confused way—the laity sometimes suffer in peace and pocket, with a bad grace, and DO grumble very much. Then this respectability of Mr. Vholes is brought into powerful play against them. "Repeal this statute, my good sir?" says Mr. Kenge to a smarting client. "Repeal it, my dear sir? Never, with my consent. Alter this law, sir, and what will be the effect of your rash proceeding on a class of practitioners very worthily represented, allow me to say to you, by the opposite attorney in the case, Mr. Vholes? Sir, that class of practitioners would be swept from the face of the earth. Now you cannot afford—I will say, the social system cannot afford—to lose an order of men like Mr. Vholes. Diligent, persevering, steady, acute in business. My dear sir, I understand your present feelings against the existing state of things, which I grant to be a little hard in your case; but I can never raise my voice for the demolition of a class of men like Mr. Vholes." The respectability of Mr. Vholes has even been cited with crushing effect before Parliamentary committees, as in the following blue minutes of a distinguished attorney's evidence. "Question (number five hundred and seventeen thousand eight hundred and sixty-nine): If I understand you, these forms of practice indisputably occasion delay? Answer: Yes, some delay. Question: And great expense? Answer: Most assuredly they cannot be gone through for nothing. Question: And unspeakable vexation? Answer: I am not prepared to say that. They have never given ME any vexation; quite the contrary. Question: But you think that their abolition would damage a class of practitioners? Answer: I have no doubt of it. Question: Can you instance any type of that class? Answer: Yes. I would unhesitatingly mention Mr. Vholes. He would be ruined. Question: Mr. Vholes is considered, in the profession, a respectable man? Answer:"—which proved fatal to the inquiry for ten years—"Mr. Vholes is considered, in the profession, a MOST respectable man."

So in familiar conversation, private authorities no less disinterested will remark that they don't know what this age is coming to, that we are plunging down precipices, that now here is something else gone, that these changes are death to people like Vholes—a man of undoubted respectability, with a father in the Vale of Taunton, and three daughters at home. Take a few steps more in this direction, say they, and what is to become of Vholes's father? Is he to perish? And of Vholes's daughters? Are they to be shirt-makers, or governesses? As though, Mr. Vholes and his relations being minor cannibal chiefs and it being proposed to abolish cannibalism, indignant champions were to put the case thus: Make man-eating unlawful, and you starve the Vholeses!

In a word, Mr. Vholes, with his three daughters and his father in the Vale of Taunton, is continually doing duty, like a piece of timber, to shore up some decayed foundation that has become a pitfall and a nuisance. And with a great many people in a great many instances, the question is never one of a change from wrong to right (which is quite an extraneous consideration), but is always one of injury or advantage to that eminently respectable legion, Vholes.

The Chancellor is, within these ten minutes, "up" for the long vacation. Mr. Vholes, and his young client, and several blue bags hastily stuffed out of all regularity of form, as the larger sort of serpents are in their first gorged state, have returned to the official den. Mr. Vholes, quiet and unmoved, as a man of so much respectability ought to be, takes off his close black gloves as if he were skinning his hands, lifts off his tight hat as if he were scalping himself, and sits down at his desk. The client throws his hat and gloves upon the ground—tosses them anywhere, without looking after them or caring where they go; flings himself into a chair, half sighing and half groaning; rests his aching head upon his hand and looks the portrait of young despair.

"Again nothing done!" says Richard. "Nothing, nothing done!"

"Don't say nothing done, sir," returns the placid Vholes. "That is scarcely fair, sir, scarcely fair!"

"Why, what IS done?" says Richard, turning gloomily upon him.

"That may not be the whole question," returns Vholes, "The question may branch off into what is doing, what is doing?"

"And what is doing?" asks the moody client.

Vholes, sitting with his arms on the desk, quietly bringing the tips of his five right fingers to meet the tips of his five left fingers, and quietly separating them again, and fixedly and slowly looking at his client, replies, "A good deal is doing, sir. We have put our shoulders to the wheel, Mr. Carstone, and the wheel is going round."

"Yes, with Ixion on it. How am I to get through the next four or five accursed months?" exclaims the young man, rising from his chair and walking about the room.

"Mr. C.," returns Vholes, following him close with his eyes wherever he goes, "your spirits are hasty, and I am sorry for it on your account. Excuse me if I recommend you not to chafe so much, not to be so impetuous, not to wear yourself out so. You should have more patience. You should sustain yourself better."

"I ought to imitate you, in fact, Mr. Vholes?" says Richard, sitting down again with an impatient laugh and beating the devil's tattoo with his boot on the patternless carpet.

"Sir," returns Vholes, always looking at the client as if he were making a lingering meal of him with his eyes as well as with his professional appetite. "Sir," returns Vholes with his inward manner of speech and his bloodless quietude, "I should not have had the presumption to propose myself as a model for your imitation or any man's. Let me but leave the good name to my three daughters, and that is enough for me; I am not a self-seeker. But since you mention me so pointedly, I will acknowledge that I should like to impart to you a little of my—come, sir, you are disposed to call it insensibility, and I am sure I have no objection—say insensibility—a little of my insensibility."

"Mr. Vholes," explains the client, somewhat abashed, "I had no intention to accuse you of insensibility."

"I think you had, sir, without knowing it," returns the equable Vholes. "Very naturally. It is my duty to attend to your interests with a cool head, and I can quite understand that to your excited feelings I may appear, at such times as the present, insensible. My daughters may know me better; my aged father may know me better. But they have known me much longer than you have, and the confiding eye of affection is not the distrustful eye of business. Not that I complain, sir, of the eye of business being distrustful; quite the contrary. In attending to your interests, I wish to have all possible checks upon me; it is right that I should have them; I court inquiry. But your interests demand that I should be cool and methodical, Mr. Carstone; and I cannot be otherwise—no, sir, not even to please you."

Mr. Vholes, after glancing at the official cat who is patiently watching a mouse's hole, fixes his charmed gaze again on his young client and proceeds in his buttoned-up, half-audible voice as if there were an unclean spirit in him that will neither come out nor speak out, "What are you to do, sir, you inquire, during the vacation. I should hope you gentlemen of the army may find many means of amusing yourselves if you give your minds to it. If you had asked me what I was to do during the vacation, I could have answered you more readily. I am to attend to your interests. I am to be found here, day by day, attending to your interests. That is my duty, Mr. C., and term-time or vacation makes no difference to me. If you wish to consult me as to your interests, you will find me here at all times alike. Other professional men go out of town. I don't. Not that I blame them for going; I merely say I don't go. This desk is your rock, sir!"

Mr. Vholes gives it a rap, and it sounds as hollow as a coffin. Not to Richard, though. There is encouragement in the sound to him. Perhaps Mr. Vholes knows there is.

"I am perfectly aware, Mr. Vholes," says Richard, more familiarly and good-humouredly, "that you are the most reliable fellow in the world and that to have to do with you is to have to do with a man of business who is not to be hoodwinked. But put yourself in my case, dragging on this dislocated life, sinking deeper and deeper into difficulty every day, continually hoping and continually disappointed, conscious of change upon change for the worse in myself, and of no change for the better in anything else, and you will find it a dark-looking case sometimes, as I do."

"You know," says Mr. Vholes, "that I never give hopes, sir. I told you from the first, Mr. C., that I never give hopes. Particularly in a case like this, where the greater part of the costs comes out of the estate, I should not be considerate of my good name if I gave hopes. It might seem as if costs were my object. Still, when you say there is no change for the better, I must, as a bare matter of fact, deny that."

"Aye?" returns Richard, brightening. "But how do you make it out?"

"Mr. Carstone, you are represented by—"

"You said just now—a rock."

"Yes, sir," says Mr. Vholes, gently shaking his head and rapping the hollow desk, with a sound as if ashes were falling on ashes, and dust on dust, "a rock. That's something. You are separately represented, and no longer hidden and lost in the interests of others. THAT'S something. The suit does not sleep; we wake it up, we air it, we walk it about. THAT'S something. It's not all Jarndyce, in fact as well as in name. THAT'S something. Nobody has it all his own way now, sir. And THAT'S something, surely."

Richard, his face flushing suddenly, strikes the desk with his clenched hand.

"Mr. Vholes! If any man had told me when I first went to John Jarndyce's house that he was anything but the disinterested friend he seemed—that he was what he has gradually turned out to be—I could have found no words strong enough to repel the slander; I could not have defended him too ardently. So little did I know of the world! Whereas now I do declare to you that he becomes to me the embodiment of the suit; that in place of its being an abstraction, it is John Jarndyce; that the more I suffer, the more indignant I am with him; that every new delay and every new disappointment is only a new injury from John Jarndyce's hand."

"No, no," says Vholes. "Don't say so. We ought to have patience, all of us. Besides, I never disparage, sir. I never disparage."

"Mr. Vholes," returns the angry client. "You know as well as I that he would have strangled the suit if he could."

"He was not active in it," Mr. Vholes admits with an appearance of reluctance. "He certainly was not active in it. But however, but however, he might have had amiable intentions. Who can read the heart, Mr. C.!"

"You can," returns Richard.

"I, Mr. C.?"

"Well enough to know what his intentions were. Are or are not our interests conflicting? Tell—me—that!" says Richard, accompanying his last three words with three raps on his rock of trust.

"Mr. C.," returns Vholes, immovable in attitude and never winking his hungry eyes, "I should be wanting in my duty as your professional adviser, I should be departing from my fidelity to your interests, if I represented those interests as identical with the interests of Mr. Jarndyce. They are no such thing, sir. I never impute motives; I both have and am a father, and I never impute motives. But I must not shrink from a professional duty, even if it sows dissensions in families. I understand you to be now consulting me professionally as to your interests? You are so? I reply, then, they are not identical with those of Mr. Jarndyce."

"Of course they are not!" cries Richard. "You found that out long ago."

"Mr. C.," returns Vholes, "I wish to say no more of any third party than is necessary. I wish to leave my good name unsullied, together with any little property of which I may become possessed through industry and perseverance, to my daughters Emma, Jane, and Caroline. I also desire to live in amity with my professional brethren. When Mr. Skimpole did me the honour, sir—I will not say the very high honour, for I never stoop to flattery—of bringing us together in this room, I mentioned to you that I could offer no opinion or advice as to your interests while those interests were entrusted to another member of the profession. And I spoke in such terms as I was bound to speak of Kenge and Carboy's office, which stands high. You, sir, thought fit to withdraw your interests from that keeping nevertheless and to offer them to me. You brought them with clean hands, sir, and I accepted them with clean hands. Those interests are now paramount in this office. My digestive functions, as you may have heard me mention, are not in a good state, and rest might improve them; but I shall not rest, sir, while I am your representative. Whenever you want me, you will find me here. Summon me anywhere, and I will come. During the long vacation, sir, I shall devote my leisure to studying your interests more and more closely and to making arrangements for moving heaven and earth (including, of course, the Chancellor) after Michaelmas term; and when I ultimately congratulate you, sir," says Mr. Vholes with the severity of a determined man, "when I ultimately congratulate you, sir, with all my heart, on your accession to fortune—which, but that I never give hopes, I might say something further about—you will owe me nothing beyond whatever little balance may be then outstanding of the costs as between solicitor and client not included in the taxed costs allowed out of the estate. I pretend to no claim upon you, Mr. C., but for the zealous and active discharge—not the languid and routine discharge, sir: that much credit I stipulate for—of my professional duty. My duty prosperously ended, all between us is ended."

Vholes finally adds, by way of rider to this declaration of his principles, that as Mr. Carstone is about to rejoin his regiment, perhaps Mr. C. will favour him with an order on his agent for twenty pounds on account.

"For there have been many little consultations and attendances of late, sir," observes Vholes, turning over the leaves of his diary, "and these things mount up, and I don't profess to be a man of capital. When we first entered on our present relations I stated to you openly—it is a principle of mine that there never can be too much openness between solicitor and client—that I was not a man of capital and that if capital was your object you had better leave your papers in Kenge's office. No, Mr. C., you will find none of the advantages or disadvantages of capital here, sir. This," Vholes gives the desk one hollow blow again, "is your rock; it pretends to be nothing more."

The client, with his dejection insensibly relieved and his vague hopes rekindled, takes pen and ink and writes the draft, not without perplexed consideration and calculation of the date it may bear, implying scant effects in the agent's hands. All the while, Vholes, buttoned up in body and mind, looks at him attentively. All the while, Vholes's official cat watches the mouse's hole.

Lastly, the client, shaking hands, beseeches Mr. Vholes, for heaven's sake and earth's sake, to do his utmost to "pull him through" the Court of Chancery. Mr. Vholes, who never gives hopes, lays his palm upon the client's shoulder and answers with a smile, "Always here, sir. Personally, or by letter, you will always find me here, sir, with my shoulder to the wheel." Thus they part, and Vholes, left alone, employs himself in carrying sundry little matters out of his diary into his draft bill book for the ultimate behoof of his three daughters. So might an industrious fox or bear make up his account of chickens or stray travellers with an eye to his cubs, not to disparage by that word the three raw-visaged, lank, and buttoned-up maidens who dwell with the parent Vholes in an earthy cottage situated in a damp garden at Kennington.

Richard, emerging from the heavy shade of Symond's Inn into the sunshine of Chancery Lane—for there happens to be sunshine there to-day—walks thoughtfully on, and turns into Lincoln's Inn, and passes under the shadow of the Lincoln's Inn trees. On many such loungers have the speckled shadows of those trees often fallen; on the like bent head, the bitten nail, the lowering eye, the lingering step, the purposeless and dreamy air, the good consuming and consumed, the life turned sour. This lounger is not shabby yet, but that may come. Chancery, which knows no wisdom but in precedent, is very rich in such precedents; and why should one be different from ten thousand?

Yet the time is so short since his depreciation began that as he saunters away, reluctant to leave the spot for some long months together, though he hates it, Richard himself may feel his own case as if it were a startling one. While his heart is heavy with corroding care, suspense, distrust, and doubt, it may have room for some sorrowful wonder when he recalls how different his first visit there, how different he, how different all the colours of his mind. But injustice breeds injustice; the fighting with shadows and being defeated by them necessitates the setting up of substances to combat; from the impalpable suit which no man alive can understand, the time for that being long gone by, it has become a gloomy relief to turn to the palpable figure of the friend who would have saved him from this ruin and make HIM his enemy. Richard has told Vholes the truth. Is he in a hardened or a softened mood, he still lays his injuries equally at that door; he was thwarted, in that quarter, of a set purpose, and that purpose could only originate in the one subject that is resolving his existence into itself; besides, it is a justification to him in his own eyes to have an embodied antagonist and oppressor.

Is Richard a monster in all this, or would Chancery be found rich in such precedents too if they could be got for citation from the Recording Angel?

Two pairs of eyes not unused to such people look after him, as, biting his nails and brooding, he crosses the square and is swallowed up by the shadow of the southern gateway. Mr. Guppy and Mr. Weevle are the possessors of those eyes, and they have been leaning in conversation against the low stone parapet under the trees. He passes close by them, seeing nothing but the ground.

"William," says Mr. Weevle, adjusting his whiskers, "there's combustion going on there! It's not a case of spontaneous, but it's smouldering combustion it is."

"Ah!" says Mr. Guppy. "He wouldn't keep out of Jarndyce, and I suppose he's over head and ears in debt. I never knew much of him. He was as high as the monument when he was on trial at our place. A good riddance to me, whether as clerk or client! Well, Tony, that as I was mentioning is what they're up to."

Mr. Guppy, refolding his arms, resettles himself against the parapet, as resuming a conversation of interest.

"They are still up to it, sir," says Mr. Guppy, "still taking stock, still examining papers, still going over the heaps and heaps of rubbish. At this rate they'll be at it these seven years."

"And Small is helping?"

"Small left us at a week's notice. Told Kenge his grandfather's business was too much for the old gentleman and he could better himself by undertaking it. There had been a coolness between myself and Small on account of his being so close. But he said you and I began it, and as he had me there—for we did—I put our acquaintance on the old footing. That's how I come to know what they're up to."

"You haven't looked in at all?"

"Tony," says Mr. Guppy, a little disconcerted, "to be unreserved with you, I don't greatly relish the house, except in your company, and therefore I have not; and therefore I proposed this little appointment for our fetching away your things. There goes the hour by the clock! Tony"—Mr. Guppy becomes mysteriously and tenderly eloquent—"it is necessary that I should impress upon your mind once more that circumstances over which I have no control have made a melancholy alteration in my most cherished plans and in that unrequited image which I formerly mentioned to you as a friend. That image is shattered, and that idol is laid low. My only wish now in connexion with the objects which I had an idea of carrying out in the court with your aid as a friend is to let 'em alone and bury 'em in oblivion. Do you think it possible, do you think it at all likely (I put it to you, Tony, as a friend), from your knowledge of that capricious and deep old character who fell a prey to the—spontaneous element, do you, Tony, think it at all likely that on second thoughts he put those letters away anywhere, after you saw him alive, and that they were not destroyed that night?"

Mr. Weevle reflects for some time. Shakes his head. Decidedly thinks not.

"Tony," says Mr. Guppy as they walk towards the court, "once again understand me, as a friend. Without entering into further explanations, I may repeat that the idol is down. I have no purpose to serve now but burial in oblivion. To that I have pledged myself. I owe it to myself, and I owe it to the shattered image, as also to the circumstances over which I have no control. If you was to express to me by a gesture, by a wink, that you saw lying anywhere in your late lodgings any papers that so much as looked like the papers in question, I would pitch them into the fire, sir, on my own responsibility."

Mr. Weevle nods. Mr. Guppy, much elevated in his own opinion by having delivered these observations, with an air in part forensic and in part romantic—this gentleman having a passion for conducting anything in the form of an examination, or delivering anything in the form of a summing up or a speech—accompanies his friend with dignity to the court.

Never since it has been a court has it had such a Fortunatus' purse of gossip as in the proceedings at the rag and bottle shop. Regularly, every morning at eight, is the elder Mr. Smallweed brought down to the corner and carried in, accompanied by Mrs. Smallweed, Judy, and Bart; and regularly, all day, do they all remain there until nine at night, solaced by gipsy dinners, not abundant in quantity, from the cook's shop, rummaging and searching, digging, delving, and diving among the treasures of the late lamented. What those treasures are they keep so secret that the court is maddened. In its delirium it imagines guineas pouring out of teapots, crown-pieces overflowing punch-bowls, old chairs and mattresses stuffed with Bank of England notes. It possesses itself of the sixpenny history (with highly coloured folding frontispiece) of Mr. Daniel Dancer and his sister, and also of Mr. Elwes, of Suffolk, and transfers all the facts from those authentic narratives to Mr. Krook. Twice when the dustman is called in to carry off a cartload of old paper, ashes, and broken bottles, the whole court assembles and pries into the baskets as they come forth. Many times the two gentlemen who write with the ravenous little pens on the tissue-paper are seen prowling in the neighbourhood—shy of each other, their late partnership being dissolved. The Sol skilfully carries a vein of the prevailing interest through the Harmonic nights. Little Swills, in what are professionally known as "patter" allusions to the subject, is received with loud applause; and the same vocalist "gags" in the regular business like a man inspired. Even Miss M. Melvilleson, in the revived Caledonian melody of "We're a-Nodding," points the sentiment that "the dogs love broo" (whatever the nature of that refreshment may be) with such archness and such a turn of the head towards next door that she is immediately understood to mean Mr. Smallweed loves to find money, and is nightly honoured with a double encore. For all this, the court discovers nothing; and as Mrs. Piper and Mrs. Perkins now communicate to the late lodger whose appearance is the signal for a general rally, it is in one continual ferment to discover everything, and more.

Mr. Weevle and Mr. Guppy, with every eye in the court's head upon them, knock at the closed door of the late lamented's house, in a high state of popularity. But being contrary to the court's expectation admitted, they immediately become unpopular and are considered to mean no good.

The shutters are more or less closed all over the house, and the ground-floor is sufficiently dark to require candles. Introduced into the back shop by Mr. Smallweed the younger, they, fresh from the sunlight, can at first see nothing save darkness and shadows; but they gradually discern the elder Mr. Smallweed seated in his chair upon the brink of a well or grave of waste-paper, the virtuous Judy groping therein like a female sexton, and Mrs. Smallweed on the level ground in the vicinity snowed up in a heap of paper fragments, print, and manuscript which would appear to be the accumulated compliments that have been sent flying at her in the course of the day. The whole party, Small included, are blackened with dust and dirt and present a fiendish appearance not relieved by the general aspect of the room. There is more litter and lumber in it than of old, and it is dirtier if possible; likewise, it is ghostly with traces of its dead inhabitant and even with his chalked writing on the wall.

On the entrance of visitors, Mr. Smallweed and Judy simultaneously fold their arms and stop in their researches.

"Aha!" croaks the old gentleman. "How de do, gentlemen, how de do! Come to fetch your property, Mr. Weevle? That's well, that's well. Ha! Ha! We should have been forced to sell you up, sir, to pay your warehouse room if you had left it here much longer. You feel quite at home here again, I dare say? Glad to see you, glad to see you!"

Mr. Weevle, thanking him, casts an eye about. Mr. Guppy's eye follows Mr. Weevle's eye. Mr. Weevle's eye comes back without any new intelligence in it. Mr. Guppy's eye comes back and meets Mr. Smallweed's eye. That engaging old gentleman is still murmuring, like some wound-up instrument running down, "How de do, sir—how de—how—" And then having run down, he lapses into grinning silence, as Mr. Guppy starts at seeing Mr. Tulkinghorn standing in the darkness opposite with his hands behind him.

"Gentleman so kind as to act as my solicitor," says Grandfather Smallweed. "I am not the sort of client for a gentleman of such note, but he is so good!"

Mr. Guppy, slightly nudging his friend to take another look, makes a shuffling bow to Mr. Tulkinghorn, who returns it with an easy nod. Mr. Tulkinghorn is looking on as if he had nothing else to do and were rather amused by the novelty.

"A good deal of property here, sir, I should say," Mr. Guppy observes to Mr. Smallweed.

"Principally rags and rubbish, my dear friend! Rags and rubbish! Me and Bart and my granddaughter Judy are endeavouring to make out an inventory of what's worth anything to sell. But we haven't come to much as yet; we—haven't—come—to—hah!"

Mr. Smallweed has run down again, while Mr. Weevle's eye, attended by Mr. Guppy's eye, has again gone round the room and come back.

"Well, sir," says Mr. Weevle. "We won't intrude any longer if you'll allow us to go upstairs."

"Anywhere, my dear sir, anywhere! You're at home. Make yourself so, pray!"

As they go upstairs, Mr. Guppy lifts his eyebrows inquiringly and looks at Tony. Tony shakes his head. They find the old room very dull and dismal, with the ashes of the fire that was burning on that memorable night yet in the discoloured grate. They have a great disinclination to touch any object, and carefully blow the dust from it first. Nor are they desirous to prolong their visit, packing the few movables with all possible speed and never speaking above a whisper.

"Look here," says Tony, recoiling. "Here's that horrible cat coming in!"

Mr. Guppy retreats behind a chair. "Small told me of her. She went leaping and bounding and tearing about that night like a dragon, and got out on the house-top, and roamed about up there for a fortnight, and then came tumbling down the chimney very thin. Did you ever see such a brute? Looks as if she knew all about it, don't she? Almost looks as if she was Krook. Shoohoo! Get out, you goblin!"

Lady Jane, in the doorway, with her tiger snarl from ear to ear and her club of a tail, shows no intention of obeying; but Mr. Tulkinghorn stumbling over her, she spits at his rusty legs, and swearing wrathfully, takes her arched back upstairs. Possibly to roam the house-tops again and return by the chimney.

"Mr. Guppy," says Mr. Tulkinghorn, "could I have a word with you?"

Mr. Guppy is engaged in collecting the Galaxy Gallery of British Beauty from the wall and depositing those works of art in their old ignoble band-box. "Sir," he returns, reddening, "I wish to act with courtesy towards every member of the profession, and especially, I am sure, towards a member of it so well known as yourself—I will truly add, sir, so distinguished as yourself. Still, Mr. Tulkinghorn, sir, I must stipulate that if you have any word with me, that word is spoken in the presence of my friend."

"Oh, indeed?" says Mr. Tulkinghorn.

"Yes, sir. My reasons are not of a personal nature at all, but they are amply sufficient for myself."

"No doubt, no doubt." Mr. Tulkinghorn is as imperturbable as the hearth-stone to which he has quietly walked. "The matter is not of that consequence that I need put you to the trouble of making any conditions, Mr. Guppy." He pauses here to smile, and his smile is as dull and rusty as his pantaloons. "You are to be congratulated, Mr. Guppy; you are a fortunate young man, sir."

"Pretty well so, Mr. Tulkinghorn; I don't complain."

"Complain? High friends, free admission to great houses, and access to elegant ladies! Why, Mr. Guppy, there are people in London who would give their ears to be you."

Mr. Guppy, looking as if he would give his own reddening and still reddening ears to be one of those people at present instead of himself, replies, "Sir, if I attend to my profession and do what is right by Kenge and Carboy, my friends and acquaintances are of no consequence to them nor to any member of the profession, not excepting Mr. Tulkinghorn of the Fields. I am not under any obligation to explain myself further; and with all respect for you, sir, and without offence—I repeat, without offence—"

"Oh, certainly!"

"—I don't intend to do it."

"Quite so," says Mr. Tulkinghorn with a calm nod. "Very good; I see by these portraits that you take a strong interest in the fashionable great, sir?"

He addresses this to the astounded Tony, who admits the soft impeachment.

"A virtue in which few Englishmen are deficient," observes Mr. Tulkinghorn. He has been standing on the hearthstone with his back to the smoked chimney-piece, and now turns round with his glasses to his eyes. "Who is this? 'Lady Dedlock.' Ha! A very good likeness in its way, but it wants force of character. Good day to you, gentlemen; good day!"

When he has walked out, Mr. Guppy, in a great perspiration, nerves himself to the hasty completion of the taking down of the Galaxy Gallery, concluding with Lady Dedlock.

"Tony," he says hurriedly to his astonished companion, "let us be quick in putting the things together and in getting out of this place. It were in vain longer to conceal from you, Tony, that between myself and one of the members of a swan-like aristocracy whom I now hold in my hand, there has been undivulged communication and association. The time might have been when I might have revealed it to you. It never will be more. It is due alike to the oath I have taken, alike to the shattered idol, and alike to circumstances over which I have no control, that the whole should be buried in oblivion. I charge you as a friend, by the interest you have ever testified in the fashionable intelligence, and by any little advances with which I may have been able to accommodate you, so to bury it without a word of inquiry!"

This charge Mr. Guppy delivers in a state little short of forensic lunacy, while his friend shows a dazed mind in his whole head of hair and even in his cultivated whiskers.

CHAPTER XL
NATIONAL AND DOMESTIC

England has been in a dreadful state for some weeks. Lord Coodle would go out, Sir Thomas Doodle wouldn't come in, and there being nobody in Great Britain (to speak of) except Coodle and Doodle, there has been no government. It is a mercy that the hostile meeting between those two great men, which at one time seemed inevitable, did not come off, because if both pistols had taken effect, and Coodle and Doodle had killed each other, it is to be presumed that England must have waited to be governed until young Coodle and young Doodle, now in frocks and long stockings, were grown up. This stupendous national calamity, however, was averted by Lord Coodle's making the timely discovery that if in the heat of debate he had said that he scorned and despised the whole ignoble career of Sir Thomas Doodle, he had merely meant to say that party differences should never induce him to withhold from it the tribute of his warmest admiration; while it as opportunely turned out, on the other hand, that Sir Thomas Doodle had in his own bosom expressly booked Lord Coodle to go down to posterity as the mirror of virtue and honour. Still England has been some weeks in the dismal strait of having no pilot (as was well observed by Sir Leicester Dedlock) to weather the storm; and the marvellous part of the matter is that England has not appeared to care very much about it, but has gone on eating and drinking and marrying and giving in marriage as the old world did in the days before the flood. But Coodle knew the danger, and Doodle knew the danger, and all their followers and hangers-on had the clearest possible perception of the danger. At last Sir Thomas Doodle has not only condescended to come in, but has done it handsomely, bringing in with him all his nephews, all his male cousins, and all his brothers-in-law. So there is hope for the old ship yet.

Doodle has found that he must throw himself upon the country, chiefly in the form of sovereigns and beer. In this metamorphosed state he is available in a good many places simultaneously and can throw himself upon a considerable portion of the country at one time. Britannia being much occupied in pocketing Doodle in the form of sovereigns, and swallowing Doodle in the form of beer, and in swearing herself black in the face that she does neither—plainly to the advancement of her glory and morality—the London season comes to a sudden end, through all the Doodleites and Coodleites dispersing to assist Britannia in those religious exercises.

Hence Mrs. Rouncewell, housekeeper at Chesney Wold, foresees, though no instructions have yet come down, that the family may shortly be expected, together with a pretty large accession of cousins and others who can in any way assist the great Constitutional work. And hence the stately old dame, taking Time by the forelock, leads him up and down the staircases, and along the galleries and passages, and through the rooms, to witness before he grows any older that everything is ready, that floors are rubbed bright, carpets spread, curtains shaken out, beds puffed and patted, still-room and kitchen cleared for action—all things prepared as beseems the Dedlock dignity.

This present summer evening, as the sun goes down, the preparations are complete. Dreary and solemn the old house looks, with so many appliances of habitation and with no inhabitants except the pictured forms upon the walls. So did these come and go, a Dedlock in possession might have ruminated passing along; so did they see this gallery hushed and quiet, as I see it now; so think, as I think, of the gap that they would make in this domain when they were gone; so find it, as I find it, difficult to believe that it could be without them; so pass from my world, as I pass from theirs, now closing the reverberating door; so leave no blank to miss them, and so die.

Through some of the fiery windows beautiful from without, and set, at this sunset hour, not in dull-grey stone but in a glorious house of gold, the light excluded at other windows pours in rich, lavish, overflowing like the summer plenty in the land. Then do the frozen Dedlocks thaw. Strange movements come upon their features as the shadows of leaves play there. A dense justice in a corner is beguiled into a wink. A staring baronet, with a truncheon, gets a dimple in his chin. Down into the bosom of a stony shepherdess there steals a fleck of light and warmth that would have done it good a hundred years ago. One ancestress of Volumnia, in high-heeled shoes, very like her—casting the shadow of that virgin event before her full two centuries—shoots out into a halo and becomes a saint. A maid of honour of the court of Charles the Second, with large round eyes (and other charms to correspond), seems to bathe in glowing water, and it ripples as it glows.

But the fire of the sun is dying. Even now the floor is dusky, and shadow slowly mounts the walls, bringing the Dedlocks down like age and death. And now, upon my Lady's picture over the great chimney-piece, a weird shade falls from some old tree, that turns it pale, and flutters it, and looks as if a great arm held a veil or hood, watching an opportunity to draw it over her. Higher and darker rises shadow on the wall—now a red gloom on the ceiling—now the fire is out.

All that prospect, which from the terrace looked so near, has moved solemnly away and changed—not the first nor the last of beautiful things that look so near and will so change—into a distant phantom. Light mists arise, and the dew falls, and all the sweet scents in the garden are heavy in the air. Now the woods settle into great masses as if they were each one profound tree. And now the moon rises to separate them, and to glimmer here and there in horizontal lines behind their stems, and to make the avenue a pavement of light among high cathedral arches fantastically broken.

Now the moon is high; and the great house, needing habitation more than ever, is like a body without life. Now it is even awful, stealing through it, to think of the live people who have slept in the solitary bedrooms, to say nothing of the dead. Now is the time for shadow, when every corner is a cavern and every downward step a pit, when the stained glass is reflected in pale and faded hues upon the floors, when anything and everything can be made of the heavy staircase beams excepting their own proper shapes, when the armour has dull lights upon it not easily to be distinguished from stealthy movement, and when barred helmets are frightfully suggestive of heads inside. But of all the shadows in Chesney Wold, the shadow in the long drawing-room upon my Lady's picture is the first to come, the last to be disturbed. At this hour and by this light it changes into threatening hands raised up and menacing the handsome face with every breath that stirs.

"She is not well, ma'am," says a groom in Mrs. Rouncewell's audience-chamber.

"My Lady not well! What's the matter?"

"Why, my Lady has been but poorly, ma'am, since she was last here—I don't mean with the family, ma'am, but when she was here as a bird of passage like. My Lady has not been out much, for her, and has kept her room a good deal."

"Chesney Wold, Thomas," rejoins the housekeeper with proud complacency, "will set my Lady up! There is no finer air and no healthier soil in the world!"

Thomas may have his own personal opinions on this subject, probably hints them in his manner of smoothing his sleek head from the nape of his neck to his temples, but he forbears to express them further and retires to the servants' hall to regale on cold meat-pie and ale.

This groom is the pilot-fish before the nobler shark. Next evening, down come Sir Leicester and my Lady with their largest retinue, and down come the cousins and others from all the points of the compass. Thenceforth for some weeks backward and forward rush mysterious men with no names, who fly about all those particular parts of the country on which Doodle is at present throwing himself in an auriferous and malty shower, but who are merely persons of a restless disposition and never do anything anywhere.

On these national occasions Sir Leicester finds the cousins useful. A better man than the Honourable Bob Stables to meet the Hunt at dinner, there could not possibly be. Better got up gentlemen than the other cousins to ride over to polling-booths and hustings here and there, and show themselves on the side of England, it would be hard to find. Volumnia is a little dim, but she is of the true descent; and there are many who appreciate her sprightly conversation, her French conundrums so old as to have become in the cycles of time almost new again, the honour of taking the fair Dedlock in to dinner, or even the privilege of her hand in the dance. On these national occasions dancing may be a patriotic service, and Volumnia is constantly seen hopping about for the good of an ungrateful and unpensioning country.

My Lady takes no great pains to entertain the numerous guests, and being still unwell, rarely appears until late in the day. But at all the dismal dinners, leaden lunches, basilisk balls, and other melancholy pageants, her mere appearance is a relief. As to Sir Leicester, he conceives it utterly impossible that anything can be wanting, in any direction, by any one who has the good fortune to be received under that roof; and in a state of sublime satisfaction, he moves among the company, a magnificent refrigerator.

Daily the cousins trot through dust and canter over roadside turf, away to hustings and polling-booths (with leather gloves and hunting-whips for the counties and kid gloves and riding-canes for the boroughs), and daily bring back reports on which Sir Leicester holds forth after dinner. Daily the restless men who have no occupation in life present the appearance of being rather busy. Daily Volumnia has a little cousinly talk with Sir Leicester on the state of the nation, from which Sir Leicester is disposed to conclude that Volumnia is a more reflecting woman than he had thought her.

"How are we getting on?" says Miss Volumnia, clasping her hands. "ARE we safe?"

The mighty business is nearly over by this time, and Doodle will throw himself off the country in a few days more. Sir Leicester has just appeared in the long drawing-room after dinner, a bright particular star surrounded by clouds of cousins.

"Volumnia," replies Sir Leicester, who has a list in his hand, "we are doing tolerably."

"Only tolerably!"

Although it is summer weather, Sir Leicester always has his own particular fire in the evening. He takes his usual screened seat near it and repeats with much firmness and a little displeasure, as who should say, I am not a common man, and when I say tolerably, it must not be understood as a common expression, "Volumnia, we are doing tolerably."

"At least there is no opposition to YOU," Volumnia asserts with confidence.

"No, Volumnia. This distracted country has lost its senses in many respects, I grieve to say, but—"

"It is not so mad as that. I am glad to hear it!"

Volumnia's finishing the sentence restores her to favour. Sir Leicester, with a gracious inclination of his head, seems to say to himself, "A sensible woman this, on the whole, though occasionally precipitate."

In fact, as to this question of opposition, the fair Dedlock's observation was superfluous, Sir Leicester on these occasions always delivering in his own candidateship, as a kind of handsome wholesale order to be promptly executed. Two other little seats that belong to him he treats as retail orders of less importance, merely sending down the men and signifying to the tradespeople, "You will have the goodness to make these materials into two members of Parliament and to send them home when done."

"I regret to say, Volumnia, that in many places the people have shown a bad spirit, and that this opposition to the government has been of a most determined and most implacable description."

"W-r-retches!" says Volumnia.

"Even," proceeds Sir Leicester, glancing at the circumjacent cousins on sofas and ottomans, "even in many—in fact, in most—of those places in which the government has carried it against a faction—"

(Note, by the way, that the Coodleites are always a faction with the Doodleites, and that the Doodleites occupy exactly the same position towards the Coodleites.)

"—Even in them I am shocked, for the credit of Englishmen, to be constrained to inform you that the party has not triumphed without being put to an enormous expense. Hundreds," says Sir Leicester, eyeing the cousins with increasing dignity and swelling indignation, "hundreds of thousands of pounds!"

If Volumnia have a fault, it is the fault of being a trifle too innocent, seeing that the innocence which would go extremely well with a sash and tucker is a little out of keeping with the rouge and pearl necklace. Howbeit, impelled by innocence, she asks, "What for?"

"Volumnia," remonstrates Sir Leicester with his utmost severity. "Volumnia!"

"No, no, I don't mean what for," cries Volumnia with her favourite little scream. "How stupid I am! I mean what a pity!"

"I am glad," returns Sir Leicester, "that you do mean what a pity."

Volumnia hastens to express her opinion that the shocking people ought to be tried as traitors and made to support the party.

"I am glad, Volumnia," repeats Sir Leicester, unmindful of these mollifying sentiments, "that you do mean what a pity. It is disgraceful to the electors. But as you, though inadvertently and without intending so unreasonable a question, asked me 'what for?' let me reply to you. For necessary expenses. And I trust to your good sense, Volumnia, not to pursue the subject, here or elsewhere."

Sir Leicester feels it incumbent on him to observe a crushing aspect towards Volumnia because it is whispered abroad that these necessary expenses will, in some two hundred election petitions, be unpleasantly connected with the word bribery, and because some graceless jokers have consequently suggested the omission from the Church service of the ordinary supplication in behalf of the High Court of Parliament and have recommended instead that the prayers of the congregation be requested for six hundred and fifty-eight gentlemen in a very unhealthy state.

"I suppose," observes Volumnia, having taken a little time to recover her spirits after her late castigation, "I suppose Mr. Tulkinghorn has been worked to death."

"I don't know," says Sir Leicester, opening his eyes, "why Mr. Tulkinghorn should be worked to death. I don't know what Mr. Tulkinghorn's engagements may be. He is not a candidate."

Volumnia had thought he might have been employed. Sir Leicester could desire to know by whom, and what for. Volumnia, abashed again, suggests, by somebody—to advise and make arrangements. Sir Leicester is not aware that any client of Mr. Tulkinghorn has been in need of his assistance.

Lady Dedlock, seated at an open window with her arm upon its cushioned ledge and looking out at the evening shadows falling on the park, has seemed to attend since the lawyer's name was mentioned.

A languid cousin with a moustache in a state of extreme debility now observes from his couch that man told him ya'as'dy that Tulkinghorn had gone down t' that iron place t' give legal 'pinion 'bout something, and that contest being over t' day, 'twould be highly jawlly thing if Tulkinghorn should 'pear with news that Coodle man was floored.

Mercury in attendance with coffee informs Sir Leicester, hereupon, that Mr. Tulkinghorn has arrived and is taking dinner. My Lady turns her head inward for the moment, then looks out again as before.

Volumnia is charmed to hear that her delight is come. He is so original, such a stolid creature, such an immense being for knowing all sorts of things and never telling them! Volumnia is persuaded that he must be a Freemason. Is sure he is at the head of a lodge, and wears short aprons, and is made a perfect idol of with candlesticks and trowels. These lively remarks the fair Dedlock delivers in her youthful manner, while making a purse.

"He has not been here once," she adds, "since I came. I really had some thoughts of breaking my heart for the inconstant creature. I had almost made up my mind that he was dead."

It may be the gathering gloom of evening, or it may be the darker gloom within herself, but a shade is on my Lady's face, as if she thought, "I would he were!"

"Mr. Tulkinghorn," says Sir Leicester, "is always welcome here and always discreet wheresoever he is. A very valuable person, and deservedly respected."

The debilitated cousin supposes he is "'normously rich fler."

"He has a stake in the country," says Sir Leicester, "I have no doubt. He is, of course, handsomely paid, and he associates almost on a footing of equality with the highest society."

Everybody starts. For a gun is fired close by.

"Good gracious, what's that?" cries Volumnia with her little withered scream.

"A rat," says my Lady. "And they have shot him."

Enter Mr. Tulkinghorn, followed by Mercuries with lamps and candles.

"No, no," says Sir Leicester, "I think not. My Lady, do you object to the twilight?"

On the contrary, my Lady prefers it.

"Volumnia?"

Oh! Nothing is so delicious to Volumnia as to sit and talk in the dark.

"Then take them away," says Sir Leicester. "Tulkinghorn, I beg your pardon. How do you do?"

Mr. Tulkinghorn with his usual leisurely ease advances, renders his passing homage to my Lady, shakes Sir Leicester's hand, and subsides into the chair proper to him when he has anything to communicate, on the opposite side of the Baronet's little newspaper-table. Sir Leicester is apprehensive that my Lady, not being very well, will take cold at that open window. My Lady is obliged to him, but would rather sit there for the air. Sir Leicester rises, adjusts her scarf about her, and returns to his seat. Mr. Tulkinghorn in the meanwhile takes a pinch of snuff.

"Now," says Sir Leicester. "How has that contest gone?"

"Oh, hollow from the beginning. Not a chance. They have brought in both their people. You are beaten out of all reason. Three to one."

It is a part of Mr. Tulkinghorn's policy and mastery to have no political opinions; indeed, NO opinions. Therefore he says "you" are beaten, and not "we."

Sir Leicester is majestically wroth. Volumnia never heard of such a thing. 'The debilitated cousin holds that it's sort of thing that's sure tapn slongs votes—giv'n—Mob.

"It's the place, you know," Mr. Tulkinghorn goes on to say in the fast-increasing darkness when there is silence again, "where they wanted to put up Mrs. Rouncewell's son."

"A proposal which, as you correctly informed me at the time, he had the becoming taste and perception," observes Sir Leicester, "to decline. I cannot say that I by any means approve of the sentiments expressed by Mr. Rouncewell when he was here for some half-hour in this room, but there was a sense of propriety in his decision which I am glad to acknowledge."

"Ha!" says Mr. Tulkinghorn. "It did not prevent him from being very active in this election, though."

Sir Leicester is distinctly heard to gasp before speaking. "Did I understand you? Did you say that Mr. Rouncewell had been very active in this election?"

"Uncommonly active."

"Against—"

"Oh, dear yes, against you. He is a very good speaker. Plain and emphatic. He made a damaging effect, and has great influence. In the business part of the proceedings he carried all before him."

It is evident to the whole company, though nobody can see him, that Sir Leicester is staring majestically.

"And he was much assisted," says Mr. Tulkinghorn as a wind-up, "by his son."

"By his son, sir?" repeats Sir Leicester with awful politeness.

"By his son."

"The son who wished to marry the young woman in my Lady's service?"

"That son. He has but one."

"Then upon my honour," says Sir Leicester after a terrific pause during which he has been heard to snort and felt to stare, "then upon my honour, upon my life, upon my reputation and principles, the floodgates of society are burst open, and the waters have—a—obliterated the landmarks of the framework of the cohesion by which things are held together!"

General burst of cousinly indignation. Volumnia thinks it is really high time, you know, for somebody in power to step in and do something strong. Debilitated cousin thinks—country's going—Dayvle—steeple-chase pace.

"I beg," says Sir Leicester in a breathless condition, "that we may not comment further on this circumstance. Comment is superfluous. My Lady, let me suggest in reference to that young woman—"

"I have no intention," observes my Lady from her window in a low but decided tone, "of parting with her."

"That was not my meaning," returns Sir Leicester. "I am glad to hear you say so. I would suggest that as you think her worthy of your patronage, you should exert your influence to keep her from these dangerous hands. You might show her what violence would be done in such association to her duties and principles, and you might preserve her for a better fate. You might point out to her that she probably would, in good time, find a husband at Chesney Wold by whom she would not be—" Sir Leicester adds, after a moment's consideration, "dragged from the altars of her forefathers."

These remarks he offers with his unvarying politeness and deference when he addresses himself to his wife. She merely moves her head in reply. The moon is rising, and where she sits there is a little stream of cold pale light, in which her head is seen.

"It is worthy of remark," says Mr. Tulkinghorn, "however, that these people are, in their way, very proud."

"Proud?" Sir Leicester doubts his hearing.

"I should not be surprised if they all voluntarily abandoned the girl—yes, lover and all—instead of her abandoning them, supposing she remained at Chesney Wold under such circumstances."

"Well!" says Sir Leicester tremulously. "Well! You should know, Mr. Tulkinghorn. You have been among them."

"Really, Sir Leicester," returns the lawyer, "I state the fact. Why, I could tell you a story—with Lady Dedlock's permission."

Her head concedes it, and Volumnia is enchanted. A story! Oh, he is going to tell something at last! A ghost in it, Volumnia hopes?

"No. Real flesh and blood." Mr. Tulkinghorn stops for an instant and repeats with some little emphasis grafted upon his usual monotony, "Real flesh and blood, Miss Dedlock. Sir Leicester, these particulars have only lately become known to me. They are very brief. They exemplify what I have said. I suppress names for the present. Lady Dedlock will not think me ill-bred, I hope?"

By the light of the fire, which is low, he can be seen looking towards the moonlight. By the light of the moon Lady Dedlock can be seen, perfectly still.

"A townsman of this Mrs. Rouncewell, a man in exactly parallel circumstances as I am told, had the good fortune to have a daughter who attracted the notice of a great lady. I speak of really a great lady, not merely great to him, but married to a gentleman of your condition, Sir Leicester."

Sir Leicester condescendingly says, "Yes, Mr. Tulkinghorn," implying that then she must have appeared of very considerable moral dimensions indeed in the eyes of an iron-master.

"The lady was wealthy and beautiful, and had a liking for the girl, and treated her with great kindness, and kept her always near her. Now this lady preserved a secret under all her greatness, which she had preserved for many years. In fact, she had in early life been engaged to marry a young rake—he was a captain in the army—nothing connected with whom came to any good. She never did marry him, but she gave birth to a child of which he was the father."

By the light of the fire he can be seen looking towards the moonlight. By the moonlight, Lady Dedlock can be seen in profile, perfectly still.

"The captain in the army being dead, she believed herself safe; but a train of circumstances with which I need not trouble you led to discovery. As I received the story, they began in an imprudence on her own part one day when she was taken by surprise, which shows how difficult it is for the firmest of us (she was very firm) to be always guarded. There was great domestic trouble and amazement, you may suppose; I leave you to imagine, Sir Leicester, the husband's grief. But that is not the present point. When Mr. Rouncewell's townsman heard of the disclosure, he no more allowed the girl to be patronized and honoured than he would have suffered her to be trodden underfoot before his eyes. Such was his pride, that he indignantly took her away, as if from reproach and disgrace. He had no sense of the honour done him and his daughter by the lady's condescension; not the least. He resented the girl's position, as if the lady had been the commonest of commoners. That is the story. I hope Lady Dedlock will excuse its painful nature."

There are various opinions on the merits, more or less conflicting with Volumnia's. That fair young creature cannot believe there ever was any such lady and rejects the whole history on the threshold. The majority incline to the debilitated cousin's sentiment, which is in few words—"no business—Rouncewell's fernal townsman." Sir Leicester generally refers back in his mind to Wat Tyler and arranges a sequence of events on a plan of his own.

There is not much conversation in all, for late hours have been kept at Chesney Wold since the necessary expenses elsewhere began, and this is the first night in many on which the family have been alone. It is past ten when Sir Leicester begs Mr. Tulkinghorn to ring for candles. Then the stream of moonlight has swelled into a lake, and then Lady Dedlock for the first time moves, and rises, and comes forward to a table for a glass of water. Winking cousins, bat-like in the candle glare, crowd round to give it; Volumnia (always ready for something better if procurable) takes another, a very mild sip of which contents her; Lady Dedlock, graceful, self-possessed, looked after by admiring eyes, passes away slowly down the long perspective by the side of that nymph, not at all improving her as a question of contrast.

CHAPTER XLI
IN MR. TULKINGHORN'S ROOM

Mr. Tulkinghorn arrives in his turret-room a little breathed by the journey up, though leisurely performed. There is an expression on his face as if he had discharged his mind of some grave matter and were, in his close way, satisfied. To say of a man so severely and strictly self-repressed that he is triumphant would be to do him as great an injustice as to suppose him troubled with love or sentiment or any romantic weakness. He is sedately satisfied. Perhaps there is a rather increased sense of power upon him as he loosely grasps one of his veinous wrists with his other hand and holding it behind his back walks noiselessly up and down.

There is a capacious writing-table in the room on which is a pretty large accumulation of papers. The green lamp is lighted, his reading-glasses lie upon the desk, the easy-chair is wheeled up to it, and it would seem as though he had intended to bestow an hour or so upon these claims on his attention before going to bed. But he happens not to be in a business mind. After a glance at the documents awaiting his notice—with his head bent low over the table, the old man's sight for print or writing being defective at night—he opens the French window and steps out upon the leads. There he again walks slowly up and down in the same attitude, subsiding, if a man so cool may have any need to subside, from the story he has related downstairs.

The time was once when men as knowing as Mr. Tulkinghorn would walk on turret-tops in the starlight and look up into the sky to read their fortunes there. Hosts of stars are visible to-night, though their brilliancy is eclipsed by the splendour of the moon. If he be seeking his own star as he methodically turns and turns upon the leads, it should be but a pale one to be so rustily represented below. If he be tracing out his destiny, that may be written in other characters nearer to his hand.

As he paces the leads with his eyes most probably as high above his thoughts as they are high above the earth, he is suddenly stopped in passing the window by two eyes that meet his own. The ceiling of his room is rather low; and the upper part of the door, which is opposite the window, is of glass. There is an inner baize door, too, but the night being warm he did not close it when he came upstairs. These eyes that meet his own are looking in through the glass from the corridor outside. He knows them well. The blood has not flushed into his face so suddenly and redly for many a long year as when he recognizes Lady Dedlock.

He steps into the room, and she comes in too, closing both the doors behind her. There is a wild disturbance—is it fear or anger?—in her eyes. In her carriage and all else she looks as she looked downstairs two hours ago.

Is it fear or is it anger now? He cannot be sure. Both might be as pale, both as intent.

"Lady Dedlock?"

She does not speak at first, nor even when she has slowly dropped into the easy-chair by the table. They look at each other, like two pictures.

"Why have you told my story to so many persons?"

"Lady Dedlock, it was necessary for me to inform you that I knew it."

"How long have you known it?"

"I have suspected it a long while—fully known it a little while."

"Months?"

"Days."

He stands before her with one hand on a chair-back and the other in his old-fashioned waistcoat and shirt-frill, exactly as he has stood before her at any time since her marriage. The same formal politeness, the same composed deference that might as well be defiance; the whole man the same dark, cold object, at the same distance, which nothing has ever diminished.

"Is this true concerning the poor girl?"

He slightly inclines and advances his head as not quite understanding the question.

"You know what you related. Is it true? Do her friends know my story also? Is it the town-talk yet? Is it chalked upon the walls and cried in the streets?"

So! Anger, and fear, and shame. All three contending. What power this woman has to keep these raging passions down! Mr. Tulkinghorn's thoughts take such form as he looks at her, with his ragged grey eyebrows a hair's breadth more contracted than usual under her gaze.

"No, Lady Dedlock. That was a hypothetical case, arising out of Sir Leicester's unconsciously carrying the matter with so high a hand. But it would be a real case if they knew—what we know."

"Then they do not know it yet?"

"No."

"Can I save the poor girl from injury before they know it?"

"Really, Lady Dedlock," Mr. Tulkinghorn replies, "I cannot give a satisfactory opinion on that point."

And he thinks, with the interest of attentive curiosity, as he watches the struggle in her breast, "The power and force of this woman are astonishing!"

"Sir," she says, for the moment obliged to set her lips with all the energy she has, that she may speak distinctly, "I will make it plainer. I do not dispute your hypothetical case. I anticipated it, and felt its truth as strongly as you can do, when I saw Mr. Rouncewell here. I knew very well that if he could have had the power of seeing me as I was, he would consider the poor girl tarnished by having for a moment been, although most innocently, the subject of my great and distinguished patronage. But I have an interest in her, or I should rather say—no longer belonging to this place—I had, and if you can find so much consideration for the woman under your foot as to remember that, she will be very sensible of your mercy."

Mr. Tulkinghorn, profoundly attentive, throws this off with a shrug of self-depreciation and contracts his eyebrows a little more.

"You have prepared me for my exposure, and I thank you for that too. Is there anything that you require of me? Is there any claim that I can release or any charge or trouble that I can spare my husband in obtaining HIS release by certifying to the exactness of your discovery? I will write anything, here and now, that you will dictate. I am ready to do it."

And she would do it, thinks the lawyer, watchful of the firm hand with which she takes the pen!

"I will not trouble you, Lady Dedlock. Pray spare yourself."

"I have long expected this, as you know. I neither wish to spare myself nor to be spared. You can do nothing worse to me than you have done. Do what remains now."

"Lady Dedlock, there is nothing to be done. I will take leave to say a few words when you have finished."

Their need for watching one another should be over now, but they do it all this time, and the stars watch them both through the opened window. Away in the moonlight lie the woodland fields at rest, and the wide house is as quiet as the narrow one. The narrow one! Where are the digger and the spade, this peaceful night, destined to add the last great secret to the many secrets of the Tulkinghorn existence? Is the man born yet, is the spade wrought yet? Curious questions to consider, more curious perhaps not to consider, under the watching stars upon a summer night.

"Of repentance or remorse or any feeling of mine," Lady Dedlock presently proceeds, "I say not a word. If I were not dumb, you would be deaf. Let that go by. It is not for your ears."

He makes a feint of offering a protest, but she sweeps it away with her disdainful hand.

"Of other and very different things I come to speak to you. My jewels are all in their proper places of keeping. They will be found there. So, my dresses. So, all the valuables I have. Some ready money I had with me, please to say, but no large amount. I did not wear my own dress, in order that I might avoid observation. I went to be henceforward lost. Make this known. I leave no other charge with you."

"Excuse me, Lady Dedlock," says Mr. Tulkinghorn, quite unmoved. "I am not sure that I understand you. You want—"

"To be lost to all here. I leave Chesney Wold to-night. I go this hour."

Mr. Tulkinghorn shakes his head. She rises, but he, without moving hand from chair-back or from old-fashioned waistcoat and shirt-frill, shakes his head.

"What? Not go as I have said?"

"No, Lady Dedlock," he very calmly replies.

"Do you know the relief that my disappearance will be? Have you forgotten the stain and blot upon this place, and where it is, and who it is?"

"No, Lady Dedlock, not by any means."

Without deigning to rejoin, she moves to the inner door and has it in her hand when he says to her, without himself stirring hand or foot or raising his voice, "Lady Dedlock, have the goodness to stop and hear me, or before you reach the staircase I shall ring the alarm-bell and rouse the house. And then I must speak out before every guest and servant, every man and woman, in it."

He has conquered her. She falters, trembles, and puts her hand confusedly to her head. Slight tokens these in any one else, but when so practised an eye as Mr. Tulkinghorn's sees indecision for a moment in such a subject, he thoroughly knows its value.

He promptly says again, "Have the goodness to hear me, Lady Dedlock," and motions to the chair from which she has risen. She hesitates, but he motions again, and she sits down.

"The relations between us are of an unfortunate description, Lady Dedlock; but as they are not of my making, I will not apologize for them. The position I hold in reference to Sir Leicester is so well known to you that I can hardly imagine but that I must long have appeared in your eyes the natural person to make this discovery."

"Sir," she returns without looking up from the ground on which her eyes are now fixed, "I had better have gone. It would have been far better not to have detained me. I have no more to say."

"Excuse me, Lady Dedlock, if I add a little more to hear."

"I wish to hear it at the window, then. I can't breathe where I am."

His jealous glance as she walks that way betrays an instant's misgiving that she may have it in her thoughts to leap over, and dashing against ledge and cornice, strike her life out upon the terrace below. But a moment's observation of her figure as she stands in the window without any support, looking out at the stars—not up—gloomily out at those stars which are low in the heavens, reassures him. By facing round as she has moved, he stands a little behind her.

"Lady Dedlock, I have not yet been able to come to a decision satisfactory to myself on the course before me. I am not clear what to do or how to act next. I must request you, in the meantime, to keep your secret as you have kept it so long and not to wonder that I keep it too."

He pauses, but she makes no reply.

"Pardon me, Lady Dedlock. This is an important subject. You are honouring me with your attention?"

"I am."

"Thank you. I might have known it from what I have seen of your strength of character. I ought not to have asked the question, but I have the habit of making sure of my ground, step by step, as I go on. The sole consideration in this unhappy case is Sir Leicester."

"Then why," she asks in a low voice and without removing her gloomy look from those distant stars, "do you detain me in his house?"

"Because he IS the consideration. Lady Dedlock, I have no occasion to tell you that Sir Leicester is a very proud man, that his reliance upon you is implicit, that the fall of that moon out of the sky would not amaze him more than your fall from your high position as his wife."

She breathes quickly and heavily, but she stands as unflinchingly as ever he has seen her in the midst of her grandest company.

"I declare to you, Lady Dedlock, that with anything short of this case that I have, I would as soon have hoped to root up by means of my own strength and my own hands the oldest tree on this estate as to shake your hold upon Sir Leicester and Sir Leicester's trust and confidence in you. And even now, with this case, I hesitate. Not that he could doubt (that, even with him, is impossible), but that nothing can prepare him for the blow."

"Not my flight?" she returned. "Think of it again."

"Your flight, Lady Dedlock, would spread the whole truth, and a hundred times the whole truth, far and wide. It would be impossible to save the family credit for a day. It is not to be thought of."

There is a quiet decision in his reply which admits of no remonstrance.

"When I speak of Sir Leicester being the sole consideration, he and the family credit are one. Sir Leicester and the baronetcy, Sir Leicester and Chesney Wold, Sir Leicester and his ancestors and his patrimony"—Mr. Tulkinghorn very dry here—"are, I need not say to you, Lady Dedlock, inseparable."

"Go on!"

"Therefore," says Mr. Tulkinghorn, pursuing his case in his jog-trot style, "I have much to consider. This is to be hushed up if it can be. How can it be, if Sir Leicester is driven out of his wits or laid upon a death-bed? If I inflicted this shock upon him to-morrow morning, how could the immediate change in him be accounted for? What could have caused it? What could have divided you? Lady Dedlock, the wall-chalking and the street-crying would come on directly, and you are to remember that it would not affect you merely (whom I cannot at all consider in this business) but your husband, Lady Dedlock, your husband."

He gets plainer as he gets on, but not an atom more emphatic or animated.

"There is another point of view," he continues, "in which the case presents itself. Sir Leicester is devoted to you almost to infatuation. He might not be able to overcome that infatuation, even knowing what we know. I am putting an extreme case, but it might be so. If so, it were better that he knew nothing. Better for common sense, better for him, better for me. I must take all this into account, and it combines to render a decision very difficult."

She stands looking out at the same stars without a word. They are beginning to pale, and she looks as if their coldness froze her.

"My experience teaches me," says Mr. Tulkinghorn, who has by this time got his hands in his pockets and is going on in his business consideration of the matter like a machine. "My experience teaches me, Lady Dedlock, that most of the people I know would do far better to leave marriage alone. It is at the bottom of three fourths of their troubles. So I thought when Sir Leicester married, and so I always have thought since. No more about that. I must now be guided by circumstances. In the meanwhile I must beg you to keep your own counsel, and I will keep mine."

"I am to drag my present life on, holding its pains at your pleasure, day by day?" she asks, still looking at the distant sky.

"Yes, I am afraid so, Lady Dedlock."

"It is necessary, you think, that I should be so tied to the stake?"

"I am sure that what I recommend is necessary."

"I am to remain on this gaudy platform on which my miserable deception has been so long acted, and it is to fall beneath me when you give the signal?" she said slowly.

"Not without notice, Lady Dedlock. I shall take no step without forewarning you."

She asks all her questions as if she were repeating them from memory or calling them over in her sleep.

"We are to meet as usual?"

"Precisely as usual, if you please."

"And I am to hide my guilt, as I have done so many years?"

"As you have done so many years. I should not have made that reference myself, Lady Dedlock, but I may now remind you that your secret can be no heavier to you than it was, and is no worse and no better than it was. I know it certainly, but I believe we have never wholly trusted each other."

She stands absorbed in the same frozen way for some little time before asking, "Is there anything more to be said to-night?"

"Why," Mr. Tulkinghorn returns methodically as he softly rubs his hands, "I should like to be assured of your acquiescence in my arrangements, Lady Dedlock."

"You may be assured of it."

"Good. And I would wish in conclusion to remind you, as a business precaution, in case it should be necessary to recall the fact in any communication with Sir Leicester, that throughout our interview I have expressly stated my sole consideration to be Sir Leicester's feelings and honour and the family reputation. I should have been happy to have made Lady Dedlock a prominent consideration, too, if the case had admitted of it; but unfortunately it does not."

"I can attest your fidelity, sir."

Both before and after saying it she remains absorbed, but at length moves, and turns, unshaken in her natural and acquired presence, towards the door. Mr. Tulkinghorn opens both the doors exactly as he would have done yesterday, or as he would have done ten years ago, and makes his old-fashioned bow as she passes out. It is not an ordinary look that he receives from the handsome face as it goes into the darkness, and it is not an ordinary movement, though a very slight one, that acknowledges his courtesy. But as he reflects when he is left alone, the woman has been putting no common constraint upon herself.

He would know it all the better if he saw the woman pacing her own rooms with her hair wildly thrown from her flung-back face, her hands clasped behind her head, her figure twisted as if by pain. He would think so all the more if he saw the woman thus hurrying up and down for hours, without fatigue, without intermission, followed by the faithful step upon the Ghost's Walk. But he shuts out the now chilled air, draws the window-curtain, goes to bed, and falls asleep. And truly when the stars go out and the wan day peeps into the turret-chamber, finding him at his oldest, he looks as if the digger and the spade were both commissioned and would soon be digging.

The same wan day peeps in at Sir Leicester pardoning the repentant country in a majestically condescending dream; and at the cousins entering on various public employments, principally receipt of salary; and at the chaste Volumnia, bestowing a dower of fifty thousand pounds upon a hideous old general with a mouth of false teeth like a pianoforte too full of keys, long the admiration of Bath and the terror of every other community. Also into rooms high in the roof, and into offices in court-yards, and over stables, where humbler ambition dreams of bliss, in keepers' lodges, and in holy matrimony with Will or Sally. Up comes the bright sun, drawing everything up with it—the Wills and Sallys, the latent vapour in the earth, the drooping leaves and flowers, the birds and beasts and creeping things, the gardeners to sweep the dewy turf and unfold emerald velvet where the roller passes, the smoke of the great kitchen fire wreathing itself straight and high into the lightsome air. Lastly, up comes the flag over Mr. Tulkinghorn's unconscious head cheerfully proclaiming that Sir Leicester and Lady Dedlock are in their happy home and that there is hospitality at the place in Lincolnshire.

CHAPTER XLII
IN MR. TULKINGHORN'S CHAMBERS

From the verdant undulations and the spreading oaks of the Dedlock property, Mr. Tulkinghorn transfers himself to the stale heat and dust of London. His manner of coming and going between the two places is one of his impenetrabilities. He walks into Chesney Wold as if it were next door to his chambers and returns to his chambers as if he had never been out of Lincoln's Inn Fields. He neither changes his dress before the journey nor talks of it afterwards. He melted out of his turret-room this morning, just as now, in the late twilight, he melts into his own square.

Like a dingy London bird among the birds at roost in these pleasant fields, where the sheep are all made into parchment, the goats into wigs, and the pasture into chaff, the lawyer, smoke-dried and faded, dwelling among mankind but not consorting with them, aged without experience of genial youth, and so long used to make his cramped nest in holes and corners of human nature that he has forgotten its broader and better range, comes sauntering home. In the oven made by the hot pavements and hot buildings, he has baked himself dryer than usual; and he has in his thirsty mind his mellowed port-wine half a century old.

The lamplighter is skipping up and down his ladder on Mr. Tulkinghorn's side of the Fields when that high-priest of noble mysteries arrives at his own dull court-yard. He ascends the door-steps and is gliding into the dusky hall when he encounters, on the top step, a bowing and propitiatory little man.

"Is that Snagsby?"

"Yes, sir. I hope you are well, sir. I was just giving you up, sir, and going home."

"Aye? What is it? What do you want with me?"

"Well, sir," says Mr. Snagsby, holding his hat at the side of his head in his deference towards his best customer, "I was wishful to say a word to you, sir."

"Can you say it here?"

"Perfectly, sir."

"Say it then." The lawyer turns, leans his arms on the iron railing at the top of the steps, and looks at the lamplighter lighting the court-yard.

"It is relating," says Mr. Snagsby in a mysterious low voice, "it is relating—not to put too fine a point upon it—to the foreigner, sir!"

Mr. Tulkinghorn eyes him with some surprise. "What foreigner?"

"The foreign female, sir. French, if I don't mistake? I am not acquainted with that language myself, but I should judge from her manners and appearance that she was French; anyways, certainly foreign. Her that was upstairs, sir, when Mr. Bucket and me had the honour of waiting upon you with the sweeping-boy that night."

"Oh! Yes, yes. Mademoiselle Hortense."

"Indeed, sir?" Mr. Snagsby coughs his cough of submission behind his hat. "I am not acquainted myself with the names of foreigners in general, but I have no doubt it WOULD be that." Mr. Snagsby appears to have set out in this reply with some desperate design of repeating the name, but on reflection coughs again to excuse himself.

"And what can you have to say, Snagsby," demands Mr. Tulkinghorn, "about her?"

"Well, sir," returns the stationer, shading his communication with his hat, "it falls a little hard upon me. My domestic happiness is very great—at least, it's as great as can be expected, I'm sure—but my little woman is rather given to jealousy. Not to put too fine a point upon it, she is very much given to jealousy. And you see, a foreign female of that genteel appearance coming into the shop, and hovering—I should be the last to make use of a strong expression if I could avoid it, but hovering, sir—in the court—you know it is—now ain't it? I only put it to yourself, sir."

Mr. Snagsby, having said this in a very plaintive manner, throws in a cough of general application to fill up all the blanks.

"Why, what do you mean?" asks Mr. Tulkinghorn.

"Just so, sir," returns Mr. Snagsby; "I was sure you would feel it yourself and would excuse the reasonableness of MY feelings when coupled with the known excitableness of my little woman. You see, the foreign female—which you mentioned her name just now, with quite a native sound I am sure—caught up the word Snagsby that night, being uncommon quick, and made inquiry, and got the direction and come at dinner-time. Now Guster, our young woman, is timid and has fits, and she, taking fright at the foreigner's looks—which are fierce—and at a grinding manner that she has of speaking—which is calculated to alarm a weak mind—gave way to it, instead of bearing up against it, and tumbled down the kitchen stairs out of one into another, such fits as I do sometimes think are never gone into, or come out of, in any house but ours. Consequently there was by good fortune ample occupation for my little woman, and only me to answer the shop. When she DID say that Mr. Tulkinghorn, being always denied to her by his employer (which I had no doubt at the time was a foreign mode of viewing a clerk), she would do herself the pleasure of continually calling at my place until she was let in here. Since then she has been, as I began by saying, hovering, hovering, sir"—Mr. Snagsby repeats the word with pathetic emphasis—"in the court. The effects of which movement it is impossible to calculate. I shouldn't wonder if it might have already given rise to the painfullest mistakes even in the neighbours' minds, not mentioning (if such a thing was possible) my little woman. Whereas, goodness knows," says Mr. Snagsby, shaking his head, "I never had an idea of a foreign female, except as being formerly connected with a bunch of brooms and a baby, or at the present time with a tambourine and earrings. I never had, I do assure you, sir!"

Mr. Tulkinghorn had listened gravely to this complaint and inquires when the stationer has finished, "And that's all, is it, Snagsby?"

"Why yes, sir, that's all," says Mr. Snagsby, ending with a cough that plainly adds, "and it's enough too—for me."

"I don't know what Mademoiselle Hortense may want or mean, unless she is mad," says the lawyer.

"Even if she was, you know, sir," Mr. Snagsby pleads, "it wouldn't be a consolation to have some weapon or another in the form of a foreign dagger planted in the family."

"No," says the other. "Well, well! This shall be stopped. I am sorry you have been inconvenienced. If she comes again, send her here."

Mr. Snagsby, with much bowing and short apologetic coughing, takes his leave, lightened in heart. Mr. Tulkinghorn goes upstairs, saying to himself, "These women were created to give trouble the whole earth over. The mistress not being enough to deal with, here's the maid now! But I will be short with THIS jade at least!"

So saying, he unlocks his door, gropes his way into his murky rooms, lights his candles, and looks about him. It is too dark to see much of the Allegory overhead there, but that importunate Roman, who is for ever toppling out of the clouds and pointing, is at his old work pretty distinctly. Not honouring him with much attention, Mr. Tulkinghorn takes a small key from his pocket, unlocks a drawer in which there is another key, which unlocks a chest in which there is another, and so comes to the cellar-key, with which he prepares to descend to the regions of old wine. He is going towards the door with a candle in his hand when a knock comes.

"Who's this? Aye, aye, mistress, it's you, is it? You appear at a good time. I have just been hearing of you. Now! What do you want?"

He stands the candle on the chimney-piece in the clerk's hall and taps his dry cheek with the key as he addresses these words of welcome to Mademoiselle Hortense. That feline personage, with her lips tightly shut and her eyes looking out at him sideways, softly closes the door before replying.

"I have had great deal of trouble to find you, sir."

"HAVE you!"

"I have been here very often, sir. It has always been said to me, he is not at home, he is engage, he is this and that, he is not for you."

"Quite right, and quite true."

"Not true. Lies!"

At times there is a suddenness in the manner of Mademoiselle Hortense so like a bodily spring upon the subject of it that such subject involuntarily starts and fails back. It is Mr. Tulkinghorn's case at present, though Mademoiselle Hortense, with her eyes almost shut up (but still looking out sideways), is only smiling contemptuously and shaking her head.

"Now, mistress," says the lawyer, tapping the key hastily upon the chimney-piece. "If you have anything to say, say it, say it."

"Sir, you have not use me well. You have been mean and shabby."

"Mean and shabby, eh?" returns the lawyer, rubbing his nose with the key.

"Yes. What is it that I tell you? You know you have. You have attrapped me—catched me—to give you information; you have asked me to show you the dress of mine my Lady must have wore that night, you have prayed me to come in it here to meet that boy. Say! Is it not?" Mademoiselle Hortense makes another spring.

"You are a vixen, a vixen!" Mr. Tulkinghorn seems to meditate as he looks distrustfully at her, then he replies, "Well, wench, well. I paid you."

"You paid me!" she repeats with fierce disdain. "Two sovereign! I have not change them, I re-fuse them, I des-pise them, I throw them from me!" Which she literally does, taking them out of her bosom as she speaks and flinging them with such violence on the floor that they jerk up again into the light before they roll away into corners and slowly settle down there after spinning vehemently.

"Now!" says Mademoiselle Hortense, darkening her large eyes again. "You have paid me? Eh, my God, oh yes!"

Mr. Tulkinghorn rubs his head with the key while she entertains herself with a sarcastic laugh.

"You must be rich, my fair friend," he composedly observes, "to throw money about in that way!"

"I AM rich," she returns. "I am very rich in hate. I hate my Lady, of all my heart. You know that."

"Know it? How should I know it?"

"Because you have known it perfectly before you prayed me to give you that information. Because you have known perfectly that I was en-r-r-r-raged!" It appears impossible for mademoiselle to roll the letter "r" sufficiently in this word, notwithstanding that she assists her energetic delivery by clenching both her hands and setting all her teeth.

"Oh! I knew that, did I?" says Mr. Tulkinghorn, examining the wards of the key.

"Yes, without doubt. I am not blind. You have made sure of me because you knew that. You had reason! I det-est her." Mademoiselle Hortense folds her arms and throws this last remark at him over one of her shoulders.

"Having said this, have you anything else to say, mademoiselle?"

"I am not yet placed. Place me well. Find me a good condition! If you cannot, or do not choose to do that, employ me to pursue her, to chase her, to disgrace and to dishonour her. I will help you well, and with a good will. It is what YOU do. Do I not know that?"

"You appear to know a good deal," Mr. Tulkinghorn retorts.

"Do I not? Is it that I am so weak as to believe, like a child, that I come here in that dress to rec-eive that boy only to decide a little bet, a wager? Eh, my God, oh yes!" In this reply, down to the word "wager" inclusive, mademoiselle has been ironically polite and tender, then as suddenly dashed into the bitterest and most defiant scorn, with her black eyes in one and the same moment very nearly shut and staringly wide open.

"Now, let us see," says Mr. Tulkinghorn, tapping his chin with the key and looking imperturbably at her, "how this matter stands."

"Ah! Let us see," mademoiselle assents, with many angry and tight nods of her head.

"You come here to make a remarkably modest demand, which you have just stated, and it not being conceded, you will come again."

"And again," says mademoiselle with more tight and angry nods. "And yet again. And yet again. And many times again. In effect, for ever!"

"And not only here, but you will go to Mr. Snagsby's too, perhaps? That visit not succeeding either, you will go again perhaps?"

"And again," repeats mademoiselle, cataleptic with determination. "And yet again. And yet again. And many times again. In effect, for ever!"

"Very well. Now, Mademoiselle Hortense, let me recommend you to take the candle and pick up that money of yours. I think you will find it behind the clerk's partition in the corner yonder."

She merely throws a laugh over her shoulder and stands her ground with folded arms.

"You will not, eh?"

"No, I will not!"

"So much the poorer you; so much the richer I! Look, mistress, this is the key of my wine-cellar. It is a large key, but the keys of prisons are larger. In this city there are houses of correction (where the treadmills are, for women), the gates of which are very strong and heavy, and no doubt the keys too. I am afraid a lady of your spirit and activity would find it an inconvenience to have one of those keys turned upon her for any length of time. What do you think?"

"I think," mademoiselle replies without any action and in a clear, obliging voice, "that you are a miserable wretch."

"Probably," returns Mr. Tulkinghorn, quietly blowing his nose. "But I don't ask what you think of myself; I ask what you think of the prison."

"Nothing. What does it matter to me?"

"Why, it matters this much, mistress," says the lawyer, deliberately putting away his handkerchief and adjusting his frill; "the law is so despotic here that it interferes to prevent any of our good English citizens from being troubled, even by a lady's visits against his desire. And on his complaining that he is so troubled, it takes hold of the troublesome lady and shuts her up in prison under hard discipline. Turns the key upon her, mistress." Illustrating with the cellar-key.

"Truly?" returns mademoiselle in the same pleasant voice. "That is droll! But—my faith!—still what does it matter to me?"

"My fair friend," says Mr. Tulkinghorn, "make another visit here, or at Mr. Snagsby's, and you shall learn."

"In that case you will send me to the prison, perhaps?"

"Perhaps."

It would be contradictory for one in mademoiselle's state of agreeable jocularity to foam at the mouth, otherwise a tigerish expansion thereabouts might look as if a very little more would make her do it.

"In a word, mistress," says Mr. Tulkinghorn, "I am sorry to be unpolite, but if you ever present yourself uninvited here—or there—again, I will give you over to the police. Their gallantry is great, but they carry troublesome people through the streets in an ignominious manner, strapped down on a board, my good wench."

"I will prove you," whispers mademoiselle, stretching out her hand, "I will try if you dare to do it!"

"And if," pursues the lawyer without minding her, "I place you in that good condition of being locked up in jail, it will be some time before you find yourself at liberty again."

"I will prove you," repeats mademoiselle in her former whisper.

"And now," proceeds the lawyer, still without minding her, "you had better go. Think twice before you come here again."

"Think you," she answers, "twice two hundred times!"

"You were dismissed by your lady, you know," Mr. Tulkinghorn observes, following her out upon the staircase, "as the most implacable and unmanageable of women. Now turn over a new leaf and take warning by what I say to you. For what I say, I mean; and what I threaten, I will do, mistress."

She goes down without answering or looking behind her. When she is gone, he goes down too, and returning with his cobweb-covered bottle, devotes himself to a leisurely enjoyment of its contents, now and then, as he throws his head back in his chair, catching sight of the pertinacious Roman pointing from the ceiling.

CHAPTER XLIII
ESTHER'S NARRATIVE

It matters little now how much I thought of my living mother who had told me evermore to consider her dead. I could not venture to approach her or to communicate with her in writing, for my sense of the peril in which her life was passed was only to be equalled by my fears of increasing it. Knowing that my mere existence as a living creature was an unforeseen danger in her way, I could not always conquer that terror of myself which had seized me when I first knew the secret. At no time did I dare to utter her name. I felt as if I did not even dare to hear it. If the conversation anywhere, when I was present, took that direction, as it sometimes naturally did, I tried not to hear: I mentally counted, repeated something that I knew, or went out of the room. I am conscious now that I often did these things when there can have been no danger of her being spoken of, but I did them in the dread I had of hearing anything that might lead to her betrayal, and to her betrayal through me.

It matters little now how often I recalled the tones of my mother's voice, wondered whether I should ever hear it again as I so longed to do, and thought how strange and desolate it was that it should be so new to me. It matters little that I watched for every public mention of my mother's name; that I passed and repassed the door of her house in town, loving it, but afraid to look at it; that I once sat in the theatre when my mother was there and saw me, and when we were so wide asunder before the great company of all degrees that any link or confidence between us seemed a dream. It is all, all over. My lot has been so blest that I can relate little of myself which is not a story of goodness and generosity in others. I may well pass that little and go on.

When we were settled at home again, Ada and I had many conversations with my guardian of which Richard was the theme. My dear girl was deeply grieved that he should do their kind cousin so much wrong, but she was so faithful to Richard that she could not bear to blame him even for that. My guardian was assured of it, and never coupled his name with a word of reproof. "Rick is mistaken, my dear," he would say to her. "Well, well! We have all been mistaken over and over again. We must trust to you and time to set him right."

We knew afterwards what we suspected then, that he did not trust to time until he had often tried to open Richard's eyes. That he had written to him, gone to him, talked with him, tried every gentle and persuasive art his kindness could devise. Our poor devoted Richard was deaf and blind to all. If he were wrong, he would make amends when the Chancery suit was over. If he were groping in the dark, he could not do better than do his utmost to clear away those clouds in which so much was confused and obscured. Suspicion and misunderstanding were the fault of the suit? Then let him work the suit out and come through it to his right mind. This was his unvarying reply. Jarndyce and Jarndyce had obtained such possession of his whole nature that it was impossible to place any consideration before him which he did not, with a distorted kind of reason, make a new argument in favour of his doing what he did. "So that it is even more mischievous," said my guardian once to me, "to remonstrate with the poor dear fellow than to leave him alone."

I took one of these opportunities of mentioning my doubts of Mr. Skimpole as a good adviser for Richard.

"Adviser!" returned my guardian, laughing, "My dear, who would advise with Skimpole?"

"Encourager would perhaps have been a better word," said I.

"Encourager!" returned my guardian again. "Who could be encouraged by Skimpole?"

"Not Richard?" I asked.

"No," he replied. "Such an unworldly, uncalculating, gossamer creature is a relief to him and an amusement. But as to advising or encouraging or occupying a serious station towards anybody or anything, it is simply not to be thought of in such a child as Skimpole."

"Pray, cousin John," said Ada, who had just joined us and now looked over my shoulder, "what made him such a child?"

"What made him such a child?" inquired my guardian, rubbing his head, a little at a loss.

"Yes, cousin John."

"Why," he slowly replied, roughening his head more and more, "he is all sentiment, and—and susceptibility, and—and sensibility, and—and imagination. And these qualities are not regulated in him, somehow. I suppose the people who admired him for them in his youth attached too much importance to them and too little to any training that would have balanced and adjusted them, and so he became what he is. Hey?" said my guardian, stopping short and looking at us hopefully. "What do you think, you two?"

Ada, glancing at me, said she thought it was a pity he should be an expense to Richard.

"So it is, so it is," returned my guardian hurriedly. "That must not be. We must arrange that. I must prevent it. That will never do."

And I said I thought it was to be regretted that he had ever introduced Richard to Mr. Vholes for a present of five pounds.

"Did he?" said my guardian with a passing shade of vexation on his face. "But there you have the man. There you have the man! There is nothing mercenary in that with him. He has no idea of the value of money. He introduces Rick, and then he is good friends with Mr. Vholes and borrows five pounds of him. He means nothing by it and thinks nothing of it. He told you himself, I'll be bound, my dear?"

"Oh, yes!" said I.

"Exactly!" cried my guardian, quite triumphant. "There you have the man! If he had meant any harm by it or was conscious of any harm in it, he wouldn't tell it. He tells it as he does it in mere simplicity. But you shall see him in his own home, and then you'll understand him better. We must pay a visit to Harold Skimpole and caution him on these points. Lord bless you, my dears, an infant, an infant!"

In pursuance of this plan, we went into London on an early day and presented ourselves at Mr. Skimpole's door.

He lived in a place called the Polygon, in Somers Town, where there were at that time a number of poor Spanish refugees walking about in cloaks, smoking little paper cigars. Whether he was a better tenant than one might have supposed, in consequence of his friend Somebody always paying his rent at last, or whether his inaptitude for business rendered it particularly difficult to turn him out, I don't know; but he had occupied the same house some years. It was in a state of dilapidation quite equal to our expectation. Two or three of the area railings were gone, the water-butt was broken, the knocker was loose, the bell-handle had been pulled off a long time to judge from the rusty state of the wire, and dirty footprints on the steps were the only signs of its being inhabited.

A slatternly full-blown girl who seemed to be bursting out at the rents in her gown and the cracks in her shoes like an over-ripe berry answered our knock by opening the door a very little way and stopping up the gap with her figure. As she knew Mr. Jarndyce (indeed Ada and I both thought that she evidently associated him with the receipt of her wages), she immediately relented and allowed us to pass in. The lock of the door being in a disabled condition, she then applied herself to securing it with the chain, which was not in good action either, and said would we go upstairs?

We went upstairs to the first floor, still seeing no other furniture than the dirty footprints. Mr. Jarndyce without further ceremony entered a room there, and we followed. It was dingy enough and not at all clean, but furnished with an odd kind of shabby luxury, with a large footstool, a sofa, and plenty of cushions, an easy-chair, and plenty of pillows, a piano, books, drawing materials, music, newspapers, and a few sketches and pictures. A broken pane of glass in one of the dirty windows was papered and wafered over, but there was a little plate of hothouse nectarines on the table, and there was another of grapes, and another of sponge-cakes, and there was a bottle of light wine. Mr. Skimpole himself reclined upon the sofa in a dressing-gown, drinking some fragrant coffee from an old china cup—it was then about mid-day—and looking at a collection of wallflowers in the balcony.

He was not in the least disconcerted by our appearance, but rose and received us in his usual airy manner.

"Here I am, you see!" he said when we were seated, not without some little difficulty, the greater part of the chairs being broken. "Here I am! This is my frugal breakfast. Some men want legs of beef and mutton for breakfast; I don't. Give me my peach, my cup of coffee, and my claret; I am content. I don't want them for themselves, but they remind me of the sun. There's nothing solar about legs of beef and mutton. Mere animal satisfaction!"

"This is our friend's consulting-room (or would be, if he ever prescribed), his sanctum, his studio," said my guardian to us.

"Yes," said Mr. Skimpole, turning his bright face about, "this is the bird's cage. This is where the bird lives and sings. They pluck his feathers now and then and clip his wings, but he sings, he sings!"

He handed us the grapes, repeating in his radiant way, "He sings! Not an ambitious note, but still he sings."

"These are very fine," said my guardian. "A present?"

"No," he answered. "No! Some amiable gardener sells them. His man wanted to know, when he brought them last evening, whether he should wait for the money. 'Really, my friend,' I said, 'I think not—if your time is of any value to you.' I suppose it was, for he went away."

My guardian looked at us with a smile, as though he asked us, "Is it possible to be worldly with this baby?"

"This is a day," said Mr. Skimpole, gaily taking a little claret in a tumbler, "that will ever be remembered here. We shall call it Saint Clare and Saint Summerson day. You must see my daughters. I have a blue-eyed daughter who is my Beauty daughter, I have a Sentiment daughter, and I have a Comedy daughter. You must see them all. They'll be enchanted."

He was going to summon them when my guardian interposed and asked him to pause a moment, as he wished to say a word to him first. "My dear Jarndyce," he cheerfully replied, going back to his sofa, "as many moments as you please. Time is no object here. We never know what o'clock it is, and we never care. Not the way to get on in life, you'll tell me? Certainly. But we DON'T get on in life. We don't pretend to do it."

My guardian looked at us again, plainly saying, "You hear him?"

"Now, Harold," he began, "the word I have to say relates to Rick."

"The dearest friend I have!" returned Mr. Skimpole cordially. "I suppose he ought not to be my dearest friend, as he is not on terms with you. But he is, I can't help it; he is full of youthful poetry, and I love him. If you don't like it, I can't help it. I love him."

The engaging frankness with which he made this declaration really had a disinterested appearance and captivated my guardian, if not, for the moment, Ada too.

"You are welcome to love him as much as you like," returned Mr. Jarndyce, "but we must save his pocket, Harold."

"Oh!" said Mr. Skimpole. "His pocket? Now you are coming to what I don't understand." Taking a little more claret and dipping one of the cakes in it, he shook his head and smiled at Ada and me with an ingenuous foreboding that he never could be made to understand.

"If you go with him here or there," said my guardian plainly, "you must not let him pay for both."

"My dear Jarndyce," returned Mr. Skimpole, his genial face irradiated by the comicality of this idea, "what am I to do? If he takes me anywhere, I must go. And how can I pay? I never have any money. If I had any money, I don't know anything about it. Suppose I say to a man, how much? Suppose the man says to me seven and sixpence? I know nothing about seven and sixpence. It is impossible for me to pursue the subject with any consideration for the man. I don't go about asking busy people what seven and sixpence is in Moorish—which I don't understand. Why should I go about asking them what seven and sixpence is in Money—which I don't understand?"

"Well," said my guardian, by no means displeased with this artless reply, "if you come to any kind of journeying with Rick, you must borrow the money of me (never breathing the least allusion to that circumstance), and leave the calculation to him."

"My dear Jarndyce," returned Mr. Skimpole, "I will do anything to give you pleasure, but it seems an idle form—a superstition. Besides, I give you my word, Miss Clare and my dear Miss Summerson, I thought Mr. Carstone was immensely rich. I thought he had only to make over something, or to sign a bond, or a draft, or a cheque, or a bill, or to put something on a file somewhere, to bring down a shower of money."

"Indeed it is not so, sir," said Ada. "He is poor."

"No, really?" returned Mr. Skimpole with his bright smile. "You surprise me.

"And not being the richer for trusting in a rotten reed," said my guardian, laying his hand emphatically on the sleeve of Mr. Skimpole's dressing-gown, "be you very careful not to encourage him in that reliance, Harold."

"My dear good friend," returned Mr. Skimpole, "and my dear Miss Summerson, and my dear Miss Clare, how can I do that? It's business, and I don't know business. It is he who encourages me. He emerges from great feats of business, presents the brightest prospects before me as their result, and calls upon me to admire them. I do admire them—as bright prospects. But I know no more about them, and I tell him so."

The helpless kind of candour with which he presented this before us, the light-hearted manner in which he was amused by his innocence, the fantastic way in which he took himself under his own protection and argued about that curious person, combined with the delightful ease of everything he said exactly to make out my guardian's case. The more I saw of him, the more unlikely it seemed to me, when he was present, that he could design, conceal, or influence anything; and yet the less likely that appeared when he was not present, and the less agreeable it was to think of his having anything to do with any one for whom I cared.

Hearing that his examination (as he called it) was now over, Mr. Skimpole left the room with a radiant face to fetch his daughters (his sons had run away at various times), leaving my guardian quite delighted by the manner in which he had vindicated his childish character. He soon came back, bringing with him the three young ladies and Mrs. Skimpole, who had once been a beauty but was now a delicate high-nosed invalid suffering under a complication of disorders.

"This," said Mr. Skimpole, "is my Beauty daughter, Arethusa—plays and sings odds and ends like her father. This is my Sentiment daughter, Laura—plays a little but don't sing. This is my Comedy daughter, Kitty—sings a little but don't play. We all draw a little and compose a little, and none of us have any idea of time or money."

Mrs. Skimpole sighed, I thought, as if she would have been glad to strike out this item in the family attainments. I also thought that she rather impressed her sigh upon my guardian and that she took every opportunity of throwing in another.

"It is pleasant," said Mr. Skimpole, turning his sprightly eyes from one to the other of us, "and it is whimsically interesting to trace peculiarities in families. In this family we are all children, and I am the youngest."

The daughters, who appeared to be very fond of him, were amused by this droll fact, particularly the Comedy daughter.

"My dears, it is true," said Mr. Skimpole, "is it not? So it is, and so it must be, because like the dogs in the hymn, 'it is our nature to.' Now, here is Miss Summerson with a fine administrative capacity and a knowledge of details perfectly surprising. It will sound very strange in Miss Summerson's ears, I dare say, that we know nothing about chops in this house. But we don't, not the least. We can't cook anything whatever. A needle and thread we don't know how to use. We admire the people who possess the practical wisdom we want, but we don't quarrel with them. Then why should they quarrel with us? Live and let live, we say to them. Live upon your practical wisdom, and let us live upon you!"

He laughed, but as usual seemed quite candid and really to mean what he said.

"We have sympathy, my roses," said Mr. Skimpole, "sympathy for everything. Have we not?"

"Oh, yes, papa!" cried the three daughters.

"In fact, that is our family department," said Mr. Skimpole, "in this hurly-burly of life. We are capable of looking on and of being interested, and we DO look on, and we ARE interested. What more can we do? Here is my Beauty daughter, married these three years. Now I dare say her marrying another child, and having two more, was all wrong in point of political economy, but it was very agreeable. We had our little festivities on those occasions and exchanged social ideas. She brought her young husband home one day, and they and their young fledglings have their nest upstairs. I dare say at some time or other Sentiment and Comedy will bring THEIR husbands home and have THEIR nests upstairs too. So we get on, we don't know how, but somehow."

She looked very young indeed to be the mother of two children, and I could not help pitying both her and them. It was evident that the three daughters had grown up as they could and had had just as little haphazard instruction as qualified them to be their father's playthings in his idlest hours. His pictorial tastes were consulted, I observed, in their respective styles of wearing their hair, the Beauty daughter being in the classic manner, the Sentiment daughter luxuriant and flowing, and the Comedy daughter in the arch style, with a good deal of sprightly forehead, and vivacious little curls dotted about the corners of her eyes. They were dressed to correspond, though in a most untidy and negligent way.

Ada and I conversed with these young ladies and found them wonderfully like their father. In the meanwhile Mr. Jarndyce (who had been rubbing his head to a great extent, and hinted at a change in the wind) talked with Mrs. Skimpole in a corner, where we could not help hearing the chink of money. Mr. Skimpole had previously volunteered to go home with us and had withdrawn to dress himself for the purpose.

"My roses," he said when he came back, "take care of mama. She is poorly to-day. By going home with Mr. Jarndyce for a day or two, I shall hear the larks sing and preserve my amiability. It has been tried, you know, and would be tried again if I remained at home."

"That bad man!" said the Comedy daughter.

"At the very time when he knew papa was lying ill by his wallflowers, looking at the blue sky," Laura complained.

"And when the smell of hay was in the air!" said Arethusa.

"It showed a want of poetry in the man," Mr. Skimpole assented, but with perfect good humour. "It was coarse. There was an absence of the finer touches of humanity in it! My daughters have taken great offence," he explained to us, "at an honest man—"

"Not honest, papa. Impossible!" they all three protested.

"At a rough kind of fellow—a sort of human hedgehog rolled up," said Mr. Skimpole, "who is a baker in this neighbourhood and from whom we borrowed a couple of arm-chairs. We wanted a couple of arm-chairs, and we hadn't got them, and therefore of course we looked to a man who HAD got them, to lend them. Well! This morose person lent them, and we wore them out. When they were worn out, he wanted them back. He had them back. He was contented, you will say. Not at all. He objected to their being worn. I reasoned with him, and pointed out his mistake. I said, 'Can you, at your time of life, be so headstrong, my friend, as to persist that an arm-chair is a thing to put upon a shelf and look at? That it is an object to contemplate, to survey from a distance, to consider from a point of sight? Don't you KNOW that these arm-chairs were borrowed to be sat upon?' He was unreasonable and unpersuadable and used intemperate language. Being as patient as I am at this minute, I addressed another appeal to him. I said, 'Now, my good man, however our business capacities may vary, we are all children of one great mother, Nature. On this blooming summer morning here you see me' (I was on the sofa) 'with flowers before me, fruit upon the table, the cloudless sky above me, the air full of fragrance, contemplating Nature. I entreat you, by our common brotherhood, not to interpose between me and a subject so sublime, the absurd figure of an angry baker!' But he did," said Mr. Skimpole, raising his laughing eyes in playful astonishment; "he did interpose that ridiculous figure, and he does, and he will again. And therefore I am very glad to get out of his way and to go home with my friend Jarndyce."

It seemed to escape his consideration that Mrs. Skimpole and the daughters remained behind to encounter the baker, but this was so old a story to all of them that it had become a matter of course. He took leave of his family with a tenderness as airy and graceful as any other aspect in which he showed himself and rode away with us in perfect harmony of mind. We had an opportunity of seeing through some open doors, as we went downstairs, that his own apartment was a palace to the rest of the house.

I could have no anticipation, and I had none, that something very startling to me at the moment, and ever memorable to me in what ensued from it, was to happen before this day was out. Our guest was in such spirits on the way home that I could do nothing but listen to him and wonder at him; nor was I alone in this, for Ada yielded to the same fascination. As to my guardian, the wind, which had threatened to become fixed in the east when we left Somers Town, veered completely round before we were a couple of miles from it.

Whether of questionable childishness or not in any other matters, Mr. Skimpole had a child's enjoyment of change and bright weather. In no way wearied by his sallies on the road, he was in the drawing-room before any of us; and I heard him at the piano while I was yet looking after my housekeeping, singing refrains of barcaroles and drinking songs, Italian and German, by the score.

We were all assembled shortly before dinner, and he was still at the piano idly picking out in his luxurious way little strains of music, and talking between whiles of finishing some sketches of the ruined old Verulam wall to-morrow, which he had begun a year or two ago and had got tired of, when a card was brought in and my guardian read aloud in a surprised voice, "Sir Leicester Dedlock!"

The visitor was in the room while it was yet turning round with me and before I had the power to stir. If I had had it, I should have hurried away. I had not even the presence of mind, in my giddiness, to retire to Ada in the window, or to see the window, or to know where it was. I heard my name and found that my guardian was presenting me before I could move to a chair.

"Pray be seated, Sir Leicester."

"Mr. Jarndyce," said Sir Leicester in reply as he bowed and seated himself, "I do myself the honour of calling here—"

"You do ME the honour, Sir Leicester."

"Thank you—of calling here on my road from Lincolnshire to express my regret that any cause of complaint, however strong, that I may have against a gentleman who—who is known to you and has been your host, and to whom therefore I will make no farther reference, should have prevented you, still more ladies under your escort and charge, from seeing whatever little there may be to gratify a polite and refined taste at my house, Chesney Wold."

"You are exceedingly obliging, Sir Leicester, and on behalf of those ladies (who are present) and for myself, I thank you very much."

"It is possible, Mr. Jarndyce, that the gentleman to whom, for the reasons I have mentioned, I refrain from making further allusion—it is possible, Mr. Jarndyce, that that gentleman may have done me the honour so far to misapprehend my character as to induce you to believe that you would not have been received by my local establishment in Lincolnshire with that urbanity, that courtesy, which its members are instructed to show to all ladies and gentlemen who present themselves at that house. I merely beg to observe, sir, that the fact is the reverse."

My guardian delicately dismissed this remark without making any verbal answer.

"It has given me pain, Mr. Jarndyce," Sir Leicester weightily proceeded. "I assure you, sir, it has given—me—pain—to learn from the housekeeper at Chesney Wold that a gentleman who was in your company in that part of the county, and who would appear to possess a cultivated taste for the fine arts, was likewise deterred by some such cause from examining the family pictures with that leisure, that attention, that care, which he might have desired to bestow upon them and which some of them might possibly have repaid." Here he produced a card and read, with much gravity and a little trouble, through his eye-glass, "Mr. Hirrold—Herald—Harold—Skampling—Skumpling—I beg your pardon—Skimpole."

"This is Mr. Harold Skimpole," said my guardian, evidently surprised.

"Oh!" exclaimed Sir Leicester, "I am happy to meet Mr. Skimpole and to have the opportunity of tendering my personal regrets. I hope, sir, that when you again find yourself in my part of the county, you will be under no similar sense of restraint."

"You are very obliging, Sir Leicester Dedlock. So encouraged, I shall certainly give myself the pleasure and advantage of another visit to your beautiful house. The owners of such places as Chesney Wold," said Mr. Skimpole with his usual happy and easy air, "are public benefactors. They are good enough to maintain a number of delightful objects for the admiration and pleasure of us poor men; and not to reap all the admiration and pleasure that they yield is to be ungrateful to our benefactors."

Sir Leicester seemed to approve of this sentiment highly. "An artist, sir?"

"No," returned Mr. Skimpole. "A perfectly idle man. A mere amateur."

Sir Leicester seemed to approve of this even more. He hoped he might have the good fortune to be at Chesney Wold when Mr. Skimpole next came down into Lincolnshire. Mr. Skimpole professed himself much flattered and honoured.

"Mr. Skimpole mentioned," pursued Sir Leicester, addressing himself again to my guardian, "mentioned to the housekeeper, who, as he may have observed, is an old and attached retainer of the family—"

("That is, when I walked through the house the other day, on the occasion of my going down to visit Miss Summerson and Miss Clare," Mr. Skimpole airily explained to us.)

"—That the friend with whom he had formerly been staying there was Mr. Jarndyce." Sir Leicester bowed to the bearer of that name. "And hence I became aware of the circumstance for which I have professed my regret. That this should have occurred to any gentleman, Mr. Jarndyce, but especially a gentleman formerly known to Lady Dedlock, and indeed claiming some distant connexion with her, and for whom (as I learn from my Lady herself) she entertains a high respect, does, I assure you, give—me—pain."

"Pray say no more about it, Sir Leicester," returned my guardian. "I am very sensible, as I am sure we all are, of your consideration. Indeed the mistake was mine, and I ought to apologize for it."

I had not once looked up. I had not seen the visitor and had not even appeared to myself to hear the conversation. It surprises me to find that I can recall it, for it seemed to make no impression on me as it passed. I heard them speaking, but my mind was so confused and my instinctive avoidance of this gentleman made his presence so distressing to me that I thought I understood nothing, through the rushing in my head and the beating of my heart.

"I mentioned the subject to Lady Dedlock," said Sir Leicester, rising, "and my Lady informed me that she had had the pleasure of exchanging a few words with Mr. Jarndyce and his wards on the occasion of an accidental meeting during their sojourn in the vicinity. Permit me, Mr. Jarndyce, to repeat to yourself, and to these ladies, the assurance I have already tendered to Mr. Skimpole. Circumstances undoubtedly prevent my saying that it would afford me any gratification to hear that Mr. Boythorn had favoured my house with his presence, but those circumstances are confined to that gentleman himself and do not extend beyond him."

"You know my old opinion of him," said Mr. Skimpole, lightly appealing to us. "An amiable bull who is determined to make every colour scarlet!"

Sir Leicester Dedlock coughed as if he could not possibly hear another word in reference to such an individual and took his leave with great ceremony and politeness. I got to my own room with all possible speed and remained there until I had recovered my self-command. It had been very much disturbed, but I was thankful to find when I went downstairs again that they only rallied me for having been shy and mute before the great Lincolnshire baronet.

By that time I had made up my mind that the period was come when I must tell my guardian what I knew. The possibility of my being brought into contact with my mother, of my being taken to her house, even of Mr. Skimpole's, however distantly associated with me, receiving kindnesses and obligations from her husband, was so painful that I felt I could no longer guide myself without his assistance.

When we had retired for the night, and Ada and I had had our usual talk in our pretty room, I went out at my door again and sought my guardian among his books. I knew he always read at that hour, and as I drew near I saw the light shining out into the passage from his reading-lamp.

"May I come in, guardian?"

"Surely, little woman. What's the matter?"

"Nothing is the matter. I thought I would like to take this quiet time of saying a word to you about myself."

He put a chair for me, shut his book, and put it by, and turned his kind attentive face towards me. I could not help observing that it wore that curious expression I had observed in it once before—on that night when he had said that he was in no trouble which I could readily understand.

"What concerns you, my dear Esther," said he, "concerns us all. You cannot be more ready to speak than I am to hear."

"I know that, guardian. But I have such need of your advice and support. Oh! You don't know how much need I have to-night."

He looked unprepared for my being so earnest, and even a little alarmed.

"Or how anxious I have been to speak to you," said I, "ever since the visitor was here to-day."

"The visitor, my dear! Sir Leicester Dedlock?"

"Yes."

He folded his arms and sat looking at me with an air of the profoundest astonishment, awaiting what I should say next. I did not know how to prepare him.

"Why, Esther," said he, breaking into a smile, "our visitor and you are the two last persons on earth I should have thought of connecting together!"

"Oh, yes, guardian, I know it. And I too, but a little while ago."

The smile passed from his face, and he became graver than before. He crossed to the door to see that it was shut (but I had seen to that) and resumed his seat before me.

"Guardian," said I, "do you remember, when we were overtaken by the thunder-storm, Lady Dedlock's speaking to you of her sister?"

"Of course. Of course I do."

"And reminding you that she and her sister had differed, had gone their several ways?"

"Of course."

"Why did they separate, guardian?"

His face quite altered as he looked at me. "My child, what questions are these! I never knew. No one but themselves ever did know, I believe. Who could tell what the secrets of those two handsome and proud women were! You have seen Lady Dedlock. If you had ever seen her sister, you would know her to have been as resolute and haughty as she."

"Oh, guardian, I have seen her many and many a time!"

"Seen her?"

He paused a little, biting his lip. "Then, Esther, when you spoke to me long ago of Boythorn, and when I told you that he was all but married once, and that the lady did not die, but died to him, and that that time had had its influence on his later life—did you know it all, and know who the lady was?"

"No, guardian," I returned, fearful of the light that dimly broke upon me. "Nor do I know yet."

"Lady Dedlock's sister."

"And why," I could scarcely ask him, "why, guardian, pray tell me why were THEY parted?"

"It was her act, and she kept its motives in her inflexible heart. He afterwards did conjecture (but it was mere conjecture) that some injury which her haughty spirit had received in her cause of quarrel with her sister had wounded her beyond all reason, but she wrote him that from the date of that letter she died to him—as in literal truth she did—and that the resolution was exacted from her by her knowledge of his proud temper and his strained sense of honour, which were both her nature too. In consideration for those master points in him, and even in consideration for them in herself, she made the sacrifice, she said, and would live in it and die in it. She did both, I fear; certainly he never saw her, never heard of her from that hour. Nor did any one."

"Oh, guardian, what have I done!" I cried, giving way to my grief; "what sorrow have I innocently caused!"

"You caused, Esther?"

"Yes, guardian. Innocently, but most surely. That secluded sister is my first remembrance."

"No, no!" he cried, starting.

"Yes, guardian, yes! And HER sister is my mother!"

I would have told him all my mother's letter, but he would not hear it then. He spoke so tenderly and wisely to me, and he put so plainly before me all I had myself imperfectly thought and hoped in my better state of mind, that, penetrated as I had been with fervent gratitude towards him through so many years, I believed I had never loved him so dearly, never thanked him in my heart so fully, as I did that night. And when he had taken me to my room and kissed me at the door, and when at last I lay down to sleep, my thought was how could I ever be busy enough, how could I ever be good enough, how in my little way could I ever hope to be forgetful enough of myself, devoted enough to him, and useful enough to others, to show him how I blessed and honoured him.

CHAPTER XLIV
THE LETTER AND THE ANSWER

My guardian called me into his room next morning, and then I told him what had been left untold on the previous night. There was nothing to be done, he said, but to keep the secret and to avoid another such encounter as that of yesterday. He understood my feeling and entirely shared it. He charged himself even with restraining Mr. Skimpole from improving his opportunity. One person whom he need not name to me, it was not now possible for him to advise or help. He wished it were, but no such thing could be. If her mistrust of the lawyer whom she had mentioned were well-founded, which he scarcely doubted, he dreaded discovery. He knew something of him, both by sight and by reputation, and it was certain that he was a dangerous man. Whatever happened, he repeatedly impressed upon me with anxious affection and kindness, I was as innocent of as himself and as unable to influence.

"Nor do I understand," said he, "that any doubts tend towards you, my dear. Much suspicion may exist without that connexion."

"With the lawyer," I returned. "But two other persons have come into my mind since I have been anxious. Then I told him all about Mr. Guppy, who I feared might have had his vague surmises when I little understood his meaning, but in whose silence after our last interview I expressed perfect confidence.

"Well," said my guardian. "Then we may dismiss him for the present. Who is the other?"

I called to his recollection the French maid and the eager offer of herself she had made to me.

"Ha!" he returned thoughtfully. "That is a more alarming person than the clerk. But after all, my dear, it was but seeking for a new service. She had seen you and Ada a little while before, and it was natural that you should come into her head. She merely proposed herself for your maid, you know. She did nothing more."

"Her manner was strange," said I.

"Yes, and her manner was strange when she took her shoes off and showed that cool relish for a walk that might have ended in her death-bed," said my guardian. "It would be useless self-distress and torment to reckon up such chances and possibilities. There are very few harmless circumstances that would not seem full of perilous meaning, so considered. Be hopeful, little woman. You can be nothing better than yourself; be that, through this knowledge, as you were before you had it. It is the best you can do for everybody's sake. I, sharing the secret with you—"

"And lightening it, guardian, so much," said I.

"—will be attentive to what passes in that family, so far as I can observe it from my distance. And if the time should come when I can stretch out a hand to render the least service to one whom it is better not to name even here, I will not fail to do it for her dear daughter's sake."

I thanked him with my whole heart. What could I ever do but thank him! I was going out at the door when he asked me to stay a moment. Quickly turning round, I saw that same expression on his face again; and all at once, I don't know how, it flashed upon me as a new and far-off possibility that I understood it.

"My dear Esther," said my guardian, "I have long had something in my thoughts that I have wished to say to you."

"Indeed?"

"I have had some difficulty in approaching it, and I still have. I should wish it to be so deliberately said, and so deliberately considered. Would you object to my writing it?"

"Dear guardian, how could I object to your writing anything for ME to read?"

"Then see, my love," said he with his cheery smile, "am I at this moment quite as plain and easy—do I seem as open, as honest and old-fashioned—as I am at any time?"

I answered in all earnestness, "Quite." With the strictest truth, for his momentary hesitation was gone (it had not lasted a minute), and his fine, sensible, cordial, sterling manner was restored.

"Do I look as if I suppressed anything, meant anything but what I said, had any reservation at all, no matter what?" said he with his bright clear eyes on mine.

I answered, most assuredly he did not.

"Can you fully trust me, and thoroughly rely on what I profess, Esther?"

"Most thoroughly," said I with my whole heart.

"My dear girl," returned my guardian, "give me your hand."

He took it in his, holding me lightly with his arm, and looking down into my face with the same genuine freshness and faithfulness of manner—the old protecting manner which had made that house my home in a moment—said, "You have wrought changes in me, little woman, since the winter day in the stage-coach. First and last you have done me a world of good since that time."

"Ah, guardian, what have you done for me since that time!"

"But," said he, "that is not to be remembered now."

"It never can be forgotten."

"Yes, Esther," said he with a gentle seriousness, "it is to be forgotten now, to be forgotten for a while. You are only to remember now that nothing can change me as you know me. Can you feel quite assured of that, my dear?"

"I can, and I do," I said.

"That's much," he answered. "That's everything. But I must not take that at a word. I will not write this something in my thoughts until you have quite resolved within yourself that nothing can change me as you know me. If you doubt that in the least degree, I will never write it. If you are sure of that, on good consideration, send Charley to me this night week—'for the letter.' But if you are not quite certain, never send. Mind, I trust to your truth, in this thing as in everything. If you are not quite certain on that one point, never send!"

"Guardian," said I, "I am already certain, I can no more be changed in that conviction than you can be changed towards me. I shall send Charley for the letter."

He shook my hand and said no more. Nor was any more said in reference to this conversation, either by him or me, through the whole week. When the appointed night came, I said to Charley as soon as I was alone, "Go and knock at Mr. Jarndyce's door, Charley, and say you have come from me—'for the letter.'" Charley went up the stairs, and down the stairs, and along the passages—the zig-zag way about the old-fashioned house seemed very long in my listening ears that night—and so came back, along the passages, and down the stairs, and up the stairs, and brought the letter. "Lay it on the table, Charley," said I. So Charley laid it on the table and went to bed, and I sat looking at it without taking it up, thinking of many things.

I began with my overshadowed childhood, and passed through those timid days to the heavy time when my aunt lay dead, with her resolute face so cold and set, and when I was more solitary with Mrs. Rachael than if I had had no one in the world to speak to or to look at. I passed to the altered days when I was so blest as to find friends in all around me, and to be beloved. I came to the time when I first saw my dear girl and was received into that sisterly affection which was the grace and beauty of my life. I recalled the first bright gleam of welcome which had shone out of those very windows upon our expectant faces on that cold bright night, and which had never paled. I lived my happy life there over again, I went through my illness and recovery, I thought of myself so altered and of those around me so unchanged; and all this happiness shone like a light from one central figure, represented before me by the letter on the table.

I opened it and read it. It was so impressive in its love for me, and in the unselfish caution it gave me, and the consideration it showed for me in every word, that my eyes were too often blinded to read much at a time. But I read it through three times before I laid it down. I had thought beforehand that I knew its purport, and I did. It asked me, would I be the mistress of Bleak House.

It was not a love letter, though it expressed so much love, but was written just as he would at any time have spoken to me. I saw his face, and heard his voice, and felt the influence of his kind protecting manner in every line. It addressed me as if our places were reversed, as if all the good deeds had been mine and all the feelings they had awakened his. It dwelt on my being young, and he past the prime of life; on his having attained a ripe age, while I was a child; on his writing to me with a silvered head, and knowing all this so well as to set it in full before me for mature deliberation. It told me that I would gain nothing by such a marriage and lose nothing by rejecting it, for no new relation could enhance the tenderness in which he held me, and whatever my decision was, he was certain it would be right. But he had considered this step anew since our late confidence and had decided on taking it, if it only served to show me through one poor instance that the whole world would readily unite to falsify the stern prediction of my childhood. I was the last to know what happiness I could bestow upon him, but of that he said no more, for I was always to remember that I owed him nothing and that he was my debtor, and for very much. He had often thought of our future, and foreseeing that the time must come, and fearing that it might come soon, when Ada (now very nearly of age) would leave us, and when our present mode of life must be broken up, had become accustomed to reflect on this proposal. Thus he made it. If I felt that I could ever give him the best right he could have to be my protector, and if I felt that I could happily and justly become the dear companion of his remaining life, superior to all lighter chances and changes than death, even then he could not have me bind myself irrevocably while this letter was yet so new to me, but even then I must have ample time for reconsideration. In that case, or in the opposite case, let him be unchanged in his old relation, in his old manner, in the old name by which I called him. And as to his bright Dame Durden and little housekeeper, she would ever be the same, he knew.

This was the substance of the letter, written throughout with a justice and a dignity as if he were indeed my responsible guardian impartially representing the proposal of a friend against whom in his integrity he stated the full case.

But he did not hint to me that when I had been better looking he had had this same proceeding in his thoughts and had refrained from it. That when my old face was gone from me, and I had no attractions, he could love me just as well as in my fairer days. That the discovery of my birth gave him no shock. That his generosity rose above my disfigurement and my inheritance of shame. That the more I stood in need of such fidelity, the more firmly I might trust in him to the last.

But I knew it, I knew it well now. It came upon me as the close of the benignant history I had been pursuing, and I felt that I had but one thing to do. To devote my life to his happiness was to thank him poorly, and what had I wished for the other night but some new means of thanking him?

Still I cried very much, not only in the fullness of my heart after reading the letter, not only in the strangeness of the prospect—for it was strange though I had expected the contents—but as if something for which there was no name or distinct idea were indefinitely lost to me. I was very happy, very thankful, very hopeful; but I cried very much.

By and by I went to my old glass. My eyes were red and swollen, and I said, "Oh, Esther, Esther, can that be you!" I am afraid the face in the glass was going to cry again at this reproach, but I held up my finger at it, and it stopped.

"That is more like the composed look you comforted me with, my dear, when you showed me such a change!" said I, beginning to let down my hair. "When you are mistress of Bleak House, you are to be as cheerful as a bird. In fact, you are always to be cheerful; so let us begin for once and for all."

I went on with my hair now, quite comfortably. I sobbed a little still, but that was because I had been crying, not because I was crying then.

"And so Esther, my dear, you are happy for life. Happy with your best friends, happy in your old home, happy in the power of doing a great deal of good, and happy in the undeserved love of the best of men."

I thought, all at once, if my guardian had married some one else, how should I have felt, and what should I have done! That would have been a change indeed. It presented my life in such a new and blank form that I rang my housekeeping keys and gave them a kiss before I laid them down in their basket again.

Then I went on to think, as I dressed my hair before the glass, how often had I considered within myself that the deep traces of my illness and the circumstances of my birth were only new reasons why I should be busy, busy, busy—useful, amiable, serviceable, in all honest, unpretending ways. This was a good time, to be sure, to sit down morbidly and cry! As to its seeming at all strange to me at first (if that were any excuse for crying, which it was not) that I was one day to be the mistress of Bleak House, why should it seem strange? Other people had thought of such things, if I had not. "Don't you remember, my plain dear," I asked myself, looking at the glass, "what Mrs. Woodcourt said before those scars were there about your marrying—"

Perhaps the name brought them to my remembrance. The dried remains of the flowers. It would be better not to keep them now. They had only been preserved in memory of something wholly past and gone, but it would be better not to keep them now.

They were in a book, and it happened to be in the next room—our sitting-room, dividing Ada's chamber from mine. I took a candle and went softly in to fetch it from its shelf. After I had it in my hand, I saw my beautiful darling, through the open door, lying asleep, and I stole in to kiss her.

It was weak in me, I know, and I could have no reason for crying; but I dropped a tear upon her dear face, and another, and another. Weaker than that, I took the withered flowers out and put them for a moment to her lips. I thought about her love for Richard, though, indeed, the flowers had nothing to do with that. Then I took them into my own room and burned them at the candle, and they were dust in an instant.

On entering the breakfast-room next morning, I found my guardian just as usual, quite as frank, as open, and free. There being not the least constraint in his manner, there was none (or I think there was none) in mine. I was with him several times in the course of the morning, in and out, when there was no one there, and I thought it not unlikely that he might speak to me about the letter, but he did not say a word.

So, on the next morning, and the next, and for at least a week, over which time Mr. Skimpole prolonged his stay. I expected, every day, that my guardian might speak to me about the letter, but he never did.

I thought then, growing uneasy, that I ought to write an answer. I tried over and over again in my own room at night, but I could not write an answer that at all began like a good answer, so I thought each night I would wait one more day. And I waited seven more days, and he never said a word.

At last, Mr. Skimpole having departed, we three were one afternoon going out for a ride; and I, being dressed before Ada and going down, came upon my guardian, with his back towards me, standing at the drawing-room window looking out.

He turned on my coming in and said, smiling, "Aye, it's you, little woman, is it?" and looked out again.

I had made up my mind to speak to him now. In short, I had come down on purpose. "Guardian," I said, rather hesitating and trembling, "when would you like to have the answer to the letter Charley came for?"

"When it's ready, my dear," he replied.

"I think it is ready," said I.

"Is Charley to bring it?" he asked pleasantly.

"No. I have brought it myself, guardian," I returned.

I put my two arms round his neck and kissed him, and he said was this the mistress of Bleak House, and I said yes; and it made no difference presently, and we all went out together, and I said nothing to my precious pet about it.

CHAPTER XLV
IN TRUST

One morning when I had done jingling about with my baskets of keys, as my beauty and I were walking round and round the garden I happened to turn my eyes towards the house and saw a long thin shadow going in which looked like Mr. Vholes. Ada had been telling me only that morning of her hopes that Richard might exhaust his ardour in the Chancery suit by being so very earnest in it; and therefore, not to damp my dear girl's spirits, I said nothing about Mr. Vholes's shadow.

Presently came Charley, lightly winding among the bushes and tripping along the paths, as rosy and pretty as one of Flora's attendants instead of my maid, saying, "Oh, if you please, miss, would you step and speak to Mr. Jarndyce!"

It was one of Charley's peculiarities that whenever she was charged with a message she always began to deliver it as soon as she beheld, at any distance, the person for whom it was intended. Therefore I saw Charley asking me in her usual form of words to "step and speak" to Mr. Jarndyce long before I heard her. And when I did hear her, she had said it so often that she was out of breath.

I told Ada I would make haste back and inquired of Charley as we went in whether there was not a gentleman with Mr. Jarndyce. To which Charley, whose grammar, I confess to my shame, never did any credit to my educational powers, replied, "Yes, miss. Him as come down in the country with Mr. Richard."

A more complete contrast than my guardian and Mr. Vholes I suppose there could not be. I found them looking at one another across a table, the one so open and the other so close, the one so broad and upright and the other so narrow and stooping, the one giving out what he had to say in such a rich ringing voice and the other keeping it in in such a cold-blooded, gasping, fish-like manner that I thought I never had seen two people so unmatched.

"You know Mr. Vholes, my dear," said my guardian. Not with the greatest urbanity, I must say.

Mr. Vholes rose, gloved and buttoned up as usual, and seated himself again, just as he had seated himself beside Richard in the gig. Not having Richard to look at, he looked straight before him.

"Mr. Vholes," said my guardian, eyeing his black figure as if he were a bird of ill omen, "has brought an ugly report of our most unfortunate Rick." Laying a marked emphasis on "most unfortunate" as if the words were rather descriptive of his connexion with Mr. Vholes.

I sat down between them; Mr. Vholes remained immovable, except that he secretly picked at one of the red pimples on his yellow face with his black glove.

"And as Rick and you are happily good friends, I should like to know," said my guardian, "what you think, my dear. Would you be so good as to—as to speak up, Mr. Vholes?"

Doing anything but that, Mr. Vholes observed, "I have been saying that I have reason to know, Miss Summerson, as Mr. C.'s professional adviser, that Mr. C.'s circumstances are at the present moment in an embarrassed state. Not so much in point of amount as owing to the peculiar and pressing nature of liabilities Mr. C. has incurred and the means he has of liquidating or meeting the same. I have staved off many little matters for Mr. C., but there is a limit to staving off, and we have reached it. I have made some advances out of pocket to accommodate these unpleasantnesses, but I necessarily look to being repaid, for I do not pretend to be a man of capital, and I have a father to support in the Vale of Taunton, besides striving to realize some little independence for three dear girls at home. My apprehension is, Mr. C.'s circumstances being such, lest it should end in his obtaining leave to part with his commission, which at all events is desirable to be made known to his connexions."

Mr. Vholes, who had looked at me while speaking, here emerged into the silence he could hardly be said to have broken, so stifled was his tone, and looked before him again.

"Imagine the poor fellow without even his present resource," said my guardian to me. "Yet what can I do? You know him, Esther. He would never accept of help from me now. To offer it or hint at it would be to drive him to an extremity, if nothing else did."

Mr. Vholes hereupon addressed me again.

"What Mr. Jarndyce remarks, miss, is no doubt the case, and is the difficulty. I do not see that anything is to be done. I do not say that anything is to be done. Far from it. I merely come down here under the seal of confidence and mention it in order that everything may be openly carried on and that it may not be said afterwards that everything was not openly carried on. My wish is that everything should be openly carried on. I desire to leave a good name behind me. If I consulted merely my own interests with Mr. C., I should not be here. So insurmountable, as you must well know, would be his objections. This is not a professional attendance. This can he charged to nobody. I have no interest in it except as a member of society and a father—AND a son," said Mr. Vholes, who had nearly forgotten that point.

It appeared to us that Mr. Vholes said neither more nor less than the truth in intimating that he sought to divide the responsibility, such as it was, of knowing Richard's situation. I could only suggest that I should go down to Deal, where Richard was then stationed, and see him, and try if it were possible to avert the worst. Without consulting Mr. Vholes on this point, I took my guardian aside to propose it, while Mr. Vholes gauntly stalked to the fire and warmed his funeral gloves.

The fatigue of the journey formed an immediate objection on my guardian's part, but as I saw he had no other, and as I was only too happy to go, I got his consent. We had then merely to dispose of Mr. Vholes.

"Well, sir," said Mr. Jarndyce, "Miss Summerson will communicate with Mr. Carstone, and you can only hope that his position may be yet retrievable. You will allow me to order you lunch after your journey, sir."

"I thank you, Mr. Jarndyce," said Mr. Vholes, putting out his long black sleeve to check the ringing of the bell, "not any. I thank you, no, not a morsel. My digestion is much impaired, and I am but a poor knife and fork at any time. If I was to partake of solid food at this period of the day, I don't know what the consequences might be. Everything having been openly carried on, sir, I will now with your permission take my leave."

"And I would that you could take your leave, and we could all take our leave, Mr. Vholes," returned my guardian bitterly, "of a cause you know of."

Mr. Vholes, whose black dye was so deep from head to foot that it had quite steamed before the fire, diffusing a very unpleasant perfume, made a short one-sided inclination of his head from the neck and slowly shook it.

"We whose ambition it is to be looked upon in the light of respectable practitioners, sir, can but put our shoulders to the wheel. We do it, sir. At least, I do it myself; and I wish to think well of my professional brethren, one and all. You are sensible of an obligation not to refer to me, miss, in communicating with Mr. C.?"

I said I would be careful not to do it.

"Just so, miss. Good morning. Mr. Jarndyce, good morning, sir." Mr. Vholes put his dead glove, which scarcely seemed to have any hand in it, on my fingers, and then on my guardian's fingers, and took his long thin shadow away. I thought of it on the outside of the coach, passing over all the sunny landscape between us and London, chilling the seed in the ground as it glided along.

Of course it became necessary to tell Ada where I was going and why I was going, and of course she was anxious and distressed. But she was too true to Richard to say anything but words of pity and words of excuse, and in a more loving spirit still—my dear devoted girl!—she wrote him a long letter, of which I took charge.

Charley was to be my travelling companion, though I am sure I wanted none and would willingly have left her at home. We all went to London that afternoon, and finding two places in the mail, secured them. At our usual bed-time, Charley and I were rolling away seaward with the Kentish letters.

It was a night's journey in those coach times, but we had the mail to ourselves and did not find the night very tedious. It passed with me as I suppose it would with most people under such circumstances. At one while my journey looked hopeful, and at another hopeless. Now I thought I should do some good, and now I wondered how I could ever have supposed so. Now it seemed one of the most reasonable things in the world that I should have come, and now one of the most unreasonable. In what state I should find Richard, what I should say to him, and what he would say to me occupied my mind by turns with these two states of feeling; and the wheels seemed to play one tune (to which the burden of my guardian's letter set itself) over and over again all night.

At last we came into the narrow streets of Deal, and very gloomy they were upon a raw misty morning. The long flat beach, with its little irregular houses, wooden and brick, and its litter of capstans, and great boats, and sheds, and bare upright poles with tackle and blocks, and loose gravelly waste places overgrown with grass and weeds, wore as dull an appearance as any place I ever saw. The sea was heaving under a thick white fog; and nothing else was moving but a few early ropemakers, who, with the yarn twisted round their bodies, looked as if, tired of their present state of existence, they were spinning themselves into cordage.

But when we got into a warm room in an excellent hotel and sat down, comfortably washed and dressed, to an early breakfast (for it was too late to think of going to bed), Deal began to look more cheerful. Our little room was like a ship's cabin, and that delighted Charley very much. Then the fog began to rise like a curtain, and numbers of ships that we had had no idea were near appeared. I don't know how many sail the waiter told us were then lying in the downs. Some of these vessels were of grand size—one was a large Indiaman just come home; and when the sun shone through the clouds, making silvery pools in the dark sea, the way in which these ships brightened, and shadowed, and changed, amid a bustle of boats pulling off from the shore to them and from them to the shore, and a general life and motion in themselves and everything around them, was most beautiful.

The large Indiaman was our great attraction because she had come into the downs in the night. She was surrounded by boats, and we said how glad the people on board of her must be to come ashore. Charley was curious, too, about the voyage, and about the heat in India, and the serpents and the tigers; and as she picked up such information much faster than grammar, I told her what I knew on those points. I told her, too, how people in such voyages were sometimes wrecked and cast on rocks, where they were saved by the intrepidity and humanity of one man. And Charley asking how that could be, I told her how we knew at home of such a case.

I had thought of sending Richard a note saying I was there, but it seemed so much better to go to him without preparation. As he lived in barracks I was a little doubtful whether this was feasible, but we went out to reconnoitre. Peeping in at the gate of the barrack-yard, we found everything very quiet at that time in the morning, and I asked a sergeant standing on the guard-house-steps where he lived. He sent a man before to show me, who went up some bare stairs, and knocked with his knuckles at a door, and left us.

"Now then!" cried Richard from within. So I left Charley in the little passage, and going on to the half-open door, said, "Can I come in, Richard? It's only Dame Durden."

He was writing at a table, with a great confusion of clothes, tin cases, books, boots, brushes, and portmanteaus strewn all about the floor. He was only half dressed—in plain clothes, I observed, not in uniform—and his hair was unbrushed, and he looked as wild as his room. All this I saw after he had heartily welcomed me and I was seated near him, for he started upon hearing my voice and caught me in his arms in a moment. Dear Richard! He was ever the same to me. Down to—ah, poor poor fellow!—to the end, he never received me but with something of his old merry boyish manner.

"Good heaven, my dear little woman," said he, "how do you come here? Who could have thought of seeing you! Nothing the matter? Ada is well?"

"Quite well. Lovelier than ever, Richard!"

"Ah!" he said, leaning back in his chair. "My poor cousin! I was writing to you, Esther."

So worn and haggard as he looked, even in the fullness of his handsome youth, leaning back in his chair and crushing the closely written sheet of paper in his hand!

"Have you been at the trouble of writing all that, and am I not to read it after all?" I asked.

"Oh, my dear," he returned with a hopeless gesture. "You may read it in the whole room. It is all over here."

I mildly entreated him not to be despondent. I told him that I had heard by chance of his being in difficulty and had come to consult with him what could best be done.

"Like you, Esther, but useless, and so NOT like you!" said he with a melancholy smile. "I am away on leave this day—should have been gone in another hour—and that is to smooth it over, for my selling out. Well! Let bygones be bygones. So this calling follows the rest. I only want to have been in the church to have made the round of all the professions."

"Richard," I urged, "it is not so hopeless as that?"

"Esther," he returned, "it is indeed. I am just so near disgrace as that those who are put in authority over me (as the catechism goes) would far rather be without me than with me. And they are right. Apart from debts and duns and all such drawbacks, I am not fit even for this employment. I have no care, no mind, no heart, no soul, but for one thing. Why, if this bubble hadn't broken now," he said, tearing the letter he had written into fragments and moodily casting them away, by driblets, "how could I have gone abroad? I must have been ordered abroad, but how could I have gone? How could I, with my experience of that thing, trust even Vholes unless I was at his back!"

I suppose he knew by my face what I was about to say, but he caught the hand I had laid upon his arm and touched my own lips with it to prevent me from going on.

"No, Dame Durden! Two subjects I forbid—must forbid. The first is John Jarndyce. The second, you know what. Call it madness, and I tell you I can't help it now, and can't be sane. But it is no such thing; it is the one object I have to pursue. It is a pity I ever was prevailed upon to turn out of my road for any other. It would be wisdom to abandon it now, after all the time, anxiety, and pains I have bestowed upon it! Oh, yes, true wisdom. It would be very agreeable, too, to some people; but I never will."

He was in that mood in which I thought it best not to increase his determination (if anything could increase it) by opposing him. I took out Ada's letter and put it in his hand.

"Am I to read it now?" he asked.

As I told him yes, he laid it on the table, and resting his head upon his hand, began. He had not read far when he rested his head upon his two hands—to hide his face from me. In a little while he rose as if the light were bad and went to the window. He finished reading it there, with his back towards me, and after he had finished and had folded it up, stood there for some minutes with the letter in his hand. When he came back to his chair, I saw tears in his eyes.

"Of course, Esther, you know what she says here?" He spoke in a softened voice and kissed the letter as he asked me.

"Yes, Richard."

"Offers me," he went on, tapping his foot upon the floor, "the little inheritance she is certain of so soon—just as little and as much as I have wasted—and begs and prays me to take it, set myself right with it, and remain in the service."

"I know your welfare to be the dearest wish of her heart," said I. "And, oh, my dear Richard, Ada's is a noble heart."

"I am sure it is. I—I wish I was dead!"

He went back to the window, and laying his arm across it, leaned his head down on his arm. It greatly affected me to see him so, but I hoped he might become more yielding, and I remained silent. My experience was very limited; I was not at all prepared for his rousing himself out of this emotion to a new sense of injury.

"And this is the heart that the same John Jarndyce, who is not otherwise to be mentioned between us, stepped in to estrange from me," said he indignantly. "And the dear girl makes me this generous offer from under the same John Jarndyce's roof, and with the same John Jarndyce's gracious consent and connivance, I dare say, as a new means of buying me off."

"Richard!" I cried out, rising hastily. "I will not hear you say such shameful words!" I was very angry with him indeed, for the first time in my life, but it only lasted a moment. When I saw his worn young face looking at me as if he were sorry, I put my hand on his shoulder and said, "If you please, my dear Richard, do not speak in such a tone to me. Consider!"

He blamed himself exceedingly and told me in the most generous manner that he had been very wrong and that he begged my pardon a thousand times. At that I laughed, but trembled a little too, for I was rather fluttered after being so fiery.

"To accept this offer, my dear Esther," said he, sitting down beside me and resuming our conversation, "—once more, pray, pray forgive me; I am deeply grieved—to accept my dearest cousin's offer is, I need not say, impossible. Besides, I have letters and papers that I could show you which would convince you it is all over here. I have done with the red coat, believe me. But it is some satisfaction, in the midst of my troubles and perplexities, to know that I am pressing Ada's interests in pressing my own. Vholes has his shoulder to the wheel, and he cannot help urging it on as much for her as for me, thank God!"

His sanguine hopes were rising within him and lighting up his features, but they made his face more sad to me than it had been before.

"No, no!" cried Richard exultingly. "If every farthing of Ada's little fortune were mine, no part of it should be spent in retaining me in what I am not fit for, can take no interest in, and am weary of. It should be devoted to what promises a better return, and should be used where she has a larger stake. Don't be uneasy for me! I shall now have only one thing on my mind, and Vholes and I will work it. I shall not be without means. Free of my commission, I shall be able to compound with some small usurers who will hear of nothing but their bond now—Vholes says so. I should have a balance in my favour anyway, but that would swell it. Come, come! You shall carry a letter to Ada from me, Esther, and you must both of you be more hopeful of me and not believe that I am quite cast away just yet, my dear."

I will not repeat what I said to Richard. I know it was tiresome, and nobody is to suppose for a moment that it was at all wise. It only came from my heart. He heard it patiently and feelingly, but I saw that on the two subjects he had reserved it was at present hopeless to make any representation to him. I saw too, and had experienced in this very interview, the sense of my guardian's remark that it was even more mischievous to use persuasion with him than to leave him as he was.

Therefore I was driven at last to asking Richard if he would mind convincing me that it really was all over there, as he had said, and that it was not his mere impression. He showed me without hesitation a correspondence making it quite plain that his retirement was arranged. I found, from what he told me, that Mr. Vholes had copies of these papers and had been in consultation with him throughout. Beyond ascertaining this, and having been the bearer of Ada's letter, and being (as I was going to be) Richard's companion back to London, I had done no good by coming down. Admitting this to myself with a reluctant heart, I said I would return to the hotel and wait until he joined me there, so he threw a cloak over his shoulders and saw me to the gate, and

Charley and I went back along the beach.

There was a concourse of people in one spot, surrounding some naval officers who were landing from a boat, and pressing about them with unusual interest. I said to Charley this would be one of the great Indiaman's boats now, and we stopped to look.

The gentlemen came slowly up from the waterside, speaking good-humouredly to each other and to the people around and glancing about them as if they were glad to be in England again. "Charley, Charley," said I, "come away!" And I hurried on so swiftly that my little maid was surprised.

It was not until we were shut up in our cabin-room and I had had time to take breath that I began to think why I had made such haste. In one of the sunburnt faces I had recognized Mr. Allan Woodcourt, and I had been afraid of his recognizing me. I had been unwilling that he should see my altered looks. I had been taken by surprise, and my courage had quite failed me.

But I knew this would not do, and I now said to myself, "My dear, there is no reason—there is and there can be no reason at all—why it should be worse for you now than it ever has been. What you were last month, you are to-day; you are no worse, you are no better. This is not your resolution; call it up, Esther, call it up!" I was in a great tremble—with running—and at first was quite unable to calm myself; but I got better, and I was very glad to know it.

The party came to the hotel. I heard them speaking on the staircase. I was sure it was the same gentlemen because I knew their voices again—I mean I knew Mr. Woodcourt's. It would still have been a great relief to me to have gone away without making myself known, but I was determined not to do so. "No, my dear, no. No, no, no!"

I untied my bonnet and put my veil half up—I think I mean half down, but it matters very little—and wrote on one of my cards that I happened to be there with Mr. Richard Carstone, and I sent it in to Mr. Woodcourt. He came immediately. I told him I was rejoiced to be by chance among the first to welcome him home to England. And I saw that he was very sorry for me.

"You have been in shipwreck and peril since you left us, Mr. Woodcourt," said I, "but we can hardly call that a misfortune which enabled you to be so useful and so brave. We read of it with the truest interest. It first came to my knowledge through your old patient, poor Miss Flite, when I was recovering from my severe illness."

"Ah! Little Miss Flite!" he said. "She lives the same life yet?"

"Just the same."

I was so comfortable with myself now as not to mind the veil and to be able to put it aside.

"Her gratitude to you, Mr. Woodcourt, is delightful. She is a most affectionate creature, as I have reason to say."

"You—you have found her so?" he returned. "I—I am glad of that." He was so very sorry for me that he could scarcely speak.

"I assure you," said I, "that I was deeply touched by her sympathy and pleasure at the time I have referred to."

"I was grieved to hear that you had been very ill."

"I was very ill."

"But you have quite recovered?"

"I have quite recovered my health and my cheerfulness," said I. "You know how good my guardian is and what a happy life we lead, and I have everything to be thankful for and nothing in the world to desire."

I felt as if he had greater commiseration for me than I had ever had for myself. It inspired me with new fortitude and new calmness to find that it was I who was under the necessity of reassuring him. I spoke to him of his voyage out and home, and of his future plans, and of his probable return to India. He said that was very doubtful. He had not found himself more favoured by fortune there than here. He had gone out a poor ship's surgeon and had come home nothing better. While we were talking, and when I was glad to believe that I had alleviated (if I may use such a term) the shock he had had in seeing me, Richard came in. He had heard downstairs who was with me, and they met with cordial pleasure.

I saw that after their first greetings were over, and when they spoke of Richard's career, Mr. Woodcourt had a perception that all was not going well with him. He frequently glanced at his face as if there were something in it that gave him pain, and more than once he looked towards me as though he sought to ascertain whether I knew what the truth was. Yet Richard was in one of his sanguine states and in good spirits and was thoroughly pleased to see Mr. Woodcourt again, whom he had always liked.

Richard proposed that we all should go to London together; but Mr. Woodcourt, having to remain by his ship a little longer, could not join us. He dined with us, however, at an early hour, and became so much more like what he used to be that I was still more at peace to think I had been able to soften his regrets. Yet his mind was not relieved of Richard. When the coach was almost ready and Richard ran down to look after his luggage, he spoke to me about him.

I was not sure that I had a right to lay his whole story open, but I referred in a few words to his estrangement from Mr Jarndyce and to his being entangled in the ill-fated Chancery suit. Mr. Woodcourt listened with interest and expressed his regret.

"I saw you observe him rather closely," said I, "Do you think him so changed?"

"He is changed," he returned, shaking his head.

I felt the blood rush into my face for the first time, but it was only an instantaneous emotion. I turned my head aside, and it was gone.

"It is not," said Mr. Woodcourt, "his being so much younger or older, or thinner or fatter, or paler or ruddier, as there being upon his face such a singular expression. I never saw so remarkable a look in a young person. One cannot say that it is all anxiety or all weariness; yet it is both, and like ungrown despair."

"You do not think he is ill?" said I.

No. He looked robust in body.

"That he cannot be at peace in mind, we have too much reason to know," I proceeded. "Mr. Woodcourt, you are going to London?"

"To-morrow or the next day."

"There is nothing Richard wants so much as a friend. He always liked you. Pray see him when you get there. Pray help him sometimes with your companionship if you can. You do not know of what service it might be. You cannot think how Ada, and Mr. Jarndyce, and even I—how we should all thank you, Mr. Woodcourt!"

"Miss Summerson," he said, more moved than he had been from the first, "before heaven, I will be a true friend to him! I will accept him as a trust, and it shall be a sacred one!"

"God bless you!" said I, with my eyes filling fast; but I thought they might, when it was not for myself. "Ada loves him—we all love him, but Ada loves him as we cannot. I will tell her what you say. Thank you, and God bless you, in her name!"

Richard came back as we finished exchanging these hurried words and gave me his arm to take me to the coach.

"Woodcourt," he said, unconscious with what application, "pray let us meet in London!"

"Meet?" returned the other. "I have scarcely a friend there now but you. Where shall I find you?"

"Why, I must get a lodging of some sort," said Richard, pondering. "Say at Vholes's, Symond's Inn."

"Good! Without loss of time."

They shook hands heartily. When I was seated in the coach and Richard was yet standing in the street, Mr. Woodcourt laid his friendly hand on Richard's shoulder and looked at me. I understood him and waved mine in thanks.

And in his last look as we drove away, I saw that he was very sorry for me. I was glad to see it. I felt for my old self as the dead may feel if they ever revisit these scenes. I was glad to be tenderly remembered, to be gently pitied, not to be quite forgotten.

CHAPTER XLVI
STOP HIM!

Darkness rests upon Tom-All-Alone's. Dilating and dilating since the sun went down last night, it has gradually swelled until it fills every void in the place. For a time there were some dungeon lights burning, as the lamp of life hums in Tom-all-Alone's, heavily, heavily, in the nauseous air, and winking—as that lamp, too, winks in Tom-all-Alone's—at many horrible things. But they are blotted out. The moon has eyed Tom with a dull cold stare, as admitting some puny emulation of herself in his desert region unfit for life and blasted by volcanic fires; but she has passed on and is gone. The blackest nightmare in the infernal stables grazes on Tom-all-Alone's, and Tom is fast asleep.

Much mighty speech-making there has been, both in and out of Parliament, concerning Tom, and much wrathful disputation how Tom shall be got right. Whether he shall be put into the main road by constables, or by beadles, or by bell-ringing, or by force of figures, or by correct principles of taste, or by high church, or by low church, or by no church; whether he shall be set to splitting trusses of polemical straws with the crooked knife of his mind or whether he shall be put to stone-breaking instead. In the midst of which dust and noise there is but one thing perfectly clear, to wit, that Tom only may and can, or shall and will, be reclaimed according to somebody's theory but nobody's practice. And in the hopeful meantime, Tom goes to perdition head foremost in his old determined spirit.

But he has his revenge. Even the winds are his messengers, and they serve him in these hours of darkness. There is not a drop of Tom's corrupted blood but propagates infection and contagion somewhere. It shall pollute, this very night, the choice stream (in which chemists on analysis would find the genuine nobility) of a Norman house, and his Grace shall not be able to say nay to the infamous alliance. There is not an atom of Tom's slime, not a cubic inch of any pestilential gas in which he lives, not one obscenity or degradation about him, not an ignorance, not a wickedness, not a brutality of his committing, but shall work its retribution through every order of society up to the proudest of the proud and to the highest of the high. Verily, what with tainting, plundering, and spoiling, Tom has his revenge.

It is a moot point whether Tom-all-Alone's be uglier by day or by night, but on the argument that the more that is seen of it the more shocking it must be, and that no part of it left to the imagination is at all likely to be made so bad as the reality, day carries it. The day begins to break now; and in truth it might be better for the national glory even that the sun should sometimes set upon the British dominions than that it should ever rise upon so vile a wonder as Tom.

A brown sunburnt gentleman, who appears in some inaptitude for sleep to be wandering abroad rather than counting the hours on a restless pillow, strolls hitherward at this quiet time. Attracted by curiosity, he often pauses and looks about him, up and down the miserable by-ways. Nor is he merely curious, for in his bright dark eye there is compassionate interest; and as he looks here and there, he seems to understand such wretchedness and to have studied it before.

On the banks of the stagnant channel of mud which is the main street of Tom-all-Alone's, nothing is to be seen but the crazy houses, shut up and silent. No waking creature save himself appears except in one direction, where he sees the solitary figure of a woman sitting on a door-step. He walks that way. Approaching, he observes that she has journeyed a long distance and is footsore and travel-stained. She sits on the door-step in the manner of one who is waiting, with her elbow on her knee and her head upon her hand. Beside her is a canvas bag, or bundle, she has carried. She is dozing probably, for she gives no heed to his steps as he comes toward her.

The broken footway is so narrow that when Allan Woodcourt comes to where the woman sits, he has to turn into the road to pass her. Looking down at her face, his eye meets hers, and he stops.

"What is the matter?"

"Nothing, sir."

"Can't you make them hear? Do you want to be let in?"

"I'm waiting till they get up at another house—a lodging-house—not here," the woman patiently returns. "I'm waiting here because there will be sun here presently to warm me."

"I am afraid you are tired. I am sorry to see you sitting in the street."

"Thank you, sir. It don't matter."

A habit in him of speaking to the poor and of avoiding patronage or condescension or childishness (which is the favourite device, many people deeming it quite a subtlety to talk to them like little spelling books) has put him on good terms with the woman easily.

"Let me look at your forehead," he says, bending down. "I am a doctor. Don't be afraid. I wouldn't hurt you for the world."

He knows that by touching her with his skilful and accustomed hand he can soothe her yet more readily. She makes a slight objection, saying, "It's nothing"; but he has scarcely laid his fingers on the wounded place when she lifts it up to the light.

"Aye! A bad bruise, and the skin sadly broken. This must be very sore."

"It do ache a little, sir," returns the woman with a started tear upon her cheek.

"Let me try to make it more comfortable. My handkerchief won't hurt you."

"Oh, dear no, sir, I'm sure of that!"

He cleanses the injured place and dries it, and having carefully examined it and gently pressed it with the palm of his hand, takes a small case from his pocket, dresses it, and binds it up. While he is thus employed, he says, after laughing at his establishing a surgery in the street, "And so your husband is a brickmaker?"

"How do you know that, sir?" asks the woman, astonished.

"Why, I suppose so from the colour of the clay upon your bag and on your dress. And I know brickmakers go about working at piecework in different places. And I am sorry to say I have known them cruel to their wives too."

The woman hastily lifts up her eyes as if she would deny that her injury is referable to such a cause. But feeling the hand upon her forehead, and seeing his busy and composed face, she quietly drops them again.

"Where is he now?" asks the surgeon.

"He got into trouble last night, sir; but he'll look for me at the lodging-house."

"He will get into worse trouble if he often misuses his large and heavy hand as he has misused it here. But you forgive him, brutal as he is, and I say no more of him, except that I wish he deserved it. You have no young child?"

The woman shakes her head. "One as I calls mine, sir, but it's Liz's."

"Your own is dead. I see! Poor little thing!"

By this time he has finished and is putting up his case. "I suppose you have some settled home. Is it far from here?" he asks, good-humouredly making light of what he has done as she gets up and curtsys.

"It's a good two or three and twenty mile from here, sir. At Saint Albans. You know Saint Albans, sir? I thought you gave a start like, as if you did."

"Yes, I know something of it. And now I will ask you a question in return. Have you money for your lodging?"

"Yes, sir," she says, "really and truly." And she shows it. He tells her, in acknowledgment of her many subdued thanks, that she is very welcome, gives her good day, and walks away. Tom-all-Alone's is still asleep, and nothing is astir.

Yes, something is! As he retraces his way to the point from which he descried the woman at a distance sitting on the step, he sees a ragged figure coming very cautiously along, crouching close to the soiled walls—which the wretchedest figure might as well avoid—and furtively thrusting a hand before it. It is the figure of a youth whose face is hollow and whose eyes have an emaciated glare. He is so intent on getting along unseen that even the apparition of a stranger in whole garments does not tempt him to look back. He shades his face with his ragged elbow as he passes on the other side of the way, and goes shrinking and creeping on with his anxious hand before him and his shapeless clothes hanging in shreds. Clothes made for what purpose, or of what material, it would be impossible to say. They look, in colour and in substance, like a bundle of rank leaves of swampy growth that rotted long ago.

Allan Woodcourt pauses to look after him and note all this, with a shadowy belief that he has seen the boy before. He cannot recall how or where, but there is some association in his mind with such a form. He imagines that he must have seen it in some hospital or refuge, still, cannot make out why it comes with any special force on his remembrance.

He is gradually emerging from Tom-all-Alone's in the morning light, thinking about it, when he hears running feet behind him, and looking round, sees the boy scouring towards him at great speed, followed by the woman.

"Stop him, stop him!" cries the woman, almost breathless. "Stop him, sir!"

He darts across the road into the boy's path, but the boy is quicker than he, makes a curve, ducks, dives under his hands, comes up half-a-dozen yards beyond him, and scours away again. Still the woman follows, crying, "Stop him, sir, pray stop him!" Allan, not knowing but that he has just robbed her of her money, follows in chase and runs so hard that he runs the boy down a dozen times, but each time he repeats the curve, the duck, the dive, and scours away again. To strike at him on any of these occasions would be to fell and disable him, but the pursuer cannot resolve to do that, and so the grimly ridiculous pursuit continues. At last the fugitive, hard-pressed, takes to a narrow passage and a court which has no thoroughfare. Here, against a hoarding of decaying timber, he is brought to bay and tumbles down, lying gasping at his pursuer, who stands and gasps at him until the woman comes up.

"Oh, you, Jo!" cries the woman. "What? I have found you at last!"

"Jo," repeats Allan, looking at him with attention, "Jo! Stay. To be sure! I recollect this lad some time ago being brought before the coroner."

"Yes, I see you once afore at the inkwhich," whimpers Jo. "What of that? Can't you never let such an unfortnet as me alone? An't I unfortnet enough for you yet? How unfortnet do you want me fur to be? I've been a-chivied and a-chivied, fust by one on you and nixt by another on you, till I'm worritted to skins and bones. The inkwhich warn't MY fault. I done nothink. He wos wery good to me, he wos; he wos the only one I knowed to speak to, as ever come across my crossing. It ain't wery likely I should want him to be inkwhiched. I only wish I wos, myself. I don't know why I don't go and make a hole in the water, I'm sure I don't."

He says it with such a pitiable air, and his grimy tears appear so real, and he lies in the corner up against the hoarding so like a growth of fungus or any unwholesome excrescence produced there in neglect and impurity, that Allan Woodcourt is softened towards him. He says to the woman, "Miserable creature, what has he done?"

To which she only replies, shaking her head at the prostrate figure more amazedly than angrily, "Oh, you Jo, you Jo. I have found you at last!"

"What has he done?" says Allan. "Has he robbed you?"

"No, sir, no. Robbed me? He did nothing but what was kind-hearted by me, and that's the wonder of it."

Allan looks from Jo to the woman, and from the woman to Jo, waiting for one of them to unravel the riddle.

"But he was along with me, sir," says the woman. "Oh, you Jo! He was along with me, sir, down at Saint Albans, ill, and a young lady, Lord bless her for a good friend to me, took pity on him when I durstn't, and took him home—"

Allan shrinks back from him with a sudden horror.

"Yes, sir, yes. Took him home, and made him comfortable, and like a thankless monster he ran away in the night and never has been seen or heard of since till I set eyes on him just now. And that young lady that was such a pretty dear caught his illness, lost her beautiful looks, and wouldn't hardly be known for the same young lady now if it wasn't for her angel temper, and her pretty shape, and her sweet voice. Do you know it? You ungrateful wretch, do you know that this is all along of you and of her goodness to you?" demands the woman, beginning to rage at him as she recalls it and breaking into passionate tears.

The boy, in rough sort stunned by what he hears, falls to smearing his dirty forehead with his dirty palm, and to staring at the ground, and to shaking from head to foot until the crazy hoarding against which he leans rattles.

Allan restrains the woman, merely by a quiet gesture, but effectually.

"Richard told me—" He falters. "I mean, I have heard of this—don't mind me for a moment, I will speak presently."

He turns away and stands for a while looking out at the covered passage. When he comes back, he has recovered his composure, except that he contends against an avoidance of the boy, which is so very remarkable that it absorbs the woman's attention.

"You hear what she says. But get up, get up!"

Jo, shaking and chattering, slowly rises and stands, after the manner of his tribe in a difficulty, sideways against the hoarding, resting one of his high shoulders against it and covertly rubbing his right hand over his left and his left foot over his right.

"You hear what she says, and I know it's true. Have you been here ever since?"

"Wishermaydie if I seen Tom-all-Alone's till this blessed morning," replies Jo hoarsely.

"Why have you come here now?"

Jo looks all round the confined court, looks at his questioner no higher than the knees, and finally answers, "I don't know how to do nothink, and I can't get nothink to do. I'm wery poor and ill, and I thought I'd come back here when there warn't nobody about, and lay down and hide somewheres as I knows on till arter dark, and then go and beg a trifle of Mr. Snagsby. He wos allus willin fur to give me somethink he wos, though Mrs. Snagsby she was allus a-chivying on me—like everybody everywheres."

"Where have you come from?"

Jo looks all round the court again, looks at his questioner's knees again, and concludes by laying his profile against the hoarding in a sort of resignation.

"Did you hear me ask you where you have come from?"

"Tramp then," says Jo.

"Now tell me," proceeds Allan, making a strong effort to overcome his repugnance, going very near to him, and leaning over him with an expression of confidence, "tell me how it came about that you left that house when the good young lady had been so unfortunate as to pity you and take you home."

Jo suddenly comes out of his resignation and excitedly declares, addressing the woman, that he never known about the young lady, that he never heern about it, that he never went fur to hurt her, that he would sooner have hurt his own self, that he'd sooner have had his unfortnet ed chopped off than ever gone a-nigh her, and that she wos wery good to him, she wos. Conducting himself throughout as if in his poor fashion he really meant it, and winding up with some very miserable sobs.

Allan Woodcourt sees that this is not a sham. He constrains himself to touch him. "Come, Jo. Tell me."

"No. I dustn't," says Jo, relapsing into the profile state. "I dustn't, or I would."

"But I must know," returns the other, "all the same. Come, Jo."

After two or three such adjurations, Jo lifts up his head again, looks round the court again, and says in a low voice, "Well, I'll tell you something. I was took away. There!"

"Took away? In the night?"

"Ah!" Very apprehensive of being overheard, Jo looks about him and even glances up some ten feet at the top of the hoarding and through the cracks in it lest the object of his distrust should be looking over or hidden on the other side.

"Who took you away?"

"I dustn't name him," says Jo. "I dustn't do it, sir.

"But I want, in the young lady's name, to know. You may trust me. No one else shall hear."

"Ah, but I don't know," replies Jo, shaking his head fearfully, "as he DON'T hear."

"Why, he is not in this place."

"Oh, ain't he though?" says Jo. "He's in all manner of places, all at wanst."

Allan looks at him in perplexity, but discovers some real meaning and good faith at the bottom of this bewildering reply. He patiently awaits an explicit answer; and Jo, more baffled by his patience than by anything else, at last desperately whispers a name in his ear.

"Aye!" says Allan. "Why, what had you been doing?"

"Nothink, sir. Never done nothink to get myself into no trouble, 'sept in not moving on and the inkwhich. But I'm a-moving on now. I'm a-moving on to the berryin ground—that's the move as I'm up to."

"No, no, we will try to prevent that. But what did he do with you?"

"Put me in a horsepittle," replied Jo, whispering, "till I was discharged, then giv me a little money—four half-bulls, wot you may call half-crowns—and ses 'Hook it! Nobody wants you here,' he ses. 'You hook it. You go and tramp,' he ses. 'You move on,' he ses. 'Don't let me ever see you nowheres within forty mile of London, or you'll repent it.' So I shall, if ever he doos see me, and he'll see me if I'm above ground," concludes Jo, nervously repeating all his former precautions and investigations.

Allan considers a little, then remarks, turning to the woman but keeping an encouraging eye on Jo, "He is not so ungrateful as you supposed. He had a reason for going away, though it was an insufficient one."

"Thankee, sir, thankee!" exclaims Jo. "There now! See how hard you wos upon me. But ony you tell the young lady wot the genlmn ses, and it's all right. For YOU wos wery good to me too, and I knows it."

"Now, Jo," says Allan, keeping his eye upon him, "come with me and I will find you a better place than this to lie down and hide in. If I take one side of the way and you the other to avoid observation, you will not run away, I know very well, if you make me a promise."

"I won't, not unless I wos to see HIM a-coming, sir."

"Very well. I take your word. Half the town is getting up by this time, and the whole town will be broad awake in another hour. Come along. Good day again, my good woman."

"Good day again, sir, and I thank you kindly many times again."

She has been sitting on her bag, deeply attentive, and now rises and takes it up. Jo, repeating, "Ony you tell the young lady as I never went fur to hurt her and wot the genlmn ses!" nods and shambles and shivers, and smears and blinks, and half laughs and half cries, a farewell to her, and takes his creeping way along after Allan Woodcourt, close to the houses on the opposite side of the street. In this order, the two come up out of Tom-all-Alone's into the broad rays of the sunlight and the purer air.

CHAPTER XLVII
JO'S WILL

As Allan Woodcourt and Jo proceed along the streets where the high church spires and the distances are so near and clear in the morning light that the city itself seems renewed by rest, Allan revolves in his mind how and where he shall bestow his companion. "It surely is a strange fact," he considers, "that in the heart of a civilized world this creature in human form should be more difficult to dispose of than an unowned dog." But it is none the less a fact because of its strangeness, and the difficulty remains.

At first he looks behind him often to assure himself that Jo is still really following. But look where he will, he still beholds him close to the opposite houses, making his way with his wary hand from brick to brick and from door to door, and often, as he creeps along, glancing over at him watchfully. Soon satisfied that the last thing in his thoughts is to give him the slip, Allan goes on, considering with a less divided attention what he shall do.

A breakfast-stall at a street-corner suggests the first thing to be done. He stops there, looks round, and beckons Jo. Jo crosses and comes halting and shuffling up, slowly scooping the knuckles of his right hand round and round in the hollowed palm of his left, kneading dirt with a natural pestle and mortar. What is a dainty repast to Jo is then set before him, and he begins to gulp the coffee and to gnaw the bread and butter, looking anxiously about him in all directions as he eats and drinks, like a scared animal.

But he is so sick and miserable that even hunger has abandoned him. "I thought I was amost a-starvin, sir," says Jo, soon putting down his food, "but I don't know nothink—not even that. I don't care for eating wittles nor yet for drinking on 'em." And Jo stands shivering and looking at the breakfast wonderingly.

Allan Woodcourt lays his hand upon his pulse and on his chest. "Draw breath, Jo!" "It draws," says Jo, "as heavy as a cart." He might add, "And rattles like it," but he only mutters, "I'm a-moving on, sir."

Allan looks about for an apothecary's shop. There is none at hand, but a tavern does as well or better. He obtains a little measure of wine and gives the lad a portion of it very carefully. He begins to revive almost as soon as it passes his lips. "We may repeat that dose, Jo," observes Allan after watching him with his attentive face. "So! Now we will take five minutes' rest, and then go on again."

Leaving the boy sitting on the bench of the breakfast-stall, with his back against an iron railing, Allan Woodcourt paces up and down in the early sunshine, casting an occasional look towards him without appearing to watch him. It requires no discernment to perceive that he is warmed and refreshed.

If a face so shaded can brighten, his face brightens somewhat; and by little and little he eats the slice of bread he had so hopelessly laid down. Observant of these signs of improvement, Allan engages him in conversation and elicits to his no small wonder the adventure of the lady in the veil, with all its consequences. Jo slowly munches as he slowly tells it. When he has finished his story and his bread, they go on again.

Intending to refer his difficulty in finding a temporary place of refuge for the boy to his old patient, zealous little Miss Flite, Allan leads the way to the court where he and Jo first foregathered. But all is changed at the rag and bottle shop; Miss Flite no longer lodges there; it is shut up; and a hard-featured female, much obscured by dust, whose age is a problem, but who is indeed no other than the interesting Judy, is tart and spare in her replies. These sufficing, however, to inform the visitor that Miss Flite and her birds are domiciled with a Mrs. Blinder, in Bell Yard, he repairs to that neighbouring place, where Miss Flite (who rises early that she may be punctual at the divan of justice held by her excellent friend the Chancellor) comes running downstairs with tears of welcome and with open arms.

"My dear physician!" cries Miss Flite. "My meritorious, distinguished, honourable officer!" She uses some odd expressions, but is as cordial and full of heart as sanity itself can be—more so than it often is. Allan, very patient with her, waits until she has no more raptures to express, then points out Jo, trembling in a doorway, and tells her how he comes there.

"Where can I lodge him hereabouts for the present? Now, you have a fund of knowledge and good sense and can advise me."

Miss Flite, mighty proud of the compliment, sets herself to consider; but it is long before a bright thought occurs to her. Mrs. Blinder is entirely let, and she herself occupies poor Gridley's room. "Gridley!" exclaims Miss Flite, clapping her hands after a twentieth repetition of this remark. "Gridley! To be sure! Of course! My dear physician! General George will help us out."

It is hopeless to ask for any information about General George, and would be, though Miss Flite had not already run upstairs to put on her pinched bonnet and her poor little shawl and to arm herself with her reticule of documents. But as she informs her physician in her disjointed manner on coming down in full array that General George, whom she often calls upon, knows her dear Fitz Jarndyce and takes a great interest in all connected with her, Allan is induced to think that they may be in the right way. So he tells Jo, for his encouragement, that this walking about will soon be over now; and they repair to the general's. Fortunately it is not far.

From the exterior of George's Shooting Gallery, and the long entry, and the bare perspective beyond it, Allan Woodcourt augurs well. He also descries promise in the figure of Mr. George himself, striding towards them in his morning exercise with his pipe in his mouth, no stock on, and his muscular arms, developed by broadsword and dumbbell, weightily asserting themselves through his light shirt-sleeves.

"Your servant, sir," says Mr. George with a military salute. Good-humouredly smiling all over his broad forehead up into his crisp hair, he then defers to Miss Flite, as, with great stateliness, and at some length, she performs the courtly ceremony of presentation. He winds it up with another "Your servant, sir!" and another salute.

"Excuse me, sir. A sailor, I believe?" says Mr. George.

"I am proud to find I have the air of one," returns Allan; "but I am only a sea-going doctor."

"Indeed, sir! I should have thought you was a regular blue-jacket myself."

Allan hopes Mr. George will forgive his intrusion the more readily on that account, and particularly that he will not lay aside his pipe, which, in his politeness, he has testified some intention of doing. "You are very good, sir," returns the trooper. "As I know by experience that it's not disagreeable to Miss Flite, and since it's equally agreeable to yourself—" and finishes the sentence by putting it between his lips again. Allan proceeds to tell him all he knows about Jo, unto which the trooper listens with a grave face.

"And that's the lad, sir, is it?" he inquires, looking along the entry to where Jo stands staring up at the great letters on the whitewashed front, which have no meaning in his eyes.

"That's he," says Allan. "And, Mr. George, I am in this difficulty about him. I am unwilling to place him in a hospital, even if I could procure him immediate admission, because I foresee that he would not stay there many hours if he could be so much as got there. The same objection applies to a workhouse, supposing I had the patience to be evaded and shirked, and handed about from post to pillar in trying to get him into one, which is a system that I don't take kindly to."

"No man does, sir," returns Mr. George.

"I am convinced that he would not remain in either place, because he is possessed by an extraordinary terror of this person who ordered him to keep out of the way; in his ignorance, he believes this person to be everywhere, and cognizant of everything."

"I ask your pardon, sir," says Mr. George. "But you have not mentioned that party's name. Is it a secret, sir?"

"The boy makes it one. But his name is Bucket."

"Bucket the detective, sir?"

"The same man."

"The man is known to me, sir," returns the trooper after blowing out a cloud of smoke and squaring his chest, "and the boy is so far correct that he undoubtedly is a—rum customer." Mr. George smokes with a profound meaning after this and surveys Miss Flite in silence.

"Now, I wish Mr. Jarndyce and Miss Summerson at least to know that this Jo, who tells so strange a story, has reappeared, and to have it in their power to speak with him if they should desire to do so. Therefore I want to get him, for the present moment, into any poor lodging kept by decent people where he would be admitted. Decent people and Jo, Mr. George," says Allan, following the direction of the trooper's eyes along the entry, "have not been much acquainted, as you see. Hence the difficulty. Do you happen to know any one in this neighbourhood who would receive him for a while on my paying for him beforehand?"

As he puts the question, he becomes aware of a dirty-faced little man standing at the trooper's elbow and looking up, with an oddly twisted figure and countenance, into the trooper's face. After a few more puffs at his pipe, the trooper looks down askant at the little man, and the little man winks up at the trooper.

"Well, sir," says Mr. George, "I can assure you that I would willingly be knocked on the head at any time if it would be at all agreeable to Miss Summerson, and consequently I esteem it a privilege to do that young lady any service, however small. We are naturally in the vagabond way here, sir, both myself and Phil. You see what the place is. You are welcome to a quiet corner of it for the boy if the same would meet your views. No charge made, except for rations. We are not in a flourishing state of circumstances here, sir. We are liable to be tumbled out neck and crop at a moment's notice. However, sir, such as the place is, and so long as it lasts, here it is at your service."

With a comprehensive wave of his pipe, Mr. George places the whole building at his visitor's disposal.

"I take it for granted, sir," he adds, "you being one of the medical staff, that there is no present infection about this unfortunate subject?"

Allan is quite sure of it.

"Because, sir," says Mr. George, shaking his head sorrowfully, "we have had enough of that."

His tone is no less sorrowfully echoed by his new acquaintance. "Still I am bound to tell you," observes Allan after repeating his former assurance, "that the boy is deplorably low and reduced and that he may be—I do not say that he is—too far gone to recover."

"Do you consider him in present danger, sir?" inquires the trooper.

"Yes, I fear so."

"Then, sir," returns the trooper in a decisive manner, "it appears to me—being naturally in the vagabond way myself—that the sooner he comes out of the street, the better. You, Phil! Bring him in!"

Mr. Squod tacks out, all on one side, to execute the word of command; and the trooper, having smoked his pipe, lays it by. Jo is brought in. He is not one of Mrs. Pardiggle's Tockahoopo Indians; he is not one of Mrs. Jellyby's lambs, being wholly unconnected with Borrioboola-Gha; he is not softened by distance and unfamiliarity; he is not a genuine foreign-grown savage; he is the ordinary home-made article. Dirty, ugly, disagreeable to all the senses, in body a common creature of the common streets, only in soul a heathen. Homely filth begrimes him, homely parasites devour him, homely sores are in him, homely rags are on him; native ignorance, the growth of English soil and climate, sinks his immortal nature lower than the beasts that perish. Stand forth, Jo, in uncompromising colours! From the sole of thy foot to the crown of thy head, there is nothing interesting about thee.

He shuffles slowly into Mr. George's gallery and stands huddled together in a bundle, looking all about the floor. He seems to know that they have an inclination to shrink from him, partly for what he is and partly for what he has caused. He, too, shrinks from them. He is not of the same order of things, not of the same place in creation. He is of no order and no place, neither of the beasts nor of humanity.

"Look here, Jo!" says Allan. "This is Mr. George."

Jo searches the floor for some time longer, then looks up for a moment, and then down again.

"He is a kind friend to you, for he is going to give you lodging room here."

Jo makes a scoop with one hand, which is supposed to be a bow. After a little more consideration and some backing and changing of the foot on which he rests, he mutters that he is "wery thankful."

"You are quite safe here. All you have to do at present is to be obedient and to get strong. And mind you tell us the truth here, whatever you do, Jo."

"Wishermaydie if I don't, sir," says Jo, reverting to his favourite declaration. "I never done nothink yit, but wot you knows on, to get myself into no trouble. I never was in no other trouble at all, sir, 'sept not knowin' nothink and starwation."

"I believe it, now attend to Mr. George. I see he is going to speak to you."

"My intention merely was, sir," observes Mr. George, amazingly broad and upright, "to point out to him where he can lie down and get a thorough good dose of sleep. Now, look here." As the trooper speaks, he conducts them to the other end of the gallery and opens one of the little cabins. "There you are, you see! Here is a mattress, and here you may rest, on good behaviour, as long as Mr., I ask your pardon, sir"—he refers apologetically to the card Allan has given him—"Mr. Woodcourt pleases. Don't you be alarmed if you hear shots; they'll be aimed at the target, and not you. Now, there's another thing I would recommend, sir," says the trooper, turning to his visitor. "Phil, come here!"

Phil bears down upon them according to his usual tactics. "Here is a man, sir, who was found, when a baby, in the gutter. Consequently, it is to be expected that he takes a natural interest in this poor creature. You do, don't you, Phil?"

"Certainly and surely I do, guv'ner," is Phil's reply.

"Now I was thinking, sir," says Mr. George in a martial sort of confidence, as if he were giving his opinion in a council of war at a drum-head, "that if this man was to take him to a bath and was to lay out a few shillings in getting him one or two coarse articles—"

"Mr. George, my considerate friend," returns Allan, taking out his purse, "it is the very favour I would have asked."

Phil Squod and Jo are sent out immediately on this work of improvement. Miss Flite, quite enraptured by her success, makes the best of her way to court, having great fears that otherwise her friend the Chancellor may be uneasy about her or may give the judgment she has so long expected in her absence, and observing "which you know, my dear physician, and general, after so many years, would be too absurdly unfortunate!" Allan takes the opportunity of going out to procure some restorative medicines, and obtaining them near at hand, soon returns to find the trooper walking up and down the gallery, and to fall into step and walk with him.

"I take it, sir," says Mr. George, "that you know Miss Summerson pretty well?"

Yes, it appears.

"Not related to her, sir?"

No, it appears.

"Excuse the apparent curiosity," says Mr. George. "It seemed to me probable that you might take more than a common interest in this poor creature because Miss Summerson had taken that unfortunate interest in him. 'Tis MY case, sir, I assure you."

"And mine, Mr. George."

The trooper looks sideways at Allan's sunburnt cheek and bright dark eye, rapidly measures his height and build, and seems to approve of him.

"Since you have been out, sir, I have been thinking that I unquestionably know the rooms in Lincoln's Inn Fields, where Bucket took the lad, according to his account. Though he is not acquainted with the name, I can help you to it. It's Tulkinghorn. That's what it is."

Allan looks at him inquiringly, repeating the name.

"Tulkinghorn. That's the name, sir. I know the man, and know him to have been in communication with Bucket before, respecting a deceased person who had given him offence. I know the man, sir. To my sorrow."

Allan naturally asks what kind of man he is.

"What kind of man! Do you mean to look at?"

"I think I know that much of him. I mean to deal with. Generally, what kind of man?"

"Why, then I'll tell you, sir," returns the trooper, stopping short and folding his arms on his square chest so angrily that his face fires and flushes all over; "he is a confoundedly bad kind of man. He is a slow-torturing kind of man. He is no more like flesh and blood than a rusty old carbine is. He is a kind of man—by George!—that has caused me more restlessness, and more uneasiness, and more dissatisfaction with myself than all other men put together. That's the kind of man Mr. Tulkinghorn is!"

"I am sorry," says Allan, "to have touched so sore a place."

"Sore?" The trooper plants his legs wider apart, wets the palm of his broad right hand, and lays it on the imaginary moustache. "It's no fault of yours, sir; but you shall judge. He has got a power over me. He is the man I spoke of just now as being able to tumble me out of this place neck and crop. He keeps me on a constant see-saw. He won't hold off, and he won't come on. If I have a payment to make him, or time to ask him for, or anything to go to him about, he don't see me, don't hear me—passes me on to Melchisedech's in Clifford's Inn, Melchisedech's in Clifford's Inn passes me back again to him—he keeps me prowling and dangling about him as if I was made of the same stone as himself. Why, I spend half my life now, pretty well, loitering and dodging about his door. What does he care? Nothing. Just as much as the rusty old carbine I have compared him to. He chafes and goads me till—Bah! Nonsense! I am forgetting myself. Mr. Woodcourt," the trooper resumes his march, "all I say is, he is an old man; but I am glad I shall never have the chance of setting spurs to my horse and riding at him in a fair field. For if I had that chance, in one of the humours he drives me into—he'd go down, sir!"

Mr. George has been so excited that he finds it necessary to wipe his forehead on his shirt-sleeve. Even while he whistles his impetuosity away with the national anthem, some involuntary shakings of his head and heavings of his chest still linger behind, not to mention an occasional hasty adjustment with both hands of his open shirt-collar, as if it were scarcely open enough to prevent his being troubled by a choking sensation. In short, Allan Woodcourt has not much doubt about the going down of Mr. Tulkinghorn on the field referred to.

Jo and his conductor presently return, and Jo is assisted to his mattress by the careful Phil, to whom, after due administration of medicine by his own hands, Allan confides all needful means and instructions. The morning is by this time getting on apace. He repairs to his lodgings to dress and breakfast, and then, without seeking rest, goes away to Mr. Jarndyce to communicate his discovery.

With him Mr. Jarndyce returns alone, confidentially telling him that there are reasons for keeping this matter very quiet indeed and showing a serious interest in it. To Mr. Jarndyce, Jo repeats in substance what he said in the morning, without any material variation. Only that cart of his is heavier to draw, and draws with a hollower sound.

"Let me lay here quiet and not be chivied no more," falters Jo, "and be so kind any person as is a-passin nigh where I used fur to sleep, as jist to say to Mr. Sangsby that Jo, wot he known once, is a-moving on right forards with his duty, and I'll be wery thankful. I'd be more thankful than I am aready if it wos any ways possible for an unfortnet to be it."

He makes so many of these references to the law-stationer in the course of a day or two that Allan, after conferring with Mr. Jarndyce, good-naturedly resolves to call in Cook's Court, the rather, as the cart seems to be breaking down.

To Cook's Court, therefore, he repairs. Mr. Snagsby is behind his counter in his grey coat and sleeves, inspecting an indenture of several skins which has just come in from the engrosser's, an immense desert of law-hand and parchment, with here and there a resting-place of a few large letters to break the awful monotony and save the traveller from despair. Mr Snagsby puts up at one of these inky wells and greets the stranger with his cough of general preparation for business.

"You don't remember me, Mr. Snagsby?"

The stationer's heart begins to thump heavily, for his old apprehensions have never abated. It is as much as he can do to answer, "No, sir, I can't say I do. I should have considered—not to put too fine a point upon it—that I never saw you before, sir."

"Twice before," says Allan Woodcourt. "Once at a poor bedside, and once—"

"It's come at last!" thinks the afflicted stationer, as recollection breaks upon him. "It's got to a head now and is going to burst!" But he has sufficient presence of mind to conduct his visitor into the little counting-house and to shut the door.

"Are you a married man, sir?"

"No, I am not."

"Would you make the attempt, though single," says Mr. Snagsby in a melancholy whisper, "to speak as low as you can? For my little woman is a-listening somewheres, or I'll forfeit the business and five hundred pound!"

In deep dejection Mr. Snagsby sits down on his stool, with his back against his desk, protesting, "I never had a secret of my own, sir. I can't charge my memory with ever having once attempted to deceive my little woman on my own account since she named the day. I wouldn't have done it, sir. Not to put too fine a point upon it, I couldn't have done it, I dursn't have done it. Whereas, and nevertheless, I find myself wrapped round with secrecy and mystery, till my life is a burden to me."

His visitor professes his regret to hear it and asks him does he remember Jo. Mr. Snagsby answers with a suppressed groan, oh, don't he!

"You couldn't name an individual human being—except myself—that my little woman is more set and determined against than Jo," says Mr. Snagsby.

Allan asks why.

"Why?" repeats Mr. Snagsby, in his desperation clutching at the clump of hair at the back of his bald head. "How should I know why? But you are a single person, sir, and may you long be spared to ask a married person such a question!"

With this beneficent wish, Mr. Snagsby coughs a cough of dismal resignation and submits himself to hear what the visitor has to communicate.

"There again!" says Mr. Snagsby, who, between the earnestness of his feelings and the suppressed tones of his voice is discoloured in the face. "At it again, in a new direction! A certain person charges me, in the solemnest way, not to talk of Jo to any one, even my little woman. Then comes another certain person, in the person of yourself, and charges me, in an equally solemn way, not to mention Jo to that other certain person above all other persons. Why, this is a private asylum! Why, not to put too fine a point upon it, this is Bedlam, sir!" says Mr. Snagsby.

But it is better than he expected after all, being no explosion of the mine below him or deepening of the pit into which he has fallen. And being tender-hearted and affected by the account he hears of Jo's condition, he readily engages to "look round" as early in the evening as he can manage it quietly. He looks round very quietly when the evening comes, but it may turn out that Mrs. Snagsby is as quiet a manager as he.

Jo is very glad to see his old friend and says, when they are left alone, that he takes it uncommon kind as Mr. Sangsby should come so far out of his way on accounts of sich as him. Mr. Snagsby, touched by the spectacle before him, immediately lays upon the table half a crown, that magic balsam of his for all kinds of wounds.

"And how do you find yourself, my poor lad?" inquires the stationer with his cough of sympathy.

"I am in luck, Mr. Sangsby, I am," returns Jo, "and don't want for nothink. I'm more cumfbler nor you can't think. Mr. Sangsby! I'm wery sorry that I done it, but I didn't go fur to do it, sir."

The stationer softly lays down another half-crown and asks him what it is that he is sorry for having done.

"Mr. Sangsby," says Jo, "I went and giv a illness to the lady as wos and yit as warn't the t'other lady, and none of 'em never says nothink to me for having done it, on accounts of their being ser good and my having been s'unfortnet. The lady come herself and see me yesday, and she ses, 'Ah, Jo!' she ses. 'We thought we'd lost you, Jo!' she ses. And she sits down a-smilin so quiet, and don't pass a word nor yit a look upon me for having done it, she don't, and I turns agin the wall, I doos, Mr. Sangsby. And Mr. Jarnders, I see him a-forced to turn away his own self. And Mr. Woodcot, he come fur to giv me somethink fur to ease me, wot he's allus a-doin' on day and night, and wen he come a-bending over me and a-speakin up so bold, I see his tears a-fallin, Mr. Sangsby."

The softened stationer deposits another half-crown on the table. Nothing less than a repetition of that infallible remedy will relieve his feelings.

"Wot I was a-thinkin on, Mr. Sangsby," proceeds Jo, "wos, as you wos able to write wery large, p'raps?"

"Yes, Jo, please God," returns the stationer.

"Uncommon precious large, p'raps?" says Jo with eagerness.

"Yes, my poor boy."

Jo laughs with pleasure. "Wot I wos a-thinking on then, Mr. Sangsby, wos, that when I wos moved on as fur as ever I could go and couldn't be moved no furder, whether you might be so good p'raps as to write out, wery large so that any one could see it anywheres, as that I wos wery truly hearty sorry that I done it and that I never went fur to do it, and that though I didn't know nothink at all, I knowd as Mr. Woodcot once cried over it and wos allus grieved over it, and that I hoped as he'd be able to forgive me in his mind. If the writin could be made to say it wery large, he might."

"It shall say it, Jo. Very large."

Jo laughs again. "Thankee, Mr. Sangsby. It's wery kind of you, sir, and it makes me more cumfbler nor I was afore."

The meek little stationer, with a broken and unfinished cough, slips down his fourth half-crown—he has never been so close to a case requiring so many—and is fain to depart. And Jo and he, upon this little earth, shall meet no more. No more.

For the cart so hard to draw is near its journey's end and drags over stony ground. All round the clock it labours up the broken steps, shattered and worn. Not many times can the sun rise and behold it still upon its weary road.

Phil Squod, with his smoky gunpowder visage, at once acts as nurse and works as armourer at his little table in a corner, often looking round and saying with a nod of his green-baize cap and an encouraging elevation of his one eyebrow, "Hold up, my boy! Hold up!" There, too, is Mr. Jarndyce many a time, and Allan Woodcourt almost always, both thinking, much, how strangely fate has entangled this rough outcast in the web of very different lives. There, too, the trooper is a frequent visitor, filling the doorway with his athletic figure and, from his superfluity of life and strength, seeming to shed down temporary vigour upon Jo, who never fails to speak more robustly in answer to his cheerful words.

Jo is in a sleep or in a stupor to-day, and Allan Woodcourt, newly arrived, stands by him, looking down upon his wasted form. After a while he softly seats himself upon the bedside with his face towards him—just as he sat in the law-writer's room—and touches his chest and heart. The cart had very nearly given up, but labours on a little more.

The trooper stands in the doorway, still and silent. Phil has stopped in a low clinking noise, with his little hammer in his hand. Mr. Woodcourt looks round with that grave professional interest and attention on his face, and glancing significantly at the trooper, signs to Phil to carry his table out. When the little hammer is next used, there will be a speck of rust upon it.

"Well, Jo! What is the matter? Don't be frightened."

"I thought," says Jo, who has started and is looking round, "I thought I was in Tom-all-Alone's agin. Ain't there nobody here but you, Mr. Woodcot?"

"Nobody."

"And I ain't took back to Tom-all-Alone's. Am I, sir?"

"No." Jo closes his eyes, muttering, "I'm wery thankful."

After watching him closely a little while, Allan puts his mouth very near his ear and says to him in a low, distinct voice, "Jo! Did you ever know a prayer?"

"Never knowd nothink, sir."

"Not so much as one short prayer?"

"No, sir. Nothink at all. Mr. Chadbands he wos a-prayin wunst at Mr. Sangsby's and I heerd him, but he sounded as if he wos a-speakin to hisself, and not to me. He prayed a lot, but I couldn't make out nothink on it. Different times there was other genlmen come down Tom-all-Alone's a-prayin, but they all mostly sed as the t'other 'wuns prayed wrong, and all mostly sounded to be a-talking to theirselves, or a-passing blame on the t'others, and not a-talkin to us. WE never knowd nothink. I never knowd what it wos all about."

It takes him a long time to say this, and few but an experienced and attentive listener could hear, or, hearing, understand him. After a short relapse into sleep or stupor, he makes, of a sudden, a strong effort to get out of bed.

"Stay, Jo! What now?"

"It's time for me to go to that there berryin ground, sir," he returns with a wild look.

"Lie down, and tell me. What burying ground, Jo?"

"Where they laid him as wos wery good to me, wery good to me indeed, he wos. It's time fur me to go down to that there berryin ground, sir, and ask to be put along with him. I wants to go there and be berried. He used fur to say to me, 'I am as poor as you to-day, Jo,' he ses. I wants to tell him that I am as poor as him now and have come there to be laid along with him."

"By and by, Jo. By and by."

"Ah! P'raps they wouldn't do it if I wos to go myself. But will you promise to have me took there, sir, and laid along with him?"

"I will, indeed."

"Thankee, sir. Thankee, sir. They'll have to get the key of the gate afore they can take me in, for it's allus locked. And there's a step there, as I used for to clean with my broom. It's turned wery dark, sir. Is there any light a-comin?"

"It is coming fast, Jo."

Fast. The cart is shaken all to pieces, and the rugged road is very near its end.

"Jo, my poor fellow!"

"I hear you, sir, in the dark, but I'm a-gropin—a-gropin—let me catch hold of your hand."

"Jo, can you say what I say?"

"I'll say anythink as you say, sir, for I knows it's good."

"Our Father."

"Our Father! Yes, that's wery good, sir."

"Which art in heaven."

"Art in heaven—is the light a-comin, sir?"

"It is close at hand. Hallowed be thy name!"

"Hallowed be—thy—"

The light is come upon the dark benighted way. Dead!

Dead, your Majesty. Dead, my lords and gentlemen. Dead, right reverends and wrong reverends of every order. Dead, men and women, born with heavenly compassion in your hearts. And dying thus around us every day.

CHAPTER XLVIII
CLOSING IN

The place in Lincolnshire has shut its many eyes again, and the house in town is awake. In Lincolnshire the Dedlocks of the past doze in their picture-frames, and the low wind murmurs through the long drawing-room as if they were breathing pretty regularly. In town the Dedlocks of the present rattle in their fire-eyed carriages through the darkness of the night, and the Dedlock Mercuries, with ashes (or hair-powder) on their heads, symptomatic of their great humility, loll away the drowsy mornings in the little windows of the hall. The fashionable world—tremendous orb, nearly five miles round—is in full swing, and the solar system works respectfully at its appointed distances.

Where the throng is thickest, where the lights are brightest, where all the senses are ministered to with the greatest delicacy and refinement, Lady Dedlock is. From the shining heights she has scaled and taken, she is never absent. Though the belief she of old reposed in herself as one able to reserve whatsoever she would under her mantle of pride is beaten down, though she has no assurance that what she is to those around her she will remain another day, it is not in her nature when envious eyes are looking on to yield or to droop. They say of her that she has lately grown more handsome and more haughty. The debilitated cousin says of her that she's beauty nough—tsetup shopofwomen—but rather larming kind—remindingmanfact—inconvenient woman—who WILL getoutofbedandbawthstahlishment—Shakespeare.

Mr. Tulkinghorn says nothing, looks nothing. Now, as heretofore, he is to be found in doorways of rooms, with his limp white cravat loosely twisted into its old-fashioned tie, receiving patronage from the peerage and making no sign. Of all men he is still the last who might be supposed to have any influence upon my Lady. Of all women she is still the last who might be supposed to have any dread of him.

One thing has been much on her mind since their late interview in his turret-room at Chesney Wold. She is now decided, and prepared to throw it off.

It is morning in the great world, afternoon according to the little sun. The Mercuries, exhausted by looking out of window, are reposing in the hall and hang their heavy heads, the gorgeous creatures, like overblown sunflowers. Like them, too, they seem to run to a deal of seed in their tags and trimmings. Sir Leicester, in the library, has fallen asleep for the good of the country over the report of a Parliamentary committee. My Lady sits in the room in which she gave audience to the young man of the name of Guppy. Rosa is with her and has been writing for her and reading to her. Rosa is now at work upon embroidery or some such pretty thing, and as she bends her head over it, my

Lady watches her in silence. Not for the first time to-day.

"Rosa."

The pretty village face looks brightly up. Then, seeing how serious my Lady is, looks puzzled and surprised.

"See to the door. Is it shut?"

Yes. She goes to it and returns, and looks yet more surprised.

"I am about to place confidence in you, child, for I know I may trust your attachment, if not your judgment. In what I am going to do, I will not disguise myself to you at least. But I confide in you. Say nothing to any one of what passes between us."

The timid little beauty promises in all earnestness to be trustworthy.

"Do you know," Lady Dedlock asks her, signing to her to bring her chair nearer, "do you know, Rosa, that I am different to you from what I am to any one?"

"Yes, my Lady. Much kinder. But then I often think I know you as you really are."

"You often think you know me as I really am? Poor child, poor child!"

She says it with a kind of scorn—though not of Rosa—and sits brooding, looking dreamily at her.

"Do you think, Rosa, you are any relief or comfort to me? Do you suppose your being young and natural, and fond of me and grateful to me, makes it any pleasure to me to have you near me?"

"I don't know, my Lady; I can scarcely hope so. But with all my heart, I wish it was so."

"It is so, little one."

The pretty face is checked in its flush of pleasure by the dark expression on the handsome face before it. It looks timidly for an explanation.

"And if I were to say to-day, 'Go! Leave me!' I should say what would give me great pain and disquiet, child, and what would leave me very solitary."

"My Lady! Have I offended you?"

"In nothing. Come here."

Rosa bends down on the footstool at my Lady's feet. My Lady, with that motherly touch of the famous ironmaster night, lays her hand upon her dark hair and gently keeps it there.

"I told you, Rosa, that I wished you to be happy and that I would make you so if I could make anybody happy on this earth. I cannot. There are reasons now known to me, reasons in which you have no part, rendering it far better for you that you should not remain here. You must not remain here. I have determined that you shall not. I have written to the father of your lover, and he will be here to-day. All this I have done for your sake."

The weeping girl covers her hand with kisses and says what shall she do, what shall she do, when they are separated! Her mistress kisses her on the cheek and makes no other answer.

"Now, be happy, child, under better circumstances. Be beloved and happy!"

"Ah, my Lady, I have sometimes thought—forgive my being so free—that YOU are not happy."

"I!"

"Will you be more so when you have sent me away? Pray, pray, think again. Let me stay a little while!"

"I have said, my child, that what I do, I do for your sake, not my own. It is done. What I am towards you, Rosa, is what I am now—not what I shall be a little while hence. Remember this, and keep my confidence. Do so much for my sake, and thus all ends between us!"

She detaches herself from her simple-hearted companion and leaves the room. Late in the afternoon, when she next appears upon the staircase, she is in her haughtiest and coldest state. As indifferent as if all passion, feeling, and interest had been worn out in the earlier ages of the world and had perished from its surface with its other departed monsters.

Mercury has announced Mr. Rouncewell, which is the cause of her appearance. Mr. Rouncewell is not in the library, but she repairs to the library. Sir Leicester is there, and she wishes to speak to him first.

"Sir Leicester, I am desirous—but you are engaged."

Oh, dear no! Not at all. Only Mr. Tulkinghorn.

Always at hand. Haunting every place. No relief or security from him for a moment.

"I beg your pardon, Lady Dedlock. Will you allow me to retire?"

With a look that plainly says, "You know you have the power to remain if you will," she tells him it is not necessary and moves towards a chair. Mr. Tulkinghorn brings it a little forward for her with his clumsy bow and retires into a window opposite. Interposed between her and the fading light of day in the now quiet street, his shadow falls upon her, and he darkens all before her. Even so does he darken her life.

It is a dull street under the best conditions, where the two long rows of houses stare at each other with that severity that half-a-dozen of its greatest mansions seem to have been slowly stared into stone rather than originally built in that material. It is a street of such dismal grandeur, so determined not to condescend to liveliness, that the doors and windows hold a gloomy state of their own in black paint and dust, and the echoing mews behind have a dry and massive appearance, as if they were reserved to stable the stone chargers of noble statues. Complicated garnish of iron-work entwines itself over the flights of steps in this awful street, and from these petrified bowers, extinguishers for obsolete flambeaux gasp at the upstart gas. Here and there a weak little iron hoop, through which bold boys aspire to throw their friends' caps (its only present use), retains its place among the rusty foliage, sacred to the memory of departed oil. Nay, even oil itself, yet lingering at long intervals in a little absurd glass pot, with a knob in the bottom like an oyster, blinks and sulks at newer lights every night, like its high and dry master in the House of Lords.

Therefore there is not much that Lady Dedlock, seated in her chair, could wish to see through the window in which Mr. Tulkinghorn stands. And yet—and yet—she sends a look in that direction as if it were her heart's desire to have that figure moved out of the way.

Sir Leicester begs his Lady's pardon. She was about to say?

"Only that Mr. Rouncewell is here (he has called by my appointment) and that we had better make an end of the question of that girl. I am tired to death of the matter."

"What can I do—to—assist?" demands Sir Leicester in some considerable doubt.

"Let us see him here and have done with it. Will you tell them to send him up?"

"Mr. Tulkinghorn, be so good as to ring. Thank you. Request," says Sir Leicester to Mercury, not immediately remembering the business term, "request the iron gentleman to walk this way."

Mercury departs in search of the iron gentleman, finds, and produces him. Sir Leicester receives that ferruginous person graciously.

"I hope you are well, Mr. Rouncewell. Be seated. (My solicitor, Mr. Tulkinghorn.) My Lady was desirous, Mr. Rouncewell," Sir Leicester skilfully transfers him with a solemn wave of his hand, "was desirous to speak with you. Hem!"

"I shall be very happy," returns the iron gentleman, "to give my best attention to anything Lady Dedlock does me the honour to say."

As he turns towards her, he finds that the impression she makes upon him is less agreeable than on the former occasion. A distant supercilious air makes a cold atmosphere about her, and there is nothing in her bearing, as there was before, to encourage openness.

"Pray, sir," says Lady Dedlock listlessly, "may I be allowed to inquire whether anything has passed between you and your son respecting your son's fancy?"

It is almost too troublesome to her languid eyes to bestow a look upon him as she asks this question.

"If my memory serves me, Lady Dedlock, I said, when I had the pleasure of seeing you before, that I should seriously advise my son to conquer that—fancy." The ironmaster repeats her expression with a little emphasis.

"And did you?"

"Oh! Of course I did."

Sir Leicester gives a nod, approving and confirmatory. Very proper. The iron gentleman, having said that he would do it, was bound to do it. No difference in this respect between the base metals and the precious. Highly proper.

"And pray has he done so?"

"Really, Lady Dedlock, I cannot make you a definite reply. I fear not. Probably not yet. In our condition of life, we sometimes couple an intention with our—our fancies which renders them not altogether easy to throw off. I think it is rather our way to be in earnest."

Sir Leicester has a misgiving that there may be a hidden Wat Tylerish meaning in this expression, and fumes a little. Mr. Rouncewell is perfectly good-humoured and polite, but within such limits, evidently adapts his tone to his reception.

"Because," proceeds my Lady, "I have been thinking of the subject, which is tiresome to me."

"I am very sorry, I am sure."

"And also of what Sir Leicester said upon it, in which I quite concur"—Sir Leicester flattered—"and if you cannot give us the assurance that this fancy is at an end, I have come to the conclusion that the girl had better leave me."

"I can give no such assurance, Lady Dedlock. Nothing of the kind."

"Then she had better go."

"Excuse me, my Lady," Sir Leicester considerately interposes, "but perhaps this may be doing an injury to the young woman which she has not merited. Here is a young woman," says Sir Leicester, magnificently laying out the matter with his right hand like a service of plate, "whose good fortune it is to have attracted the notice and favour of an eminent lady and to live, under the protection of that eminent lady, surrounded by the various advantages which such a position confers, and which are unquestionably very great—I believe unquestionably very great, sir—for a young woman in that station of life. The question then arises, should that young woman be deprived of these many advantages and that good fortune simply because she has"—Sir Leicester, with an apologetic but dignified inclination of his head towards the ironmaster, winds up his sentence—"has attracted the notice of Mr Rouncewell's son? Now, has she deserved this punishment? Is this just towards her? Is this our previous understanding?"

"I beg your pardon," interposes Mr. Rouncewell's son's father. "Sir Leicester, will you allow me? I think I may shorten the subject. Pray dismiss that from your consideration. If you remember anything so unimportant—which is not to be expected—you would recollect that my first thought in the affair was directly opposed to her remaining here."

Dismiss the Dedlock patronage from consideration? Oh! Sir Leicester is bound to believe a pair of ears that have been handed down to him through such a family, or he really might have mistrusted their report of the iron gentleman's observations.

"It is not necessary," observes my Lady in her coldest manner before he can do anything but breathe amazedly, "to enter into these matters on either side. The girl is a very good girl; I have nothing whatever to say against her, but she is so far insensible to her many advantages and her good fortune that she is in love—or supposes she is, poor little fool—and unable to appreciate them."

Sir Leicester begs to observe that wholly alters the case. He might have been sure that my Lady had the best grounds and reasons in support of her view. He entirely agrees with my Lady. The young woman had better go.

"As Sir Leicester observed, Mr. Rouncewell, on the last occasion when we were fatigued by this business," Lady Dedlock languidly proceeds, "we cannot make conditions with you. Without conditions, and under present circumstances, the girl is quite misplaced here and had better go. I have told her so. Would you wish to have her sent back to the village, or would you like to take her with you, or what would you prefer?"

"Lady Dedlock, if I may speak plainly— "

"By all means."

"—I should prefer the course which will the soonest relieve you of the incumbrance and remove her from her present position."

"And to speak as plainly," she returns with the same studied carelessness, "so should I. Do I understand that you will take her with you?"

The iron gentleman makes an iron bow.

"Sir Leicester, will you ring?" Mr. Tulkinghorn steps forward from his window and pulls the bell. "I had forgotten you. Thank you." He makes his usual bow and goes quietly back again. Mercury, swift-responsive, appears, receives instructions whom to produce, skims away, produces the aforesaid, and departs.

Rosa has been crying and is yet in distress. On her coming in, the ironmaster leaves his chair, takes her arm in his, and remains with her near the door ready to depart.

"You are taken charge of, you see," says my Lady in her weary manner, "and are going away well protected. I have mentioned that you are a very good girl, and you have nothing to cry for."

"She seems after all," observes Mr. Tulkinghorn, loitering a little forward with his hands behind him, "as if she were crying at going away."

"Why, she is not well-bred, you see," returns Mr. Rouncewell with some quickness in his manner, as if he were glad to have the lawyer to retort upon, "and she is an inexperienced little thing and knows no better. If she had remained here, sir, she would have improved, no doubt."

"No doubt," is Mr. Tulkinghorn's composed reply.

Rosa sobs out that she is very sorry to leave my Lady, and that she was happy at Chesney Wold, and has been happy with my Lady, and that she thanks my Lady over and over again. "Out, you silly little puss!" says the ironmaster, checking her in a low voice, though not angrily. "Have a spirit, if you're fond of Watt!" My Lady merely waves her off with indifference, saying, "There, there, child! You are a good girl. Go away!" Sir Leicester has magnificently disengaged himself from the subject and retired into the sanctuary of his blue coat. Mr. Tulkinghorn, an indistinct form against the dark street now dotted with lamps, looms in my Lady's view, bigger and blacker than before.

"Sir Leicester and Lady Dedlock," says Mr. Rouncewell after a pause of a few moments, "I beg to take my leave, with an apology for having again troubled you, though not of my own act, on this tiresome subject. I can very well understand, I assure you, how tiresome so small a matter must have become to Lady Dedlock. If I am doubtful of my dealing with it, it is only because I did not at first quietly exert my influence to take my young friend here away without troubling you at all. But it appeared to me—I dare say magnifying the importance of the thing—that it was respectful to explain to you how the matter stood and candid to consult your wishes and convenience. I hope you will excuse my want of acquaintance with the polite world."

Sir Leicester considers himself evoked out of the sanctuary by these remarks. "Mr. Rouncewell," he returns, "do not mention it. Justifications are unnecessary, I hope, on either side."

"I am glad to hear it, Sir Leicester; and if I may, by way of a last word, revert to what I said before of my mother's long connexion with the family and the worth it bespeaks on both sides, I would point out this little instance here on my arm who shows herself so affectionate and faithful in parting and in whom my mother, I dare say, has done something to awaken such feelings—though of course Lady Dedlock, by her heartfelt interest and her genial condescension, has done much more."

If he mean this ironically, it may be truer than he thinks. He points it, however, by no deviation from his straightforward manner of speech, though in saying it he turns towards that part of the dim room where my Lady sits. Sir Leicester stands to return his parting salutation, Mr. Tulkinghorn again rings, Mercury takes another flight, and Mr. Rouncewell and Rosa leave the house.

Then lights are brought in, discovering Mr. Tulkinghorn still standing in his window with his hands behind him and my Lady still sitting with his figure before her, closing up her view of the night as well as of the day. She is very pale. Mr. Tulkinghorn, observing it as she rises to retire, thinks, "Well she may be! The power of this woman is astonishing. She has been acting a part the whole time." But he can act a part too—his one unchanging character—and as he holds the door open for this woman, fifty pairs of eyes, each fifty times sharper than Sir Leicester's pair, should find no flaw in him.

Lady Dedlock dines alone in her own room to-day. Sir Leicester is whipped in to the rescue of the Doodle Party and the discomfiture of the Coodle Faction. Lady Dedlock asks on sitting down to dinner, still deadly pale (and quite an illustration of the debilitated cousin's text), whether he is gone out? Yes. Whether Mr. Tulkinghorn is gone yet? No. Presently she asks again, is he gone YET? No. What is he doing? Mercury thinks he is writing letters in the library. Would my Lady wish to see him? Anything but that.

But he wishes to see my Lady. Within a few more minutes he is reported as sending his respects, and could my Lady please to receive him for a word or two after her dinner? My Lady will receive him now. He comes now, apologizing for intruding, even by her permission, while she is at table. When they are alone, my Lady waves her hand to dispense with such mockeries.

"What do you want, sir?"

"Why, Lady Dedlock," says the lawyer, taking a chair at a little distance from her and slowly rubbing his rusty legs up and down, up and down, up and down, "I am rather surprised by the course you have taken."

"Indeed?"

"Yes, decidedly. I was not prepared for it. I consider it a departure from our agreement and your promise. It puts us in a new position, Lady Dedlock. I feel myself under the necessity of saying that I don't approve of it."

He stops in his rubbing and looks at her, with his hands on his knees. Imperturbable and unchangeable as he is, there is still an indefinable freedom in his manner which is new and which does not escape this woman's observation.

"I do not quite understand you."

"Oh, yes you do, I think. I think you do. Come, come, Lady Dedlock, we must not fence and parry now. You know you like this girl."

"Well, sir?"

"And you know—and I know—that you have not sent her away for the reasons you have assigned, but for the purpose of separating her as much as possible from—excuse my mentioning it as a matter of business—any reproach and exposure that impend over yourself."

"Well, sir?"

"Well, Lady Dedlock," returns the lawyer, crossing his legs and nursing the uppermost knee. "I object to that. I consider that a dangerous proceeding. I know it to be unnecessary and calculated to awaken speculation, doubt, rumour, I don't know what, in the house. Besides, it is a violation of our agreement. You were to be exactly what you were before. Whereas, it must be evident to yourself, as it is to me, that you have been this evening very different from what you were before. Why, bless my soul, Lady Dedlock, transparently so!"

"If, sir," she begins, "in my knowledge of my secret—" But he interrupts her.

"Now, Lady Dedlock, this is a matter of business, and in a matter of business the ground cannot be kept too clear. It is no longer your secret. Excuse me. That is just the mistake. It is my secret, in trust for Sir Leicester and the family. If it were your secret, Lady Dedlock, we should not be here holding this conversation."

"That is very true. If in my knowledge of THE secret I do what I can to spare an innocent girl (especially, remembering your own reference to her when you told my story to the assembled guests at Chesney Wold) from the taint of my impending shame, I act upon a resolution I have taken. Nothing in the world, and no one in the world, could shake it or could move me." This she says with great deliberation and distinctness and with no more outward passion than himself. As for him, he methodically discusses his matter of business as if she were any insensible instrument used in business.

"Really? Then you see, Lady Dedlock," he returns, "you are not to be trusted. You have put the case in a perfectly plain way, and according to the literal fact; and that being the case, you are not to be trusted."

"Perhaps you may remember that I expressed some anxiety on this same point when we spoke at night at Chesney Wold?"

"Yes," says Mr. Tulkinghorn, coolly getting up and standing on the hearth. "Yes. I recollect, Lady Dedlock, that you certainly referred to the girl, but that was before we came to our arrangement, and both the letter and the spirit of our arrangement altogether precluded any action on your part founded upon my discovery. There can be no doubt about that. As to sparing the girl, of what importance or value is she? Spare! Lady Dedlock, here is a family name compromised. One might have supposed that the course was straight on—over everything, neither to the right nor to the left, regardless of all considerations in the way, sparing nothing, treading everything under foot."

She has been looking at the table. She lifts up her eyes and looks at him. There is a stern expression on her face and a part of her lower lip is compressed under her teeth. "This woman understands me," Mr. Tulkinghorn thinks as she lets her glance fall again. "SHE cannot be spared. Why should she spare others?"

For a little while they are silent. Lady Dedlock has eaten no dinner, but has twice or thrice poured out water with a steady hand and drunk it. She rises from table, takes a lounging-chair, and reclines in it, shading her face. There is nothing in her manner to express weakness or excite compassion. It is thoughtful, gloomy, concentrated. "This woman," thinks Mr. Tulkinghorn, standing on the hearth, again a dark object closing up her view, "is a study."

He studies her at his leisure, not speaking for a time. She too studies something at her leisure. She is not the first to speak, appearing indeed so unlikely to be so, though he stood there until midnight, that even he is driven upon breaking silence.

"Lady Dedlock, the most disagreeable part of this business interview remains, but it is business. Our agreement is broken. A lady of your sense and strength of character will be prepared for my now declaring it void and taking my own course."

"I am quite prepared."

Mr. Tulkinghorn inclines his head. "That is all I have to trouble you with, Lady Dedlock."

She stops him as he is moving out of the room by asking, "This is the notice I was to receive? I wish not to misapprehend you."

"Not exactly the notice you were to receive, Lady Dedlock, because the contemplated notice supposed the agreement to have been observed. But virtually the same, virtually the same. The difference is merely in a lawyer's mind."

"You intend to give me no other notice?"

"You are right. No."

"Do you contemplate undeceiving Sir Leicester to-night?"

"A home question!" says Mr. Tulkinghorn with a slight smile and cautiously shaking his head at the shaded face. "No, not to-night."

"To-morrow?"

"All things considered, I had better decline answering that question, Lady Dedlock. If I were to say I don't know when, exactly, you would not believe me, and it would answer no purpose. It may be to-morrow. I would rather say no more. You are prepared, and I hold out no expectations which circumstances might fail to justify. I wish you good evening."

She removes her hand, turns her pale face towards him as he walks silently to the door, and stops him once again as he is about to open it.

"Do you intend to remain in the house any time? I heard you were writing in the library. Are you going to return there?"

"Only for my hat. I am going home."

She bows her eyes rather than her head, the movement is so slight and curious, and he withdraws. Clear of the room he looks at his watch but is inclined to doubt it by a minute or thereabouts. There is a splendid clock upon the staircase, famous, as splendid clocks not often are, for its accuracy. "And what do YOU say," Mr. Tulkinghorn inquires, referring to it. "What do you say?"

If it said now, "Don't go home!" What a famous clock, hereafter, if it said to-night of all the nights that it has counted off, to this old man of all the young and old men who have ever stood before it, "Don't go home!" With its sharp clear bell it strikes three quarters after seven and ticks on again. "Why, you are worse than I thought you," says Mr. Tulkinghorn, muttering reproof to his watch. "Two minutes wrong? At this rate you won't last my time." What a watch to return good for evil if it ticked in answer, "Don't go home!"

He passes out into the streets and walks on, with his hands behind him, under the shadow of the lofty houses, many of whose mysteries, difficulties, mortgages, delicate affairs of all kinds, are treasured up within his old black satin waistcoat. He is in the confidence of the very bricks and mortar. The high chimney-stacks telegraph family secrets to him. Yet there is not a voice in a mile of them to whisper, "Don't go home!"

Through the stir and motion of the commoner streets; through the roar and jar of many vehicles, many feet, many voices; with the blazing shop-lights lighting him on, the west wind blowing him on, and the crowd pressing him on, he is pitilessly urged upon his way, and nothing meets him murmuring, "Don't go home!" Arrived at last in his dull room to light his candles, and look round and up, and see the Roman pointing from the ceiling, there is no new significance in the Roman's hand to-night or in the flutter of the attendant groups to give him the late warning, "Don't come here!"

It is a moonlight night, but the moon, being past the full, is only now rising over the great wilderness of London. The stars are shining as they shone above the turret-leads at Chesney Wold. This woman, as he has of late been so accustomed to call her, looks out upon them. Her soul is turbulent within her; she is sick at heart and restless. The large rooms are too cramped and close. She cannot endure their restraint and will walk alone in a neighbouring garden.

Too capricious and imperious in all she does to be the cause of much surprise in those about her as to anything she does, this woman, loosely muffled, goes out into the moonlight. Mercury attends with the key. Having opened the garden-gate, he delivers the key into his Lady's hands at her request and is bidden to go back. She will walk there some time to ease her aching head. She may be an hour, she may be more. She needs no further escort. The gate shuts upon its spring with a clash, and he leaves her passing on into the dark shade of some trees.

A fine night, and a bright large moon, and multitudes of stars. Mr. Tulkinghorn, in repairing to his cellar and in opening and shutting those resounding doors, has to cross a little prison-like yard. He looks up casually, thinking what a fine night, what a bright large moon, what multitudes of stars! A quiet night, too.

A very quiet night. When the moon shines very brilliantly, a solitude and stillness seem to proceed from her that influence even crowded places full of life. Not only is it a still night on dusty high roads and on hill-summits, whence a wide expanse of country may be seen in repose, quieter and quieter as it spreads away into a fringe of trees against the sky with the grey ghost of a bloom upon them; not only is it a still night in gardens and in woods, and on the river where the water-meadows are fresh and green, and the stream sparkles on among pleasant islands, murmuring weirs, and whispering rushes; not only does the stillness attend it as it flows where houses cluster thick, where many bridges are reflected in it, where wharves and shipping make it black and awful, where it winds from these disfigurements through marshes whose grim beacons stand like skeletons washed ashore, where it expands through the bolder region of rising grounds, rich in cornfield wind-mill and steeple, and where it mingles with the ever-heaving sea; not only is it a still night on the deep, and on the shore where the watcher stands to see the ship with her spread wings cross the path of light that appears to be presented to only him; but even on this stranger's wilderness of London there is some rest. Its steeples and towers and its one great dome grow more ethereal; its smoky house-tops lose their grossness in the pale effulgence; the noises that arise from the streets are fewer and are softened, and the footsteps on the pavements pass more tranquilly away. In these fields of Mr. Tulkinghorn's inhabiting, where the shepherds play on Chancery pipes that have no stop, and keep their sheep in the fold by hook and by crook until they have shorn them exceeding close, every noise is merged, this moonlight night, into a distant ringing hum, as if the city were a vast glass, vibrating.

What's that? Who fired a gun or pistol? Where was it?

The few foot-passengers start, stop, and stare about them. Some windows and doors are opened, and people come out to look. It was a loud report and echoed and rattled heavily. It shook one house, or so a man says who was passing. It has aroused all the dogs in the neighbourhood, who bark vehemently. Terrified cats scamper across the road. While the dogs are yet barking and howling—there is one dog howling like a demon—the church-clocks, as if they were startled too, begin to strike. The hum from the streets, likewise, seems to swell into a shout. But it is soon over. Before the last clock begins to strike ten, there is a lull. When it has ceased, the fine night, the bright large moon, and multitudes of stars, are left at peace again.

Has Mr. Tulkinghorn been disturbed? His windows are dark and quiet, and his door is shut. It must be something unusual indeed to bring him out of his shell. Nothing is heard of him, nothing is seen of him. What power of cannon might it take to shake that rusty old man out of his immovable composure?

For many years the persistent Roman has been pointing, with no particular meaning, from that ceiling. It is not likely that he has any new meaning in him to-night. Once pointing, always pointing—like any Roman, or even Briton, with a single idea. There he is, no doubt, in his impossible attitude, pointing, unavailingly, all night long. Moonlight, darkness, dawn, sunrise, day. There he is still, eagerly pointing, and no one minds him.

But a little after the coming of the day come people to clean the rooms. And either the Roman has some new meaning in him, not expressed before, or the foremost of them goes wild, for looking up at his outstretched hand and looking down at what is below it, that person shrieks and flies. The others, looking in as the first one looked, shriek and fly too, and there is an alarm in the street.

What does it mean? No light is admitted into the darkened chamber, and people unaccustomed to it enter, and treading softly but heavily, carry a weight into the bedroom and lay it down. There is whispering and wondering all day, strict search of every corner, careful tracing of steps, and careful noting of the disposition of every article of furniture. All eyes look up at the Roman, and all voices murmur, "If he could only tell what he saw!"

He is pointing at a table with a bottle (nearly full of wine) and a glass upon it and two candles that were blown out suddenly soon after being lighted. He is pointing at an empty chair and at a stain upon the ground before it that might be almost covered with a hand. These objects lie directly within his range. An excited imagination might suppose that there was something in them so terrific as to drive the rest of the composition, not only the attendant big-legged boys, but the clouds and flowers and pillars too—in short, the very body and soul of Allegory, and all the brains it has—stark mad. It happens surely that every one who comes into the darkened room and looks at these things looks up at the Roman and that he is invested in all eyes with mystery and awe, as if he were a paralysed dumb witness.

So it shall happen surely, through many years to come, that ghostly stories shall be told of the stain upon the floor, so easy to be covered, so hard to be got out, and that the Roman, pointing from the ceiling shall point, so long as dust and damp and spiders spare him, with far greater significance than he ever had in Mr. Tulkinghorn's time, and with a deadly meaning. For Mr. Tulkinghorn's time is over for evermore, and the Roman pointed at the murderous hand uplifted against his life, and pointed helplessly at him, from night to morning, lying face downward on the floor, shot through the heart.

CHAPTER XLIX
DUTIFUL FRIENDSHIP

A great annual occasion has come round in the establishment of Mr. Matthew Bagnet, otherwise Lignum Vitae, ex-artilleryman and present bassoon-player. An occasion of feasting and festival. The celebration of a birthday in the family.

It is not Mr. Bagnet's birthday. Mr. Bagnet merely distinguishes that epoch in the musical instrument business by kissing the children with an extra smack before breakfast, smoking an additional pipe after dinner, and wondering towards evening what his poor old mother is thinking about it—a subject of infinite speculation, and rendered so by his mother having departed this life twenty years. Some men rarely revert to their father, but seem, in the bank-books of their remembrance, to have transferred all the stock of filial affection into their mother's name. Mr. Bagnet is one of these. Perhaps his exalted appreciation of the merits of the old girl causes him usually to make the noun-substantive "goodness" of the feminine gender.

It is not the birthday of one of the three children. Those occasions are kept with some marks of distinction, but they rarely overleap the bounds of happy returns and a pudding. On young Woolwich's last birthday, Mr. Bagnet certainly did, after observing on his growth and general advancement, proceed, in a moment of profound reflection on the changes wrought by time, to examine him in the catechism, accomplishing with extreme accuracy the questions number one and two, "What is your name?" and "Who gave you that name?" but there failing in the exact precision of his memory and substituting for number three the question "And how do you like that name?" which he propounded with a sense of its importance, in itself so edifying and improving as to give it quite an orthodox air. This, however, was a speciality on that particular birthday, and not a general solemnity.

It is the old girl's birthday, and that is the greatest holiday and reddest-letter day in Mr. Bagnet's calendar. The auspicious event is always commemorated according to certain forms settled and prescribed by Mr. Bagnet some years since. Mr. Bagnet, being deeply convinced that to have a pair of fowls for dinner is to attain the highest pitch of imperial luxury, invariably goes forth himself very early in the morning of this day to buy a pair; he is, as invariably, taken in by the vendor and installed in the possession of the oldest inhabitants of any coop in Europe. Returning with these triumphs of toughness tied up in a clean blue and white cotton handkerchief (essential to the arrangements), he in a casual manner invites Mrs. Bagnet to declare at breakfast what she would like for dinner. Mrs. Bagnet, by a coincidence never known to fail, replying fowls, Mr. Bagnet instantly produces his bundle from a place of concealment amidst general amazement and rejoicing. He further requires that the old girl shall do nothing all day long but sit in her very best gown and be served by himself and the young people. As he is not illustrious for his cookery, this may be supposed to be a matter of state rather than enjoyment on the old girl's part, but she keeps her state with all imaginable cheerfulness.

On this present birthday, Mr. Bagnet has accomplished the usual preliminaries. He has bought two specimens of poultry, which, if there be any truth in adages, were certainly not caught with chaff, to be prepared for the spit; he has amazed and rejoiced the family by their unlooked-for production; he is himself directing the roasting of the poultry; and Mrs. Bagnet, with her wholesome brown fingers itching to prevent what she sees going wrong, sits in her gown of ceremony, an honoured guest.

Quebec and Malta lay the cloth for dinner, while Woolwich, serving, as beseems him, under his father, keeps the fowls revolving. To these young scullions Mrs. Bagnet occasionally imparts a wink, or a shake of the head, or a crooked face, as they made mistakes.

"At half after one." Says Mr. Bagnet. "To the minute. They'll be done."

Mrs. Bagnet, with anguish, beholds one of them at a standstill before the fire and beginning to burn.

"You shall have a dinner, old girl," says Mr. Bagnet. "Fit for a queen."

Mrs. Bagnet shows her white teeth cheerfully, but to the perception of her son, betrays so much uneasiness of spirit that he is impelled by the dictates of affection to ask her, with his eyes, what is the matter, thus standing, with his eyes wide open, more oblivious of the fowls than before, and not affording the least hope of a return to consciousness. Fortunately his elder sister perceives the cause of the agitation in Mrs. Bagnet's breast and with an admonitory poke recalls him. The stopped fowls going round again, Mrs. Bagnet closes her eyes in the intensity of her relief.

"George will look us up," says Mr. Bagnet. "At half after four. To the moment. How many years, old girl. Has George looked us up. This afternoon?"

"Ah, Lignum, Lignum, as many as make an old woman of a young one, I begin to think. Just about that, and no less," returns Mrs. Bagnet, laughing and shaking her head.

"Old girl," says Mr. Bagnet, "never mind. You'd be as young as ever you was. If you wasn't younger. Which you are. As everybody knows."

Quebec and Malta here exclaim, with clapping of hands, that Bluffy is sure to bring mother something, and begin to speculate on what it will be.

"Do you know, Lignum," says Mrs. Bagnet, casting a glance on the table-cloth, and winking "salt!" at Malta with her right eye, and shaking the pepper away from Quebec with her head, "I begin to think George is in the roving way again.

"George," returns Mr. Bagnet, "will never desert. And leave his old comrade. In the lurch. Don't be afraid of it."

"No, Lignum. No. I don't say he will. I don't think he will. But if he could get over this money trouble of his, I believe he would be off."

Mr. Bagnet asks why.

"Well," returns his wife, considering, "George seems to me to be getting not a little impatient and restless. I don't say but what he's as free as ever. Of course he must be free or he wouldn't be George, but he smarts and seems put out."

"He's extra-drilled," says Mr. Bagnet. "By a lawyer. Who would put the devil out."

"There's something in that," his wife assents; "but so it is, Lignum."

Further conversation is prevented, for the time, by the necessity under which Mr. Bagnet finds himself of directing the whole force of his mind to the dinner, which is a little endangered by the dry humour of the fowls in not yielding any gravy, and also by the made gravy acquiring no flavour and turning out of a flaxen complexion. With a similar perverseness, the potatoes crumble off forks in the process of peeling, upheaving from their centres in every direction, as if they were subject to earthquakes. The legs of the fowls, too, are longer than could be desired, and extremely scaly. Overcoming these disadvantages to the best of his ability, Mr. Bagnet at last dishes and they sit down at table, Mrs. Bagnet occupying the guest's place at his right hand.

It is well for the old girl that she has but one birthday in a year, for two such indulgences in poultry might be injurious. Every kind of finer tendon and ligament that is in the nature of poultry to possess is developed in these specimens in the singular form of guitar-strings. Their limbs appear to have struck roots into their breasts and bodies, as aged trees strike roots into the earth. Their legs are so hard as to encourage the idea that they must have devoted the greater part of their long and arduous lives to pedestrian exercises and the walking of matches. But Mr. Bagnet, unconscious of these little defects, sets his heart on Mrs. Bagnet eating a most severe quantity of the delicacies before her; and as that good old girl would not cause him a moment's disappointment on any day, least of all on such a day, for any consideration, she imperils her digestion fearfully. How young Woolwich cleans the drum-sticks without being of ostrich descent, his anxious mother is at a loss to understand.

The old girl has another trial to undergo after the conclusion of the repast in sitting in state to see the room cleared, the hearth swept, and the dinner-service washed up and polished in the backyard. The great delight and energy with which the two young ladies apply themselves to these duties, turning up their skirts in imitation of their mother and skating in and out on little scaffolds of pattens, inspire the highest hopes for the future, but some anxiety for the present. The same causes lead to confusion of tongues, a clattering of crockery, a rattling of tin mugs, a whisking of brooms, and an expenditure of water, all in excess, while the saturation of the young ladies themselves is almost too moving a spectacle for Mrs. Bagnet to look upon with the calmness proper to her position. At last the various cleansing processes are triumphantly completed; Quebec and Malta appear in fresh attire, smiling and dry; pipes, tobacco, and something to drink are placed upon the table; and the old girl enjoys the first peace of mind she ever knows on the day of this delightful entertainment.

When Mr. Bagnet takes his usual seat, the hands of the clock are very near to half-past four; as they mark it accurately, Mr. Bagnet announces, "George! Military time."

It is George, and he has hearty congratulations for the old girl (whom he kisses on the great occasion), and for the children, and for Mr. Bagnet. "Happy returns to all!" says Mr. George.

"But, George, old man!" cries Mrs. Bagnet, looking at him curiously. "What's come to you?"

"Come to me?"

"Ah! You are so white, George—for you—and look so shocked. Now don't he, Lignum?"

"George," says Mr. Bagnet, "tell the old girl. What's the matter."

"I didn't know I looked white," says the trooper, passing his hand over his brow, "and I didn't know I looked shocked, and I'm sorry I do. But the truth is, that boy who was taken in at my place died yesterday afternoon, and it has rather knocked me over."

"Poor creetur!" says Mrs. Bagnet with a mother's pity. "Is he gone? Dear, dear!"

"I didn't mean to say anything about it, for it's not birthday talk, but you have got it out of me, you see, before I sit down. I should have roused up in a minute," says the trooper, making himself speak more gaily, "but you're so quick, Mrs. Bagnet."

"You're right. The old girl," says Mr. Bagnet. "Is as quick. As powder."

"And what's more, she's the subject of the day, and we'll stick to her," cries Mr. George. "See here, I have brought a little brooch along with me. It's a poor thing, you know, but it's a keepsake. That's all the good it is, Mrs. Bagnet."

Mr. George produces his present, which is greeted with admiring leapings and clappings by the young family, and with a species of reverential admiration by Mr. Bagnet. "Old girl," says Mr. Bagnet. "Tell him my opinion of it."

"Why, it's a wonder, George!" Mrs. Bagnet exclaims. "It's the beautifullest thing that ever was seen!"

"Good!" says Mr. Bagnet. "My opinion."

"It's so pretty, George," cries Mrs. Bagnet, turning it on all sides and holding it out at arm's length, "that it seems too choice for me."

"Bad!" says Mr. Bagnet. "Not my opinion."

"But whatever it is, a hundred thousand thanks, old fellow," says Mrs. Bagnet, her eyes sparkling with pleasure and her hand stretched out to him; "and though I have been a crossgrained soldier's wife to you sometimes, George, we are as strong friends, I am sure, in reality, as ever can be. Now you shall fasten it on yourself, for good luck, if you will, George."

The children close up to see it done, and Mr. Bagnet looks over young Woolwich's head to see it done with an interest so maturely wooden, yet pleasantly childish, that Mrs. Bagnet cannot help laughing in her airy way and saying, "Oh, Lignum, Lignum, what a precious old chap you are!" But the trooper fails to fasten the brooch. His hand shakes, he is nervous, and it falls off. "Would any one believe this?" says he, catching it as it drops and looking round. "I am so out of sorts that I bungle at an easy job like this!"

Mrs. Bagnet concludes that for such a case there is no remedy like a pipe, and fastening the brooch herself in a twinkling, causes the trooper to be inducted into his usual snug place and the pipes to be got into action. "If that don't bring you round, George," says she, "just throw your eye across here at your present now and then, and the two together MUST do it."

"You ought to do it of yourself," George answers; "I know that very well, Mrs. Bagnet. I'll tell you how, one way and another, the blues have got to be too many for me. Here was this poor lad. 'Twas dull work to see him dying as he did, and not be able to help him."

"What do you mean, George? You did help him. You took him under your roof."

"I helped him so far, but that's little. I mean, Mrs. Bagnet, there he was, dying without ever having been taught much more than to know his right hand from his left. And he was too far gone to be helped out of that."

"Ah, poor creetur!" says Mrs. Bagnet.

"Then," says the trooper, not yet lighting his pipe, and passing his heavy hand over his hair, "that brought up Gridley in a man's mind. His was a bad case too, in a different way. Then the two got mixed up in a man's mind with a flinty old rascal who had to do with both. And to think of that rusty carbine, stock and barrel, standing up on end in his corner, hard, indifferent, taking everything so evenly—it made flesh and blood tingle, I do assure you."

"My advice to you," returns Mrs. Bagnet, "is to light your pipe and tingle that way. It's wholesomer and comfortabler, and better for the health altogether."

"You're right," says the trooper, "and I'll do it."

So he does it, though still with an indignant gravity that impresses the young Bagnets, and even causes Mr. Bagnet to defer the ceremony of drinking Mrs. Bagnet's health, always given by himself on these occasions in a speech of exemplary terseness. But the young ladies having composed what Mr. Bagnet is in the habit of calling "the mixtur," and George's pipe being now in a glow, Mr. Bagnet considers it his duty to proceed to the toast of the evening. He addresses the assembled company in the following terms.

"George. Woolwich. Quebec. Malta. This is her birthday. Take a day's march. And you won't find such another. Here's towards her!"

The toast having been drunk with enthusiasm, Mrs. Bagnet returns thanks in a neat address of corresponding brevity. This model composition is limited to the three words "And wishing yours!" which the old girl follows up with a nod at everybody in succession and a well-regulated swig of the mixture. This she again follows up, on the present occasion, by the wholly unexpected exclamation, "Here's a man!"

Here IS a man, much to the astonishment of the little company, looking in at the parlour-door. He is a sharp-eyed man—a quick keen man—and he takes in everybody's look at him, all at once, individually and collectively, in a manner that stamps him a remarkable man.

"George," says the man, nodding, "how do you find yourself?"

"Why, it's Bucket!" cries Mr. George.

"Yes," says the man, coming in and closing the door. "I was going down the street here when I happened to stop and look in at the musical instruments in the shop-window—a friend of mine is in want of a second-hand wiolinceller of a good tone—and I saw a party enjoying themselves, and I thought it was you in the corner; I thought I couldn't be mistaken. How goes the world with you, George, at the present moment? Pretty smooth? And with you, ma'am? And with you, governor? And Lord," says Mr. Bucket, opening his arms, "here's children too! You may do anything with me if you only show me children. Give us a kiss, my pets. No occasion to inquire who YOUR father and mother is. Never saw such a likeness in my life!"

Mr. Bucket, not unwelcome, has sat himself down next to Mr. George and taken Quebec and Malta on his knees. "You pretty dears," says Mr. Bucket, "give us another kiss; it's the only thing I'm greedy in. Lord bless you, how healthy you look! And what may be the ages of these two, ma'am? I should put 'em down at the figures of about eight and ten."

"You're very near, sir," says Mrs. Bagnet.

"I generally am near," returns Mr. Bucket, "being so fond of children. A friend of mine has had nineteen of 'em, ma'am, all by one mother, and she's still as fresh and rosy as the morning. Not so much so as yourself, but, upon my soul, she comes near you! And what do you call these, my darling?" pursues Mr. Bucket, pinching Malta's cheeks. "These are peaches, these are. Bless your heart! And what do you think about father? Do you think father could recommend a second-hand wiolinceller of a good tone for Mr. Bucket's friend, my dear? My name's Bucket. Ain't that a funny name?"

These blandishments have entirely won the family heart. Mrs. Bagnet forgets the day to the extent of filling a pipe and a glass for Mr. Bucket and waiting upon him hospitably. She would be glad to receive so pleasant a character under any circumstances, but she tells him that as a friend of George's she is particularly glad to see him this evening, for George has not been in his usual spirits.

"Not in his usual spirits?" exclaims Mr. Bucket. "Why, I never heard of such a thing! What's the matter, George? You don't intend to tell me you've been out of spirits. What should you be out of spirits for? You haven't got anything on your mind, you know."

"Nothing particular," returns the trooper.

"I should think not," rejoins Mr. Bucket. "What could you have on your mind, you know! And have these pets got anything on THEIR minds, eh? Not they, but they'll be upon the minds of some of the young fellows, some of these days, and make 'em precious low-spirited. I ain't much of a prophet, but I can tell you that, ma'am."

Mrs. Bagnet, quite charmed, hopes Mr. Bucket has a family of his own.

"There, ma'am!" says Mr. Bucket. "Would you believe it? No, I haven't. My wife and a lodger constitute my family. Mrs. Bucket is as fond of children as myself and as wishful to have 'em, but no. So it is. Worldly goods are divided unequally, and man must not repine. What a very nice backyard, ma'am! Any way out of that yard, now?"

There is no way out of that yard.

"Ain't there really?" says Mr. Bucket. "I should have thought there might have been. Well, I don't know as I ever saw a backyard that took my fancy more. Would you allow me to look at it? Thank you. No, I see there's no way out. But what a very good-proportioned yard it is!"

Having cast his sharp eye all about it, Mr. Bucket returns to his chair next his friend Mr. George and pats Mr. George affectionately on the shoulder.

"How are your spirits now, George?"

"All right now," returns the trooper.

"That's your sort!" says Mr. Bucket. "Why should you ever have been otherwise? A man of your fine figure and constitution has no right to be out of spirits. That ain't a chest to be out of spirits, is it, ma'am? And you haven't got anything on your mind, you know, George; what could you have on your mind!"

Somewhat harping on this phrase, considering the extent and variety of his conversational powers, Mr. Bucket twice or thrice repeats it to the pipe he lights, and with a listening face that is particularly his own. But the sun of his sociality soon recovers from this brief eclipse and shines again.

"And this is brother, is it, my dears?" says Mr. Bucket, referring to Quebec and Malta for information on the subject of young Woolwich. "And a nice brother he is—half-brother I mean to say. For he's too old to be your boy, ma'am."

"I can certify at all events that he is not anybody else's," returns Mrs. Bagnet, laughing.

"Well, you do surprise me! Yet he's like you, there's no denying. Lord, he's wonderfully like you! But about what you may call the brow, you know, THERE his father comes out!" Mr. Bucket compares the faces with one eye shut up, while Mr. Bagnet smokes in stolid satisfaction.

This is an opportunity for Mrs. Bagnet to inform him that the boy is George's godson.

"George's godson, is he?" rejoins Mr. Bucket with extreme cordiality. "I must shake hands over again with George's godson. Godfather and godson do credit to one another. And what do you intend to make of him, ma'am? Does he show any turn for any musical instrument?"

Mr. Bagnet suddenly interposes, "Plays the fife. Beautiful."

"Would you believe it, governor," says Mr. Bucket, struck by the coincidence, "that when I was a boy I played the fife myself? Not in a scientific way, as I expect he does, but by ear. Lord bless you! 'British Grenadiers'—there's a tune to warm an Englishman up! COULD you give us 'British Grenadiers,' my fine fellow?"

Nothing could be more acceptable to the little circle than this call upon young Woolwich, who immediately fetches his fife and performs the stirring melody, during which performance Mr. Bucket, much enlivened, beats time and never fails to come in sharp with the burden, "British Gra-a-anadeers!" In short, he shows so much musical taste that Mr. Bagnet actually takes his pipe from his lips to express his conviction that he is a singer. Mr. Bucket receives the harmonious impeachment so modestly, confessing how that he did once chaunt a little, for the expression of the feelings of his own bosom, and with no presumptuous idea of entertaining his friends, that he is asked to sing. Not to be behindhand in the sociality of the evening, he complies and gives them "Believe Me, if All Those Endearing Young Charms." This ballad, he informs Mrs. Bagnet, he considers to have been his most powerful ally in moving the heart of Mrs. Bucket when a maiden, and inducing her to approach the altar—Mr. Bucket's own words are "to come up to the scratch."

This sparkling stranger is such a new and agreeable feature in the evening that Mr. George, who testified no great emotions of pleasure on his entrance, begins, in spite of himself, to be rather proud of him. He is so friendly, is a man of so many resources, and so easy to get on with, that it is something to have made him known there. Mr. Bagnet becomes, after another pipe, so sensible of the value of his acquaintance that he solicits the honour of his company on the old girl's next birthday. If anything can more closely cement and consolidate the esteem which Mr. Bucket has formed for the family, it is the discovery of the nature of the occasion. He drinks to Mrs. Bagnet with a warmth approaching to rapture, engages himself for that day twelvemonth more than thankfully, makes a memorandum of the day in a large black pocket-book with a girdle to it, and breathes a hope that Mrs. Bucket and Mrs. Bagnet may before then become, in a manner, sisters. As he says himself, what is public life without private ties? He is in his humble way a public man, but it is not in that sphere that he finds happiness. No, it must be sought within the confines of domestic bliss.

It is natural, under these circumstances, that he, in his turn, should remember the friend to whom he is indebted for so promising an acquaintance. And he does. He keeps very close to him. Whatever the subject of the conversation, he keeps a tender eye upon him. He waits to walk home with him. He is interested in his very boots and observes even them attentively as Mr. George sits smoking cross-legged in the chimney-corner.

At length Mr. George rises to depart. At the same moment Mr. Bucket, with the secret sympathy of friendship, also rises. He dotes upon the children to the last and remembers the commission he has undertaken for an absent friend.

"Respecting that second-hand wiolinceller, governor—could you recommend me such a thing?"

"Scores," says Mr. Bagnet.

"I am obliged to you," returns Mr. Bucket, squeezing his hand. "You're a friend in need. A good tone, mind you! My friend is a regular dab at it. Ecod, he saws away at Mozart and Handel and the rest of the big-wigs like a thorough workman. And you needn't," says Mr. Bucket in a considerate and private voice, "you needn't commit yourself to too low a figure, governor. I don't want to pay too large a price for my friend, but I want you to have your proper percentage and be remunerated for your loss of time. That is but fair. Every man must live, and ought to it."

Mr. Bagnet shakes his head at the old girl to the effect that they have found a jewel of price.

"Suppose I was to give you a look in, say, at half arter ten to-morrow morning. Perhaps you could name the figures of a few wiolincellers of a good tone?" says Mr. Bucket.

Nothing easier. Mr. and Mrs. Bagnet both engage to have the requisite information ready and even hint to each other at the practicability of having a small stock collected there for approval.

"Thank you," says Mr. Bucket, "thank you. Good night, ma'am. Good night, governor. Good night, darlings. I am much obliged to you for one of the pleasantest evenings I ever spent in my life."

They, on the contrary, are much obliged to him for the pleasure he has given them in his company; and so they part with many expressions of goodwill on both sides. "Now George, old boy," says Mr. Bucket, taking his arm at the shop-door, "come along!" As they go down the little street and the Bagnets pause for a minute looking after them, Mrs. Bagnet remarks to the worthy Lignum that Mr. Bucket "almost clings to George like, and seems to be really fond of him."

The neighbouring streets being narrow and ill-paved, it is a little inconvenient to walk there two abreast and arm in arm. Mr. George therefore soon proposes to walk singly. But Mr. Bucket, who cannot make up his mind to relinquish his friendly hold, replies, "Wait half a minute, George. I should wish to speak to you first." Immediately afterwards, he twists him into a public-house and into a parlour, where he confronts him and claps his own back against the door.

"Now, George," says Mr. Bucket, "duty is duty, and friendship is friendship. I never want the two to clash if I can help it. I have endeavoured to make things pleasant to-night, and I put it to you whether I have done it or not. You must consider yourself in custody, George."

"Custody? What for?" returns the trooper, thunderstruck.

"Now, George," says Mr. Bucket, urging a sensible view of the case upon him with his fat forefinger, "duty, as you know very well, is one thing, and conversation is another. It's my duty to inform you that any observations you may make will be liable to be used against you. Therefore, George, be careful what you say. You don't happen to have heard of a murder?"

"Murder!"

"Now, George," says Mr. Bucket, keeping his forefinger in an impressive state of action, "bear in mind what I've said to you. I ask you nothing. You've been in low spirits this afternoon. I say, you don't happen to have heard of a murder?"

"No. Where has there been a murder?"

"Now, George," says Mr. Bucket, "don't you go and commit yourself. I'm a-going to tell you what I want you for. There has been a murder in Lincoln's Inn Fields—gentleman of the name of Tulkinghorn. He was shot last night. I want you for that."

The trooper sinks upon a seat behind him, and great drops start out upon his forehead, and a deadly pallor overspreads his face.

"Bucket! It's not possible that Mr. Tulkinghorn has been killed and that you suspect ME?"

"George," returns Mr. Bucket, keeping his forefinger going, "it is certainly possible, because it's the case. This deed was done last night at ten o'clock. Now, you know where you were last night at ten o'clock, and you'll be able to prove it, no doubt."

"Last night! Last night?" repeats the trooper thoughtfully. Then it flashes upon him. "Why, great heaven, I was there last night!"

"So I have understood, George," returns Mr. Bucket with great deliberation. "So I have understood. Likewise you've been very often there. You've been seen hanging about the place, and you've been heard more than once in a wrangle with him, and it's possible—I don't say it's certainly so, mind you, but it's possible—that he may have been heard to call you a threatening, murdering, dangerous fellow."

The trooper gasps as if he would admit it all if he could speak.

"Now, George," continues Mr. Bucket, putting his hat upon the table with an air of business rather in the upholstery way than otherwise, "my wish is, as it has been all the evening, to make things pleasant. I tell you plainly there's a reward out, of a hundred guineas, offered by Sir Leicester Dedlock,

Baronet. You and me have always been pleasant together; but I have got a duty to discharge; and if that hundred guineas is to be made, it may as well be made by me as any other man. On all of which accounts, I should hope it was clear to you that I must have you, and that I'm damned if I don't have you. Am I to call in any assistance, or is the trick done?"

Mr. George has recovered himself and stands up like a soldier. "Come," he says; "I am ready."

"George," continues Mr. Bucket, "wait a bit!" With his upholsterer manner, as if the trooper were a window to be fitted up, he takes from his pocket a pair of handcuffs. "This is a serious charge, George, and such is my duty."

The trooper flushes angrily and hesitates a moment, but holds out his two hands, clasped together, and says, "There! Put them on!"

Mr. Bucket adjusts them in a moment. "How do you find them? Are they comfortable? If not, say so, for I wish to make things as pleasant as is consistent with my duty, and I've got another pair in my pocket." This remark he offers like a most respectable tradesman anxious to execute an order neatly and to the perfect satisfaction of his customer. "They'll do as they are? Very well! Now, you see, George"—he takes a cloak from a corner and begins adjusting it about the trooper's neck—"I was mindful of your feelings when I come out, and brought this on purpose. There! Who's the wiser?"

"Only I," returns the trooper, "but as I know it, do me one more good turn and pull my hat over my eyes."

"Really, though! Do you mean it? Ain't it a pity? It looks so."

"I can't look chance men in the face with these things on," Mr. George hurriedly replies. "Do, for God's sake, pull my hat forward."

So strongly entreated, Mr. Bucket complies, puts his own hat on, and conducts his prize into the streets, the trooper marching on as steadily as usual, though with his head less erect, and Mr. Bucket steering him with his elbow over the crossings and up the turnings.

CHAPTER L
ESTHER'S NARRATIVE

It happened that when I came home from Deal I found a note from Caddy Jellyby (as we always continued to call her), informing me that her health, which had been for some time very delicate, was worse and that she would be more glad than she could tell me if I would go to see her. It was a note of a few lines, written from the couch on which she lay and enclosed to me in another from her husband, in which he seconded her entreaty with much solicitude. Caddy was now the mother, and I the godmother, of such a poor little baby—such a tiny old-faced mite, with a countenance that seemed to be scarcely anything but cap-border, and a little lean, long-fingered hand, always clenched under its chin. It would lie in this attitude all day, with its bright specks of eyes open, wondering (as I used to imagine) how it came to be so small and weak. Whenever it was moved it cried, but at all other times it was so patient that the sole desire of its life appeared to be to lie quiet and think. It had curious little dark veins in its face and curious little dark marks under its eyes like faint remembrances of poor Caddy's inky days, and altogether, to those who were not used to it, it was quite a piteous little sight.

But it was enough for Caddy that SHE was used to it. The projects with which she beguiled her illness, for little Esther's education, and little Esther's marriage, and even for her own old age as the grandmother of little Esther's little Esthers, was so prettily expressive of devotion to this pride of her life that I should be tempted to recall some of them but for the timely remembrance that I am getting on irregularly as it is.

To return to the letter. Caddy had a superstition about me which had been strengthening in her mind ever since that night long ago when she had lain asleep with her head in my lap. She almost—I think I must say quite—believed that I did her good whenever I was near her. Now although this was such a fancy of the affectionate girl's that I am almost ashamed to mention it, still it might have all the force of a fact when she was really ill. Therefore I set off to Caddy, with my guardian's consent, post-haste; and she and Prince made so much of me that there never was anything like it.

Next day I went again to sit with her, and next day I went again. It was a very easy journey, for I had only to rise a little earlier in the morning, and keep my accounts, and attend to housekeeping matters before leaving home.

But when I had made these three visits, my guardian said to me, on my return at night, "Now, little woman, little woman, this will never do. Constant dropping will wear away a stone, and constant coaching will wear out a Dame Durden. We will go to London for a while and take possession of our old lodgings."

"Not for me, dear guardian," said I, "for I never feel tired," which was strictly true. I was only too happy to be in such request.

"For me then," returned my guardian, "or for Ada, or for both of us. It is somebody's birthday to-morrow, I think."

"Truly I think it is," said I, kissing my darling, who would be twenty-one to-morrow.

"Well," observed my guardian, half pleasantly, half seriously, "that's a great occasion and will give my fair cousin some necessary business to transact in assertion of her independence, and will make London a more convenient place for all of us. So to London we will go. That being settled, there is another thing—how have you left Caddy?"

"Very unwell, guardian. I fear it will be some time before she regains her health and strength."

"What do you call some time, now?" asked my guardian thoughtfully.

"Some weeks, I am afraid."

"Ah!" He began to walk about the room with his hands in his pockets, showing that he had been thinking as much. "Now, what do you say about her doctor? Is he a good doctor, my love?"

I felt obliged to confess that I knew nothing to the contrary but that Prince and I had agreed only that evening that we would like his opinion to be confirmed by some one.

"Well, you know," returned my guardian quickly, "there's Woodcourt."

I had not meant that, and was rather taken by surprise. For a moment all that I had had in my mind in connexion with Mr. Woodcourt seemed to come back and confuse me.

"You don't object to him, little woman?"

"Object to him, guardian? Oh no!"

"And you don't think the patient would object to him?"

So far from that, I had no doubt of her being prepared to have a great reliance on him and to like him very much. I said that he was no stranger to her personally, for she had seen him often in his kind attendance on Miss Flite.

"Very good," said my guardian. "He has been here to-day, my dear, and I will see him about it to-morrow."

I felt in this short conversation—though I did not know how, for she was quiet, and we interchanged no look—that my dear girl well remembered how merrily she had clasped me round the waist when no other hands than Caddy's had brought me the little parting token. This caused me to feel that I ought to tell her, and Caddy too, that I was going to be the mistress of Bleak House and that if I avoided that disclosure any longer I might become less worthy in my own eyes of its master's love. Therefore, when we went upstairs and had waited listening until the clock struck twelve in order that only I might be the first to wish my darling all good wishes on her birthday and to take her to my heart, I set before her, just as I had set before myself, the goodness and honour of her cousin John and the happy life that was in store for me. If ever my darling were fonder of me at one time than another in all our intercourse, she was surely fondest of me that night. And I was so rejoiced to know it and so comforted by the sense of having done right in casting this last idle reservation away that I was ten times happier than I had been before. I had scarcely thought it a reservation a few hours ago, but now that it was gone I felt as if I understood its nature better.

Next day we went to London. We found our old lodging vacant, and in half an hour were quietly established there, as if we had never gone away. Mr. Woodcourt dined with us to celebrate my darling's birthday, and we were as pleasant as we could be with the great blank among us that Richard's absence naturally made on such an occasion. After that day I was for some weeks—eight or nine as I remember—very much with Caddy, and thus it fell out that I saw less of Ada at this time than any other since we had first come together, except the time of my own illness. She often came to Caddy's, but our function there was to amuse and cheer her, and we did not talk in our usual confidential manner. Whenever I went home at night we were together, but Caddy's rest was broken by pain, and I often remained to nurse her.

With her husband and her poor little mite of a baby to love and their home to strive for, what a good creature Caddy was! So self-denying, so uncomplaining, so anxious to get well on their account, so afraid of giving trouble, and so thoughtful of the unassisted labours of her husband and the comforts of old Mr. Turveydrop; I had never known the best of her until now. And it seemed so curious that her pale face and helpless figure should be lying there day after day where dancing was the business of life, where the kit and the apprentices began early every morning in the ball-room, and where the untidy little boy waltzed by himself in the kitchen all the afternoon.

At Caddy's request I took the supreme direction of her apartment, trimmed it up, and pushed her, couch and all, into a lighter and more airy and more cheerful corner than she had yet occupied; then, every day, when we were in our neatest array, I used to lay my small small namesake in her arms and sit down to chat or work or read to her. It was at one of the first of these quiet times that I told Caddy about Bleak House.

We had other visitors besides Ada. First of all we had Prince, who in his hurried intervals of teaching used to come softly in and sit softly down, with a face of loving anxiety for Caddy and the very little child. Whatever Caddy's condition really was, she never failed to declare to Prince that she was all but well—which I, heaven forgive me, never failed to confirm. This would put Prince in such good spirits that he would sometimes take the kit from his pocket and play a chord or two to astonish the baby, which I never knew it to do in the least degree, for my tiny namesake never noticed it at all.

Then there was Mrs. Jellyby. She would come occasionally, with her usual distraught manner, and sit calmly looking miles beyond her grandchild as if her attention were absorbed by a young Borrioboolan on its native shores. As bright-eyed as ever, as serene, and as untidy, she would say, "Well, Caddy, child, and how do you do to-day?" And then would sit amiably smiling and taking no notice of the reply or would sweetly glide off into a calculation of the number of letters she had lately received and answered or of the coffee-bearing power of Borrioboola-Gha. This she would always do with a serene contempt for our limited sphere of action, not to be disguised.

Then there was old Mr. Turveydrop, who was from morning to night and from night to morning the subject of innumerable precautions. If the baby cried, it was nearly stifled lest the noise should make him uncomfortable. If the fire wanted stirring in the night, it was surreptitiously done lest his rest should be broken. If Caddy required any little comfort that the house contained, she first carefully discussed whether he was likely to require it too. In return for this consideration he would come into the room once a day, all but blessing it—showing a condescension, and a patronage, and a grace of manner in dispensing the light of his high-shouldered presence from which I might have supposed him (if I had not known better) to have been the benefactor of Caddy's life.

"My Caroline," he would say, making the nearest approach that he could to bending over her. "Tell me that you are better to-day."

"Oh, much better, thank you, Mr. Turveydrop," Caddy would reply.

"Delighted! Enchanted! And our dear Miss Summerson. She is not quite prostrated by fatigue?" Here he would crease up his eyelids and kiss his fingers to me, though I am happy to say he had ceased to be particular in his attentions since I had been so altered.

"Not at all," I would assure him.

"Charming! We must take care of our dear Caroline, Miss Summerson. We must spare nothing that will restore her. We must nourish her. My dear Caroline"—he would turn to his daughter-in-law with infinite generosity and protection—"want for nothing, my love. Frame a wish and gratify it, my daughter. Everything this house contains, everything my room contains, is at your service, my dear. Do not," he would sometimes add in a burst of deportment, "even allow my simple requirements to be considered if they should at any time interfere with your own, my Caroline. Your necessities are greater than mine."

He had established such a long prescriptive right to this deportment (his son's inheritance from his mother) that I several times knew both Caddy and her husband to be melted to tears by these affectionate self-sacrifices.

"Nay, my dears," he would remonstrate; and when I saw Caddy's thin arm about his fat neck as he said it, I would be melted too, though not by the same process. "Nay, nay! I have promised never to leave ye. Be dutiful and affectionate towards me, and I ask no other return. Now, bless ye! I am going to the Park."

He would take the air there presently and get an appetite for his hotel dinner. I hope I do old Mr. Turveydrop no wrong, but I never saw any better traits in him than these I faithfully record, except that he certainly conceived a liking for Peepy and would take the child out walking with great pomp, always on those occasions sending him home before he went to dinner himself, and occasionally with a halfpenny in his pocket. But even this disinterestedness was attended with no inconsiderable cost, to my knowledge, for before Peepy was sufficiently decorated to walk hand in hand with the professor of deportment, he had to be newly dressed, at the expense of Caddy and her husband, from top to toe.

Last of our visitors, there was Mr. Jellyby. Really when he used to come in of an evening, and ask Caddy in his meek voice how she was, and then sit down with his head against the wall, and make no attempt to say anything more, I liked him very much. If he found me bustling about doing any little thing, he sometimes half took his coat off, as if with an intention of helping by a great exertion; but he never got any further. His sole occupation was to sit with his head against the wall, looking hard at the thoughtful baby; and I could not quite divest my mind of a fancy that they understood one another.

I have not counted Mr. Woodcourt among our visitors because he was now Caddy's regular attendant. She soon began to improve under his care, but he was so gentle, so skilful, so unwearying in the pains he took that it is not to be wondered at, I am sure. I saw a good deal of Mr. Woodcourt during this time, though not so much as might be supposed, for knowing Caddy to be safe in his hands, I often slipped home at about the hours when he was expected. We frequently met, notwithstanding. I was quite reconciled to myself now, but I still felt glad to think that he was sorry for me, and he still WAS sorry for me I believed. He helped Mr. Badger in his professional engagements, which were numerous, and had as yet no settled projects for the future.

It was when Caddy began to recover that I began to notice a change in my dear girl. I cannot say how it first presented itself to me, because I observed it in many slight particulars which were nothing in themselves and only became something when they were pieced together. But I made it out, by putting them together, that Ada was not so frankly cheerful with me as she used to be. Her tenderness for me was as loving and true as ever; I did not for a moment doubt that; but there was a quiet sorrow about her which she did not confide to me, and in which I traced some hidden regret.

Now, I could not understand this, and I was so anxious for the happiness of my own pet that it caused me some uneasiness and set me thinking often. At length, feeling sure that Ada suppressed this something from me lest it should make me unhappy too, it came into my head that she was a little grieved—for me—by what I had told her about Bleak House.

How I persuaded myself that this was likely, I don't know. I had no idea that there was any selfish reference in my doing so. I was not grieved for myself: I was quite contented and quite happy. Still, that Ada might be thinking—for me, though I had abandoned all such thoughts—of what once was, but was now all changed, seemed so easy to believe that I believed it.

What could I do to reassure my darling (I considered then) and show her that I had no such feelings? Well! I could only be as brisk and busy as possible, and that I had tried to be all along. However, as Caddy's illness had certainly interfered, more or less, with my home duties—though I had always been there in the morning to make my guardian's breakfast, and he had a hundred times laughed and said there must be two little women, for his little woman was never missing—I resolved to be doubly diligent and gay. So I went about the house humming all the tunes I knew, and I sat working and working in a desperate manner, and I talked and talked, morning, noon, and night.

And still there was the same shade between me and my darling.

"So, Dame Trot," observed my guardian, shutting up his book one night when we were all three together, "so Woodcourt has restored Caddy Jellyby to the full enjoyment of life again?"

"Yes," I said; "and to be repaid by such gratitude as hers is to be made rich, guardian."

"I wish it was," he returned, "with all my heart."

So did I too, for that matter. I said so.

"Aye! We would make him as rich as a Jew if we knew how. Would we not, little woman?"

I laughed as I worked and replied that I was not sure about that, for it might spoil him, and he might not be so useful, and there might be many who could ill spare him. As Miss Flite, and Caddy herself, and many others.

"True," said my guardian. "I had forgotten that. But we would agree to make him rich enough to live, I suppose? Rich enough to work with tolerable peace of mind? Rich enough to have his own happy home and his own household gods—and household goddess, too, perhaps?"

That was quite another thing, I said. We must all agree in that.

"To be sure," said my guardian. "All of us. I have a great regard for Woodcourt, a high esteem for him; and I have been sounding him delicately about his plans. It is difficult to offer aid to an independent man with that just kind of pride which he possesses. And yet I would be glad to do it if I might or if I knew how. He seems half inclined for another voyage. But that appears like casting such a man away."

"It might open a new world to him," said I.

"So it might, little woman," my guardian assented. "I doubt if he expects much of the old world. Do you know I have fancied that he sometimes feels some particular disappointment or misfortune encountered in it. You never heard of anything of that sort?"

I shook my head.

"Humph," said my guardian. "I am mistaken, I dare say." As there was a little pause here, which I thought, for my dear girl's satisfaction, had better be filled up, I hummed an air as I worked which was a favourite with my guardian.

"And do you think Mr. Woodcourt will make another voyage?" I asked him when I had hummed it quietly all through.

"I don't quite know what to think, my dear, but I should say it was likely at present that he will give a long trip to another country."

"I am sure he will take the best wishes of all our hearts with him wherever he goes," said I; "and though they are not riches, he will never be the poorer for them, guardian, at least."

"Never, little woman," he replied.

I was sitting in my usual place, which was now beside my guardian's chair. That had not been my usual place before the letter, but it was now. I looked up to Ada, who was sitting opposite, and I saw, as she looked at me, that her eyes were filled with tears and that tears were falling down her face. I felt that I had only to be placid and merry once for all to undeceive my dear and set her loving heart at rest. I really was so, and I had nothing to do but to be myself.

So I made my sweet girl lean upon my shoulder—how little thinking what was heavy on her mind!—and I said she was not quite well, and put my arm about her, and took her upstairs. When we were in our own room, and when she might perhaps have told me what I was so unprepared to hear, I gave her no encouragement to confide in me; I never thought she stood in need of it.

"Oh, my dear good Esther," said Ada, "if I could only make up my mind to speak to you and my cousin John when you are together!"

"Why, my love!" I remonstrated. "Ada, why should you not speak to us!"

Ada only dropped her head and pressed me closer to her heart.

"You surely don't forget, my beauty," said I, smiling, "what quiet, old-fashioned people we are and how I have settled down to be the discreetest of dames? You don't forget how happily and peacefully my life is all marked out for me, and by whom? I am certain that you don't forget by what a noble character, Ada. That can never be."

"No, never, Esther."

"Why then, my dear," said I, "there can be nothing amiss—and why should you not speak to us?"

"Nothing amiss, Esther?" returned Ada. "Oh, when I think of all these years, and of his fatherly care and kindness, and of the old relations among us, and of you, what shall I do, what shall I do!"

I looked at my child in some wonder, but I thought it better not to answer otherwise than by cheering her, and so I turned off into many little recollections of our life together and prevented her from saying more. When she lay down to sleep, and not before, I returned to my guardian to say good night, and then I came back to Ada and sat near her for a little while.

She was asleep, and I thought as I looked at her that she was a little changed. I had thought so more than once lately. I could not decide, even looking at her while she was unconscious, how she was changed, but something in the familiar beauty of her face looked different to me. My guardian's old hopes of her and Richard arose sorrowfully in my mind, and I said to myself, "She has been anxious about him," and I wondered how that love would end.

When I had come home from Caddy's while she was ill, I had often found Ada at work, and she had always put her work away, and I had never known what it was. Some of it now lay in a drawer near her, which was not quite closed. I did not open the drawer, but I still rather wondered what the work could be, for it was evidently nothing for herself.

And I noticed as I kissed my dear that she lay with one hand under her pillow so that it was hidden.

How much less amiable I must have been than they thought me, how much less amiable than I thought myself, to be so preoccupied with my own cheerfulness and contentment as to think that it only rested with me to put my dear girl right and set her mind at peace!

But I lay down, self-deceived, in that belief. And I awoke in it next day to find that there was still the same shade between me and my darling.

CHAPTER LI
ENLIGHTENED

When Mr. Woodcourt arrived in London, he went, that very same day, to Mr. Vholes's in Symond's Inn. For he never once, from the moment when I entreated him to be a friend to Richard, neglected or forgot his promise. He had told me that he accepted the charge as a sacred trust, and he was ever true to it in that spirit.

He found Mr. Vholes in his office and informed Mr. Vholes of his agreement with Richard that he should call there to learn his address.

"Just so, sir," said Mr. Vholes. "Mr. C.'s address is not a hundred miles from here, sir, Mr. C.'s address is not a hundred miles from here. Would you take a seat, sir?"

Mr. Woodcourt thanked Mr. Vholes, but he had no business with him beyond what he had mentioned.

"Just so, sir. I believe, sir," said Mr. Vholes, still quietly insisting on the seat by not giving the address, "that you have influence with Mr. C. Indeed I am aware that you have."

"I was not aware of it myself," returned Mr. Woodcourt; "but I suppose you know best."

"Sir," rejoined Mr. Vholes, self-contained as usual, voice and all, "it is a part of my professional duty to know best. It is a part of my professional duty to study and to understand a gentleman who confides his interests to me. In my professional duty I shall not be wanting, sir, if I know it. I may, with the best intentions, be wanting in it without knowing it; but not if I know it, sir."

Mr. Woodcourt again mentioned the address.

"Give me leave, sir," said Mr. Vholes. "Bear with me for a moment. Sir, Mr. C. is playing for a considerable stake, and cannot play without—need I say what?"

"Money, I presume?"

"Sir," said Mr. Vholes, "to be honest with you (honesty being my golden rule, whether I gain by it or lose, and I find that I generally lose), money is the word. Now, sir, upon the chances of Mr. C.'s game I express to you no opinion, NO opinion. It might be highly impolitic in Mr. C., after playing so long and so high, to leave off; it might be the reverse; I say nothing. No, sir," said Mr. Vholes, bringing his hand flat down upon his desk in a positive manner, "nothing."

"You seem to forget," returned Mr. Woodcourt, "that I ask you to say nothing and have no interest in anything you say."

"Pardon me, sir!" retorted Mr. Vholes. "You do yourself an injustice. No, sir! Pardon me! You shall not—shall not in my office, if I know it—do yourself an injustice. You are interested in anything, and in everything, that relates to your friend. I know human nature much better, sir, than to admit for an instant that a gentleman of your appearance is not interested in whatever concerns his friend."

"Well," replied Mr. Woodcourt, "that may be. I am particularly interested in his address."

"The number, sir," said Mr. Vholes parenthetically, "I believe I have already mentioned. If Mr. C. is to continue to play for this considerable stake, sir, he must have funds. Understand me! There are funds in hand at present. I ask for nothing; there are funds in hand. But for the onward play, more funds must be provided, unless Mr. C. is to throw away what he has already ventured, which is wholly and solely a point for his consideration. This, sir, I take the opportunity of stating openly to you as the friend of Mr. C. Without funds I shall always be happy to appear and act for Mr. C. to the extent of all such costs as are safe to be allowed out of the estate, not beyond that. I could not go beyond that, sir, without wronging some one. I must either wrong my three dear girls or my venerable father, who is entirely dependent on me, in the Vale of Taunton; or some one. Whereas, sir, my resolution is (call it weakness or folly if you please) to wrong no one."

Mr. Woodcourt rather sternly rejoined that he was glad to hear it.

"I wish, sir," said Mr. Vholes, "to leave a good name behind me. Therefore I take every opportunity of openly stating to a friend of Mr. C. how Mr. C. is situated. As to myself, sir, the labourer is worthy of his hire. If I undertake to put my shoulder to the wheel, I do it, and I earn what I get. I am here for that purpose. My name is painted on the door outside, with that object."

"And Mr. Carstone's address, Mr. Vholes?"

"Sir," returned Mr. Vholes, "as I believe I have already mentioned, it is next door. On the second story you will find Mr. C.'s apartments. Mr. C. desires to be near his professional adviser, and I am far from objecting, for I court inquiry."

Upon this Mr. Woodcourt wished Mr. Vholes good day and went in search of Richard, the change in whose appearance he began to understand now but too well.

He found him in a dull room, fadedly furnished, much as I had found him in his barrack-room but a little while before, except that he was not writing but was sitting with a book before him, from which his eyes and thoughts were far astray. As the door chanced to be standing open, Mr. Woodcourt was in his presence for some moments without being perceived, and he told me that he never could forget the haggardness of his face and the dejection of his manner before he was aroused from his dream.

"Woodcourt, my dear fellow," cried Richard, starting up with extended hands, "you come upon my vision like a ghost."

"A friendly one," he replied, "and only waiting, as they say ghosts do, to be addressed. How does the mortal world go?" They were seated now, near together.

"Badly enough, and slowly enough," said Richard, "speaking at least for my part of it."

"What part is that?"

"The Chancery part."

"I never heard," returned Mr. Woodcourt, shaking his head, "of its going well yet."

"Nor I," said Richard moodily. "Who ever did?" He brightened again in a moment and said with his natural openness, "Woodcourt, I should be sorry to be misunderstood by you, even if I gained by it in your estimation. You must know that I have done no good this long time. I have not intended to do much harm, but I seem to have been capable of nothing else. It may be that I should have done better by keeping out of the net into which my destiny has worked me, but I think not, though I dare say you will soon hear, if you have not already heard, a very different opinion. To make short of a long story, I am afraid I have wanted an object; but I have an object now—or it has me—and it is too late to discuss it. Take me as I am, and make the best of me."

"A bargain," said Mr. Woodcourt. "Do as much by me in return."

"Oh! You," returned Richard, "you can pursue your art for its own sake, and can put your hand upon the plough and never turn, and can strike a purpose out of anything. You and I are very different creatures."

He spoke regretfully and lapsed for a moment into his weary condition.

"Well, well!" he cried, shaking it off. "Everything has an end. We shall see! So you will take me as I am, and make the best of me?"

"Aye! Indeed I will." They shook hands upon it laughingly, but in deep earnestness. I can answer for one of them with my heart of hearts.

"You come as a godsend," said Richard, "for I have seen nobody here yet but Vholes. Woodcourt, there is one subject I should like to mention, for once and for all, in the beginning of our treaty. You can hardly make the best of me if I don't. You know, I dare say, that I have an attachment to my cousin Ada?"

Mr. Woodcourt replied that I had hinted as much to him. "Now pray," returned Richard, "don't think me a heap of selfishness. Don't suppose that I am splitting my head and half breaking my heart over this miserable Chancery suit for my own rights and interests alone. Ada's are bound up with mine; they can't be separated; Vholes works for both of us. Do think of that!"

He was so very solicitous on this head that Mr. Woodcourt gave him the strongest assurances that he did him no injustice.

"You see," said Richard, with something pathetic in his manner of lingering on the point, though it was off-hand and unstudied, "to an upright fellow like you, bringing a friendly face like yours here, I cannot bear the thought of appearing selfish and mean. I want to see Ada righted, Woodcourt, as well as myself; I want to do my utmost to right her, as well as myself; I venture what I can scrape together to extricate her, as well as myself. Do, I beseech you, think of that!"

Afterwards, when Mr. Woodcourt came to reflect on what had passed, he was so very much impressed by the strength of Richard's anxiety on this point that in telling me generally of his first visit to Symond's Inn he particularly dwelt upon it. It revived a fear I had had before that my dear girl's little property would be absorbed by Mr. Vholes and that Richard's justification to himself would be sincerely this. It was just as I began to take care of Caddy that the interview took place, and I now return to the time when Caddy had recovered and the shade was still between me and my darling.

I proposed to Ada that morning that we should go and see Richard. It a little surprised me to find that she hesitated and was not so radiantly willing as I had expected.

"My dear," said I, "you have not had any difference with Richard since I have been so much away?"

"No, Esther."

"Not heard of him, perhaps?" said I.

"Yes, I have heard of him," said Ada.

Such tears in her eyes, and such love in her face. I could not make my darling out. Should I go to Richard's by myself? I said. No, Ada thought I had better not go by myself. Would she go with me? Yes, Ada thought she had better go with me. Should we go now? Yes, let us go now. Well, I could not understand my darling, with the tears in her eyes and the love in her face!

We were soon equipped and went out. It was a sombre day, and drops of chill rain fell at intervals. It was one of those colourless days when everything looks heavy and harsh. The houses frowned at us, the dust rose at us, the smoke swooped at us, nothing made any compromise about itself or wore a softened aspect. I fancied my beautiful girl quite out of place in the rugged streets, and I thought there were more funerals passing along the dismal pavements than I had ever seen before.

We had first to find out Symond's Inn. We were going to inquire in a shop when Ada said she thought it was near Chancery Lane. "We are not likely to be far out, my love, if we go in that direction," said I. So to Chancery Lane we went, and there, sure enough, we saw it written up. Symond's Inn.

We had next to find out the number. "Or Mr. Vholes's office will do," I recollected, "for Mr. Vholes's office is next door." Upon which Ada said, perhaps that was Mr. Vholes's office in the corner there. And it really was.

Then came the question, which of the two next doors? I was going for the one, and my darling was going for the other; and my darling was right again. So up we went to the second story, when we came to Richard's name in great white letters on a hearse-like panel.

I should have knocked, but Ada said perhaps we had better turn the handle and go in. Thus we came to Richard, poring over a table covered with dusty bundles of papers which seemed to me like dusty mirrors reflecting his own mind. Wherever I looked I saw the ominous words that ran in it repeated. Jarndyce and Jarndyce.

He received us very affectionately, and we sat down. "If you had come a little earlier," he said, "you would have found Woodcourt here. There never was such a good fellow as Woodcourt is. He finds time to look in between-whiles, when anybody else with half his work to do would be thinking about not being able to come. And he is so cheery, so fresh, so sensible, so earnest, so—everything that I am not, that the place brightens whenever he comes, and darkens whenever he goes again."

"God bless him," I thought, "for his truth to me!"

"He is not so sanguine, Ada," continued Richard, casting his dejected look over the bundles of papers, "as Vholes and I are usually, but he is only an outsider and is not in the mysteries. We have gone into them, and he has not. He can't be expected to know much of such a labyrinth."

As his look wandered over the papers again and he passed his two hands over his head, I noticed how sunken and how large his eyes appeared, how dry his lips were, and how his finger-nails were all bitten away.

"Is this a healthy place to live in, Richard, do you think?" said I.

"Why, my dear Minerva," answered Richard with his old gay laugh, "it is neither a rural nor a cheerful place; and when the sun shines here, you may lay a pretty heavy wager that it is shining brightly in an open spot. But it's well enough for the time. It's near the offices and near Vholes."

"Perhaps," I hinted, "a change from both—"

"Might do me good?" said Richard, forcing a laugh as he finished the sentence. "I shouldn't wonder! But it can only come in one way now—in one of two ways, I should rather say. Either the suit must be ended, Esther, or the suitor. But it shall be the suit, my dear girl, the suit, my dear girl!"

These latter words were addressed to Ada, who was sitting nearest to him. Her face being turned away from me and towards him, I could not see it.

"We are doing very well," pursued Richard. "Vholes will tell you so. We are really spinning along. Ask Vholes. We are giving them no rest. Vholes knows all their windings and turnings, and we are upon them everywhere. We have astonished them already. We shall rouse up that nest of sleepers, mark my words!"

His hopefulness had long been more painful to me than his despondency; it was so unlike hopefulness, had something so fierce in its determination to be it, was so hungry and eager, and yet so conscious of being forced and unsustainable that it had long touched me to the heart. But the commentary upon it now indelibly written in his handsome face made it far more distressing than it used to be. I say indelibly, for I felt persuaded that if the fatal cause could have been for ever terminated, according to his brightest visions, in that same hour, the traces of the premature anxiety, self-reproach, and disappointment it had occasioned him would have remained upon his features to the hour of his death.

"The sight of our dear little woman," said Richard, Ada still remaining silent and quiet, "is so natural to me, and her compassionate face is so like the face of old days—"

Ah! No, no. I smiled and shook my head.

"—So exactly like the face of old days," said Richard in his cordial voice, and taking my hand with the brotherly regard which nothing ever changed, "that I can't make pretences with her. I fluctuate a little; that's the truth. Sometimes I hope, my dear, and sometimes I—don't quite despair, but nearly. I get," said Richard, relinquishing my hand gently and walking across the room, "so tired!"

He took a few turns up and down and sunk upon the sofa. "I get," he repeated gloomily, "so tired. It is such weary, weary work!"

He was leaning on his arm saying these words in a meditative voice and looking at the ground when my darling rose, put off her bonnet, kneeled down beside him with her golden hair falling like sunlight on his head, clasped her two arms round his neck, and turned her face to me. Oh, what a loving and devoted face I saw!

"Esther, dear," she said very quietly, "I am not going home again."

A light shone in upon me all at once.

"Never any more. I am going to stay with my dear husband. We have been married above two months. Go home without me, my own Esther; I shall never go home any more!" With those words my darling drew his head down on her breast and held it there. And if ever in my life I saw a love that nothing but death could change, I saw it then before me.

"Speak to Esther, my dearest," said Richard, breaking the silence presently. "Tell her how it was."

I met her before she could come to me and folded her in my arms. We neither of us spoke, but with her cheek against my own I wanted to hear nothing. "My pet," said I. "My love. My poor, poor girl!" I pitied her so much. I was very fond of Richard, but the impulse that I had upon me was to pity her so much.

"Esther, will you forgive me? Will my cousin John forgive me?"

"My dear," said I, "to doubt it for a moment is to do him a great wrong. And as to me!" Why, as to me, what had I to forgive!

I dried my sobbing darling's eyes and sat beside her on the sofa, and Richard sat on my other side; and while I was reminded of that so different night when they had first taken me into their confidence and had gone on in their own wild happy way, they told me between them how it was.

"All I had was Richard's," Ada said; "and Richard would not take it, Esther, and what could I do but be his wife when I loved him dearly!"

"And you were so fully and so kindly occupied, excellent Dame Durden," said Richard, "that how could we speak to you at such a time! And besides, it was not a long-considered step. We went out one morning and were married."

"And when it was done, Esther," said my darling, "I was always thinking how to tell you and what to do for the best. And sometimes I thought you ought to know it directly, and sometimes I thought you ought not to know it and keep it from my cousin John; and I could not tell what to do, and I fretted very much."

How selfish I must have been not to have thought of this before! I don't know what I said now. I was so sorry, and yet I was so fond of them and so glad that they were fond of me; I pitied them so much, and yet I felt a kind of pride in their loving one another. I never had experienced such painful and pleasurable emotion at one time, and in my own heart I did not know which predominated. But I was not there to darken their way; I did not do that.

When I was less foolish and more composed, my darling took her wedding-ring from her bosom, and kissed it, and put it on. Then I remembered last night and told Richard that ever since her marriage she had worn it at night when there was no one to see. Then Ada blushingly asked me how did I know that, my dear. Then I told Ada how I had seen her hand concealed under her pillow and had little thought why, my dear. Then they began telling me how it was all over again, and I began to be sorry and glad again, and foolish again, and to hide my plain old face as much as I could lest I should put them out of heart.

Thus the time went on until it became necessary for me to think of returning. When that time arrived it was the worst of all, for then my darling completely broke down. She clung round my neck, calling me by every dear name she could think of and saying what should she do without me! Nor was Richard much better; and as for me, I should have been the worst of the three if I had not severely said to myself, "Now Esther, if you do, I'll never speak to you again!"

"Why, I declare," said I, "I never saw such a wife. I don't think she loves her husband at all. Here, Richard, take my child, for goodness' sake." But I held her tight all the while, and could have wept over her I don't know how long.

"I give this dear young couple notice," said I, "that I am only going away to come back to-morrow and that I shall be always coming backwards and forwards until Symond's Inn is tired of the sight of me. So I shall not say good-bye, Richard. For what would be the use of that, you know, when I am coming back so soon!"

I had given my darling to him now, and I meant to go; but I lingered for one more look of the precious face which it seemed to rive my heart to turn from.

So I said (in a merry, bustling manner) that unless they gave me some encouragement to come back, I was not sure that I could take that liberty, upon which my dear girl looked up, faintly smiling through her tears, and I folded her lovely face between my hands, and gave it one last kiss, and laughed, and ran away.

And when I got downstairs, oh, how I cried! It almost seemed to me that I had lost my Ada for ever. I was so lonely and so blank without her, and it was so desolate to be going home with no hope of seeing her there, that I could get no comfort for a little while as I walked up and down in a dim corner sobbing and crying.

I came to myself by and by, after a little scolding, and took a coach home. The poor boy whom I had found at St. Albans had reappeared a short time before and was lying at the point of death; indeed, was then dead, though I did not know it. My guardian had gone out to inquire about him and did not return to dinner. Being quite alone, I cried a little again, though on the whole I don't think I behaved so very, very ill.

It was only natural that I should not be quite accustomed to the loss of my darling yet. Three or four hours were not a long time after years. But my mind dwelt so much upon the uncongenial scene in which I had left her, and I pictured it as such an overshadowed stony-hearted one, and I so longed to be near her and taking some sort of care of her, that I determined to go back in the evening only to look up at her windows.

It was foolish, I dare say, but it did not then seem at all so to me, and it does not seem quite so even now. I took Charley into my confidence, and we went out at dusk. It was dark when we came to the new strange home of my dear girl, and there was a light behind the yellow blinds. We walked past cautiously three or four times, looking up, and narrowly missed encountering Mr. Vholes, who came out of his office while we were there and turned his head to look up too before going home. The sight of his lank black figure and the lonesome air of that nook in the dark were favourable to the state of my mind. I thought of the youth and love and beauty of my dear girl, shut up in such an ill-assorted refuge, almost as if it were a cruel place.

It was very solitary and very dull, and I did not doubt that I might safely steal upstairs. I left Charley below and went up with a light foot, not distressed by any glare from the feeble oil lanterns on the way. I listened for a few moments, and in the musty rotting silence of the house believed that I could hear the murmur of their young voices. I put my lips to the hearse-like panel of the door as a kiss for my dear and came quietly down again, thinking that one of these days I would confess to the visit.

And it really did me good, for though nobody but Charley and I knew anything about it, I somehow felt as if it had diminished the separation between Ada and me and had brought us together again for those moments. I went back, not quite accustomed yet to the change, but all the better for that hovering about my darling.

My guardian had come home and was standing thoughtfully by the dark window. When I went in, his face cleared and he came to his seat, but he caught the light upon my face as I took mine.

"Little woman," said he, "You have been crying."

"Why, yes, guardian," said I, "I am afraid I have been, a little. Ada has been in such distress, and is so very sorry, guardian."

I put my arm on the back of his chair, and I saw in his glance that my words and my look at her empty place had prepared him.

"Is she married, my dear?"

I told him all about it and how her first entreaties had referred to his forgiveness.

"She has no need of it," said he. "Heaven bless her and her husband!" But just as my first impulse had been to pity her, so was his. "Poor girl, poor girl! Poor Rick! Poor Ada!"

Neither of us spoke after that, until he said with a sigh, "Well, well, my dear! Bleak House is thinning fast."

"But its mistress remains, guardian." Though I was timid about saying it, I ventured because of the sorrowful tone in which he had spoken. "She will do all she can to make it happy," said I.

"She will succeed, my love!"

The letter had made no difference between us except that the seat by his side had come to be mine; it made none now. He turned his old bright fatherly look upon me, laid his hand on my hand in his old way, and said again, "She will succeed, my dear. Nevertheless, Bleak House is thinning fast, O little woman!"

I was sorry presently that this was all we said about that. I was rather disappointed. I feared I might not quite have been all I had meant to be since the letter and the answer.

CHAPTER LII
OBSTINACY

But one other day had intervened when, early in the morning as we were going to breakfast, Mr. Woodcourt came in haste with the astounding news that a terrible murder had been committed for which Mr. George had been apprehended and was in custody. When he told us that a large reward was offered by Sir Leicester Dedlock for the murderer's apprehension, I did not in my first consternation understand why; but a few more words explained to me that the murdered person was Sir Leicester's lawyer, and immediately my mother's dread of him rushed into my remembrance.

This unforeseen and violent removal of one whom she had long watched and distrusted and who had long watched and distrusted her, one for whom she could have had few intervals of kindness, always dreading in him a dangerous and secret enemy, appeared so awful that my first thoughts were of her. How appalling to hear of such a death and be able to feel no pity! How dreadful to remember, perhaps, that she had sometimes even wished the old man away who was so swiftly hurried out of life!

Such crowding reflections, increasing the distress and fear I always felt when the name was mentioned, made me so agitated that I could scarcely hold my place at the table. I was quite unable to follow the conversation until I had had a little time to recover. But when I came to myself and saw how shocked my guardian was and found that they were earnestly speaking of the suspected man and recalling every favourable impression we had formed of him out of the good we had known of him, my interest and my fears were so strongly aroused in his behalf that I was quite set up again.

"Guardian, you don't think it possible that he is justly accused?"

"My dear, I CAN'T think so. This man whom we have seen so open-hearted and compassionate, who with the might of a giant has the gentleness of a child, who looks as brave a fellow as ever lived and is so simple and quiet with it, this man justly accused of such a crime? I can't believe it. It's not that I don't or I won't. I can't!"

"And I can't," said Mr. Woodcourt. "Still, whatever we believe or know of him, we had better not forget that some appearances are against him. He bore an animosity towards the deceased gentleman. He has openly mentioned it in many places. He is said to have expressed himself violently towards him, and he certainly did about him, to my knowledge. He admits that he was alone on the scene of the murder within a few minutes of its commission. I sincerely believe him to be as innocent of any participation in it as I am, but these are all reasons for suspicion falling upon him."

"True," said my guardian. And he added, turning to me, "It would be doing him a very bad service, my dear, to shut our eyes to the truth in any of these respects."

I felt, of course, that we must admit, not only to ourselves but to others, the full force of the circumstances against him. Yet I knew withal (I could not help saying) that their weight would not induce us to desert him in his need.

"Heaven forbid!" returned my guardian. "We will stand by him, as he himself stood by the two poor creatures who are gone." He meant Mr. Gridley and the boy, to both of whom Mr. George had given shelter.

Mr. Woodcourt then told us that the trooper's man had been with him before day, after wandering about the streets all night like a distracted creature. That one of the trooper's first anxieties was that we should not suppose him guilty. That he had charged his messenger to represent his perfect innocence with every solemn assurance he could send us. That Mr. Woodcourt had only quieted the man by undertaking to come to our house very early in the morning with these representations. He added that he was now upon his way to see the prisoner himself.

My guardian said directly he would go too. Now, besides that I liked the retired soldier very much and that he liked me, I had that secret interest in what had happened which was only known to my guardian. I felt as if it came close and near to me. It seemed to become personally important to myself that the truth should be discovered and that no innocent people should be suspected, for suspicion, once run wild, might run wilder.

In a word, I felt as if it were my duty and obligation to go with them. My guardian did not seek to dissuade me, and I went.

It was a large prison with many courts and passages so like one another and so uniformly paved that I seemed to gain a new comprehension, as I passed along, of the fondness that solitary prisoners, shut up among the same staring walls from year to year, have had—as I have read—for a weed or a stray blade of grass. In an arched room by himself, like a cellar upstairs, with walls so glaringly white that they made the massive iron window-bars and iron-bound door even more profoundly black than they were, we found the trooper standing in a corner. He had been sitting on a bench there and had risen when he heard the locks and bolts turn.

When he saw us, he came forward a step with his usual heavy tread, and there stopped and made a slight bow. But as I still advanced, putting out my hand to him, he understood us in a moment.

"This is a load off my mind, I do assure you, miss and gentlemen," said he, saluting us with great heartiness and drawing a long breath. "And now I don't so much care how it ends."

He scarcely seemed to be the prisoner. What with his coolness and his soldierly bearing, he looked far more like the prison guard.

"This is even a rougher place than my gallery to receive a lady in," said Mr. George, "but I know Miss Summerson will make the best of it." As he handed me to the bench on which he had been sitting, I sat down, which seemed to give him great satisfaction.

"I thank you, miss," said he.

"Now, George," observed my guardian, "as we require no new assurances on your part, so I believe we need give you none on ours."

"Not at all, sir. I thank you with all my heart. If I was not innocent of this crime, I couldn't look at you and keep my secret to myself under the condescension of the present visit. I feel the present visit very much. I am not one of the eloquent sort, but I feel it, Miss Summerson and gentlemen, deeply."

He laid his hand for a moment on his broad chest and bent his head to us. Although he squared himself again directly, he expressed a great amount of natural emotion by these simple means.

"First," said my guardian, "can we do anything for your personal comfort, George?"

"For which, sir?" he inquired, clearing his throat.

"For your personal comfort. Is there anything you want that would lessen the hardship of this confinement?"

"Well, sir," replied George, after a little cogitation, "I am equally obliged to you, but tobacco being against the rules, I can't say that there is."

"You will think of many little things perhaps, by and by. Whenever you do, George, let us know."

"Thank you, sir. Howsoever," observed Mr. George with one of his sunburnt smiles, "a man who has been knocking about the world in a vagabond kind of a way as long as I have gets on well enough in a place like the present, so far as that goes."

"Next, as to your case," observed my guardian.

"Exactly so, sir," returned Mr. George, folding his arms upon his breast with perfect self-possession and a little curiosity.

"How does it stand now?"

"Why, sir, it is under remand at present. Bucket gives me to understand that he will probably apply for a series of remands from time to time until the case is more complete. How it is to be made more complete I don't myself see, but I dare say Bucket will manage it somehow."

"Why, heaven save us, man," exclaimed my guardian, surprised into his old oddity and vehemence, "you talk of yourself as if you were somebody else!"

"No offence, sir," said Mr. George. "I am very sensible of your kindness. But I don't see how an innocent man is to make up his mind to this kind of thing without knocking his head against the walls unless he takes it in that point of view.

"That is true enough to a certain extent," returned my guardian, softened. "But my good fellow, even an innocent man must take ordinary precautions to defend himself."

"Certainly, sir. And I have done so. I have stated to the magistrates, 'Gentlemen, I am as innocent of this charge as yourselves; what has been stated against me in the way of facts is perfectly true; I know no more about it.' I intend to continue stating that, sir. What more can I do? It's the truth."

"But the mere truth won't do," rejoined my guardian.

"Won't it indeed, sir? Rather a bad look-out for me!" Mr. George good-humouredly observed.

"You must have a lawyer," pursued my guardian. "We must engage a good one for you."

"I ask your pardon, sir," said Mr. George with a step backward. "I am equally obliged. But I must decidedly beg to be excused from anything of that sort."

"You won't have a lawyer?"

"No, sir." Mr. George shook his head in the most emphatic manner. "I thank you all the same, sir, but—no lawyer!"

"Why not?"

"I don't take kindly to the breed," said Mr. George. "Gridley didn't. And—if you'll excuse my saying so much—I should hardly have thought you did yourself, sir."

"That's equity," my guardian explained, a little at a loss; "that's equity, George."

"Is it, indeed, sir?" returned the trooper in his off-hand manner. "I am not acquainted with those shades of names myself, but in a general way I object to the breed."

Unfolding his arms and changing his position, he stood with one massive hand upon the table and the other on his hip, as complete a picture of a man who was not to be moved from a fixed purpose as ever I saw. It was in vain that we all three talked to him and endeavoured to persuade him; he listened with that gentleness which went so well with his bluff bearing, but was evidently no more shaken by our representations that his place of confinement was.

"Pray think, once more, Mr. George," said I. "Have you no wish in reference to your case?"

"I certainly could wish it to be tried, miss," he returned, "by court-martial; but that is out of the question, as I am well aware. If you will be so good as to favour me with your attention for a couple of minutes, miss, not more, I'll endeavour to explain myself as clearly as I can."

He looked at us all three in turn, shook his head a little as if he were adjusting it in the stock and collar of a tight uniform, and after a moment's reflection went on.

"You see, miss, I have been handcuffed and taken into custody and brought here. I am a marked and disgraced man, and here I am. My shooting gallery is rummaged, high and low, by Bucket; such property as I have—'tis small—is turned this way and that till it don't know itself; and (as aforesaid) here I am! I don't particular complain of that. Though I am in these present quarters through no immediately preceding fault of mine, I can very well understand that if I hadn't gone into the vagabond way in my youth, this wouldn't have happened. It HAS happened. Then comes the question how to meet it."

He rubbed his swarthy forehead for a moment with a good-humoured look and said apologetically, "I am such a short-winded talker that I must think a bit." Having thought a bit, he looked up again and resumed.

"How to meet it. Now, the unfortunate deceased was himself a lawyer and had a pretty tight hold of me. I don't wish to rake up his ashes, but he had, what I should call if he was living, a devil of a tight hold of me. I don't like his trade the better for that. If I had kept clear of his trade, I should have kept outside this place. But that's not what I mean. Now, suppose I had killed him. Suppose I really had discharged into his body any one of those pistols recently fired off that Bucket has found at my place, and dear me, might have found there any day since it has been my place. What should I have done as soon as I was hard and fast here? Got a lawyer."

He stopped on hearing some one at the locks and bolts and did not resume until the door had been opened and was shut again. For what purpose opened, I will mention presently.

"I should have got a lawyer, and he would have said (as I have often read in the newspapers), 'My client says nothing, my client reserves his defence': my client this, that, and t'other. Well, 'tis not the custom of that breed to go straight, according to my opinion, or to think that other men do. Say I am innocent and I get a lawyer. He would be as likely to believe me guilty as not; perhaps more. What would he do, whether or not? Act as if I was—shut my mouth up, tell me not to commit myself, keep circumstances back, chop the evidence small, quibble, and get me off perhaps! But, Miss Summerson, do I care for getting off in that way; or would I rather be hanged in my own way—if you'll excuse my mentioning anything so disagreeable to a lady?"

He had warmed into his subject now, and was under no further necessity to wait a bit.

"I would rather be hanged in my own way. And I mean to be! I don't intend to say," looking round upon us with his powerful arms akimbo and his dark eyebrows raised, "that I am more partial to being hanged than another man. What I say is, I must come off clear and full or not at all. Therefore, when I hear stated against me what is true, I say it's true; and when they tell me, 'whatever you say will be used,' I tell them I don't mind that; I mean it to be used. If they can't make me innocent out of the whole truth, they are not likely to do it out of anything less, or anything else. And if they are, it's worth nothing to me."

Taking a pace or two over the stone floor, he came back to the table and finished what he had to say.

"I thank you, miss and gentlemen both, many times for your attention, and many times more for your interest. That's the plain state of the matter as it points itself out to a mere trooper with a blunt broadsword kind of a mind. I have never done well in life beyond my duty as a soldier, and if the worst comes after all, I shall reap pretty much as I have sown. When I got over the first crash of being seized as a murderer—it don't take a rover who has knocked about so much as myself so very long to recover from a crash—I worked my way round to what you find me now. As such I shall remain. No relations will be disgraced by me or made unhappy for me, and—and that's all I've got to say."

The door had been opened to admit another soldier-looking man of less prepossessing appearance at first sight and a weather-tanned, bright-eyed wholesome woman with a basket, who, from her entrance, had been exceedingly attentive to all Mr. George had said. Mr. George had received them with a familiar nod and a friendly look, but without any more particular greeting in the midst of his address. He now shook them cordially by the hand and said, "Miss Summerson and gentlemen, this is an old comrade of mine, Matthew Bagnet. And this is his wife, Mrs. Bagnet."

Mr. Bagnet made us a stiff military bow, and Mrs. Bagnet dropped us a curtsy.

"Real good friends of mine, they are," sald Mr. George. "It was at their house I was taken."

"With a second-hand wiolinceller," Mr. Bagnet put in, twitching his head angrily. "Of a good tone. For a friend. That money was no object to."

"Mat," said Mr. George, "you have heard pretty well all I have been saying to this lady and these two gentlemen. I know it meets your approval?"

Mr. Bagnet, after considering, referred the point to his wife. "Old girl," said he. "Tell him. Whether or not. It meets my approval."

"Why, George," exclaimed Mrs. Bagnet, who had been unpacking her basket, in which there was a piece of cold pickled pork, a little tea and sugar, and a brown loaf, "you ought to know it don't. You ought to know it's enough to drive a person wild to hear you. You won't be got off this way, and you won't be got off that way—what do you mean by such picking and choosing? It's stuff and nonsense, George."

"Don't be severe upon me in my misfortunes, Mrs. Bagnet," said the trooper lightly.

"Oh! Bother your misfortunes," cried Mrs. Bagnet, "if they don't make you more reasonable than that comes to. I never was so ashamed in my life to hear a man talk folly as I have been to hear you talk this day to the present company. Lawyers? Why, what but too many cooks should hinder you from having a dozen lawyers if the gentleman recommended them to you."

"This is a very sensible woman," said my guardian. "I hope you will persuade him, Mrs. Bagnet."

"Persuade him, sir?" she returned. "Lord bless you, no. You don't know George. Now, there!" Mrs. Bagnet left her basket to point him out with both her bare brown hands. "There he stands! As self-willed and as determined a man, in the wrong way, as ever put a human creature under heaven out of patience! You could as soon take up and shoulder an eight and forty pounder by your own strength as turn that man when he has got a thing into his head and fixed it there. Why, don't I know him!" cried Mrs. Bagnet. "Don't I know you, George! You don't mean to set up for a new character with ME after all these years, I hope?"

Her friendly indignation had an exemplary effect upon her husband, who shook his head at the trooper several times as a silent recommendation to him to yield. Between whiles, Mrs. Bagnet looked at me; and I understood from the play of her eyes that she wished me to do something, though I did not comprehend what.

"But I have given up talking to you, old fellow, years and years," said Mrs. Bagnet as she blew a little dust off the pickled pork, looking at me again; "and when ladies and gentlemen know you as well as I do, they'll give up talking to you too. If you are not too headstrong to accept of a bit of dinner, here it is."

"I accept it with many thanks," returned the trooper.

"Do you though, indeed?" said Mrs. Bagnet, continuing to grumble on good-humouredly. "I'm sure I'm surprised at that. I wonder you don't starve in your own way also. It would only be like you. Perhaps you'll set your mind upon THAT next." Here she again looked at me, and I now perceived from her glances at the door and at me, by turns, that she wished us to retire and to await her following us outside the prison. Communicating this by similar means to my guardian and Mr. Woodcourt, I rose.

"We hope you will think better of it, Mr. George," said I, "and we shall come to see you again, trusting to find you more reasonable."

"More grateful, Miss Summerson, you can't find me," he returned.

"But more persuadable we can, I hope," said I. "And let me entreat you to consider that the clearing up of this mystery and the discovery of the real perpetrator of this deed may be of the last importance to others besides yourself."

He heard me respectfully but without much heeding these words, which I spoke a little turned from him, already on my way to the door; he was observing (this they afterwards told me) my height and figure, which seemed to catch his attention all at once.

"'Tis curious," said he. "And yet I thought so at the time!"

My guardian asked him what he meant.

"Why, sir," he answered, "when my ill fortune took me to the dead man's staircase on the night of his murder, I saw a shape so like Miss Summerson's go by me in the dark that I had half a mind to speak to it."

For an instant I felt such a shudder as I never felt before or since and hope I shall never feel again.

"It came downstairs as I went up," said the trooper, "and crossed the moonlighted window with a loose black mantle on; I noticed a deep fringe to it.

However, it has nothing to do with the present subject, excepting that Miss Summerson looked so like it at the moment that it came into my head."

I cannot separate and define the feelings that arose in me after this; it is enough that the vague duty and obligation I had felt upon me from the first of following the investigation was, without my distinctly daring to ask myself any question, increased, and that I was indignantly sure of there being no possibility of a reason for my being afraid.

We three went out of the prison and walked up and down at some short distance from the gate, which was in a retired place. We had not waited long when Mr. and Mrs. Bagnet came out too and quickly joined us.

There was a tear in each of Mrs. Bagnet's eyes, and her face was flushed and hurried. "I didn't let George see what I thought about it, you know, miss," was her first remark when she came up, "but he's in a bad way, poor old fellow!"

"Not with care and prudence and good help," said my guardian.

"A gentleman like you ought to know best, sir," returned Mrs. Bagnet, hurriedly drying her eyes on the hem of her grey cloak, "but I am uneasy for him. He has been so careless and said so much that he never meant. The gentlemen of the juries might not understand him as Lignum and me do. And then such a number of circumstances have happened bad for him, and such a number of people will be brought forward to speak against him, and Bucket is so deep."

"With a second-hand wiolinceller. And said he played the fife. When a boy," Mr. Bagnet added with great solemnity.

"Now, I tell you, miss," said Mrs. Bagnet; "and when I say miss, I mean all! Just come into the corner of the wall and I'll tell you!"

Mrs. Bagnet hurried us into a more secluded place and was at first too breathless to proceed, occasioning Mr. Bagnet to say, "Old girl! Tell 'em!"

"Why, then, miss," the old girl proceeded, untying the strings of her bonnet for more air, "you could as soon move Dover Castle as move George on this point unless you had got a new power to move him with. And I have got it!"

"You are a jewel of a woman," said my guardian. "Go on!"

"Now, I tell you, miss," she proceeded, clapping her hands in her hurry and agitation a dozen times in every sentence, "that what he says concerning no relations is all bosh. They don't know of him, but he does know of them. He has said more to me at odd times than to anybody else, and it warn't for nothing that he once spoke to my Woolwich about whitening and wrinkling mothers' heads. For fifty pounds he had seen his mother that day. She's alive and must be brought here straight!"

Instantly Mrs. Bagnet put some pins into her mouth and began pinning up her skirts all round a little higher than the level of her grey cloak, which she accomplished with surpassing dispatch and dexterity.

"Lignum," said Mrs. Bagnet, "you take care of the children, old man, and give me the umbrella! I'm away to Lincolnshire to bring that old lady here."

"But, bless the woman," cried my guardian with his hand in his pocket, "how is she going? What money has she got?"

Mrs. Bagnet made another application to her skirts and brought forth a leathern purse in which she hastily counted over a few shillings and which she then shut up with perfect satisfaction.

"Never you mind for me, miss. I'm a soldier's wife and accustomed to travel my own way. Lignum, old boy," kissing him, "one for yourself, three for the children. Now I'm away into Lincolnshire after George's mother!"

And she actually set off while we three stood looking at one another lost in amazement. She actually trudged away in her grey cloak at a sturdy pace, and turned the corner, and was gone.

"Mr. Bagnet," said my guardian. "Do you mean to let her go in that way?"

"Can't help it," he returned. "Made her way home once from another quarter of the world. With the same grey cloak. And same umbrella. Whatever the old girl says, do. Do it! Whenever the old girl says, I'LL do it. She does it."

"Then she is as honest and genuine as she looks," rejoined my guardian, "and it is impossible to say more for her."

"She's Colour-Sergeant of the Nonpareil battalion," said Mr. Bagnet, looking at us over his shoulder as he went his way also. "And there's not such another. But I never own to it before her. Discipline must be maintained."

CHAPTER LIII
THE TRACK

Mr. Bucket and his fat forefinger are much in consultation together under existing circumstances. When Mr. Bucket has a matter of this pressing interest under his consideration, the fat forefinger seems to rise, to the dignity of a familiar demon. He puts it to his ears, and it whispers information; he puts it to his lips, and it enjoins him to secrecy; he rubs it over his nose, and it sharpens his scent; he shakes it before a guilty man, and it charms him to his destruction. The Augurs of the Detective Temple invariably predict that when Mr. Bucket and that finger are in much conference, a terrible avenger will be heard of before long.

Otherwise mildly studious in his observation of human nature, on the whole a benignant philosopher not disposed to be severe upon the follies of mankind, Mr. Bucket pervades a vast number of houses and strolls about an infinity of streets, to outward appearance rather languishing for want of an object. He is in the friendliest condition towards his species and will drink with most of them. He is free with his money, affable in his manners, innocent in his conversation—but through the placid stream of his life there glides an under-current of forefinger.

Time and place cannot bind Mr. Bucket. Like man in the abstract, he is here to-day and gone to-morrow—but, very unlike man indeed, he is here again the next day. This evening he will be casually looking into the iron extinguishers at the door of Sir Leicester Dedlock's house in town; and to-morrow morning he will be walking on the leads at Chesney Wold, where erst the old man walked whose ghost is propitiated with a hundred guineas. Drawers, desks, pockets, all things belonging to him, Mr. Bucket examines. A few hours afterwards, he and the Roman will be alone together comparing forefingers.

It is likely that these occupations are irreconcilable with home enjoyment, but it is certain that Mr. Bucket at present does not go home. Though in general he highly appreciates the society of Mrs. Bucket—a lady of a natural detective genius, which if it had been improved by professional exercise, might have done great things, but which has paused at the level of a clever amateur—he holds himself aloof from that dear solace. Mrs. Bucket is dependent on their lodger (fortunately an amiable lady in whom she takes an interest) for companionship and conversation.

A great crowd assembles in Lincoln's Inn Fields on the day of the funeral. Sir Leicester Dedlock attends the ceremony in person; strictly speaking, there are only three other human followers, that is to say, Lord Doodle, William Buffy, and the debilitated cousin (thrown in as a make-weight), but the amount of inconsolable carriages is immense. The peerage contributes more four-wheeled affliction than has ever been seen in that neighbourhood. Such is the assemblage of armorial bearings on coach panels that the Herald's College might be supposed to have lost its father and mother at a blow. The Duke of Foodle sends a splendid pile of dust and ashes, with silver wheel-boxes, patent axles, all the last improvements, and three bereaved worms, six feet high, holding on behind, in a bunch of woe. All the state coachmen in London seem plunged into mourning; and if that dead old man of the rusty garb be not beyond a taste in horseflesh (which appears impossible), it must be highly gratified this day.

Quiet among the undertakers and the equipages and the calves of so many legs all steeped in grief, Mr. Bucket sits concealed in one of the inconsolable carriages and at his ease surveys the crowd through the lattice blinds. He has a keen eye for a crowd—as for what not?—and looking here and there, now from this side of the carriage, now from the other, now up at the house windows, now along the people's heads, nothing escapes him.

"And there you are, my partner, eh?" says Mr. Bucket to himself, apostrophizing Mrs. Bucket, stationed, by his favour, on the steps of the deceased's house. "And so you are. And so you are! And very well indeed you are looking, Mrs. Bucket!"

The procession has not started yet, but is waiting for the cause of its assemblage to be brought out. Mr. Bucket, in the foremost emblazoned carriage, uses his two fat forefingers to hold the lattice a hair's breadth open while he looks.

And it says a great deal for his attachment, as a husband, that he is still occupied with Mrs. B. "There you are, my partner, eh?" he murmuringly repeats. "And our lodger with you. I'm taking notice of you, Mrs. Bucket; I hope you're all right in your health, my dear!"

Not another word does Mr. Bucket say, but sits with most attentive eyes until the sacked depository of noble secrets is brought down—Where are all those secrets now? Does he keep them yet? Did they fly with him on that sudden journey?—and until the procession moves, and Mr. Bucket's view is changed. After which he composes himself for an easy ride and takes note of the fittings of the carriage in case he should ever find such knowledge useful.

Contrast enough between Mr. Tulkinghorn shut up in his dark carriage and Mr. Bucket shut up in HIS. Between the immeasurable track of space beyond the little wound that has thrown the one into the fixed sleep which jolts so heavily over the stones of the streets, and the narrow track of blood which keeps the other in the watchful state expressed in every hair of his head! But it is all one to both; neither is troubled about that.

Mr. Bucket sits out the procession in his own easy manner and glides from the carriage when the opportunity he has settled with himself arrives. He makes for Sir Leicester Dedlock's, which is at present a sort of home to him, where he comes and goes as he likes at all hours, where he is always welcome and made much of, where he knows the whole establishment, and walks in an atmosphere of mysterious greatness.

No knocking or ringing for Mr. Bucket. He has caused himself to be provided with a key and can pass in at his pleasure. As he is crossing the hall, Mercury informs him, "Here's another letter for you, Mr. Bucket, come by post," and gives it him.

"Another one, eh?" says Mr. Bucket.

If Mercury should chance to be possessed by any lingering curiosity as to Mr. Bucket's letters, that wary person is not the man to gratify it. Mr. Bucket looks at him as if his face were a vista of some miles in length and he were leisurely contemplating the same.

"Do you happen to carry a box?" says Mr. Bucket.

Unfortunately Mercury is no snuff-taker.

"Could you fetch me a pinch from anywheres?" says Mr. Bucket. "Thankee. It don't matter what it is; I'm not particular as to the kind. Thankee!"

Having leisurely helped himself from a canister borrowed from somebody downstairs for the purpose, and having made a considerable show of tasting it, first with one side of his nose and then with the other, Mr. Bucket, with much deliberation, pronounces it of the right sort and goes on, letter in hand.

Now although Mr. Bucket walks upstairs to the little library within the larger one with the face of a man who receives some scores of letters every day, it happens that much correspondence is not incidental to his life. He is no great scribe, rather handling his pen like the pocket-staff he carries about with him always convenient to his grasp, and discourages correspondence with himself in others as being too artless and direct a way of doing delicate business. Further, he often sees damaging letters produced in evidence and has occasion to reflect that it was a green thing to write them. For these reasons he has very little to do with letters, either as sender or receiver. And yet he has received a round half-dozen within the last twenty-four hours.

"And this," says Mr. Bucket, spreading it out on the table, "is in the same hand, and consists of the same two words."

What two words?

He turns the key in the door, ungirdles his black pocket-book (book of fate to many), lays another letter by it, and reads, boldly written in each, "Lady Dedlock."

"Yes, yes," says Mr. Bucket. "But I could have made the money without this anonymous information."

Having put the letters in his book of fate and girdled it up again, he unlocks the door just in time to admit his dinner, which is brought upon a goodly tray with a decanter of sherry. Mr. Bucket frequently observes, in friendly circles where there is no restraint, that he likes a toothful of your fine old brown East Inder sherry better than anything you can offer him. Consequently he fills and empties his glass with a smack of his lips and is proceeding with his refreshment when an idea enters his mind.

Mr. Bucket softly opens the door of communication between that room and the next and looks in. The library is deserted, and the fire is sinking low. Mr. Bucket's eye, after taking a pigeon-flight round the room, alights upon a table where letters are usually put as they arrive. Several letters for Sir Leicester are upon it. Mr. Bucket draws near and examines the directions. "No," he says, "there's none in that hand. It's only me as is written to. I can break it to Sir Leicester Dedlock, Baronet, to-morrow."

With that he returns to finish his dinner with a good appetite, and after a light nap, is summoned into the drawing-room. Sir Leicester has received him there these several evenings past to know whether he has anything to report. The debilitated cousin (much exhausted by the funeral) and Volumnia are in attendance.

Mr. Bucket makes three distinctly different bows to these three people. A bow of homage to Sir Leicester, a bow of gallantry to Volumnia, and a bow of recognition to the debilitated Cousin, to whom it airily says, "You are a swell about town, and you know me, and I know you." Having distributed these little specimens of his tact, Mr. Bucket rubs his hands.

"Have you anything new to communicate, officer?" inquires Sir Leicester. "Do you wish to hold any conversation with me in private?"

"Why—not to-night, Sir Leicester Dedlock, Baronet."

"Because my time," pursues Sir Leicester, "is wholly at your disposal with a view to the vindication of the outraged majesty of the law."

Mr. Bucket coughs and glances at Volumnia, rouged and necklaced, as though he would respectfully observe, "I do assure you, you're a pretty creetur. I've seen hundreds worse looking at your time of life, I have indeed."

The fair Volumnia, not quite unconscious perhaps of the humanizing influence of her charms, pauses in the writing of cocked-hat notes and meditatively adjusts the pearl necklace. Mr. Bucket prices that decoration in his mind and thinks it as likely as not that Volumnia is writing poetry.

"If I have not," pursues Sir Leicester, "in the most emphatic manner, adjured you, officer, to exercise your utmost skill in this atrocious case, I particularly desire to take the present opportunity of rectifying any omission I may have made. Let no expense be a consideration. I am prepared to defray all charges. You can incur none in pursuit of the object you have undertaken that I shall hesitate for a moment to bear."

Mr. Bucket made Sir Leicester's bow again as a response to this liberality.

"My mind," Sir Leicester adds with a generous warmth, "has not, as may be easily supposed, recovered its tone since the late diabolical occurrence. It is not likely ever to recover its tone. But it is full of indignation to-night after undergoing the ordeal of consigning to the tomb the remains of a faithful, a zealous, a devoted adherent."

Sir Leicester's voice trembles and his grey hair stirs upon his head. Tears are in his eyes; the best part of his nature is aroused.

"I declare," he says, "I solemnly declare that until this crime is discovered and, in the course of justice, punished, I almost feel as if there were a stain upon my name. A gentleman who has devoted a large portion of his life to me, a gentleman who has devoted the last day of his life to me, a gentleman who has constantly sat at my table and slept under my roof, goes from my house to his own, and is struck down within an hour of his leaving my house. I cannot say but that he may have been followed from my house, watched at my house, even first marked because of his association with my house—which may have suggested his possessing greater wealth and being altogether of greater importance than his own retiring demeanour would have indicated. If I cannot with my means and influence and my position bring all the perpetrators of such a crime to light, I fail in the assertion of my respect for that gentleman's memory and of my fidelity towards one who was ever faithful to me."

While he makes this protestation with great emotion and earnestness, looking round the room as if he were addressing an assembly, Mr. Bucket glances at him with an observant gravity in which there might be, but for the audacity of the thought, a touch of compassion.

"The ceremony of to-day," continues Sir Leicester, "strikingly illustrative of the respect in which my deceased friend"—he lays a stress upon the word, for death levels all distinctions—"was held by the flower of the land, has, I say, aggravated the shock I have received from this most horrible and audacious crime. If it were my brother who had committed it, I would not spare him."

Mr. Bucket looks very grave. Volumnia remarks of the deceased that he was the trustiest and dearest person!

"You must feel it as a deprivation to you, miss," replies Mr. Bucket soothingly, "no doubt. He was calculated to BE a deprivation, I'm sure he was."

Volumnia gives Mr. Bucket to understand, in reply, that her sensitive mind is fully made up never to get the better of it as long as she lives, that her nerves are unstrung for ever, and that she has not the least expectation of ever smiling again. Meanwhile she folds up a cocked hat for that redoubtable old general at Bath, descriptive of her melancholy condition.

"It gives a start to a delicate female," says Mr. Bucket sympathetically, "but it'll wear off."

Volumnia wishes of all things to know what is doing? Whether they are going to convict, or whatever it is, that dreadful soldier? Whether he had any accomplices, or whatever the thing is called in the law? And a great deal more to the like artless purpose.

"Why you see, miss," returns Mr. Bucket, bringing the finger into persuasive action—and such is his natural gallantry that he had almost said "my dear"—"it ain't easy to answer those questions at the present moment. Not at the present moment. I've kept myself on this case, Sir Leicester Dedlock, Baronet," whom Mr. Bucket takes into the conversation in right of his importance, "morning, noon, and night. But for a glass or two of sherry, I don't think I could have had my mind so much upon the stretch as it has been. I COULD answer your questions, miss, but duty forbids it. Sir Leicester Dedlock, Baronet, will very soon be made acquainted with all that has been traced. And I hope that he may find it"—Mr. Bucket again looks grave—"to his satisfaction."

The debilitated cousin only hopes some fler'll be executed—zample. Thinks more interest's wanted—get man hanged presentime—than get man place ten thousand a year. Hasn't a doubt—zample—far better hang wrong fler than no fler.

"YOU know life, you know, sir," says Mr. Bucket with a complimentary twinkle of his eye and crook of his finger, "and you can confirm what I've mentioned to this lady. YOU don't want to be told that from information I have received I have gone to work. You're up to what a lady can't be expected to be up to. Lord! Especially in your elevated station of society, miss," says Mr. Bucket, quite reddening at another narrow escape from "my dear."

"The officer, Volumnia," observes Sir Leicester, "is faithful to his duty, and perfectly right."

Mr. Bucket murmurs, "Glad to have the honour of your approbation, Sir Leicester Dedlock, Baronet."

"In fact, Volumnia," proceeds Sir Leicester, "it is not holding up a good model for imitation to ask the officer any such questions as you have put to him. He is the best judge of his own responsibility; he acts upon his responsibility. And it does not become us, who assist in making the laws, to impede or interfere with those who carry them into execution. Or," says Sir Leicester somewhat sternly, for Volumnia was going to cut in before he had rounded his sentence, "or who vindicate their outraged majesty."

Volumnia with all humility explains that she had not merely the plea of curiosity to urge (in common with the giddy youth of her sex in general) but that she is perfectly dying with regret and interest for the darling man whose loss they all deplore.

"Very well, Volumnia," returns Sir Leicester. "Then you cannot be too discreet."

Mr. Bucket takes the opportunity of a pause to be heard again.

"Sir Leicester Dedlock, Baronet, I have no objections to telling this lady, with your leave and among ourselves, that I look upon the case as pretty well complete. It is a beautiful case—a beautiful case—and what little is wanting to complete it, I expect to be able to supply in a few hours."

"I am very glad indeed to hear it," says Sir Leicester. "Highly creditable to you."

"Sir Leicester Dedlock, Baronet," returns Mr. Bucket very seriously, "I hope it may at one and the same time do me credit and prove satisfactory to all. When I depict it as a beautiful case, you see, miss," Mr. Bucket goes on, glancing gravely at Sir Leicester, "I mean from my point of view. As considered from other points of view, such cases will always involve more or less unpleasantness. Very strange things comes to our knowledge in families, miss; bless your heart, what you would think to be phenomenons, quite."

Volumnia, with her innocent little scream, supposes so.

"Aye, and even in gen-teel families, in high families, in great families," says Mr. Bucket, again gravely eyeing Sir Leicester aside. "I have had the honour of being employed in high families before, and you have no idea—come, I'll go so far as to say not even YOU have any idea, sir," this to the debilitated cousin, "what games goes on!"

The cousin, who has been casting sofa-pillows on his head, in a prostration of boredom yawns, "Vayli," being the used-up for "very likely."

Sir Leicester, deeming it time to dismiss the officer, here majestically interposes with the words, "Very good. Thank you!" and also with a wave of his hand, implying not only that there is an end of the discourse, but that if high families fall into low habits they must take the consequences. "You will not forget, officer," he adds with condescension, "that I am at your disposal when you please."

Mr. Bucket (still grave) inquires if to-morrow morning, now, would suit, in case he should be as for'ard as he expects to be. Sir Leicester replies, "All times are alike to me." Mr. Bucket makes his three bows and is withdrawing when a forgotten point occurs to him.

"Might I ask, by the by," he says in a low voice, cautiously returning, "who posted the reward-bill on the staircase."

"I ordered it to be put up there," replies Sir Leicester.

"Would it be considered a liberty, Sir Leicester Dedlock, Baronet, if I was to ask you why?"

"Not at all. I chose it as a conspicuous part of the house. I think it cannot be too prominently kept before the whole establishment. I wish my people to be impressed with the enormity of the crime, the determination to punish it, and the hopelessness of escape. At the same time, officer, if you in your better knowledge of the subject see any objection—"

Mr. Bucket sees none now; the bill having been put up, had better not be taken down. Repeating his three bows he withdraws, closing the door on Volumnia's little scream, which is a preliminary to her remarking that that charmingly horrible person is a perfect Blue Chamber.

In his fondness for society and his adaptability to all grades, Mr. Bucket is presently standing before the hall-fire—bright and warm on the early winter night—admiring Mercury.

"Why, you're six foot two, I suppose?" says Mr. Bucket.

"Three," says Mercury.

"Are you so much? But then, you see, you're broad in proportion and don't look it. You're not one of the weak-legged ones, you ain't. Was you ever modelled now?" Mr. Bucket asks, conveying the expression of an artist into the turn of his eye and head.

Mercury never was modelled.

"Then you ought to be, you know," says Mr. Bucket; "and a friend of mine that you'll hear of one day as a Royal Academy sculptor would stand something handsome to make a drawing of your proportions for the marble. My Lady's out, ain't she?"

"Out to dinner."

"Goes out pretty well every day, don't she?"

"Yes."

"Not to be wondered at!" says Mr. Bucket. "Such a fine woman as her, so handsome and so graceful and so elegant, is like a fresh lemon on a dinner-table, ornamental wherever she goes. Was your father in the same way of life as yourself?"

Answer in the negative.

"Mine was," says Mr. Bucket. "My father was first a page, then a footman, then a butler, then a steward, then an inn-keeper. Lived universally respected, and died lamented. Said with his last breath that he considered service the most honourable part of his career, and so it was. I've a brother in service, AND a brother-in-law. My Lady a good temper?"

Mercury replies, "As good as you can expect."

"Ah!" says Mr. Bucket. "A little spoilt? A little capricious? Lord! What can you anticipate when they're so handsome as that? And we like 'em all the better for it, don't we?"

Mercury, with his hands in the pockets of his bright peach-blossom small-clothes, stretches his symmetrical silk legs with the air of a man of gallantry and can't deny it. Come the roll of wheels and a violent ringing at the bell. "Talk of the angels," says Mr. Bucket. "Here she is!"

The doors are thrown open, and she passes through the hall. Still very pale, she is dressed in slight mourning and wears two beautiful bracelets. Either their beauty or the beauty of her arms is particularly attractive to Mr. Bucket. He looks at them with an eager eye and rattles something in his pocket—halfpence perhaps.

Noticing him at his distance, she turns an inquiring look on the other Mercury who has brought her home.

"Mr. Bucket, my Lady."

Mr. Bucket makes a leg and comes forward, passing his familiar demon over the region of his mouth.

"Are you waiting to see Sir Leicester?"

"No, my Lady, I've seen him!"

"Have you anything to say to me?"

"Not just at present, my Lady."

"Have you made any new discoveries?"

"A few, my Lady."

This is merely in passing. She scarcely makes a stop, and sweeps upstairs alone. Mr. Bucket, moving towards the staircase-foot, watches her as she goes up the steps the old man came down to his grave, past murderous groups of statuary repeated with their shadowy weapons on the wall, past the printed bill, which she looks at going by, out of view.

"She's a lovely woman, too, she really is," says Mr. Bucket, coming back to Mercury. "Don't look quite healthy though."

Is not quite healthy, Mercury informs him. Suffers much from headaches.

Really? That's a pity! Walking, Mr. Bucket would recommend for that. Well, she tries walking, Mercury rejoins. Walks sometimes for two hours when she has them bad. By night, too.

"Are you sure you're quite so much as six foot three?" asks Mr. Bucket. "Begging your pardon for interrupting you a moment?"

Not a doubt about it.

"You're so well put together that I shouldn't have thought it. But the household troops, though considered fine men, are built so straggling. Walks by night, does she? When it's moonlight, though?"

Oh, yes. When it's moonlight! Of course. Oh, of course! Conversational and acquiescent on both sides.

"I suppose you ain't in the habit of walking yourself?" says Mr. Bucket. "Not much time for it, I should say?"

Besides which, Mercury don't like it. Prefers carriage exercise.

"To be sure," says Mr. Bucket. "That makes a difference. Now I think of it," says Mr. Bucket, warming his hands and looking pleasantly at the blaze, "she went out walking the very night of this business."

"To be sure she did! I let her into the garden over the way."

"And left her there. Certainly you did. I saw you doing it."

"I didn't see YOU," says Mercury.

"I was rather in a hurry," returns Mr. Bucket, "for I was going to visit a aunt of mine that lives at Chelsea—next door but two to the old original Bun House—ninety year old the old lady is, a single woman, and got a little property. Yes, I chanced to be passing at the time. Let's see. What time might it be? It wasn't ten."

"Half-past nine."

"You're right. So it was. And if I don't deceive myself, my Lady was muffled in a loose black mantle, with a deep fringe to it?"

"Of course she was."

Of course she was. Mr. Bucket must return to a little work he has to get on with upstairs, but he must shake hands with Mercury in acknowledgment of his agreeable conversation, and will he—this is all he asks—will he, when he has a leisure half-hour, think of bestowing it on that Royal Academy sculptor, for the advantage of both parties?

CHAPTER LIV
SPRINGING A MINE

Refreshed by sleep, Mr. Bucket rises betimes in the morning and prepares for a field-day. Smartened up by the aid of a clean shirt and a wet hairbrush, with which instrument, on occasions of ceremony, he lubricates such thin locks as remain to him after his life of severe study, Mr. Bucket lays in a breakfast of two mutton chops as a foundation to work upon, together with tea, eggs, toast, and marmalade on a corresponding scale. Having much enjoyed these strengthening matters and having held subtle conference with his familiar demon, he confidently instructs Mercury "just to mention quietly to Sir Leicester Dedlock, Baronet, that whenever he's ready for me, I'm ready for him." A gracious message being returned that Sir Leicester will expedite his dressing and join Mr. Bucket in the library within ten minutes, Mr. Bucket repairs to that apartment and stands before the fire with his finger on his chin, looking at the blazing coals.

Thoughtful Mr. Bucket is, as a man may be with weighty work to do, but composed, sure, confident. From the expression of his face he might be a famous whist-player for a large stake—say a hundred guineas certain—with the game in his hand, but with a high reputation involved in his playing his hand out to the last card in a masterly way. Not in the least anxious or disturbed is Mr. Bucket when Sir Leicester appears, but he eyes the baronet aside as he comes slowly to his easy-chair with that observant gravity of yesterday in which there might have been yesterday, but for the audacity of the idea, a touch of compassion.

"I am sorry to have kept you waiting, officer, but I am rather later than my usual hour this morning. I am not well. The agitation and the indignation from which I have recently suffered have been too much for me. I am subject to—gout"—Sir Leicester was going to say indisposition and would have said it to anybody else, but Mr. Bucket palpably knows all about it—"and recent circumstances have brought it on."

As he takes his seat with some difficulty and with an air of pain, Mr. Bucket draws a little nearer, standing with one of his large hands on the library-table.

"I am not aware, officer," Sir Leicester observes; raising his eyes to his face, "whether you wish us to be alone, but that is entirely as you please. If you do, well and good. If not, Miss Dedlock would be interested—"

"Why, Sir Leicester Dedlock, Baronet," returns Mr. Bucket with his head persuasively on one side and his forefinger pendant at one ear like an earring, "we can't be too private just at present. You will presently see that we can't be too private. A lady, under the circumstances, and especially in Miss Dedlock's elevated station of society, can't but be agreeable to me, but speaking without a view to myself, I will take the liberty of assuring you that I know we can't be too private."

"That is enough."

"So much so, Sir Leicester Dedlock, Baronet," Mr. Bucket resumes, "that I was on the point of asking your permission to turn the key in the door."

"By all means." Mr. Bucket skilfully and softly takes that precaution, stooping on his knee for a moment from mere force of habit so to adjust the key in the lock as that no one shall peep in from the outerside.

"Sir Leicester Dedlock, Baronet, I mentioned yesterday evening that I wanted but a very little to complete this case. I have now completed it and collected proof against the person who did this crime."

"Against the soldier?"

"No, Sir Leicester Dedlock; not the soldier."

Sir Leicester looks astounded and inquires, "Is the man in custody?"

Mr. Bucket tells him, after a pause, "It was a woman."

Sir Leicester leans back in his chair, and breathlessly ejaculates, "Good heaven!"

"Now, Sir Leicester Dedlock, Baronet," Mr. Bucket begins, standing over him with one hand spread out on the library-table and the forefinger of the other in impressive use, "it's my duty to prepare you for a train of circumstances that may, and I go so far as to say that will, give you a shock. But Sir Leicester Dedlock, Baronet, you are a gentleman, and I know what a gentleman is and what a gentleman is capable of. A gentleman can bear a shock when it must come, boldly and steadily. A gentleman can make up his mind to stand up against almost any blow. Why, take yourself, Sir Leicester Dedlock, Baronet. If there's a blow to be inflicted on you, you naturally think of your family. You ask yourself, how would all them ancestors of yours, away to Julius Caesar—not to go beyond him at present—have borne that blow; you remember scores of them that would have borne it well; and you bear it well on their accounts, and to maintain the family credit. That's the way you argue, and that's the way you act, Sir Leicester Dedlock, Baronet."

Sir Leicester, leaning back in his chair and grasping the elbows, sits looking at him with a stony face.

"Now, Sir Leicester Dedlock," proceeds Mr. Bucket, "thus preparing you, let me beg of you not to trouble your mind for a moment as to anything having come to MY knowledge. I know so much about so many characters, high and low, that a piece of information more or less don't signify a straw. I don't suppose there's a move on the board that would surprise ME, and as to this or that move having taken place, why my knowing it is no odds at all, any possible move whatever (provided it's in a wrong direction) being a probable move according to my experience. Therefore, what I say to you, Sir Leicester Dedlock, Baronet, is, don't you go and let yourself be put out of the way because of my knowing anything of your family affairs."

"I thank you for your preparation," returns Sir Leicester after a silence, without moving hand, foot, or feature, "which I hope is not necessary; though I give it credit for being well intended. Be so good as to go on. Also"—Sir Leicester seems to shrink in the shadow of his figure—"also, to take a seat, if you have no objection."

None at all. Mr. Bucket brings a chair and diminishes his shadow. "Now, Sir Leicester Dedlock, Baronet, with this short preface I come to the point. Lady Dedlock—"

Sir Leicester raises himself in his seat and stares at him fiercely. Mr. Bucket brings the finger into play as an emollient.

"Lady Dedlock, you see she's universally admired. That's what her ladyship is; she's universally admired," says Mr. Bucket.

"I would greatly prefer, officer," Sir Leicester returns stiffly, "my Lady's name being entirely omitted from this discussion."

"So would I, Sir Leicester Dedlock, Baronet, but—it's impossible."

"Impossible?"

Mr. Bucket shakes his relentless head.

"Sir Leicester Dedlock, Baronet, it's altogether impossible. What I have got to say is about her ladyship. She is the pivot it all turns on."

"Officer," retorts Sir Leicester with a fiery eye and a quivering lip, "you know your duty. Do your duty, but be careful not to overstep it. I would not suffer it. I would not endure it. You bring my Lady's name into this communication upon your responsibility—upon your responsibility. My Lady's name is not a name for common persons to trifle with!"

"Sir Leicester Dedlock, Baronet, I say what I must say, and no more."

"I hope it may prove so. Very well. Go on. Go on, sir!" Glancing at the angry eyes which now avoid him and at the angry figure trembling from head to foot, yet striving to be still, Mr. Bucket feels his way with his forefinger and in a low voice proceeds.

"Sir Leicester Dedlock, Baronet, it becomes my duty to tell you that the deceased Mr. Tulkinghorn long entertained mistrusts and suspicions of Lady Dedlock."

"If he had dared to breathe them to me, sir—which he never did—I would have killed him myself!" exclaims Sir Leicester, striking his hand upon the table. But in the very heat and fury of the act he stops, fixed by the knowing eyes of Mr. Bucket, whose forefinger is slowly going and who, with mingled confidence and patience, shakes his head.

"Sir Leicester Dedlock, the deceased Mr. Tulkinghorn was deep and close, and what he fully had in his mind in the very beginning I can't quite take upon myself to say. But I know from his lips that he long ago suspected Lady Dedlock of having discovered, through the sight of some handwriting—in this very house, and when you yourself, Sir Leicester Dedlock, were present—the existence, in great poverty, of a certain person who had been her lover before you courted her and who ought to have been her husband." Mr. Bucket stops and deliberately repeats, "Ought to have been her husband, not a doubt about it. I know from his lips that when that person soon afterwards died, he suspected Lady Dedlock of visiting his wretched lodging and his wretched grave, alone and in secret. I know from my own inquiries and through my eyes and ears that Lady Dedlock did make such visit in the dress of her own maid, for the deceased Mr. Tulkinghorn employed me to reckon up her ladyship—if you'll excuse my making use of the term we commonly employ—and I reckoned her up, so far, completely. I confronted the maid in the chambers in Lincoln's Inn Fields with a witness who had been Lady Dedlock's guide, and there couldn't be the shadow of a doubt that she had worn the young woman's dress, unknown to her. Sir Leicester Dedlock, Baronet, I did endeavour to pave the way a little towards these unpleasant disclosures yesterday by saying that very strange things happened even in high families sometimes. All this, and more, has happened in your own family, and to and through your own Lady. It's my belief that the deceased Mr. Tulkinghorn followed up these inquiries to the hour of his death and that he and Lady Dedlock even had bad blood between them upon the matter that very night. Now, only you put that to Lady Dedlock, Sir Leicester Dedlock, Baronet, and ask her ladyship whether, even after he had left here, she didn't go down to his chambers with the intention of saying something further to him, dressed in a loose black mantle with a deep fringe to it."

Sir Leicester sits like a statue, gazing at the cruel finger that is probing the life-blood of his heart.

"You put that to her ladyship, Sir Leicester Dedlock, Baronet, from me, Inspector Bucket of the Detective. And if her ladyship makes any difficulty about admitting of it, you tell her that it's no use, that Inspector Bucket knows it and knows that she passed the soldier as you called him (though he's not in the army now) and knows that she knows she passed him on the staircase. Now, Sir Leicester Dedlock, Baronet, why do I relate all this?"

Sir Leicester, who has covered his face with his hands, uttering a single groan, requests him to pause for a moment. By and by he takes his hands away, and so preserves his dignity and outward calmness, though there is no more colour in his face than in his white hair, that Mr. Bucket is a little awed by him. Something frozen and fixed is upon his manner, over and above its usual shell of haughtiness, and Mr. Bucket soon detects an unusual slowness in his speech, with now and then a curious trouble in beginning, which occasions him to utter inarticulate sounds. With such sounds he now breaks silence, soon, however, controlling himself to say that he does not comprehend why a gentleman so faithful and zealous as the late Mr. Tulkinghorn should have communicated to him nothing of this painful, this distressing, this unlooked-for, this overwhelming, this incredible intelligence.

"Again, Sir Leicester Dedlock, Baronet," returns Mr. Bucket, "put it to her ladyship to clear that up. Put it to her ladyship, if you think it right, from Inspector Bucket of the Detective. You'll find, or I'm much mistaken, that the deceased Mr. Tulkinghorn had the intention of communicating the whole to you as soon as he considered it ripe, and further, that he had given her ladyship so to understand. Why, he might have been going to reveal it the very morning when I examined the body! You don't know what I'm going to say and do five minutes from this present time, Sir Leicester Dedlock, Baronet; and supposing I was to be picked off now, you might wonder why I hadn't done it, don't you see?"

True. Sir Leicester, avoiding, with some trouble those obtrusive sounds, says, "True." At this juncture a considerable noise of voices is heard in the hall. Mr. Bucket, after listening, goes to the library-door, softly unlocks and opens it, and listens again. Then he draws in his head and whispers hurriedly but composedly, "Sir Leicester Dedlock, Baronet, this unfortunate family affair has taken air, as I expected it might, the deceased Mr. Tulkinghorn being cut down so sudden. The chance to hush it is to let in these people now in a wrangle with your footmen. Would you mind sitting quiet—on the family account—while I reckon 'em up? And would you just throw in a nod when I seem to ask you for it?"

Sir Leicester indistinctly answers, "Officer. The best you can, the best you can!" and Mr. Bucket, with a nod and a sagacious crook of the forefinger, slips down into the hall, where the voices quickly die away. He is not long in returning; a few paces ahead of Mercury and a brother deity also powdered and in peach-blossomed smalls, who bear between them a chair in which is an incapable old man. Another man and two women come behind. Directing the pitching of the chair in an affable and easy manner, Mr. Bucket dismisses the Mercuries and locks the door again. Sir Leicester looks on at this invasion of the sacred precincts with an icy stare.

"Now, perhaps you may know me, ladies and gentlemen," says Mr. Bucket in a confidential voice. "I am Inspector Bucket of the Detective, I am; and this," producing the tip of his convenient little staff from his breast-pocket, "is my authority. Now, you wanted to see Sir Leicester Dedlock, Baronet. Well! You do see him, and mind you, it ain't every one as is admitted to that honour. Your name, old gentleman, is Smallweed; that's what your name is; I know it well."

"Well, and you never heard any harm of it!" cries Mr. Smallweed in a shrill loud voice.

"You don't happen to know why they killed the pig, do you?" retorts Mr. Bucket with a steadfast look, but without loss of temper.

"No!"

"Why, they killed him," says Mr. Bucket, "on account of his having so much cheek. Don't YOU get into the same position, because it isn't worthy of you. You ain't in the habit of conversing with a deaf person, are you?"

"Yes," snarls Mr. Smallweed, "my wife's deaf."

"That accounts for your pitching your voice so high. But as she ain't here; just pitch it an octave or two lower, will you, and I'll not only be obliged to you, but it'll do you more credit," says Mr. Bucket. "This other gentleman is in the preaching line, I think?"

"Name of Chadband," Mr. Smallweed puts in, speaking henceforth in a much lower key.

"Once had a friend and brother serjeant of the same name," says Mr. Bucket, offering his hand, "and consequently feel a liking for it. Mrs. Chadband, no doubt?"

"And Mrs. Snagsby," Mr. Smallweed introduces.

"Husband a law-stationer and a friend of my own," says Mr. Bucket. "Love him like a brother! Now, what's up?"

"Do you mean what business have we come upon?" Mr. Smallweed asks, a little dashed by the suddenness of this turn.

"Ah! You know what I mean. Let us hear what it's all about in presence of Sir Leicester Dedlock, Baronet. Come."

Mr. Smallweed, beckoning Mr. Chadband, takes a moment's counsel with him in a whisper. Mr. Chadband, expressing a considerable amount of oil from the pores of his forehead and the palms of his hands, says aloud, "Yes. You first!" and retires to his former place.

"I was the client and friend of Mr. Tulkinghorn," pipes Grandfather Smallweed then; "I did business with him. I was useful to him, and he was useful to me. Krook, dead and gone, was my brother-in-law. He was own brother to a brimstone magpie—leastways Mrs. Smallweed. I come into Krook's property. I examined all his papers and all his effects. They was all dug out under my eyes. There was a bundle of letters belonging to a dead and gone lodger as was hid away at the back of a shelf in the side of Lady Jane's bed—his cat's bed. He hid all manner of things away, everywheres. Mr. Tulkinghorn wanted 'em and got 'em, but I looked 'em over first. I'm a man of business, and I took a squint at 'em. They was letters from the lodger's sweetheart, and she signed Honoria. Dear me, that's not a common name, Honoria, is it? There's no lady in this house that signs Honoria is there? Oh, no, I don't think so! Oh, no, I don't think so! And not in the same hand, perhaps? Oh, no, I don't think so!"

Here Mr. Smallweed, seized with a fit of coughing in the midst of his triumph, breaks off to ejaculate, "Oh, dear me! Oh, Lord! I'm shaken all to pieces!"

"Now, when you're ready," says Mr. Bucket after awaiting his recovery, "to come to anything that concerns Sir Leicester Dedlock, Baronet, here the gentleman sits, you know."

"Haven't I come to it, Mr. Bucket?" cries Grandfather Smallweed. "Isn't the gentleman concerned yet? Not with Captain Hawdon, and his ever affectionate Honoria, and their child into the bargain? Come, then, I want to know where those letters are. That concerns me, if it don't concern Sir Leicester Dedlock. I will know where they are. I won't have 'em disappear so quietly. I handed 'em over to my friend and solicitor, Mr. Tulkinghorn, not to anybody else."

"Why, he paid you for them, you know, and handsome too," says Mr. Bucket.

"I don't care for that. I want to know who's got 'em. And I tell you what we want—what we all here want, Mr. Bucket. We want more painstaking and search-making into this murder. We know where the interest and the motive was, and you have not done enough. If George the vagabond dragoon had any hand in it, he was only an accomplice, and was set on. You know what I mean as well as any man."

"Now I tell you what," says Mr. Bucket, instantaneously altering his manner, coming close to him, and communicating an extraordinary fascination to the forefinger, "I am damned if I am a-going to have my case spoilt, or interfered with, or anticipated by so much as half a second of time by any human being in creation. YOU want more painstaking and search-making! YOU do? Do you see this hand, and do you think that I don't know the right time to stretch it out and put it on the arm that fired that shot?"

Such is the dread power of the man, and so terribly evident it is that he makes no idle boast, that Mr. Smallweed begins to apologize. Mr. Bucket, dismissing his sudden anger, checks him.

"The advice I give you is, don't you trouble your head about the murder. That's my affair. You keep half an eye on the newspapers, and I shouldn't wonder if you was to read something about it before long, if you look sharp. I know my business, and that's all I've got to say to you on that subject. Now about those letters. You want to know who's got 'em. I don't mind telling you. I have got 'em. Is that the packet?"

Mr. Smallweed looks, with greedy eyes, at the little bundle Mr. Bucket produces from a mysterious part of his coat, and identifies it as the same.

"What have you got to say next?" asks Mr. Bucket. "Now, don't open your mouth too wide, because you don't look handsome when you do it."

"I want five hundred pound."

"No, you don't; you mean fifty," says Mr. Bucket humorously.

It appears, however, that Mr. Smallweed means five hundred.

"That is, I am deputed by Sir Leicester Dedlock, Baronet, to consider (without admitting or promising anything) this bit of business," says Mr. Bucket—Sir Leicester mechanically bows his head—"and you ask me to consider a proposal of five hundred pounds. Why, it's an unreasonable proposal! Two fifty would be bad enough, but better than that. Hadn't you better say two fifty?"

Mr. Smallweed is quite clear that he had better not.

"Then," says Mr. Bucket, "let's hear Mr. Chadband. Lord! Many a time I've heard my old fellow-serjeant of that name; and a moderate man he was in all respects, as ever I come across!"

Thus invited, Mr. Chadband steps forth, and after a little sleek smiling and a little oil-grinding with the palms of his hands, delivers himself as follows, "My friends, we are now—Rachael, my wife, and I—in the mansions of the rich and great. Why are we now in the mansions of the rich and great, my friends? Is it because we are invited? Because we are bidden to feast with them, because we are bidden to rejoice with them, because we are bidden to play the lute with them, because we are bidden to dance with them? No. Then why are we here, my friends? Air we in possession of a sinful secret, and do we require corn, and wine, and oil, or what is much the same thing, money, for the keeping thereof? Probably so, my friends."

"You're a man of business, you are," returns Mr. Bucket, very attentive, "and consequently you're going on to mention what the nature of your secret is. You are right. You couldn't do better."

"Let us then, my brother, in a spirit of love," says Mr. Chadband with a cunning eye, "proceed unto it. Rachael, my wife, advance!"

Mrs. Chadband, more than ready, so advances as to jostle her husband into the background and confronts Mr. Bucket with a hard, frowning smile.

"Since you want to know what we know," says she, "I'll tell you. I helped to bring up Miss Hawdon, her ladyship's daughter. I was in the service of her ladyship's sister, who was very sensitive to the disgrace her ladyship brought upon her, and gave out, even to her ladyship, that the child was dead—she WAS very nearly so—when she was born. But she's alive, and I know her." With these words, and a laugh, and laying a bitter stress on the word "ladyship," Mrs. Chadband folds her arms and looks implacably at Mr. Bucket.

"I suppose now," returns that officer, "YOU will be expecting a twenty-pound note or a present of about that figure?"

Mrs. Chadband merely laughs and contemptuously tells him he can "offer" twenty pence.

"My friend the law-stationer's good lady, over there," says Mr. Bucket, luring Mrs. Snagsby forward with the finger. "What may YOUR game be, ma'am?"

Mrs. Snagsby is at first prevented, by tears and lamentations, from stating the nature of her game, but by degrees it confusedly comes to light that she is a woman overwhelmed with injuries and wrongs, whom Mr. Snagsby has habitually deceived, abandoned, and sought to keep in darkness, and whose chief comfort, under her afflictions, has been the sympathy of the late Mr. Tulkinghorn, who showed so much commiseration for her on one occasion of his calling in Cook's Court in the absence of her perjured husband that she has of late habitually carried to him all her woes. Everybody it appears, the present company excepted, has plotted against Mrs. Snagsby's peace. There is Mr. Guppy, clerk to Kenge and Carboy, who was at first as open as the sun at noon, but who suddenly shut up as close as midnight, under the influence—no doubt—of Mr. Snagsby's suborning and tampering. There is Mr. Weevle, friend of Mr. Guppy, who lived mysteriously up a court, owing to the like coherent causes. There was Krook, deceased; there was Nimrod, deceased; and there was Jo, deceased; and they were "all in it." In what, Mrs. Snagsby does not with particularity express, but she knows that Jo was Mr. Snagsby's son, "as well as if a trumpet had spoken it," and she followed Mr. Snagsby when he went on his last visit to the boy, and if he was not his son why did he go? The one occupation of her life has been, for some time back, to follow Mr. Snagsby to and fro, and up and down, and to piece suspicious circumstances together—and every circumstance that has happened has been most suspicious; and in this way she has pursued her object of detecting and confounding her false husband, night and day. Thus did it come to pass that she brought the Chadbands and Mr. Tulkinghorn together, and conferred with Mr. Tulkinghorn on the change in Mr. Guppy, and helped to turn up the circumstances in which the present company are interested, casually, by the wayside, being still and ever on the great high road that is to terminate in Mr. Snagsby's full exposure and a matrimonial separation. All this, Mrs. Snagsby, as an injured woman, and the friend of Mrs. Chadband, and the follower of Mr. Chadband, and the mourner of the late Mr. Tulkinghorn, is here to certify under the seal of confidence, with every possible confusion and involvement possible and impossible, having no pecuniary motive whatever, no scheme or project but the one mentioned, and bringing here, and taking everywhere, her own dense atmosphere of dust, arising from the ceaseless working of her mill of jealousy.

While this exordium is in hand—and it takes some time—Mr. Bucket, who has seen through the transparency of Mrs. Snagsby's vinegar at a glance, confers with his familiar demon and bestows his shrewd attention on the Chadbands and Mr. Smallweed. Sir Leicester Dedlock remains immovable, with the same icy surface upon him, except that he once or twice looks towards Mr. Bucket, as relying on that officer alone of all mankind.

"Very good," says Mr. Bucket. "Now I understand you, you know, and being deputed by Sir Leicester Dedlock, Baronet, to look into this little matter," again Sir Leicester mechanically bows in confirmation of the statement, "can give it my fair and full attention. Now I won't allude to conspiring to extort money or anything of that sort, because we are men and women of the world here, and our object is to make things pleasant. But I tell you what I DO wonder at; I am surprised that you should think of making a noise below in the hall. It was so opposed to your interests. That's what I look at."

"We wanted to get in," pleads Mr. Smallweed.

"Why, of course you wanted to get in," Mr. Bucket asserts with cheerfulness; "but for a old gentleman at your time of life—what I call truly venerable, mind you!—with his wits sharpened, as I have no doubt they are, by the loss of the use of his limbs, which occasions all his animation to mount up into his head, not to consider that if he don't keep such a business as the present as close as possible it can't be worth a mag to him, is so curious! You see your temper got the better of you; that's where you lost ground," says Mr. Bucket in an argumentative and friendly way.

"I only said I wouldn't go without one of the servants came up to Sir Leicester Dedlock," returns Mr. Smallweed.

"That's it! That's where your temper got the better of you. Now, you keep it under another time and you'll make money by it. Shall I ring for them to carry you down?"

"When are we to hear more of this?" Mrs. Chadband sternly demands.

"Bless your heart for a true woman! Always curious, your delightful sex is!" replies Mr. Bucket with gallantry. "I shall have the pleasure of giving you a call to-morrow or next day—not forgetting Mr. Smallweed and his proposal of two fifty."

"Five hundred!" exclaims Mr. Smallweed.

"All right! Nominally five hundred." Mr. Bucket has his hand on the bell-rope. "SHALL I wish you good day for the present on the part of myself and the gentleman of the house?" he asks in an insinuating tone.

Nobody having the hardihood to object to his doing so, he does it, and the party retire as they came up. Mr. Bucket follows them to the door, and returning, says with an air of serious business, "Sir Leicester Dedlock, Baronet, it's for you to consider whether or not to buy this up. I should recommend, on the whole, it's being bought up myself; and I think it may be bought pretty cheap. You see, that little pickled cowcumber of a Mrs. Snagsby has been used by all sides of the speculation and has done a deal more harm in bringing odds and ends together than if she had meant it. Mr. Tulkinghorn, deceased, he held all these horses in his hand and could have drove 'em his own way, I haven't a doubt; but he was fetched off the box head-foremost, and now they have got their legs over the traces, and are all dragging and pulling their own ways. So it is, and such is life. The cat's away, and the mice they play; the frost breaks up, and the water runs. Now, with regard to the party to be apprehended."

Sir Leicester seems to wake, though his eyes have been wide open, and he looks intently at Mr. Bucket as Mr. Bucket refers to his watch.

"The party to be apprehended is now in this house," proceeds Mr. Bucket, putting up his watch with a steady hand and with rising spirits, "and I'm about to take her into custody in your presence. Sir Leicester Dedlock, Baronet, don't you say a word nor yet stir. There'll be no noise and no disturbance at all. I'll come back in the course of the evening, if agreeable to you, and endeavour to meet your wishes respecting this unfortunate family matter and the nobbiest way of keeping it quiet. Now, Sir Leicester Dedlock, Baronet, don't you be nervous on account of the apprehension at present coming off.

You shall see the whole case clear, from first to last."

Mr. Bucket rings, goes to the door, briefly whispers Mercury, shuts the door, and stands behind it with his arms folded. After a suspense of a minute or two the door slowly opens and a Frenchwoman enters. Mademoiselle Hortense.

The moment she is in the room Mr. Bucket claps the door to and puts his back against it. The suddenness of the noise occasions her to turn, and then for the first time she sees Sir Leicester Dedlock in his chair.

"I ask you pardon," she mutters hurriedly. "They tell me there was no one here."

Her step towards the door brings her front to front with Mr. Bucket. Suddenly a spasm shoots across her face and she turns deadly pale.

"This is my lodger, Sir Leicester Dedlock," says Mr. Bucket, nodding at her. "This foreign young woman has been my lodger for some weeks back."

"What do Sir Leicester care for that, you think, my angel?" returns mademoiselle in a jocular strain.

"Why, my angel," returns Mr. Bucket, "we shall see."

Mademoiselle Hortense eyes him with a scowl upon her tight face, which gradually changes into a smile of scorn, "You are very mysterieuse. Are you drunk?"

"Tolerable sober, my angel," returns Mr. Bucket.

"I come from arriving at this so detestable house with your wife. Your wife have left me since some minutes. They tell me downstairs that your wife is here. I come here, and your wife is not here. What is the intention of this fool's play, say then?" mademoiselle demands, with her arms composedly crossed, but with something in her dark cheek beating like a clock.

Mr. Bucket merely shakes the finger at her.

"Ah, my God, you are an unhappy idiot!" cries mademoiselle with a toss of her head and a laugh. "Leave me to pass downstairs, great pig." With a stamp of her foot and a menace.

"Now, mademoiselle," says Mr. Bucket in a cool determined way, "you go and sit down upon that sofy."

"I will not sit down upon nothing," she replies with a shower of nods.

"Now, mademoiselle," repeats Mr. Bucket, making no demonstration except with the finger, "you sit down upon that sofy."

"Why?"

"Because I take you into custody on a charge of murder, and you don't need to be told it. Now, I want to be polite to one of your sex and a foreigner if I can. If I can't, I must be rough, and there's rougher ones outside. What I am to be depends on you. So I recommend you, as a friend, afore another half a blessed moment has passed over your head, to go and sit down upon that sofy."

Mademoiselle complies, saying in a concentrated voice while that something in her cheek beats fast and hard, "You are a devil."

"Now, you see," Mr. Bucket proceeds approvingly, "you're comfortable and conducting yourself as I should expect a foreign young woman of your sense to do. So I'll give you a piece of advice, and it's this, don't you talk too much. You're not expected to say anything here, and you can't keep too quiet a tongue in your head. In short, the less you PARLAY, the better, you know." Mr. Bucket is very complacent over this French explanation.

Mademoiselle, with that tigerish expansion of the mouth and her black eyes darting fire upon him, sits upright on the sofa in a rigid state, with her hands clenched—and her feet too, one might suppose—muttering, "Oh, you Bucket, you are a devil!"

"Now, Sir Leicester Dedlock, Baronet," says Mr. Bucket, and from this time forth the finger never rests, "this young woman, my lodger, was her ladyship's maid at the time I have mentioned to you; and this young woman, besides being extraordinary vehement and passionate against her ladyship after being discharged—"

"Lie!" cries mademoiselle. "I discharge myself."

"Now, why don't you take my advice?" returns Mr. Bucket in an impressive, almost in an imploring, tone. "I'm surprised at the indiscreetness you commit. You'll say something that'll be used against you, you know. You're sure to come to it. Never you mind what I say till it's given in evidence. It is not addressed to you."

"Discharge, too," cries mademoiselle furiously, "by her ladyship! Eh, my faith, a pretty ladyship! Why, I r-r-r-ruin my character by remaining with a ladyship so infame!"

"Upon my soul I wonder at you!" Mr. Bucket remonstrates. "I thought the French were a polite nation, I did, really. Yet to hear a female going on like that before Sir Leicester Dedlock, Baronet!"

"He is a poor abused!" cries mademoiselle. "I spit upon his house, upon his name, upon his imbecility," all of which she makes the carpet represent. "Oh, that he is a great man! Oh, yes, superb! Oh, heaven! Bah!"

"Well, Sir Leicester Dedlock," proceeds Mr. Bucket, "this intemperate foreigner also angrily took it into her head that she had established a claim upon Mr. Tulkinghorn, deceased, by attending on the occasion I told you of at his chambers, though she was liberally paid for her time and trouble."

"Lie!" cries mademoiselle. "I ref-use his money all togezzer."

"If you WILL PARLAY, you know," says Mr. Bucket parenthetically, "you must take the consequences. Now, whether she became my lodger, Sir Leicester Dedlock, with any deliberate intention then of doing this deed and blinding me, I give no opinion on; but she lived in my house in that capacity at the time that she was hovering about the chambers of the deceased Mr. Tulkinghorn with a view to a wrangle, and likewise persecuting and half frightening the life out of an unfortunate stationer."

"Lie!" cries mademoiselle. "All lie!"

"The murder was committed, Sir Leicester Dedlock, Baronet, and you know under what circumstances. Now, I beg of you to follow me close with your attention for a minute or two. I was sent for, and the case was entrusted to me. I examined the place, and the body, and the papers, and everything. From information I received (from a clerk in the same house) I took George into custody as having been seen hanging about there on the night, and at very nigh the time of the murder, also as having been overheard in high words with the deceased on former occasions—even threatening him, as the witness made out. If you ask me, Sir Leicester Dedlock, whether from the first I believed George to be the murderer, I tell you candidly no, but he might be, notwithstanding, and there was enough against him to make it my duty to take him and get him kept under remand. Now, observe!"

As Mr. Bucket bends forward in some excitement—for him—and inaugurates what he is going to say with one ghostly beat of his forefinger in the air, Mademoiselle Hortense fixes her black eyes upon him with a dark frown and sets her dry lips closely and firmly together.

"I went home, Sir Leicester Dedlock, Baronet, at night and found this young woman having supper with my wife, Mrs. Bucket. She had made a mighty show of being fond of Mrs. Bucket from her first offering herself as our lodger, but that night she made more than ever—in fact, overdid it. Likewise she overdid her respect, and all that, for the lamented memory of the deceased Mr. Tulkinghorn. By the living Lord it flashed upon me, as I sat opposite to her at the table and saw her with a knife in her hand, that she had done it!"

Mademoiselle is hardly audible in straining through her teeth and lips the words, "You are a devil."

"Now where," pursues Mr. Bucket, "had she been on the night of the murder? She had been to the theayter. (She really was there, I have since found, both before the deed and after it.) I knew I had an artful customer to deal with and that proof would be very difficult; and I laid a trap for her—such a trap as I never laid yet, and such a venture as I never made yet. I worked it out in my mind while I was talking to her at supper. When I went upstairs to bed, our house being small and this young woman's ears sharp, I stuffed the sheet into Mrs. Bucket's mouth that she shouldn't say a word of surprise and told her all about it. My dear, don't you give your mind to that again, or I shall link your feet together at the ankles." Mr. Bucket, breaking off, has made a noiseless descent upon mademoiselle and laid his heavy hand upon her shoulder.

"What is the matter with you now?" she asks him.

"Don't you think any more," returns Mr. Bucket with admonitory finger, "of throwing yourself out of window. That's what's the matter with me. Come! Just take my arm. You needn't get up; I'll sit down by you. Now take my arm, will you? I'm a married man, you know; you're acquainted with my wife. Just take my arm."

Vainly endeavouring to moisten those dry lips, with a painful sound she struggles with herself and complies.

"Now we're all right again. Sir Leicester Dedlock, Baronet, this case could never have been the case it is but for Mrs. Bucket, who is a woman in fifty thousand—in a hundred and fifty thousand! To throw this young woman off her guard, I have never set foot in our house since, though I've communicated with Mrs. Bucket in the baker's loaves and in the milk as often as required. My whispered words to Mrs. Bucket when she had the sheet in her mouth were, 'My dear, can you throw her off continually with natural accounts of my suspicions against George, and this, and that, and t'other? Can you do without rest and keep watch upon her night and day? Can you undertake to say, 'She shall do nothing without my knowledge, she shall be my prisoner without suspecting it, she shall no more escape from me than from death, and her life shall be my life, and her soul my soul, till I have got her, if she did this murder?' Mrs. Bucket says to me, as well as she could speak on account of the sheet, 'Bucket, I can!' And she has acted up to it glorious!"

"Lies!" mademoiselle interposes. "All lies, my friend!"

"Sir Leicester Dedlock, Baronet, how did my calculations come out under these circumstances? When I calculated that this impetuous young woman would overdo it in new directions, was I wrong or right? I was right. What does she try to do? Don't let it give you a turn? To throw the murder on her ladyship."

Sir Leicester rises from his chair and staggers down again.

"And she got encouragement in it from hearing that I was always here, which was done a-purpose. Now, open that pocket-book of mine, Sir Leicester Dedlock, if I may take the liberty of throwing it towards you, and look at the letters sent to me, each with the two words 'Lady Dedlock' in it. Open the one directed to yourself, which I stopped this very morning, and read the three words 'Lady Dedlock, Murderess' in it. These letters have been falling about like a shower of lady-birds. What do you say now to Mrs. Bucket, from her spy-place having seen them all 'written by this young woman? What do you say to Mrs. Bucket having, within this half-hour, secured the corresponding ink and paper, fellow half-sheets and what not? What do you say to Mrs. Bucket having watched the posting of 'em every one by this young woman, Sir Leicester Dedlock, Baronet?" Mr. Bucket asks, triumphant in his admiration of his lady's genius.

Two things are especially observable as Mr. Bucket proceeds to a conclusion. First, that he seems imperceptibly to establish a dreadful right of property in mademoiselle. Secondly, that the very atmosphere she breathes seems to narrow and contract about her as if a close net or a pall were being drawn nearer and yet nearer around her breathless figure.

"There is no doubt that her ladyship was on the spot at the eventful period," says Mr. Bucket, "and my foreign friend here saw her, I believe, from the upper part of the staircase. Her ladyship and George and my foreign friend were all pretty close on one another's heels. But that don't signify any more, so I'll not go into it. I found the wadding of the pistol with which the deceased Mr. Tulkinghorn was shot. It was a bit of the printed description of your house at Chesney Wold. Not much in that, you'll say, Sir Leicester Dedlock, Baronet. No. But when my foreign friend here is so thoroughly off her guard as to think it a safe time to tear up the rest of that leaf, and when Mrs. Bucket puts the pieces together and finds the wadding wanting, it begins to look like Queer Street."

"These are very long lies," mademoiselle interposes. "You prose great deal. Is it that you have almost all finished, or are you speaking always?"

"Sir Leicester Dedlock, Baronet," proceeds Mr. Bucket, who delights in a full title and does violence to himself when he dispenses with any fragment of it, "the last point in the case which I am now going to mention shows the necessity of patience in our business, and never doing a thing in a hurry. I watched this young woman yesterday without her knowledge when she was looking at the funeral, in company with my wife, who planned to take her there; and I had so much to convict her, and I saw such an expression in her face, and my mind so rose against her malice towards her ladyship, and the time was altogether such a time for bringing down what you may call retribution upon her, that if I had been a younger hand with less experience, I should have taken her, certain. Equally, last night, when her ladyship, as is so universally admired I am sure, come home looking—why, Lord, a man might almost say like Venus rising from the ocean—it was so unpleasant and inconsistent to think of her being charged with a murder of which she was innocent that I felt quite to want to put an end to the job. What should I have lost? Sir Leicester Dedlock, Baronet, I should have lost the weapon. My prisoner here proposed to Mrs. Bucket, after the departure of the funeral, that they should go per bus a little ways into the country and take tea at a very decent house of entertainment. Now, near that house of entertainment there's a piece of water. At tea, my prisoner got up to fetch her pocket handkercher from the bedroom where the bonnets was; she was rather a long time gone and came back a little out of wind. As soon as they came home this was reported to me by Mrs. Bucket, along with her observations and suspicions. I had the piece of water dragged by moonlight, in presence of a couple of our men, and the pocket pistol was brought up before it had been there half-a-dozen hours. Now, my dear, put your arm a little further through mine, and hold it steady, and I shan't hurt you!"

In a trice Mr. Bucket snaps a handcuff on her wrist. "That's one," says Mr. Bucket. "Now the other, darling. Two, and all told!"

He rises; she rises too. "Where," she asks him, darkening her large eyes until their drooping lids almost conceal them—and yet they stare, "where is your false, your treacherous, and cursed wife?"

"She's gone forrard to the Police Office," returns Mr. Bucket. "You'll see her there, my dear."

"I would like to kiss her!" exclaims Mademoiselle Hortense, panting tigress-like.

"You'd bite her, I suspect," says Mr. Bucket.

"I would!" making her eyes very large. "I would love to tear her limb from limb."

"Bless you, darling," says Mr. Bucket with the greatest composure, "I'm fully prepared to hear that. Your sex have such a surprising animosity against one another when you do differ. You don't mind me half so much, do you?"

"No. Though you are a devil still."

"Angel and devil by turns, eh?" cries Mr. Bucket. "But I am in my regular employment, you must consider. Let me put your shawl tidy. I've been lady's maid to a good many before now. Anything wanting to the bonnet? There's a cab at the door."

Mademoiselle Hortense, casting an indignant eye at the glass, shakes herself perfectly neat in one shake and looks, to do her justice, uncommonly genteel.

"Listen then, my angel," says she after several sarcastic nods. "You are very spiritual. But can you restore him back to life?"

Mr. Bucket answers, "Not exactly."

"That is droll. Listen yet one time. You are very spiritual. Can you make a honourable lady of her?"

"Don't be so malicious," says Mr. Bucket.

"Or a haughty gentleman of HIM?" cries mademoiselle, referring to Sir Leicester with ineffable disdain. "Eh! Oh, then regard him! The poor infant! Ha! Ha! Ha!"

"Come, come, why this is worse PARLAYING than the other," says Mr. Bucket. "Come along!"

"You cannot do these things? Then you can do as you please with me. It is but the death, it is all the same. Let us go, my angel. Adieu, you old man, grey. I pity you, and I despise you!"

With these last words she snaps her teeth together as if her mouth closed with a spring. It is impossible to describe how Mr. Bucket gets her out, but he accomplishes that feat in a manner so peculiar to himself, enfolding and pervading her like a cloud, and hovering away with her as if he were a homely Jupiter and she the object of his affections.

Sir Leicester, left alone, remains in the same attitude, as though he were still listening and his attention were still occupied. At length he gazes round the empty room, and finding it deserted, rises unsteadily to his feet, pushes back his chair, and walks a few steps, supporting himself by the table. Then he stops, and with more of those inarticulate sounds, lifts up his eyes and seems to stare at something.

Heaven knows what he sees. The green, green woods of Chesney Wold, the noble house, the pictures of his forefathers, strangers defacing them, officers of police coarsely handling his most precious heirlooms, thousands of fingers pointing at him, thousands of faces sneering at him. But if such shadows flit before him to his bewilderment, there is one other shadow which he can name with something like distinctness even yet and to which alone he addresses his tearing of his white hair and his extended arms.

It is she in association with whom, saving that she has been for years a main fibre of the root of his dignity and pride, he has never had a selfish thought. It is she whom he has loved, admired, honoured, and set up for the world to respect. It is she who, at the core of all the constrained formalities and conventionalities of his life, has been a stock of living tenderness and love, susceptible as nothing else is of being struck with the agony he feels. He sees her, almost to the exclusion of himself, and cannot bear to look upon her cast down from the high place she has graced so well.

And even to the point of his sinking on the ground, oblivious of his suffering, he can yet pronounce her name with something like distinctness in the midst of those intrusive sounds, and in a tone of mourning and compassion rather than reproach.

CHAPTER LV
FLIGHT

Inspector Bucket of the Detective has not yet struck his great blow, as just now chronicled, but is yet refreshing himself with sleep preparatory to his field-day, when through the night and along the freezing wintry roads a chaise and pair comes out of Lincolnshire, making its way towards London.

Railroads shall soon traverse all this country, and with a rattle and a glare the engine and train shall shoot like a meteor over the wide night-landscape, turning the moon paler; but as yet such things are non-existent in these parts, though not wholly unexpected. Preparations are afoot, measurements are made, ground is staked out. Bridges are begun, and their not yet united piers desolately look at one another over roads and streams like brick and mortar couples with an obstacle to their union; fragments of embankments are thrown up and left as precipices with torrents of rusty carts and barrows tumbling over them; tripods of tall poles appear on hilltops, where there are rumours of tunnels; everything looks chaotic and abandoned in full hopelessness. Along the freezing roads, and through the night, the post-chaise makes its way without a railroad on its mind.

Mrs. Rouncewell, so many years housekeeper at Chesney Wold, sits within the chaise; and by her side sits Mrs. Bagnet with her grey cloak and umbrella. The old girl would prefer the bar in front, as being exposed to the weather and a primitive sort of perch more in accordance with her usual course of travelling, but Mrs. Rouncewell is too thoughtful of her comfort to admit of her proposing it. The old lady cannot make enough of the old girl. She sits, in her stately manner, holding her hand, and regardless of its roughness, puts it often to her lips. "You are a mother, my dear soul," says she many times, "and you found out my George's mother!"

"Why, George," returns Mrs. Bagnet, "was always free with me, ma'am, and when he said at our house to my Woolwich that of all the things my Woolwich could have to think of when he grew to be a man, the comfortablest would be that he had never brought a sorrowful line into his mother's face or turned a hair of her head grey, then I felt sure, from his way, that something fresh had brought his own mother into his mind. I had often known him say to me, in past times, that he had behaved bad to her."

"Never, my dear!" returns Mrs. Rouncewell, bursting into tears. "My blessing on him, never! He was always fond of me, and loving to me, was my George! But he had a bold spirit, and he ran a little wild and went for a soldier. And I know he waited at first, in letting us know about himself, till he should rise to be an officer; and when he didn't rise, I know he considered himself beneath us, and wouldn't be a disgrace to us. For he had a lion heart, had my George, always from a baby!"

The old lady's hands stray about her as of yore, while she recalls, all in a tremble, what a likely lad, what a fine lad, what a gay good-humoured clever lad he was; how they all took to him down at Chesney Wold; how Sir Leicester took to him when he was a young gentleman; how the dogs took to him; how even the people who had been angry with him forgave him the moment he was gone, poor boy. And now to see him after all, and in a prison too! And the broad stomacher heaves, and the quaint upright old-fashioned figure bends under its load of affectionate distress.

Mrs. Bagnet, with the instinctive skill of a good warm heart, leaves the old housekeeper to her emotions for a little while—not without passing the back of her hand across her own motherly eyes—and presently chirps up in her cheery manner, "So I says to George when I goes to call him in to tea (he pretended to be smoking his pipe outside), 'What ails you this afternoon, George, for gracious sake? I have seen all sorts, and I have seen you pretty often in season and out of season, abroad and at home, and I never see you so melancholy penitent.' 'Why, Mrs. Bagnet,' says George, 'it's because I AM melancholy and penitent both, this afternoon, that you see me so.' 'What have you done, old fellow?' I says. 'Why, Mrs. Bagnet,' says George, shaking his head, 'what I have done has been done this many a long year, and is best not tried to be undone now. If I ever get to heaven it won't be for being a good son to a widowed mother; I say no more.' Now, ma'am, when George says to me that it's best not tried to be undone now, I have my thoughts as I have often had before, and I draw it out of George how he comes to have such things on him that afternoon. Then George tells me that he has seen by chance, at the lawyer's office, a fine old lady that has brought his mother plain before him, and he runs on about that old lady till he quite forgets himself and paints her picture to me as she used to be, years upon years back. So I says to George when he has done, who is this old lady he has seen? And George tells me it's Mrs. Rouncewell, housekeeper for more than half a century to the Dedlock family down at Chesney Wold in Lincolnshire. George has frequently told me before that he's a Lincolnshire man, and I says to my old Lignum that night, 'Lignum, that's his mother for five and for-ty pound!'"

All this Mrs. Bagnet now relates for the twentieth time at least within the last four hours. Trilling it out like a kind of bird, with a pretty high note, that it may be audible to the old lady above the hum of the wheels.

"Bless you, and thank you," says Mrs. Rouncewell. "Bless you, and thank you, my worthy soul!"

"Dear heart!" cries Mrs. Bagnet in the most natural manner. "No thanks to me, I am sure. Thanks to yourself, ma'am, for being so ready to pay 'em! And mind once more, ma'am, what you had best do on finding George to be your own son is to make him—for your sake—have every sort of help to put himself in the right and clear himself of a charge of which he is as innocent as you or me. It won't do to have truth and justice on his side; he must have law and lawyers," exclaims the old girl, apparently persuaded that the latter form a separate establishment and have dissolved partnership with truth and justice for ever and a day.

"He shall have," says Mrs. Rouncewell, "all the help that can be got for him in the world, my dear. I will spend all I have, and thankfully, to procure it. Sir Leicester will do his best, the whole family will do their best. I—I know something, my dear; and will make my own appeal, as his mother parted from him all these years, and finding him in a jail at last."

The extreme disquietude of the old housekeeper's manner in saying this, her broken words, and her wringing of her hands make a powerful impression on Mrs. Bagnet and would astonish her but that she refers them all to her sorrow for her son's condition. And yet Mrs. Bagnet wonders too why Mrs. Rouncewell should murmur so distractedly, "My Lady, my Lady, my Lady!" over and over again.

The frosty night wears away, and the dawn breaks, and the post-chaise comes rolling on through the early mist like the ghost of a chaise departed. It has plenty of spectral company in ghosts of trees and hedges, slowly vanishing and giving place to the realities of day. London reached, the travellers alight, the old housekeeper in great tribulation and confusion, Mrs. Bagnet quite fresh and collected—as she would be if her next point, with no new equipage and outfit, were the Cape of Good Hope, the Island of Ascension, Hong Kong, or any other military station.

But when they set out for the prison where the trooper is confined, the old lady has managed to draw about her, with her lavender-coloured dress, much of the staid calmness which is its usual accompaniment. A wonderfully grave, precise, and handsome piece of old china she looks, though her heart beats fast and her stomacher is ruffled more than even the remembrance of this wayward son has ruffled it these many years.

Approaching the cell, they find the door opening and a warder in the act of coming out. The old girl promptly makes a sign of entreaty to him to say nothing; assenting with a nod, he suffers them to enter as he shuts the door.

So George, who is writing at his table, supposing himself to be alone, does not raise his eyes, but remains absorbed. The old housekeeper looks at him, and those wandering hands of hers are quite enough for Mrs. Bagnet's confirmation, even if she could see the mother and the son together, knowing what she knows, and doubt their relationship.

Not a rustle of the housekeeper's dress, not a gesture, not a word betrays her. She stands looking at him as he writes on, all unconscious, and only her fluttering hands give utterance to her emotions. But they are very eloquent, very, very eloquent. Mrs. Bagnet understands them. They speak of gratitude, of joy, of grief, of hope; of inextinguishable affection, cherished with no return since this stalwart man was a stripling; of a better son loved less, and this son loved so fondly and so proudly; and they speak in such touching language that Mrs. Bagnet's eyes brim up with tears and they run glistening down her sun-brown face.

"George Rouncewell! Oh, my dear child, turn and look at me!"

The trooper starts up, clasps his mother round the neck, and falls down on his knees before her. Whether in a late repentance, whether in the first association that comes back upon him, he puts his hands together as a child does when it says its prayers, and raising them towards her breast, bows down his head, and cries.

"My George, my dearest son! Always my favourite, and my favourite still, where have you been these cruel years and years? Grown such a man too, grown such a fine strong man. Grown so like what I knew he must be, if it pleased God he was alive!"

She can ask, and he can answer, nothing connected for a time. All that time the old girl, turned away, leans one arm against the whitened wall, leans her honest forehead upon it, wipes her eyes with her serviceable grey cloak, and quite enjoys herself like the best of old girls as she is.

"Mother," says the trooper when they are more composed, "forgive me first of all, for I know my need of it."

Forgive him! She does it with all her heart and soul. She always has done it. She tells him how she has had it written in her will, these many years, that he was her beloved son George. She has never believed any ill of him, never. If she had died without this happiness—and she is an old woman now and can't look to live very long—she would have blessed him with her last breath, if she had had her senses, as her beloved son George.

"Mother, I have been an undutiful trouble to you, and I have my reward; but of late years I have had a kind of glimmering of a purpose in me too. When I left home I didn't care much, mother—I am afraid not a great deal—for leaving; and went away and 'listed, harum-scarum, making believe to think that I cared for nobody, no not I, and that nobody cared for me."

The trooper has dried his eyes and put away his handkerchief, but there is an extraordinary contrast between his habitual manner of expressing himself and carrying himself and the softened tone in which he speaks, interrupted occasionally by a half-stifled sob.

"So I wrote a line home, mother, as you too well know, to say I had 'listed under another name, and I went abroad. Abroad, at one time I thought I would write home next year, when I might be better off; and when that year was out, I thought I would write home next year, when I might be better off; and when that year was out again, perhaps I didn't think much about it. So on, from year to year, through a service of ten years, till I began to get older, and to ask myself why should I ever write."

"I don't find any fault, child—but not to ease my mind, George? Not a word to your loving mother, who was growing older too?"

This almost overturns the trooper afresh, but he sets himself up with a great, rough, sounding clearance of his throat.

"Heaven forgive me, mother, but I thought there would be small consolation then in hearing anything about me. There were you, respected and esteemed. There was my brother, as I read in chance North Country papers now and then, rising to be prosperous and famous. There was I a dragoon, roving, unsettled, not self-made like him, but self-unmade—all my earlier advantages thrown away, all my little learning unlearnt, nothing picked up but what unfitted me for most things that I could think of. What business had I to make myself known? After letting all that time go by me, what good could come of it? The worst was past with you, mother. I knew by that time (being a man) how you had mourned for me, and wept for me, and prayed for me; and the pain was over, or was softened down, and I was better in your mind as it was."

The old lady sorrowfully shakes her head, and taking one of his powerful hands, lays it lovingly upon her shoulder.

"No, I don't say that it was so, mother, but that I made it out to be so. I said just now, what good could come of it? Well, my dear mother, some good might have come of it to myself—and there was the meanness of it. You would have sought me out; you would have purchased my discharge; you would have taken me down to Chesney Wold; you would have brought me and my brother and my brother's family together; you would all have considered anxiously how to do something for me and set me up as a respectable civilian. But how could any of you feel sure of me when I couldn't so much as feel sure of myself? How could you help regarding as an incumbrance and a discredit to you an idle dragooning chap who was an incumbrance and a discredit to himself, excepting under discipline? How could I look my brother's children in the face and pretend to set them an example—I, the vagabond boy who had run away from home and been the grief and unhappiness of my mother's life? 'No, George.' Such were my words, mother, when I passed this in review before me: 'You have made your bed. Now, lie upon it.'"

Mrs. Rouncewell, drawing up her stately form, shakes her head at the old girl with a swelling pride upon her, as much as to say, "I told you so!" The old girl relieves her feelings and testifies her interest in the conversation by giving the trooper a great poke between the shoulders with her umbrella; this action she afterwards repeats, at intervals, in a species of affectionate lunacy, never failing, after the administration of each of these remonstrances, to resort to the whitened wall and the grey cloak again.

"This was the way I brought myself to think, mother, that my best amends was to lie upon that bed I had made, and die upon it. And I should have done it (though I have been to see you more than once down at Chesney Wold, when you little thought of me) but for my old comrade's wife here, who I find has been too many for me. But I thank her for it. I thank you for it, Mrs.

Bagnet, with all my heart and might."

To which Mrs. Bagnet responds with two pokes.

And now the old lady impresses upon her son George, her own dear recovered boy, her joy and pride, the light of her eyes, the happy close of her life, and every fond name she can think of, that he must be governed by the best advice obtainable by money and influence, that he must yield up his case to the greatest lawyers that can be got, that he must act in this serious plight as he shall be advised to act and must not be self-willed, however right, but must promise to think only of his poor old mother's anxiety and suffering until he is released, or he will break her heart.

"Mother, 'tis little enough to consent to," returns the trooper, stopping her with a kiss; "tell me what I shall do, and I'll make a late beginning and do it. Mrs. Bagnet, you'll take care of my mother, I know?"

A very hard poke from the old girl's umbrella.

"If you'll bring her acquainted with Mr. Jarndyce and Miss Summerson, she will find them of her way of thinking, and they will give her the best advice and assistance."

"And, George," says the old lady, "we must send with all haste for your brother. He is a sensible sound man as they tell me—out in the world beyond Chesney Wold, my dear, though I don't know much of it myself—and will be of great service."

"Mother," returns the trooper, "is it too soon to ask a favour?"

"Surely not, my dear."

"Then grant me this one great favour. Don't let my brother know."

"Not know what, my dear?"

"Not know of me. In fact, mother, I can't bear it; I can't make up my mind to it. He has proved himself so different from me and has done so much to raise himself while I've been soldiering that I haven't brass enough in my composition to see him in this place and under this charge. How could a man like him be expected to have any pleasure in such a discovery? It's impossible. No, keep my secret from him, mother; do me a greater kindness than I deserve and keep my secret from my brother, of all men."

"But not always, dear George?"

"Why, mother, perhaps not for good and all—though I may come to ask that too—but keep it now, I do entreat you. If it's ever broke to him that his rip of a brother has turned up, I could wish," says the trooper, shaking his head very doubtfully, "to break it myself and be governed as to advancing or retreating by the way in which he seems to take it."

As he evidently has a rooted feeling on this point, and as the depth of it is recognized in Mrs. Bagnet's face, his mother yields her implicit assent to what he asks. For this he thanks her kindly.

"In all other respects, my dear mother, I'll be as tractable and obedient as you can wish; on this one alone, I stand out. So now I am ready even for the lawyers. I have been drawing up," he glances at his writing on the table, "an exact account of what I knew of the deceased and how I came to be involved in this unfortunate affair. It's entered, plain and regular, like an orderly-book; not a word in it but what's wanted for the facts. I did intend to read it, straight on end, whensoever I was called upon to say anything in my defence. I hope I may be let to do it still; but I have no longer a will of my own in this case, and whatever is said or done, I give my promise not to have any."

Matters being brought to this so far satisfactory pass, and time being on the wane, Mrs. Bagnet proposes a departure. Again and again the old lady hangs upon her son's neck, and again and again the trooper holds her to his broad chest.

"Where are you going to take my mother, Mrs. Bagnet?"

"I am going to the town house, my dear, the family house. I have some business there that must be looked to directly," Mrs. Rouncewell answers.

"Will you see my mother safe there in a coach, Mrs. Bagnet? But of course I know you will. Why should I ask it!"

Why indeed, Mrs. Bagnet expresses with the umbrella.

"Take her, my old friend, and take my gratitude along with you. Kisses to Quebec and Malta, love to my godson, a hearty shake of the hand to Lignum, and this for yourself, and I wish it was ten thousand pound in gold, my dear!" So saying, the trooper puts his lips to the old girl's tanned forehead, and the door shuts upon him in his cell.

No entreaties on the part of the good old housekeeper will induce Mrs. Bagnet to retain the coach for her own conveyance home. Jumping out cheerfully at the door of the Dedlock mansion and handing Mrs. Rouncewell up the steps, the old girl shakes hands and trudges off, arriving soon afterwards in the bosom of the Bagnet family and falling to washing the greens as if nothing had happened.

My Lady is in that room in which she held her last conference with the murdered man, and is sitting where she sat that night, and is looking at the spot where he stood upon the hearth studying her so leisurely, when a tap comes at the door. Who is it? Mrs. Rouncewell. What has brought Mrs. Rouncewell to town so unexpectedly?

"Trouble, my Lady. Sad trouble. Oh, my Lady, may I beg a word with you?"

What new occurrence is it that makes this tranquil old woman tremble so? Far happier than her Lady, as her Lady has often thought, why does she falter in this manner and look at her with such strange mistrust?

"What is the matter? Sit down and take your breath."

"Oh, my Lady, my Lady. I have found my son—my youngest, who went away for a soldier so long ago. And he is in prison."

"For debt?"

"Oh, no, my Lady; I would have paid any debt, and joyful."

"For what is he in prison then?"

"Charged with a murder, my Lady, of which he is as innocent as—as I am. Accused of the murder of Mr. Tulkinghorn."

What does she mean by this look and this imploring gesture? Why does she come so close? What is the letter that she holds?

"Lady Dedlock, my dear Lady, my good Lady, my kind Lady! You must have a heart to feel for me, you must have a heart to forgive me. I was in this family before you were born. I am devoted to it. But think of my dear son wrongfully accused."

"I do not accuse him."

"No, my Lady, no. But others do, and he is in prison and in danger. Oh, Lady Dedlock, if you can say but a word to help to clear him, say it!"

What delusion can this be? What power does she suppose is in the person she petitions to avert this unjust suspicion, if it be unjust? Her Lady's handsome eyes regard her with astonishment, almost with fear.

"My Lady, I came away last night from Chesney Wold to find my son in my old age, and the step upon the Ghost's Walk was so constant and so solemn that I never heard the like in all these years. Night after night, as it has fallen dark, the sound has echoed through your rooms, but last night it was awfullest. And as it fell dark last night, my Lady, I got this letter."

"What letter is it?"

"Hush! Hush!" The housekeeper looks round and answers in a frightened whisper, "My Lady, I have not breathed a word of it, I don't believe what's written in it, I know it can't be true, I am sure and certain that it is not true. But my son is in danger, and you must have a heart to pity me. If you know of anything that is not known to others, if you have any suspicion, if you have any clue at all, and any reason for keeping it in your own breast, oh, my dear Lady, think of me, and conquer that reason, and let it be known! This is the most I consider possible. I know you are not a hard lady, but you go your own way always without help, and you are not familiar with your friends; and all who admire you—and all do—as a beautiful and elegant lady, know you to be one far away from themselves who can't be approached close. My Lady, you may have some proud or angry reasons for disdaining to utter something that you know; if so, pray, oh, pray, think of a faithful servant whose whole life has been passed in this family which she dearly loves, and relent, and help to clear my son! My Lady, my good Lady," the old housekeeper pleads with genuine simplicity, "I am so humble in my place and you are by nature so high and distant that you may not think what I feel for my child, but I feel so much that I have come here to make so bold as to beg and pray you not to be scornful of us if you can do us any right or justice at this fearful time!"

Lady Dedlock raises her without one word, until she takes the letter from her hand.

"Am I to read this?"

"When I am gone, my Lady, if you please, and then remembering the most that I consider possible."

"I know of nothing I can do. I know of nothing I reserve that can affect your son. I have never accused him."

"My Lady, you may pity him the more under a false accusation after reading the letter."

The old housekeeper leaves her with the letter in her hand. In truth she is not a hard lady naturally, and the time has been when the sight of the venerable figure suing to her with such strong earnestness would have moved her to great compassion. But so long accustomed to suppress emotion and keep down reality, so long schooled for her own purposes in that destructive school which shuts up the natural feelings of the heart like flies in amber and spreads one uniform and dreary gloss over the good and bad, the feeling and the unfeeling, the sensible and the senseless, she had subdued even her wonder until now.

She opens the letter. Spread out upon the paper is a printed account of the discovery of the body as it lay face downward on the floor, shot through the heart; and underneath is written her own name, with the word "murderess" attached.

It falls out of her hand. How long it may have lain upon the ground she knows not, but it lies where it fell when a servant stands before her announcing the young man of the name of Guppy. The words have probably been repeated several times, for they are ringing in her head before she begins to understand them.

"Let him come in!"

He comes in. Holding the letter in her hand, which she has taken from the floor, she tries to collect her thoughts. In the eyes of Mr. Guppy she is the same Lady Dedlock, holding the same prepared, proud, chilling state.

"Your ladyship may not be at first disposed to excuse this visit from one who has never been welcome to your ladyship"—which he don't complain of, for he is bound to confess that there never has been any particular reason on the face of things why he should be—"but I hope when I mention my motives to your ladyship you will not find fault with me," says Mr. Guppy.

"Do so."

"Thank your ladyship. I ought first to explain to your ladyship," Mr. Guppy sits on the edge of a chair and puts his hat on the carpet at his feet, "that Miss Summerson, whose image, as I formerly mentioned to your ladyship, was at one period of my life imprinted on my 'eart until erased by circumstances over which I had no control, communicated to me, after I had the pleasure of waiting on your ladyship last, that she particularly wished me to take no steps whatever in any manner at all relating to her. And Miss Summerson's wishes being to me a law (except as connected with circumstances over which I have no control), I consequently never expected to have the distinguished honour of waiting on your ladyship again."

And yet he is here now, Lady Dedlock moodily reminds him.

"And yet I am here now," Mr. Guppy admits. "My object being to communicate to your ladyship, under the seal of confidence, why I am here."

He cannot do so, she tells him, too plainly or too briefly. "Nor can I," Mr. Guppy returns with a sense of injury upon him, "too particularly request your ladyship to take particular notice that it's no personal affair of mine that brings me here. I have no interested views of my own to serve in coming here. If it was not for my promise to Miss Summerson and my keeping of it sacred—I, in point of fact, shouldn't have darkened these doors again, but should have seen 'em further first."

Mr. Guppy considers this a favourable moment for sticking up his hair with both hands.

"Your ladyship will remember when I mention it that the last time I was here I run against a party very eminent in our profession and whose loss we all deplore. That party certainly did from that time apply himself to cutting in against me in a way that I will call sharp practice, and did make it, at every turn and point, extremely difficult for me to be sure that I hadn't inadvertently led up to something contrary to Miss Summerson's wishes. Self-praise is no recommendation, but I may say for myself that I am not so bad a man of business neither."

Lady Dedlock looks at him in stern inquiry. Mr. Guppy immediately withdraws his eyes from her face and looks anywhere else.

"Indeed, it has been made so hard," he goes on, "to have any idea what that party was up to in combination with others that until the loss which we all deplore I was gravelled—an expression which your ladyship, moving in the higher circles, will be so good as to consider tantamount to knocked over. Small likewise—a name by which I refer to another party, a friend of mine that your ladyship is not acquainted with—got to be so close and double-faced that at times it wasn't easy to keep one's hands off his 'ead. However, what with the exertion of my humble abilities, and what with the help of a mutual friend by the name of Mr. Tony Weevle (who is of a high aristocratic turn and has your ladyship's portrait always hanging up in his room), I have now reasons for an apprehension as to which I come to put your ladyship upon your guard. First, will your ladyship allow me to ask you whether you have had any strange visitors this morning? I don't mean fashionable visitors, but such visitors, for instance, as Miss Barbary's old servant, or as a person without the use of his lower extremities, carried upstairs similarly to a guy?"

"No!"

"Then I assure your ladyship that such visitors have been here and have been received here. Because I saw them at the door, and waited at the corner of the square till they came out, and took half an hour's turn afterwards to avoid them."

"What have I to do with that, or what have you? I do not understand you.

What do you mean?"

"Your ladyship, I come to put you on your guard. There may be no occasion for it. Very well. Then I have only done my best to keep my promise to Miss Summerson. I strongly suspect (from what Small has dropped, and from what we have corkscrewed out of him) that those letters I was to have brought to your ladyship were not destroyed when I supposed they were. That if there was anything to be blown upon, it IS blown upon. That the visitors I have alluded to have been here this morning to make money of it. And that the money is made, or making."

Mr. Guppy picks up his hat and rises.

"Your ladyship, you know best whether there's anything in what I say or whether there's nothing. Something or nothing, I have acted up to Miss Summerson's wishes in letting things alone and in undoing what I had begun to do, as far as possible; that's sufficient for me. In case I should be taking a liberty in putting your ladyship on your guard when there's no necessity for it, you will endeavour, I should hope, to outlive my presumption, and I shall endeavour to outlive your disapprobation. I now take my farewell of your ladyship, and assure you that there's no danger of your ever being waited on by me again."

She scarcely acknowledges these parting words by any look, but when he has been gone a little while, she rings her bell.

"Where is Sir Leicester?"

Mercury reports that he is at present shut up in the library alone.

"Has Sir Leicester had any visitors this morning?"

Several, on business. Mercury proceeds to a description of them, which has been anticipated by Mr. Guppy. Enough; he may go.

So! All is broken down. Her name is in these many mouths, her husband knows his wrongs, her shame will be published—may be spreading while she thinks about it—and in addition to the thunderbolt so long foreseen by her, so unforeseen by him, she is denounced by an invisible accuser as the murderess of her enemy.

Her enemy he was, and she has often, often, often wished him dead. Her enemy he is, even in his grave. This dreadful accusation comes upon her like a new torment at his lifeless hand. And when she recalls how she was secretly at his door that night, and how she may be represented to have sent her favourite girl away so soon before merely to release herself from observation, she shudders as if the hangman's hands were at her neck.

She has thrown herself upon the floor and lies with her hair all wildly scattered and her face buried in the cushions of a couch. She rises up, hurries to and fro, flings herself down again, and rocks and moans. The horror that is upon her is unutterable. If she really were the murderess, it could hardly be, for the moment, more intense.

For as her murderous perspective, before the doing of the deed, however subtle the precautions for its commission, would have been closed up by a gigantic dilatation of the hateful figure, preventing her from seeing any consequences beyond it; and as those consequences would have rushed in, in an unimagined flood, the moment the figure was laid low—which always happens when a murder is done; so, now she sees that when he used to be on the watch before her, and she used to think, "if some mortal stroke would but fall on this old man and take him from my way!" it was but wishing that all he held against her in his hand might be flung to the winds and chance-sown in many places. So, too, with the wicked relief she has felt in his death. What was his death but the key-stone of a gloomy arch removed, and now the arch begins to fall in a thousand fragments, each crushing and mangling piecemeal!

Thus, a terrible impression steals upon and overshadows her that from this pursuer, living or dead—obdurate and imperturbable before her in his well-remembered shape, or not more obdurate and imperturbable in his coffin-bed—there is no escape but in death. Hunted, she flies. The complication of her shame, her dread, remorse, and misery, overwhelms her at its height; and even her strength of self-reliance is overturned and whirled away like a leaf before a mighty wind.

She hurriedly addresses these lines to her husband, seals, and leaves them on her table:

If I am sought for, or accused of, his murder, believe that I am wholly innocent. Believe no other good of me, for I am innocent of nothing else that you have heard, or will hear, laid to my charge. He prepared me, on that fatal night, for his disclosure of my guilt to you. After he had left me, I went out on pretence of walking in the garden where I sometimes walk, but really to follow him and make one last petition that he would not protract the dreadful suspense on which I have been racked by him, you do not know how long, but would mercifully strike next morning.

I found his house dark and silent. I rang twice at his door, but there was no reply, and I came home.

I have no home left. I will encumber you no more. May you, in your just resentment, be able to forget the unworthy woman on whom you have wasted a most generous devotion—who avoids you only with a deeper shame than that with which she hurries from herself—and who writes this last adieu.

She veils and dresses quickly, leaves all her jewels and her money, listens, goes downstairs at a moment when the hall is empty, opens and shuts the great door, flutters away in the shrill frosty wind.

CHAPTER LVI
PURSUIT

Impassive, as behoves its high breeding, the Dedlock town house stares at the other houses in the street of dismal grandeur and gives no outward sign of anything going wrong within. Carriages rattle, doors are battered at, the world exchanges calls; ancient charmers with skeleton throats and peachy cheeks that have a rather ghastly bloom upon them seen by daylight, when indeed these fascinating creatures look like Death and the Lady fused together, dazzle the eyes of men. Forth from the frigid mews come easily swinging carriages guided by short-legged coachmen in flaxen wigs, deep sunk into downy hammercloths, and up behind mount luscious Mercuries bearing sticks of state and wearing cocked hats broadwise, a spectacle for the angels.

The Dedlock town house changes not externally, and hours pass before its exalted dullness is disturbed within. But Volumnia the fair, being subject to the prevalent complaint of boredom and finding that disorder attacking her spirits with some virulence, ventures at length to repair to the library for change of scene. Her gentle tapping at the door producing no response, she opens it and peeps in; seeing no one there, takes possession.

The sprightly Dedlock is reputed, in that grass-grown city of the ancients, Bath, to be stimulated by an urgent curiosity which impels her on all convenient and inconvenient occasions to sidle about with a golden glass at her eye, peering into objects of every description. Certain it is that she avails herself of the present opportunity of hovering over her kinsman's letters and papers like a bird, taking a short peck at this document and a blink with her head on one side at that document, and hopping about from table to table with her glass at her eye in an inquisitive and restless manner. In the course of these researches she stumbles over something, and turning her glass in that direction, sees her kinsman lying on the ground like a felled tree.

Volumnia's pet little scream acquires a considerable augmentation of reality from this surprise, and the house is quickly in commotion. Servants tear up and down stairs, bells are violently rung, doctors are sent for, and Lady Dedlock is sought in all directions, but not found. Nobody has seen or heard her since she last rang her bell. Her letter to Sir Leicester is discovered on her table, but it is doubtful yet whether he has not received another missive from another world requiring to be personally answered, and all the living languages, and all the dead, are as one to him.

They lay him down upon his bed, and chafe, and rub, and fan, and put ice to his head, and try every means of restoration. Howbeit, the day has ebbed away, and it is night in his room before his stertorous breathing lulls or his fixed eyes show any consciousness of the candle that is occasionally passed before them. But when this change begins, it goes on; and by and by he nods or moves his eyes or even his hand in token that he hears and comprehends.

He fell down, this morning, a handsome stately gentleman, somewhat infirm, but of a fine presence, and with a well-filled face. He lies upon his bed, an aged man with sunken cheeks, the decrepit shadow of himself. His voice was rich and mellow and he had so long been thoroughly persuaded of the weight and import to mankind of any word he said that his words really had come to sound as if there were something in them. But now he can only whisper, and what he whispers sounds like what it is—mere jumble and jargon.

His favourite and faithful housekeeper stands at his bedside. It is the first act he notices, and he clearly derives pleasure from it. After vainly trying to make himself understood in speech, he makes signs for a pencil. So inexpressively that they cannot at first understand him; it is his old housekeeper who makes out what he wants and brings in a slate.

After pausing for some time, he slowly scrawls upon it in a hand that is not his, "Chesney Wold?"

No, she tells him; he is in London. He was taken ill in the library this morning. Right thankful she is that she happened to come to London and is able to attend upon him.

"It is not an illness of any serious consequence, Sir Leicester. You will be much better to-morrow, Sir Leicester. All the gentlemen say so." This, with the tears coursing down her fair old face.

After making a survey of the room and looking with particular attention all round the bed where the doctors stand, he writes, "My Lady."

"My Lady went out, Sir Leicester, before you were taken ill, and don't know of your illness yet."

He points again, in great agitation, at the two words. They all try to quiet him, but he points again with increased agitation. On their looking at one another, not knowing what to say, he takes the slate once more and writes "My Lady. For God's sake, where?" And makes an imploring moan.

It is thought better that his old housekeeper should give him Lady Dedlock's letter, the contents of which no one knows or can surmise. She opens it for him and puts it out for his perusal. Having read it twice by a great effort, he turns it down so that it shall not be seen and lies moaning. He passes into a kind of relapse or into a swoon, and it is an hour before he opens his eyes, reclining on his faithful and attached old servant's arm. The doctors know that he is best with her, and when not actively engaged about him, stand aloof.

The slate comes into requisition again, but the word he wants to write he cannot remember. His anxiety, his eagerness, and affliction at this pass are pitiable to behold. It seems as if he must go mad in the necessity he feels for haste and the inability under which he labours of expressing to do what or to fetch whom. He has written the letter B, and there stopped. Of a sudden, in the height of his misery, he puts Mr. before it. The old housekeeper suggests

Bucket. Thank heaven! That's his meaning.

Mr. Bucket is found to be downstairs, by appointment. Shall he come up?

There is no possibility of misconstruing Sir Leicester's burning wish to see him or the desire he signifies to have the room cleared of every one but the housekeeper. It is speedily done, and Mr. Bucket appears. Of all men upon earth, Sir Leicester seems fallen from his high estate to place his sole trust and reliance upon this man.

"Sir Leicester Dedlock, Baronet, I'm sorry to see you like this. I hope you'll cheer up. I'm sure you will, on account of the family credit."

Sir Leicester puts her letter in his hands and looks intently in his face while he reads it. A new intelligence comes into Mr. Bucket's eye as he reads on; with one hook of his finger, while that eye is still glancing over the words, he indicates, "Sir Leicester Dedlock, Baronet, I understand you."

Sir Leicester writes upon the slate. "Full forgiveness. Find—" Mr. Bucket stops his hand.

"Sir Leicester Dedlock, Baronet, I'll find her. But my search after her must be begun out of hand. Not a minute must be lost."

With the quickness of thought, he follows Sir Leicester Dedlock's look towards a little box upon a table.

"Bring it here, Sir Leicester Dedlock, Baronet? Certainly. Open it with one of these here keys? Certainly. The littlest key? TO be sure. Take the notes out? So I will. Count 'em? That's soon done. Twenty and thirty's fifty, and twenty's seventy, and fifty's one twenty, and forty's one sixty. Take 'em for expenses? That I'll do, and render an account of course. Don't spare money? No I won't."

The velocity and certainty of Mr. Bucket's interpretation on all these heads is little short of miraculous. Mrs. Rouncewell, who holds the light, is giddy with the swiftness of his eyes and hands as he starts up, furnished for his journey.

"You're George's mother, old lady; that's about what you are, I believe?" says Mr. Bucket aside, with his hat already on and buttoning his coat.

"Yes, sir, I am his distressed mother."

"So I thought, according to what he mentioned to me just now. Well, then, I'll tell you something. You needn't be distressed no more. Your son's all right. Now, don't you begin a-crying, because what you've got to do is to take care of Sir Leicester Dedlock, Baronet, and you won't do that by crying. As to your son, he's all right, I tell you; and he sends his loving duty, and hoping you're the same. He's discharged honourable; that's about what HE is; with no more imputation on his character than there is on yours, and yours is a tidy one, I'LL bet a pound. You may trust me, for I took your son. He conducted himself in a game way, too, on that occasion; and he's a fine-made man, and you're a fine-made old lady, and you're a mother and son, the pair of you, as might be showed for models in a caravan. Sir Leicester Dedlock, Baronet, what you've trusted to me I'll go through with. Don't you be afraid of my turning out of my way, right or left, or taking a sleep, or a wash, or a shave till I have found what I go in search of. Say everything as is kind and forgiving on your part? Sir Leicester Dedlock, Baronet, I will. And I wish you better, and these family affairs smoothed over—as, Lord, many other family affairs equally has been, and equally will be, to the end of time."

With this peroration, Mr. Bucket, buttoned up, goes quietly out, looking steadily before him as if he were already piercing the night in quest of the fugitive.

His first step is to take himself to Lady Dedlock's rooms and look all over them for any trifling indication that may help him. The rooms are in darkness now; and to see Mr. Bucket with a wax-light in his hand, holding it above his head and taking a sharp mental inventory of the many delicate objects so curiously at variance with himself, would be to see a sight—which nobody DOES see, as he is particular to lock himself in.

"A spicy boudoir, this," says Mr. Bucket, who feels in a manner furbished up in his French by the blow of the morning. "Must have cost a sight of money. Rum articles to cut away from, these; she must have been hard put to it!"

Opening and shutting table-drawers and looking into caskets and jewel-cases, he sees the reflection of himself in various mirrors, and moralizes thereon.

"One might suppose I was a-moving in the fashionable circles and getting myself up for almac's," says Mr. Bucket. "I begin to think I must be a swell in the Guards without knowing it."

Ever looking about, he has opened a dainty little chest in an inner drawer. His great hand, turning over some gloves which it can scarcely feel, they are so light and soft within it, comes upon a white handkerchief.

"Hum! Let's have a look at YOU," says Mr. Bucket, putting down the light. "What should YOU be kept by yourself for? What's YOUR motive? Are you her ladyship's property, or somebody else's? You've got a mark upon you somewheres or another, I suppose?"

He finds it as he speaks, "Esther Summerson."

"Oh!" says Mr. Bucket, pausing, with his finger at his ear. "Come, I'll take YOU."

He completes his observations as quietly and carefully as he has carried them on, leaves everything else precisely as he found it, glides away after some five minutes in all, and passes into the street. With a glance upward at the dimly lighted windows of Sir Leicester's room, he sets off, full-swing, to the nearest coach-stand, picks out the horse for his money, and directs to be driven to the shooting gallery. Mr. Bucket does not claim to be a scientific judge of horses, but he lays out a little money on the principal events in that line, and generally sums up his knowledge of the subject in the remark that when he sees a horse as can go, he knows him.

His knowledge is not at fault in the present instance. Clattering over the stones at a dangerous pace, yet thoughtfully bringing his keen eyes to bear on every slinking creature whom he passes in the midnight streets, and even on the lights in upper windows where people are going or gone to bed, and on all the turnings that he rattles by, and alike on the heavy sky, and on the earth where the snow lies thin—for something may present itself to assist him, anywhere—he dashes to his destination at such a speed that when he stops the horse half smothers him in a cloud of steam.

"Unbear him half a moment to freshen him up, and I'll be back."

He runs up the long wooden entry and finds the trooper smoking his pipe.

"I thought I should, George, after what you have gone through, my lad. I haven't a word to spare. Now, honour! All to save a woman. Miss Summerson that was here when Gridley died—that was the name, I know—all right—where does she live?"

The trooper has just come from there and gives him the address, near Oxford Street.

"You won't repent it, George. Good night!"

He is off again, with an impression of having seen Phil sitting by the frosty fire staring at him open-mouthed, and gallops away again, and gets out in a cloud of steam again.

Mr. Jarndyce, the only person up in the house, is just going to bed, rises from his book on hearing the rapid ringing at the bell, and comes down to the door in his dressing-gown.

"Don't be alarmed, sir." In a moment his visitor is confidential with him in the hall, has shut the door, and stands with his hand upon the lock. "I've had the pleasure of seeing you before. Inspector Bucket. Look at that handkerchief, sir, Miss Esther Summerson's. Found it myself put away in a drawer of Lady Dedlock's, quarter of an hour ago. Not a moment to lose. Matter of life or death. You know Lady Dedlock?"

"Yes."

"There has been a discovery there to-day. Family affairs have come out. Sir Leicester Dedlock, Baronet, has had a fit—apoplexy or paralysis—and couldn't be brought to, and precious time has been lost. Lady Dedlock disappeared this afternoon and left a letter for him that looks bad. Run your eye over it. Here it is!"

Mr. Jarndyce, having read it, asks him what he thinks.

"I don't know. It looks like suicide. Anyways, there's more and more danger, every minute, of its drawing to that. I'd give a hundred pound an hour to have got the start of the present time. Now, Mr. Jarndyce, I am employed by Sir Leicester Dedlock, Baronet, to follow her and find her, to save her and take her his forgiveness. I have money and full power, but I want something else. I want Miss Summerson."

Mr. Jarndyce in a troubled voice repeats, "Miss Summerson?"

"Now, Mr. Jarndyce"—Mr. Bucket has read his face with the greatest attention all along—"I speak to you as a gentleman of a humane heart, and under such pressing circumstances as don't often happen. If ever delay was dangerous, it's dangerous now; and if ever you couldn't afterwards forgive yourself for causing it, this is the time. Eight or ten hours, worth, as I tell you, a hundred pound apiece at least, have been lost since Lady Dedlock disappeared. I am charged to find her. I am Inspector Bucket. Besides all the rest that's heavy on her, she has upon her, as she believes, suspicion of murder. If I follow her alone, she, being in ignorance of what Sir Leicester Dedlock, Baronet, has communicated to me, may be driven to desperation. But if I follow her in company with a young lady, answering to the description of a young lady that she has a tenderness for—I ask no question, and I say no more than that—she will give me credit for being friendly. Let me come up with her and be able to have the hold upon her of putting that young lady for'ard, and I'll save her and prevail with her if she is alive. Let me come up with her alone—a hard matter—and I'll do my best, but I don't answer for what the best may be. Time flies; it's getting on for one o'clock. When one strikes, there's another hour gone, and it's worth a thousand pound now instead of a hundred."

This is all true, and the pressing nature of the case cannot be questioned. Mr. Jarndyce begs him to remain there while he speaks to Miss Summerson. Mr. Bucket says he will, but acting on his usual principle, does no such thing, following upstairs instead and keeping his man in sight. So he remains, dodging and lurking about in the gloom of the staircase while they confer. In a very little time Mr. Jarndyce comes down and tells him that Miss Summerson will join him directly and place herself under his protection to accompany him where he pleases. Mr. Bucket, satisfied, expresses high approval and awaits her coming at the door.

There he mounts a high tower in his mind and looks out far and wide. Many solitary figures he perceives creeping through the streets; many solitary figures out on heaths, and roads, and lying under haystacks. But the figure that he seeks is not among them. Other solitaries he perceives, in nooks of bridges, looking over; and in shadowed places down by the river's level; and a dark, dark, shapeless object drifting with the tide, more solitary than all, clings with a drowning hold on his attention.

Where is she? Living or dead, where is she? If, as he folds the handkerchief and carefully puts it up, it were able with an enchanted power to bring before him the place where she found it and the night-landscape near the cottage where it covered the little child, would he descry her there? On the waste where the brick-kilns are burning with a pale blue flare, where the straw-roofs of the wretched huts in which the bricks are made are being scattered by the wind, where the clay and water are hard frozen and the mill in which the gaunt blind horse goes round all day looks like an instrument of human torture—traversing this deserted, blighted spot there is a lonely figure with the sad world to itself, pelted by the snow and driven by the wind, and cast out, it would seem, from all companionship. It is the figure of a woman, too; but it is miserably dressed, and no such clothes ever came through the hall and out at the great door of the Dedlock mansion.

CHAPTER LVII
ESTHER'S NARRATIVE

I had gone to bed and fallen asleep when my guardian knocked at the door of my room and begged me to get up directly. On my hurrying to speak to him and learn what had happened, he told me, after a word or two of preparation, that there had been a discovery at Sir Leicester Dedlock's. That my mother had fled, that a person was now at our door who was empowered to convey to her the fullest assurances of affectionate protection and forgiveness if he could possibly find her, and that I was sought for to accompany him in the hope that my entreaties might prevail upon her if his failed. Something to this general purpose I made out, but I was thrown into such a tumult of alarm, and hurry and distress, that in spite of every effort I could make to subdue my agitation, I did not seem, to myself, fully to recover my right mind until hours had passed.

But I dressed and wrapped up expeditiously without waking Charley or any one and went down to Mr. Bucket, who was the person entrusted with the secret. In taking me to him my guardian told me this, and also explained how it was that he had come to think of me. Mr. Bucket, in a low voice, by the light of my guardian's candle, read to me in the hall a letter that my mother had left upon her table; and I suppose within ten minutes of my having been aroused I was sitting beside him, rolling swiftly through the streets.

His manner was very keen, and yet considerate when he explained to me that a great deal might depend on my being able to answer, without confusion, a few questions that he wished to ask me. These were, chiefly, whether I had had much communication with my mother (to whom he only referred as Lady Dedlock), when and where I had spoken with her last, and how she had become possessed of my handkerchief. When I had satisfied him on these points, he asked me particularly to consider—taking time to think—whether within my knowledge there was any one, no matter where, in whom she might be at all likely to confide under circumstances of the last necessity. I could think of no one but my guardian. But by and by I mentioned Mr. Boythorn. He came into my mind as connected with his old chivalrous manner of mentioning my mother's name and with what my guardian had informed me of his engagement to her sister and his unconscious connexion with her unhappy story.

My companion had stopped the driver while we held this conversation, that we might the better hear each other. He now told him to go on again and said to me, after considering within himself for a few moments, that he had made up his mind how to proceed. He was quite willing to tell me what his plan was, but I did not feel clear enough to understand it.

We had not driven very far from our lodgings when we stopped in a by-street at a public-looking place lighted up with gas. Mr. Bucket took me in and sat me in an arm-chair by a bright fire. It was now past one, as I saw by the clock against the wall. Two police officers, looking in their perfectly neat uniform not at all like people who were up all night, were quietly writing at a desk; and the place seemed very quiet altogether, except for some beating and calling out at distant doors underground, to which nobody paid any attention.

A third man in uniform, whom Mr. Bucket called and to whom he whispered his instructions, went out; and then the two others advised together while one wrote from Mr. Bucket's subdued dictation. It was a description of my mother that they were busy with, for Mr. Bucket brought it to me when it was done and read it in a whisper. It was very accurate indeed.

The second officer, who had attended to it closely, then copied it out and called in another man in uniform (there were several in an outer room), who took it up and went away with it. All this was done with the greatest dispatch and without the waste of a moment; yet nobody was at all hurried. As soon as the paper was sent out upon its travels, the two officers resumed their former quiet work of writing with neatness and care. Mr. Bucket thoughtfully came and warmed the soles of his boots, first one and then the other, at the fire.

"Are you well wrapped up, Miss Summerson?" he asked me as his eyes met mine. "It's a desperate sharp night for a young lady to be out in."

I told him I cared for no weather and was warmly clothed.

"It may be a long job," he observed; "but so that it ends well, never mind, miss."

"I pray to heaven it may end well!" said I.

He nodded comfortingly. "You see, whatever you do, don't you go and fret yourself. You keep yourself cool and equal for anything that may happen, and it'll be the better for you, the better for me, the better for Lady Dedlock, and the better for Sir Leicester Dedlock, Baronet."

He was really very kind and gentle, and as he stood before the fire warming his boots and rubbing his face with his forefinger, I felt a confidence in his sagacity which reassured me. It was not yet a quarter to two when I heard horses' feet and wheels outside. "Now, Miss Summerson," said he, "we are off, if you please!"

He gave me his arm, and the two officers courteously bowed me out, and we found at the door a phaeton or barouche with a postilion and post horses. Mr. Bucket handed me in and took his own seat on the box. The man in uniform whom he had sent to fetch this equipage then handed him up a dark lantern at his request, and when he had given a few directions to the driver, we rattled away.

I was far from sure that I was not in a dream. We rattled with great rapidity through such a labyrinth of streets that I soon lost all idea where we were, except that we had crossed and re-crossed the river, and still seemed to be traversing a low-lying, waterside, dense neighbourhood of narrow thoroughfares chequered by docks and basins, high piles of warehouses, swing-bridges, and masts of ships. At length we stopped at the corner of a little slimy turning, which the wind from the river, rushing up it, did not purify; and I saw my companion, by the light of his lantern, in conference with several men who looked like a mixture of police and sailors. Against the mouldering wall by which they stood, there was a bill, on which I could discern the words, "Found Drowned"; and this and an inscription about drags possessed me with the awful suspicion shadowed forth in our visit to that place.

I had no need to remind myself that I was not there by the indulgence of any feeling of mine to increase the difficulties of the search, or to lessen its hopes, or enhance its delays. I remained quiet, but what I suffered in that dreadful spot I never can forget. And still it was like the horror of a dream. A man yet dark and muddy, in long swollen sodden boots and a hat like them, was called out of a boat and whispered with Mr. Bucket, who went away with him down some slippery steps—as if to look at something secret that he had to show. They came back, wiping their hands upon their coats, after turning over something wet; but thank God it was not what I feared!

After some further conference, Mr. Bucket (whom everybody seemed to know and defer to) went in with the others at a door and left me in the carriage, while the driver walked up and down by his horses to warm himself. The tide was coming in, as I judged from the sound it made, and I could hear it break at the end of the alley with a little rush towards me. It never did so—and I thought it did so, hundreds of times, in what can have been at the most a quarter of an hour, and probably was less—but the thought shuddered through me that it would cast my mother at the horses' feet.

Mr. Bucket came out again, exhorting the others to be vigilant, darkened his lantern, and once more took his seat. "Don't you be alarmed, Miss Summerson, on account of our coming down here," he said, turning to me. "I only want to have everything in train and to know that it is in train by looking after it myself. Get on, my lad!"

We appeared to retrace the way we had come. Not that I had taken note of any particular objects in my perturbed state of mind, but judging from the general character of the streets. We called at another office or station for a minute and crossed the river again. During the whole of this time, and during the whole search, my companion, wrapped up on the box, never relaxed in his vigilance a single moment; but when we crossed the bridge he seemed, if possible, to be more on the alert than before. He stood up to look over the parapet, he alighted and went back after a shadowy female figure that flitted past us, and he gazed into the profound black pit of water with a face that made my heart die within me. The river had a fearful look, so overcast and secret, creeping away so fast between the low flat lines of shore—so heavy with indistinct and awful shapes, both of substance and shadow; so deathlike and mysterious. I have seen it many times since then, by sunlight and by moonlight, but never free from the impressions of that journey. In my memory the lights upon the bridge are always burning dim, the cutting wind is eddying round the homeless woman whom we pass, the monotonous wheels are whirling on, and the light of the carriage-lamps reflected back looks palely in upon me—a face rising out of the dreaded water.

Clattering and clattering through the empty streets, we came at length from the pavement on to dark smooth roads and began to leave the houses behind us. After a while I recognized the familiar way to Saint Albans. At Barnet fresh horses were ready for us, and we changed and went on. It was very cold indeed, and the open country was white with snow, though none was falling then.

"An old acquaintance of yours, this road, Miss Summerson," said Mr. Bucket cheerfully.

"Yes," I returned. "Have you gathered any intelligence?"

"None that can be quite depended on as yet," he answered, "but it's early times as yet."

He had gone into every late or early public-house where there was a light (they were not a few at that time, the road being then much frequented by drovers) and had got down to talk to the turnpike-keepers. I had heard him ordering drink, and chinking money, and making himself agreeable and merry everywhere; but whenever he took his seat upon the box again, his face resumed its watchful steady look, and he always said to the driver in the same business tone, "Get on, my lad!"

With all these stoppages, it was between five and six o'clock and we were yet a few miles short of Saint Albans when he came out of one of these houses and handed me in a cup of tea.

"Drink it, Miss Summerson, it'll do you good. You're beginning to get more yourself now, ain't you?"

I thanked him and said I hoped so.

"You was what you may call stunned at first," he returned; "and Lord, no wonder! Don't speak loud, my dear. It's all right. She's on ahead."

I don't know what joyful exclamation I made or was going to make, but he put up his finger and I stopped myself.

"Passed through here on foot this evening about eight or nine. I heard of her first at the archway toll, over at Highgate, but couldn't make quite sure. Traced her all along, on and off. Picked her up at one place, and dropped her at another; but she's before us now, safe. Take hold of this cup and saucer, ostler. Now, if you wasn't brought up to the butter trade, look out and see if you can catch half a crown in your t'other hand. One, two, three, and there you are! Now, my lad, try a gallop!"

We were soon in Saint Albans and alighted a little before day, when I was just beginning to arrange and comprehend the occurrences of the night and really to believe that they were not a dream. Leaving the carriage at the posting-house and ordering fresh horses to be ready, my companion gave me his arm, and we went towards home.

"As this is your regular abode, Miss Summerson, you see," he observed, "I should like to know whether you've been asked for by any stranger answering the description, or whether Mr. Jarndyce has. I don't much expect it, but it might be."

As we ascended the hill, he looked about him with a sharp eye—the day was now breaking—and reminded me that I had come down it one night, as I had reason for remembering, with my little servant and poor Jo, whom he called Toughey.

I wondered how he knew that.

"When you passed a man upon the road, just yonder, you know," said Mr. Bucket.

Yes, I remembered that too, very well.

"That was me," said Mr. Bucket.

Seeing my surprise, he went on, "I drove down in a gig that afternoon to look after that boy. You might have heard my wheels when you came out to look after him yourself, for I was aware of you and your little maid going up when I was walking the horse down. Making an inquiry or two about him in the town, I soon heard what company he was in and was coming among the brick-fields to look for him when I observed you bringing him home here."

"Had he committed any crime?" I asked.

"None was charged against him," said Mr. Bucket, coolly lifting off his hat, "but I suppose he wasn't over-particular. No. What I wanted him for was in connexion with keeping this very matter of Lady Dedlock quiet. He had been making his tongue more free than welcome as to a small accidental service he had been paid for by the deceased Mr. Tulkinghorn; and it wouldn't do, at any sort of price, to have him playing those games. So having warned him out of London, I made an afternoon of it to warn him to keep out of it now he WAS away, and go farther from it, and maintain a bright look-out that I didn't catch him coming back again."

"Poor creature!" said I.

"Poor enough," assented Mr. Bucket, "and trouble enough, and well enough away from London, or anywhere else. I was regularly turned on my back when I found him taken up by your establishment, I do assure you."

I asked him why. "Why, my dear?" said Mr. Bucket. "Naturally there was no end to his tongue then. He might as well have been born with a yard and a half of it, and a remnant over."

Although I remember this conversation now, my head was in confusion at the time, and my power of attention hardly did more than enable me to understand that he entered into these particulars to divert me. With the same kind intention, manifestly, he often spoke to me of indifferent things, while his face was busy with the one object that we had in view. He still pursued this subject as we turned in at the garden-gate.

"Ah!" said Mr. Bucket. "Here we are, and a nice retired place it is. Puts a man in mind of the country house in the Woodpecker-tapping, that was known by the smoke which so gracefully curled. They're early with the kitchen fire, and that denotes good servants. But what you've always got to be careful of with servants is who comes to see 'em; you never know what they're up to if you don't know that. And another thing, my dear. Whenever you find a young man behind the kitchen-door, you give that young man in charge on suspicion of being secreted in a dwelling-house with an unlawful purpose."

We were now in front of the house; he looked attentively and closely at the gravel for footprints before he raised his eyes to the windows.

"Do you generally put that elderly young gentleman in the same room when he's on a visit here, Miss Summerson?" he inquired, glancing at Mr. Skimpole's usual chamber.

"You know Mr. Skimpole!" said I.

"What do you call him again?" returned Mr. Bucket, bending down his ear. "Skimpole, is it? I've often wondered what his name might be. Skimpole. Not John, I should say, nor yet Jacob?"

"Harold," I told him.

"Harold. Yes. He's a queer bird is Harold," said Mr. Bucket, eyeing me with great expression.

"He is a singular character," said I.

"No idea of money," observed Mr. Bucket. "He takes it, though!"

I involuntarily returned for answer that I perceived Mr. Bucket knew him.

"Why, now I'll tell you, Miss Summerson," he replied. "Your mind will be all the better for not running on one point too continually, and I'll tell you for a change. It was him as pointed out to me where Toughey was. I made up my mind that night to come to the door and ask for Toughey, if that was all; but willing to try a move or so first, if any such was on the board, I just pitched up a morsel of gravel at that window where I saw a shadow. As soon as Harold opens it and I have had a look at him, thinks I, you're the man for me. So I smoothed him down a bit about not wanting to disturb the family after they was gone to bed and about its being a thing to be regretted that charitable young ladies should harbour vagrants; and then, when I pretty well understood his ways, I said I should consider a fypunnote well bestowed if I could relieve the premises of Toughey without causing any noise or trouble. Then says he, lifting up his eyebrows in the gayest way, 'It's no use mentioning a fypunnote to me, my friend, because I'm a mere child in such matters and have no idea of money.' Of course I understood what his taking it so easy meant; and being now quite sure he was the man for me, I wrapped the note round a little stone and threw it up to him. Well! He laughs and beams, and looks as innocent as you like, and says, 'But I don't know the value of these things. What am I to DO with this?' 'Spend it, sir,' says I. 'But I shall be taken in,' he says, 'they won't give me the right change, I shall lose it, it's no use to me.' Lord, you never saw such a face as he carried it with! Of course he told me where to find Toughey, and I found him."

I regarded this as very treacherous on the part of Mr. Skimpole towards my guardian and as passing the usual bounds of his childish innocence.

"Bounds, my dear?" returned Mr. Bucket. "Bounds? Now, Miss Summerson, I'll give you a piece of advice that your husband will find useful when you are happily married and have got a family about you. Whenever a person says to you that they are as innocent as can be in all concerning money, look well after your own money, for they are dead certain to collar it if they can. Whenever a person proclaims to you 'In worldly matters I'm a child,' you consider that that person is only a-crying off from being held accountable and that you have got that person's number, and it's Number One. Now, I am not a poetical man myself, except in a vocal way when it goes round a company, but I'm a practical one, and that's my experience. So's this rule. Fast and loose in one thing, fast and loose in everything. I never knew it fail. No more will you. Nor no one. With which caution to the unwary, my dear, I take the liberty of pulling this here bell, and so go back to our business."

I believe it had not been for a moment out of his mind, any more than it had been out of my mind, or out of his face. The whole household were amazed to see me, without any notice, at that time in the morning, and so accompanied; and their surprise was not diminished by my inquiries. No one, however, had been there. It could not be doubted that this was the truth.

"Then, Miss Summerson," said my companion, "we can't be too soon at the cottage where those brickmakers are to be found. Most inquiries there I leave to you, if you'll be so good as to make 'em. The naturalest way is the best way, and the naturalest way is your own way."

We set off again immediately. On arriving at the cottage, we found it shut up and apparently deserted, but one of the neighbours who knew me and who came out when I was trying to make some one hear informed me that the two women and their husbands now lived together in another house, made of loose rough bricks, which stood on the margin of the piece of ground where the kilns were and where the long rows of bricks were drying. We lost no time in repairing to this place, which was within a few hundred yards; and as the door stood ajar, I pushed it open.

There were only three of them sitting at breakfast, the child lying asleep on a bed in the corner. It was Jenny, the mother of the dead child, who was absent. The other woman rose on seeing me; and the men, though they were, as usual, sulky and silent, each gave me a morose nod of recognition. A look passed between them when Mr. Bucket followed me in, and I was surprised to see that the woman evidently knew him.

I had asked leave to enter of course. Liz (the only name by which I knew her) rose to give me her own chair, but I sat down on a stool near the fire, and Mr. Bucket took a corner of the bedstead. Now that I had to speak and was among people with whom I was not familiar, I became conscious of being hurried and giddy. It was very difficult to begin, and I could not help bursting into tears.

"Liz," said I, "I have come a long way in the night and through the snow to inquire after a lady—"

"Who has been here, you know," Mr. Bucket struck in, addressing the whole group with a composed propitiatory face; "that's the lady the young lady means. The lady that was here last night, you know."

"And who told YOU as there was anybody here?" inquired Jenny's husband, who had made a surly stop in his eating to listen and now measured him with his eye.

"A person of the name of Michael Jackson, with a blue welveteen waistcoat with a double row of mother of pearl buttons," Mr. Bucket immediately answered.

"He had as good mind his own business, whoever he is," growled the man.

"He's out of employment, I believe," said Mr. Bucket apologetically for Michael Jackson, "and so gets talking."

The woman had not resumed her chair, but stood faltering with her hand upon its broken back, looking at me. I thought she would have spoken to me privately if she had dared. She was still in this attitude of uncertainty when her husband, who was eating with a lump of bread and fat in one hand and his clasp-knife in the other, struck the handle of his knife violently on the table and told her with an oath to mind HER own business at any rate and sit down.

"I should like to have seen Jenny very much," said I, "for I am sure she would have told me all she could about this lady, whom I am very anxious indeed—you cannot think how anxious—to overtake. Will Jenny be here soon? Where is she?"

The woman had a great desire to answer, but the man, with another oath, openly kicked at her foot with his heavy boot. He left it to Jenny's husband to say what he chose, and after a dogged silence the latter turned his shaggy head towards me.

"I'm not partial to gentlefolks coming into my place, as you've heerd me say afore now, I think, miss. I let their places be, and it's curious they can't let my place be. There'd be a pretty shine made if I was to go a-wisitin THEM, I think. Howsoever, I don't so much complain of you as of some others, and I'm agreeable to make you a civil answer, though I give notice that I'm not a-going to be drawed like a badger. Will Jenny be here soon? No she won't. Where is she? She's gone up to Lunnun."

"Did she go last night?" I asked.

"Did she go last night? Ah! She went last night," he answered with a sulky jerk of his head.

"But was she here when the lady came? And what did the lady say to her? And where is the lady gone? I beg and pray you to be so kind as to tell me," said I, "for I am in great distress to know."

"If my master would let me speak, and not say a word of harm—" the woman timidly began.

"Your master," said her husband, muttering an imprecation with slow emphasis, "will break your neck if you meddle with wot don't concern you."

After another silence, the husband of the absent woman, turning to me again, answered me with his usual grumbling unwillingness.

"Wos Jenny here when the lady come? Yes, she wos here when the lady come. Wot did the lady say to her? Well, I'll tell you wot the lady said to her. She said, 'You remember me as come one time to talk to you about the young lady as had been a-wisiting of you? You remember me as give you somethink handsome for a handkercher wot she had left?' Ah, she remembered. So we all did. Well, then, wos that young lady up at the house now? No, she warn't up at the house now. Well, then, lookee here. The lady was upon a journey all alone, strange as we might think it, and could she rest herself where you're a setten for a hour or so. Yes she could, and so she did. Then she went—it might be at twenty minutes past eleven, and it might be at twenty minutes past twelve; we ain't got no watches here to know the time by, nor yet clocks. Where did she go? I don't know where she go'd. She went one way, and Jenny went another; one went right to Lunnun, and t'other went right from it. That's all about it. Ask this man. He heerd it all, and see it all. He knows."

The other man repeated, "That's all about it."

"Was the lady crying?" I inquired.

"Devil a bit," returned the first man. "Her shoes was the worse, and her clothes was the worse, but she warn't—not as I see."

The woman sat with her arms crossed and her eyes upon the ground. Her husband had turned his seat a little so as to face her and kept his hammer-like hand upon the table as if it were in readiness to execute his threat if she disobeyed him.

"I hope you will not object to my asking your wife," said I, "how the lady looked."

"Come, then!" he gruffly cried to her. "You hear what she says. Cut it short and tell her."

"Bad," replied the woman. "Pale and exhausted. Very bad."

"Did she speak much?"

"Not much, but her voice was hoarse."

She answered, looking all the while at her husband for leave.

"Was she faint?" said I. "Did she eat or drink here?"

"Go on!" said the husband in answer to her look. "Tell her and cut it short."

"She had a little water, miss, and Jenny fetched her some bread and tea. But she hardly touched it."

"And when she went from here," I was proceeding, when Jenny's husband impatiently took me up.

"When she went from here, she went right away nor'ard by the high road. Ask on the road if you doubt me, and see if it warn't so. Now, there's the end. That's all about it."

I glanced at my companion, and finding that he had already risen and was ready to depart, thanked them for what they had told me, and took my leave. The woman looked full at Mr. Bucket as he went out, and he looked full at her.

"Now, Miss Summerson," he said to me as we walked quickly away. "They've got her ladyship's watch among 'em. That's a positive fact."

"You saw it?" I exclaimed.

"Just as good as saw it," he returned. "Else why should he talk about his 'twenty minutes past' and about his having no watch to tell the time by? Twenty minutes! He don't usually cut his time so fine as that. If he comes to half-hours, it's as much as HE does. Now, you see, either her ladyship gave him that watch or he took it. I think she gave it him. Now, what should she give it him for? What should she give it him for?"

He repeated this question to himself several times as we hurried on, appearing to balance between a variety of answers that arose in his mind.

"If time could be spared," said Mr. Bucket, "which is the only thing that can't be spared in this case, I might get it out of that woman; but it's too doubtful a chance to trust to under present circumstances. They are up to keeping a close eye upon her, and any fool knows that a poor creetur like her, beaten and kicked and scarred and bruised from head to foot, will stand by the husband that ill uses her through thick and thin. There's something kept back. It's a pity but what we had seen the other woman."

I regretted it exceedingly, for she was very grateful, and I felt sure would have resisted no entreaty of mine.

"It's possible, Miss Summerson," said Mr. Bucket, pondering on it, "that her ladyship sent her up to London with some word for you, and it's possible that her husband got the watch to let her go. It don't come out altogether so plain as to please me, but it's on the cards. Now, I don't take kindly to laying out the money of Sir Leicester Dedlock, Baronet, on these roughs, and I don't see my way to the usefulness of it at present. No! So far our road, Miss Summerson, is for'ard—straight ahead—and keeping everything quiet!"

We called at home once more that I might send a hasty note to my guardian, and then we hurried back to where we had left the carriage. The horses were brought out as soon as we were seen coming, and we were on the road again in a few minutes.

It had set in snowing at daybreak, and it now snowed hard. The air was so thick with the darkness of the day and the density of the fall that we could see but a very little way in any direction. Although it was extremely cold, the snow was but partially frozen, and it churned—with a sound as if it were a beach of small shells—under the hoofs of the horses into mire and water. They sometimes slipped and floundered for a mile together, and we were obliged to come to a standstill to rest them. One horse fell three times in this first stage, and trembled so and was so shaken that the driver had to dismount from his saddle and lead him at last.

I could eat nothing and could not sleep, and I grew so nervous under those delays and the slow pace at which we travelled that I had an unreasonable desire upon me to get out and walk. Yielding to my companion's better sense, however, I remained where I was. All this time, kept fresh by a certain enjoyment of the work in which he was engaged, he was up and down at every house we came to, addressing people whom he had never beheld before as old acquaintances, running in to warm himself at every fire he saw, talking and drinking and shaking hands at every bar and tap, friendly with every waggoner, wheelwright, blacksmith, and toll-taker, yet never seeming to lose time, and always mounting to the box again with his watchful, steady face and his business-like "Get on, my lad!"

When we were changing horses the next time, he came from the stable-yard, with the wet snow encrusted upon him and dropping off him—plashing and crashing through it to his wet knees as he had been doing frequently since we left Saint Albans—and spoke to me at the carriage side.

"Keep up your spirits. It's certainly true that she came on here, Miss Summerson. There's not a doubt of the dress by this time, and the dress has been seen here."

"Still on foot?" said I.

"Still on foot. I think the gentleman you mentioned must be the point she's aiming at, and yet I don't like his living down in her own part of the country neither."

"I know so little," said I. "There may be some one else nearer here, of whom I never heard."

"That's true. But whatever you do, don't you fall a-crying, my dear; and don't you worry yourself no more than you can help. Get on, my lad!"

The sleet fell all that day unceasingly, a thick mist came on early, and it never rose or lightened for a moment. Such roads I had never seen. I sometimes feared we had missed the way and got into the ploughed grounds or the marshes. If I ever thought of the time I had been out, it presented itself as an indefinite period of great duration, and I seemed, in a strange way, never to have been free from the anxiety under which I then laboured.

As we advanced, I began to feel misgivings that my companion lost confidence. He was the same as before with all the roadside people, but he looked graver when he sat by himself on the box. I saw his finger uneasily going across and across his mouth during the whole of one long weary stage. I overheard that he began to ask the drivers of coaches and other vehicles coming towards us what passengers they had seen in other coaches and vehicles that were in advance. Their replies did not encourage him. He always gave me a reassuring beck of his finger and lift of his eyelid as he got upon the box again, but he seemed perplexed now when he said, "Get on, my lad!"

At last, when we were changing, he told me that he had lost the track of the dress so long that he began to be surprised. It was nothing, he said, to lose such a track for one while, and to take it up for another while, and so on; but it had disappeared here in an unaccountable manner, and we had not come upon it since. This corroborated the apprehensions I had formed, when he began to look at direction-posts, and to leave the carriage at cross roads for a quarter of an hour at a time while he explored them. But I was not to be down-hearted, he told me, for it was as likely as not that the next stage might set us right again.

The next stage, however, ended as that one ended; we had no new clue. There was a spacious inn here, solitary, but a comfortable substantial building, and as we drove in under a large gateway before I knew it, where a landlady and her pretty daughters came to the carriage-door, entreating me to alight and refresh myself while the horses were making ready, I thought it would be uncharitable to refuse. They took me upstairs to a warm room and left me there.

It was at the corner of the house, I remember, looking two ways. On one side to a stable-yard open to a by-road, where the ostlers were unharnessing the splashed and tired horses from the muddy carriage, and beyond that to the by-road itself, across which the sign was heavily swinging; on the other side to a wood of dark pine-trees. Their branches were encumbered with snow, and it silently dropped off in wet heaps while I stood at the window. Night was setting in, and its bleakness was enhanced by the contrast of the pictured fire glowing and gleaming in the window-pane. As I looked among the stems of the trees and followed the discoloured marks in the snow where the thaw was sinking into it and undermining it, I thought of the motherly face brightly set off by daughters that had just now welcomed me and of MY mother lying down in such a wood to die.

I was frightened when I found them all about me, but I remembered that before I fainted I tried very hard not to do it; and that was some little comfort. They cushioned me up on a large sofa by the fire, and then the comely landlady told me that I must travel no further to-night, but must go to bed. But this put me into such a tremble lest they should detain me there that she soon recalled her words and compromised for a rest of half an hour.

A good endearing creature she was. She and her three fair girls, all so busy about me. I was to take hot soup and broiled fowl, while Mr. Bucket dried himself and dined elsewhere; but I could not do it when a snug round table was presently spread by the fireside, though I was very unwilling to disappoint them. However, I could take some toast and some hot negus, and as I really enjoyed that refreshment, it made some recompense.

Punctual to the time, at the half-hour's end the carriage came rumbling under the gateway, and they took me down, warmed, refreshed, comforted by kindness, and safe (I assured them) not to faint any more. After I had got in and had taken a grateful leave of them all, the youngest daughter—a blooming girl of nineteen, who was to be the first married, they had told me—got upon the carriage step, reached in, and kissed me. I have never seen her, from that hour, but I think of her to this hour as my friend.

The transparent windows with the fire and light, looking so bright and warm from the cold darkness out of doors, were soon gone, and again we were crushing and churning the loose snow. We went on with toil enough, but the dismal roads were not much worse than they had been, and the stage was only nine miles. My companion smoking on the box—I had thought at the last inn of begging him to do so when I saw him standing at a great fire in a comfortable cloud of tobacco—was as vigilant as ever and as quickly down and up again when we came to any human abode or any human creature. He had lighted his little dark lantern, which seemed to be a favourite with him, for we had lamps to the carriage; and every now and then he turned it upon me to see that I was doing well. There was a folding-window to the carriage-head, but I never closed it, for it seemed like shutting out hope.

We came to the end of the stage, and still the lost trace was not recovered. I looked at him anxiously when we stopped to change, but I knew by his yet graver face as he stood watching the ostlers that he had heard nothing. Almost in an instant afterwards, as I leaned back in my seat, he looked in, with his lighted lantern in his hand, an excited and quite different man.

"What is it?" said I, starting. "Is she here?"

"No, no. Don't deceive yourself, my dear. Nobody's here. But I've got it!"

The crystallized snow was in his eyelashes, in his hair, lying in ridges on his dress. He had to shake it from his face and get his breath before he spoke to me.

"Now, Miss Summerson," said he, beating his finger on the apron, "don't you be disappointed at what I'm a-going to do. You know me. I'm Inspector Bucket, and you can trust me. We've come a long way; never mind. Four horses out there for the next stage up! Quick!"

There was a commotion in the yard, and a man came running out of the stables to know if he meant up or down.

"Up, I tell you! Up! Ain't it English? Up!"

"Up?" said I, astonished. "To London! Are we going back?"

"Miss Summerson," he answered, "back. Straight back as a die. You know me. Don't be afraid. I'll follow the other, by G——"

"The other?" I repeated. "Who?"

"You called her Jenny, didn't you? I'll follow her. Bring those two pair out here for a crown a man. Wake up, some of you!"

"You will not desert this lady we are in search of; you will not abandon her on such a night and in such a state of mind as I know her to be in!" said I, in an agony, and grasping his hand.

"You are right, my dear, I won't. But I'll follow the other. Look alive here with them horses. Send a man for'ard in the saddle to the next stage, and let him send another for'ard again, and order four on, up, right through. My darling, don't you be afraid!"

These orders and the way in which he ran about the yard urging them caused a general excitement that was scarcely less bewildering to me than the sudden change. But in the height of the confusion, a mounted man galloped away to order the relays, and our horses were put to with great speed.

"My dear," said Mr. Bucket, jumping to his seat and looking in again, "—you'll excuse me if I'm too familiar—don't you fret and worry yourself no more than you can help. I say nothing else at present; but you know me, my dear; now, don't you?"

I endeavoured to say that I knew he was far more capable than I of deciding what we ought to do, but was he sure that this was right? Could I not go forward by myself in search of—I grasped his hand again in my distress and whispered it to him—of my own mother.

"My dear," he answered, "I know, I know, and would I put you wrong, do you think? Inspector Bucket. Now you know me, don't you?"

What could I say but yes!

"Then you keep up as good a heart as you can, and you rely upon me for standing by you, no less than by Sir Leicester Dedlock, Baronet. Now, are you right there?"

"All right, sir!"

"Off she goes, then. And get on, my lads!"

We were again upon the melancholy road by which we had come, tearing up the miry sleet and thawing snow as if they were torn up by a waterwheel.

CHAPTER LVIII
A WINTRY DAY AND NIGHT

Still impassive, as behoves its breeding, the Dedlock town house carries itself as usual towards the street of dismal grandeur. There are powdered heads from time to time in the little windows of the hall, looking out at the untaxed powder falling all day from the sky; and in the same conservatory there is peach blossom turning itself exotically to the great hall fire from the nipping weather out of doors. It is given out that my Lady has gone down into Lincolnshire, but is expected to return presently.

Rumour, busy overmuch, however, will not go down into Lincolnshire. It persists in flitting and chattering about town. It knows that that poor unfortunate man, Sir Leicester, has been sadly used. It hears, my dear child, all sorts of shocking things. It makes the world of five miles round quite merry. Not to know that there is something wrong at the Dedlocks' is to augur yourself unknown. One of the peachy-cheeked charmers with the skeleton throats is already apprised of all the principal circumstances that will come out before the Lords on Sir Leicester's application for a bill of divorce.

At Blaze and Sparkle's the jewellers and at Sheen and Gloss's the mercers, it is and will be for several hours the topic of the age, the feature of the century. The patronesses of those establishments, albeit so loftily inscrutable, being as nicely weighed and measured there as any other article of the stock-in-trade, are perfectly understood in this new fashion by the rawest hand behind the counter. "Our people, Mr. Jones," said Blaze and Sparkle to the hand in question on engaging him, "our people, sir, are sheep—mere sheep. Where two or three marked ones go, all the rest follow. Keep those two or three in your eye, Mr. Jones, and you have the flock." So, likewise, Sheen and Gloss to THEIR Jones, in reference to knowing where to have the fashionable people and how to bring what they (Sheen and Gloss) choose into fashion. On similar unerring principles, Mr. Sladdery the librarian, and indeed the great farmer of gorgeous sheep, admits this very day, "Why yes, sir, there certainly ARE reports concerning Lady Dedlock, very current indeed among my high connexion, sir. You see, my high connexion must talk about something, sir; and it's only to get a subject into vogue with one or two ladies I could name to make it go down with the whole. Just what I should have done with those ladies, sir, in the case of any novelty you had left to me to bring in, they have done of themselves in this case through knowing Lady Dedlock and being perhaps a little innocently jealous of her too, sir. You'll find, sir, that this topic will be very popular among my high connexion. If it had been a speculation, sir, it would have brought money. And when I say so, you may trust to my being right, sir, for I have made it my business to study my high connexion and to be able to wind it up like a clock, sir."

Thus rumour thrives in the capital, and will not go down into Lincolnshire. By half-past five, post meridian, Horse Guards' time, it has even elicited a new remark from the Honourable Mr. Stables, which bids fair to outshine the old one, on which he has so long rested his colloquial reputation. This sparkling sally is to the effect that although he always knew she was the best-groomed woman in the stud, he had no idea she was a bolter. It is immensely received in turf-circles.

At feasts and festivals also, in firmaments she has often graced, and among constellations she outshone but yesterday, she is still the prevalent subject. What is it? Who is it? When was it? Where was it? How was it? She is discussed by her dear friends with all the genteelest slang in vogue, with the last new word, the last new manner, the last new drawl, and the perfection of polite indifference. A remarkable feature of the theme is that it is found to be so inspiring that several people come out upon it who never came out before—positively say things! William Buffy carries one of these smartnesses from the place where he dines down to the House, where the Whip for his party hands it about with his snuff-box to keep men together who want to be off, with such effect that the Speaker (who has had it privately insinuated into his own ear under the corner of his wig) cries, "Order at the bar!" three times without making an impression.

And not the least amazing circumstance connected with her being vaguely the town talk is that people hovering on the confines of Mr. Sladdery's high connexion, people who know nothing and ever did know nothing about her, think it essential to their reputation to pretend that she is their topic too, and to retail her at second-hand with the last new word and the last new manner, and the last new drawl, and the last new polite indifference, and all the rest of it, all at second-hand but considered equal to new in inferior systems and to fainter stars. If there be any man of letters, art, or science among these little dealers, how noble in him to support the feeble sisters on such majestic crutches!

So goes the wintry day outside the Dedlock mansion. How within it?

Sir Leicester, lying in his bed, can speak a little, though with difficulty and indistinctness. He is enjoined to silence and to rest, and they have given him some opiate to lull his pain, for his old enemy is very hard with him. He is never asleep, though sometimes he seems to fall into a dull waking doze. He caused his bedstead to be moved out nearer to the window when he heard it was such inclement weather, and his head to be so adjusted that he could see the driving snow and sleet. He watches it as it falls, throughout the whole wintry day.

Upon the least noise in the house, which is kept hushed, his hand is at the pencil. The old housekeeper, sitting by him, knows what he would write and whispers, "No, he has not come back yet, Sir Leicester. It was late last night when he went. He has been but a little time gone yet."

He withdraws his hand and falls to looking at the sleet and snow again until they seem, by being long looked at, to fall so thick and fast that he is obliged to close his eyes for a minute on the giddy whirl of white flakes and icy blots.

He began to look at them as soon as it was light. The day is not yet far spent when he conceives it to be necessary that her rooms should be prepared for her. It is very cold and wet. Let there be good fires. Let them know that she is expected. Please see to it yourself. He writes to this purpose on his slate, and Mrs. Rouncewell with a heavy heart obeys.

"For I dread, George," the old lady says to her son, who waits below to keep her company when she has a little leisure, "I dread, my dear, that my Lady will never more set foot within these walls."

"That's a bad presentiment, mother."

"Nor yet within the walls of Chesney Wold, my dear."

"That's worse. But why, mother?"

"When I saw my Lady yesterday, George, she looked to me—and I may say at me too—as if the step on the Ghost's Walk had almost walked her down."

"Come, come! You alarm yourself with old-story fears, mother."

"No I don't, my dear. No I don't. It's going on for sixty year that I have been in this family, and I never had any fears for it before. But it's breaking up, my dear; the great old Dedlock family is breaking up."

"I hope not, mother."

"I am thankful I have lived long enough to be with Sir Leicester in this illness and trouble, for I know I am not too old nor too useless to be a welcomer sight to him than anybody else in my place would be. But the step on the Ghost's Walk will walk my Lady down, George; it has been many a day behind her, and now it will pass her and go on."

"Well, mother dear, I say again, I hope not."

"Ah, so do I, George," the old lady returns, shaking her head and parting her folded hands. "But if my fears come true, and he has to know it, who will tell him!"

"Are these her rooms?"

"These are my Lady's rooms, just as she left them."

"Why, now," says the trooper, glancing round him and speaking in a lower voice, "I begin to understand how you come to think as you do think, mother. Rooms get an awful look about them when they are fitted up, like these, for one person you are used to see in them, and that person is away under any shadow, let alone being God knows where."

He is not far out. As all partings foreshadow the great final one, so, empty rooms, bereft of a familiar presence, mournfully whisper what your room and what mine must one day be. My Lady's state has a hollow look, thus gloomy and abandoned; and in the inner apartment, where Mr. Bucket last night made his secret perquisition, the traces of her dresses and her ornaments, even the mirrors accustomed to reflect them when they were a portion of herself, have a desolate and vacant air. Dark and cold as the wintry day is, it is darker and colder in these deserted chambers than in many a hut that will barely exclude the weather; and though the servants heap fires in the grates and set the couches and the chairs within the warm glass screens that let their ruddy light shoot through to the furthest corners, there is a heavy cloud upon the rooms which no light will dispel.

The old housekeeper and her son remain until the preparations are complete, and then she returns upstairs. Volumnia has taken Mrs. Rouncewell's place in the meantime, though pearl necklaces and rouge pots, however calculated to embellish Bath, are but indifferent comforts to the invalid under present circumstances. Volumnia, not being supposed to know (and indeed not knowing) what is the matter, has found it a ticklish task to offer appropriate observations and consequently has supplied their place with distracting smoothings of the bed-linen, elaborate locomotion on tiptoe, vigilant peeping at her kinsman's eyes, and one exasperating whisper to herself of, "He is asleep." In disproof of which superfluous remark Sir Leicester has indignantly written on the slate, "I am not."

Yielding, therefore, the chair at the bedside to the quaint old housekeeper, Volumnia sits at a table a little removed, sympathetically sighing. Sir Leicester watches the sleet and snow and listens for the returning steps that he expects. In the ears of his old servant, looking as if she had stepped out of an old picture-frame to attend a summoned Dedlock to another world, the silence is fraught with echoes of her own words, "Who will tell him!"

He has been under his valet's hands this morning to be made presentable and is as well got up as the circumstances will allow. He is propped with pillows, his grey hair is brushed in its usual manner, his linen is arranged to a nicety, and he is wrapped in a responsible dressing-gown. His eye-glass and his watch are ready to his hand. It is necessary—less to his own dignity now perhaps than for her sake—that he should be seen as little disturbed and as much himself as may be. Women will talk, and Volumnia, though a Dedlock, is no exceptional case. He keeps her here, there is little doubt, to prevent her talking somewhere else. He is very ill, but he makes his present stand against distress of mind and body most courageously.

The fair Volumnia, being one of those sprightly girls who cannot long continue silent without imminent peril of seizure by the dragon Boredom, soon indicates the approach of that monster with a series of undisguisable yawns. Finding it impossible to suppress those yawns by any other process than conversation, she compliments Mrs. Rouncewell on her son, declaring that he positively is one of the finest figures she ever saw and as soldierly a looking person, she should think, as what's his name, her favourite Life Guardsman—the man she dotes on, the dearest of creatures—who was killed at Waterloo.

Sir Leicester hears this tribute with so much surprise and stares about him in such a confused way that Mrs. Rouncewell feels it necessary to explain.

"Miss Dedlock don't speak of my eldest son, Sir Leicester, but my youngest. I have found him. He has come home."

Sir Leicester breaks silence with a harsh cry. "George? Your son George come home, Mrs. Rouncewell?"

The old housekeeper wipes her eyes. "Thank God. Yes, Sir Leicester."

Does this discovery of some one lost, this return of some one so long gone, come upon him as a strong confirmation of his hopes? Does he think, "Shall I not, with the aid I have, recall her safely after this, there being fewer hours in her case than there are years in his?"

It is of no use entreating him; he is determined to speak now, and he does. In a thick crowd of sounds, but still intelligibly enough to be understood.

"Why did you not tell me, Mrs. Rouncewell?"

"It happened only yesterday, Sir Leicester, and I doubted your being well enough to be talked to of such things."

Besides, the giddy Volumnia now remembers with her little scream that nobody was to have known of his being Mrs. Rouncewell's son and that she was not to have told. But Mrs. Rouncewell protests, with warmth enough to swell the stomacher, that of course she would have told Sir Leicester as soon as he got better.

"Where is your son George, Mrs. Rouncewell?" asks Sir Leicester,

Mrs. Rouncewell, not a little alarmed by his disregard of the doctor's injunctions, replies, in London.

"Where in London?"

Mrs. Rouncewell is constrained to admit that he is in the house.

"Bring him here to my room. Bring him directly."

The old lady can do nothing but go in search of him. Sir Leicester, with such power of movement as he has, arranges himself a little to receive him. When he has done so, he looks out again at the falling sleet and snow and listens again for the returning steps. A quantity of straw has been tumbled down in the street to deaden the noises there, and she might be driven to the door perhaps without his hearing wheels.

He is lying thus, apparently forgetful of his newer and minor surprise, when the housekeeper returns, accompanied by her trooper son. Mr. George approaches softly to the bedside, makes his bow, squares his chest, and stands, with his face flushed, very heartily ashamed of himself.

"Good heaven, and it is really George Rouncewell!" exclaims Sir Leicester. "Do you remember me, George?"

The trooper needs to look at him and to separate this sound from that sound before he knows what he has said, but doing this and being a little helped by his mother, he replies, "I must have a very bad memory, indeed, Sir Leicester, if I failed to remember you."

"When I look at you, George Rouncewell," Sir Leicester observes with difficulty, "I see something of a boy at Chesney Wold—I remember well—very well."

He looks at the trooper until tears come into his eyes, and then he looks at the sleet and snow again.

"I ask your pardon, Sir Leicester," says the trooper, "but would you accept of my arms to raise you up? You would lie easier, Sir Leicester, if you would allow me to move you."

"If you please, George Rouncewell; if you will be so good."

The trooper takes him in his arms like a child, lightly raises him, and turns him with his face more towards the window. "Thank you. You have your mother's gentleness," returns Sir Leicester, "and your own strength. Thank you."

He signs to him with his hand not to go away. George quietly remains at the bedside, waiting to be spoken to.

"Why did you wish for secrecy?" It takes Sir Leicester some time to ask this.

"Truly I am not much to boast of, Sir Leicester, and I—I should still, Sir Leicester, if you was not so indisposed—which I hope you will not be long—I should still hope for the favour of being allowed to remain unknown in general. That involves explanations not very hard to be guessed at, not very well timed here, and not very creditable to myself. However opinions may differ on a variety of subjects, I should think it would be universally agreed, Sir Leicester, that I am not much to boast of."

"You have been a soldier," observes Sir Leicester, "and a faithful one."

George makes his military bow. "As far as that goes, Sir Leicester, I have done my duty under discipline, and it was the least I could do."

"You find me," says Sir Leicester, whose eyes are much attracted towards him, "far from well, George Rouncewell."

"I am very sorry both to hear it and to see it, Sir Leicester."

"I am sure you are. No. In addition to my older malady, I have had a sudden and bad attack. Something that deadens," making an endeavour to pass one hand down one side, "and confuses," touching his lips.

George, with a look of assent and sympathy, makes another bow. The different times when they were both young men (the trooper much the younger of the two) and looked at one another down at Chesney Wold arise before them both and soften both.

Sir Leicester, evidently with a great determination to say, in his own manner, something that is on his mind before relapsing into silence, tries to raise himself among his pillows a little more. George, observant of the action, takes him in his arms again and places him as he desires to be. "Thank you, George. You are another self to me. You have often carried my spare gun at Chesney Wold, George. You are familiar to me in these strange circumstances, very familiar." He has put Sir Leicester's sounder arm over his shoulder in lifting him up, and Sir Leicester is slow in drawing it away again as he says these words.

"I was about to add," he presently goes on, "I was about to add, respecting this attack, that it was unfortunately simultaneous with a slight misunderstanding between my Lady and myself. I do not mean that there was any difference between us (for there has been none), but that there was a misunderstanding of certain circumstances important only to ourselves, which deprives me, for a little while, of my Lady's society. She has found it necessary to make a journey—I trust will shortly return. Volumnia, do I make myself intelligible? The words are not quite under my command in the manner of pronouncing them."

Volumnia understands him perfectly, and in truth he delivers himself with far greater plainness than could have been supposed possible a minute ago. The effort by which he does so is written in the anxious and labouring expression of his face. Nothing but the strength of his purpose enables him to make it.

"Therefore, Volumnia, I desire to say in your presence—and in the presence of my old retainer and friend, Mrs. Rouncewell, whose truth and fidelity no one can question, and in the presence of her son George, who comes back like a familiar recollection of my youth in the home of my ancestors at Chesney Wold—in case I should relapse, in case I should not recover, in case I should lose both my speech and the power of writing, though I hope for better things—"

The old housekeeper weeping silently; Volumnia in the greatest agitation, with the freshest bloom on her cheeks; the trooper with his arms folded and his head a little bent, respectfully attentive.

"Therefore I desire to say, and to call you all to witness—beginning, Volumnia, with yourself, most solemnly—that I am on unaltered terms with Lady Dedlock. That I assert no cause whatever of complaint against her. That I have ever had the strongest affection for her, and that I retain it undiminished. Say this to herself, and to every one. If you ever say less than this, you will be guilty of deliberate falsehood to me."

Volumnia tremblingly protests that she will observe his injunctions to the letter.

"My Lady is too high in position, too handsome, too accomplished, too superior in most respects to the best of those by whom she is surrounded, not to have her enemies and traducers, I dare say. Let it be known to them, as I make it known to you, that being of sound mind, memory, and understanding, I revoke no disposition I have made in her favour. I abridge nothing I have ever bestowed upon her. I am on unaltered terms with her, and I recall—having the full power to do it if I were so disposed, as you see—no act I have done for her advantage and happiness."

His formal array of words might have at any other time, as it has often had, something ludicrous in it, but at this time it is serious and affecting. His noble earnestness, his fidelity, his gallant shielding of her, his generous conquest of his own wrong and his own pride for her sake, are simply honourable, manly, and true. Nothing less worthy can be seen through the lustre of such qualities in the commonest mechanic, nothing less worthy can be seen in the best-born gentleman. In such a light both aspire alike, both rise alike, both children of the dust shine equally.

Overpowered by his exertions, he lays his head back on his pillows and closes his eyes for not more than a minute, when he again resumes his watching of the weather and his attention to the muffled sounds. In the rendering of those little services, and in the manner of their acceptance, the trooper has become installed as necessary to him. Nothing has been said, but it is quite understood. He falls a step or two backward to be out of sight and mounts guard a little behind his mother's chair.

The day is now beginning to decline. The mist and the sleet into which the snow has all resolved itself are darker, and the blaze begins to tell more vividly upon the room walls and furniture. The gloom augments; the bright gas springs up in the streets; and the pertinacious oil lamps which yet hold their ground there, with their source of life half frozen and half thawed, twinkle gaspingly like fiery fish out of water—as they are. The world, which has been rumbling over the straw and pulling at the bell, "to inquire," begins to go home, begins to dress, to dine, to discuss its dear friend with all the last new modes, as already mentioned.

Now does Sir Leicester become worse, restless, uneasy, and in great pain. Volumnia, lighting a candle (with a predestined aptitude for doing something objectionable), is bidden to put it out again, for it is not yet dark enough. Yet it is very dark too, as dark as it will be all night. By and by she tries again. No! Put it out. It is not dark enough yet.

His old housekeeper is the first to understand that he is striving to uphold the fiction with himself that it is not growing late.

"Dear Sir Leicester, my honoured master," she softly whispers, "I must, for your own good, and my duty, take the freedom of begging and praying that you will not lie here in the lone darkness watching and waiting and dragging through the time. Let me draw the curtains, and light the candles, and make things more comfortable about you. The church-clocks will strike the hours just the same, Sir Leicester, and the night will pass away just the same. My Lady will come back, just the same."

"I know it, Mrs. Rouncewell, but I am weak—and she has been so long gone."

"Not so very long, Sir Leicester. Not twenty-four hours yet."

"But that is a long time. Oh, it is a long time!"

He says it with a groan that wrings her heart.

She knows that this is not a period for bringing the rough light upon him; she thinks his tears too sacred to be seen, even by her. Therefore she sits in the darkness for a while without a word, then gently begins to move about, now stirring the fire, now standing at the dark window looking out. Finally he tells her, with recovered self-command, "As you say, Mrs. Rouncewell, it is no worse for being confessed. It is getting late, and they are not come. Light the room!" When it is lighted and the weather shut out, it is only left to him to listen.

But they find that however dejected and ill he is, he brightens when a quiet pretence is made of looking at the fires in her rooms and being sure that everything is ready to receive her. Poor pretence as it is, these allusions to her being expected keep up hope within him.

Midnight comes, and with it the same blank. The carriages in the streets are few, and other late sounds in that neighbourhood there are none, unless a man so very nomadically drunk as to stray into the frigid zone goes brawling and bellowing along the pavement. Upon this wintry night it is so still that listening to the intense silence is like looking at intense darkness. If any distant sound be audible in this case, it departs through the gloom like a feeble light in that, and all is heavier than before.

The corporation of servants are dismissed to bed (not unwilling to go, for they were up all last night), and only Mrs. Rouncewell and George keep watch in Sir Leicester's room. As the night lags tardily on—or rather when it seems to stop altogether, at between two and three o'clock—they find a restless craving on him to know more about the weather, now he cannot see it. Hence George, patrolling regularly every half-hour to the rooms so carefully looked after, extends his march to the hall-door, looks about him, and brings back the best report he can make of the worst of nights, the sleet still falling and even the stone footways lying ankle-deep in icy sludge.

Volumnia, in her room up a retired landing on the staircase—the second turning past the end of the carving and gilding, a cousinly room containing a fearful abortion of a portrait of Sir Leicester banished for its crimes, and commanding in the day a solemn yard planted with dried-up shrubs like antediluvian specimens of black tea—is a prey to horrors of many kinds. Not last nor least among them, possibly, is a horror of what may befall her little income in the event, as she expresses it, "of anything happening" to Sir Leicester. Anything, in this sense, meaning one thing only; and that the last thing that can happen to the consciousness of any baronet in the known world.

An effect of these horrors is that Volumnia finds she cannot go to bed in her own room or sit by the fire in her own room, but must come forth with her fair head tied up in a profusion of shawl, and her fair form enrobed in drapery, and parade the mansion like a ghost, particularly haunting the rooms, warm and luxurious, prepared for one who still does not return. Solitude under such circumstances being not to be thought of, Volumnia is attended by her maid, who, impressed from her own bed for that purpose, extremely cold, very sleepy, and generally an injured maid as condemned by circumstances to take office with a cousin, when she had resolved to be maid to nothing less than ten thousand a year, has not a sweet expression of countenance.

The periodical visits of the trooper to these rooms, however, in the course of his patrolling is an assurance of protection and company both to mistress and maid, which renders them very acceptable in the small hours of the night. Whenever he is heard advancing, they both make some little decorative preparation to receive him; at other times they divide their watches into short scraps of oblivion and dialogues not wholly free from acerbity, as to whether Miss Dedlock, sitting with her feet upon the fender, was or was not falling into the fire when rescued (to her great displeasure) by her guardian genius the maid.

"How is Sir Leicester now, Mr. George?" inquires Volumnia, adjusting her cowl over her head.

"Why, Sir Leicester is much the same, miss. He is very low and ill, and he even wanders a little sometimes."

"Has he asked for me?" inquires Volumnia tenderly.

"Why, no, I can't say he has, miss. Not within my hearing, that is to say."

"This is a truly sad time, Mr. George."

"It is indeed, miss. Hadn't you better go to bed?"

"You had a deal better go to bed, Miss Dedlock," quoth the maid sharply.

But Volumnia answers No! No! She may be asked for, she may be wanted at a moment's notice. She never should forgive herself "if anything was to happen" and she was not on the spot. She declines to enter on the question, mooted by the maid, how the spot comes to be there, and not in her room (which is nearer to Sir Leicester's), but staunchly declares that on the spot she will remain. Volumnia further makes a merit of not having "closed an eye"—as if she had twenty or thirty—though it is hard to reconcile this statement with her having most indisputably opened two within five minutes.

But when it comes to four o'clock, and still the same blank, Volumnia's constancy begins to fail her, or rather it begins to strengthen, for she now considers that it is her duty to be ready for the morrow, when much may be expected of her, that, in fact, howsoever anxious to remain upon the spot, it may be required of her, as an act of self-devotion, to desert the spot. So when the trooper reappears with his, "Hadn't you better go to bed, miss?" and when the maid protests, more sharply than before, "You had a deal better go to bed, Miss Dedlock!" she meekly rises and says, "Do with me what you think best!"

Mr. George undoubtedly thinks it best to escort her on his arm to the door of her cousinly chamber, and the maid as undoubtedly thinks it best to hustle her into bed with mighty little ceremony. Accordingly, these steps are taken; and now the trooper, in his rounds, has the house to himself.

There is no improvement in the weather. From the portico, from the eaves, from the parapet, from every ledge and post and pillar, drips the thawed snow. It has crept, as if for shelter, into the lintels of the great door—under it, into the corners of the windows, into every chink and crevice of retreat, and there wastes and dies. It is falling still; upon the roof, upon the skylight, even through the skylight, and drip, drip, drip, with the regularity of the Ghost's Walk, on the stone floor below.

The trooper, his old recollections awakened by the solitary grandeur of a great house—no novelty to him once at Chesney Wold—goes up the stairs and through the chief rooms, holding up his light at arm's length. Thinking of his varied fortunes within the last few weeks, and of his rustic boyhood, and of the two periods of his life so strangely brought together across the wide intermediate space; thinking of the murdered man whose image is fresh in his mind; thinking of the lady who has disappeared from these very rooms and the tokens of whose recent presence are all here; thinking of the master of the house upstairs and of the foreboding, "Who will tell him!" he looks here and looks there, and reflects how he MIGHT see something now, which it would tax his boldness to walk up to, lay his hand upon, and prove to be a fancy. But it is all blank, blank as the darkness above and below, while he goes up the great staircase again, blank as the oppressive silence.

"All is still in readiness, George Rouncewell?"

"Quite orderly and right, Sir Leicester."

"No word of any kind?"

The trooper shakes his head.

"No letter that can possibly have been overlooked?"

But he knows there is no such hope as that and lays his head down without looking for an answer.

Very familiar to him, as he said himself some hours ago, George Rouncewell lifts him into easier positions through the long remainder of the blank wintry night, and equally familiar with his unexpressed wish, extinguishes the light and undraws the curtains at the first late break of day. The day comes like a phantom. Cold, colourless, and vague, it sends a warning streak before it of a deathlike hue, as if it cried out, "Look what I am bringing you who watch there! Who will tell him!"

CHAPTER LIX
ESTHER'S NARRATIVE

It was three o'clock in the morning when the houses outside London did at last begin to exclude the country and to close us in with streets. We had made our way along roads in a far worse condition than when we had traversed them by daylight, both the fall and the thaw having lasted ever since; but the energy of my companion never slackened. It had only been, as I thought, of less assistance than the horses in getting us on, and it had often aided them. They had stopped exhausted half-way up hills, they had been driven through streams of turbulent water, they had slipped down and become entangled with the harness; but he and his little lantern had been always ready, and when the mishap was set right, I had never heard any variation in his cool, "Get on, my lads!"

The steadiness and confidence with which he had directed our journey back I could not account for. Never wavering, he never even stopped to make an inquiry until we were within a few miles of London. A very few words, here and there, were then enough for him; and thus we came, at between three and four o'clock in the morning, into Islington.

I will not dwell on the suspense and anxiety with which I reflected all this time that we were leaving my mother farther and farther behind every minute. I think I had some strong hope that he must be right and could not fail to have a satisfactory object in following this woman, but I tormented myself with questioning it and discussing it during the whole journey. What was to ensue when we found her and what could compensate us for this loss of time were questions also that I could not possibly dismiss; my mind was quite tortured by long dwelling on such reflections when we stopped.

We stopped in a high-street where there was a coach-stand. My companion paid our two drivers, who were as completely covered with splashes as if they had been dragged along the roads like the carriage itself, and giving them some brief direction where to take it, lifted me out of it and into a hackney-coach he had chosen from the rest.

"Why, my dear!" he said as he did this. "How wet you are!"

I had not been conscious of it. But the melted snow had found its way into the carriage, and I had got out two or three times when a fallen horse was plunging and had to be got up, and the wet had penetrated my dress. I assured him it was no matter, but the driver, who knew him, would not be dissuaded by me from running down the street to his stable, whence he brought an armful of clean dry straw. They shook it out and strewed it well about me, and I found it warm and comfortable.

"Now, my dear," said Mr. Bucket, with his head in at the window after I was shut up. "We're a-going to mark this person down. It may take a little time, but you don't mind that. You're pretty sure that I've got a motive. Ain't you?"

I little thought what it was, little thought in how short a time I should understand it better, but I assured him that I had confidence in him.

"So you may have, my dear," he returned. "And I tell you what! If you only repose half as much confidence in me as I repose in you after what I've experienced of you, that'll do. Lord! You're no trouble at all. I never see a young woman in any station of society—and I've seen many elevated ones too—conduct herself like you have conducted yourself since you was called out of your bed. You're a pattern, you know, that's what you are," said Mr. Bucket warmly; "you're a pattern."

I told him I was very glad, as indeed I was, to have been no hindrance to him, and that I hoped I should be none now.

"My dear," he returned, "when a young lady is as mild as she's game, and as game as she's mild, that's all I ask, and more than I expect. She then becomes a queen, and that's about what you are yourself."

With these encouraging words—they really were encouraging to me under those lonely and anxious circumstances—he got upon the box, and we once more drove away. Where we drove I neither knew then nor have ever known since, but we appeared to seek out the narrowest and worst streets in London. Whenever I saw him directing the driver, I was prepared for our descending into a deeper complication of such streets, and we never failed to do so.

Sometimes we emerged upon a wider thoroughfare or came to a larger building than the generality, well lighted. Then we stopped at offices like those we had visited when we began our journey, and I saw him in consultation with others. Sometimes he would get down by an archway or at a street corner and mysteriously show the light of his little lantern. This would attract similar lights from various dark quarters, like so many insects, and a fresh consultation would be held. By degrees we appeared to contract our search within narrower and easier limits. Single police-officers on duty could now tell Mr. Bucket what he wanted to know and point to him where to go. At last we stopped for a rather long conversation between him and one of these men, which I supposed to be satisfactory from his manner of nodding from time to time. When it was finished he came to me looking very busy and very attentive.

"Now, Miss Summerson," he said to me, "you won't be alarmed whatever comes off, I know. It's not necessary for me to give you any further caution than to tell you that we have marked this person down and that you may be of use to me before I know it myself. I don't like to ask such a thing, my dear, but would you walk a little way?"

Of course I got out directly and took his arm.

"It ain't so easy to keep your feet," said Mr. Bucket, "but take time."

Although I looked about me confusedly and hurriedly as we crossed the street, I thought I knew the place. "Are we in Holborn?" I asked him.

"Yes," said Mr. Bucket. "Do you know this turning?"

"It looks like Chancery Lane."

"And was christened so, my dear," said Mr. Bucket.

We turned down it, and as we went shuffling through the sleet, I heard the clocks strike half-past five. We passed on in silence and as quickly as we could with such a foot-hold, when some one coming towards us on the narrow pavement, wrapped in a cloak, stopped and stood aside to give me room. In the same moment I heard an exclamation of wonder and my own name from Mr. Woodcourt. I knew his voice very well.

It was so unexpected and so—I don't know what to call it, whether pleasant or painful—to come upon it after my feverish wandering journey, and in the midst of the night, that I could not keep back the tears from my eyes. It was like hearing his voice in a strange country.

"My dear Miss Summerson, that you should be out at this hour, and in such weather!"

He had heard from my guardian of my having been called away on some uncommon business and said so to dispense with any explanation. I told him that we had but just left a coach and were going—but then I was obliged to look at my companion.

"Why, you see, Mr. Woodcourt"—he had caught the name from me—"we are a-going at present into the next street. Inspector Bucket."

Mr. Woodcourt, disregarding my remonstrances, had hurriedly taken off his cloak and was putting it about me. "That's a good move, too," said Mr. Bucket, assisting, "a very good move."

"May I go with you?" said Mr. Woodcourt. I don't know whether to me or to my companion.

"Why, Lord!" exclaimed Mr. Bucket, taking the answer on himself. "Of course you may."

It was all said in a moment, and they took me between them, wrapped in the cloak.

"I have just left Richard," said Mr. Woodcourt. "I have been sitting with him since ten o'clock last night."

"Oh, dear me, he is ill!"

"No, no, believe me; not ill, but not quite well. He was depressed and faint—you know he gets so worried and so worn sometimes—and Ada sent to me of course; and when I came home I found her note and came straight here. Well! Richard revived so much after a little while, and Ada was so happy and so convinced of its being my doing, though God knows I had little enough to do with it, that I remained with him until he had been fast asleep some hours. As fast asleep as she is now, I hope!"

His friendly and familiar way of speaking of them, his unaffected devotion to them, the grateful confidence with which I knew he had inspired my darling, and the comfort he was to her; could I separate all this from his promise to me? How thankless I must have been if it had not recalled the words he said to me when he was so moved by the change in my appearance: "I will accept him as a trust, and it shall be a sacred one!"

We now turned into another narrow street. "Mr. Woodcourt," said Mr. Bucket, who had eyed him closely as we came along, "our business takes us to a law-stationer's here, a certain Mr. Snagsby's. What, you know him, do you?" He was so quick that he saw it in an instant.

"Yes, I know a little of him and have called upon him at this place."

"Indeed, sir?" said Mr. Bucket. "Then you will be so good as to let me leave Miss Summerson with you for a moment while I go and have half a word with him?"

The last police-officer with whom he had conferred was standing silently behind us. I was not aware of it until he struck in on my saying I heard some one crying.

"Don't be alarmed, miss," he returned. "It's Snagsby's servant."

"Why, you see," said Mr. Bucket, "the girl's subject to fits, and has 'em bad upon her to-night. A most contrary circumstance it is, for I want certain information out of that girl, and she must be brought to reason somehow."

"At all events, they wouldn't be up yet if it wasn't for her, Mr. Bucket," said the other man. "She's been at it pretty well all night, sir."

"Well, that's true," he returned. "My light's burnt out. Show yours a moment."

All this passed in a whisper a door or two from the house in which I could faintly hear crying and moaning. In the little round of light produced for the purpose, Mr. Bucket went up to the door and knocked. The door was opened after he had knocked twice, and he went in, leaving us standing in the street.

"Miss Summerson," said Mr. Woodcourt, "if without obtruding myself on your confidence I may remain near you, pray let me do so."

"You are truly kind," I answered. "I need wish to keep no secret of my own from you; if I keep any, it is another's."

"I quite understand. Trust me, I will remain near you only so long as I can fully respect it."

"I trust implicitly to you," I said. "I know and deeply feel how sacredly you keep your promise."

After a short time the little round of light shone out again, and Mr. Bucket advanced towards us in it with his earnest face. "Please to come in, Miss Summerson," he said, "and sit down by the fire. Mr. Woodcourt, from information I have received I understand you are a medical man. Would you look to this girl and see if anything can be done to bring her round. She has a letter somewhere that I particularly want. It's not in her box, and I think it must be about her; but she is so twisted and clenched up that she is difficult to handle without hurting."

We all three went into the house together; although it was cold and raw, it smelt close too from being up all night. In the passage behind the door stood a scared, sorrowful-looking little man in a grey coat who seemed to have a naturally polite manner and spoke meekly.

"Downstairs, if you please, Mr. Bucket," said he. "The lady will excuse the front kitchen; we use it as our workaday sitting-room. The back is Guster's bedroom, and in it she's a-carrying on, poor thing, to a frightful extent!"

We went downstairs, followed by Mr. Snagsby, as I soon found the little man to be. In the front kitchen, sitting by the fire, was Mrs. Snagsby, with very red eyes and a very severe expression of face.

"My little woman," said Mr. Snagsby, entering behind us, "to wave—not to put too fine a point upon it, my dear—hostilities for one single moment in the course of this prolonged night, here is Inspector Bucket, Mr. Woodcourt, and a lady."

She looked very much astonished, as she had reason for doing, and looked particularly hard at me.

"My little woman," said Mr. Snagsby, sitting down in the remotest corner by the door, as if he were taking a liberty, "it is not unlikely that you may inquire of me why Inspector Bucket, Mr. Woodcourt, and a lady call upon us in Cook's Court, Cursitor Street, at the present hour. I don't know. I have not the least idea. If I was to be informed, I should despair of understanding, and I'd rather not be told."

He appeared so miserable, sitting with his head upon his hand, and I appeared so unwelcome, that I was going to offer an apology when Mr. Bucket took the matter on himself.

"Now, Mr. Snagsby," said he, "the best thing you can do is to go along with Mr. Woodcourt to look after your Guster—"

"My Guster, Mr. Bucket!" cried Mr. Snagsby. "Go on, sir, go on. I shall be charged with that next."

"And to hold the candle," pursued Mr. Bucket without correcting himself, "or hold her, or make yourself useful in any way you're asked. Which there's not a man alive more ready to do, for you're a man of urbanity and suavity, you know, and you've got the sort of heart that can feel for another. Mr. Woodcourt, would you be so good as see to her, and if you can get that letter from her, to let me have it as soon as ever you can?"

As they went out, Mr. Bucket made me sit down in a corner by the fire and take off my wet shoes, which he turned up to dry upon the fender, talking all the time.

"Don't you be at all put out, miss, by the want of a hospitable look from Mrs. Snagsby there, because she's under a mistake altogether. She'll find that out sooner than will be agreeable to a lady of her generally correct manner of forming her thoughts, because I'm a-going to explain it to her." Here, standing on the hearth with his wet hat and shawls in his hand, himself a pile of wet, he turned to Mrs. Snagsby. "Now, the first thing that I say to you, as a married woman possessing what you may call charms, you know—'Believe Me, if All Those Endearing,' and cetrer—you're well acquainted with the song, because it's in vain for you to tell me that you and good society are strangers—charms—attractions, mind you, that ought to give you confidence in yourself—is, that you've done it."

Mrs. Snagsby looked rather alarmed, relented a little and faltered, what did Mr. Bucket mean.

"What does Mr. Bucket mean?" he repeated, and I saw by his face that all the time he talked he was listening for the discovery of the letter, to my own great agitation, for I knew then how important it must be; "I'll tell you what he means, ma'am. Go and see Othello acted. That's the tragedy for you."

Mrs. Snagsby consciously asked why.

"Why?" said Mr. Bucket. "Because you'll come to that if you don't look out. Why, at the very moment while I speak, I know what your mind's not wholly free from respecting this young lady. But shall I tell you who this young lady is? Now, come, you're what I call an intellectual woman—with your soul too large for your body, if you come to that, and chafing it—and you know me, and you recollect where you saw me last, and what was talked of in that circle. Don't you? Yes! Very well. This young lady is that young lady."

Mrs. Snagsby appeared to understand the reference better than I did at the time.

"And Toughey—him as you call Jo—was mixed up in the same business, and no other; and the law-writer that you know of was mixed up in the same business, and no other; and your husband, with no more knowledge of it than your great grandfather, was mixed up (by Mr. Tulkinghorn, deceased, his best customer) in the same business, and no other; and the whole bileing of people was mixed up in the same business, and no other. And yet a married woman, possessing your attractions, shuts her eyes (and sparklers too), and goes and runs her delicate-formed head against a wall. Why, I am ashamed of you! (I expected Mr. Woodcourt might have got it by this time.)"

Mrs. Snagsby shook her head and put her handkerchief to her eyes.

"Is that all?" said Mr. Bucket excitedly. "No. See what happens. Another person mixed up in that business and no other, a person in a wretched state, comes here to-night and is seen a-speaking to your maid-servant; and between her and your maid-servant there passes a paper that I would give a hundred pound for, down. What do you do? You hide and you watch 'em, and you pounce upon that maid-servant—knowing what she's subject to and what a little thing will bring 'em on—in that surprising manner and with that severity that, by the Lord, she goes off and keeps off, when a life may be hanging upon that girl's words!"

He so thoroughly meant what he said now that I involuntarily clasped my hands and felt the room turning away from me. But it stopped. Mr. Woodcourt came in, put a paper into his hand, and went away again.

"Now, Mrs. Snagsby, the only amends you can make," said Mr. Bucket, rapidly glancing at it, "is to let me speak a word to this young lady in private here. And if you know of any help that you can give to that gentleman in the next kitchen there or can think of any one thing that's likelier than another to bring the girl round, do your swiftest and best!" In an instant she was gone, and he had shut the door. "Now my dear, you're steady and quite sure of yourself?"

"Quite," said I.

"Whose writing is that?"

It was my mother's. A pencil-writing, on a crushed and torn piece of paper, blotted with wet. Folded roughly like a letter, and directed to me at my guardian's.

"You know the hand," he said, "and if you are firm enough to read it to me, do! But be particular to a word."

It had been written in portions, at different times. I read what follows:

I came to the cottage with two objects. First, to see the dear one, if I could, once more—but only to see her—not to speak to her or let her know that I was near. The other object, to elude pursuit and to be lost. Do not blame the mother for her share. The assistance that she rendered me, she rendered on my strongest assurance that it was for the dear one's good. You remember her dead child. The men's consent I bought, but her help was freely given.

"'I came.' That was written," said my companion, "when she rested there. It bears out what I made of it. I was right."

The next was written at another time:

I have wandered a long distance, and for many hours, and I know that I must soon die. These streets! I have no purpose but to die. When I left, I had a worse, but I am saved from adding that guilt to the rest. Cold, wet, and fatigue are sufficient causes for my being found dead, but I shall die of others, though I suffer from these. It was right that all that had sustained me should give way at once and that I should die of terror and my conscience.

"Take courage," said Mr. Bucket. "There's only a few words more."

Those, too, were written at another time. To all appearance, almost in the dark:

I have done all I could do to be lost. I shall be soon forgotten so, and shall disgrace him least. I have nothing about me by which I can be recognized. This paper I part with now. The place where I shall lie down, if I can get so far, has been often in my mind. Farewell. Forgive.

Mr. Bucket, supporting me with his arm, lowered me gently into my chair. "Cheer up! Don't think me hard with you, my dear, but as soon as ever you feel equal to it, get your shoes on and be ready."

I did as he required, but I was left there a long time, praying for my unhappy mother. They were all occupied with the poor girl, and I heard Mr. Woodcourt directing them and speaking to her often. At length he came in with Mr. Bucket and said that as it was important to address her gently, he thought it best that I should ask her for whatever information we desired to obtain. There was no doubt that she could now reply to questions if she were soothed and not alarmed. The questions, Mr. Bucket said, were how she came by the letter, what passed between her and the person who gave her the letter, and where the person went. Holding my mind as steadily as I could to these points, I went into the next room with them. Mr. Woodcourt would have remained outside, but at my solicitation went in with us.

The poor girl was sitting on the floor where they had laid her down. They stood around her, though at a little distance, that she might have air. She was not pretty and looked weak and poor, but she had a plaintive and a good face, though it was still a little wild. I kneeled on the ground beside her and put her poor head upon my shoulder, whereupon she drew her arm round my neck and burst into tears.

"My poor girl," said I, laying my face against her forehead, for indeed I was crying too, and trembling, "it seems cruel to trouble you now, but more depends on our knowing something about this letter than I could tell you in an hour."

She began piteously declaring that she didn't mean any harm, she didn't mean any harm, Mrs. Snagsby!

"We are all sure of that," said I. "But pray tell me how you got it."

"Yes, dear lady, I will, and tell you true. I'll tell true, indeed, Mrs. Snagsby."

"I am sure of that," said I. "And how was it?"

"I had been out on an errand, dear lady—long after it was dark—quite late; and when I came home, I found a common-looking person, all wet and muddy, looking up at our house. When she saw me coming in at the door, she called me back and said did I live here. And I said yes, and she said she knew only one or two places about here, but had lost her way and couldn't find them. Oh, what shall I do, what shall I do! They won't believe me! She didn't say any harm to me, and I didn't say any harm to her, indeed, Mrs. Snagsby!"

It was necessary for her mistress to comfort her—which she did, I must say, with a good deal of contrition—before she could be got beyond this.

"She could not find those places," said I.

"No!" cried the girl, shaking her head. "No! Couldn't find them. And she was so faint, and lame, and miserable, Oh so wretched, that if you had seen her, Mr. Snagsby, you'd have given her half a crown, I know!"

"Well, Guster, my girl," said he, at first not knowing what to say. "I hope I should."

"And yet she was so well spoken," said the girl, looking at me with wide open eyes, "that it made a person's heart bleed. And so she said to me, did I know the way to the burying ground? And I asked her which burying ground. And she said, the poor burying ground. And so I told her I had been a poor child myself, and it was according to parishes. But she said she meant a poor burying ground not very far from here, where there was an archway, and a step, and an iron gate."

As I watched her face and soothed her to go on, I saw that Mr. Bucket received this with a look which I could not separate from one of alarm.

"Oh, dear, dear!" cried the girl, pressing her hair back with her hands. "What shall I do, what shall I do! She meant the burying ground where the man was buried that took the sleeping-stuff—that you came home and told us of, Mr. Snagsby—that frightened me so, Mrs. Snagsby. Oh, I am frightened again. Hold me!"

"You are so much better now," said I. "Pray, pray tell me more."

"Yes I will, yes I will! But don't be angry with me, that's a dear lady, because I have been so ill."

Angry with her, poor soul!

"There! Now I will, now I will. So she said, could I tell her how to find it, and I said yes, and I told her; and she looked at me with eyes like almost as if she was blind, and herself all waving back. And so she took out the letter, and showed it me, and said if she was to put that in the post-office, it would be rubbed out and not minded and never sent; and would I take it from her, and send it, and the messenger would be paid at the house. And so I said yes, if it was no harm, and she said no—no harm. And so I took it from her, and she said she had nothing to give me, and I said I was poor myself and consequently wanted nothing. And so she said God bless you, and went."

"And did she go—"

"Yes," cried the girl, anticipating the inquiry. "Yes! She went the way I had shown her. Then I came in, and Mrs. Snagsby came behind me from somewhere and laid hold of me, and I was frightened."

Mr. Woodcourt took her kindly from me. Mr. Bucket wrapped me up, and immediately we were in the street. Mr. Woodcourt hesitated, but I said, "Don't leave me now!" and Mr. Bucket added, "You'll be better with us, we may want you; don't lose time!"

I have the most confused impressions of that walk. I recollect that it was neither night nor day, that morning was dawning but the street-lamps were not yet put out, that the sleet was still falling and that all the ways were deep with it. I recollect a few chilled people passing in the streets. I recollect the wet house-tops, the clogged and bursting gutters and water-spouts, the mounds of blackened ice and snow over which we passed, the narrowness of the courts by which we went. At the same time I remember that the poor girl seemed to be yet telling her story audibly and plainly in my hearing, that I could feel her resting on my arm, that the stained house-fronts put on human shapes and looked at me, that great water-gates seemed to be opening and closing in my head or in the air, and that the unreal things were more substantial than the real.

At last we stood under a dark and miserable covered way, where one lamp was burning over an iron gate and where the morning faintly struggled in. The gate was closed. Beyond it was a burial ground—a dreadful spot in which the night was very slowly stirring, but where I could dimly see heaps of dishonoured graves and stones, hemmed in by filthy houses with a few dull lights in their windows and on whose walls a thick humidity broke out like a disease. On the step at the gate, drenched in the fearful wet of such a place, which oozed and splashed down everywhere, I saw, with a cry of pity and horror, a woman lying—Jenny, the mother of the dead child.

I ran forward, but they stopped me, and Mr. Woodcourt entreated me with the greatest earnestness, even with tears, before I went up to the figure to listen for an instant to what Mr. Bucket said. I did so, as I thought. I did so, as I am sure.

"Miss Summerson, you'll understand me, if you think a moment. They changed clothes at the cottage."

They changed clothes at the cottage. I could repeat the words in my mind, and I knew what they meant of themselves, but I attached no meaning to them in any other connexion.

"And one returned," said Mr. Bucket, "and one went on. And the one that went on only went on a certain way agreed upon to deceive and then turned across country and went home. Think a moment!"

I could repeat this in my mind too, but I had not the least idea what it meant. I saw before me, lying on the step, the mother of the dead child. She lay there with one arm creeping round a bar of the iron gate and seeming to embrace it. She lay there, who had so lately spoken to my mother. She lay there, a distressed, unsheltered, senseless creature. She who had brought my mother's letter, who could give me the only clue to where my mother was; she, who was to guide us to rescue and save her whom we had sought so far, who had come to this condition by some means connected with my mother that I could not follow, and might be passing beyond our reach and help at that moment; she lay there, and they stopped me! I saw but did not comprehend the solemn and compassionate look in Mr. Woodcourt's face. I saw but did not comprehend his touching the other on the breast to keep him back. I saw him stand uncovered in the bitter air, with a reverence for something. But my understanding for all this was gone.

I even heard it said between them, "Shall she go?"

"She had better go. Her hands should be the first to touch her. They have a higher right than ours."

I passed on to the gate and stooped down. I lifted the heavy head, put the long dank hair aside, and turned the face. And it was my mother, cold and dead.

CHAPTER LX
PERSPECTIVE

I proceed to other passages of my narrative. From the goodness of all about me I derived such consolation as I can never think of unmoved. I have already said so much of myself, and so much still remains, that I will not dwell upon my sorrow. I had an illness, but it was not a long one; and I would avoid even this mention of it if I could quite keep down the recollection of their sympathy.

I proceed to other passages of my narrative.

During the time of my illness, we were still in London, where Mrs. Woodcourt had come, on my guardian's invitation, to stay with us. When my guardian thought me well and cheerful enough to talk with him in our old way—though I could have done that sooner if he would have believed me—I resumed my work and my chair beside his. He had appointed the time himself, and we were alone.

"Dame Trot," said he, receiving me with a kiss, "welcome to the growlery again, my dear. I have a scheme to develop, little woman. I propose to remain here, perhaps for six months, perhaps for a longer time—as it may be. Quite to settle here for a while, in short."

"And in the meanwhile leave Bleak House?" said I.

"Aye, my dear? Bleak House," he returned, "must learn to take care of itself."

I thought his tone sounded sorrowful, but looking at him, I saw his kind face lighted up by its pleasantest smile.

"Bleak House," he repeated—and his tone did NOT sound sorrowful, I found—"must learn to take care of itself. It is a long way from Ada, my dear, and Ada stands much in need of you."

"It's like you, guardian," said I, "to have been taking that into consideration for a happy surprise to both of us."

"Not so disinterested either, my dear, if you mean to extol me for that virtue, since if you were generally on the road, you could be seldom with me. And besides, I wish to hear as much and as often of Ada as I can in this condition of estrangement from poor Rick. Not of her alone, but of him too, poor fellow."

"Have you seen Mr. Woodcourt, this morning, guardian?"

"I see Mr. Woodcourt every morning, Dame Durden."

"Does he still say the same of Richard?"

"Just the same. He knows of no direct bodily illness that he has; on the contrary, he believes that he has none. Yet he is not easy about him; who CAN be?"

My dear girl had been to see us lately every day, some times twice in a day. But we had foreseen, all along, that this would only last until I was quite myself. We knew full well that her fervent heart was as full of affection and gratitude towards her cousin John as it had ever been, and we acquitted Richard of laying any injunctions upon her to stay away; but we knew on the other hand that she felt it a part of her duty to him to be sparing of her visits at our house. My guardian's delicacy had soon perceived this and had tried to convey to her that he thought she was right.

"Dear, unfortunate, mistaken Richard," said I. "When will he awake from his delusion!"

"He is not in the way to do so now, my dear," replied my guardian. "The more he suffers, the more averse he will be to me, having made me the principal representative of the great occasion of his suffering."

I could not help adding, "So unreasonably!"

"Ah, Dame Trot, Dame Trot," returned my guardian, "what shall we find reasonable in Jarndyce and Jarndyce! Unreason and injustice at the top, unreason and injustice at the heart and at the bottom, unreason and injustice from beginning to end—if it ever has an end—how should poor Rick, always hovering near it, pluck reason out of it? He no more gathers grapes from thorns or figs from thistles than older men did in old times."

His gentleness and consideration for Richard whenever we spoke of him touched me so that I was always silent on this subject very soon.

"I suppose the Lord Chancellor, and the Vice Chancellors, and the whole Chancery battery of great guns would be infinitely astonished by such unreason and injustice in one of their suitors," pursued my guardian. "When those learned gentlemen begin to raise moss-roses from the powder they sow in their wigs, I shall begin to be astonished too!"

He checked himself in glancing towards the window to look where the wind was and leaned on the back of my chair instead.

"Well, well, little woman! To go on, my dear. This rock we must leave to time, chance, and hopeful circumstance. We must not shipwreck Ada upon it. She cannot afford, and he cannot afford, the remotest chance of another separation from a friend. Therefore I have particularly begged of Woodcourt, and I now particularly beg of you, my dear, not to move this subject with Rick. Let it rest. Next week, next month, next year, sooner or later, he will see me with clearer eyes. I can wait."

But I had already discussed it with him, I confessed; and so, I thought, had Mr. Woodcourt.

"So he tells me," returned my guardian. "Very good. He has made his protest, and Dame Durden has made hers, and there is nothing more to be said about it. Now I come to Mrs. Woodcourt. How do you like her, my dear?"

In answer to this question, which was oddly abrupt, I said I liked her very much and thought she was more agreeable than she used to be.

"I think so too," said my guardian. "Less pedigree? Not so much of Morgan ap—what's his name?"

That was what I meant, I acknowledged, though he was a very harmless person, even when we had had more of him.

"Still, upon the whole, he is as well in his native mountains," said my guardian. "I agree with you. Then, little woman, can I do better for a time than retain Mrs. Woodcourt here?"

No. And yet—

My guardian looked at me, waiting for what I had to say.

I had nothing to say. At least I had nothing in my mind that I could say. I had an undefined impression that it might have been better if we had had some other inmate, but I could hardly have explained why even to myself. Or, if to myself, certainly not to anybody else.

"You see," said my guardian, "our neighbourhood is in Woodcourt's way, and he can come here to see her as often as he likes, which is agreeable to them both; and she is familiar to us and fond of you."

Yes. That was undeniable. I had nothing to say against it. I could not have suggested a better arrangement, but I was not quite easy in my mind. Esther, Esther, why not? Esther, think!

"It is a very good plan indeed, dear guardian, and we could not do better."

"Sure, little woman?"

Quite sure. I had had a moment's time to think, since I had urged that duty on myself, and I was quite sure.

"Good," said my guardian. "It shall be done. Carried unanimously."

"Carried unanimously," I repeated, going on with my work.

It was a cover for his book-table that I happened to be ornamenting. It had been laid by on the night preceding my sad journey and never resumed. I showed it to him now, and he admired it highly. After I had explained the pattern to him and all the great effects that were to come out by and by, I thought I would go back to our last theme.

"You said, dear guardian, when we spoke of Mr. Woodcourt before Ada left us, that you thought he would give a long trial to another country. Have you been advising him since?"

"Yes, little woman, pretty often."

"Has he decided to do so?"

"I rather think not."

"Some other prospect has opened to him, perhaps?" said I.

"Why—yes—perhaps," returned my guardian, beginning his answer in a very deliberate manner. "About half a year hence or so, there is a medical attendant for the poor to be appointed at a certain place in Yorkshire. It is a thriving place, pleasantly situated—streams and streets, town and country, mill and moor—and seems to present an opening for such a man. I mean a man whose hopes and aims may sometimes lie (as most men's sometimes do, I dare say) above the ordinary level, but to whom the ordinary level will be high enough after all if it should prove to be a way of usefulness and good service leading to no other. All generous spirits are ambitious, I suppose, but the ambition that calmly trusts itself to such a road, instead of spasmodically trying to fly over it, is of the kind I care for. It is Woodcourt's kind."

"And will he get this appointment?" I asked.

"Why, little woman," returned my guardian, smiling, "not being an oracle, I cannot confidently say, but I think so. His reputation stands very high; there were people from that part of the country in the shipwreck; and strange to say, I believe the best man has the best chance. You must not suppose it to be a fine endowment. It is a very, very commonplace affair, my dear, an appointment to a great amount of work and a small amount of pay; but better things will gather about it, it may be fairly hoped."

"The poor of that place will have reason to bless the choice if it falls on Mr. Woodcourt, guardian."

"You are right, little woman; that I am sure they will."

We said no more about it, nor did he say a word about the future of Bleak House. But it was the first time I had taken my seat at his side in my mourning dress, and that accounted for it, I considered.

I now began to visit my dear girl every day in the dull dark corner where she lived. The morning was my usual time, but whenever I found I had an hour or so to spare, I put on my bonnet and bustled off to Chancery Lane. They were both so glad to see me at all hours, and used to brighten up so when they heard me opening the door and coming in (being quite at home, I never knocked), that I had no fear of becoming troublesome just yet.

On these occasions I frequently found Richard absent. At other times he would be writing or reading papers in the cause at that table of his, so covered with papers, which was never disturbed. Sometimes I would come upon him lingering at the door of Mr. Vholes's office. Sometimes I would meet him in the neighbourhood lounging about and biting his nails. I often met him wandering in Lincoln's Inn, near the place where I had first seen him, oh how different, how different!

That the money Ada brought him was melting away with the candles I used to see burning after dark in Mr. Vholes's office I knew very well. It was not a large amount in the beginning, he had married in debt, and I could not fail to understand, by this time, what was meant by Mr. Vholes's shoulder being at the wheel—as I still heard it was. My dear made the best of housekeepers and tried hard to save, but I knew that they were getting poorer and poorer every day.

She shone in the miserable corner like a beautiful star. She adorned and graced it so that it became another place. Paler than she had been at home, and a little quieter than I had thought natural when she was yet so cheerful and hopeful, her face was so unshadowed that I half believed she was blinded by her love for Richard to his ruinous career.

I went one day to dine with them while I was under this impression. As I turned into Symond's Inn, I met little Miss Flite coming out. She had been to make a stately call upon the wards in Jarndyce, as she still called them, and had derived the highest gratification from that ceremony. Ada had already told me that she called every Monday at five o'clock, with one little extra white bow in her bonnet, which never appeared there at any other time, and with her largest reticule of documents on her arm.

"My dear!" she began. "So delighted! How do you do! So glad to see you. And you are going to visit our interesting Jarndyce wards? TO be sure! Our beauty is at home, my dear, and will be charmed to see you."

"Then Richard is not come in yet?" said I. "I am glad of that, for I was afraid of being a little late."

"No, he is not come in," returned Miss Flite. "He has had a long day in court. I left him there with Vholes. You don't like Vholes, I hope? DON'T like Vholes. Dan-gerous man!"

"I am afraid you see Richard oftener than ever now," said I.

"My dearest," returned Miss Flite, "daily and hourly. You know what I told you of the attraction on the Chancellor's table? My dear, next to myself he is the most constant suitor in court. He begins quite to amuse our little party. Ve-ry friendly little party, are we not?"

It was miserable to hear this from her poor mad lips, though it was no surprise.

"In short, my valued friend," pursued Miss Flite, advancing her lips to my ear with an air of equal patronage and mystery, "I must tell you a secret. I have made him my executor. Nominated, constituted, and appointed him. In my will. Ye-es."

"Indeed?" said I.

"Ye-es," repeated Miss Flite in her most genteel accents, "my executor, administrator, and assign. (Our Chancery phrases, my love.) I have reflected that if I should wear out, he will be able to watch that judgment. Being so very regular in his attendance."

It made me sigh to think of him.

"I did at one time mean," said Miss Flite, echoing the sigh, "to nominate, constitute, and appoint poor Gridley. Also very regular, my charming girl. I assure you, most exemplary! But he wore out, poor man, so I have appointed his successor. Don't mention it. This is in confidence."

She carefully opened her reticule a little way and showed me a folded piece of paper inside as the appointment of which she spoke.

"Another secret, my dear. I have added to my collection of birds."

"Really, Miss Flite?" said I, knowing how it pleased her to have her confidence received with an appearance of interest.

She nodded several times, and her face became overcast and gloomy. "Two more. I call them the Wards in Jarndyce. They are caged up with all the others.

With Hope, Joy, Youth, Peace, Rest, Life, Dust, Ashes, Waste, Want, Ruin, Despair, Madness, Death, Cunning, Folly, Words, Wigs, Rags, Sheepskin, Plunder, Precedent, Jargon, Gammon, and Spinach!"

The poor soul kissed me with the most troubled look I had ever seen in her and went her way. Her manner of running over the names of her birds, as if she were afraid of hearing them even from her own lips, quite chilled me.

This was not a cheering preparation for my visit, and I could have dispensed with the company of Mr. Vholes, when Richard (who arrived within a minute or two after me) brought him to share our dinner. Although it was a very plain one, Ada and Richard were for some minutes both out of the room together helping to get ready what we were to eat and drink. Mr. Vholes took that opportunity of holding a little conversation in a low voice with me. He came to the window where I was sitting and began upon Symond's Inn.

"A dull place, Miss Summerson, for a life that is not an official one," said Mr. Vholes, smearing the glass with his black glove to make it clearer for me.

"There is not much to see here," said I.

"Nor to hear, miss," returned Mr. Vholes. "A little music does occasionally stray in, but we are not musical in the law and soon eject it. I hope Mr. Jarndyce is as well as his friends could wish him?"

I thanked Mr. Vholes and said he was quite well.

"I have not the pleasure to be admitted among the number of his friends myself," said Mr. Vholes, "and I am aware that the gentlemen of our profession are sometimes regarded in such quarters with an unfavourable eye. Our plain course, however, under good report and evil report, and all kinds of prejudice (we are the victims of prejudice), is to have everything openly carried on. How do you find Mr. C. looking, Miss Summerson?"

"He looks very ill. Dreadfully anxious."

"Just so," said Mr. Vholes.

He stood behind me with his long black figure reaching nearly to the ceiling of those low rooms, feeling the pimples on his face as if they were ornaments and speaking inwardly and evenly as though there were not a human passion or emotion in his nature.

"Mr. Woodcourt is in attendance upon Mr. C., I believe?" he resumed.

"Mr. Woodcourt is his disinterested friend," I answered.

"But I mean in professional attendance, medical attendance."

"That can do little for an unhappy mind," said I.

"Just so," said Mr. Vholes.

So slow, so eager, so bloodless and gaunt, I felt as if Richard were wasting away beneath the eyes of this adviser and there were something of the vampire in him.

"Miss Summerson," said Mr. Vholes, very slowly rubbing his gloved hands, as if, to his cold sense of touch, they were much the same in black kid or out of it, "this was an ill-advised marriage of Mr. C.'s."

I begged he would excuse me from discussing it. They had been engaged when they were both very young, I told him (a little indignantly) and when the prospect before them was much fairer and brighter. When Richard had not yielded himself to the unhappy influence which now darkened his life.

"Just so," assented Mr. Vholes again. "Still, with a view to everything being openly carried on, I will, with your permission, Miss Summerson, observe to you that I consider this a very ill-advised marriage indeed. I owe the opinion not only to Mr. C.'s connexions, against whom I should naturally wish to protect myself, but also to my own reputation—dear to myself as a professional man aiming to keep respectable; dear to my three girls at home, for whom I am striving to realize some little independence; dear, I will even say, to my aged father, whom it is my privilege to support."

"It would become a very different marriage, a much happier and better marriage, another marriage altogether, Mr. Vholes," said I, "if Richard were persuaded to turn his back on the fatal pursuit in which you are engaged with him."

Mr. Vholes, with a noiseless cough—or rather gasp—into one of his black gloves, inclined his head as if he did not wholly dispute even that.

"Miss Summerson," he said, "it may be so; and I freely admit that the young lady who has taken Mr. C.'s name upon herself in so ill-advised a manner—you will I am sure not quarrel with me for throwing out that remark again, as a duty I owe to Mr. C.'s connexions—is a highly genteel young lady. Business has prevented me from mixing much with general society in any but a professional character; still I trust I am competent to perceive that she is a highly genteel young lady. As to beauty, I am not a judge of that myself, and I never did give much attention to it from a boy, but I dare say the young lady is equally eligible in that point of view. She is considered so (I have heard) among the clerks in the Inn, and it is a point more in their way than in mine. In reference to Mr. C.'s pursuit of his interests—"

"Oh! His interests, Mr. Vholes!"

"Pardon me," returned Mr. Vholes, going on in exactly the same inward and dispassionate manner. "Mr. C. takes certain interests under certain wills disputed in the suit. It is a term we use. In reference to Mr. C.'s pursuit of his interests, I mentioned to you, Miss Summerson, the first time I had the pleasure of seeing you, in my desire that everything should be openly carried on—I used those words, for I happened afterwards to note them in my diary, which is producible at any time—I mentioned to you that Mr. C. had laid down the principle of watching his own interests, and that when a client of mine laid down a principle which was not of an immoral (that is to say, unlawful) nature, it devolved upon me to carry it out. I HAVE carried it out; I do carry it out. But I will not smooth things over to any connexion of Mr. C.'s on any account. As open as I was to Mr. Jarndyce, I am to you. I regard it in the light of a professional duty to be so, though it can be charged to no one.

I openly say, unpalatable as it may be, that I consider Mr. C.'s affairs in a very bad way, that I consider Mr. C. himself in a very bad way, and that I regard this as an exceedingly ill-advised marriage. Am I here, sir? Yes, I thank you; I am here, Mr. C., and enjoying the pleasure of some agreeable conversation with Miss Summerson, for which I have to thank you very much, sir!"

He broke off thus in answer to Richard, who addressed him as he came into the room. By this time I too well understood Mr. Vholes's scrupulous way of saving himself and his respectability not to feel that our worst fears did but keep pace with his client's progress.

We sat down to dinner, and I had an opportunity of observing Richard, anxiously. I was not disturbed by Mr. Vholes (who took off his gloves to dine), though he sat opposite to me at the small table, for I doubt if, looking up at all, he once removed his eyes from his host's face. I found Richard thin and languid, slovenly in his dress, abstracted in his manner, forcing his spirits now and then, and at other intervals relapsing into a dull thoughtfulness. About his large bright eyes that used to be so merry there was a wanness and a restlessness that changed them altogether. I cannot use the expression that he looked old. There is a ruin of youth which is not like age, and into such a ruin Richard's youth and youthful beauty had all fallen away.

He ate little and seemed indifferent what it was, showed himself to be much more impatient than he used to be, and was quick even with Ada. I thought at first that his old light-hearted manner was all gone, but it shone out of him sometimes as I had occasionally known little momentary glimpses of my own old face to look out upon me from the glass. His laugh had not quite left him either, but it was like the echo of a joyful sound, and that is always sorrowful.

Yet he was as glad as ever, in his old affectionate way, to have me there, and we talked of the old times pleasantly. These did not appear to be interesting to Mr. Vholes, though he occasionally made a gasp which I believe was his smile. He rose shortly after dinner and said that with the permission of the ladies he would retire to his office.

"Always devoted to business, Vholes!" cried Richard.

"Yes, Mr. C.," he returned, "the interests of clients are never to be neglected, sir. They are paramount in the thoughts of a professional man like myself, who wishes to preserve a good name among his fellow-practitioners and society at large. My denying myself the pleasure of the present agreeable conversation may not be wholly irrespective of your own interests, Mr. C."

Richard expressed himself quite sure of that and lighted Mr. Vholes out. On his return he told us, more than once, that Vholes was a good fellow, a safe fellow, a man who did what he pretended to do, a very good fellow indeed! He was so defiant about it that it struck me he had begun to doubt Mr. Vholes.

Then he threw himself on the sofa, tired out; and Ada and I put things to rights, for they had no other servant than the woman who attended to the chambers. My dear girl had a cottage piano there and quietly sat down to sing some of Richard's favourites, the lamp being first removed into the next room, as he complained of its hurting his eyes.

I sat between them, at my dear girl's side, and felt very melancholy listening to her sweet voice. I think Richard did too; I think he darkened the room for that reason. She had been singing some time, rising between whiles to bend over him and speak to him, when Mr. Woodcourt came in. Then he sat down by Richard and half playfully, half earnestly, quite naturally and easily, found out how he felt and where he had been all day. Presently he proposed to accompany him in a short walk on one of the bridges, as it was a moonlight airy night; and Richard readily consenting, they went out together.

They left my dear girl still sitting at the piano and me still sitting beside her. When they were gone out, I drew my arm round her waist. She put her left hand in mine (I was sitting on that side), but kept her right upon the keys, going over and over them without striking any note.

"Esther, my dearest," she said, breaking silence, "Richard is never so well and I am never so easy about him as when he is with Allan Woodcourt. We have to thank you for that."

I pointed out to my darling how this could scarcely be, because Mr. Woodcourt had come to her cousin John's house and had known us all there, and because he had always liked Richard, and Richard had always liked him, and—and so forth.

"All true," said Ada, "but that he is such a devoted friend to us we owe to you."

I thought it best to let my dear girl have her way and to say no more about it. So I said as much. I said it lightly, because I felt her trembling.

"Esther, my dearest, I want to be a good wife, a very, very good wife indeed. You shall teach me."

I teach! I said no more, for I noticed the hand that was fluttering over the keys, and I knew that it was not I who ought to speak, that it was she who had something to say to me.

"When I married Richard I was not insensible to what was before him. I had been perfectly happy for a long time with you, and I had never known any trouble or anxiety, so loved and cared for, but I understood the danger he was in, dear Esther."

"I know, I know, my darling."

"When we were married I had some little hope that I might be able to convince him of his mistake, that he might come to regard it in a new way as my husband and not pursue it all the more desperately for my sake—as he does. But if I had not had that hope, I would have married him just the same, Esther. Just the same!"

In the momentary firmness of the hand that was never still—a firmness inspired by the utterance of these last words, and dying away with them—I saw the confirmation of her earnest tones.

"You are not to think, my dearest Esther, that I fail to see what you see and fear what you fear. No one can understand him better than I do. The greatest wisdom that ever lived in the world could scarcely know Richard better than my love does."

She spoke so modestly and softly and her trembling hand expressed such agitation as it moved to and fro upon the silent notes! My dear, dear girl!

"I see him at his worst every day. I watch him in his sleep. I know every change of his face. But when I married Richard I was quite determined, Esther, if heaven would help me, never to show him that I grieved for what he did and so to make him more unhappy. I want him, when he comes home, to find no trouble in my face. I want him, when he looks at me, to see what he loved in me. I married him to do this, and this supports me."

I felt her trembling more. I waited for what was yet to come, and I now thought I began to know what it was.

"And something else supports me, Esther."

She stopped a minute. Stopped speaking only; her hand was still in motion.

"I look forward a little while, and I don't know what great aid may come to me. When Richard turns his eyes upon me then, there may be something lying on my breast more eloquent than I have been, with greater power than mine to show him his true course and win him back."

Her hand stopped now. She clasped me in her arms, and I clasped her in mine.

"If that little creature should fail too, Esther, I still look forward. I look forward a long while, through years and years, and think that then, when I am growing old, or when I am dead perhaps, a beautiful woman, his daughter, happily married, may be proud of him and a blessing to him. Or that a generous brave man, as handsome as he used to be, as hopeful, and far more happy, may walk in the sunshine with him, honouring his grey head and saying to himself, 'I thank God this is my father! Ruined by a fatal inheritance, and restored through me!'"

Oh, my sweet girl, what a heart was that which beat so fast against me!

"These hopes uphold me, my dear Esther, and I know they will. Though sometimes even they depart from me before a dread that arises when I look at Richard."

I tried to cheer my darling, and asked her what it was. Sobbing and weeping, she replied, "That he may not live to see his child."

CHAPTER LXI
A DISCOVERY

The days when I frequented that miserable corner which my dear girl brightened can never fade in my remembrance. I never see it, and I never wish to see it now; I have been there only once since, but in my memory there is a mournful glory shining on the place which will shine for ever.

Not a day passed without my going there, of course. At first I found Mr. Skimpole there, on two or three occasions, idly playing the piano and talking in his usual vivacious strain. Now, besides my very much mistrusting the probability of his being there without making Richard poorer, I felt as if there were something in his careless gaiety too inconsistent with what I knew of the depths of Ada's life. I clearly perceived, too, that Ada shared my feelings. I therefore resolved, after much thinking of it, to make a private visit to Mr. Skimpole and try delicately to explain myself. My dear girl was the great consideration that made me bold.

I set off one morning, accompanied by Charley, for Somers Town. As I approached the house, I was strongly inclined to turn back, for I felt what a desperate attempt it was to make an impression on Mr. Skimpole and how extremely likely it was that he would signally defeat me. However, I thought that being there, I would go through with it. I knocked with a trembling hand at Mr. Skimpole's door—literally with a hand, for the knocker was gone—and after a long parley gained admission from an Irishwoman, who was in the area when I knocked, breaking up the lid of a water-butt with a poker to light the fire with.

Mr. Skimpole, lying on the sofa in his room, playing the flute a little, was enchanted to see me. Now, who should receive me, he asked. Who would I prefer for mistress of the ceremonies? Would I have his Comedy daughter, his Beauty daughter, or his Sentiment daughter? Or would I have all the daughters at once in a perfect nosegay?

I replied, half defeated already, that I wished to speak to himself only if he would give me leave.

"My dear Miss Summerson, most joyfully! Of course," he said, bringing his chair nearer mine and breaking into his fascinating smile, "of course it's not business. Then it's pleasure!"

I said it certainly was not business that I came upon, but it was not quite a pleasant matter.

"Then, my dear Miss Summerson," said he with the frankest gaiety, "don't allude to it. Why should you allude to anything that is NOT a pleasant matter? I never do. And you are a much pleasanter creature, in every point of view, than I. You are perfectly pleasant; I am imperfectly pleasant; then, if I never allude to an unpleasant matter, how much less should you! So that's disposed of, and we will talk of something else."

Although I was embarrassed, I took courage to intimate that I still wished to pursue the subject.

"I should think it a mistake," said Mr. Skimpole with his airy laugh, "if I thought Miss Summerson capable of making one. But I don't!"

"Mr. Skimpole," said I, raising my eyes to his, "I have so often heard you say that you are unacquainted with the common affairs of life—"

"Meaning our three banking-house friends, L, S, and who's the junior partner? D?" said Mr. Skimpole, brightly. "Not an idea of them!"

"—That perhaps," I went on, "you will excuse my boldness on that account. I think you ought most seriously to know that Richard is poorer than he was."

"Dear me!" said Mr. Skimpole. "So am I, they tell me."

"And in very embarrassed circumstances."

"Parallel case, exactly!" said Mr. Skimpole with a delighted countenance.

"This at present naturally causes Ada much secret anxiety, and as I think she is less anxious when no claims are made upon her by visitors, and as Richard has one uneasiness always heavy on his mind, it has occurred to me to take the liberty of saying that—if you would—not—"

I was coming to the point with great difficulty when he took me by both hands and with a radiant face and in the liveliest way anticipated it.

"Not go there? Certainly not, my dear Miss Summerson, most assuredly not. Why SHOULD I go there? When I go anywhere, I go for pleasure. I don't go anywhere for pain, because I was made for pleasure. Pain comes to ME when it wants me. Now, I have had very little pleasure at our dear Richard's lately, and your practical sagacity demonstrates why. Our young friends, losing the youthful poetry which was once so captivating in them, begin to think, 'This is a man who wants pounds.' So I am; I always want pounds; not for myself, but because tradespeople always want them of me. Next, our young friends begin to think, becoming mercenary, 'This is the man who HAD pounds, who borrowed them,' which I did. I always borrow pounds. So our young friends, reduced to prose (which is much to be regretted), degenerate in their power of imparting pleasure to me. Why should I go to see them, therefore? Absurd!"

Through the beaming smile with which he regarded me as he reasoned thus, there now broke forth a look of disinterested benevolence quite astonishing.

"Besides," he said, pursuing his argument in his tone of light-hearted conviction, "if I don't go anywhere for pain—which would be a perversion of the intention of my being, and a monstrous thing to do—why should I go anywhere to be the cause of pain? If I went to see our young friends in their present ill-regulated state of mind, I should give them pain. The associations with me would be disagreeable. They might say, 'This is the man who had pounds and who can't pay pounds,' which I can't, of course; nothing could be more out of the question! Then kindness requires that I shouldn't go near them—and I won't."

He finished by genially kissing my hand and thanking me. Nothing but Miss Summerson's fine tact, he said, would have found this out for him.

I was much disconcerted, but I reflected that if the main point were gained, it mattered little how strangely he perverted everything leading to it. I had determined to mention something else, however, and I thought I was not to be put off in that.

"Mr. Skimpole," said I, "I must take the liberty of saying before I conclude my visit that I was much surprised to learn, on the best authority, some little time ago, that you knew with whom that poor boy left Bleak House and that you accepted a present on that occasion. I have not mentioned it to my guardian, for I fear it would hurt him unnecessarily; but I may say to you that I was much surprised."

"No? Really surprised, my dear Miss Summerson?" he returned inquiringly, raising his pleasant eyebrows.

"Greatly surprised."

He thought about it for a little while with a highly agreeable and whimsical expression of face, then quite gave it up and said in his most engaging manner, "You know what a child I am. Why surprised?"

I was reluctant to enter minutely into that question, but as he begged I would, for he was really curious to know, I gave him to understand in the gentlest words I could use that his conduct seemed to involve a disregard of several moral obligations. He was much amused and interested when he heard this and said, "No, really?" with ingenuous simplicity.

"You know I don't intend to be responsible. I never could do it. Responsibility is a thing that has always been above me—or below me," said Mr. Skimpole. "I don't even know which; but as I understand the way in which my dear Miss Summerson (always remarkable for her practical good sense and clearness) puts this case, I should imagine it was chiefly a question of money, do you know?"

I incautiously gave a qualified assent to this.

"Ah! Then you see," said Mr. Skimpole, shaking his head, "I am hopeless of understanding it."

I suggested, as I rose to go, that it was not right to betray my guardian's confidence for a bribe.

"My dear Miss Summerson," he returned with a candid hilarity that was all his own, "I can't be bribed."

"Not by Mr. Bucket?" said I.

"No," said he. "Not by anybody. I don't attach any value to money. I don't care about it, I don't know about it, I don't want it, I don't keep it—it goes away from me directly. How can I be bribed?"

I showed that I was of a different opinion, though I had not the capacity for arguing the question.

"On the contrary," said Mr. Skimpole, "I am exactly the man to be placed in a superior position in such a case as that. I am above the rest of mankind in such a case as that. I can act with philosophy in such a case as that. I am not warped by prejudices, as an Italian baby is by bandages. I am as free as the air. I feel myself as far above suspicion as Caesar's wife."

Anything to equal the lightness of his manner and the playful impartiality with which he seemed to convince himself, as he tossed the matter about like a ball of feathers, was surely never seen in anybody else!

"Observe the case, my dear Miss Summerson. Here is a boy received into the house and put to bed in a state that I strongly object to. The boy being in bed, a man arrives—like the house that Jack built. Here is the man who demands the boy who is received into the house and put to bed in a state that I strongly object to. Here is a bank-note produced by the man who demands the boy who is received into the house and put to bed in a state that I strongly object to. Here is the Skimpole who accepts the bank-note produced by the man who demands the boy who is received into the house and put to bed in a state that I strongly object to. Those are the facts. Very well. Should the Skimpole have refused the note? WHY should the Skimpole have refused the note? Skimpole protests to Bucket, 'What's this for? I don't understand it, it is of no use to me, take it away.' Bucket still entreats Skimpole to accept it. Are there reasons why Skimpole, not being warped by prejudices, should accept it? Yes. Skimpole perceives them. What are they? Skimpole reasons with himself, this is a tamed lynx, an active police-officer, an intelligent man, a person of a peculiarly directed energy and great subtlety both of conception and execution, who discovers our friends and enemies for us when they run away, recovers our property for us when we are robbed, avenges us comfortably when we are murdered. This active police-officer and intelligent man has acquired, in the exercise of his art, a strong faith in money; he finds it very useful to him, and he makes it very useful to society. Shall I shake that faith in Bucket because I want it myself; shall I deliberately blunt one of Bucket's weapons; shall I positively paralyse Bucket in his next detective operation? And again. If it is blameable in Skimpole to take the note, it is blameable in Bucket to offer the note—much more blameable in Bucket, because he is the knowing man. Now, Skimpole wishes to think well of Bucket; Skimpole deems it essential, in its little place, to the general cohesion of things, that he SHOULD think well of Bucket. The state expressly asks him to trust to Bucket. And he does. And that's all he does!"

I had nothing to offer in reply to this exposition and therefore took my leave. Mr. Skimpole, however, who was in excellent spirits, would not hear of my returning home attended only by "Little Coavinses," and accompanied me himself. He entertained me on the way with a variety of delightful conversation and assured me, at parting, that he should never forget the fine tact with which I had found that out for him about our young friends.

As it so happened that I never saw Mr. Skimpole again, I may at once finish what I know of his history. A coolness arose between him and my guardian, based principally on the foregoing grounds and on his having heartlessly disregarded my guardian's entreaties (as we afterwards learned from Ada) in reference to Richard. His being heavily in my guardian's debt had nothing to do with their separation. He died some five years afterwards and left a diary behind him, with letters and other materials towards his life, which was published and which showed him to have been the victim of a combination on the part of mankind against an amiable child. It was considered very pleasant reading, but I never read more of it myself than the sentence on which I chanced to light on opening the book. It was this: "Jarndyce, in common with most other men I have known, is the incarnation of selfishness."

And now I come to a part of my story touching myself very nearly indeed, and for which I was quite unprepared when the circumstance occurred. Whatever little lingerings may have now and then revived in my mind associated with my poor old face had only revived as belonging to a part of my life that was gone—gone like my infancy or my childhood. I have suppressed none of my many weaknesses on that subject, but have written them as faithfully as my memory has recalled them. And I hope to do, and mean to do, the same down to the last words of these pages, which I see now not so very far before me.

The months were gliding away, and my dear girl, sustained by the hopes she had confided in me, was the same beautiful star in the miserable corner. Richard, more worn and haggard, haunted the court day after day, listlessly sat there the whole day long when he knew there was no remote chance of the suit being mentioned, and became one of the stock sights of the place. I wonder whether any of the gentlemen remembered him as he was when he first went there.

So completely was he absorbed in his fixed idea that he used to avow in his cheerful moments that he should never have breathed the fresh air now "but for Woodcourt." It was only Mr. Woodcourt who could occasionally divert his attention for a few hours at a time and rouse him, even when he sunk into a lethargy of mind and body that alarmed us greatly, and the returns of which became more frequent as the months went on. My dear girl was right in saying that he only pursued his errors the more desperately for her sake. I have no doubt that his desire to retrieve what he had lost was rendered the more intense by his grief for his young wife, and became like the madness of a gamester.

I was there, as I have mentioned, at all hours. When I was there at night, I generally went home with Charley in a coach; sometimes my guardian would meet me in the neighbourhood, and we would walk home together. One evening he had arranged to meet me at eight o'clock. I could not leave, as I usually did, quite punctually at the time, for I was working for my dear girl and had a few stitches more to do to finish what I was about; but it was within a few minutes of the hour when I bundled up my little work-basket, gave my darling my last kiss for the night, and hurried downstairs. Mr. Woodcourt went with me, as it was dusk.

When we came to the usual place of meeting—it was close by, and Mr. Woodcourt had often accompanied me before—my guardian was not there. We waited half an hour, walking up and down, but there were no signs of him. We agreed that he was either prevented from coming or that he had come and gone away, and Mr. Woodcourt proposed to walk home with me.

It was the first walk we had ever taken together, except that very short one to the usual place of meeting. We spoke of Richard and Ada the whole way. I did not thank him in words for what he had done—my appreciation of it had risen above all words then—but I hoped he might not be without some understanding of what I felt so strongly.

Arriving at home and going upstairs, we found that my guardian was out and that Mrs. Woodcourt was out too. We were in the very same room into which I had brought my blushing girl when her youthful lover, now her so altered husband, was the choice of her young heart, the very same room from which my guardian and I had watched them going away through the sunlight in the fresh bloom of their hope and promise.

We were standing by the opened window looking down into the street when Mr. Woodcourt spoke to me. I learned in a moment that he loved me. I learned in a moment that my scarred face was all unchanged to him. I learned in a moment that what I had thought was pity and compassion was devoted, generous, faithful love. Oh, too late to know it now, too late, too late. That was the first ungrateful thought I had. Too late.

"When I returned," he told me, "when I came back, no richer than when I went away, and found you newly risen from a sick bed, yet so inspired by sweet consideration for others and so free from a selfish thought—"

"Oh, Mr. Woodcourt, forbear, forbear!" I entreated him. "I do not deserve your high praise. I had many selfish thoughts at that time, many!"

"Heaven knows, beloved of my life," said he, "that my praise is not a lover's praise, but the truth. You do not know what all around you see in Esther Summerson, how many hearts she touches and awakens, what sacred admiration and what love she wins."

"Oh, Mr. Woodcourt," cried I, "it is a great thing to win love, it is a great thing to win love! I am proud of it, and honoured by it; and the hearing of it causes me to shed these tears of mingled joy and sorrow—joy that I have won it, sorrow that I have not deserved it better; but I am not free to think of yours."

I said it with a stronger heart, for when he praised me thus and when I heard his voice thrill with his belief that what he said was true, I aspired to be more worthy of it. It was not too late for that. Although I closed this unforeseen page in my life to-night, I could be worthier of it all through my life. And it was a comfort to me, and an impulse to me, and I felt a dignity rise up within me that was derived from him when I thought so.

He broke the silence.

"I should poorly show the trust that I have in the dear one who will evermore be as dear to me as now"—and the deep earnestness with which he said it at once strengthened me and made me weep—"if, after her assurance that she is not free to think of my love, I urged it. Dear Esther, let me only tell you that the fond idea of you which I took abroad was exalted to the heavens when I came home. I have always hoped, in the first hour when I seemed to stand in any ray of good fortune, to tell you this. I have always feared that I should tell it you in vain. My hopes and fears are both fulfilled to-night. I distress you. I have said enough."

Something seemed to pass into my place that was like the angel he thought me, and I felt so sorrowful for the loss he had sustained! I wished to help him in his trouble, as I had wished to do when he showed that first commiseration for me.

"Dear Mr. Woodcourt," said I, "before we part to-night, something is left for me to say. I never could say it as I wish—I never shall—but—"

I had to think again of being more deserving of his love and his affliction before I could go on.

"—I am deeply sensible of your generosity, and I shall treasure its remembrance to my dying hour. I know full well how changed I am, I know you are not unacquainted with my history, and I know what a noble love that is which is so faithful. What you have said to me could have affected me so much from no other lips, for there are none that could give it such a value to me. It shall not be lost. It shall make me better."

He covered his eyes with his hand and turned away his head. How could I ever be worthy of those tears?

"If, in the unchanged intercourse we shall have together—in tending Richard and Ada, and I hope in many happier scenes of life—you ever find anything in me which you can honestly think is better than it used to be, believe that it will have sprung up from to-night and that I shall owe it to you. And never believe, dear dear Mr. Woodcourt, never believe that I forget this night or that while my heart beats it can be insensible to the pride and joy of having been beloved by you."

He took my hand and kissed it. He was like himself again, and I felt still more encouraged.

"I am induced by what you said just now," said I, "to hope that you have succeeded in your endeavour."

"I have," he answered. "With such help from Mr. Jarndyce as you who know him so well can imagine him to have rendered me, I have succeeded."

"Heaven bless him for it," said I, giving him my hand; "and heaven bless you in all you do!"

"I shall do it better for the wish," he answered; "it will make me enter on these new duties as on another sacred trust from you."

"Ah! Richard!" I exclaimed involuntarily, "What will he do when you are gone!"

"I am not required to go yet; I would not desert him, dear Miss Summerson, even if I were."

One other thing I felt it needful to touch upon before he left me. I knew that I should not be worthier of the love I could not take if I reserved it.

"Mr. Woodcourt," said I, "you will be glad to know from my lips before I say good night that in the future, which is clear and bright before me, I am most happy, most fortunate, have nothing to regret or desire."

It was indeed a glad hearing to him, he replied.

"From my childhood I have been," said I, "the object of the untiring goodness of the best of human beings, to whom I am so bound by every tie of attachment, gratitude, and love, that nothing I could do in the compass of a life could express the feelings of a single day."

"I share those feelings," he returned. "You speak of Mr. Jarndyce."

"You know his virtues well," said I, "but few can know the greatness of his character as I know it. All its highest and best qualities have been revealed to me in nothing more brightly than in the shaping out of that future in which I am so happy. And if your highest homage and respect had not been his already—which I know they are—they would have been his, I think, on this assurance and in the feeling it would have awakened in you towards him for my sake."

He fervently replied that indeed indeed they would have been. I gave him my hand again.

"Good night," I said, "Good-bye."

"The first until we meet to-morrow, the second as a farewell to this theme between us for ever."

"Yes."

"Good night; good-bye."

He left me, and I stood at the dark window watching the street. His love, in all its constancy and generosity, had come so suddenly upon me that he had not left me a minute when my fortitude gave way again and the street was blotted out by my rushing tears.

But they were not tears of regret and sorrow. No. He had called me the beloved of his life and had said I would be evermore as dear to him as I was then, and I felt as if my heart would not hold the triumph of having heard those words. My first wild thought had died away. It was not too late to hear them, for it was not too late to be animated by them to be good, true, grateful, and contented. How easy my path, how much easier than his!

CHAPTER LXII
ANOTHER DISCOVERY

I had not the courage to see any one that night. I had not even the courage to see myself, for I was afraid that my tears might a little reproach me. I went up to my room in the dark, and prayed in the dark, and lay down in the dark to sleep. I had no need of any light to read my guardian's letter by, for I knew it by heart. I took it from the place where I kept it, and repeated its contents by its own clear light of integrity and love, and went to sleep with it on my pillow.

I was up very early in the morning and called Charley to come for a walk. We bought flowers for the breakfast-table, and came back and arranged them, and were as busy as possible. We were so early that I had a good time still for Charley's lesson before breakfast; Charley (who was not in the least improved in the old defective article of grammar) came through it with great applause; and we were altogether very notable. When my guardian appeared he said, "Why, little woman, you look fresher than your flowers!" And Mrs. Woodcourt repeated and translated a passage from the Mewlinnwillinwodd expressive of my being like a mountain with the sun upon it.

This was all so pleasant that I hope it made me still more like the mountain than I had been before. After breakfast I waited my opportunity and peeped about a little until I saw my guardian in his own room—the room of last night—by himself. Then I made an excuse to go in with my housekeeping keys, shutting the door after me.

"Well, Dame Durden?" said my guardian; the post had brought him several letters, and he was writing. "You want money?"

"No, indeed, I have plenty in hand."

"There never was such a Dame Durden," said my guardian, "for making money last."

He had laid down his pen and leaned back in his chair looking at me. I have often spoken of his bright face, but I thought I had never seen it look so bright and good. There was a high happiness upon it which made me think, "He has been doing some great kindness this morning."

"There never was," said my guardian, musing as he smiled upon me, "such a Dame Durden for making money last."

He had never yet altered his old manner. I loved it and him so much that when I now went up to him and took my usual chair, which was always put at his side—for sometimes I read to him, and sometimes I talked to him, and sometimes I silently worked by him—I hardly liked to disturb it by laying my hand on his breast. But I found I did not disturb it at all.

"Dear guardian," said I, "I want to speak to you. Have I been remiss in anything?"

"Remiss in anything, my dear!"

"Have I not been what I have meant to be since—I brought the answer to your letter, guardian?"

"You have been everything I could desire, my love."

"I am very glad indeed to hear that," I returned. "You know, you said to me, was this the mistress of Bleak House. And I said, yes."

"Yes," said my guardian, nodding his head. He had put his arm about me as if there were something to protect me from and looked in my face, smiling.

"Since then," said I, "we have never spoken on the subject except once."

"And then I said Bleak House was thinning fast; and so it was, my dear."

"And I said," I timidly reminded him, "but its mistress remained."

He still held me in the same protecting manner and with the same bright goodness in his face.

"Dear guardian," said I, "I know how you have felt all that has happened, and how considerate you have been. As so much time has passed, and as you spoke only this morning of my being so well again, perhaps you expect me to renew the subject. Perhaps I ought to do so. I will be the mistress of Bleak House when you please."

"See," he returned gaily, "what a sympathy there must be between us! I have had nothing else, poor Rick excepted—it's a large exception—in my mind. When you came in, I was full of it. When shall we give Bleak House its mistress, little woman?"

"When you please."

"Next month?"

"Next month, dear guardian."

"The day on which I take the happiest and best step of my life—the day on which I shall be a man more exulting and more enviable than any other man in the world—the day on which I give Bleak House its little mistress—shall be next month then," said my guardian.

I put my arms round his neck and kissed him just as I had done on the day when I brought my answer.

A servant came to the door to announce Mr. Bucket, which was quite unnecessary, for Mr. Bucket was already looking in over the servant's shoulder. "Mr. Jarndyce and Miss Summerson," said he, rather out of breath, "with all apologies for intruding, WILL you allow me to order up a person that's on the stairs and that objects to being left there in case of becoming the subject of observations in his absence? Thank you. Be so good as chair that there member in this direction, will you?" said Mr. Bucket, beckoning over the banisters.

This singular request produced an old man in a black skull-cap, unable to walk, who was carried up by a couple of bearers and deposited in the room near the door. Mr. Bucket immediately got rid of the bearers, mysteriously shut the door, and bolted it.

"Now you see, Mr. Jarndyce," he then began, putting down his hat and opening his subject with a flourish of his well-remembered finger, "you know me, and Miss Summerson knows me. This gentleman likewise knows me, and his name is Smallweed. The discounting line is his line principally, and he's what you may call a dealer in bills. That's about what YOU are, you know, ain't you?" said Mr. Bucket, stopping a little to address the gentleman in question, who was exceedingly suspicious of him.

He seemed about to dispute this designation of himself when he was seized with a violent fit of coughing.

"Now, moral, you know!" said Mr. Bucket, improving the accident. "Don't you contradict when there ain't no occasion, and you won't be took in that way. Now, Mr. Jarndyce, I address myself to you. I've been negotiating with this gentleman on behalf of Sir Leicester Dedlock, Baronet, and one way and another I've been in and out and about his premises a deal. His premises are the premises formerly occupied by Krook, marine store dealer—a relation of this gentleman's that you saw in his lifetime if I don't mistake?"

My guardian replied, "Yes."

"Well! You are to understand," said Mr. Bucket, "that this gentleman he come into Krook's property, and a good deal of magpie property there was. Vast lots of waste-paper among the rest. Lord bless you, of no use to nobody!"

The cunning of Mr. Bucket's eye and the masterly manner in which he contrived, without a look or a word against which his watchful auditor could protest, to let us know that he stated the case according to previous agreement and could say much more of Mr. Smallweed if he thought it advisable, deprived us of any merit in quite understanding him. His difficulty was increased by Mr. Smallweed's being deaf as well as suspicious and watching his face with the closest attention.

"Among them odd heaps of old papers, this gentleman, when he comes into the property, naturally begins to rummage, don't you see?" said Mr. Bucket.

"To which? Say that again," cried Mr. Smallweed in a shrill, sharp voice.

"To rummage," repeated Mr. Bucket. "Being a prudent man and accustomed to take care of your own affairs, you begin to rummage among the papers as you have come into; don't you?"

"Of course I do," cried Mr. Smallweed.

"Of course you do," said Mr. Bucket conversationally, "and much to blame you would be if you didn't. And so you chance to find, you know," Mr. Bucket went on, stooping over him with an air of cheerful raillery which Mr. Smallweed by no means reciprocated, "and so you chance to find, you know, a paper with the signature of Jarndyce to it. Don't you?"

Mr. Smallweed glanced with a troubled eye at us and grudgingly nodded assent.

"And coming to look at that paper at your full leisure and convenience—all in good time, for you're not curious to read it, and why should you be?—what do you find it to be but a will, you see. That's the drollery of it," said Mr.

Bucket with the same lively air of recalling a joke for the enjoyment of Mr. Smallweed, who still had the same crest-fallen appearance of not enjoying it at all; "what do you find it to be but a will?"

"I don't know that it's good as a will or as anything else," snarled Mr. Smallweed.

Mr. Bucket eyed the old man for a moment—he had slipped and shrunk down in his chair into a mere bundle—as if he were much disposed to pounce upon him; nevertheless, he continued to bend over him with the same agreeable air, keeping the corner of one of his eyes upon us.

"Notwithstanding which," said Mr. Bucket, "you get a little doubtful and uncomfortable in your mind about it, having a very tender mind of your own."

"Eh? What do you say I have got of my own?" asked Mr. Smallweed with his hand to his ear.

"A very tender mind."

"Ho! Well, go on," said Mr. Smallweed.

"And as you've heard a good deal mentioned regarding a celebrated Chancery will case of the same name, and as you know what a card Krook was for buying all manner of old pieces of furniter, and books, and papers, and what not, and never liking to part with 'em, and always a-going to teach himself to read, you begin to think—and you never was more correct in your born days—'Ecod, if I don't look about me, I may get into trouble regarding this will.'"

"Now, mind how you put it, Bucket," cried the old man anxiously with his hand at his ear. "Speak up; none of your brimstone tricks. Pick me up; I want to hear better. Oh, Lord, I am shaken to bits!"

Mr. Bucket had certainly picked him up at a dart. However, as soon as he could be heard through Mr. Smallweed's coughing and his vicious ejaculations of "Oh, my bones! Oh, dear! I've no breath in my body! I'm worse than the chattering, clattering, brimstone pig at home!" Mr. Bucket proceeded in the same convivial manner as before.

"So, as I happen to be in the habit of coming about your premises, you take me into your confidence, don't you?"

I think it would be impossible to make an admission with more ill will and a worse grace than Mr. Smallweed displayed when he admitted this, rendering it perfectly evident that Mr. Bucket was the very last person he would have thought of taking into his confidence if he could by any possibility have kept him out of it.

"And I go into the business with you—very pleasant we are over it; and I confirm you in your well-founded fears that you will get yourself into a most precious line if you don't come out with that there will," said Mr. Bucket emphatically; "and accordingly you arrange with me that it shall be delivered up to this present Mr. Jarndyce, on no conditions. If it should prove to be valuable, you trusting yourself to him for your reward; that's about where it is, ain't it?"

"That's what was agreed," Mr. Smallweed assented with the same bad grace.

"In consequence of which," said Mr. Bucket, dismissing his agreeable manner all at once and becoming strictly business-like, "you've got that will upon your person at the present time, and the only thing that remains for you to do is just to out with it!"

Having given us one glance out of the watching corner of his eye, and having given his nose one triumphant rub with his forefinger, Mr. Bucket stood with his eyes fastened on his confidential friend and his hand stretched forth ready to take the paper and present it to my guardian. It was not produced without much reluctance and many declarations on the part of Mr. Smallweed that he was a poor industrious man and that he left it to Mr. Jarndyce's honour not to let him lose by his honesty. Little by little he very slowly took from a breast-pocket a stained, discoloured paper which was much singed upon the outside and a little burnt at the edges, as if it had long ago been thrown upon a fire and hastily snatched off again. Mr. Bucket lost no time in transferring this paper, with the dexterity of a conjuror, from Mr. Smallweed to Mr. Jarndyce. As he gave it to my guardian, he whispered behind his fingers, "Hadn't settled how to make their market of it. Quarrelled and hinted about it. I laid out twenty pound upon it. First the avaricious grandchildren split upon him on account of their objections to his living so unreasonably long, and then they split on one another. Lord! There ain't one of the family that wouldn't sell the other for a pound or two, except the old lady—and she's only out of it because she's too weak in her mind to drive a bargain."

"Mr Bucket," said my guardian aloud, "whatever the worth of this paper may be to any one, my obligations are great to you; and if it be of any worth, I hold myself bound to see Mr. Smallweed remunerated accordingly."

"Not according to your merits, you know," said Mr. Bucket in friendly explanation to Mr. Smallweed. "Don't you be afraid of that. According to its value."

"That is what I mean," said my guardian. "You may observe, Mr. Bucket, that I abstain from examining this paper myself. The plain truth is, I have forsworn and abjured the whole business these many years, and my soul is sick of it. But Miss Summerson and I will immediately place the paper in the hands of my solicitor in the cause, and its existence shall be made known without delay to all other parties interested."

"Mr. Jarndyce can't say fairer than that, you understand," observed Mr. Bucket to his fellow-visitor. "And it being now made clear to you that nobody's a-going to be wronged—which must be a great relief to YOUR mind—we may proceed with the ceremony of chairing you home again."

He unbolted the door, called in the bearers, wished us good morning, and with a look full of meaning and a crook of his finger at parting went his way.

We went our way too, which was to Lincoln's Inn, as quickly as possible. Mr. Kenge was disengaged, and we found him at his table in his dusty room with the inexpressive-looking books and the piles of papers. Chairs having been placed for us by Mr. Guppy, Mr. Kenge expressed the surprise and gratification he felt at the unusual sight of Mr. Jarndyce in his office. He turned over his double eye-glass as he spoke and was more Conversation Kenge than ever.

"I hope," said Mr. Kenge, "that the genial influence of Miss Summerson," he bowed to me, "may have induced Mr. Jarndyce," he bowed to him, "to forego some little of his animosity towards a cause and towards a court which are—shall I say, which take their place in the stately vista of the pillars of our profession?"

"I am inclined to think," returned my guardian, "that Miss Summerson has seen too much of the effects of the court and the cause to exert any influence in their favour. Nevertheless, they are a part of the occasion of my being here. Mr. Kenge, before I lay this paper on your desk and have done with it, let me tell you how it has come into my hands."

He did so shortly and distinctly.

"It could not, sir," said Mr. Kenge, "have been stated more plainly and to the purpose if it had been a case at law."

"Did you ever know English law, or equity either, plain and to the purpose?" said my guardian.

"Oh, fie!" said Mr. Kenge.

At first he had not seemed to attach much importance to the paper, but when he saw it he appeared more interested, and when he had opened and read a little of it through his eye-glass, he became amazed. "Mr. Jarndyce," he said, looking off it, "you have perused this?"

"Not I!" returned my guardian.

"But, my dear sir," said Mr. Kenge, "it is a will of later date than any in the suit. It appears to be all in the testator's handwriting. It is duly executed and attested. And even if intended to be cancelled, as might possibly be supposed to be denoted by these marks of fire, it is NOT cancelled. Here it is, a perfect instrument!"

"Well!" said my guardian. "What is that to me?"

"Mr. Guppy!" cried Mr. Kenge, raising his voice. "I beg your pardon, Mr. Jarndyce."

"Sir."

"Mr. Vholes of Symond's Inn. My compliments. Jarndyce and Jarndyce. Glad to speak with him."

Mr. Guppy disappeared.

"You ask me what is this to you, Mr. Jarndyce. If you had perused this document, you would have seen that it reduces your interest considerably, though still leaving it a very handsome one, still leaving it a very handsome one," said Mr. Kenge, waving his hand persuasively and blandly. "You would further have seen that the interests of Mr. Richard Carstone and of Miss Ada Clare, now Mrs. Richard Carstone, are very materially advanced by it."

"Kenge," said my guardian, "if all the flourishing wealth that the suit brought into this vile court of Chancery could fall to my two young cousins, I should be well contented. But do you ask ME to believe that any good is to come of Jarndyce and Jarndyce?"

"Oh, really, Mr. Jarndyce! Prejudice, prejudice. My dear sir, this is a very great country, a very great country. Its system of equity is a very great system, a very great system. Really, really!"

My guardian said no more, and Mr. Vholes arrived. He was modestly impressed by Mr. Kenge's professional eminence.

"How do you do, Mr. Vholes? Will you be so good as to take a chair here by me and look over this paper?"

Mr. Vholes did as he was asked and seemed to read it every word. He was not excited by it, but he was not excited by anything. When he had well examined it, he retired with Mr. Kenge into a window, and shading his mouth with his black glove, spoke to him at some length. I was not surprised to observe Mr. Kenge inclined to dispute what he said before he had said much, for I knew that no two people ever did agree about anything in Jarndyce and Jarndyce. But he seemed to get the better of Mr. Kenge too in a conversation that sounded as if it were almost composed of the words "Receiver-General," "Accountant-General," "report," "estate," and "costs." When they had finished, they came back to Mr. Kenge's table and spoke aloud.

"Well! But this is a very remarkable document, Mr. Vholes," said Mr. Kenge.

Mr. Vholes said, "Very much so."

"And a very important document, Mr. Vholes," said Mr. Kenge.

Again Mr. Vholes said, "Very much so."

"And as you say, Mr. Vholes, when the cause is in the paper next term, this document will be an unexpected and interesting feature in it," said Mr. Kenge, looking loftily at my guardian.

Mr. Vholes was gratified, as a smaller practitioner striving to keep respectable, to be confirmed in any opinion of his own by such an authority.

"And when," asked my guardian, rising after a pause, during which Mr. Kenge had rattled his money and Mr. Vholes had picked his pimples, "when is next term?"

"Next term, Mr. Jarndyce, will be next month," said Mr. Kenge. "Of course we shall at once proceed to do what is necessary with this document and to collect the necessary evidence concerning it; and of course you will receive our usual notification of the cause being in the paper."

"To which I shall pay, of course, my usual attention."

"Still bent, my dear sir," said Mr. Kenge, showing us through the outer office to the door, "still bent, even with your enlarged mind, on echoing a popular prejudice? We are a prosperous community, Mr. Jarndyce, a very prosperous community. We are a great country, Mr. Jarndyce, we are a very great country. This is a great system, Mr. Jarndyce, and would you wish a great country to have a little system? Now, really, really!"

He said this at the stair-head, gently moving his right hand as if it were a silver trowel with which to spread the cement of his words on the structure of the system and consolidate it for a thousand ages.

CHAPTER LXIII
STEEL AND IRON

George's Shooting Gallery is to let, and the stock is sold off, and George himself is at Chesney Wold attending on Sir Leicester in his rides and riding very near his bridle-rein because of the uncertain hand with which he guides his horse. But not to-day is George so occupied. He is journeying to-day into the iron country farther north to look about him.

As he comes into the iron country farther north, such fresh green woods as those of Chesney Wold are left behind; and coal pits and ashes, high chimneys and red bricks, blighted verdure, scorching fires, and a heavy never-lightening cloud of smoke become the features of the scenery. Among such objects rides the trooper, looking about him and always looking for something he has come to find.

At last, on the black canal bridge of a busy town, with a clang of iron in it, and more fires and more smoke than he has seen yet, the trooper, swart with the dust of the coal roads, checks his horse and asks a workman does he know the name of Rouncewell thereabouts.

"Why, master," quoth the workman, "do I know my own name?"

"'Tis so well known here, is it, comrade?" asks the trooper.

"Rouncewell's? Ah! You're right."

"And where might it be now?" asks the trooper with a glance before him.

"The bank, the factory, or the house?" the workman wants to know.

"Hum! Rouncewell's is so great apparently," mutters the trooper, stroking his chin, "that I have as good as half a mind to go back again. Why, I don't know which I want. Should I find Mr. Rouncewell at the factory, do you think?"

"Tain't easy to say where you'd find him—at this time of the day you might find either him or his son there, if he's in town; but his contracts take him away."

And which is the factory? Why, he sees those chimneys—the tallest ones! Yes, he sees THEM. Well! Let him keep his eye on those chimneys, going on as straight as ever he can, and presently he'll see 'em down a turning on the left, shut in by a great brick wall which forms one side of the street. That's Rouncewell's.

The trooper thanks his informant and rides slowly on, looking about him. He does not turn back, but puts up his horse (and is much disposed to groom him too) at a public-house where some of Rouncewell's hands are dining, as the ostler tells him. Some of Rouncewell's hands have just knocked off for dinner-time and seem to be invading the whole town. They are very sinewy and strong, are Rouncewell's hands—a little sooty too.

He comes to a gateway in the brick wall, looks in, and sees a great perplexity of iron lying about in every stage and in a vast variety of shapes—in bars, in wedges, in sheets; in tanks, in boilers, in axles, in wheels, in cogs, in cranks, in rails; twisted and wrenched into eccentric and perverse forms as separate parts of machinery; mountains of it broken up, and rusty in its age; distant furnaces of it glowing and bubbling in its youth; bright fireworks of it showering about under the blows of the steam-hammer; red-hot iron, white-hot iron, cold-black iron; an iron taste, an iron smell, and a Babel of iron sounds.

"This is a place to make a man's head ache too!" says the trooper, looking about him for a counting-house. "Who comes here? This is very like me before I was set up. This ought to be my nephew, if likenesses run in families. Your servant, sir."

"Yours, sir. Are you looking for any one?"

"Excuse me. Young Mr. Rouncewell, I believe?"

"Yes."

"I was looking for your father, sir. I wish to have a word with him."

The young man, telling him he is fortunate in his choice of a time, for his father is there, leads the way to the office where he is to be found. "Very like me before I was set up—devilish like me!" thinks the trooper as he follows. They come to a building in the yard with an office on an upper floor. At sight of the gentleman in the office, Mr. George turns very red.

"What name shall I say to my father?" asks the young man.

George, full of the idea of iron, in desperation answers "Steel," and is so presented. He is left alone with the gentleman in the office, who sits at a table with account-books before him and some sheets of paper blotted with hosts of figures and drawings of cunning shapes. It is a bare office, with bare windows, looking on the iron view below. Tumbled together on the table are some pieces of iron, purposely broken to be tested at various periods of their service, in various capacities. There is iron-dust on everything; and the smoke is seen through the windows rolling heavily out of the tall chimneys to mingle with the smoke from a vaporous Babylon of other chimneys.

"I am at your service, Mr. Steel," says the gentleman when his visitor has taken a rusty chair.

"Well, Mr. Rouncewell," George replies, leaning forward with his left arm on his knee and his hat in his hand, and very chary of meeting his brother's eye, "I am not without my expectations that in the present visit I may prove to be more free than welcome. I have served as a dragoon in my day, and a comrade of mine that I was once rather partial to was, if I don't deceive myself, a brother of yours. I believe you had a brother who gave his family some trouble, and ran away, and never did any good but in keeping away?"

"Are you quite sure," returns the ironmaster in an altered voice, "that your name is Steel?"

The trooper falters and looks at him. His brother starts up, calls him by his name, and grasps him by both hands.

"You are too quick for me!" cries the trooper with the tears springing out of his eyes. "How do you do, my dear old fellow? I never could have thought you would have been half so glad to see me as all this. How do you do, my dear old fellow, how do you do!"

They shake hands and embrace each other over and over again, the trooper still coupling his "How do you do, my dear old fellow!" with his protestation that he never thought his brother would have been half so glad to see him as all this!

"So far from it," he declares at the end of a full account of what has preceded his arrival there, "I had very little idea of making myself known. I thought if you took by any means forgivingly to my name I might gradually get myself up to the point of writing a letter. But I should not have been surprised, brother, if you had considered it anything but welcome news to hear of me."

"We will show you at home what kind of news we think it, George," returns his brother. "This is a great day at home, and you could not have arrived, you bronzed old soldier, on a better. I make an agreement with my son Watt to-day that on this day twelvemonth he shall marry as pretty and as good a girl as you have seen in all your travels. She goes to Germany to-morrow with one of your nieces for a little polishing up in her education. We make a feast of the event, and you will be made the hero of it."

Mr. George is so entirely overcome at first by this prospect that he resists the proposed honour with great earnestness. Being overborne, however, by his brother and his nephew—concerning whom he renews his protestations that he never could have thought they would have been half so glad to see him—he is taken home to an elegant house in all the arrangements of which there is to be observed a pleasant mixture of the originally simple habits of the father and mother with such as are suited to their altered station and the higher fortunes of their children. Here Mr. George is much dismayed by the graces and accomplishments of his nieces that are and by the beauty of Rosa, his niece that is to be, and by the affectionate salutations of these young ladies, which he receives in a sort of dream. He is sorely taken aback, too, by the dutiful behaviour of his nephew and has a woeful consciousness upon him of being a scapegrace. However, there is great rejoicing and a very hearty company and infinite enjoyment, and Mr. George comes bluff and martial through it all, and his pledge to be present at the marriage and give away the bride is received with universal favour. A whirling head has Mr. George that night when he lies down in the state-bed of his brother's house to think of all these things and to see the images of his nieces (awful all the evening in their floating muslins) waltzing, after the German manner, over his counterpane.

The brothers are closeted next morning in the ironmaster's room, where the elder is proceeding, in his clear sensible way, to show how he thinks he may best dispose of George in his business, when George squeezes his hand and stops him.

"Brother, I thank you a million times for your more than brotherly welcome, and a million times more to that for your more than brotherly intentions. But my plans are made. Before I say a word as to them, I wish to consult you upon one family point. How," says the trooper, folding his arms and looking with indomitable firmness at his brother, "how is my mother to be got to scratch me?"

"I am not sure that I understand you, George," replies the ironmaster.

"I say, brother, how is my mother to be got to scratch me? She must be got to do it somehow."

"Scratch you out of her will, I think you mean?"

"Of course I do. In short," says the trooper, folding his arms more resolutely yet, "I mean—TO—scratch me!"

"My dear George," returns his brother, "is it so indispensable that you should undergo that process?"

"Quite! Absolutely! I couldn't be guilty of the meanness of coming back without it. I should never be safe not to be off again. I have not sneaked home to rob your children, if not yourself, brother, of your rights. I, who forfeited mine long ago! If I am to remain and hold up my head, I must be scratched. Come. You are a man of celebrated penetration and intelligence, and you can tell me how it's to be brought about."

"I can tell you, George," replies the ironmaster deliberately, "how it is not to be brought about, which I hope may answer the purpose as well. Look at our mother, think of her, recall her emotion when she recovered you. Do you believe there is a consideration in the world that would induce her to take such a step against her favourite son? Do you believe there is any chance of her consent, to balance against the outrage it would be to her (loving dear old lady!) to propose it? If you do, you are wrong. No, George! You must make up your mind to remain UNscratched, I think." There is an amused smile on the ironmaster's face as he watches his brother, who is pondering, deeply disappointed. "I think you may manage almost as well as if the thing were done, though."

"How, brother?"

"Being bent upon it, you can dispose by will of anything you have the misfortune to inherit in any way you like, you know."

"That's true!" says the trooper, pondering again. Then he wistfully asks, with his hand on his brother's, "Would you mind mentioning that, brother, to your wife and family?"

"Not at all."

"Thank you. You wouldn't object to say, perhaps, that although an undoubted vagabond, I am a vagabond of the harum-scarum order, and not of the mean sort?"

The ironmaster, repressing his amused smile, assents.

"Thank you. Thank you. It's a weight off my mind," says the trooper with a heave of his chest as he unfolds his arms and puts a hand on each leg, "though I had set my heart on being scratched, too!"

The brothers are very like each other, sitting face to face; but a certain massive simplicity and absence of usage in the ways of the world is all on the trooper's side.

"Well," he proceeds, throwing off his disappointment, "next and last, those plans of mine. You have been so brotherly as to propose to me to fall in here and take my place among the products of your perseverance and sense. I thank you heartily. It's more than brotherly, as I said before, and I thank you heartily for it," shaking him a long time by the hand. "But the truth is, brother, I am a—I am a kind of a weed, and it's too late to plant me in a regular garden."

"My dear George," returns the elder, concentrating his strong steady brow upon him and smiling confidently, "leave that to me, and let me try."

George shakes his head. "You could do it, I have not a doubt, if anybody could; but it's not to be done. Not to be done, sir! Whereas it so falls out, on the other hand, that I am able to be of some trifle of use to Sir Leicester Dedlock since his illness—brought on by family sorrows—and that he would rather have that help from our mother's son than from anybody else."

"Well, my dear George," returns the other with a very slight shade upon his open face, "if you prefer to serve in Sir Leicester Dedlock's household brigade—"

"There it is, brother," cries the trooper, checking him, with his hand upon his knee again; "there it is! You don't take kindly to that idea; I don't mind it. You are not used to being officered; I am. Everything about you is in perfect order and discipline; everything about me requires to be kept so. We are not accustomed to carry things with the same hand or to look at 'em from the same point. I don't say much about my garrison manners because I found myself pretty well at my ease last night, and they wouldn't be noticed here, I dare say, once and away. But I shall get on best at Chesney Wold, where there's more room for a weed than there is here; and the dear old lady will be made happy besides. Therefore I accept of Sir Leicester Dedlock's proposals. When I come over next year to give away the bride, or whenever I come, I shall have the sense to keep the household brigade in ambuscade and not to manoeuvre it on your ground. I thank you heartily again and am proud to think of the Rouncewells as they'll be founded by you."

"You know yourself, George," says the elder brother, returning the grip of his hand, "and perhaps you know me better than I know myself. Take your way. So that we don't quite lose one another again, take your way."

"No fear of that!" returns the trooper. "Now, before I turn my horse's head homewards, brother, I will ask you—if you'll be so good—to look over a letter for me. I brought it with me to send from these parts, as Chesney Wold might be a painful name just now to the person it's written to. I am not much accustomed to correspondence myself, and I am particular respecting this present letter because I want it to be both straightforward and delicate."

Herewith he hands a letter, closely written in somewhat pale ink but in a neat round hand, to the ironmaster, who reads as follows:

Miss Esther Summerson,

A communication having been made to me by Inspector Bucket of a letter to myself being found among the papers of a certain person, I take the liberty to make known to you that it was but a few lines of instruction from abroad, when, where, and how to deliver an enclosed letter to a young and beautiful lady, then unmarried, in England. I duly observed the same.

I further take the liberty to make known to you that it was got from me as a proof of handwriting only and that otherwise I would not have given it up, as appearing to be the most harmless in my possession, without being previously shot through the heart.

I further take the liberty to mention that if I could have supposed a certain unfortunate gentleman to have been in existence, I never could and never would have rested until I had discovered his retreat and shared my last farthing with him, as my duty and my inclination would have equally been. But he was (officially) reported drowned, and assuredly went over the side of a transport-ship at night in an Irish harbour within a few hours of her arrival from the West Indies, as I have myself heard both from officers and men on board, and know to have been (officially) confirmed.

I further take the liberty to state that in my humble quality as one of the rank and file, I am, and shall ever continue to be, your thoroughly devoted and admiring servant and that I esteem the qualities you possess above all others far beyond the limits of the present dispatch.

I have the honour to be,
George

"A little formal," observes the elder brother, refolding it with a puzzled face.

"But nothing that might not be sent to a pattern young lady?" asks the younger.

"Nothing at all."

Therefore it is sealed and deposited for posting among the iron correspondence of the day. This done, Mr. George takes a hearty farewell of the family party and prepares to saddle and mount. His brother, however, unwilling to part with him so soon, proposes to ride with him in a light open carriage to the place where he will bait for the night, and there remain with him until morning, a servant riding for so much of the journey on the thoroughbred old grey from Chesney Wold. The offer, being gladly accepted, is followed by a pleasant ride, a pleasant dinner, and a pleasant breakfast, all in brotherly communion. Then they once more shake hands long and heartily and part, the ironmaster turning his face to the smoke and fires, and the trooper to the green country. Early in the afternoon the subdued sound of his heavy military trot is heard on the turf in the avenue as he rides on with imaginary clank and jingle of accoutrements under the old elm-trees.

CHAPTER LXIV
ESTHER'S NARRATIVE

Soon after I had that conversation with my guardian, he put a sealed paper in my hand one morning and said, "This is for next month, my dear." I found in it two hundred pounds.

I now began very quietly to make such preparations as I thought were necessary. Regulating my purchases by my guardian's taste, which I knew very well of course, I arranged my wardrobe to please him and hoped I should be highly successful. I did it all so quietly because I was not quite free from my old apprehension that Ada would be rather sorry and because my guardian was so quiet himself. I had no doubt that under all the circumstances we should be married in the most private and simple manner. Perhaps I should only have to say to Ada, "Would you like to come and see me married to-morrow, my pet?" Perhaps our wedding might even be as unpretending as her own, and I might not find it necessary to say anything about it until it was over. I thought that if I were to choose, I would like this best.

The only exception I made was Mrs. Woodcourt. I told her that I was going to be married to my guardian and that we had been engaged some time. She highly approved. She could never do enough for me and was remarkably softened now in comparison with what she had been when we first knew her. There was no trouble she would not have taken to have been of use to me, but I need hardly say that I only allowed her to take as little as gratified her kindness without tasking it.

Of course this was not a time to neglect my guardian, and of course it was not a time for neglecting my darling. So I had plenty of occupation, which I was glad of; and as to Charley, she was absolutely not to be seen for needlework. To surround herself with great heaps of it—baskets full and tables full—and do a little, and spend a great deal of time in staring with her round eyes at what there was to do, and persuade herself that she was going to do it, were Charley's great dignities and delights.

Meanwhile, I must say, I could not agree with my guardian on the subject of the will, and I had some sanguine hopes of Jarndyce and Jarndyce. Which of us was right will soon appear, but I certainly did encourage expectations. In Richard, the discovery gave occasion for a burst of business and agitation that buoyed him up for a little time, but he had lost the elasticity even of hope now and seemed to me to retain only its feverish anxieties. From something my guardian said one day when we were talking about this, I understood that my marriage would not take place until after the term-time we had been told to look forward to; and I thought the more, for that, how rejoiced I should be if I could be married when Richard and Ada were a little more prosperous.

The term was very near indeed when my guardian was called out of town and went down into Yorkshire on Mr. Woodcourt's business. He had told me beforehand that his presence there would be necessary. I had just come in one night from my dear girl's and was sitting in the midst of all my new clothes, looking at them all around me and thinking, when a letter from my guardian was brought to me. It asked me to join him in the country and mentioned by what stage-coach my place was taken and at what time in the morning I should have to leave town. It added in a postscript that I would not be many hours from Ada.

I expected few things less than a journey at that time, but I was ready for it in half an hour and set off as appointed early next morning. I travelled all day, wondering all day what I could be wanted for at such a distance; now I thought it might be for this purpose, and now I thought it might be for that purpose, but I was never, never, never near the truth.

It was night when I came to my journey's end and found my guardian waiting for me. This was a great relief, for towards evening I had begun to fear (the more so as his letter was a very short one) that he might be ill. However, there he was, as well as it was possible to be; and when I saw his genial face again at its brightest and best, I said to myself, he has been doing some other great kindness. Not that it required much penetration to say that, because I knew that his being there at all was an act of kindness.

Supper was ready at the hotel, and when we were alone at table he said, "Full of curiosity, no doubt, little woman, to know why I have brought you here?"

"Well, guardian," said I, "without thinking myself a Fatima or you a Blue Beard, I am a little curious about it."

"Then to ensure your night's rest, my love," he returned gaily, "I won't wait until to-morrow to tell you. I have very much wished to express to Woodcourt, somehow, my sense of his humanity to poor unfortunate Jo, his inestimable services to my young cousins, and his value to us all. When it was decided that he should settle here, it came into my head that I might ask his acceptance of some unpretending and suitable little place to lay his own head in. I therefore caused such a place to be looked out for, and such a place was found on very easy terms, and I have been touching it up for him and making it habitable. However, when I walked over it the day before yesterday and it was reported ready, I found that I was not housekeeper enough to know whether things were all as they ought to be. So I sent off for the best little housekeeper that could possibly be got to come and give me her advice and opinion. And here she is," said my guardian, "laughing and crying both together!"

Because he was so dear, so good, so admirable. I tried to tell him what I thought of him, but I could not articulate a word.

"Tut, tut!" said my guardian. "You make too much of it, little woman. Why, how you sob, Dame Durden, how you sob!"

"It is with exquisite pleasure, guardian—with a heart full of thanks."

"Well, well," said he. "I am delighted that you approve. I thought you would. I meant it as a pleasant surprise for the little mistress of Bleak House."

I kissed him and dried my eyes. "I know now!" said I. "I have seen this in your face a long while."

"No; have you really, my dear?" said he. "What a Dame Durden it is to read a face!"

He was so quaintly cheerful that I could not long be otherwise, and was almost ashamed of having been otherwise at all. When I went to bed, I cried. I am bound to confess that I cried; but I hope it was with pleasure, though I am not quite sure it was with pleasure. I repeated every word of the letter twice over.

A most beautiful summer morning succeeded, and after breakfast we went out arm in arm to see the house of which I was to give my mighty housekeeping opinion. We entered a flower-garden by a gate in a side wall, of which he had the key, and the first thing I saw was that the beds and flowers were all laid out according to the manner of my beds and flowers at home.

"You see, my dear," observed my guardian, standing still with a delighted face to watch my looks, "knowing there could be no better plan, I borrowed yours."

We went on by a pretty little orchard, where the cherries were nestling among the green leaves and the shadows of the apple-trees were sporting on the grass, to the house itself—a cottage, quite a rustic cottage of doll's rooms; but such a lovely place, so tranquil and so beautiful, with such a rich and smiling country spread around it; with water sparkling away into the distance, here all overhung with summer-growth, there turning a humming mill; at its nearest point glancing through a meadow by the cheerful town, where cricket-players were assembling in bright groups and a flag was flying from a white tent that rippled in the sweet west wind. And still, as we went through the pretty rooms, out at the little rustic verandah doors, and underneath the tiny wooden colonnades garlanded with woodbine, jasmine, and honey-suckle, I saw in the papering on the walls, in the colours of the furniture, in the arrangement of all the pretty objects, MY little tastes and fancies, MY little methods and inventions which they used to laugh at while they praised them, my odd ways everywhere.

I could not say enough in admiration of what was all so beautiful, but one secret doubt arose in my mind when I saw this, I thought, oh, would he be the happier for it! Would it not have been better for his peace that I should not have been so brought before him? Because although I was not what he thought me, still he loved me very dearly, and it might remind him mournfully of what be believed he had lost. I did not wish him to forget me—perhaps he might not have done so, without these aids to his memory—but my way was easier than his, and I could have reconciled myself even to that so that he had been the happier for it.

"And now, little woman," said my guardian, whom I had never seen so proud and joyful as in showing me these things and watching my appreciation of them, "now, last of all, for the name of this house."

"What is it called, dear guardian?"

"My child," said he, "come and see,"

He took me to the porch, which he had hitherto avoided, and said, pausing before we went out, "My dear child, don't you guess the name?"

"No!" said I.

We went out of the porch and he showed me written over it, Bleak House.

He led me to a seat among the leaves close by, and sitting down beside me and taking my hand in his, spoke to me thus, "My darling girl, in what there has been between us, I have, I hope, been really solicitous for your happiness. When I wrote you the letter to which you brought the answer," smiling as he referred to it, "I had my own too much in view; but I had yours too. Whether, under different circumstances, I might ever have renewed the old dream I sometimes dreamed when you were very young, of making you my wife one day, I need not ask myself. I did renew it, and I wrote my letter, and you brought your answer. You are following what I say, my child?"

I was cold, and I trembled violently, but not a word he uttered was lost. As I sat looking fixedly at him and the sun's rays descended, softly shining through the leaves upon his bare head, I felt as if the brightness on him must be like the brightness of the angels.

"Hear me, my love, but do not speak. It is for me to speak now. When it was that I began to doubt whether what I had done would really make you happy is no matter. Woodcourt came home, and I soon had no doubt at all."

I clasped him round the neck and hung my head upon his breast and wept. "Lie lightly, confidently here, my child," said he, pressing me gently to him. "I am your guardian and your father now. Rest confidently here."

Soothingly, like the gentle rustling of the leaves; and genially, like the ripening weather; and radiantly and beneficently, like the sunshine, he went on.

"Understand me, my dear girl. I had no doubt of your being contented and happy with me, being so dutiful and so devoted; but I saw with whom you would be happier. That I penetrated his secret when Dame Durden was blind to it is no wonder, for I knew the good that could never change in her better far than she did. Well! I have long been in Allan Woodcourt's confidence, although he was not, until yesterday, a few hours before you came here, in mine. But I would not have my Esther's bright example lost; I would not have a jot of my dear girl's virtues unobserved and unhonoured; I would not have her admitted on sufferance into the line of Morgan ap-Kerrig, no, not for the weight in gold of all the mountains in Wales!"

He stopped to kiss me on the forehead, and I sobbed and wept afresh. For

I felt as if I could not bear the painful delight of his praise.

"Hush, little woman! Don't cry; this is to be a day of joy. I have looked forward to it," he said exultingly, "for months on months! A few words more, Dame Trot, and I have said my say. Determined not to throw away one atom of my Esther's worth, I took Mrs. Woodcourt into a separate confidence. 'Now, madam,' said I, 'I clearly perceive—and indeed I know, to boot—that your son loves my ward. I am further very sure that my ward loves your son, but will sacrifice her love to a sense of duty and affection, and will sacrifice it so completely, so entirely, so religiously, that you should never suspect it though you watched her night and day.' Then I told her all our story—ours—yours and mine. 'Now, madam,' said I, 'come you, knowing this, and live with us. Come you, and see my child from hour to hour; set what you see against her pedigree, which is this, and this'—for I scorned to mince it—'and tell me what is the true legitimacy when you shall have quite made up your mind on that subject.' Why, honour to her old Welsh blood, my dear," cried my guardian with enthusiasm, "I believe the heart it animates beats no less warmly, no less admiringly, no less lovingly, towards Dame Durden than my own!"

He tenderly raised my head, and as I clung to him, kissed me in his old fatherly way again and again. What a light, now, on the protecting manner I had thought about!

"One more last word. When Allan Woodcourt spoke to you, my dear, he spoke with my knowledge and consent—but I gave him no encouragement, not I, for these surprises were my great reward, and I was too miserly to part with a scrap of it. He was to come and tell me all that passed, and he did. I have no more to say. My dearest, Allan Woodcourt stood beside your father when he lay dead—stood beside your mother. This is Bleak House. This day I give this house its little mistress; and before God, it is the brightest day in all my life!"

He rose and raised me with him. We were no longer alone. My husband—I have called him by that name full seven happy years now—stood at my side.

"Allan," said my guardian, "take from me a willing gift, the best wife that ever man had. What more can I say for you than that I know you deserve her! Take with her the little home she brings you. You know what she will make it, Allan; you know what she has made its namesake. Let me share its felicity sometimes, and what do I sacrifice? Nothing, nothing."

He kissed me once again, and now the tears were in his eyes as he said more softly, "Esther, my dearest, after so many years, there is a kind of parting in this too. I know that my mistake has caused you some distress. Forgive your old guardian, in restoring him to his old place in your affections; and blot it out of your memory. Allan, take my dear."

He moved away from under the green roof of leaves, and stopping in the sunlight outside and turning cheerfully towards us, said, "I shall be found about here somewhere. It's a west wind, little woman, due west! Let no one thank me any more, for I am going to revert to my bachelor habits, and if anybody disregards this warning, I'll run away and never come back!"

What happiness was ours that day, what joy, what rest, what hope, what gratitude, what bliss! We were to be married before the month was out, but when we were to come and take possession of our own house was to depend on Richard and Ada.

We all three went home together next day. As soon as we arrived in town, Allan went straight to see Richard and to carry our joyful news to him and my darling. Late as it was, I meant to go to her for a few minutes before lying down to sleep, but I went home with my guardian first to make his tea for him and to occupy the old chair by his side, for I did not like to think of its being empty so soon.

When we came home we found that a young man had called three times in the course of that one day to see me and that having been told on the occasion of his third call that I was not expected to return before ten o'clock at night, he had left word that he would call about then. He had left his card three times. Mr. Guppy.

As I naturally speculated on the object of these visits, and as I always associated something ludicrous with the visitor, it fell out that in laughing about Mr. Guppy I told my guardian of his old proposal and his subsequent retraction. "After that," said my guardian, "we will certainly receive this hero." So instructions were given that Mr. Guppy should be shown in when he came again, and they were scarcely given when he did come again.

He was embarrassed when he found my guardian with me, but recovered himself and said, "How de do, sir?"

"How do you do, sir?" returned my guardian.

"Thank you, sir, I am tolerable," returned Mr. Guppy. "Will you allow me to introduce my mother, Mrs. Guppy of the Old Street Road, and my particular friend, Mr. Weevle. That is to say, my friend has gone by the name of Weevle, but his name is really and truly Jobling."

My guardian begged them to be seated, and they all sat down.

"Tony," said Mr. Guppy to his friend after an awkward silence. "Will you open the case?"

"Do it yourself," returned the friend rather tartly.

"Well, Mr. Jarndyce, sir," Mr. Guppy, after a moment's consideration, began, to the great diversion of his mother, which she displayed by nudging Mr. Jobling with her elbow and winking at me in a most remarkable manner, "I had an idea that I should see Miss Summerson by herself and was not quite prepared for your esteemed presence. But Miss Summerson has mentioned to you, perhaps, that something has passed between us on former occasions?"

"Miss Summerson," returned my guardian, smiling, "has made a communication to that effect to me."

"That," said Mr. Guppy, "makes matters easier. Sir, I have come out of my articles at Kenge and Carboy's, and I believe with satisfaction to all parties. I am now admitted (after undergoing an examination that's enough to badger a man blue, touching a pack of nonsense that he don't want to know) on the roll of attorneys and have taken out my certificate, if it would be any satisfaction to you to see it."

"Thank you, Mr. Guppy," returned my guardian. "I am quite willing—I believe I use a legal phrase—to admit the certificate."

Mr. Guppy therefore desisted from taking something out of his pocket and proceeded without it.

"I have no capital myself, but my mother has a little property which takes the form of an annuity"—here Mr. Guppy's mother rolled her head as if she never could sufficiently enjoy the observation, and put her handkerchief to her mouth, and again winked at me—"and a few pounds for expenses out of pocket in conducting business will never be wanting, free of interest, which is an advantage, you know," said Mr. Guppy feelingly.

"Certainly an advantage," returned my guardian.

"I HAVE some connexion," pursued Mr. Guppy, "and it lays in the direction of Walcot Square, Lambeth. I have therefore taken a 'ouse in that locality, which, in the opinion of my friends, is a hollow bargain (taxes ridiculous, and use of fixtures included in the rent), and intend setting up professionally for myself there forthwith."

Here Mr. Guppy's mother fell into an extraordinary passion of rolling her head and smiling waggishly at anybody who would look at her.

"It's a six-roomer, exclusive of kitchens," said Mr. Guppy, "and in the opinion of my friends, a commodious tenement. When I mention my friends, I refer principally to my friend Jobling, who I believe has known me," Mr. Guppy looked at him with a sentimental air, "from boyhood's hour."

Mr. Jobling confirmed this with a sliding movement of his legs.

"My friend Jobling will render me his assistance in the capacity of clerk and will live in the 'ouse," said Mr. Guppy. "My mother will likewise live in the 'ouse when her present quarter in the Old Street Road shall have ceased and expired; and consequently there will be no want of society. My friend Jobling is naturally aristocratic by taste, and besides being acquainted with the movements of the upper circles, fully backs me in the intentions I am now developing."

Mr. Jobling said "Certainly" and withdrew a little from the elbow of Mr Guppy's mother.

"Now, I have no occasion to mention to you, sir, you being in the confidence of Miss Summerson," said Mr. Guppy, "(mother, I wish you'd be so good as to keep still), that Miss Summerson's image was formerly imprinted on my 'eart and that I made her a proposal of marriage."

"That I have heard," returned my guardian.

"Circumstances," pursued Mr. Guppy, "over which I had no control, but quite the contrary, weakened the impression of that image for a time. At which time Miss Summerson's conduct was highly genteel; I may even add, magnanimous."

My guardian patted me on the shoulder and seemed much amused.

"Now, sir," said Mr. Guppy, "I have got into that state of mind myself that I wish for a reciprocity of magnanimous behaviour. I wish to prove to Miss Summerson that I can rise to a heighth of which perhaps she hardly thought me capable. I find that the image which I did suppose had been eradicated from my 'eart is NOT eradicated. Its influence over me is still tremenjous, and yielding to it, I am willing to overlook the circumstances over which none of us have had any control and to renew those proposals to Miss Summerson which I had the honour to make at a former period. I beg to lay the 'ouse in Walcot Square, the business, and myself before Miss Summerson for her acceptance."

"Very magnanimous indeed, sir," observed my guardian.

"Well, sir," replied Mr. Guppy with candour, "my wish is to BE magnanimous. I do not consider that in making this offer to Miss Summerson I am by any means throwing myself away; neither is that the opinion of my friends. Still, there are circumstances which I submit may be taken into account as a set off against any little drawbacks of mine, and so a fair and equitable balance arrived at."

"I take upon myself, sir," said my guardian, laughing as he rang the bell, "to reply to your proposals on behalf of Miss Summerson. She is very sensible of your handsome intentions, and wishes you good evening, and wishes you well."

"Oh!" said Mr. Guppy with a blank look. "Is that tantamount, sir, to acceptance, or rejection, or consideration?"

"To decided rejection, if you please," returned my guardian.

Mr. Guppy looked incredulously at his friend, and at his mother, who suddenly turned very angry, and at the floor, and at the ceiling.

"Indeed?" said he. "Then, Jobling, if you was the friend you represent yourself, I should think you might hand my mother out of the gangway instead of allowing her to remain where she ain't wanted."

But Mrs. Guppy positively refused to come out of the gangway. She wouldn't hear of it. "Why, get along with you," said she to my guardian, "what do you mean? Ain't my son good enough for you? You ought to be ashamed of yourself. Get out with you!"

"My good lady," returned my guardian, "it is hardly reasonable to ask me to get out of my own room."

"I don't care for that," said Mrs. Guppy. "Get out with you. If we ain't good enough for you, go and procure somebody that is good enough. Go along and find 'em."

I was quite unprepared for the rapid manner in which Mrs. Guppy's power of jocularity merged into a power of taking the profoundest offence.

"Go along and find somebody that's good enough for you," repeated Mrs. Guppy. "Get out!" Nothing seemed to astonish Mr. Guppy's mother so much and to make her so very indignant as our not getting out. "Why don't you get out?" said Mrs. Guppy. "What are you stopping here for?"

"Mother," interposed her son, always getting before her and pushing her back with one shoulder as she sidled at my guardian, "WILL you hold your tongue?"

"No, William," she returned, "I won't! Not unless he gets out, I won't!"

However, Mr. Guppy and Mr. Jobling together closed on Mr. Guppy's mother (who began to be quite abusive) and took her, very much against her will, downstairs, her voice rising a stair higher every time her figure got a stair lower, and insisting that we should immediately go and find somebody who was good enough for us, and above all things that we should get out.

CHAPTER LXV
BEGINNING THE WORLD

The term had commenced, and my guardian found an intimation from Mr. Kenge that the cause would come on in two days. As I had sufficient hopes of the will to be in a flutter about it, Allan and I agreed to go down to the court that morning. Richard was extremely agitated and was so weak and low, though his illness was still of the mind, that my dear girl indeed had sore occasion to be supported. But she looked forward—a very little way now—to the help that was to come to her, and never drooped.

It was at Westminster that the cause was to come on. It had come on there, I dare say, a hundred times before, but I could not divest myself of an idea that it MIGHT lead to some result now. We left home directly after breakfast to be at Westminster Hall in good time and walked down there through the lively streets—so happily and strangely it seemed!—together.

As we were going along, planning what we should do for Richard and Ada, I heard somebody calling "Esther! My dear Esther! Esther!" And there was Caddy Jellyby, with her head out of the window of a little carriage which she hired now to go about in to her pupils (she had so many), as if she wanted to embrace me at a hundred yards' distance. I had written her a note to tell her of all that my guardian had done, but had not had a moment to go and see her. Of course we turned back, and the affectionate girl was in that state of rapture, and was so overjoyed to talk about the night when she brought me the flowers, and was so determined to squeeze my face (bonnet and all) between her hands, and go on in a wild manner altogether, calling me all kinds of precious names, and telling Allan I had done I don't know what for her, that I was just obliged to get into the little carriage and calm her down by letting her say and do exactly what she liked. Allan, standing at the window, was as pleased as Caddy; and I was as pleased as either of them; and I wonder that I got away as I did, rather than that I came off laughing, and red, and anything but tidy, and looking after Caddy, who looked after us out of the coach-window as long as she could see us.

This made us some quarter of an hour late, and when we came to Westminster Hall we found that the day's business was begun. Worse than that, we found such an unusual crowd in the Court of Chancery that it was full to the door, and we could neither see nor hear what was passing within. It appeared to be something droll, for occasionally there was a laugh and a cry of "Silence!" It appeared to be something interesting, for every one was pushing and striving to get nearer. It appeared to be something that made the professional gentlemen very merry, for there were several young counsellors in wigs and whiskers on the outside of the crowd, and when one of them told the others about it, they put their hands in their pockets, and quite doubled themselves up with laughter, and went stamping about the pavement of the Hall.

We asked a gentleman by us if he knew what cause was on. He told us Jarndyce and Jarndyce. We asked him if he knew what was doing in it. He said really, no he did not, nobody ever did, but as well as he could make out, it was over. Over for the day? we asked him. No, he said, over for good.

Over for good!

When we heard this unaccountable answer, we looked at one another quite lost in amazement. Could it be possible that the will had set things right at last and that Richard and Ada were going to be rich? It seemed too good to be true. Alas it was!

Our suspense was short, for a break-up soon took place in the crowd, and the people came streaming out looking flushed and hot and bringing a quantity of bad air with them. Still they were all exceedingly amused and were more like people coming out from a farce or a juggler than from a court of justice. We stood aside, watching for any countenance we knew, and presently great bundles of paper began to be carried out—bundles in bags, bundles too large to be got into any bags, immense masses of papers of all shapes and no shapes, which the bearers staggered under, and threw down for the time being, anyhow, on the Hall pavement, while they went back to bring out more. Even these clerks were laughing. We glanced at the papers, and seeing Jarndyce and Jarndyce everywhere, asked an official-looking person who was standing in the midst of them whether the cause was over. Yes, he said, it was all up with it at last, and burst out laughing too.

At this juncture we perceived Mr. Kenge coming out of court with an affable dignity upon him, listening to Mr. Vholes, who was deferential and carried his own bag. Mr. Vholes was the first to see us. "Here is Miss Summerson, sir," he said. "And Mr. Woodcourt."

"Oh, indeed! Yes. Truly!" said Mr. Kenge, raising his hat to me with polished politeness. "How do you do? Glad to see you. Mr. Jarndyce is not here?"

No. He never came there, I reminded him.

"Really," returned Mr. Kenge, "it is as well that he is NOT here to-day, for his—shall I say, in my good friend's absence, his indomitable singularity of opinion?—might have been strengthened, perhaps; not reasonably, but might have been strengthened."

"Pray what has been done to-day?" asked Allan.

"I beg your pardon?" said Mr. Kenge with excessive urbanity.

"What has been done to-day?"

"What has been done," repeated Mr. Kenge. "Quite so. Yes. Why, not much has been done; not much. We have been checked—brought up suddenly, I would say—upon the—shall I term it threshold?"

"Is this will considered a genuine document, sir?" said Allan. "Will you tell us that?"

"Most certainly, if I could," said Mr. Kenge; "but we have not gone into that, we have not gone into that."

"We have not gone into that," repeated Mr. Vholes as if his low inward voice were an echo.

"You are to reflect, Mr. Woodcourt," observed Mr. Kenge, using his silver trowel persuasively and smoothingly, "that this has been a great cause, that this has been a protracted cause, that this has been a complex cause. Jarndyce and Jarndyce has been termed, not inaptly, a monument of Chancery practice."

"And patience has sat upon it a long time," said Allan.

"Very well indeed, sir," returned Mr. Kenge with a certain condescending laugh he had. "Very well! You are further to reflect, Mr. Woodcourt," becoming dignified almost to severity, "that on the numerous difficulties, contingencies, masterly fictions, and forms of procedure in this great cause, there has been expended study, ability, eloquence, knowledge, intellect, Mr. Woodcourt, high intellect. For many years, the—a—I would say the flower of the bar, and the—a—I would presume to add, the matured autumnal fruits of the woolsack—have been lavished upon Jarndyce and Jarndyce. If the public have the benefit, and if the country have the adornment, of this great grasp, it must be paid for in money or money's worth, sir."

"Mr. Kenge," said Allan, appearing enlightened all in a moment. "Excuse me, our time presses. Do I understand that the whole estate is found to have been absorbed in costs?"

"Hem! I believe so," returned Mr. Kenge. "Mr. Vholes, what do YOU say?"

"I believe so," said Mr. Vholes.

"And that thus the suit lapses and melts away?"

"Probably," returned Mr. Kenge. "Mr. Vholes?"

"Probably," said Mr. Vholes.

"My dearest life," whispered Allan, "this will break Richard's heart!"

There was such a shock of apprehension in his face, and he knew Richard so perfectly, and I too had seen so much of his gradual decay, that what my dear girl had said to me in the fullness of her foreboding love sounded like a knell in my ears.

"In case you should be wanting Mr. C., sir," said Mr. Vholes, coming after us, "you'll find him in court. I left him there resting himself a little. Good day, sir; good day, Miss Summerson." As he gave me that slowly devouring look of his, while twisting up the strings of his bag before he hastened with it after Mr. Kenge, the benignant shadow of whose conversational presence he seemed afraid to leave, he gave one gasp as if he had swallowed the last morsel of his client, and his black buttoned-up unwholesome figure glided away to the low door at the end of the Hall.

"My dear love," said Allan, "leave to me, for a little while, the charge you gave me. Go home with this intelligence and come to Ada's by and by!"

I would not let him take me to a coach, but entreated him to go to Richard without a moment's delay and leave me to do as he wished. Hurrying home, I found my guardian and told him gradually with what news I had returned. "Little woman," said he, quite unmoved for himself, "to have done with the suit on any terms is a greater blessing than I had looked for. But my poor young cousins!"

We talked about them all the morning and discussed what it was possible to do. In the afternoon my guardian walked with me to Symond's Inn and left me at the door. I went upstairs. When my darling heard my footsteps, she came out into the small passage and threw her arms round my neck, but she composed herself directly and said that Richard had asked for me several times. Allan had found him sitting in the corner of the court, she told me, like a stone figure. On being roused, he had broken away and made as if he would have spoken in a fierce voice to the judge. He was stopped by his mouth being full of blood, and Allan had brought him home.

He was lying on a sofa with his eyes closed when I went in. There were restoratives on the table; the room was made as airy as possible, and was darkened, and was very orderly and quiet. Allan stood behind him watching him gravely. His face appeared to me to be quite destitute of colour, and now that I saw him without his seeing me, I fully saw, for the first time, how worn away he was. But he looked handsomer than I had seen him look for many a day.

I sat down by his side in silence. Opening his eyes by and by, he said in a weak voice, but with his old smile, "Dame Durden, kiss me, my dear!"

It was a great comfort and surprise to me to find him in his low state cheerful and looking forward. He was happier, he said, in our intended marriage than he could find words to tell me. My husband had been a guardian angel to him and Ada, and he blessed us both and wished us all the joy that life could yield us. I almost felt as if my own heart would have broken when I saw him take my husband's hand and hold it to his breast.

We spoke of the future as much as possible, and he said several times that he must be present at our marriage if he could stand upon his feet. Ada would contrive to take him, somehow, he said. "Yes, surely, dearest Richard!" But as my darling answered him thus hopefully, so serene and beautiful, with the help that was to come to her so near—I knew—I knew!

It was not good for him to talk too much, and when he was silent, we were silent too. Sitting beside him, I made a pretence of working for my dear, as he had always been used to joke about my being busy. Ada leaned upon his pillow, holding his head upon her arm. He dozed often, and whenever he awoke without seeing him, said first of all, "Where is Woodcourt?"

Evening had come on when I lifted up my eyes and saw my guardian standing in the little hall. "Who is that, Dame Durden?" Richard asked me. The door was behind him, but he had observed in my face that some one was there.

I looked to Allan for advice, and as he nodded "Yes," bent over Richard and told him. My guardian saw what passed, came softly by me in a moment, and laid his hand on Richard's. "Oh, sir," said Richard, "you are a good man, you are a good man!" and burst into tears for the first time.

My guardian, the picture of a good man, sat down in my place, keeping his hand on Richard's.

"My dear Rick," said he, "the clouds have cleared away, and it is bright now. We can see now. We were all bewildered, Rick, more or less. What matters! And how are you, my dear boy?"

"I am very weak, sir, but I hope I shall be stronger. I have to begin the world."

"Aye, truly; well said!" cried my guardian.

"I will not begin it in the old way now," said Richard with a sad smile. "I have learned a lesson now, sir. It was a hard one, but you shall be assured, indeed, that I have learned it."

"Well, well," said my guardian, comforting him; "well, well, well, dear boy!"

"I was thinking, sir," resumed Richard, "that there is nothing on earth I should so much like to see as their house—Dame Durden's and Woodcourt's house. If I could be removed there when I begin to recover my strength, I feel as if I should get well there sooner than anywhere."

"Why, so have I been thinking too, Rick," said my guardian, "and our little woman likewise; she and I have been talking of it this very day. I dare say her husband won't object. What do you think?"

Richard smiled and lifted up his arm to touch him as he stood behind the head of the couch.

"I say nothing of Ada," said Richard, "but I think of her, and have thought of her very much. Look at her! See her here, sir, bending over this pillow when she has so much need to rest upon it herself, my dear love, my poor girl!"

He clasped her in his arms, and none of us spoke. He gradually released her, and she looked upon us, and looked up to heaven, and moved her lips.

"When I get down to Bleak House," said Richard, "I shall have much to tell you, sir, and you will have much to show me. You will go, won't you?"

"Undoubtedly, dear Rick."

"Thank you; like you, like you," said Richard. "But it's all like you. They have been telling me how you planned it and how you remembered all Esther's familiar tastes and ways. It will be like coming to the old Bleak House again."

"And you will come there too, I hope, Rick. I am a solitary man now, you know, and it will be a charity to come to me. A charity to come to me, my love!" he repeated to Ada as he gently passed his hand over her golden hair and put a lock of it to his lips. (I think he vowed within himself to cherish her if she were left alone.)

"It was a troubled dream?" said Richard, clasping both my guardian's hands eagerly.

"Nothing more, Rick; nothing more."

"And you, being a good man, can pass it as such, and forgive and pity the dreamer, and be lenient and encouraging when he wakes?"

"Indeed I can. What am I but another dreamer, Rick?"

"I will begin the world!" said Richard with a light in his eyes.

My husband drew a little nearer towards Ada, and I saw him solemnly lift up his hand to warn my guardian.

"When shall I go from this place to that pleasant country where the old times are, where I shall have strength to tell what Ada has been to me, where I shall be able to recall my many faults and blindnesses, where I shall prepare myself to be a guide to my unborn child?" said Richard. "When shall I go?"

"Dear Rick, when you are strong enough," returned my guardian.

"Ada, my darling!"

He sought to raise himself a little. Allan raised him so that she could hold him on her bosom, which was what he wanted.

"I have done you many wrongs, my own. I have fallen like a poor stray shadow on your way, I have married you to poverty and trouble, I have scattered your means to the winds. You will forgive me all this, my Ada, before I begin the world?"

A smile irradiated his face as she bent to kiss him. He slowly laid his face down upon her bosom, drew his arms closer round her neck, and with one parting sob began the world. Not this world, oh, not this! The world that sets this right.

When all was still, at a late hour, poor crazed Miss Flite came weeping to me and told me she had given her birds their liberty.

CHAPTER LXVI
DOWN IN LINCOLNSHIRE

There is a hush upon Chesney Wold in these altered days, as there is upon a portion of the family history. The story goes that Sir Leicester paid some who could have spoken out to hold their peace; but it is a lame story, feebly whispering and creeping about, and any brighter spark of life it shows soon dies away. It is known for certain that the handsome Lady Dedlock lies in the mausoleum in the park, where the trees arch darkly overhead, and the owl is heard at night making the woods ring; but whence she was brought home to be laid among the echoes of that solitary place, or how she died, is all mystery. Some of her old friends, principally to be found among the peachy-cheeked charmers with the skeleton throats, did once occasionally say, as they toyed in a ghastly manner with large fans—like charmers reduced to flirting with grim death, after losing all their other beaux—did once occasionally say, when the world assembled together, that they wondered the ashes of the Dedlocks, entombed in the mausoleum, never rose against the profanation of her company. But the dead-and-gone Dedlocks take it very calmly and have never been known to object.

Up from among the fern in the hollow, and winding by the bridle-road among the trees, comes sometimes to this lonely spot the sound of horses' hoofs. Then may be seen Sir Leicester—invalided, bent, and almost blind, but of worthy presence yet—riding with a stalwart man beside him, constant to his bridle-rein. When they come to a certain spot before the mausoleum-door, Sir Leicester's accustomed horse stops of his own accord, and Sir Leicester, pulling off his hat, is still for a few moments before they ride away.

War rages yet with the audacious Boythorn, though at uncertain intervals, and now hotly, and now coolly, flickering like an unsteady fire. The truth is said to be that when Sir Leicester came down to Lincolnshire for good, Mr. Boythorn showed a manifest desire to abandon his right of way and do whatever Sir Leicester would, which Sir Leicester, conceiving to be a condescension to his illness or misfortune, took in such high dudgeon, and was so magnificently aggrieved by, that Mr. Boythorn found himself under the necessity of committing a flagrant trespass to restore his neighbour to himself. Similarly, Mr. Boythorn continues to post tremendous placards on the disputed thoroughfare and (with his bird upon his head) to hold forth vehemently against Sir Leicester in the sanctuary of his own home; similarly, also, he defies him as of old in the little church by testifying a bland unconsciousness of his existence. But it is whispered that when he is most ferocious towards his old foe, he is really most considerate, and that Sir Leicester, in the dignity of being implacable, little supposes how much he is humoured. As little does he think how near together he and his antagonist have suffered in the fortunes of two sisters, and his antagonist, who knows it now, is not the man to tell him. So the quarrel goes on to the satisfaction of both.

In one of the lodges of the park—that lodge within sight of the house where, once upon a time, when the waters were out down in Lincolnshire, my Lady used to see the keeper's child—the stalwart man, the trooper formerly, is housed. Some relics of his old calling hang upon the walls, and these it is the chosen recreation of a little lame man about the stable-yard to keep gleaming bright. A busy little man he always is, in the polishing at harness-house doors, of stirrup-irons, bits, curb-chains, harness bosses, anything in the way of a stable-yard that will take a polish, leading a life of friction. A shaggy little damaged man, withal, not unlike an old dog of some mongrel breed, who has been considerably knocked about. He answers to the name of Phil.

A goodly sight it is to see the grand old housekeeper (harder of hearing now) going to church on the arm of her son and to observe—which few do, for the house is scant of company in these times—the relations of both towards Sir Leicester, and his towards them. They have visitors in the high summer weather, when a grey cloak and umbrella, unknown to Chesney Wold at other periods, are seen among the leaves; when two young ladies are occasionally found gambolling in sequestered saw-pits and such nooks of the park; and when the smoke of two pipes wreathes away into the fragrant evening air from the trooper's door. Then is a fife heard trolling within the lodge on the inspiring topic of the "British Grenadiers"; and as the evening closes in, a gruff inflexible voice is heard to say, while two men pace together up and down, "But I never own to it before the old girl. Discipline must be maintained."

The greater part of the house is shut up, and it is a show-house no longer; yet Sir Leicester holds his shrunken state in the long drawing-room for all that, and reposes in his old place before my Lady's picture. Closed in by night with broad screens, and illumined only in that part, the light of the drawing-room seems gradually contracting and dwindling until it shall be no more. A little more, in truth, and it will be all extinguished for Sir Leicester; and the damp door in the mausoleum which shuts so tight, and looks so obdurate, will have opened and received him.

Volumnia, growing with the flight of time pinker as to the red in her face, and yellower as to the white, reads to Sir Leicester in the long evenings and is driven to various artifices to conceal her yawns, of which the chief and most efficacious is the insertion of the pearl necklace between her rosy lips. Long-winded treatises on the Buffy and Boodle question, showing how Buffy is immaculate and Boodle villainous, and how the country is lost by being all Boodle and no Buffy, or saved by being all Buffy and no Boodle (it must be one of the two, and cannot be anything else), are the staple of her reading. Sir Leicester is not particular what it is and does not appear to follow it very closely, further than that he always comes broad awake the moment Volumnia ventures to leave off, and sonorously repeating her last words, begs with some displeasure to know if she finds herself fatigued. However, Volumnia, in the course of her bird-like hopping about and pecking at papers, has alighted on a memorandum concerning herself in the event of "anything happening" to her kinsman, which is handsome compensation for an extensive course of reading and holds even the dragon Boredom at bay.

The cousins generally are rather shy of Chesney Wold in its dullness, but take to it a little in the shooting season, when guns are heard in the plantations, and a few scattered beaters and keepers wait at the old places of appointment for low-spirited twos and threes of cousins. The debilitated cousin, more debilitated by the dreariness of the place, gets into a fearful state of depression, groaning under penitential sofa-pillows in his gunless hours and protesting that such fernal old jail's—nough t'sew fler up—frever.

The only great occasions for Volumnia in this changed aspect of the place in Lincolnshire are those occasions, rare and widely separated, when something is to be done for the county or the country in the way of gracing a public ball. Then, indeed, does the tuckered sylph come out in fairy form and proceed with joy under cousinly escort to the exhausted old assembly-room, fourteen heavy miles off, which, during three hundred and sixty-four days and nights of every ordinary year, is a kind of antipodean lumber-room full of old chairs and tables upside down. Then, indeed, does she captivate all hearts by her condescension, by her girlish vivacity, and by her skipping about as in the days when the hideous old general with the mouth too full of teeth had not cut one of them at two guineas each. Then does she twirl and twine, a pastoral nymph of good family, through the mazes of the dance. Then do the swains appear with tea, with lemonade, with sandwiches, with homage. Then is she kind and cruel, stately and unassuming, various, beautifully wilful. Then is there a singular kind of parallel between her and the little glass chandeliers of another age embellishing that assembly-room, which, with their meagre stems, their spare little drops, their disappointing knobs where no drops are, their bare little stalks from which knobs and drops have both departed, and their little feeble prismatic twinkling, all seem Volumnias.

For the rest, Lincolnshire life to Volumnia is a vast blank of overgrown house looking out upon trees, sighing, wringing their hands, bowing their heads, and casting their tears upon the window-panes in monotonous depressions. A labyrinth of grandeur, less the property of an old family of human beings and their ghostly likenesses than of an old family of echoings and thunderings which start out of their hundred graves at every sound and go resounding through the building. A waste of unused passages and staircases in which to drop a comb upon a bedroom floor at night is to send a stealthy footfall on an errand through the house. A place where few people care to go about alone, where a maid screams if an ash drops from the fire, takes to crying at all times and seasons, becomes the victim of a low disorder of the spirits, and gives warning and departs.

Thus Chesney Wold. With so much of itself abandoned to darkness and vacancy; with so little change under the summer shining or the wintry lowering; so sombre and motionless always—no flag flying now by day, no rows of lights sparkling by night; with no family to come and go, no visitors to be the souls of pale cold shapes of rooms, no stir of life about it—passion and pride, even to the stranger's eye, have died away from the place in Lincolnshire and yielded it to dull repose.

CHAPTER LXVII
THE CLOSE OF ESTHER'S NARRATIVE

Full seven happy years I have been the mistress of Bleak House. The few words that I have to add to what I have written are soon penned; then I and the unknown friend to whom I write will part for ever. Not without much dear remembrance on my side. Not without some, I hope, on his or hers.

They gave my darling into my arms, and through many weeks I never left her. The little child who was to have done so much was born before the turf was planted on its father's grave. It was a boy; and I, my husband, and my guardian gave him his father's name.

The help that my dear counted on did come to her, though it came, in the eternal wisdom, for another purpose. Though to bless and restore his mother, not his father, was the errand of this baby, its power was mighty to do it. When I saw the strength of the weak little hand and how its touch could heal my darling's heart and raised hope within her, I felt a new sense of the goodness and the tenderness of God.

They throve, and by degrees I saw my dear girl pass into my country garden and walk there with her infant in her arms. I was married then. I was the happiest of the happy.

It was at this time that my guardian joined us and asked Ada when she would come home.

"Both houses are your home, my dear," said he, "but the older Bleak House claims priority. When you and my boy are strong enough to do it, come and take possession of your home."

Ada called him "her dearest cousin, John." But he said, no, it must be guardian now. He was her guardian henceforth, and the boy's; and he had an old association with the name. So she called him guardian, and has called him guardian ever since. The children know him by no other name. I say the children; I have two little daughters.

It is difficult to believe that Charley (round-eyed still, and not at all grammatical) is married to a miller in our neighbourhood; yet so it is; and even now, looking up from my desk as I write early in the morning at my summer window, I see the very mill beginning to go round. I hope the miller will not spoil Charley; but he is very fond of her, and Charley is rather vain of such a match, for he is well to do and was in great request. So far as my small maid is concerned, I might suppose time to have stood for seven years as still as the mill did half an hour ago, since little Emma, Charley's sister, is exactly what Charley used to be. As to Tom, Charley's brother, I am really afraid to say what he did at school in ciphering, but I think it was decimals. He is apprenticed to the miller, whatever it was, and is a good bashful fellow, always falling in love with somebody and being ashamed of it.

Caddy Jellyby passed her very last holidays with us and was a dearer creature than ever, perpetually dancing in and out of the house with the children as if she had never given a dancing-lesson in her life. Caddy keeps her own little carriage now instead of hiring one, and lives full two miles further westward than Newman Street. She works very hard, her husband (an excellent one) being lame and able to do very little. Still, she is more than contented and does all she has to do with all her heart. Mr. Jellyby spends his evenings at her new house with his head against the wall as he used to do in her old one. I have heard that Mrs. Jellyby was understood to suffer great mortification from her daughter's ignoble marriage and pursuits, but I hope she got over it in time. She has been disappointed in Borrioboola-Gha, which turned out a failure in consequence of the king of Borrioboola wanting to sell everybody—who survived the climate—for rum, but she has taken up with the rights of women to sit in Parliament, and Caddy tells me it is a mission involving more correspondence than the old one. I had almost forgotten Caddy's poor little girl. She is not such a mite now, but she is deaf and dumb. I believe there never was a better mother than Caddy, who learns, in her scanty intervals of leisure, innumerable deaf and dumb arts to soften the affliction of her child.

As if I were never to have done with Caddy, I am reminded here of Peepy and old Mr. Turveydrop. Peepy is in the Custom House, and doing extremely well. Old Mr. Turveydrop, very apoplectic, still exhibits his deportment about town, still enjoys himself in the old manner, is still believed in in the old way. He is constant in his patronage of Peepy and is understood to have bequeathed him a favourite French clock in his dressing-room—which is not his property.

With the first money we saved at home, we added to our pretty house by throwing out a little growlery expressly for my guardian, which we inaugurated with great splendour the next time he came down to see us. I try to write all this lightly, because my heart is full in drawing to an end, but when I write of him, my tears will have their way.

I never look at him but I hear our poor dear Richard calling him a good man. To Ada and her pretty boy, he is the fondest father; to me he is what he has ever been, and what name can I give to that? He is my husband's best and dearest friend, he is our children's darling, he is the object of our deepest love and veneration. Yet while I feel towards him as if he were a superior being, I am so familiar with him and so easy with him that I almost wonder at myself. I have never lost my old names, nor has he lost his; nor do I ever, when he is with us, sit in any other place than in my old chair at his side, Dame Trot, Dame Durden, Little Woman—all just the same as ever; and I answer, "Yes, dear guardian!" just the same.

I have never known the wind to be in the east for a single moment since the day when he took me to the porch to read the name. I remarked to him once that the wind seemed never in the east now, and he said, no, truly; it had finally departed from that quarter on that very day.

I think my darling girl is more beautiful than ever. The sorrow that has been in her face—for it is not there now—seems to have purified even its innocent expression and to have given it a diviner quality. Sometimes when I raise my eyes and see her in the black dress that she still wears, teaching my Richard, I feel—it is difficult to express—as if it were so good to know that she remembers her dear Esther in her prayers.

I call him my Richard! But he says that he has two mamas, and I am one.

We are not rich in the bank, but we have always prospered, and we have quite enough. I never walk out with my husband but I hear the people bless him. I never go into a house of any degree but I hear his praises or see them in grateful eyes. I never lie down at night but I know that in the course of that day he has alleviated pain and soothed some fellow-creature in the time of need. I know that from the beds of those who were past recovery, thanks have often, often gone up, in the last hour, for his patient ministration. Is not this to be rich?

The people even praise me as the doctor's wife. The people even like me as I go about, and make so much of me that I am quite abashed. I owe it all to him, my love, my pride! They like me for his sake, as I do everything I do in life for his sake.

A night or two ago, after bustling about preparing for my darling and my guardian and little Richard, who are coming to-morrow, I was sitting out in the porch of all places, that dearly memorable porch, when Allan came home. So he said, "My precious little woman, what are you doing here?" And I said, "The moon is shining so brightly, Allan, and the night is so delicious, that I have been sitting here thinking."

"What have you been thinking about, my dear?" said Allan then.

"How curious you are!" said I. "I am almost ashamed to tell you, but I will. I have been thinking about my old looks—such as they were."

"And what have you been thinking about THEM, my busy bee?" said Allan.

"I have been thinking that I thought it was impossible that you COULD have loved me any better, even if I had retained them."

"'Such as they were'?" said Allan, laughing.

"Such as they were, of course."

"My dear Dame Durden," said Allan, drawing my arm through his, "do you ever look in the glass?"

"You know I do; you see me do it."

"And don't you know that you are prettier than you ever were?"

"I did not know that; I am not certain that I know it now. But I know that my dearest little pets are very pretty, and that my darling is very beautiful, and that my husband is very handsome, and that my guardian has the brightest and most benevolent face that ever was seen, and that they can very well do without much beauty in me—even supposing—."

Charles Dickens Biography

Charles Dickens, renowned author of iconic tales such as *Tale of Two Cities* and *Great Expectations*, has cemented himself in the literary hall of fame. His stories, many of which have been reimagined countless times for theatre, film and even television, are a captivating and often bleak vision into 19th century England. They were lauded by the rich and poor alike and earned him a celebrity reputation in his time. Though he ended his life as one of the most highly regarded writers of his time, like many of the children of the Victorian age, Dickens spent parts of his childhood living in poverty and working on a factory floor.

Charles Dickens was one of eight children born to Elizabeth and John Dickens in Portsmouth and initially had a comfortable child-hood. His father, who worked as a naval clerk, was able to afford Charles a few years of private education and he developed a passion for reading and writing from a young age. His father was eventually hauled off to prison however, after accumulating a substantial amount of debt. Charles would work in a factory and his experience of the conditions and the working-class folk that he got to know would become an important catalyst for much of his later work.

Dicken began to attract attention in his twenties. He worked as a journalist for several publications, including work as a political commentator for *The Morning Chronicle*, and began forming important professional connections across London. His real passion was for fiction however and in 1836 he released the first edition of *The Pickwick Papers*. Envisioned as a series of adventures to be released in a serial format, much like a magazine (or episodes of a television show), *The Pickwick Papers* helped him rise to fame, especially considering the final edition sold over 40,000 copies. Dickens was a pioneer of serialised writing. This format allowed him to work with cliff-hangers and register the readers reactions to his stories in order to devise shocking moments. Not unlike how the world of television works in the modern world.

After *The Pickwick Papers*, Dickens soon began releasing monthly instalments of a story the world now recognises, *Oliver Twist*, from 1837 - 1839. A young Queen Victoria was famously enamoured with this publication and it marked the first Victorian novel with a child protagonist. Charles Dickens was working on numerous serialised stories at this time, such as *The Old Curiosity Shop* and *Nicholas Nickleby*. He developed a reputation for his satirical outlook and sharp social commentary on Victorian England and London. He also got married to one Catherine Dickens, who he would remain legally married with until his death in 1870, though they were eventually separated due to Dickens infatuation with another woman in 1857, actress Ellen Ternan.

After spending a brief stint in New York, giving lectures on international copyright laws and developing a strong disapproval of slavery, Dickens returned home and released his first major Christmas novella, *A Christmas*

Carol, in 1843. This story is one that has been retold and reimagined countless times since it's release and Ebenezer Scrooge is one of the most recognised literary characters of all time. It was well received at the time and was a celebration of Christmas for the less wealthy to experience. It sold out on Christmas Eve.

Dickens continued to produce novels and serials over the next couple of decades at an alarming pace. *David Copperfield* was released in 1849 which he later commented that it was the story he was most fond of. While he resided in his famous London home, Tavistock House, he wrote the serial *Bleak House* from 1852-1853 and the novel, *Hard Times*, in 1954. The latter was his shortest and the only novel not to include any scenes set in London. He would put on amateur performances at Tavistock House and it was there where he fell in love with the actress, Ellen Ternan, during a production of his play, *The Frozen Deep*. Him and his wife would separate and his relationship with Ternan remains speculative to this day but she was definitely a companion of some regard in his later years

Two of his most famous novels were written over the next few years. *A Tale of Two Cities* was released in 1859, a story that takes place in both London and Paris during the French Revolution, and is regarded as one of his best works. Dickens spent many family holidays in France and the inspiration was clear in this work of historical fiction. *Great Expectations* was written as Dickens approached his fiftieth birthday. Initially released in a serialized format, *Great Expectation*, is now one of his most famous works, in part because of the 1947 Oscar-nominated film adaption.

As his health deteriorated during the 1860s, Dickens gave a series of farewell readings across the country, still driven towards the end of his life. He died in June 1970 after suffering another stroke. He was 58 at the time and his extensive bibliography by then included around twenty novels and novellas, hundreds of short stories and a magazine published weekly for over thirty years (continuing after his death) called *All The Year Round*. He would be remembered by fellow writers at the time and by the world in 2020. His works are being constantly recreated for theatre and film and his iconic serialized format for writing would pave way writers such as Wilkie Collins & Arthur Conan Doyle, the latter of whom created Sherlock Holmes.

Charles Dickens is one of the most famous names in literature but also one of the first early authors to appeal to the rich and poor alike; fictionalising both sides of the coin in his works. Originally an art-form reserved for the wealthy in England, the illiterate working class in London used to pay a halfpenny to have his work read out to them and through this he single-handedly pulled a whole new class into the world of literature, despite ending up well above the bread-line himself. The term *Dickensian* has been coined in reference to his affinity for raising awareness about lower social class conditions. Charles Dickens will be remembered as one of the most widely influential Victorian writers of all time

Enjoy Other Sastrugi Press Charles Dickens Books

A Christmas Carol

Charles Dickens's timeless Christmas classic inspires readers to look at their lives with a vision of the future.

www.sastrugipress.com/classics/a-christmas-carol/

A Tale of Two Cities

A story of a man who is imprisoned in the Bastille, a French prison, for eighteen years and is able to reunite with his daughter in London who he has never met.

www.sastrugipress.com/classics/a-tale-of-two-cities/

Bleak House

Bleak House is considered one of Dickens's best works due to the witty, poignant critique of the convoluted British legal system that a family becomes trapped in.

www.sastrugipress.com/classics/bleak-house/

David Copperfield

This coming-of-age tale follows the adventures of David Copperfield and his friends as he grows and matures out of his cruel circumstances.

www.sastrugipress.com/classics/david-copperfield/

Dombey and Son

Charles Dickens's lesser-known novel follows the tumultuous journey of the Dombey family and their eventual road to forgiveness and acceptance.

www.sastrugipress.com/classics/dombey-and-son/

Great Expectations

A modern classic that explores poverty, love, rejection, wealth, and the consequences of our actions in a Victorian England setting.
www.sastrugipress.com/classics/great-expectations/

Hard Times

Charles Dickens's haunting novel explores socio-economical theories and philosophies of 19th-century England. Rich descriptions and characterizations make this work a classic, asking questions of morality, truth, and status.
www.sastrugipress.com/classics/hard-times/

Oliver Twist

Charles Dickens's unromantic description of the industrial age of Britain gives insight into the cruelties born by children.
www.sastrugipress.com/classics/oliver-twist/

Little Dorrit

Dickens satirizes both the society and government of the Victorian era, particularly the lack of social safety net.
www.sastrugipress.com/classics/little-dorrit/

Use your smart device to scan the QR codes for website links.

Visit www.sastrugipress.com/large-print-classics/ for more classic large print books from your favorite authors. Thank you for purchasing a Sastrugi Press Large Print Classic!

www.ingramcontent.com/pod-product-compliance
Lightning Source LLC
LaVergne TN
LVHW041050080826
845145LV00007B/1523

* 9 7 8 1 6 4 9 2 2 1 0 2 5 *